Cock-a-Hoop

Cock-a-Hoop

The adventures, mostly, of Neill Rhymer

COREY MESLER

WHISK(E)Y TIT
NYC & VT

Published in the United States by Whisk(e)y Tit: www.whiskeytit.com. If you wish to use or reproduce all or part of this book for any means, please let the author and publisher know. You're pretty much required to, legally.

ISBN 978-1-952600-10-4

Cover art by Amanda Bearden.

for Cheryl, always the hours

*And in memory of Susan Verner
Wells
1955-2018
and
Susan Pipkin
1955-2020*

"Oh God the privacies he had seen. He felt the strangeness of unbound flesh
strongly. They ought to be kept hidden, these vulnerabilities, these oddities
and organs soft as a snail's body or its tender horns, the exposure of them
was monstrous, he wanted to recase hers in the pretty white things that
hung around the car like festoons, and yet even as he thought this he began
to rise again."
— John Crowley

"Well, happiness to their sheets!"
— William Shakespeare

The Main Characters

Neill Rhymer, our protagonist, bookseller and writer

His family

Max, father
Lolly, mother
Brack, brother
AJ, sister
Dan Johnson, later AJ's husband.
   In New York and Canada: Aunts July, Lane, Queue, etc.
Uncles Tulip, Ron, Larry, Ron, Bart, etc.
Great Uncle Frank
Maternal Grandparents: Ema and Opel "Open" Graves

On Kenneth Street

The neighbors: The Reids, Mr. and Henny, and the girls Evening and Lessa
The Porch boys: Robert, Lafayette, Chino, Truck
New kid: Hawker Mikar
Mick Allen

At Bartlett High School

Greg Borneo
Bucky (he came from Spain)
Rita Houston (a Beauty like Truth and Justice)
Reverend Kif
Sam Onides

At Waldenbooks

Joy Johns Dun—the boss
Pam– had strawberry blond hair and skin like ice cream

At The Bookshelf

Ianthe and Maude—the owners
Iago—a co-worker
Smithy—she deserves more ink

Disclaimer: Though rich with the blood of real life, this is totally a work of fiction, and all persons herein products of the author's wiggy imagination. Or, as Robertson Davies said, "None of the characters in the book are portraits of living people. Fiction may be portrait painting but if it is any good it is not photography."

"A little autobiography and a lot of imagination is best."
— Raymond Carver
"I'm cock-a-hoop and I feel alright."
— Manfred Mann

Prologue

"Idle reader: Without my swearing to it, you can believe that I would like this book, the child of my understanding, to be the most beautiful, the most brilliant, and the most discreet that anyone could imagine."
— Cervantes, from Don Quixote (Edith Grossman, trans.)

"After all, the membrum virile is like a human being. One must not judge it by size alone. It is the tout ensemble which counts. By that I mean...not only the sculptural elegance, the silkiness of texture and the richness of content, but also the whole chiaroscuro of responsiveness, intensity, and general playfulness."
— Fredric Prokosch

BOOK I: FOREPLAY

"Doctor, I can't stand any more being frightened like this over nothing! Bless me with manhood! Make me brave! Make me strong! Make me whole!"
— Philip Roth

Peepees

When he was five years old, Neill Rhymer was caught comparing peepees with the young girl down the street. Her name was Alix Naughty. When Alix bared her little round bottom something like a small pebble in Neill fell from the top of his brain, caromed down through his limbic system, bounced off a kidney and touched the innermost part of his urinary tract. They were standing in an open area between houses, as exposed as God's worst secret, and Neill's Aunt Lane, who lived next door, ratted him out to his mother. Neill's mother, Lolly, sputtered with anger, hot as monkeys. Neill was deeply ashamed and embarrassed and sick in his heart. He wept the tears of the criminal, the penitent, the sinner.

He was five. His life was over.

Soon though, perhaps only days later, Neill couldn't wait to do it again.

Neill was moony and mooncow simple.

We Were Not There. We Tell the Story as it Was Told to Us.

It will move with a lurch and a jump, a lurch and a pause, like a slinky, but it will move, inevitably, downward (not to imply anything negative about that direction; it is the way we will all go eventually).

The Family Rhymers

In 1960, the family Rhymers moved from Niagara Falls, New York (cold, snow deeper than rooftops, handmade Sears-kit-home in suburban Lewiston) to Memphis, Tennessee (hot, snaky, brand-spanking-new home on a brand-spanking-new street of gravel in heavily-wooded, suburban Raleigh), between the jarring change of kindergarten for Neill to the jarring new city, jarring first grade at a new school, collywobbles and stomach aches and a neighborhood so nascent there was only one other family nearby.

Let's set the table at the Rhymers': Max Rhymer, the father, engineering estimator for DuPont du Nemours (*Better Living Through Chemistry*), premature gray, stolid and quiet, and solid as a principal (soft inside but not yet); Lolly Rhymer (nee Graves), two years younger than her husband, a Canadian beauty from a family as large as the Mormon Tabernacle Choir, a family of 8 strapping men and 8 lovely women, who made Niagara Falls, Ontario, their own playground, breeding ground, launching ground (hidden depressives but not yet, or not as much so yet); Brack Rhymer, oldest son, eleven at the time of the move, sweet natured except when he's not, ball player, groovy as Donovan on acid (but not yet); AJ Rhymer, youngest child, towhead girl, only 7 months old at the time of the move South, anon, anon.

And our hero Neill. Only five soon to be six on arrival in Memphis. Small, wispy, blond, thin-limbed, shy to the point of wanting to disappear, already convinced life is unfair ever since he found out that *everyone* dies. Even George Reeves. Even Neill Rhymer. What a sucky idea! Already convinced that seeing the neighbor's peepee back in Lewiston was as good as life gets, already convinced that it held the secret if there was a secret, which, at this time, Neill believes there is. (Should we talk here about thanatos and eros? Should we try to shoehorn that in? Make much of it as a Janus head, the opposite sides of the same worn coin [or coinage]? Maybe later...maybe later.) Almost effeminate, but not quite. Bullied and frightened. The opposite of rough and tumble. Ambisinister. The good student. The mother's boy. Called pansy but before that word meant homosexual. Called sullen, brooding, and too delicate. Phrases he is known by (so far, so far); "I've got a stomach ache," his catch-phrase. Tries, he really tries. Let's give him that if he's going to be our hero. He tries.

Transplanted into the Land of the Hottentots

Imagine: Max Rhymer looks out over the property he has just purchased. He has moved his (relatively) young family away from kith and kin and resettled into an area of America that must have seemed to him like Borneo. (The Klan! Whites only bathrooms! Heat like the surface of the sun! Elvis Presley! The Merrymobile!) The small lot on which his house sat also contained 72 trees. 72 trees! He must have looked at it and said, I am no lumberjack (though his father-in-law, Lolly's father Opel ("Open") Graves, was exactly that...there are photographs of Opel at his Canadian lumber camp in the late days of the 19th c.). But I will carve from this suburban tract a yard, a play area, a place for wiffle ball and basketball court and above-ground pool. I will make the Rhymers happy here. As much, as much as it is in my power, amen.

Lolly frets and swears, swears and frets. "For crying in the sink," she cries. "Who will deliver me from this hellhole?" She does not take change well. She thinks perhaps the world is stacked against her. "I swannee to the goodness," she cries. "I didn't want these children. No one here cares if I live or die." She passes this particularly tasty gene down to her middle son. Brack swaggers and goes exploring. It's injun territory! AJ is only the size and shape of a good pungent meatloaf. What she knows or thinks is a mystery akin to the serpent crest of the king's crown on the pillars of Egypt.

And our hero: he weeps and feels sorry for himself. He does not like the heat. He does not like the gravel road (Kenneth Street, dubbed after the builder's oldest son). He does not like feeling that his street is a street unborn, a place where anything could happen, anything dark and dangerous and full of bloodless murder. He has nightmares. He sleeps in his parents' bed often. He shares a room with Brack, who, six years older, might as well be another adult. Or a game show host. Or an astronaut. Our hero feels alone. This is the start of something big. This is the start of something insidious and invasive, and like a worm inside the apple, if we can envision this scrawny little half-Canuck as a piece of thin-skinned fruit. (We do not mean "fruit" in its later context. See "pansy" above.)

Mrs. Legree

For Neill, school at Coleman Elementary is a basket of sores. He is heart-broken. (What do you mean I have to leave home *every day*?) He is frightened of everything. He cries daily. (In his bath he would douse himself with Johnson and Johnson baby shampoo with its promise of 'No More Tears.') He is estranged. He is unmoored and cast adrift and bereft. He weeps. He sits at his little blond desk and weeps. The teacher is not amused. Her name is Mrs. Legree. This is how the leaky boat of memory wants her named. She calls Neill out in front of the class. She says these words, which live inside Neill for the rest of his life, hurtful words that carry with them the weight of the unjust world, the weight of not being in control: *I'll give you something to cry about.*

She takes Neill into the hall and paddles him. He believes he is dying. He feels each stroke of the paddle as if it is jolts of electricity from Thomas Edison's Furniture. He has been taken from his place of refuge and comfort, bussed across wild neighborhood avenues, dumped onto an asphalt place of retribution, over which is an arch with these words in filigree iron: "*Lasciate ogni speranza, voi ch'entrate.*"

He has been thrown out of paradise and jailed in Hell.

Lolly is livid. Lolly, to her credit, wants to jugulate Mrs. Legree.

Still. The lack of justice sits on little Neill like a coat of scobs.

There is consolation, though, small consolation but nevertheless consolation enough to make Neill Rhymer believe in consolation. There is a dark-haired girl with gray eyes, the prettiest girl in the class, and occasionally Neill can see her white panties inside her new school clothes. He spends much time craning his young neck for a repeat of that view. (One would be tempted to say that those white panties were Neill's sexual awakening but, in actuality, this occurred while watching *The Parent Trap* with his parents. When the rear of Hayley Mills' dress is cut away and her white underwear revealed, Neill felt something being born within him for which he had no name, something frightening, something primordial, something fascinating. *This*, he said, I want to explore.) (Ok, maybe that's a little much, but he did feel a noteworthy stirring.) (Later it was Jeannie's navelless midriff and Laura Petrie's undercupping that first set the bugs loose in Neill...whatever.) This schoolgirl with the white panties that make Neill feel hot and a little queasy and insanely curious has a name and that name is Akin Upspins. She is so pretty Neill never talks to her. Neill talks to no one, practically. He misses so much school he almost doesn't pass first grade. The school tells Lolly this. Lolly frets. But pass he does, with all As. Thus, begins a pattern. School is dreadful yet there Neill Rhymer excels. The world is made of such shoddy irony.

The Reids Arrive

The second family on Kenneth Street arrived. Their names: The Reids. They were made to fit the Rhymers the way a crab's shell is made to fit the crab. There was a Mr. and Mrs. There was an older sister named Evening. Really, her name was Evening Reid. She was Brack's age. There was a younger sister named Lessa. Lessa was the same age as Neill. How about that!

As far as the narrators of this story know, Brack and Evening never did much together. Evening may not have been good looking enough for Brack, or vice versa. This is lost to the mist of time.

More important to this tale: Neill and Lessa were inseparable. They fell together like lifelong pals, or as lifelong as six years count. They played together, sometimes games, sometimes with dolls. Neill enjoyed Barbie because of all her accouterment and for her groovy pad. It was cooler than anything G. I Joe had. Neill didn't particularly care for G. I. Joe. Truth be told, Neill didn't care for war stories, even though his father fought in the big Dubya Dubya Dos. Neill didn't like *Rat Patrol* or *Combat*. He liked *Wild Wild West* and *Dick Van Dyke* and *Man from UNCLE* and *The Twilight Zone*, and the Saturday night locally produced monster movie show, *Fantastic Features* with Sivad, your Monster of Ceremonies.

Soon, Neill and Lessa found times and places to show each other their naked bodies. They may have poked or stroked in a very minor way. The thrill was mostly visual.

And, lo! Mrs. Reid, also called Henny, became Lolly's best friend. Henny was from England and Lolly was from Canada, and that may or may not have had anything to do with the friendship. They spent all their time together. Fathers went to work. Mothers stayed home and did housework and minded children and sat at kitchen tables talking about housework and children and President Eisenhower. They loved President Eisenhower.

Henny later died of cancer. It was terrible. She went into the hospital right after she and Evening had had a big blowout fight, which ended with Evening putting her fist through the window in the kitchen door, and then running away. When she returned, bandaged and contrite her mother was in the hospital never to come out. This was a few years later but it needed mentioning now in case events conspire to fog it over.

The Neighborhood

The neighborhood quickly filled with young families much like the Rhymers and Reids, that is, families that were perhaps buying their first or second homes, families just beginning their journey together, and what better place than in a brand-new subdivision. New houses, new lives. New streets, new pathways. New businesses, new consumerism. This is Amerika under the gray bumbershoot of Cold War freedom. Anything can happen! The Land of Opportunity! Don't be a skiver! The Ship of Endless Possibility! Everybody climb aboard!

And because of this there were many children the same age as the Rhymer children. Our hero soon fell in with a grand mob of rough and tumble boys who turned woodland hikes into adventures worthy of Jungle Jim, who played street football and corkball and whiffle ball and basketball. And Neill, neither rough nor tumble, neither athletic nor tough, neither nimble nor confident, was nevertheless taken into the fold. These were wonderful young American males! They made the outsider feel secure. They taught instead of taunted. Let us name them.

There were the Porch boys, four of them. Robert, Lafayette, Chino and Truck. Robert was three years older than Neill and three years younger than Brack. He would become the leader of the gang because he was tough and smart and full of the devil. Lafayette was a gifted athlete, bigger and stronger and just as kind. Chino was closer to Neill's temperament. He did not want to play sports so he stayed inside mostly watching magic shows and reading comic books. Later Chino, as an adult, came out of the closet and, horrors, died of AIDs in California. (We can't even imagine such a thing here in the early 1960s in suburbia so we will let it pass. It is dark and webby and outside our simple ken. *Requiescat in pace.*) And Truck was—surprise!—the same age as AJ. They became fast friends. Their friendship would last the rest of their lives.

So, this neighborhood, this verdant Raleigh on the side of whopping, boisterous Memphis, was a playground designed by seraphim who still understood childhood. There were meandering gravel streets (soon to be paved). There were construction sites where all kinds of gewgaws could be found: nails, lumber, tar bubbles, melted steel, cigarettes, wire, metal slugs to put in Coke machines in lieu of actual lucre, and, best of all, empty pop bottles which could be changed in at Walgreens for *actual* lucre. It became a neighborhood tradition to gather a wagonload of bottles, haul them a sweaty mile to the strip shopping center where there was a Walgreens, get some coins in return and use that money to buy a griddle-fried burger and deep-fried French fries at the Kress counter a few doors down. Once, when Neill needed a sleeping bag to camp out with the Porch boys, the whole group—what grand friends! — collected bottles, wagonload upon wagonload, like a miniature virtuous wagon train, and within a week, the moneys collected were taken to the Western Auto, just a few doors down from Walgreens in the opposite direction, and a beautiful $7 sleeping bag was purchased and hauled back home. Neill was, naturally, so proud of his acquisition that he made a mental note about money: *it buys things.*

The Hobby Shop

In the small township of Raleigh there were places of deep delight: Raleigh Drugs, Rexall Drugs (not quite as great as Raleigh Drugs, where you could get a vanilla coke for a nickel [Neill was renowned for plunging his straw right away into the bottom soup of syrup and gasping with deliriousness at the rich flavor and wondering why he couldn't have a glass with *just* vanilla syrup] and see visiting celebrities like the Duncan Yo-yo Champ and later where you could buy the newest 45s of The Beatles, The Young Rascals, The Bee Gees, The Animals), and, best of all, The Hobby Shop. It was every child's dream emporium. Later, Neill took art classes there (pencil, pen and ink, pastels, water colors) for 3 years, from Ms. Percy Johnson, who was legendary in Raleigh.

But, in his youth, he and the Kenneth Street boys walked the mile to The Hobby Shop because they sought Aurora modeling kits of ships and planes and monsters (Wolfman, Frankenstein, Dracula, The Mummy, The Creature from the Black Lagoon) and The Men from UNCLE. They sought little bottles of paint, also from Aurora, each about the size of a communion glass. And they sought candy and wax lips and greenie stickem caps, plastic sparking guns, Wishniks, Monster Magnets, Jigglers, trick suction cup eyes, kaleidoscopes and Whistling Whizzers and plastic bugs, water rockets, Marx Nutty Mads, modeling clay, and birds that drank from a glass of water — *perpetually*, Slinkys and slingshots and marbles, pencil erasers shaped like cartoon characters, India rubber balls and *Mad Magazines*, Silly

Soap and Soakies, plastic Ratfinks and Matchbox cars, and games like Dexterity Puzzles and Shape Games and Magic Beard. It was a small funky corner of paradise, right next to DeShazzo's Big Star, where mothers bought their weekly groceries and necessities.

The Lord and Neill Rhymer

Not long after the Rhymers settled into their new Southern suburb, Max Rhymer helped Pastor Plenty start Loving Womb Lutheran Church, high on a hill near the intersection of Stage and Austin Peay Highway. (It's still there. Go look!) Max became Vice President of the Church (an office with more responsibilities and duties than its counterpart in national government) and the whole family attended, uh, religiously.

Neill was often moved by church. Just as often he was bored.

Once in his unformed mind he thought that he would like to be a Lutheran minister. He even talked this over with Pastor Plenty.

"What draws you to the ministry," he asked young Neill.

"You only work one day a week," Neill said.

Pastor Plenty laughed. Neill thought he'd given a clever answer until this comment turned up in the pastor's Sunday sermon and Neill burned with humiliation. He never trusted PP again.

Religious training, however, sticks to you no matter whither you go henceforth.

For Neill the idea of the afterlife, the idea that you are being watched and judged, was what stuck. Even through his atheist, his agnostic, his satanic (not really) stages, though he would sometimes deny God, Neill always felt he was being watched. He didn't pray but he believed (to a certain degree) that good acts were rewarded and bad acts punished, even if the punishment was only something earthly like acne, or having to poo when your favorite TV show was on.

This became Neill's vision of God as Cinematic Eye. Consequently, Neill's whole life was a movie with himself as the hero. It was a heady thought. Neill tried his damnedest to be the best Neill Rhymer the comedy/drama required.

Jimbo

"The only thing I wanted to be was grown up. Because I was a terrible flop as a child. You cannot be a successful boy in America if you cannot throw or catch a ball." –Jules Feiffer

One Saturday a classmate, Jimbo, invited Neill to his house. Jimbo was one of the cool kids, a rugged and boisterous boy, who could run fast and jump high. Neill didn't understand why Jimbo had invited him over but he wanted to make the best of it. In-with Jimbo carried a certain status.

In the attic at Jimbo's house things went well. The boys took the motor from Jimbo's Erector Set and stuck it through the bottom of a cardboard bowl. Their idea was that if it spun the bowl fast enough they could throw sugar in there and make cotton candy. They exhausted a good hour just with prep time. Of course, the sugar stayed sugar. The bowl tossed it uselessly around. They didn't understand failure because failure was an adult concept. They moved on with only a small nagging disappointment.

In the afternoon Jimbo wanted to fly his new kite. It was a spectacular kite, a box kite, the first one of its kind Neill had seen. The afternoon was cold and overcast. Jimbo ran through a nearby field, which stretched for eons to the north and south, and the kite soared like a hawk. The sky was a swirl of pewter and moon-shade.

"Here," Jimbo said, handing the string to Neill.

Neill's hands shook. The kite was higher than high.

Neill ran in his fashion, tripping over the uneven ground, his switch-thin legs splaying outward. The kite, a mere half-minute after Neill took control, crashed into the trees, never to be seen again.

That afternoon, when Neill returned home, he dashed to his room and slammed the door. He lay across the bed, weeping for his own ineptitude, for a world which did not welcome him, for the lost possibility of ever being one of the cool kids.

Neill's father came in to comfort him, but Neill couldn't make his father understand what was so awful, so life-ending awful. Young Neill was disconsolate.

Neill and His First Pornography

One day at school one of the coarser boys had a picture. Word spread through the 4th grade that the picture was of something astonishing, almost beyond human comprehension.

It was not described this way. Instead the words used were "a whole naked lady."

Neill did not know the boy well. He saw a small group gathered outside the bathroom in front of the drinking fountain.

Neill sidled over. He was honestly a little frightened.

There were giggles and hushed sounds of admiration and incredulity.

In the group was a boy Neill knew better, a boy who was generally nice.

"Rhymer, come here. Look at this."

Neill offered a brave smile. The boy actually let Neill hold the picture in his hand.

It was black and white. The woman was heavy set but she wore a smile a pastor's wife would have been proud of. She was posed on a shabby couch.

Neill looked for about 3 seconds. He turned away, handed the picture to another boy.

"Thanks," he said, and walked away alone.

Neill had learned something from the picture. Women had hair...*down there.*

It was a revelation. It made Neill a little bilious. It also greased the cogs and wheels, which first began turning when Hayley Mills' underpants entered Neill's concupiscent consciousness.

Innocent Neill, naïve Neill, told his mother about the picture.

"Neill!" Lolly snapped. "Did you look at it?"

Suddenly Neill was as afraid as he had ever been. Tears were threatening to further disgrace him.

"No, Ma," Neill lied. "Some of the other boys told me."

"I've half a mind to go down to that school and have that boy pulled out."

"No! Ma, you can't do that!" Neill was horrified.

"It's illegal what that boy was doing. Did you know that?"

"No, ma'am. Illegal?"

"It's called pornography. I should report the boy."

Pornography, thought Neill. A new word. A word connoting something criminal and—*bewitching*.

"Please don't," a dazed Neill said.

"I won't but don't ever look at a picture like that again, you hear me?"

It was impractical, a Captain Queeg order.

"I won't, Ma," Neill lied.

A Grand Day Out

One Winter Saturday Neill, along with Robert and Lafayette, went on an all-day adventure. Beyond their neighborhood, just South and not too far from where Kenneth Street dead-ended at Stage Road, was cleared land, vast and muddy, and beyond the fields woods, dense and dusky and snaky. This was a darker, wider, wilder place than Bluefield Woods, where the boys had built huts and holes to catch beasts. They hiked southeast through wet, cold woodland. For miles they trudged, never sure where they were going, exploring for the sheer hell of it, for the thrill of feeling unfettered. Like Odysseus, they *wanted* to get lost. They stopped now and then to watch some wildlife, hawks and bobolinks, turtles and moccasins. They stopped briefly at a crude shed at the edge of the woods. There was a lock on the door but it was broken. Inside was a narrow bed with cheap blankets on top. There was a shaky wooden chair and a camp stove.

"Whoa," Robert said.

"I know what this is," Lafayette said.

"What? What?" Neill said, always the student of the Porch boys, who were as intrepid as the Hardys.

"This is where Diomedes brings Winnie Prew to fuck her," Lafayette said.

"Yes," Robert said. "Look he's carved his name on the door."

Neill looked at the crappy bed as if he were seeing the inner hall of Caligula's lair. To have a girl there, even on so narrow a bed. And to touch her everywhere, and to have her touch you, and to put your tally into her slushy, it was more than Neill could comprehend. (This cabin would haunt Neill for the rest of his life and become a symbol for sexual wantonness and desire and freedom.)

The plucky boys walked on and on. It was woods, deep woods, and they had no compass, interior or pocket. They were free and were awfully proud of themselves, b-b guns on shoulders, visions of Tom and Huck in their cloudy sensoria.

Neill was beginning to feel it was the best day of his life so far. He really was maturing. He was one of the boys. He was on a carefree adventure.

Then, as if moving in like a slow storm system, Neill began to feel the edges of a headache, one whose punishing pain would ruin the day. Even as it started to sprinkle and the boys found themselves near open sewer pipes their spirits kept them hiking, undaunted. But Neill was suffering. The headache was obliterating pleasure. It was, in short, ruining the best day of his life.

And here Neill began to suspect that he was the victim of a capricious God, one who would never let Neill have a purely pleasurable day. There would always be a fly in the yogurt. There would always be a smudge to the undergarments. There would always be a cloud behind every silver lining. Neill began to hate the world and his part in it.

Even as the boys emerged from the sewers onto Summer Avenue, miles from their home, and even as they gained admittance to a little diner with a dark interior and rustic chairs and tables, and even as they were served Cokes and griddle-fried hamburgers as if they were adults, Neill was sunk inside himself, ruing his fate, hating his head, his ache, himself.

6th Grade and Dino Danelli

In sixth grade two things conspired to make Neill think he should be a rock and roll musician.

He fell in love with the Rascals (called The Young Rascals at this time) and especially their bombastic drummer, Dino Danelli. Neill went to his first live rock show, at the Mid-South Coliseum. Whoever was the warm-up act is lost to time, but between it and The Rascals, Neill and his friend, Kip, wandered over to the area of seating directly behind the stage. From that vantage point one could look down at the group readying themselves, with preening and herbs, to take the stage. And there, below Kip and Neill stood the Young Rascals. Neill recognized Dino Danelli right off.

"Dino!" he squealed like a girl.

Dino Danelli looked up and waved a drumstick at Neill. Neill was sanctified.

And the second thing was when Neill's brother Brack told Neill that rock musicians get all the girls. He convinced the a-musical Neill that, even though he could never learn music or the intricacies of guitar, electric, acoustic or even bass, he could learn to play the drums. Like all little brothers, Neill thought his big brother was as wise as Solomon and as cool as Jean-Paul Belmondo, so in part to please Brack, this idea took hold.

Neill went once a week to Guitar and Drum City on Summer Avenue and took drum lessons from the drummer of the Gentrys (then enjoying the success of having a record on the radio, "Keep on Dancing"). Neill was awful. He learned to keep a 4/4 beat and that was about all. His parents, meaning well, bought Neill a Sears drumkit, which Neill loved to bang on (much to the chagrin of his across the backyard fence neighbor Mrs. Harp, who called every time, *every* single time Neill "practiced").

Later Neill's second teacher was the drummer of The Shortkuts (then enjoying the success of having a record on the radio, "Your Eyes May Shine"). After about 6 months Neill abandoned the drums and his dreams of getting a girl via the necromancy of rock and roll.

(Later still, Brack told Neill that after rock musicians, writers got the most tail. This was about the time Neill stopped listening to Brack.

Neill Knew it was Supposed to do Something Outré

When Neill was 12 or so his curiosity about sex began to ferment like a saucepan of milk left on the boil. From TV shows and movies he had gleaned some offhand misinformation and half-formed ideas about what went on in the boudoir and he knew it was something that he wanted to do and he wanted to do it badly and better and more often than anyone else.

The only trouble was Neill hardly knew what it was that he wanted to do.

He knew it involved Little Neill. His Little Brother. His Little Man. His *Dick*.

So one afternoon, when no one was home, Neill lay back on his twin bed and thought about girls. He thought about their underwear. He thought about Joey Heatherton's legs. He thought about Faye Dunaway's eyes. He thought about Lola Falana's stomach. He thought about Jeannie's breasts. He thought about Marilyn Monroe, all of Marilyn Monroe.

Nothing much happened.

He thought of Hayley Mills.

It was pleasant and all thinking about these things, but nothing happened. He pulled down his shorts and looked at his equipment. Maybe he didn't have the right equipment. If this were the case, what then? It would be just his luck. His equipment didn't do the job.

Neill held Little Neill gently between two fingers. He had to pee.

So, it was then that Neill had his first fully autonomous sexual experience. He peed on his own stomach.

It was warm and felt pleasant enough as it flowed off his stomach and down his thighs.

He cleaned up with a handkerchief, threw the handkerchief in the dirty clothes basket, and went to watch a Tarzan movie on television.

"Eh," he thought.

The Eighth Grade Dance of Life

One of the local churches, Bartlett United Methodist (BUM), held dances for kids age 13-18. Did they know what they were doing? For Neill it was an opportunity to slow dance and hold a girl in his arms, a girl suffering the same kind of hormone growth occurring naturally inside Neill. Neill attended in both 8th and 9th grade and then quit, partly out of embarrassment (Neill's dancing was akin to the proverbial headless chicken crossed with St. Vitus, his flailing must have occasioned great amusement among the onlookers.) At the time Neill didn't care. He wanted to do his flailing time in order to earn his slow-dance time.

Also, at this occasion some nudniks had discovered mace, not the spice but the cop spray. At numerous dances the basement had to be cleared because someone had let a mace bomb go. It was funny unless you were nearby. It hurt like bejesus.

But, Neill's fondest memories of these dances, was of a young woman named Terri, who, apparently was enamored of Neill. She was plain-faced, with indifferent brown hair, a sweet smile and a body normally reserved for older gals. They sat together when they weren't dancing (sometimes while Neill was fantasizing about dancing with Rita Houston) and chatted and petted. Neill never kissed her but she let his hands roam. Neill could hardly (heh heh) believe his luck.

Pantyhose were popular. Neill would lean toward Terri and talk close to her face and his hand would move up her thigh. Neill thought it was a game. Lord knows what Terri thought. Neill's hand crept upward, seemingly of its own volition, until the dark band at the top of the pantyhose was revealed. Terri smiled and burbled and made small cooing answers to Neill's inane conversation, which was only taking place so Neill could make his heavenly climb, up the beanstalk, toward the giant's riches.

Would Terri have let Neill go all the way to her crotch? Neill would never know because Neill chickened out in his own game of chicken. (See headless chicken above.)

Neill would get exuberant hard-ons from this play and then he and Terri would take the dance floor, and Neill would press his erection against her and let his hands roam over her ass (if caught the church sponsors could kick you out) and he would wonder and wonder what was going on in Terri's 13-year-old brain and, naturally, inside her 13-year-old chemistry set body.

Let's Skip Ahead

Let's skip ahead to Nicholas Blackwell High School in nearby Bartlett, Tennessee (usually referred to as Bartlett High School), where the two Rhymer boys matriculated. If we think of something else about childhood we'll toss it in. We're all friends here. We don't have to be so formal. *Capiche?*

Six years ahead of his younger brother, Brack started high school in 1964 while Neill was next door in Bartlett Elementary in an experimental program called The AT Program, AT standing for Academically Talented. Wherein Neill would be taught by teachers who introduced youngsters on the cusp of puberty using Tom Lehrer records, John Birch Society Meetings, Charles Addams cartoon collections, discussions of films like *Bonnie and Clyde*, the drawing of blood in front of the class (Neill, unafraid of needles, though afraid of almost everything else) was the most willing participant, "spelling baseball" (Neill hit a triple with "Mississippi") and anything else the wild and wide-ranging teachers could think of to stretch young minds. It was a heady time and in that program, instead of taking about *Tom Sawyer* and class projects on fallen empires, Neill invented his first phony anima: Neill wanted to be a hood. His best friend, Pat, was a hood. Pat smoked in 6th grade. All the girls loved Pat. Neill craved such attention. But, where Pat was Belmondo handsome, Neill was only Opie cute.

Deferments and Germination

When Neill was in 8th grade his brother Brack graduated from Nicholas Blackwell High

School. It was 1967, the school's golden anniversary. His girlfriend Rona was still in 10th grade. Rona looked like the Darling daughter on Andy Griffith and came from a similarly sophisticated background.

Brack went away to college at the University of Tennessee at Martin. This would be like saying, "I went to Yale....Yale Barber College." Sorry....Martin is a fine little college, but really, Brack was more interested in getting a student deferment and staying home from that ugly little loblolly known as the Vietnam War than he was interested in being a student. (Apparently, on the other side of the world young men were being fed into a meat grinder, all in the name of an abstract concept, which Neill did not understand [if anyone did].) Brack was, however, heartsick at being separated from Rona.

Brack didn't do well at Martin. He snuck home a lot to see his gal. She mattered more to him than Anthropology or the Romantic Poets.

Of course she got pregnant.

At the time this was a crisis, in the Rhymer household, similar to the Missiles of October. To young Neill it was disturbing on a level that he was a long way from being mature enough to understand. To Brack it was the end of the world. He was 19 and he had to quit college to marry Rona who had to quit high school.

And, guess what? His student deferment went kaput. It fell like a soufflé after a loud noise, the noise, say, of machine-gun fire. Could he file another deferment, this time for being a young father and husband? No such thing as a backup deferment, our government, in their infinite empathy informed him. Brack was working for $1 an hour at an Esso station. He had a pregnant wife and a room in his parents' home, where there was little, if any privacy, and the prospect of Vietnam (or as Kenny Roger's called it "that old crazy Asian war") staring at him. Scary shit, right?

The night the parents drove out to inform Rona's unrefined (country as a yellow egg) family that their son had impregnated their 16 year old daughter the atmosphere in the Buick was something like the waiting room to Hell. No one spoke. Everyone was sick with fear. Hell is other people, Brack might have thought if he had read No Exit by that time (he had not). And, a really specific hell is other people who are related to you and whom you have disappointed.

Outside Rona's home Brack and Max stood, leaning against the car. The night ticked around them like a dusty clock. Inside the house Lolly and Rona were still sitting over weak coffee and stale store-bought cookies, commiserating, shaking their heads, trying to waggle the Etch-a-Sketch into making a new picture.

Brack felt his father's silence as if it were inside his lungs. A steely, gray silence. Thunderheads inside Brack's torso.

Then Max's head moved slightly in Brack's direction. Brack braced himself. He thought his heart was about to be pierced. And it was, but not in the way he had expected.

Max slapped a backhand to Brack's chest and said this, in a tone miraculously light:

"You did it this time, didn't you?"

Father was smiling. Son let out a year's worth of air. Brack let out all the air he had in him. Brack found new air and let it out, too. Brack, though airless, was experiencing something close to salvation: the love of a parent for a child, regardless of how dire the circumstance.

To cut to the chase, a neighbor, who somehow had strings to pull, got Brack into the Air

Force. This meant overseas but probably not Vietnam (Brack did a year in Thailand later). This meant life instead of death, perhaps. The next thing that happened was that the draft board called and said, "Hey, Bud, here's your ticket to the Gulf of Tonkin. Have a nice trip!" To which Brack replied: "Thanks ever so much, but my family and I are going to San Antonio, Texas, Lackland Air Force Base, for my basic training."

And, they did.

Seriously, Let's Skip Ahead

Entering 9th grade, having graduated next door from Bartlett Elementary, Neill was full of trepidation. The high school was so much larger. The students were so much larger. The halls in the main building (un-air-conditioned, built in 1917, it looked like a cross between San Simeon and the Munster's house) were dusky and dusty and the crowds between classes could crush you, could run you over like a bunny on a country lane. Neill was full of trepidation.

Now, let's clarify something if it's not already clear. Neill had a rough childhood, partly, due to his being wee and pusillanimous and the bullies who attend such young American males. But, in 7th and 8th grade a few things happened which helped Neill grow a spine. It helped him get over himself a bit. One, he was given a position on the boys' basketball team. The position was the end of the bench but that didn't matter. The forward-thinking coach, Kirby Gann, allowed any boy willing to go through his rigorous practices to stay on the team. Neill could shoot a bit, but he could not dribble and other players made him nervous. He coughed up the rock like a cat coughs up hairballs. In short, he was horrible. But he stuck with the team and the team stuck with him and at the end of the year he got a letter, a fabric "B" which is now lost to time, like those great Beatles Capitol 45s his mom sold in a carport sale. This gave Neill a modicum of confidence. (The team thing and the letter thing, not the loss of his 45s.)

Also, Neill discovered another way to be popular. Listen: In the 60s, in The United States of America, boys were one way or they were thrown outside into the wagon-rutted street. They should be tough. Athletic tough. Nothing else mattered. Since Neill wasn't, he spent a long time in the dust of the street while gunslingers walked past him as if he were horse dung. But, things began to loosen up when Neill discovered he could gain some cachet with a smartass mouth. So, he became a class clown. He became a sarcastic, caustic, mordant, sardonic, acerbic, ironic, weisenheimering, captious smartass. Girls laughed. Girls laughed and talked to him after class. This was the beginning of something both splendid and troublesome. Many things in life are both splendid and troublesome. This, which began, was one of them.

So, Neill survives 9th grade. He's even made some friends who would remain friends for the rest of his life. Imagine that.

One of these friends is Thistle Sharer. Thistle sat in front of Neill in the 9th grade English class where Neill would first start to think about books and authors and how writing poems might get him into girls' pantaloons. And, one of Neill's memorable japes from this English class was to write little love notes on the straps of Thistle's bras through the holes in her lacy shirts. You might question how such a sophomoric (nay, Freshmanic) joke would be memorable but if you were to ask Thistle about it today she would still laugh. God bless her.

Thistle and Neill became inseparable. She became, quite simply, his best friend. Neill had always been drawn to female best friends and Thistle, we might say, is the template for these. She is the ur-female friend. And around these two friends many friends gathered. You'll see.

More About Thistle Sharer

The Sharers lived just up the street from the Rhymers, straight ahead, jog right, jog left, on Joslyn Street. There were 4 girl children and two delightful parents. There was a rec room (sometimes called 'The Secret Cave' as if they were in a Nancy Drew mystery) set aside for the girls and their friends. This room, this inner sanctum, became the unofficial (maybe even official) meeting place for the many young men and women drawn into the charmed circle of the Sharer household and its denizens. Mrs. Sharer taught at Bartlett High School, what was called Football Player English, where she was loved like the Sun by the Heavens. Mr. Sharer was the stern end of all questions, like many men of his generation. He frightened some of the gatherers. Mostly not. Most saw through his gruff demeanor to the jokester within.

The group, anywhere from 6 to 18 folks, was made up of a pretty heady bunch of high schoolers, whip-smart and funny, and really quite lovely young people. The talk was lively, the laughter raucous and sincere. Fellow feeling ran high, even though no one suffered a fool and this sometimes intimidated Neill. It also helped Neill to realize a sort of personal uprightness and integrity that he carried with him for the rest of his life. There was a catch-phrase the group employed like a cauterizing flame: *are we acting?* This was often said when it appeared someone had climbed too high on his or her horse, or if someone spoke, ingenuously about just about anything: books, politics, love, drugs, if he or she was not embodying authenticity, in word and deed. *Are we acting?* And suddenly you were thrust into a powerful self-examination, even if your ego was bruised, your embarrassment profound. Neill felt lucky to have fallen into this particular nest. And, the relationship with Thistle was *mostly* asexual. (More later.)

The other sisters were as follows: Laney, one year older than Thistle. Sadie, one year younger than Thistle, and where all the Sharer females were lovely, Sadie was as sexy as a flame. And the youngest Roo, who had youngest child syndrome and was often not in the rec room proper when new LPs were being played (The Doors, Fever Tree, King Crimson, Jethro Tull, Tommy, Jesus Christ Superstar) and new games begun (hearts, Yahtzee, backgammon, Monopoly).

Some hot summer afternoons in The Secret Cave it was only Neill and Thistle and Sadie. Neill, horny as an alley cat, often went in hopes of one of the sisters being as curious about sex as he. Neill (to his shame later) used to wear shorts with loose leg holes. He would position himself opposite Thistle or Sadie or both and part his legs in a lotus sitting position and conspire to make sure his testicles could be seen. He kept waiting for this to arouse something excitable in the sisters' furtive places. Alas, the summer passed and no one wanted to stroke Neill's Arabian goggles.

There was amongst this group a young man whom we will call Jeff. Perhaps his name really was Jeff. He lived around the corner from the Sharers and was about to enter Bartlett High

School as a freshman. Hence, he was Sadie's age. Jeff was popular in the Sharer household. He was loud and nice and funny and the kind of rough and tumble fella the gals go fer. Neill liked him immediately, even sensing in him an opposite, a complementary personality.

It was one sere summer afternoon in The Secret Cave. Cards were being played. Perhaps it was hearts. Perhaps it was a game concerning a less precarious organ. Conversations began, broke off, ran aground, circled for a landing, sputtered. Jeff had brought his 8th grade annual from Brownsville Road School, a feeder for Bartlett High. Jeff was showing Neill some of the young people who would soon be freshmen to his sophomore. Neill aimlessly glanced at the young, young faces. Children.

Until he was arrested by one bright, shiny face. Arrested like a second-story man stuck on the first story. This bright shiny face belonged to a young lass named Candy Markham. She had eyes. She had a sloppy-mouthed smile. She had blond hair and little side curls like Jews wear. She was, in short, as pretty as the surface of the sea.

"Who is she?" Neill asked. He stabbed the picture with his pointer. He didn't even try to tamp down his enthusiasm. He was among friends.

"Candy," Jeff (we think his name was Jeff) said. "Yes. She's quite cute."

"Cute doesn't touch it. Cute, standing on an OED and tiptoes doesn't touch it. She is Aphrodite," Neill said.

"I know where she lives," Jeff said.

And hence began something else that would come to define Neill's young manhood: he was a bold marauder. If he saw a female who transfixed him he did not feign a non-transfixed state. He went after her like Clete Boyer after a hot grounder. Candy was a hot grounder.

I Want Candy

Neill places himself on the Markham's doorstep one summer evening. He rings the bell with all the swagger of a pirate or Mormon. The door opens and it is a woman, an older woman. Neill rightly believes her to be Candy's mother.

The bold marauder. (We'll return to this theme later.)

"Hi," our Neill says. "Is Candy home?"

"Yes," the pretty mother says, still holding the door, smiling at Neill, waiting for something else. Neill doesn't know what the something else is. He feels, for the first time, a strum of nervousness behind his sternum. Perhaps this was a bad idea. Perhaps he will be arrested. Perhaps adults can read the minds of 14 year old boys and Neill will be rightly condemned.

"Come in," the smiling mother now says.

Neill exhales.

Neill is shown into the living room, the very first room in the house, just to the right of the front door. Not to foreshadow too heavy-handedly, Neill remembers this room in the Markham's house for the rest of his life and he often looks back and thinks, I never made it past that living room, as if the rest of the house implied some sort of intimacy denied him.

Candy Markham now stands before him, a figure from the mist like the transformed Kim Novak materializing from the mist of Jimmy Stewart's impassioned desires. Neill rises from the couch. The look on Candy's face is sphinxlike. Her jaw is set. But her pretty gleeps are sparkling. She is even cuter in person though she looks exactly like her annual photo.

"Do I know you?" she manages.

"I am a friend of Jeff's (that is his name)," Neill says, a clownish smile on his mug. "Neill."

"Oh," Candy Markham says.

"I better explain."

"Ok," Candy Markham says.

"Can we sit?"

They sit. Neill back on the couch. Candy on a chair a safe distance away in case Neill is an alien species and something like a toothy maw will open in his chest and will attempt to swallow Candy.

"I saw your picture in Jeff's annual. I know you are gonna be a freshman at Bartlett next year. That is the extent of my knowledge of you. I will be a sophomore."

Neill waits. The first sentence is out. The clock is still ticking.

"I sort of fell for your picture." Neill is proud of the phrasing. He waits.

Slowly, a smile spreads across Candy's sloppy mouth. She really has the most deliciously sloppy mouth.

"Are you for real?" she asks.

Candy and Neill

Readers, he kissed her. His first real osculation. On her parents' couch in that little living room just off the foyer. He put his mouth on her sloppy, wet, big-lipped, soft mouth and he moved it around a bit and she moved hers around a bit. This was the most erotic thing that had ever happened to Neill. And, oh, he fell hard. She was so pretty! Those eyes! Those Jewish curls! Her mop of blond hair!

(This smoodge was not that first meeting but later, after some phoning and some cajoling.)

Many nights followed. More osculation. What else were they going to do? Neither were old enough to drive. There were no summer parties to go to. So, they sat on that couch and rubbed lips for a fortnight or more. Neill was gaga.

Not so much Candy, apparently. Before school started she begged out of the "relationship" though they had done little relating. Neither knew much about the other. Except that making out was a gas. It was heavenly.

Candy broke it off because, she said, her parents didn't like how often they were together. If they knew they were licking each other's lips they would have broken it off sooner.

Neill sans Candy

So, tenth grade started with Neill adrift, Neill atrabilious, Neill heartbroken and sure the world stood unified against him. This was one of Neill's most prominent personalities. Hangdog. Dead, hanged dog. Killed by the world's indifference and Candy Markham's insouciance.

We may sigh at such drama now. When you're 15 such drama is your life. It consumes you. And it makes the tale sorta sticky and sad. We don't want to read too much about sticky and sad.

There was another young woman. Jeff introduced them.

She was also a freshman. Her name was Brooks Shock.

Brooks was gorgeous and she dressed better than most ninth-grade girls. She had style. It was a sexy style, too. And, Brooks had beautiful legs.

Jeff told Neill that Brooks was rather theatrical. Neill instead found her to be friendly and warm and funny and spicy. And Neill loved her legs, which she showed a lot. It was the era of short skirts and hotpants. Hot pants. Hot. Pants.

Neill and Brooks (and Sly)

Second verse, same as the first. A little bit flashier and a little bit worse.

Neill walked to Brooks' house many nights. The walk took him through Raleigh's circuitous streets. It took him through a crab apple orchard. Listen to this, if no one has told you before: the idea of the crab apple is better than the taste of the crab apple.

Neill's trek to Brooks' house was the same trek he had been making much of his life. It was on the way to Raleigh, to Walgreens and Kress and Western Auto.

The Shocks' house was much like the Markham's. There was a couch in a living room. There was a record player where Brooks and Neill listened to new platters by this new heavy group called Led Zeppelin. And to Crosby Stills and Nash. And to The Zombies.

Kissing Brooks was pure gratulation. She was palpably sexy. And she put her tongue in Neill's mouth! This was a first! Neill didn't know what to think. Naïve Neil thought perhaps this meant that Brooks was fast. Did he want a girlfriend who was *fast*? Was she fast? He didn't know whom to ask.

Enter Neill's new best friend, whom he first met in The Secret Cave. His name was Sly Jawell. He was large, where Neill was small. He was dark where Neill was light. He was loud and funny, where Neill was quiet and funny. They loved each other immediately. Sly came from a large, intellectual family and trips to Sly's house could be both stimulating and fear-provoking. Neill, never that confident about his own smarts, tended to stay quiet and listen. More about this later.

And Sly was a year older than Neill, though they were both sophomores in high school, Sly at Raleigh Egypt because he lived one street outside the Bartlett jurisdiction. So, Sly could drive. He could drive his family's second car, a Pokey-orange Pinto. It was Freedom! It was Adventure!

"Brooks puts her tongue in my mouth," Neill says.

"Fantastic!"

"Yes," Neill hedges. "I should probably put mine in hers as well."

"Yes," Sly says, thoughtfully. "It seems only fair."

"I guess I like it when she does that."

"Yes, I can see that."

"I'll put my tongue in her mouth tonight."

And Neill did. And it all went swimmingly. And Neill was having the time of his life with young Brooks Shock.

A Surprise!

This surprise should have been mentioned earlier though it is not germane, narratively, until now. Remember Akin Upspins, the prettiest girl in first grade at Coleman Elementary? She is also a sophomore at Bartlett High School. Actually, she was a freshman there too and Neill was aware of her but also a little shy about approaching her. She lived only one street over from the Sharers but she was not part of The Secret Cave. There is no good reason why she wasn't. Relationships cohere or they do not. They collect moss or momentum, or turn from a snowball into an avalanche, or they do not.

Suddenly, Neill is very aware of her. She is making eyes at him. She is initiating conversations with him, wherein she fumbles with her words and casts her eyes to East West North and South and does not meet Neill's. Neill, though naïve as we've already discovered, understood that Akin had a crush on him.

In the hierarchy of high school everyone knows, relatively, where they stand and who stands on top and who forms the base of the pyramid. Akin Upspins was a cheerleader, or she became one sometime during her sophomore year. Neill, watching her cheer, felt a new stirring within him. This young woman, this Akin Upspins, this cheerleader, this upper floor dweller, this prettiest-first-grader, had a crush on him. How about that?

However, there was still Brooks. Still Brooks ran deep. Neill didn't know what to do. He went to Sly.

"I think this cheerleader, this Akin Upspins, has a crush on me."

"I've seen her. She's prettier than an ewer."

"I know. And, she's a cheerleader."

"So you said."

"I am a boyfriend already."

"That is a dilemma."

The two friends studied the situation, separately, quietly.

"I'll break up with Brooks," Neill responded.

"I think that would be best," Sly responded.

Neill is a Heel

Neill broke things off with Brooks. He did it with little regret at the time. I mean, this was Akin Upspins, the prettiest girl in first grade, the cheerleader with eyes the color of the sea at dusk.

The conversation probably went something like this:

"Brooks, I'm sorry. I won't be coming over anymore."

"Wha?"

"You know, we're young. I gotta move around some. Find myself."

"Are you shipping out with the Merchant Marine?"

"Well, no, no, nothing like that?"

"Spiritual journey? Two years on a bike in short sleeves and a tie?"

"No, Brooks. I'm sorry."

"You said that."

"I just, you know, I just think it's too early to be tied down. I can't even drive a car yet."

"You found a better girlfriend."

"Better? How do you mean better?"

"Better for your standing in high school. Better for your rep."

"Brooks."

"Forget it. Move on. I expected you to."

"You did."

"Sure. You liked the kissing well enough."

"I did."

"You only put your tongue in my mouth once."

"I don't understand."

"Forget it."

"I'm sor—"

"Just leave, Neill."

"Brooks."

"I'll find out who the next girl is shortly, I am sure."

And, of course, she did. Neill went from Brooks' house to Akin's. He asked Akin if she wanted to go for a walk. Akin did. That was how it started, the first major love affair of Neill's life.

One More Thing about Sophomore Year

There was a teacher of English composition named Ms. McGoff. She looked like a slightly homelier Catherine Deneuve. She tried hard, Ms. McGoff did, but she was a bit of a goof. She misused the language she was trying to fine-tune for a bunch of whelked teens.

She teetered between a military bearing and a nearly sexual desire for acceptance.

But.

But she also started something Day One Sophomore Year, something that was like a seed spilled upon dry ground that nevertheless found a small foothold, if you can stand those mixed metaphors. She asked each student to keep a journal and twice a week to put something inside it. Something, anything, as Todd Rundgren said.

Indolent Neill, most weeks, copied down Beatle lyrics. Or jokes he had heard on television.

However.

However also Neill sometimes scribbled little verses in his journal, verses based on renowned poems and song lyrics and filtered through his burgeoning sexuality and milk-fed awkwardness.

This was Neill Emergent. The beggarly, amorphous commencement of Neill as Writer.

Neill and Akin, Commencement

"The sixteen year old girl was not the Woman with Golden Hair, but the boys didn't know that. They saw what they saw: they saw the Track of the Moon on the Water and were deliciously confused."Robert Bly

Now, Neill split his evenings between The Secret Cave and Akin's house. Akin's parents were strict as Sultans and they didn't really want Neill coming around. A compromise was reached and he was given permission to visit every other night and on weekend nights. Sometimes, weekend nights ended up being outings with Sly or with the Porch brothers, Robert and Lafayette. And, on Kenneth Street, a new boy had arrived, the same age as both Neill and Lafayette, another sophomore now at Bartlett. Kenneth Street was a magnet for boys Neill's age. (Why?)

This new boy was named Hawker Mikart. He was from someplace like Tupelo or Indianola or Bugtussle. He was athletic, even a better basketballer than Lafayette, and he was as handsome as a mastodon. He had Paul Newman blue eyes and was indeed known as 'Our Paul Newman,' or 'Bartlett's Paul Newman.' He was also funny and as kind as autumn twilight.

Let's say this: Neill always preferred going to Akin's. Even over the heady confabs in The Secret Cave. And here's why: Neill was a girl watcher. He had always been. Nothing was as pretty as a pretty girl to Neill, not even an eighteen-foot jump shot. And now there was something new going on: Neill and Akin were petting pretty heavily. Neill now understood that the tongue in the mouth was a prerequisite and a nice spur to warmer attentions.

Neill's naiveté was losing ground to his experience.

One could do worse than a cheerleader for one's first sex. Their bodies are compact and strong and full of the kind of energy wasted on mortals. Neill loved Akin's gray eyes, her pert mouth, her darkling hair. And now Neill had something new to love: Akin let Neill cup her breasts. At first just over the bra. They were little wonders! About the size of a kitten's head and that soft, with little nipply nipples. Neill thought this was just about the greatest thing that had ever happened to him. He was feeling a cheerleader's wubbly little breasts!

Now, let's clarify this about Neill. The only orgasms he had experienced so far were nocturnal emissions during dirty dreams, from which he awoke feeling shameful and sullied. Literally sullied since he had to clean himself and stuff the underwear deep in the laundry basket. What if his mother found out he had done *that* while asleep? What if she told the pastor of the church? What if she told Neill's dad? He was certain Lolly would send him to the Snake Pit. It was too awful to contemplate.

So, when Neill became erect while kissing Akin Upspins he was sure she would be horrified if she knew. Have we mentioned Neill's simplicity before? Neill had only recently learned how copulation worked. And how had he learned? He read it in *Everything You Always Wanted to*

Know About Sex but Were Afraid to Ask. Up until then he thought men entered a woman's anus. He thought that was what was going on with dogs. Once he had asked his parents point blank: How is it that once people get married they have babies? Is it something to do with the church service?

And his parents looked at each other. They looked at each other a couple times. Neill's father put down his John D. MacDonald novel. "Ahem," he said. Neill's mother rested her knitting hands over her wool. She looked at the wool. It might have come from one of the Savior's lambs. Then Neill's mother spoke to break what was an unbearable chasm of silence:

"You'll find out one day."

Hooray! Neill thought. A mystery that only adults knew. A mystery so mysterious adults could not even impart the answer to children.

Ok, back to the story: Neill did, by this time, understand what went where and why. He was terribly nervous about it, though. He wasn't sure he really wanted to put himself inside someone else and he was certain that the girl wouldn't like it.

So, here he is, making out with Akin on her parents' couch in the downstairs den. Her parents went to bed early. What did they think the kids were doing downstairs alone in the dark? Whatever could they think?

They were doing this: tongue kissing and breast squeezing.

Meanwhile Back at the Cave

Meanwhile, Neill was still spending a lot of time at the Sharer's. One Friday night, when Akin was forced to attend something with her family, her little brother Tiny's piano recital or some such, Neill walked to the Sharer's after having commensal time with his family.

Since it was a Friday the usual gathering had expanded by half. Besides every Sharer daughter, Sly and his brother Gulley were there; Sweeney Waterman, Sam Onides, the president of the Bartlett Student Council; Lindley Crouse, Thistle's best friend; Jeff; Boot Romney (later head of the Memphis branch of The Moral Majority, later still jailed for 'transporting zoo animals across state lines for immoral purposes'); Sadie Sharer's boyfriend, Topsy; some guy from Laney's church, who was wearing a beret, a white dress shirt and a dickey, and a nametag that said "Sophocles." No one ever really got the full story on who he was. At the end of the evening Laney said to Gulley, "I thought he came with you."

This was the kind of gathering that normally sent Neill into his shell of silence. Sam Onides was a big bear of a man, Greek and swarthy and full of brio and good will, with a wit as sharp as a poniard. He and Gulley were close. Gulley was big, too, but taller and athletic. He played quarterback for the Bartlett Panthers, while Sam played center. Gulley was Nick Nolte handsome. He was quiet, unlike his brother Sly, but when Gulley spoke it usually withered someone nearby. Sweeney Waterman was heavy-set but not fat, smart as Shakespeare and almost as funny. His wit was caustic, cynical, way past cool. For some reason he liked Neill and Neill thought Sweeney Waterman was the steeliest human being he had, up to this point, called friend. But, Neill was also cowed by these three magnificos. He let them be the show.

Sly laughed and goofed around with them, sometimes joining them in, *mostly*, good natured ribbing of Neill. Neill burned, smiled and burned.

But, on this Friday night Neill was feeling a bit more like a functioning male human being. It was the nearness of the sexual act instilling him with self-assurance and loosening his normally reluctant tongue.

After the Sharer parents went to bed the party moved to the den because *Mr. Roberts* was coming on the late show. The Jawel family (there were 3 other siblings) took this movie personally and no one was allowed to talk during the show except during commercials. A significant quantity of Ding Dongs, Nacho Doritos, popcorn and other salty or sweet snacks were consumed.

During one exchange between Jack Lemmon and Powell, Topsy asked if he could see what else was on. Everyone in the room froze. Sadie tried to hide behind a pillow.

Gulley fixed Topsy with a crushing scan. Sam started to speak as well, but Gulley was faster.

"There *is* something else on, Pressed Rat. It's on back at your house," Gulley said.

There was one snigger. Two.

There was a brief snort. A near laugh.

And then, general merriment spread around the room, like a wave. In the end even Topsy laughed and sat back down by Sadie, who looked at him as if he was a puppy that had just shit on the carpet. After the movie, the conversation swirled freely and there was camaraderie in the room that was infectious and joyful.

"Tell everyone what you and Akin Upspins have been up to," Sly said at one point.

"Naw, now," Neill said. "No one—"

"But we would, we do want to hear. What about you and the lithe cheerleader? Tell us all," Sly said.

Neill's blood flowed through his veins. It must have gone near his brain. It must have flowed into and out of his heart like a potent brew.

"I can't kiss and tell," Neill said, even as Thistle seemed to draw away from him. "But let's just say that a cheerleader's flexibility is not a bad testing ground for a young swain's newborn proclivities."

This may be what Neill said. Perhaps he didn't use those exact words. Still he had opened up his intimate gemstone box and let the gang observe. Later he was both proud and ashamed. Because he is human. Neill is human. A human, he (or she) can be simultaneously proud and ashamed. Indeed, maybe the two at times go hand in hand, or fist in glove.

Things Heat Up as Things Will

It's later. School has been a blur, even more so than usual. Neill hiked the halls lost in the joy that is like a treasure hid in a field. His little noggin was full of Akin. And she was heavily smitten, too, though Neill was not sure why. Remember: Neill has a poor self-image. Ok.

On Wednesday evening Akin's parents were monopolizing the downstairs. They had fed Neill and they expected the young people to hang around and converse. Neill never could think of something appropriate to say to Akin's parents. Possibly because all he wanted to do was experiment with Akin's fragrant form.

The youngsters were trying to expand their sensual accomplishments, with no real knowledge of what to do, and with great disquiet. They pushed the envelope in strange and myriad ways. Was there a reliable manual or what to do when and how? Their making out, which could take place on the couch, in the car, even on the front porch, was proceeding along some fairly eccentric lines. Ever since Neill discovered that the tongue was one of his best implements he wanted to put it everywhere. They had already explored each other's oral cavities at great length, the orbicularis oris, upper gum, lower gum, hard palate, soft palate, incisors, molars, the palatine uvula. They had tongued each other's ears, necks and, finally, nostrils. This was a ferocious experiment (and something never repeated in all the years of concupiscence Neill was to experience later) and they were somewhat proud of this novel undertaking. Their tongues spoke a new language: *can I go in here?*

But, on this mousy autumn evening, the pair found themselves in the Upspins' back yard, backs against the brick wall directly underneath the kitchen window. They were sitting on cruel, cold concrete. Akin's mother was washing dishes directly over their heads and the yellow glim fell just beyond their outstretched legs. They felt cloaked in darkness. They felt alone in the world. They were Adam and Eve. The starshine twinkled above them; they twinkled below.

They were licking each other as always and their hands were also trying to expand the repertoire. On this particular evening Neill was able to unsnap Akin's bra and let it fall away from her round little bobbers, underneath her velvety sweater. Her breasts were soft as the gospels and they were capped by little acorn nipples. Neill bent himself into an awkward position, head sideways burrowing insensate through coats and other garments, so that he could suck there. What pleasure! What electricity ran straight through Neill and Akin both!

When Neill popped back up his mouth was wet and rident. He was so delighted!

Akin smiled, too. And she must have felt challenged because what she did next was bold as love.

Neill was wearing thin double-knit slacks. He was doubly cold on the unforgiving patio concrete. He also had a bonk-on that, if it hadn't been dark, would have stood like a beacon for lost clippers. He was still unsure whether this was a good thing or a bad thing. Should he try to hide it from Akin? Would she be appalled?

No, Akin was not appalled.

Before Neill could catch his breath after breastfeeding Akin's sweet cheerleader hand was rubbing the front of his pants. His dofunny leapt forward like a dik-dik. Oh, the pleasure that coursed through it! Did Akin know what she was doing? Did Neill? Do humans ever?

Neill began to pant. He began to shimmy and shake. Akin was excited. She rubbed and rubbed, knuckled the bulge, pulled on it, pounded it with her palm. Neither knew if this was the right way to go about this. But, soon, too soon, Neill shot off inside his pants and a spreading moist spot grew and grew, like a magical stain, like Rapunzel's hair unloosed. His pants were soaked from snap to knee.

"What happened?" Akin said.

"I squirted sperm from my penis," Neill responded.

"Wow," Akin responded.

"I know."

"Now what?"

"I don't know. I guess I better go home and change clothes."

"Ok."

"I'll see you tomorrow first thing, outside Mrs. Appleby's room."

"Ok. Did I do it right?" Akin said.

"It would appear so," Neill said, earnestly. And he kissed her hard.

Walking home, the evening air chilly on his saturated crotch, Neill thought that he had entered a brave new world. This was what it was all about. This is life. This is why we are here, to make each other come.

Interleaving

Wait: There is a progression. It should be addressed. The thrill of first contact, that sweaty hand on thigh, the initial moist kiss, the stroke of a cheek, that full body embrace: these are elements of courtship both eternal and fleeting, both spectacular and fragile, both long-lasting and, oh so transitory. Because the hand on the thigh—how it thrills that first time—once it has drunk its fill it must desire to move. To move higher, closer, deeper, *inside*. It wants inside because we want inside. We are wired that way. Innocence is quickly abandoned for more thrills, richer pleasures, further venturing into unexplored areas. The kisser must necessarily long to be the maker-of-love, the fellatrix, the penetrator, eventually desiring nothing more than the furthest corners of taboo. We cannot mourn the loss of the sweet, fleeting pleasure of the first kiss, the first hand on the small of the back. We must celebrate the lovers who eventually find how they fit together, limb to limb, mouth to mouth, genitalia to genitalia. The same way once you have success in your chosen field, success you never thought would be yours, you celebrate, congratulate yourself, rest on your laurels a bit and then—*then*—you want more success, whatever the next step up the ladder is. We are not satisfied with stasis in any aspect of our lives and, sexually, this is truer than most other precepts.

How are We Gonna Keep Them in Class After They Have Tasted the Nectar of Immortality?

Now, each school day was only to be endured until the dark should come and free the young folks to once again experience that overarching bliss. Now, the regulations the Upspins put on the couple's time together seemed cruel and unusual punishment. The night immediately after the night of their first orgasm became a pitched dinner-time battle between Akin and her parents. In the end, in tears, Akin won out and Neill was granted the extra school night visit. When he heard the good news he could barely finish his own dinner. He may have had homework that night. If he did, it went hasta la bye-bye.

Skin was on his mind.

The walk to Akin's was practically a sprint. It was less than a mile but it seemed to take most of the evening. Feet don't fail me now, Neill sang to himself. We only have these few hours to live.

Once at the Upspins it was all Neill could do to greet the parental units and move into some place of privacy away from them with his love, his *chere amie*, his bizzo, his sexual partner, the gray-eyed cheerleader of his dreams. Underneath the kitchen window now seemed like a foolish idea, dodgy, because they knew now what they were hiding.

They walked the cove in which the Upspins' home resided. It was all homes and lawns and porch lights. Except.

Except there was a little copse of trees near the opening of the cove where it joined the larger road, Scheibler. There was a small plot of land that the landscapers and urban planners had failed to fit into the subdivision's plans. It was neither lawn nor public park. It was a piece of leftover turf with a group of trees making about 20 square feet of darkness. Sweet leafy, shrubby, scrubby, fertile, lush, thriving darkness. Into this boscage they skipped like Hansel and Gretel (without the incest that implies), holding sweaty hands, hearts beating like the brain of Haste. Forgive them for they knew not what they were doing.

They lay among leaves and shadowy branches on ground only slightly softer than the macadam streets. Slim traces of starlight fell through the trees like gossamer. Their autumn jackets were cumbersome. Their limbs were straining to make more connection to their main frames. They wrestled and snorted and slobbered and their hands ran wild.

Neill unbuttoned Akin's glossy white shirt. He unsnapped her bra and pulled it away, laying it gently beside them. It was the fullest look he had had of his love's white boosiasms. They were the size and exact shape, each of half a whiffle ball. Their young nipples winked at him in the dim. He sucked there like a young calf. Akin was panting. Neill was pretty sure this was good. He wasted no more time above. He knew where he wanted to go. He unsnapped her jeans and, with Akin's initially reluctant help, pulled them to her knees. He ran his hand fully over her panties front and rear. Her thin-sheathed beam felt as fine as anything he had ever felt. She was taut and firm from cheering, and her thighs and ass were both soft and firm. The front of her panties, between those ripe little thighs, was wet (Had she had an accident? Neill would understand if she had.) Now Akin was panting to beat the band.

Neill slipped the panties down to meet the pants. Akin drew in a breath. She was shaking, perhaps from cold, perhaps from fear.

It was dark but Neill could see her black pubic hair against her white skin. He ran his hand through it. It was soft! Neill had the idea that it might be wiry. And then—then—his fingers found the source of the dampness. Her hole was dripping wet! Neill put a finger inside her. She bucked as if he had introduced electricity into her nether regions. He moved the finger in and out. She bucked some more. This was a fine game! He moved his finger in and out, rapidly, slowly. He waggled it around inside her as if he were mixing chocolate milk. She was gasping and—perhaps—trying to speak.

"N-n-n—"she was saying.

Neill was bent to his work like a mad scientist. Suddenly, Akin went stiff and arched her back and went completely silent. It scared hell out of Neill. He stopped. He looked into her eyes except they were squeezed shut.

"Akin," he said, softly.

She was silent.

Oh, my God, I've killed her, Neill thought. But, no, she was breathing. Neill watched her small snowy breasts rising and falling. Then, Akin's eyes popped open.

"You ok?" Neill asked.

"Y-yes," Akin said. She was gathering herself. "I think I had an orgasm. Just like you."

"Wow," Neill said.

They lay there in silence for a few moments. Then Akin pulled her panties and jeans back up but did not secure them.

"Now you," she said.

"Really?" Neill asked, but he was already unbuckling his pants. Akin waited as if he was prepping the area for her assault.

Neill pulled his pants down past his knees so he could open his thighs, but he left his underwear on.

"Should I pull those down too?" he asked.

"I think so," Akin said.

He did. And his erection seemed intent on finding the North Star through the branches of the surrounding oaks and elms and hackberry saplings.

Akin put her hand around it. The lid of Neill's head came off. He grabbed it and re-positioned it atop his skull.

"Like this?" Akin said, moving her hand up and down.

Neill had no idea. He didn't even know how to make himself come. But he understood immediately that, for tonight anyway, anything she did would be hunky-dory.

"It's hot," she said.

"Mm," Neill answered, seriously.

"And, it's so hard. It's as hard as my baton."

"Mm."

Akin moved her right hand to Neill's balls and her left hand to his cock. She juggled the balls between her fingers like a table magician walking a quarter.

"Jesus," Neill said. And right then he shot off. Pop, pop, pop. His spume went a full 3 yards into the air, did a series of aeronautic maneuvers and fell down like acid rain onto Akin's hand, arm and cheek. There was a copious supply of it. It was quite a spectacle.

"It's like a roman candle," Akin said.

"Feel this," Neill huffed. His breathing was coming in fits and starts.

"It's like jelly," Akin said, wiping it from her cheek and studying the bit on her hand. "It's warm, too, like your, your—" She did not have a word for it yet. She sniffed it. She took a small taste.

"OH MY GOD," Neill said.

And that was that night.

The Young Couple, Not Yet Returned to Earth

Now, friends, we should talk a little more about high school and Neill's friends and Akin's friends, their activities, and even how their classes were going. Something should be added here about high school in general, some sociological fillip. We should leave the young neo-lovers to their bliss and talk about communal life in high school. Akin was a cheerleader. Neill had been put up for a post on the Student Council. Voting for that was fast approaching and his opponent was—Jeff. From the Cave Jeff. We're pretty sure it was Jeff.

We should talk (and later, we will at greater length) about Neill's best friends at Bartlett, Greg Borneo and Mick Allen. They were wonderful companions. Mick lived across the street from Neill with his Marine Corps lifer dad, his sweet mom, and his two younger larrikin brothers. He became a Kenneth Street Bum shortly after he moved in, which was shortly after Hawker Mikart. And Greg Borneo lived a couple neighborhoods east, about midpoint between the high school and Kenneth Street. Greg drove a beat-up, army green Mustang. In that Mustang things happened. *Later.* There was an 8-track tape player in it, for one thing. Ok, *later.* Greg started giving Neill a ride to school most mornings, even though it meant doubling back and wasting precious gas. To teenage boys with driver's licenses gas and the money to buy it are as precious as Sibyl's leaves.

Also, something else occurred that eventful autumn. Neill turned 16 on October 3 and he got his driver's license right away. This meant that Neill had access to his parents' Buick LeSabre, a veritable double bed on Firestones. His first outing in the car: he drove to Akin's. Of course he did.

After the preliminaries, the awkward talk with the folks, the offer of homemade ice cream graciously refused, Neill took Akin for a drive. Her parents were left standing in the foyer with an expression similar to the one Claus von Stauffenberg wore after the bomb in the Wolf's Lair failed to kill Mr. Hitler.

Where do young swains take their turtle-doves for their first-time parking? They find unfinished subdivisions. They find dark coves in unfinished subdivisions. Now, at this point in time, after Raleigh Springs Mall had opened to great fanfare right between Austin Peay Highway and the aforementioned Scheibler Street, there were not as many darkened coves as before. The young couple had to drive a few miles out of their way.

Neill's hands were sweating on the steering wheel, not just because he sensed something momentous about to occur, but because Neill was scared to death to be driving a 4000 pound machine, and one he was not yet comfortable with. (Neill never did become a great driver. He was timid here, also.)

Cove located, the car parked and engine turned off, Neill and Akin went at each other like feral beavers. Akin's shirt was the first thing to go, then her bra. And, lo! what is this? Akin was wearing a skirt! O precocious gal! What foresight! Soon, Akin was wearing only the skirt and her socks. Neill's hands went everywhere at once. He couldn't calm himself. He couldn't pace himself. He wanted to touch every inch of her simultaneously.

Slowly, they fell into dance steps and events slowed, but only slightly. Akin lay back against the passenger side door and opened her legs. Neill saw it all. What wonders therein! What dark, chthonic secrets within! Neill put a finger in and then two. Akin was squirming. Then

Neill had an inspiration. Drawing on his memories of tonguing places seemingly not made for tonguing he had a sudden impulse to put his tongue–*there!*

And he did. Akin squeaked like an old door in a black and white haunted house movie. This was it! This was the good stuff, Neill thought. And it was a pleasant place to put one's mouth, even if the scent was a little off-putting at first. It was so *soft*...and so oozy and warm. And soon, Neill felt his girlfriend come hard against his jaw. She let go small, frantic breaths, and then a slow whine like the air escaping from a blowup Sinclair Dino. Neill was holding Akin by the fundament, a hand on each, sweet cheek. And he was, well, eating her. There it is. After a while Akin sat up. Her eyes glinted like sparks off gun-metal gray.

Neill pulled his own pants down and let them pool around his ankles, awkwardly complicating the feet, pants, pedals correlation. It didn't matter. His tinkler stood straight up.

Akin put her hands around him, one on the shaft and one on the balls. It was a repeat performance, because it worked so well the first time, but it was only a warm up. Only the cover band before the main attraction. She engaged Neill's eyes briefly and moved her head, slowly, inexorably toward the erection. The descent took months. Then, she began licking it the way a cow licks its salt. She was unsure what to do, but anything seemed right. She put it in her mouth. That's all. She just put it in her mouth. It lay against her tongue like a dowel. It then occurred to her that it was called "sucking off." She sucked at it. She sucked too hard at it. It didn't matter. (One must be grateful that the term "blowjob" hadn't flashed across her inner screen first.)

Neill felt something for the first time that he would spend the rest of his life trying to repeat. He felt his engorgement surrounded by the sweet, soft mouth of a lover. Neill came fairly quickly after this, so quickly it surprised them both. Neill thought he was going to scream. Akin thought, *what the hell?*

Akin raised her head. Sperm was dripping from her mouth. Her expression was perplexed. Neill was suddenly worried. What if it were poisonous? Even slightly poisonous? He tried to read the perplexity on Akin's lovely visage. He could not.

"Did we just do something awful?" Akin asked.

Hawker

Weekend nights meant, often, a voyage outwards, each of the Kenneth Street Bums Ulysses in his own mythology. Often Hawker drove. He was the only one who owned a car, a battered Corvair.

Hawker was a hoarder of gasoline. He actually had a job as a sacker at Hi-Lo and he used that money solely to fill his gas tank, or on dates with any of the high school lovelies who lined his way.

Hawker was the school's Paul Newman (or Cary Grant), its Lothario, its Irresistible Male. He had had most of the cheerleaders (so it was said) and most of the Keyettes (female eye-candy pseudo-members of the Key Club) (so it was said) and even–so it was said–Baby Sweetcurd, the Home-Ec teacher. Baby was small and sort of mousy but built like a Titian nude. She wore smocks, we think they were called, light blue gingham (we think it's called) dresses of her own construction. Sometimes, when one passed the Home-Ec room, she would be sitting on her desk delivering sewing instructions to a room humming like a hive and her knee-length smock (if that's what it's called) would be hiked up and one would be allotted a glimpse of a tanned, shapely, almost muscular hamhock. Rumor also had it that her foremost lover was the shop teacher, Mr. Dribble. This seemed preposterous since Mr. Dribble looked like the banker on *The BeverlyHillbillies*, but who can fathom the bewildering ways of the human heart or groin?

Where were we? Oh, yes, Hawker and his Hawkmobile.

When Hawker and Neill and Lafayette and Robert and Mick (and occasionally Bucky, who was also new, who hailed from, of all places, Spain) gathered in the tight but glorious interior of Hawker's Corvair (sometimes called the Bum Mobile, for obvious reasons, and sometimes called Der Fuhrer, for more obscure reasons), there was much anticipation. It was a Friday night and eligible young men were ready for action in a jalopy running on Flubber. Anything could happen! Love! Adventure! Romance! Drive-in movies! Fare Four Food! Aliens dressed as Earth Women!

But, first there was The Stall.

Around the corner on Jocelyn Street Hawker would pull over and cut the engine.

"Anyone got gas money?" he'd inquire.

There was a silence like four gems upcurled in the recess of a pearly shell.

A few tokens emerged from linty pockets. A few groans.

Still they sat.

"We gotta have some plan before I restart the car. I'm not burning gas on pointless driving around."

"Eh—" Mick said.

"We're not gonna drive by the Grabenhorst's a few dozen times in hopes that the young lass inside will come out and shine her nocturnal light upon us."

Mick sulked.

So they sat.

They sat on the side of the road waiting for inspiration. It was not unlike a Quaker service. No one was to speak until a brilliant destination was delimited. Waiting for God to move one to speech is a tiring business.

We shall leave them there for now. Some nights they moved on. Some nights they went back to their beds sleepless of soul as wind or wave or fire.

A Pause

Life in high school doesn't progress so much. It doesn't move along a straight continuum. Instead it accumulates. Its construction is similar to the way you make a gothic cathedral at the beach by dripping wet sand through your hand as if through a cake icer.

Neill's sophomore year had served him well. He was moderately popular and this gave him new confidence. He began to see a new Neill, one who was attractive enough to have a cheerleader for a girlfriend and funny and quick enough to garner male companionship. As the Student Council elections rolled around Neill was beginning to cultivate some friendships with some of the school's best and brightest. This was a good thing. Still, in a group of eggheads, Neill tended to clam up. Better to be thought deep than open his mouth and reveal the vast chasms of his ignorance, or the slowing clockwork of his mechanical orange.

In the hallways, bright with chattering apes, Neill was sometimes cowed and sometimes bold. Sometimes upperclassmen and women spoke to him. This meant the world to Neill. Neill knew it was perhaps shallow. A small pond. A medium-sized fish. A shallow pond. Where Neill could still drown in his own spittle, or roast on his own spit.

His friendship with Thistle Sharer grew in importance. She was his chief confidante. Thistle was smarter than the angel of mercy and, like the tops of mountains her intellect was the first to catch the sun. Neill began to rely on her for commiseration and smarts and cordiality. Neill often warmed himself near her even as he pursued a fresh reputation, one jangly and kicky, and all about the pretty limbs of pretty young women.

Also, after school became a time for visiting friends and walking about in his mushrooming neighborhood to see the houses of his classmates, to meet parents, to ingratiate himself into newer homes and families and groups of people. The Sharers were still home base, but Neill also spent time at Lindsey Crouse's, or Rita Houston's, when he wasn't playing driveway basketball with the Kenneth Street Bums. Wait. We should have talked about Rita before now. Damn. Keeping this thing linear is like wrestling a bag full of weasels. Ok. Wait.

Rita Houston

Neill and Rita had been friends since 4th grade. They went through the AT Program together 5th through 7th grade. And, in all that time, no matter what school or class size, no matter who was added or subtracted or multiplied through each grade, Rita Houston was always the prettiest girl in the class.

How to describe her? How to write about the sun? She looked something like Lee Remick. She was wide-hipped and small breasted, and her face was the face Botticelli and those cats had in mind. And she had a laugh like bright copper and freckles that could find Tom Sawyer's heart and pull it from his rascally little chest and set it on the counter to dry out before eating. Oh, and she was so nice no one hated her for being the prettiest girl (later young woman, later woman) in the class.

Was Neill smitten with her? Was he not male? If pricked, did he not prick back? Of course he was smitten with her and would remain so for the rest of his life. Alas, though, alas and alack, he was destined, time and time again, to play a tertiary role: Rita's boyfriend's best friend.

In 6th grade, naturally Rita was Pat's girl. Precocious Pat, a hood before his time. He was the toughest kid in 6thgrade, so he won Rita's heart with swagger and expectoration. Even in 6th grade Rita had a flankey like Brigitte Bardot, though most of us didn't know why that excited us when it did. Later, we craved it. Later, we believed that between Rita's burnished thighs ran a river or warm honey and soft gold. Seriously.

So, Neill. Sidekick. Kick him aside. Poor Neill. (Later, Neill decided he was just attractive enough to win some very pretty gal's hearts but not the A list. This was useful information even if frustrating and even if he didn't always try to fish in the pool meant for him.)

There were times when they were alone, Neill and Rita. After all they were allies, or "buds" in Rita's argot. O, some Saturday afternoons over the new Cat Stevens or James Taylor albums, over lemonade Kool-Aid they would sit and talk and laugh and punch each other's biceps in friendly fun fun fun. And, all that time, Neill was thinking...if only I could kiss her. If only I could kiss her. Only that. I know I am not Pyramus to her Thisbe (nor even Steed to her Peel) but one kiss would make me happy until, decades from now, I should die and on my death whisper...it was all so awful...*but I kissed Rita Houston.*

She is the princess in this story. Ok?

Neill is the jester.

The princess will always end up with the prince.

We didn't make the rules.

We Now Continue More or Less Where we Left Off before the Rita Houston Dividend

On brittle autumn afternoons, after school, if there was no cheerleader practice and if the Rhymer Buick was available (Max did carpool to DuPont twice a week), Neill and Akin would drive out into the country. The air was golden. The fields were made of plush mud and dung and yellow allergens which floated in the air like ticker tape. The temperature outside was just what the doctor ordered, if the doctor were Dr. Ruth, and the temperature inside the car was potent.

Neill and Akin looked for places to park in the daytime.

Surprisingly, there was a lot of country left in Raleigh, Tennessee, at this time, especially out beyond Bartlett, into Ellendale and yonder. Still, daytime parking was risky and fraught with endangerment. That didn't matter, of course, if you were really horny.

Once they docked that land boat in a rutted, dirt driveway, off Ellendale Road. A quarter mile ahead, across the rutted drive and manure fields, there was a quaint house. No, it wasn't quaint. It was a shack. But people lived there and there were signs of life in the yard, abandoned toys, a rope swing from a tree branch and the cliché clunker car, sitting on its rims, hood up.

Neill and Akin stopped about ten yards from the road. Did this seem secure? Nah. Onward, and caution be damned. There were bodily juices surging.

Their pants hit the floor. Their hands hit the high spots. They groped. They swung. They tickled and pushed and prodded and rubbed and abraded and inserted and stroked. It had become a routine of sorts, if routine doesn't make it sound boring. They were not bored.

But Act III, the act right before the curtain came down, was always The Blowjob. Now, for those unfamiliar with teen sex, at least teen sex at this point in human development, little attention was given to female orgasm. This is awful. We admit it now. Neill had no idea if Akin had orgasms or, indeed, what that would be like if she did. She panted and sweated and made little piggy noises in her throat. Sometimes she said she came and sometimes she was too shy to even utter such a profoundly lusty statement. It seemed mutually rewarding, inasmuch as Neill was aware of mutuality.

So: Act III. Akin, with her hand on Neill's member, looked him in the eyes. Sweet gray-eyed Akin.

"You want me to suck you again?"

Neill smiled. Yet, there was a little pluck of trouble in his chest. The "again" seemed unnecessary, as if it were a task, as if Akin was balking at the play's finale, as if she wanted to rewrite Act III.

She went down on him. It only took a moment, as aforementioned. Neill shot off in Akin's sweet, wet mouth. As soon as he did Akin raised her face. The expression was one that usually accompanied something like medicine or alum. She smiled a half-smile. A bit of come ran from her mouth. She flung it from her chin with her fingers and it made a small, gloomy blemish on the passenger side window.

Neill reached over her and wiped it away with his coat sleeve.

He smiled. She returned the smile. Neill put the car in reverse.

That night at dinner Neill's parents asked where he had gone with the car.

"Out for a drive. It was a beautiful day."

"Looking for a place to park in the daylight?" Mr. Rhymer asked.

Mein Gott! Neill thought. His father is clairvoyant! Or maybe Neill hadn't cleaned the window well enough.

"Huh," Neill said.

It wasn't Neill's best memory that afternoon. Something, like an itch in his giddy-up, revealed itself hypogeally. Things fall apart.

Neill Always Suspected that at Some Point He Would be Unmasked as a Fake Intellectual

(Develop as a theme?)

[Cut this?]

The Doobie Discovery

Between sophomore and junior year something else happened.

In this loose conglom of friends and acquaintances and funny folk and orphans and sportsmen and girls so smart and pretty they make your heart hurt, there was a fellow whom we won't name because, well, after his high school days this fellow renounced his wild prankster past and became a Baptist preacher. He might have been a teacher for a while before that. Then a Baptist preacher. It was an agley path, whichever fashion.

Anyway.

This fellow, let's call him Reverend Kif, invited Neill and Greg to a camping party, just the three of them, out in the woods beyond Ellendale, a place Reverend Kif knew about that was so private even nearby cows did not know its whereabouts. The cows heard rumors, some bragged about going there, but really, it was all bovine bluff.

Reverend Kif took Neill and Greg into this secluded spot and they had sleeping bags and little else, except the makings of a campfire, and a couple cans of Vienna Sausages. They made a campfire.

Then Reverend Kif brought out something else, something that Greg and Neill had only heard about, a new (by Bartlett's standards and wiggly timeline) medicinal called by many names, an herbal tool to nirvana or at least a couple of rest stops down the turnpike from nirvana. Grass. This was the name Reverend Kif preferred and forever after it would be what Neill called it.

Bhang. Cannabis. Dope. Ganja. Hash Hashish Hemp. Joint. Weed. Reefer. Sinsemilla Tea Weed. *Grass.*

Why did Reverend Kif do this for the boys? Let's look at Reverend Kif for a minute and see if we can discern.

He was a star running back on the Panthers' weak football team. He was handsome like Pernell Roberts. He was a thespian (Lancelot in the school's funky production of *Camelot*, Andy Hobart in *The Star Spangled Girl*). He was as popular as water. Neill and Greg could only admire him from a few rungs down.

Yet. Yet, he found it in his heart to change their lives forever and always.

"Whoa," Neill said. "This is my first time."

"Mine, too," Greg allowed.

Reverend Kif smiled like the flowers of Eden. He rolled a thin rocket, stuck it entire into his maw, an almost sexual rite, removed it and rolled it tighter. It looked puissant, like papyrus pixie dust.

Around their bantam campfire they sat and Reverend Kif still held the small, neatly rolled missile between two fingers. Greg and Neill waited. Did they know their lives were about to change? Sure. Sorta. They sat like Grasshoppers before Master Po.

In Neill's case, there was in him a certain recklessness, a certain courting of the shadow that had begun way back on the bullies' playground. Neill had a tough time during certain periods of his youth. He didn't think his square peg fit into life's lopsided round hole. Neill, as aforementioned, already feared death and, in so fearing it, he told himself, let it come. If it will, let it come.

This was not suicidal. This was passivity bordering on clinical depression. More later.

Neill was ready, ready for anything, even if a bit dangerous, a bit dicey, a bit illegal. (Of course, the concomitant emotion residing in our Neill was the horrible dread of being caught. He had the hood's savoir faire but the chickenshit's fear of figures of authority. He would probably lose control of his bowels [weakened already, already a small plague] if a cop ever did take him in for possession.)

As for Greg, he was just wild-ass.

They Drew Reveries Deep into their Lungs

They drew reveries deep into their lungs. They knew not what to expect.

After two joints (Joint! Neill thought. What a great term. I will use it often, Neill thought), the boys looked to the Reverend Kif the way Siddhartha looked to his teacher, a darkened man not quite so handsome as Reverend Kif but as inscrutable.

"Wha?" Neill asked.

"Hurk?" Greg asked.

"Don't expect the godhead your first time out. Ease into it. Turn off your mind, relax and float downstream."

"Huh," Neill said.

"Huh," Greg parroted.

They smoked another spliff and then they just talked.

Reverend Kif told the boys a bit about football ("Joe Don was so drunk one game that when he dropped back into the pocket he urped a little onto the front of his uniform and goddamn idjit still completed the pass") and a little about acting ("I ain't a natural actor, but I've got a nice voice and I know how to walk"). Greg asked Reverend Kif if he knew anything about the rumor that Bartlett was starting a tennis team.

"Heard talk of it," Reverend Kif said, settling back against his rolled-up sleeping bag. "Family from Spain coming in is what I heard. Tennis pros. The mother once beat Billy Jean King."

"Damn," Greg said.

Neill wanted badly to participate in the confab. Greg was connecting better to Reverend Kif and this made Neill jealous.

"I'd like to act," he said finally.

Both of the others let the silence settle around them in a way conducive to further elucidation. Neill tried to come up with further elucidation.

"Shakespeare. Arthur Miller. Eugene O'Neill," he said. "Laugh-In."

"Laugh-In?" Reverend Kif asked, around a goblin's smile. There was a laughter underneath the boys' foregut like naughty peristalsis. It wanted out.

Some other kind of silence settled over the campers.

"I—" Neill started and then broke into a whinnying laugh that set them all off. It broke over them like a storm. The laughter came out in torrents. They laughed like loons; they laughed like Senators; they laughed like Robin Goodfellow. They laughed like macaws; they laughed like beech leaves; they laughed like rusty hinges. The cows politely moved further away.

(Some say [and it's not us] that for years the milk from those cows offered a gentle whirr to partakers, sending kids off to school with muttonhead grins.)

Later, sometime in that night that either lasted 42 hours or 42 minutes, they ended up at Steak and Egg and consumed what Neill still swears to this day was the best patty melt and hash browns he'd ever eaten. He tried numerous times for the rest of his life to duplicate that joy, but he could only approximate it.

Later, sometime in that night that either lasted 42 hours or 42 minutes, the boys ended up on Jim Somebody's bedroom floor. Jim was a fellow actor and, for some reason, Reverend Kif knew his floor would welcome the new cosmonauts. It didn't occur to anyone that they had started the evening with sleeping bags.

Through the years Neill tried numerous times to find the spot where they camped. He wanted to retrieve the sleeping bags. He wanted to mark it in the map of his mind with an X for Xtasy. The spot was as gone as Brigadoon.

Years later, it is said, a drunk freshman from BHS, looking for a place to sleep or piss or both, stumbled into a crude clearing in the woods and found a blacked circle that was mysteriously still warm and still redolent of what seemed to him a burning of exotic woods. It is said that this poor gowk found the sleeping bags, crawled into one and was never heard of again. His name even now has gone extinct and his, what were once called *permanent* records, were also inexplicably missing from the high school's files.

The Summer Wore On, Off and On

Meanwhile, if not playing basketball with the Bums, or getting high with any of his several friends who all seemed to come to grass concurrently, he was with Akin. Some hot summer afternoons they went for their long country-road rambles in search of private spaces in which to show each other their privates. Or, at night, they recklessly had sex in places so close to parents that it amazes them both to look back over the years and remember that they did it on Akin's front porch, on Akin's living room floor with parents and brother asleep upstairs (or maybe not even asleep) (including the evening Akin licked Neill's asshole for the first and last time causing him to come against the living room carpet, a rough substitute for soft human skin) and once, O God the chutzpah!, Akin sucked Neill off in his parent's living room which was wide open on both sides, one arched entranceway leading to the bedrooms and den where both parents were and one arched entranceway leading to the kitchen and then to the den where both parents were. Anyone could have walked in! O youth, Wild as the vulture's cry! O Youth, all green sap and promise!

Yet, something else had entered in. Some new reticence.

Both Akin and Neill were afraid of "going all the way." Both were fairly ignorant how it would even work, if it worked, or if it would work for them. Even though their tongues and fingers had boldly gone where no girl or boy had gone before, they were frightened of Neill's penis seeking out Akin's vagina.

Then Akin started asking Neill not to come in her mouth. This was a cheerless decision. Neill grew tired of it, the battle between orgasm and blueballs. Akin would lower her pretty face to his johnny and envelop it with her soft and wet lips and tongue, take the whole length of it into her mouth (O astonishing knack!), and still ask Neill not to come.

Neill wanted to say, "Are you crazy?"

Instead he pouted and sometimes fumed. Neill was 16.

One night in the Buick, in front of Akin's house, Neill had just finished bringing Akin off with as much skillful digitation as he could muster. She hung onto Neill's neck and whispered her love to him. Have we mentioned before that the young couple used the L word and frequently?

Oh yes. (Perhaps go back and add endearments, examples of affectionate and emotional tête-à -têtes.)

(Akin had even written in Neill's annual what her married name would be, what their daughter would be called, etc. Neill was only slightly more restrained. He really believed he loved Akin. He did.)

So, after bringing her off and her clinging to his neck and saying "I will love you forever," Akin sat back in the car seat.

Naturally, Neill thought this a premature ending to the night's pleasures.

"Ahem," he might have said.

Akin was staring at the tan roof of the Buick as if it contained constellations numerous and indecipherable. She was dreamy-eyed.

Neill undid his belt.

"Neill," Akin said quickly, her voice with a soft catch in it.

"Yes?" we think Neill said.

"Can we not do that tonight?"

Neill sat stock still. His short life offered him no answers to this. No conversational skills he had ever marshaled helped in this stroppy exchange.

"You mean no orgasm for Neill?" Neill said, using the third person for the first time.

"Neill," Akin said again and her gray eyes were watery with either emotion or obduracy or fear.

Neill slumped back in his seat. He stewed.

Then, he put his seatbelt on.

"Good night," he said.

"Neill," she tried one more time. Then, she cried.

Neill was unmoved. He stared through the darkened windshield at the suburban street with its silvery shadows and overarching trees and attractive American cars and its neat lawns. He could hold this sphinxlike pose all night if necessary. He was miles away.

Akin put her hand on Neill's thigh.

Akin rubbed Neill's thigh.

Neill feigned indifference.

Akin's fingers brushed up against Neill's scrotum through his thin Bermuda shorts.

Akin's fingers moved underneath the hem of Neill's thin Bermuda shorts.

Akin cupped Neill's balls through his underwear.

Neill turned toward Akin a look full of moonlight.

Akin took her hand out of Neill's shorts and undid his belt and unzipped his zipper and pulled his underwear down. Neill's bobbed bishop stood up ready to sermonize in the night air.

Akin began a sincere, studied handjob.

Neill's leg began to kick like a scratched dog's.

Akin sighed and took the thing into her mouth.

Neill came in Akin's mouth. He came quite a lot into Akin's mouth.

Later, he was glad he came quite a lot into Akin's mouth, because it was the last time. He did not know it that night but perhaps his libido did. The ways of the libido are arcane and unpredictable and certainly beyond Man's artless jurisdiction.

Vap-o-Rub

Neill had read about professional masturbators who used gels and petroleum jelly to aid in their self-love. One night, alone, lonely, having just seen Joey Heatherton on television, Neill felt particularly transgressive, or bold, or brave, or just plain horny.

Akin had been ill one night and on another resisted the front seat of the Rhymer's boat-sized Buick.

He carried his Joey Heatherton erection into the bathroom. It was a particularly insistent erection and it wanted Neill to play nice and to play quickly, quickly, man!

Neill dropped his shorts and pulled his shirt off and stood naked in the bathroom. This was already good. He looked down at his medium-sized gadso and smiled. It smiled back.

He went into the medicine cabinet and there was no petroleum jelly or any other kind of jelly, not even the ubiquitous grape. Instead he spotted a jar of Vix Vap-o-Rub. He shrugged. His gadso shrugged.

Neill sat on the toilet, leaned back for a good one, and dipped his fingers into the vaporizing vat. At first it felt pretty good, the lubrication nice and his hand worked with a new fever.

Then, a newer fever struck.

This is horrible. We can't continue. Let this stand as a warning.

Setting the head of your penis on fire is not a good idea.

The Junior Year

It was the year Neill was elected to the student council. Commissioner of Student Activities. A meaningless title for a meaningless position. Neill did absolutely zero while COSA. He may have attended meetings. He may have attended meetings stoned. This was also the year Neill went to school stoned many, many days (unlike Senior Year when it was *most* days). He and Greg would meet on the pitcher's mound before school and sit like Native American chiefs facing each other, passing around a thickly packed joint.

They could see for miles, outward miles, not the inward miles the herb offered them. Their thinking was that if anyone was coming toward them they would see them a long time before they arrived. There was a country mile between the pitcher's mound and school. There was a country mile in the other direction, where a dim neighborhood existed in the distance. And they only brought one joint each morning, so it could be eaten if indeed the fuzz came. The fuzz never came. (Newly added position at the school that year: Officer Sisson. What did Officer Sisson do all day? Lost to the vaporous climes of time.)

Often Neill walked the crowded morning halls in a violet haze, smiling like the kangaroo Sylvester thought was a mouse. Some of Neill's friends, especially Thistle, who treated Neill like a little brother sometimes, showed open displeasure when Neill was goofy. She was disappointed in him. Other times she treated him like a would-be lover, but the results would still be the same: disappointment whenever Neill was spaced-out. And loopy Neill thought he could cleverly disguise his dopey daydreamness. (Though, truth be told, he wanted others to know he smoked weed. He wanted to be thought of as an outlaw. [see 6th grade].)

And, also, readers, Akin was of that ilk which hated Neill's newfound herbal habit. This led to some heated fights. And this led to Neill spending more time driving around with Greg or Hawker or Sly weekend nights, stoned as boiled owls, restless and horny and full of that intoxicating admixture of teen angst and teen cockiness. Sly and Neill in particular spent many weekend nights visiting various young women, which initiated some elaborate and mostly unconvincing lying to Akin.

"You and Akin having some rocky times?" Sly said, squinting around a deep toke.

"Mmm," Neill answered, squinting around another.

"You got the running blues, running away...."

"Yeah, something like that. I mean, you know, Akin is so great, so sweet, so pretty, so loving."

"Yeah, that sounds awful."

"I know."

"Let's visit Kathy."

"Yes, let's. And maybe Kathy's little sister Bo will be there."

"Jesus. Have you seen her? She's a freshman now."

"I see her almost every morning after homeroom. I am usually stoned as a raw oyster, but not too stoned to notice her really short shorts and precocious nildi."

"Nildi. Great one."

"Your word, wasn't it?"

"I thought it was yours."

"I thought it was yours."

"I thought it was yours."

"I thought it was yours. Or Ricky Nelson's."

"Ricky Nelson. Great one."

"Yeah."

"Shit."

"What—what are you doing?"

"I dropped the joint."

And they both dived under Sly's crotch in search of the still burning doobie. Meanwhile, Sly's Pokey-orange Pinto crossed the oncoming lane and rode rough into the ditch alongside the road. Sly had enough acuity left to hit the break while Neill scooped up the glowing cigarette.

"We're sideways," Neill said.

"Great one," Sly said.

The New Girls

Junior year also meant new girls. Neill and his male cohorts made extensive studies of all new females, classes 74 and 75. We compared notes. We analyzed. We took our analyses home separately and masturbated. It was the year of hot pants. As if males of high school age needed help with their hormones, as if they needed jump starts. Hotpants were jump starts, often more potent than Janet Leigh in a black bra.

Neill eyed a few young women from the class of 75 particularly. Their legs drove Neill mad. Their smiles, their breasts, their giddy girlishness drove Neill mad.

There was a group of them and they all seemed to be named Cindy, and some were cheerleaders and some were party girls and some were immature and silly, and some were as hot as martyrs' visions.

In this group there was a young woman from Barstow, California named Orbit Unborn. She had legs that started with round and tender thighs shooting out from a butt that looked particularly fetching and led down a tapering path to thin shins. Her legs, her ass were enough. But, there was this also: Orbit Unborn had the biggest nubbies Neill had ever seen in his young days. She was, as young men learned to name it, *stacked.*

Stacked as a cord of wood. Stacked as a pile of poker chips.

But, still, Neill was tethered to Akin. And Akin, in those days, was not happy.

Neill Goes to Work (A chapter wherein exclamation points abound like birds that o'er the forest play)

In 1970, a few blocks from the Rhymer's home on Kenneth Street, there opened a shopping mecca called Raleigh Springs Mall. The "springs" part refers to ancient history concerning Raleigh, Tennessee, when, apparently, there were healing waters abounding in the area. There was an inn, a spa. A tramline for the rich nabobs to come from the Big City.

Anyway, the opening of this mall, the biggest in the Southeast at the time, was greeted with great whoops of joy and expectancy. Just walking its fresh tiled floor was like entering an enchanted story, something from Scheherazade or Rabelais. It was market day in the plaza! All around the awestruck itinerants were sparkling and varied emporia of goods from around the world. The names of these enchanted establishments rang out like a tintinnabulation of adrenalin, bursting in frontal lobes like the beginning of love: Sears! Goldsmiths! Spencer Gifts! Magnavox! JoAnn's Fabrics (where Neill's mom worked!)!, Waldenbooks! Konee's! JCPenney's, where they had a lollipop tree! Carousel Snack Bar! J. Riggings! Paul's (who was Paul?) Shoes! Foxmoor Casuals! Waldenbooks! Shoney's, home of the Big Boy. Walgreens and its grill, where you could get the best chicken fried steak and mashed potatoes in the whole of Raleigh!

Waldenbooks!

And, available for the picking, were gewgaws and trinkets and foodstuffs and effluvia and raiment beforetime reserved for the riches of kings. Long playing records! Paperback novels! Crushed velvet suits! Sausage and cheese and pickles as big as the dofunnies of porn stars! Vests and vestments and investments! Organs and tam-tams and pianos and zithers! Sinapisms and nostrums! Soft pretzels seemingly made for Gog and Magog, slathered in mustard! Slushies! Chili dogs! Vibrators and kicksies and spicy dice! Toby-jugs and toy roosters! Bijou and bijouterie! Tuxedos in white and pastels and dirt brown with chocolate velvet lapels, and with frilly shirts that looked like rejects from Paul Revere and the Raiders!

Paperback books!

And what else did this Astrodome of Commerce bring to backwater Raleigh, Tennessee? Jobs, my friends. O lucky Neill! O lucky babyboomers! As soon as they were of age, Neill and his peers all went to Raleigh Springs Mall and filled out little forms that asked for name, age, social security number, previous employment (leave blank if necessary), criminal record (if any), and available hours to work. It was dreamland! It was opportunity! It was the first step onto the moving floor that leads to Hell's outer office (where the leggy secretary is a hooker with a heart of ash), Free Market Capitalism.

And Neill, a callow lad of 16, his driver's license in his corduroy pocket, found his first paying job as a busboy at Konee's (Home of the Konee Dog!) making $1 an hour. He worked about 12 hours a week and so brought home a weekly check of around $10. It was a windfall! And what did Neill spend his hard-earned specie on? Not gas. Not books. Not even food. He spent almost all of it on long playing records. Neill was mad for music. (Mention before this?) (Beatles, Stones, Kinks, Dylan, The Monkees, Jefferson Airplane, Buffalo Springfield, Who, Leonard Cohen, Joni Mitchell, Velvet Underground, Moody Blues, Jethro Tull, Frank Zappa?)

Neill loved Konee's. The boss liked him and he had friends who worked there too, and at night, with the appetite of a teenager, before he dumped dishes into his bus bin, he picked uneaten morsels off the customer's plates, fried clams being an especial delicacy. Neill ate off strangers' plates, their castoff food. Is this the worst thing we will reveal about Neill? Hardly.

It Was in This Mall that Fate Intervened

It was in this mall that fate intervened. Who knew fate was a conspicuous consumer? (Fate has consumed many, says Satan.) One afternoon between school and his job at Konee's Neill was sauntering around the fountain in the center of the mall, eyeing the cute brunette who worked at the information booth, setting his sights on Camelot Records. There was a great cut-out bin there and many of Neill's Konee dollars were spent on $2 LPs. Sometimes Neill bought music by people he'd never heard of if he liked the covers. Over the years he discovered some wonderful artists this way (Barbara Keith, Chris Williamson) and sometimes he got dogs.

And there, in Neill's path, the path to the music, moving like geese toward a summer lake, was a gaggle of sophomore females. Faces as cute as kinked-up ostrich feathers, bodies fresh and wholesome, and extending from the briefest of hotpants, young pipestem legs that called to Neill as if they were a shepherd and Neill a border collie. And there, cachinnating hard enough to make her walk catawampus, was the new girl from California, Orbit Unborn.

They moved toward Neill like a cloud made of sex.

Neill stopped. His grin was a cut in the bark of a tree.

The gaggle stopped.

"Hello, Neill Rhymer," one cutie said. Neill thought her name was Pinky.

"Ladies," Neill said, bowing like a bulrush.

And this new girl, this Californian, was smiling a secret smile in Neill's direction. Neill recognized the secret behind the smile. He thought he recognized it.

"I'm Orbit," Orbit said.

"I am in orbit," Neill said.

"First time I've heard that."

"Oh. Right. Because it's not. Because I am not original, nor am I clever."

"No, literally. No one has ever said that."

Some of the gaggle giggled, some smirked.

"What are y'all doing?" Neill inquired.

"Roaming," Pinky said. "Malling."

"Great one," Neill said.

"What about you, Neill-boy," said a petite redhead named Britomart. She was cute, skinny as a rake, but with boobs like rounded vowels.

"Wasting precious moments of my young life walking back and forth, to and fro, hither and thither and yon, mostly yon, before I have to work for my shekels."

"Wanna take a picture with us? We were gonna see if we can all get in the photo booth."

"Can't miss that," Neill said. And Neill thought only this: young females in my lap. He made a quick head count and it came to five including him. That was a lot of young female flesh. Four female fleshes.

They proceeded to the booth, and laughing like parrots at a bagpiper, they crowded in. The skinny gal squeezed in last.

"I'm just naturally thin," she said, grinning.

"If you who are naturally thin should keep it to your sylph."

Neill's hands had no idea whose thighs they squeezed, whose waists they encircled. Neither did his thighs know whose ripe buttocks rested on them. They mugged and hooted and squealed and crepitated as the lights flashed, one, two, three, four times.

They tumbled out of the booth, practically sprawling on the cold tile floor, polished like a facet on a gemstone.

"Neill Rhymer," one of the gals expostulated between guffaws, "You got the wandering hands, bub."

They laughed harder.

And then she was standing right there as if conjured by the imps of the perverse. Standing right there in Raleigh Springs Mall on the cold tile floor, polished like the facet of a gemstone next to Neill and his pile of female friends.

Akin Upspin. Neill's Akin.

And she was not smiling or laughing. She was not angry either. Her face wore an expression somewhere between perplexity and abject terror. Her face wore this queer expression the way a bum wears a castoff coat. It didn't fit but it was hers.

Neill was to see this expression often in the coming weeks.

At School a Hell

Akin dragged herself around the halls of Nicholas Blackwell High School, a bedraggled spirit, a haint. She wore a yoke of dejection and dolor that could break the heart of an executioner. Her eyes were red-rimmed. Her step a sludge. Her hair unwashed and her cheerleader's cheers cheerless. She crept like the wraith of the woman from Usher's Well.

She walked the halls of high school weeping like a walrus over the waning moon.

Neill felt awful. He also felt the way we all have felt at times like this: unshackled. He asked Rita to meet him at the library to talk. Rita wore her queen's smile, sweet and patient. Neill barely had to speak before Rita sang, "You wanna be free..."

It was still the time of The Monkees.

Rita and Akin were best friends, but Rita understood. She understood because she was wise and good-natured and all around groovy. Neill hugged her. Rita hugged back. Neill wished they were naked.

Sweeney Waterman

The soundtrack was also David Bowie and Mott the Hoople. Everyone sang "Ziggy Stardust." Everyone sang "All the Way from Memphis."

Sweeney Waterman invited Neill to camp out with him one Saturday night. The plan was to pitch a tent in an empty lot in a neighborhood not too near theirs and sleep on hard dirt and drink wine. It was male bonding perhaps. Or perhaps Sweeney was still testing Neill. Or perhaps, Sweeney really did love Neill and wanted to spend time with him. It's complex, isn't it? The human psyche, human emotions. The heart is about as reliable a barometer as a can of Beenie Weenies. The heart is unpredictable, like a shadow.

They pitched their pup tent (O, for the days of the pup tent, which you had to be an engineer to get to stand up right! Backyard pup tents spotted the 1960s like acne. Once Neill thought he saw Sputnik while he was camping in his own backyard. It might have been an alien vessel or a bit of space junk) on the packed dirt of a corner lot in a half-built subdivision a few miles south of Raleigh and Bartlett. Sweeney brought a jug of cheap wine. (What was it called? *Look this up.* Boone's Farm?) They built a small smoldering fire from twigs and candy bar wrappers and motor oil.

"I haven't had much alcohol," Neill said. He tried not to sound like Opie. He sounded like Opie.

"Why we're here," Sweeney said.

"Right."

Neill once again wondered why Sweeney Waterman, the wit, the bon vivant, the raconteur, a card-carrying member of the clerisy, found Neill interesting.

"Screwtop wine. Nothing finer," Sweeney said, uncapping the glass jug and tipping a healthy amount down his gullet. (Boone's Farm? *Look that up.*)

He passed it to Neill.

Neill tried to mimic his friend's motion, spilling plonk down the front of his shirt (what will he tell his mother?!) and sloshing some down his own throat. Neill's eyes stung. He made a concerted effort not to choke, not to sound like Opie again.

"Thas good," Neill said, setting the jug between them.

Sweeney Waterman was looking at a piece of grass in his hand. He was studying it as if it were the Torah.

"Quack grass, I think," he said.

Neill looked at him. How does one respond to that?

"To see the world in a blade of grass," Neill said.

"I think the expression is a grain of sand."

"Of course it is."

"Live in the moment, as the Zen purists say, right?"

"Right. I try to do that."

"I have a problem with 'live each moment' and 'one day at a time,' which are basically the same thing except one is a little more lenient. The problem is what if it's a bad moment or a bad day? And, similarly, there is the frightening corrective, every moment is new. There is no preparation for even *one damn moment*."

Neill thought he was going to cry.

The rest of the night was warmer. The conversation loosened up with the aid of pressed grapes, if they use pressed grapes for rotgut wine. Neither boy slept much, though they both feigned being real outdoorsmen.

As Rosy Fingers and Her New Day crept over their squinched faces and dirty wine-soaked chests they both felt bereft of love and gentleness and human kindness. They both felt as lonely as Crusoe. They both felt upchuck (the Technicolor yawn) rising in them like a phoenix from their once seething campfire.

(This was Neill's penultimate camping trip. He tried only one other time in his life to enjoy these difficult pleasures and that was with a young woman with eyes like a bush baby and a bush like the eyes of a peacock's tail whom Neill thought he could lay only if he proved himself a rough and tumble sort. That trip went about as well as this one. No sleep. No sex. And similar morning exuberation.)

Barbara Hershey, Mick Jagger, et al

There is an expression. Perhaps you've heard it. Nobody promised you a rose garden.

Neill knew the expression but assumed it referred to everyone else. Life was full of possibility, and where there is possibility, there must be reward. Neill wanted reward only. This was immature of him, of course.

Except that he felt like this, somewhat, for the rest of his life. This formula for disappointment could equally be applied to the upper stratum of beautiful women who would never give Neill a sniff. (Mention Rita Houston here?)

For example: one of Neill's favorite TV shows was *The Monroes*, but he had to stop watching it. Every time they showed a close-up of Barbara Hershey, it put him into a profound funk. What kind of world is it where you can fall in love with someone and desire them to the point of mania and not get to enjoy them? Neill loved Barbara Hershey. Her beauty turned a key in Neill. There are hundreds, perhaps thousands, of people one encounters in one's life that one is attracted to ('One' sounds awfully clumsy if one uses 'one' too much.), but there are only a handful who turn this key.

Hence, Neill could not watch *The Monroes*.

Throughout his life this same disappointment with the world would crop up. Some of the movie stars he could not watch: Jenny Agutter, Julie Delpy, Jean Seberg, Lesley Ann Warren, Twiggy.

There is another expression. The Stones gave it to us: you can't always get what you want (though one assumes Mick Jagger did just that). Neill didn't buy it.

Neill sans Akin

Now, Neill discovered what countless lovers before him discovered–that being free was both tantalizing (I can try to get off with ANY girl with no guilt) and lonely (where the hell are all the girls?).

They were there. In their flowering sexuality and hotpants and cheerleader outfits and tight blue jeans and flowery perfumes. Neill wanted them all. He also only wanted one. One who would take him places Akin feared.

Conversation on the Pitcher's Mound, Before Class, Between Tokes

"So, you and Akin are quitsville."

"Yes. I'm not sure I've ever been to Quitsville."

"Nice place to visit. Wouldn't want to live there."

"Nice in a touristy, glitzy, tacky sort of way."

"Nice in a West Memphis truck-stop, Greasy Diner with Great Biscuits kind of way."

"Maybe you have been there."

"Maybe I have."

"Akin is going to cry so much she is going to dissolve."

"What's that from?"

"What?"

"Something that cries so much it dissolves."

"Tolkien?"

"I don't think so."

"It's a Twilight Zone. Or Outer Limits."

"Is it?"

"I'm pretty sure."

"It's like this thing that lives in the woods and at night you can hear it crying when the wind is just right and it disturbs all the townspeople's sleep and they go to find it and it has cried so much it is only a pile of damp salt."

"Huh."

"I'm pretty sure that's right."

"So then the townspeople sleep better though the mystery of the crying is never solved?"

"I think so."

"Huh."

"And the town learns that one should never seek the solution to middle of the night mysteries."

"The whole town learns that."

"Yeah, sure. Everyone. Even the little freckled-face boy who hangs around the smithy's."

"Huh."

"Even the barber who is from that other show. The one with the woman who was in that UFO movie."

"*Earth vs. The Flying Saucers.*"

"Nah."

"*The Blob?*"

"I think so."

"She lives in that town?"

"I think so. Wait, what town?"

"The one we were talking about."

"Quitsville?"

"I think so."

Quickly Through Junior Year and into the Summer of 1972

Junior year Neill spent a lot of time doing various school activities that had nothing to do with academics. His figurehead position on the student council was brainless time-wasting. He spent a lot of time in the Student Council Room, an idea certainly dreamed up by some witless teacher who had no idea what was really on the minds of teenagers. This was a room in the eastern annex, a space entirely for students. And to make matters more absurd it had a lock *on the inside.* Neill took part in decorating the room, which consisted in finding an old moldy couch, posters of Bowie and Zappa, and for education's sake, Dr. Edwin Corey.

Neill also was part of the regular pot-smokers who gathered behind its locked door until Mr. Bellamy discovered what was going on and "raided" the room one day. A dozen young men and women spilled from the room's front-facing windows into the sticker bushes below. Laughing like fools, they skipped away across the lawn and parking lot, high as magpies and twice as smug.

Neill also had a series of girlfriends. He was constantly surprised at how little time it took dating someone before she let him put his hands under her clothes. Sometimes 2 dates, sometimes 3.

There was the young lass from Ellendale with the ass as soft as Lempster wool. Neill slid off rain-soaked streets one night speeding to her house, that behind in the forefront of his consciousness, landing his parents Buick in a three foot-deep ditch. He, luckily, managed to back the behemoth out.

There was the blond, dumb as sleep, who gave Neill a handjob within an hour of his arrival at her house. She loved the handjob. Neill dated her eight times. A perfect eight handjobs.

There was the sister of a football player (a man-mountain named Rump, whom Neill had never spoken to, but who struck fear in everyone including his sister) (well, nor had Neill spoken to the sister prior to this one evening [her name was Glory, we think]) who, at an otherwise lackluster party, took Neill outside to her (or somebody's) Chevrolet and sucked on his tongue so hard Neill barely could feel her hand squeezing his dickie to orgasm. The next day Neill's tongue wore a purple bruise like a vulgar sport coat.

There was the brunette who worked with Neill at Konee's who took her chewing gum out right before she gave him a blowjob behind the mall one night. Neill, forevermore, would recall the stench of the nearby waste bins whenever her name came up, or her face swam into Neill's pre-sleep dreaming. She swallowed, re-mouthed her gum, and said, "Ta-ta."

And so on.

Yet, commencing the summer of 1972, Neill was still, strictly speaking, a virgin. He had never put his eikel into a young woman's jing-jang. It was something to look forward to. It was something to fret about.

The summer of 1972 would be about marijuana, tennis and cruising by girl's houses. It would be about playing hearts at the Sharer's, midnight snacks at Lindsey Crouse's (part of the mystery, the draw of the Crouse's house was Lindsey two older hippie siblings, Rake and Paste [because of whom Neill first heard Frank Zappa's masterpiece, *We're Only in it For the Money*], [Rake also had a bookshelf where Neill found radical texts that he only thumbed, but by thumbing, inhaled certain radical tendencies, books with titles like *Ringolevio*, *Really the Blues*, and *Revolution for the Hell of It*, and books of essays with provocative titles like "The Student as Nigger"], and Mr. Crouse who polished rocks in the family carport. He had display cases like in a museum and his rocks shone like the Jewels of Opar), basketball with the Kenneth Street bums, marijuana and woolgathering nights. It would be about longing and fear and love. It would be about betrayal.

On the Dark and Winding Midnight Roads of Shelby County, Tennessee

Often, summer nights meant cruising by the homes of young women, some known, some not known at all, some only made of dreamstuff. It was part of the teen lothario's confidence and bluster (read: foolishness) that he could just show up at a girl's house and she would be there waiting and eager to learn a new male landscape.

Once a father barred the door. His reasoning was simple and concise. "Come back when you cut your hair," he said, his mouth set like Ward Cleaver's, without any of Ward's worldly insouciance. Neill could still remember the young lass's name, though he never talked to her: Maven Styes. Neill, for the rest of his life, could remember the map of freckles on her pert nose, a map to Erewhon.

Maven Styes haunted him because he never got close. She never even learned his name.

Also many nights before this outrageous courting behavior, or after it, Sly and Neill took long drives out into the county, traveling highways black as the father of lies, getting high on whatever was available (one feeble evening the only thing the pair could get their hands on was cheap cough syrup, which they drank to no effect [except they didn't cough for a month] but they feigned a kick anyway).

While driving, Sly would pick his nose and fart and then say, "You wouldn't think the two were connected."

Once on Highway 70, sometime around 2 a.m., they noticed a police car was following awfully close. The radio slithered fluently from "Ride, Captain, Ride" to the Moody Blues' "Question." (This was back when one could still hear interesting things on commercial radio.)

"Damn," Sly said. "How long has he been back there?"

Neill tried to make a s-l-o-o-o-w-w head turn.

"Damn," Neill said. "How long has he been back there?"

"And what does he want?"

The air in the car grew thick. Silence reigned like the Heat Miser.

"Sly," Neill said, after a few minutes which seemed like hours, "You're only going 20 miles an hour.

One Such Peripatetic Late-Night Conversation

This is a delicate part of the tale and must be told delicately. You may skip it if you want, but we think you should hear it. As the Pharisees said to Judas about the blood money, "You might as well take it. We think that you should."

The joint was rocked, smoked to a clip's worth of roach.

"I'm horny," Neill said.

"Mm, me, too. Wanna drop in unannounced somewhere?"

"Not likely to take care of the horniness."

"Right enough."

"Know anyone who knows a hooker?"

"Guy on the football team, I think."

"What's his name?"

"Harding, I think."

"Harding would help us?"

"I doubt it."

"Know where he lives?"

"Naw."

"Right."

Some time passed. It might have been a half hour. It might have been chronometrically beyond measure.

"I'm horny," Neill said.

"Me, too," Sly said again.

"I would love to be rolling around with some twisty chickling right now."

"You had any since Akin?"

"Not really. Close. Not really. Blow job. I think.

"She was good though."

"Yes."

"Really quite good."

"Uh huh."

"I have to tell you."

"—"

"I have to tell you, I've spent some time with her, consoling her, you know. She is still pretty broken up over you."

"Yeah, I know."

"She and I have become pretty close."

"Uh huh."

Let's say Neill's density is pot-induced.

"She and I have, uh, fooled around a bit."

Some vomitus rose in Neill's throat.

"Seriously?"

"Yeah. I hope that's ok."

It wasn't.

"Sure. I'm not seeing her anymore."

"She blew me a few times."

"Great one."

"Yeah."

"Glad you're having a good time."

"Yeah. She said you were a premature ejaculator."

"She said that?"

"Well, no, I mean, in comparison."

"Uh huh."

"Actually, she said you would come as soon as she touched you."

(Develop this as a theme?)

At the Sharers

At the Sharers, that summer, there were many gatherings, many games of cards or Ping-Pong, many discussions, arguments and jokes. It was the usual reckless and intoxicating mix of hi-jinx and high (or low) culture. Some of our participants actually read books. Some were more comfortable talking movies (it was the Seventies and the Castor and Pollux of international cinema, Bergman and Fellini, excited many a young American heart) or music (was Jim Morrison really a poet or just a poseur? was Fever Tree the best unknown group in rock music? were the Monkees fakes or talented flash-in-the-pans, or talented fakes? was Melanie really as hot as she seemed? was David Bowie really bi-sexual?).

Some of the congregate were moving on to college, though Sly and Thistle and Neill were all about to be seniors (Sly, actually a year older than Neill had to repeat a grade in grade school, feeding further his youngest child syndrome that made him try harder, run faster, talk louder, beat every boy's time with every girl). Those moving on to college took on a professorial air and were, indeed, seemingly more sophisticated than those left behind. Sam Onides outdid them all. He was off to Harvard on full scholarship (and later received a rare two Fulbright Scholarships to study in Japan and translate Japanese art books into English while teaching bright young Japanese kids to read and speak the Kinks' English).

Neill still talked little when some of this older crowd attended. He was more comfortable when it was just himself and Thistle and Sadie. Once he and Sadie snuck off to make out in one of the empty bedrooms. It was a highlight of Neill's summer. Sadie was as desirable as Sleeping Beauty, even in her braces. Her braces were erotic. Neill was afraid of catching a lip on them. Neill wanted to catch a lip on them. Neill wanted to be trapped against Sadie's mouth forever.

Senior Year

Senior year began for Neill with a new mode of transportation. Junior year rides to school had been spotty; sometimes Neill walked or hitchhiked the 2 miles between his home on Kenneth Street and Nicholas Blackwell High School. Now Greg picked up Neill in his rattle-trap Mustang, the one with the 8-track player, the player with its *Ziggy Stardust* and *Mott* and *Abbey Road*. Sometimes they burned a doobie on the way. Sometimes they waited till they could get to the pitcher's mound. Sometimes, O valiant youth!, they endured schooldays as straight as knights of old.

And Neill was, in a word, popular.

He had his dear friends. He had the respect of some of his classmates. He was the target for some of his more venomous classmates.

And, besides being Vice President of the Senior Class, Neill was also Vice President of the Spanish Club, a member of The Key Club, The Beta Club, Mu Alpha Theta, The Rosicrucians, The Apathy Club (if you showed up for the meetings you were out), The Pep Club, and "Mr. Editorial" on the staff of the school newspaper, *The Gleaner*.

It was writing for *The Gleaner*, coupled with the support of an inspiring teacher, Mrs. Imogene Reid, that really sent Neill toward what would be his lifelong passion: books. And it was Mrs. Reid who first told Neill he was a writer, in a sense, giving him *permission* to be a writer.

And something about Neill at this time, his budding confidence, the glamour of being "Mr. Editorial," or simply his jerrybuilt charm, made him a bit of a lothario (high-school version, lower case 'l'). He had a few dalliances. And then, bang, Orbit Unborn stood in his path. She of the breasts like bolsters.

Suddenly, Neill was spending a lot of time at Orbit's house. She lived between Kenneth Street and the high school, and on nights when the family car was tied up, Neill was happy to walk there. Why? Because of the sex, of course.

Orbit fancied herself an actress. She was Tigger in the school play (the musical *Pooh!*, freely adapted by the drama teacher, the elegant and slightly dotty Enola Crastins) (or was she Morgiana in the obscure French play *Nothing is Worse and Some Things are Better?* [or perhaps it was her sophomore year role as Becky in *Harold Pinter in Wonderland* we're thinking of?]). (Later Orbit would, appropriately, head to Hollywood and involve herself in a lot of big talk and bluster of a particular ilk that only Hollywood fashioned, but that's another story.) She had a coquettish smile and laugh that was at times so charming you wanted to taste her and at times so phony one wondered what really went on under the curvaceous skin of Orbit Unborn. But, honestly, it was that skin, stretched taut and youthful in just the right places, that drew Neill as the moon draws the lenocinant sea.

It started on the couch in her parents' living room (there was a heavy, abdominous father who wore wife-beater t-shirts, and there was a step-mother, a gray battleship of a woman, who never smiled, never laughed, never spoke, and there was an apple-doll grannie somewhere, perhaps in the attic leaning against boxes of old toys) as heavy petting as soon as the adults went upstairs. What secret do teens possess that allows them to have all manner of illicit contact right under the very noses of authority? What secret power is perhaps more the question? Do they think they are invisible as long as they are quiet? It's similar to the child who covers his eyes so adults can't see him.

Neill and Orbit wrestled a few nights before the night Neill decided he was going for the gold. The gold, of course, being those Bobbsey Twins under Orbit's shirt. They were there. They were waiting. Neill knew he faced little resistance. He also knew that once there he would have to live there for a long time. Orbit Unborn, it was generally agreed, had the best masobs (nildi) at Bartlett High. (Was this more of Neill's wanting only the very best, feeling he was *entitled to* only the very best?) (Develop as a theme, or would it alienate the reader concerning our hero?)

The shirt was opened during a particularly forceful French kiss.

The bra was unsnapped (Oh, blessed nabob who invented the front loader, here we sing your praises!) while Neill sucked an eggplant into the side of Orbit's neck.

The first feel of their heft came as Orbit panted in Neill's ear. (She was turned on!).

And the first complete sighting and simultaneous rubbing happened when Neill had to sit up to really gauge what he had uncovered. And what he had uncovered were perhaps the best breasts he would ever fondle in his long life.

They were impeccable, powerful, as full of royalty as a pack of cards, as wondrous as an eclipse, as deep as mirrors held up to the inspection of one's very soul.

Neill couldn't open his eyes wide enough.

Orbit giggled.

"They're big, aren't they?" she said, only slightly demurely. She knew their power.

"They are all I want in life," Neill said.

Further Explorations with Orbit Unborn

Things proceeded apace. Because how else are they going to proceed?

Neill was not long content to only caress Orbit's spectacular breasts. (typo: beasts. Keep?) Soon his hands ran amok under her clothing. Orbit's silky hotpants let Neill's girlish fingers slide easily enough underneath. He found he could insert his entire forefinger into her bazoo simply by pushing the hem aside. And O how it made Orbit squirm. Orbit grew wet easily. Orbit was orgasmic; she was quickly orgasmic.

And, of course, she reciprocated (because all teenage girls do). Neill was only too happy, after fingering his now-she-can-be-called-girlfriend into orgasm, to lower his own shorts and skivvies so that Orbit could jerk his little Corey. She was good. She was almost expert. And, O holy cats, could Orbit Unborn give a blowjob. She must have taken classes. She must have read up on it. The very first blowjob was right on the money. Orbit kneeled for Neill. She bent over him like a firmament. Her breasts brushed his thighs and occasionally his balls. Her mouth worked with such gentle yet firm suction that small fizgigs went off behind Neill's eyes. And he came in quarts, as the joke goes. Orbit sat up with an expression on her face almost cartoonly. Sperm ran from the corners of her grimalkin smile.

"So, that's what happens!" she said.

"Gurf," Neill said.

And the next night, for the first time in his life, Neill would come twice in one night and return home to his parent's house, spent like stars extinguished in the firmament, spent like a first paycheck.

Obviously, our two enthusiasts are headed toward uncharted territories. They had found the map and they thought they understood its compass rose and its legend, its scale, its colors, its topography. They thought they understood the area between its neatlines.

They were unafraid.

Interlocution in the Obscurity

"Is this road always this dark?

"You said that last week."

"Did I?"

"Yeah. It's always this dark. It's the effing country."

"We were on this road last week?"

"I don't know."

Sly took a toke so deep the roach glowed like a song well-sung.

"Don't bogart that joint, my friend. Pass it over to me," Neill sang (not well, not well).

"You and this Orbit," Sly said. "You're getting in deep."

"I think so."

"That's wonderful. I like to see you happy."

"Thanks, Buddy."

"I love you, you know?"

"Yes. It's mutual. Thanks. Orbit is...she is..."

"W/E. Well-endowed."

"Like a cathedral."

"Like a swarming hive."

"Like an ivy league school."

"What?"

"I dunno. She is though."

"You've been there?"

"Oh, yes."

"Jesus. I bet they're great."

"Oh, yes."

"I bet they are better than Akin's."

"Well—"

"Sorry, that wasn't right."

"Ok. They are great. And Orbit, she's, what, she's fun to be with. She's kinda somewhere between immature and foxy."

"Between immature and Sly."

"Ha. Yeah. And can she give head."

"Shit. Really?"

"Unbelievable."

"Have you—you know–?"

"No. But we're real close."

"Jesus. I wanted to be first. I am a year older."

"Get busy, Buddy."

"Right. I wonder if Akin—"

"Is that really happening?" Even so, Neill felt the tightening of his throat and chest.

"I doubt it."

"Sorry," Neill said. He wasn't.

Interlocution with Thistle

"Are you working on an editorial for *The Gleaner*? We go to press this Friday?"

"Go to press? Who are you, Perry White?"

"Are you working on the editorial?"

"I have some ideas."

"Sheesh, Neill. Come on. Gimme a topic or I'll give you one."

"Racism."

"Right."

"No?"

"Are you serious?"

"I think so." Suddenly he was.

"That's a big topic. And a touchy one. It's only been two years since bussing began."

"So, it's time."

Between Neill's freshman and sophomore years Bartlett High School experienced what thousands of schools across the South were experiencing. They accepted black kids from a rural school, in this case a school called Shadowlawn (no kidding). BHS went from about 15% black to almost 50%. There was a rough period of adjustment, one still not entirely reconciled (and in some of the meaner corners the move was despised and the n word found new voice).

Neill had something of a reputation as a liberal, in as much as he understood the term. Some of that meaner element and even some of his oldest friends spoke of him with that affectionate term, *nigger lover*. Neill wasn't entirely comfortable with black people. He didn't possess any higher form of evolutionary development that made him see the world as all one people. It still made him nervous to talk to some of the new black students, but he did befriend a couple of guys on the basketball team (Neill did sports for *The Gleaner* during his sophomore year.) One of these guys, Malcolm was his name (check this), was the team's star, gifted with silky smooth ball handling skills and a jump shot designed by Giotto. Truth be told, Neill's parents, while banning the n word from their home, were not the most egalitarian folks. They were staunch supporters of the Republican Party. They even believed Nixon.

But, still, Neill saw things in a simpler light. Neill's heart told him what was right. This can be said for Neill.

One day, in the walkway to the Eastern Annex, a couple large black fellas cornered Neill, pushed him up against the windows. What they desired was unclear to Neill. Perhaps just to put him in his place. Perhaps just to scare the pee out of him. Neill's pee was scared out of him (not literally...we don't think).

Suddenly, just walking by casually, in a calf-length crushed velvet coat and a purple turtleneck with a gold medallion hanging in front of it, Malcolm appeared. He barely broke stride. He lightly tapped one of Neill's oppressors on the shoulder and leaned their way.

"Not Rhymer," was all he said. He didn't even meet Neill's anxious eyes.

The bullies walked away without another word said.

"I think I can do it," Neill said.

"Go for it. I'm proud of you," Thistle said, and bussed Neill's cheek.

So, Back to Orbit's

Sorry for the interjected sections. *Coitus interruptus literati.*

Orbit, with her Playboy bunny body, was the first young woman Neill saw completely naked, polished toenails to princess crown. She was spectacular. Her breasts looked even better against the soft flesh background of her chest and shoulders and arms. So large. So firm. As many men before him proclaimed, Neill proclaimed, I'd rip my own head off to see breasts like these. (Naked scene coming up soon. Patience.)

But Neill didn't have to rip his own head off. Orbit loved him. They told each other they loved each other. Imagine that. *Love* again.

In High School Clothes

In high school clothes are of the utmost importance, like subject-verb, like blooming libidos, like dope.

They are especially important to someone like Neill whose credo was, "Clothes are not important."

See Neill wear a crushed velvet winter coat. (Emulating Malcolm?)

See Neill with a Nehru jacket.

See Neill—O!—with a neckerchief.

See Neill try to dress like The Young Rascals.

See Neill try to dress like Malcolm. (Take off that damn crushed velvet coat. [At home there were pants to match. Neill wore them only once.])

See Neill in cowboy boots...with, wait for it...spurs!

See Neill eschew blue jeans because everyone wore blue jeans. (Neill's pretension went by the name of pretensionlessness.)

See Neill, then, in corduroy pants.

See Neill in double knit.

See Neill, years later, burning pictures from his high school years.

And we didn't even mention the white tux and lilac frilly shirt.

Into the Forest Primeval

Once Neill and Orbit took a drive out to Meeman-Shelby Forest Park, that great natural habitat just north of Memphis. Shelby Forest borders the Mississippi River and covers over 13,000 acres. It is old wood, as old as the pagan muses, and it was named for some conservationist named Ed Meeman. Who cares? It is also haunted. At night the woods are full of haints and duendes and spooks and banshees and wraiths.

Our juvenescent couple had had a small spat that day. Sometimes Orbit feigned indifference. It was as if Neill were looking into a face he was familiar with but that had placed over it a stolid clear plastic mask. Orbit, at times, seemed to be a planet spinning away from him. This hurt Neill. Neill was not the most secure of young men, even though he was having some romantic success, and any little wrong note could send him spiraling off course, out of Orbit, down into that secret place of self-loathing.

Anyway.

That day, a brisk fall day, they were both clad in bulky winter coats that prevented not only access to each other's bodies but were singularly unattractive enough to wilt the member of Casanova himself. They walked along a path made of subfuscous orange and brown. There was a tea-colored light in the trees. There were animal sounds around them.

Neill reached for Orbit's hand. She gave it to him and there was some peace established.

At one point there was a fallen tree above a deep ravine. Orbit wanted to skip across it. Neill knew he would never make it, nor would he ever live down shimmying across it on his ampersand.

"Hey, look over there," he diverted. "That little open area."

Orbit had already placed one foot on the log bridge. She turned and walked back to Neill, who was pointing like a dog.

"Yeah, so," Orbit said. Was this more ice? Neill tried to skate over it.

"Let's go inside. It's like a natural little living room."

This appealed to Orbit. Neill sometimes won the day with poetic invention.

Once inside the little thicket it really did feel like a private room, though it was only two yards off the path.

"Our own little nest," Neill said.

Orbit gave Neill one of those smiles that bunched her cheeks. Neill was a sucker for them. The teens kissed. Then they kissed harder, their tongues active. White kisses, red kisses, deep throating tongues and lips wet as palm leaves.

"Are you hard?" Orbit said, though she knew the answer, pressing her jeans against Neill's.

"Kiss me more," Neill said.

She did.

"I'm sorry," Orbit said, breaking away.

"What?" Neill rightly inquired.

"I am sorry I was a bitch earlier."

"Oh," Neill said, exhaling. "That's ok."

"Really. Sweetheart," Orbit said. Neill was trying to remember if she had ever called him sweetheart before. He was trying to remember if anyone had.

"Ok. I love you, Orbit," Neill said.

"You want a blowjob?"

"Always."

Neill leaned against a tree. It could have been the bo-tree. He thought later that it was.

Orbit kneeled beneath him and moving around in her heavy coat like an animal wearing a saddle she unzipped his jeans and let them fall to his ankles. She similarly lowered his briefs.

And right there, in the forest primeval, with birdsong crackling around them, Orbit swirled her juicy mouth around on Neill's young cock. She squeezed his balls. She took his langolee deep into her mouth. And soon, O soon, Neill was pumping into her mouth all the day's frustrations and all the Cyrus sap his young, semi-denuded, chilly, vigorous body could manufacture.

At Nicholas Blackwell with the Son of the Monster Magnet

Mrs. Reid one day asked Neill to stay a few minutes after everyone else had gone. Mrs. Reid placed something on Neill's desk. It was a mimeographed invitation to write an essay to be entitled "I Believe in Memphis." It was a citywide competition for seniors from every high school. Neill gave it a cursory look and Mrs. Reid a goofy grin.

"I want you to enter this," Mrs. Reid said.

Neill loved Mrs. Reid. He only wanted to please her.

"Ok," Neill said.

A week later Mrs. Reid asked Neill how the essay was shaping up.

"Oh, yes, yes," Neill hemmed. "The essay."

"Neill Rhymer, you haven't written one word," Mrs. Reid said.

"It's percolating," Neill said. "I have a title. The Return of the Son of the Monster Magnet."

Neill saw this outlandish title on a Frank Zappa album that belonged to Sly's older brother Gulley.

"Neill, the title is already a given. It's to be called 'I Believe in Memphis.'"

"Oh, right, right," Neill hemmed.

"I'll ask you again in 3 days."

Three days later Mrs. Reid asked Neill again about the progress of the essay.

Neill hung his head. If he could have he would have used a noose.

"Stay after today and write it. At your desk. I will sit here until you are finished."

That afternoon Neill sat and for the first time in his life stared at a blank sheet of paper, while inside his conk demons and angels and naked females cavorted, capered and capsized. He could not think of one English word. He could not think of one Elvish word either but that didn't matter. It wasn't like writing a poem, an activity he had begun attempting lately, basing his rhythms on pop songs. He couldn't fake this because it was prose and there were rules. (Neill believed there were no rules in poetry. He read somewhere that someone called poetry "TEGWAR: The Exciting Game Without Any Rules.") He looked up at Mrs. Reid. She was watching his consternation as if it were a pot of water on the fire.

"Ahem" Neill said aloud. He put the nib of the pen on the first line.

"Four score," he thought.

"When shall we three meet again?" he thought.

"The sea is calm tonight," he thought.

And once more he thought: "The wind was a torrent of darkness among the gusty trees."

This was harder even than his 6th grade report on *Champion Dog, Prince Tom.*

Then, something clicked, like the sound a pencil makes rolling off the desk and striking the linoleum floor. A small door opened. Neill looked in. There was a lambent light within. Neill's pen began to move. And it moved for a full 28 minutes until it stopped. At the end there were the words, "Inasmuch as I believe in freedom I believe in Memphis."

He lifted his head. Mrs. Reid was staring at him as if he were a hippogriff. A smile curled at the corner of her mouth.

"I guess this is it," Neill said.

"Ok," Mrs. Reid said and shook Neill's hand before taking the pages away from him.

And, readers, if there are any left: Neill won the damn thing. For the whole city. He won $500 and he got to meet the half mayor (it was unclear why it wasn't the full mayor) and he got his picture on the television and in the newspaper. And, at this time, in these early hours of human development and higher education, $500 paid for a full year at Memphis State, with a few dollars left over each semester for a couple LPs.

Neill was elated. This was the start of something, he thought. The start of *something.*

Orbit congratulated him. Then, she lowered her mask. It was inexplicable like the tides and the moon. Like the fucking tides and the moon.

Still...

Still, despite the fluctuations of Orbit's moods and, seemingly love, there was the sex. The youngsters were eager to pursue this mischievous sprite until they had exhausted it, or it them.

One Saturday Orbit's father and shrewish stepmother and granny took a day trip to Hot Springs, Arkansas. This meant one thing and one thing only: for the first time Orbit and Neill would be all alone in an adult house and they were free to pursue adult endeavors, up to and including the loss of virginity of both.

Hang on.

Neill had never seen Orbit, or, of course, any female, completely naked. And here was the opportunity of opportunities. He would not only see a female completely naked and at close range but that female was Orbit Unborn, whose body was every boy's wet dream.

And, lo it came to pass.

They went to the adult bed in the adult house. It was as large as an inland sea and it had that extra frisson of forbiddingness to it that only spurred our miscreants on. This was her father's bed!

While Neill lay nervously upon their brummagem orlon bedspread, which was prickly like a mohair sweater, Orbit prepared herself in the bathroom. Neill had stripped down to a t-shirt and briefs. He couldn't imagine what Orbit was up to. (This would not be the last time that Neill could not imagine what a woman was doing while he waited to penetrate her.) After what seemed hours but was really only eleven minutes, Orbit emerged wearing a bathrobe.

"Hi," she said.

"Hi," Neill said.

It was a slow start. Both their young hearts beat like dog's tongues licking a dish.

Neill had an Irish toothache anyway.

"You have an er—" Orbit said.

"Election," Neill said, cleared his throat of its imp, and corrected, "Erecting."

They both laughed nervously.

"Guess what I have on under this robe?" Orbit said.

Neill tried to remember every picture he had ever seen of women's underwear. His memory, even his imagination, was failing him. Bustle? he thought. Corset? Bodice? Camiknickers? Crinolines?

"I don't know," Neill said. "A Catwoman costume?"

Orbit laughed.

"Nothing, silly," she assured him.

This did not assure him. He was as nervous as smoke.

Orbit opened the robe. Her body shone like the treasures of Ancient Egypt. Her breasts really were dumbfounding. And her stomach was young and taut and thin, her curves seemingly imagined by Titian. And there was that pubic badge Neill had only gotten shadowy, fleeting views of. Orbit shifted nervously from foot to foot.

"Say something," she said.

"Come here," Neill said. And then quick on the draw, added, "You are so beautiful."

"Aw, Neill," Orbit said and in one deft capriole shed the robe and her inhibitions and joined Neill on the bed.

They tongue-kissed for a few moments but both knew what they were there for. Important matters called. Tongue-kissing was for kids. They had met at this place of consolation and risk to go beyond the pale. They were there to be initiated into the adult world of the non-virgin. They were there for the old goose and duck.

Orbit pulled Neill's t-shirt over his head where it stuck on his nose and then aggravated his Roger Daltry hair into a static-electric storm. Orbit pulled Neill's briefs off almost savagely. She grabbed his plonker and pulled. Neill's mind was bursting like a lab experiment taken out of his hands. His beakers were all boiling. His admixtures were all unstable.

Orbit leaned over Neill and took him into her mouth. Her breasts brushed his stomach. He ran a hand down her back over her bumbo and into her crack. She was totally, absolutely, unconditionally, undeniably, utterly, completely naked!

Neill felt the storm coming. And pulled Orbit's head up. No more sucking or there would be no fucking, Neill rhymed inside his never-quiet conker.

Now, it was up to Neill to do something he had only approximated before. (The term dry-humping is an inelegant term and will be used sparingly.) He had to learn to go down on a woman the way they so kindly went down on him. Orbit lay back upon her father's pillow. She spread her thighs soft as love's first word. Her body from the vantage point of her vantage point was unspeakably grand. Her breasts really were whole planets. They neither sagged nor spread. They were as full as the porches of cathedrals.

Neill put his mouth to her moistened shock. It had a rather unpleasant odor. Neill thought he might gag. This was unexpected. Still, he did his best and his best made Orbit squimmy. That was the point, right?

And now the moment came. Neill was no longer nervous. This was as inevitable as Shakespeare. It was what he was there for, at that moment, in that place. That delicious place.

Neill and Orbit only knew about the missionary position. So, that was what they did. Neill entered her. It was tight as if she were resisting him. He didn't know it would be tough. It hurt willy's head.

Then suddenly it wasn't tight anymore and Orbit made a sound like a tire puncture. Neill did what he thought he was supposed to do. He moved a bit.

It was very enlivening.

Neill, almost far away in his concentration, thought to look up. Orbit's face was squinched tight, her eyes closed (in ecstasy? in distress?), but her breasts were all Neill needed. They were moving like the wings of cherubim. They looked like Playboy Bunny breasts except that they were moving in a fleshly, titillating, hypnotic foxtrot.

It finished Neill. He shot off inside his girlfriend.

Then he collapsed on top of her. They were naked and lying together. That goddamn whoosh after-effect lasted for some time. Then suddenly they were filled with fear. Post-coital training would have to be learned at a later date. Suddenly they felt like Adam and Eve right before the snake exited stage left and left them there to take the rap.

Neill had no idea whether Orbit came (it would be decades before he knew...remind us to tell you about that when the time is appropriate, that is, when it is part of this chronology).

And there was another budding worry busy being born: what if Orbit got pregnant?

"Phew," Neill said, like many a clueless male before him.

"I love you," Orbit said.

"I meant, I love you," Neill said.

"You took my cherry," Orbit said.

Neill smiled wistfully. Now fully dressed but still holding each other, Neill was free to contemplate what the world would be like with a non-virginal Neill Rhymer in it. It looked a little bit like paradise.

More About Sly and Neill and the Car

Neill and Sly drove around a lot. They spent hours in cars, nights, smoking weed, listening to rock radio ("Sunshine of Your Love," Cocker's "Cry Me a River," "Tiny Dancer,") cruising the homes of the fairest of the land, wending their way through suburban streets dark yet shiny, or out country highways into the soft tree black.

Neill didn't spend every evening with Orbit, because Orbit's father was playing the father game.

Neill and Sly developed their own driving patois. They had phrases that meant something only to them (cf. "nildi"). For instance, when turning while using another car between yours and oncoming traffic was called "a screen play." Sitting behind someone at a red light who doesn't drive on quick enough brought this classic meme: "It's not gonna get any greener." And it was transmogrified into something different after the lads saw the Karen Black movie *Day of theLocust*. It became "It's not gonna get Faye Greener," which was her name in that film.

Once they passed a corner near Lake Windermere where someone had piled fresh cut grass. The dampness apparently worked an olfactory miracle on the grass: it smelled just like cum. This brought the boys up short. They stopped. They looked in each other's eyes.

"Cum, right?" Neill said.

"Exactly."

So they added the cum grass to their peregrinations. And every damn night the smell was there, like something out of a kinky version of *The 1000 and One Nights*.

Most of this was pure stoner talk, of course. Yet, we are tempted to say here: these phrases acted, even decades later, as a shorthand to talking about the past, as a sort of tacky glue which still bound Neill and Sly to each other, though the years battered their friendship like a keg in a gale at sea.

And Then the Snake Returned

It didn't occur to either of our young lovers until they had exited the bedroom and were in the kitchen, suddenly famished and thirsty, that Neill had squirted the oil of man inside Orbit's crankshaft. Who knew if one of Neill's brave little spermlets was at that very moment heading for some innocent egg, just sitting there with its yolk hanging open. They were heating up a frozen pizza to which they had added bologna, and drinking Orange Crush.

"This is how people get pregnant," Neill said as they waited for the pizza.

This seemed profound to Orbit.

"I think you're right," she said.

They took meditative sips of Orange Crush.

"We should have used something," Orbit said.

"What?" Neill asked, seriously. He really was clueless, poor sap.

"I don't know," Orbit said. "I had my period last week."

"Next time we will," Neill said, feigning maturity. "Use something."

"Right."

"Do you think you're pregnant now?" Neill asked.

"I have no idea."

The timer went off.

As they ate their pizza Neill had a brilliant idea.

"Let's call a doctor."

"Which doctor?" Orbit said. Little worry lines crept across her brow like cracks in ice.

"Any doctor," Neill said.

"Random doctor."

"Right."

"Just pick one. They should all know, right?"

"Exactly."

They got the yellow pages and flipped through the listings of MDs. They didn't even know enough to look specifically for an OB-GYN. They closed their eyes and flipped the pages and Neill stabbed a finger down on one page.

"Dr. Ed Jock Trolly," Orbit read.

"Call him," Neill said.

"Me?"

"Well, I don't know what to say about, you know, your period, and what, you know, we want to know."

Orbit dialed the number. She hung up.

"I can't do it," she said.

Neill puffed out his chest. He was Tarzan protecting his Jane.

Neill dialed the number.

"Hello," an elderly male voice said.

"Dr. Trolly?"

"Yes, that's right."

"You don't know me. Listen, I just came inside my girlfriend without any kind of, you know, birth control. She had her period last week. Are we safe?"

There was a silence like the silence inside a seashell that humans mistake for the universe caring.

"You were foolish," the good doctor said.

"Granted," Neill admitted.

"You're never safe without a rubber. Your dad tell you that?"

"Yes, sir." (He hadn't.)

"You're safer than if you had done it next week but not quite as safe as doing it while she was on her period."

"Uh huh," Neill said.

That silence again.

"Ok, thanks, Doc," Neill said jauntily.

"Be careful, youngster."

Neill smiled at Orbit. He said, "We are fine. "

It was approximately the truth.

Admiral Byrd

"Where's Orbit, tonight?"

"I'm not sure. Cousin's something or other."

"She tell you?"

"Yes, I remember her telling me."

"You don't really listen to other people, do you?"

"What?"

"Funny. So, you have anything to tell me?"

"No. Just assume I do, though."

"Bastard."

"Well—it was—*inevitable*."

"Right. Like death and sitcoms."

"And milkshakes and landing on Luxury Tax."

"Like sequels and sequins."

"Like making lists."

"Like making similes."

"Lists of similes."

"Great one."

"So, Sly, old sinsemilla pal. Tell me again whose apartment this is."

"Friend of my oldest brother. Kinda scary guy. Don't worry. My brother'll be there."

"Ok. And there are mob ties?"

"Reputed. Not this guy but his dad. Supposedly in prison for murder, a contract kill."

"Yeah, I'm real comfortable with this."

"It'll be ok. Fast in, fast out."

"We'd better."

Of course, they weren't. This apartment, a 2nd story off Jackson Avenue, was bleak for a guy making good money dealing drugs. Nothing on the walls. Large, crappy coffee table covered with piles of grass. Shag carpeting. And, against one wall, garbage bags full of pot.

Garbage bags full.

And the guy, an Argonaut in a tight t-shirt and tight Italian pants, was as frightening as a drunk dentist. Let them come tonight, Neill said. Let the police come tonight and my life is over. At least, I won't die a virgin.

"Sly and Neill are here for pot," Sly's oldest brother said.

"Got lots," the dangerous guy said.

"Just a lid," Sly said. He grinned like he did this sort of thing all the time. It was almost comforting to Neill. Sly paid for the lid and they still sat. Neill's heart was beating like a cop's fist on a cheap apartment door.

Sly's oldest brother said, "How bout we give the boys a taste of Admiral Byrd before we send them off into the night?"

The dangerous guy said, "Yes, indeed. A treat for the kiddies."

He went deeper into the crappy hallways of the crappy apartment and returned a minute later with an elaborate machine mounted on a piece of double plywood. It looked like a diabolic Mousetrap game. Or a science project by Timothy Leary.

What it was was an electric bong. It plugged into a wall socket like a toaster. And, once plugged in, it started to hum.

It hummed, "One Toke Over the Line, Sweet Jesus."

Sly's oldest brother explained how it worked. Basically, it sent the smoke through the usual bong apparatus (this one filled with a sugary Freckle Face Strawberry ade) but then, using some kind of miniature air cannon, it shot the smoke out the end of a hookah pipe in condensed jets.

"Once those jets start flying don't waste any. They are concentrated gold, baby."

Sly took it first. His head bowed. Admiral Byrd hummed and puffed and shot Sly's mouth 3 or 4 intense jets of smoke. Sly fell back.

"Whoa," he said.

Neill approached it as if it were going to sever a pinky, or turn his brain into that stuff that came out of the meteor.

When the smoke jets hit Neill's mouth it was all he could do to not choke them back. He was proud of himself later for holding his hits. Later, days later, when he remembered, he was proud. He didn't embarrass himself in front of the grown-up druggies.

The boys said thanks and goodbye to Sly's oldest brother and the dangerous guy.

"Hey, you boys are a-right," the dangerous guy said. "Next time I give you little treat. Not hash, no. Not coke, no. We give you some fine opium."

"Jesus," Neill thought.

"Great one," Neill said.

"Hey, he does talk," the dangerous guy said to Sly's oldest brother.

On the ride home Neill and Sly were quiet for a long time. The radio played "Season of the Witch" 42 times straight.

"I'm the guy in the Tidy-bol commercial," Sly said. "The guy in the little boat inside the tank of the toilet."

They were quiet for another day or two. The radio played "In-a-Gadda-Da-Vida" for 72 hours straight.

"I'm Nipsey Russell," Neill said.

"Great one."

Tripping with the Universal Fish

So Sly and Neill, high as the silver trumpet's martial noise, still made their rounds. Like drunken mailmen they made their rounds. They went by Susie's, they went by Jane's. They went by Orbit's, they went by Rita's, they went by Thistle's. They went by Ellie's and Thelma Lou's. They went by the homes of their freshmen females. Each of them, now at the wizened age of 18, had designated one freshman girl theirs to conquer. (One memorably nicknamed 'Fancy McWokwok' [wok wok being the boys' personal vernacular for beating off].) It was a diversion. It was ego.

"I got something special," Sly said one night.

"Big one?"

"Yes, but not for you."

"Great one."

"Oh. P. Um."

"You're kidding."

"Not," Sly said. He produced a small ball of tinfoil.

"Opium?" Neill said, stupidly. He was stalling.

"And you got Maxie James?" (Maxie James was their pot pipe. We'll explain later.)

"Pull over," Neill said, screwing up his courage.

They parked on a suburban street off New Allen Road.

They filled Maxie James with this new rocket fuel which looked like pre-chewed Juicy Fruit. Maxie James looked at them askance, as if to ask, Is this really what you want?

They smoked it till it was gone, passing the pipe back and forth like polite white men and skeptical Native Americans. Nothing happened.

"Hm," Sly said.

"Yeah. I feel something I think. Maybe. Something," Neill said.

"Hm," Sly said.

And then a soundless star was born inside their heads.

It was as peaceful as rose-leaves pressed in a bible. The boys floated, outward and then in again. Their hearts sang to their brains, the old songs, field chants, fife and drum.

Off Austin Peay, between Raleigh and Scenic Hills, rested a relatively new subdivision, Forest Lakes. It was as full of teen womankind as a Sophocles tragedy is full of terror, as a jail is of good company. Sam Onides also lived there, and Annie Aircraft, a housewife whose breasts Sly sucked one winter night when her husband was upstairs on the phone. It was very late, or very early. The night was silvery and glistening. Dark silver. Even without the opium. With the opium our travelers were wearing heads previously vouchsafed only to the gods.

Into this neighborhood the Pinto rolled. The boys were tired from singing. Though when, out of the ether, the disc jockey pulled out Cocker's "Cry Me a River," together, in unison, they had to count off the "1, 2, 3." Sly would really sing. Neill shrilled like an old fulcrum.

Suddenly, something was happening, something out of dreamspace. Sly let the Pinto roll to a stop.

It began, first as a sound, a rushing as of ibises lifting from a pond. Then it was more distinct. It was water. It was the sound of water rushing over stones. And then they saw it.

Moving toward them in a swirling motion was a minor brook. Otter Drive had become a streambed. The street, once familiar, had been transformed into Poseidon's realm. They were still. They were quiet. They were afraid to look at each other. They held their breaths. Maybe this is what opium did. It turned solid objects into *flow*.

"Are we seeing this?" Neill asked, his voice wee.

"Is it a river?" Sly asked.

"That's what I am seeing."

"Damn."

"I know."

"Wait. What street is this?"

"Like I would know. Sesame?"

"No, wait. We know this street. This is where Masher Steeps lives."

Masher Steeps was Sly's freshman before Raja Minute.

"Oh," Neill managed.

"It's the lake. The goddamn lake is flooding."

They squinted as if to focus. The moonlight glinted off the dark river like sparkly embroidery on a black cape.

"Let's get into it," Sly said.

They took off their shoes and socks. They rolled up their jeans. And they stepped out of their car, which had rolled into the stream tentatively, into about a foot of roiling water.

"Wow," Neill said. "It's warmish."

Sly was fording ahead. The sound of his shins breaking the waves was the sound of their hearts, opiate-spinning and open. The *swish* sound that a fetus makes in his or her own little ocean.

After about a hundred yards or so they could see the lake. For some reason the lake was emptying down the street. Well, it probably wasn't literally emptying but it did seem to be attempting a jailbreak. *No more shores*, the water shouted as it passed them.

'This is wild," Neill said.

"I've never seen anything like it. What's causing it?"

"I don't know. It's not the opium, is it?"

"How could the opium make the lake flood?"

They were silent some more. The question, perhaps metaphysical and perhaps rhetorical, remained unanswered because then it happened. The Universal Fish made its entrance, stage right. Flopping and flipping toward them the size of a muffler. Bigger. It was the size of a warhead. Bigger. It was the size of Francis Muldoon. Bigger, it grew bigger. It was the size of Yonggary, Monster from the Deep.

And it moved in a wild and frantic dance, singing as it passed them, the songs the fish sang when first God looked into the briny deeps and said, "Hmm, I need something else here."

It was the Universal Fish. It was the Carp of the Apocalypse. It was the Trout of the Bhagavad-Gita. It was the Chinese Yu. It was the Catfish of Thor and Hymir. It was The Aspidochelone. It was the Salmon of Knowledge.

The boys were agog. Together agog.

The fish passed them, its wake the roar of the Earth's resourcefulness.

With the fish gone the night settled around their shoulders. The water felt colder, clambering up their bared shins.

"You know," Sly said, his grin a jinn's, "If a fish can escape like that and come right at us, so could a snake."

Neill leapt into Sly's arms. Sly cradled him there like the ark on Ararat.

Then:

They were back in the car before they blinked. They walked on water. They discovered Jesus's best trick, how to not descend into watery depths. They were weightless. They ran on the tops of waxy wavelets.

Once back inside Pokey they reassessed. The night air shuddered as if it had just released them from onomastic incarceration.

They went home. What else could they have done? Having tasted godhead, they went home. And their dreams that night were dry dreams, dreams of the Earthbound, of the desert drifters, of the man alone enwebbed by arid introspection.

Returning to Orbit's Orbit

Now that they've seen Paris, how are you going to keep them down on the farm? In other words, once a lad (or a lass, some lasses) has gone all the way why would he ever stop? This was the 1970s and there was no AIDs. One heard vague talk about STDs, but they meant about as much as DMZ or AAA to teenagers with pistols in their pants. Neill only wanted to shoot his gun over and over and over, until something or someone made him stop.

It was hard for Neill and Orbit to find the kind of completely alone time to go all the way. They still did a lot of dry humping, fingering, oral sex. They still found pleasure in each other's bodies every time they were together. What other reason to get together? Sex was it. Sex was the top of the list, and the other items on the list (music, movies, Neill's incipient poetry) could not even see sex at the top, so far down were they. Neill wanted those tits, that ass, that pussy. He wanted them as badly as he wanted anything. He wanted to see Orbit naked every day and he wanted to orgasm with her every day. Nights when they couldn't get together were like interruptions in the fabric of time. Or like pills in the cheap blanket of time.

"I love it when you do that," Orbit said.

"What?"

"The finger thing. The two fingers—I think it's two fingers—inside me."

"Oh, yeah. That's good. That feels good."

"Do it some more."

"Yes, I will."

"I love it when you do that. I have orgasms."

"Really?"

"Of course, lunkhead. What did you think?"

"I dunno. Your orgasms are quieter than mine."

"Well, yeah. Last time you shot all over my neck while shouting '"Mother Mary, come to me'!"

"I did not."

"Practically."

"Ok."

"You wanna see?"

"See?"

"How you are when you come?"

"I do."

"Here."

"I love it when you do that."

"What?

"Juggle my balls."

"Really?"

"Yes, keep doing that."

"While I suck you?"

"Yes, keep doing that while—ah ah ah ahhh."

"Mmmffm."

"Jesus!"

"Mmmmmmmm," Orbits said, smoothing out her sounds, like a clarinet player reaching for deeper resonance.

"Oh, oh..." Neill was trying not to scream. Neill was thinking then he wasn't.

"There is a town in North Ontario...," Neill warbled in falsetto while Orbit swallowed his seed.

Afterward, she wiped her mouth, stuck her spermy tongue in Neill's mouth, pulled back grinning.

"Neil Young?" she asked.

"Right," Neill said. Now he wanted to go home and write a poem about signing Neil Young after a blowjob.

And, so...

And so senior year bumped on by. Some days Greg and Neill got stoned so that Neill took tests, answered questions aloud, talked to friends straight and crooked, and generally floated down the hallways on clouds of inattention. Some of Neill's friends, recognizing the tell-tale signs of boo haze, tsked and hmmed. Thistle was not too proud of her good friend on days when she recognized such signs.

One day Mick and Neill had gotten into Mick's mother's painkillers and that afternoon Neill showed up for Advanced Math with a new glaze to his oft-glozed features and Thistle was as angry as Mars. Another afternoon, again during Advanced Math (poor Mrs. Reed, where is she now?), the president of the class and the president of the student council showed up and announced that Neill Rhymer was needed for a student government meeting.

Neill looked quizzically at the interlopers, for he knew them but not well, and followed them down the hall, out the end of the Eastern Annex and into the parking lot. Debbie, who was a dwarf, was waiting there. She greeted Neil, who knew her but, again, not well.

"What is this?" Neill asked with the plain face of a good sport.

"Wanna go ride around and get high?"

Neill closed one eye. The sun, high up in the baby-blue sky, closed one eye. Neill pondered and Old Sol pondered, too.

"Sure," Neill said. Something about this was cock-eyed but he couldn't figure out what.

They got into the class president's AMC Javelin and began to drive around the townlet of Bartlett in broad daylight passing around a joint the size of Castro's cigar.

"Whaddya call this?" Neill asked as the smoke began to shine behind his eyes. He meant the kidnapping, but he might just have well meant the pot.

"Castro's Cigar," the president of the student council said.

They spent about a half hour at this peaceful activity and returned to campus chummy and high as Gilroy's kite. (And here these characters fade into the mist for this was their only walk-on in the stage play called Neill Rhymer's Adventures (Mostly).)

Later, discussing this unprecedented activity with Greg and Mick the theory was floated that they were testing Neill. There was much talk in these early days of pot on campus about who might be a narc, who might be working for The Man, even if The Man was only Mr. Bellamy, the guidance counselor, or Officer Sisson, the school cop. They suspected Neill was a narc!

Neill took it kind of hard. What was it about him that suggested he wasn't as "cool" (with bunny ears) as his compatriots? Perhaps his friendships with people like Thistle and Rita, and his love affair with Orbit, who knew nothing of Neill's druggy ways.

And, Orbit. She was spinning away. Some days still close (with great sex, yessir) and some days bouncing around Alpha Centauri treating Neill as if he were an astronaut passing below her atmosphere. (This metaphor sucks.)

When lovers go indifferent. There's a good chapter title. (Use it?)

Orbit was drifting like a satellite. (Better?)

In the Annual

Excerpts from the comments in Neill's senior annual. (Years later Neill was to unearth this artifact from amongst the detritus in his family's attic, under a dusty Stan Smith tennis racket and a box of photographs of people too beautiful to contemplate from the poverty of age. The parenthetical comments are his.)

(Sidebar: Neill was indeed voted "Most Ambitious" and had an extra photo in the annual under that moniker. Neill was not pleased. "Ambitious" seemed to imply that he wanted to get to the top, that he was scandent, a climber, that he would step on those below him. He really wanted "Wittiest," but his friend Jim got that. Naturally, he wanted "Best Looking," too, but honestly, he simply wasn't. This went to his fellow Kenneth Street Bum, Hawker, and rightfully so. Paul Newman eyes win every time, especially for Paul Newman. Neill would never be compared to Paul Newman. At best, Neill was, you know, the Michael Sarrazinesque sidekick.)

"Neill, you are really good looking and nice and I like you a lot. You're mean, too. Ha! Good luck, Canacee." (Who she?)

"It's not everyone in this absurd world that I not only respect but also admire but I do in your case. I have the feeling that we have seen much of the same things in life and have recognized much of the phoniness in these parts. You seem to have found some peace that I continue to search for. Although the road is dividing into many paths perhaps ours will run along side by side. Your comrade, Goffredo." (Prescience!)

"Don't loose (sic) sight of your goals. Dom."

"I've known you for years and still don't know what to say. You're such a goob. Keep your marvelous ambition (that word!) and if you don't fall too much in love with yourself you'll make it ok. Really, I love ya. Sadie." (Oh! O harden my heart, please.)

"To the greatest guy I've met. Alexey."

"Just think: one of these days when you are named poet laureate I can tell everybody—oh I knew him—he was a grand old guy. Your (sic) really a sensitive and open-minded guy with a quick to see smile. Forever remember me. Kriemhild."

"Think of me once and a while (sic). Dee."

"Well where to begin. I remember during our last year I wondered if we would ever go out again. Now I am remembering all our good times. In one year I have grown to love you more than anything else alive. You have become my one and only dream. I don't know if you're going to laugh at this or if you're going to take it seriously. I don't even know if you really care anymore. I guess this isn't the type of stuff you write in an annual. I am really proud of you. You have won so many incredible honors. I really am glad for you. People really love you, Neill. I hope we will get it together again someday but until then just remember I love you more than yesterday and less than tomorrow. Love you, Orbit." (Pass.)

"Neill, Could I possibly have dreamed last year that I would come to know you and 'to love you' as I have this year. You've been the one real spark to my teaching this year. There is nothing—absolutely nothing—that you can't do if you just pursue it. In my mind and heart I have such high hopes and desires for you. Continue to express yourself just as you do today, and the world will sit up and take notice. Much love, Mrs. Reid. (Jesus, I love that woman.)

"This is a warning: I will be waiting for you. Mike More Moore." (Thug.)

"Neill, your (sic) talented, ambitious and really I don't know quite what you are. You're someone I've admired since I was a teeny-tiny freshman and you captured my heart. For some reason I see a little of myself in you and I don't know why. I just know your (sic) someone who has influenced my life in—[ends here with not signature]" (Who is this? Where is she now?)

"To someone I don't know at all, but anyway. Dido."

"You are sweet and cool. Maybe this summer we can get together and smoke some grass. Stay smart. Stay off the hard stuff. Good luck with wine, woman and muggles. Stay cool, Launfal."

"Neill, what can I say? I know we use to be pretty good friends and whether you want to admit it or not I knew there was a time when you did like me and we could talk. (What is she talking about?) Neill, I respect you a lot. I did know you like a book but then something happened and you just weren't the same Neill Rhymer that I care about. (What the hell is she talking about?) I feel like I can't talk to you because whatever I say you cut me down. Neill, I am really gonna miss you! I love ya! Melusina." (What is this about? I was crazy about this gal. I think she dated Hawker for a while. What did I do to her?)

"2 Cool 2 B 4 Gotten. Dr. Crippen."

"Neill, I respect you so much. You'll never know how sorry I am that our friendship drifted apart. (Was I this problematic a friend?) Although I may not agree with everything you say I respect you so much for voicing your opinions and being yourself. You are truly one of the most talented people I know. I can't believe Penelope did what she did (Wha?) but the person she was referring to in the past week or so was me. I told her not to tell you because of Petruchio but I guess he and Orbit seem to be doing ok. Lots of luck and love, Thistle." (I really thought Thistle and I had an uninterrupted lifelong love. I must reassess. Who is this jerk all these folks are talking about?)

"Neill, I wish I could express in words all I feel about you. If you only knew. I wonder if you know how many times your smile brightened my day. Neill, you're such a beautiful person. I feel funny saying these words to you. It will be impossible for me to forget you. Enide." (That's more like it. Enide had a thing for me?)

"Well, I know we're not as close as we once were but you'll always have a place–should I say a reservation?–in my heart. Don't let your increasing popularity go to your head. (This seems a theme.) Thanks again for 4 years of the warmest friendship a person could ask for! Love ya always, Britomart."

"So, on to the world, Neill! It awaits you. If anyone can handle it you can. I'll always remember you as the small quiet boy who sat across from me in 4th grade at Coleman. I'll never lose my lifelong love for you. Rita." (Kee-rist, I wish she had a lifelong love for me.)

"Don't forget me. Really. Aleina, 386-4900."

"Dear Kenneth Street Bum, What can I say? I got to admire you for your accomplishments. We'll have to jive some more this summer. Hawker."

"You will always have a place in my heart. I wish I could say how I really feel. Akin." (Ah, Akin, Ah, humanity.)

And the clincher:

"Before I begin my little epic (*little* epic, Sweeney?), I want you to know and remember two things: I envy you tremendously and I sincerely love you. (Uh oh, Neill thought. He already knew that when 'friends' said they were going to be honest with you, you better duck.) However, you're turning into one of the more immoral punks I've ever known. You are bright, witty, and nothing short of brilliant. But what are you doing with it? NOTHING. And it makes me so goddamn sick! I simply can't believe it. I've always wanted to have what you have (what is *that*?). Because if I did I wouldn't be the frustrated, pessimistic, soulfully unhappy SOB I am. If I had half your brain I'd be in an Ivy league school and I'd be achieving impossible goals. I'd be known and respected by all. Well, I worked my butt off and I won't ever do those things. I just haven't got it. But you do. (WHAT?) But do you use it? Hell no! You're content to sit around that god-forsaken place called Bartlett and break the heart (something possibly more caustic crossed out) of every brainless, big tits, piece of ass you can find. Well any two-bit jerk can do that, but it takes a real man to set goals and then achieve them. So you have two choices. You can work at it and really make a name for yourself at Bartlett, and in life itself, or you can sit back and selfishly enjoy life (which sounds better to you?). If you choose the latter you sure as hell better never refer to me as your friend. What I say really doesn't matter, Neill. After-all, it's your life. From a failure to someone who's working on it. Sweeney Waterman. PS: I really do love and respect you and more than any one friend I've ever had. But I just had to say it all. I hope you understand."

Neill read this last bit once. His stomach turned. He read it twice. He looked up. There were students all around him, milling about in the hallways, chattering and going on about their studently business. Neill's eyes filled with tears.

Home, Job, Hair

During this time Neill no longer worked at Konee's bussing tables (and eating food left behind off customer's plates) but held a few part time crap jobs to pay for gas and LPs. He did maintenance at a women's clothing store (met a lass there—[may include her story here]), inventory at J. B. Hunter Department Store, and, disastrously, a stint at someplace called Gold and Silver, where Neill worked in electronics, an area he could not have been worse suited for. He spent most of his hours "on the floor" dodging customers, whose questions he could no more answer than he could explain rocket propulsion or the popularity of *Gilligan's Island*.

Raleigh Springs Mall was still the place to work and it would not be long before one particular store in the mall would change Neill for all time.

At home Neill fought the same battle being fought in households across America, if not the world: the battle over hair length. Neill wore his Roger Daltry (or Greatest American Hero, depending on you hipness) curly blond mop shoulder length.

Conversations at the dinner table went like this:

"Think it's about time you cut that hair," Dad said.

"You look like a girl," Mom said. (Mom got her best lines from television.)

"Lots of kids are wearing their hair longer. You know that."

(Insert motherly cliché here.)

"I'd like you to come to the barbershop with me this weekend," Dad said.

"I'd rather not," said Neill.

\   "Just a few inches off," Dad said.

"Dad, I should look how I wanna look, not how you think I ought to look."

"You look like a girl," Mom said.

We Think

We think we're about through with high school. Wouldn't it be great if all of us could really be through with high school? What is it about those four years that form us, thrill us, scar us and prepare us for nothing? Is it the impressionable age, as if teens were made of wax? Some folks love their high school years. Some folks look back on them as an unrelenting series of grotesque nightmares.

Neill liked high school. Even later in life he would look back on those years fondly.

Why?

Because of sex, mostly. Who doesn't remember their first sex fondly? Neill, in middle age, could still wax eloquently and passionately and affectionately about Akin and Orbit. The two girls—kids really—who initiated him into the mythic wonderland of sexuality. In a way, those two young women became templates for much of what came later.

Toward the end of senior year the cracks in his relationship became undeniable. Orbit could still make Neill feel like a chump, a loser, a sadsack, an asexual paramecium, wielding her disinterest like a ray gun. She could turn cold at the drop of a guillotine. Neill was often left feeling like the world's ugliest turd. He would go home and dream of better girlfriends. But, these were only dreams and he began to think that he would never find a better girlfriend. Certainly, Orbit's Playboy Bunny body figured heavily in this contemplation. Jesus, it was going to be hard to move on from those skookum knockers. (For the record, and this is not foreshadowing, it's just something that popped to mind: Neill was only to see one, perchance two pairs, *for the rest of his life*, that could compare to the biting majesty of Orbit's orbicular hammertons.)

And there were classes. And there were final exams. And there was a certain stress attached to that though Neill was a good enough student, even stoned, to do well, to pass. His ACT score was average. He took it on a Saturday after staying out most of Friday night with Greg drinking cheap wine and smoking boo. It didn't matter.

He took Orbit to the Senior Prom. They had a modestly entertaining evening. They ate dinner at The Four Flames. They went to the dance proper and hung out and laughed and danced. They found a place to park and Neill enjoyed the complicated tackle and gear that was Orbit's velvet prom dress. He managed to get one tit and most of her smoo uncovered. And he managed to bring Little Neill out into the night air for, what would prove to be, his last blowjob from Orbit while they were a couple. Stay tuned for why this is *qualified*.

When it came time for graduation Neill was invited to speak. He was not the Valedictorian (that was Thistle) but he had a wee reputation as a writer, or at least, a dabbler in words. Neill turned it down. He didn't want the stress. He wanted to enjoy the ceremony, maybe find a new gal to flirt with, go home early and sleep. Orbit, for reasons of her own, decided to skip Neill's graduation. Neill got the message. She was tired of The Neill Rhymer Show and wanted to put him into syndication. During the long program at The Auditorium North Hall in Downtown Memphis (don't look for the hall now, it has gone the way of the Vanished Tribes of Burma) Neill took stock of the faces around him, many he would never see again.

There was Greg, smiling a goofy marijuana smile. There was Cathy Chatterton, whom Neill didn't know very well, looking like a million dollars (it was rumored she had nothing on under her graduation gown). There was Amos Soma, wearing women's makeup and a new blond head of hair (the term homosexual was not used very often at Bartlett High School in the 1970s; no one really understood what *that* was all about). There was Casey Masterson reading a Kurt Vonnegut novel. Neill made a mental note: *Kurt Vonnegut*. There was Sif Peace, the girl with the most beautiful eyes in Christendom, and a wit as sharp as a death's lifted left finger. There was the president of the senior class and the president of the student council tripping on some California Blue. There was Garland Draper (real name), whom Neill never spoke to, though he wanted to because she seemed so mysterious, always reading a book, always with her signature hairstyle, two thin braids on each side of her wide-cheeked and lovely face, a delicate ribbon in each braid: she was as unfathomable as the Pythagorean number and hence desirable as no high school girl has a right to be. It was a good group. Neill loved these people. And, when Thistle spoke, Neill felt his heart expand. Did he love anyone more than Thistle? Probably not. Did she love anyone more than Neill? Probably not. Alas, alack.

Neill went to the dance afterward. But for some reason he was as sad as Lear. It was all ending. What would adult life be like?

Neill did dance once with Cathy Chatterton. He pulled her close and whispered in her ear: "I wish we had known each other better." She answered, "I have nothing on under my gown." Neill put a tongue in her ear. It was reflexive. She jerked back as if he had bitten her. "Gross," she said. And that was all for Cathy Chatterton.

Neill danced with Thistle. Thistle said, "I love you, you know?" And Neill said, "I love you, too, Thistle."

Then he went home.

When he arrived at home his parents were curious.

"What happened, Sport?" Neill's father asked.

"Nothing. Got tired of the dance."

"Ok," Neill's father said.

Neill went outside and got a lawn chair and pulled it up under the gas lamp that sat adjacent to his driveway. The evening air seemed scrubbed clean. There were stars where formerly there had been no stars. Neill could see for miles. He sat there for two hours. He was hoping for a miracle. He was hoping for a young woman to drive by, someone equally disenchanted with the dance, or perhaps a mysterious stranger, who would stop and say, "Neill Rhymer, let's really celebrate your graduation. Let's go to Lake Windermere and fuck."

This didn't happen. It was, admittedly, a long shot. Neill was asleep in his trundle bed by midnight.

The Second Cuckold

For those of you scoring at home you can probably guess what this chapter title portends and whom it entails. We are tempted to skip it and move ahead but there is some law of continuation which demands it be spelled out.

Orbit did not attend the graduation dance of her boyfriend Neill.

Orbit instead attended the graduation dance of Neill's best friend Sly.

Afterward Orbit and Sly went at it like woodland creatures.

How did Neill find out?

Sly told him.

Did Neill then end, unequivocally, the friendship?

He did not.

Why didn't he?

That's difficult to say. Perhaps still feeling like he not only didn't deserve Orbit's love but that he didn't deserve Sly's friendship, such as it was, either. He perhaps felt that he was lucky to have anyone who was smart and popular as a friend.

Why the perhapses?

Because humans are Steppenwolves with as many facets as a diamond. Who can figure them out? Who can figure out the need for masochistic relationships?

Later, someone would tell Neill, *Life is too short for toxic friends.*

Neill believed it then, but perhaps (sorry), his 17-year-old self would not have.

Neill ended it with Orbit. She cried. Then she said, *Fuck you.*

Pithy.

Neill did not end it with Sly.

He told Thistle and Thistle read Sly the riot act and Thistle held Neill while he cried the soft, slow tears of privation and grief.

Catching up with Brack

Recall, please, Brother Brack. Let us just catch up with him in one brief chapter.

The last time we saw him he was married with a young son and an even younger daughter, children as beautiful as timepieces. He was sent to Thailand so as not to be sent to Vietnam.

While in Thailand, his wife, a beauty along the lines of Arlene Golonka in *The Andy Griffith Show*, found herself a lover who was to prove not only a wife-stealer but a cruel fuckhead. When Brack returned from Thailand things were ok for a little while. Then the roof fell in. He headed toward that American game show from hell, *Divorce*.

They were divorced. For a while, because his wife was painted as irresponsible and imprudent and, perhaps, irrational, Mr. and Mrs. Rhymer, that is Lolly and Max, were given custody of the children. The children, ages 5 and 3, were as much a joy as a chore in the Rhymer's now cramped quarters. Brack took up his old place in the twin bed next to Neill's. Brack began taking some of Neill's things from the wall (Neill's Jethro Tull poster!) and half the dresser drawers. Neill threw a fit. This led to tears from both brothers.

"You have no idea what my life is like right now," Brack sobbed into Neill's shocked ears.

"You're overtaking mine without discussion," Neill sobbed back.

It was an ugly evening.

Nothing like the ugly evening when the children returned from a weekend with their mother and, while bathing the young girl child, Mrs. Rhymer discovered the welts on her backside. Turns out the new boyfriend was a dick, a brute, a monstrosity. His disciplines ranged from "spankings" with a small cord to locking the small, frightened children in dark closets.

Brack leaped to his feet. He looked wildly around the room. Max had to pull Brack aside and prevent him from going in search of the creep with murder in mind.

"Don't stop me again, Goddammit," Brack shouted. "No, Dad, don't! I'm gonna kill the fucker. I am going to find him and kill him."

Brack made it out the carport door with his father in pursuit.

Where was the mother during this time? You might rightly ask.

Mr. and Mrs. Rhymer, not to be trifled with, told her, the ex-Rhymer, that she would not get the children back, even on weekends, until she got her life in order. This took a long while.

Later that night, that hag-ridden night of discovery, Neill sat at the bottom of his driveway, bluer than blue, sunk into himself, tortured by a worldview that allowed for the abuse of young children. He cried quietly in the dark, in his lawn chair, at the bottom of the driveway.

A car stopped.

"What are you doing, Tuddy Jim?" a woman called from the car.

Only one chum of Neill's called him that, a beautiful woman who was a senior at Bartlett when Neill was a junior. Her name was Kiley and she had the most beautiful legs in God's world, and hair like a horse's mane. Neill and Kiley dated briefly and something came between them, something that cooled their every attempt at ardor. (Later, readers, Kiley came out of the closet. Sadly, this didn't seem possible when Kiley was a young woman.)

"I can't—" Neill said. A sob escaped like an empty speech balloon in a comic strip.

Kiley parked and went to Neill. She put her arms around him. Neill moved from the chair to the concrete driveway and Kiley sat beside him. Neill told her the story of the merciless evening at the Rhymer's.

Neill was able to add that his dad stopped Brack from murdering the asswipe. And that they were taking the youngest child to the doctor the next day to document the extent of her injuries. (Coincidentally, their family doctor was Dr. Lucas. He will appear later in a different guise.)

"Oh, Neill, oh my friend," Kiley said. She stroked his hair.

They sat there for hours. Eventually life resumed because it usually does. It doesn't always but, friends, it usually does. Now, witness the quickness with which we get along.

Eventually, the kids settled into their new surroundings. Neill loved the kids, read them stories, played on the floor with them. He also was driven near madness by their crying, especially the younger's. Looking back later Neill wished he had had more patience. He didn't understand youngsters. Till later, till later.

Which brings us up to this summer, this summer we shall enter in the next chapter.

A Breather

In relating the story of Neill Rhymer it might be appropriate to pause and say: the story of a young person's life is often told as if only full of gaiety and conversation and romantic incidents. But, to hone closer to the truth, one's life—anyone's life—is also made up of many hours of solitude, no matter how popular the anyone is. Some folks wear solitude like a jaunty cap, while for others solitude wears them like the proverbial bird beak on the mountain.

Neill's hours of solitude were, for the most part, not happy ones. Neill fell into loneliness as quickly as he fell into love. He could leave a convivial sodality of friends, who loved him and made him laugh, who entertained and enriched his life, and five minutes alone in his bedroom afterward he could fall into the blackest despair.

Some will say this is chemical. Inherited depression from the maternal side of the family. Some would say Neill thought depression romantic and embraced it as such. Whatever the reason, when the door was closed and Neill was left alone with the demons in his noggin, life could seem bleakly bleak.

Later, Neill fought this loneliness as if for his very soul. And perhaps that is the way he saw it. So, for the story's sake, many chapters shall be full of kith and kin, happy herd behavior, and joyous and thoughtful (even metaphysical) conversations that seem to deepen Neill, as if he daily fed on manna. But, let's keep in mind that each person is a secret within a secret, a *hortus conclusus*, because the heart is unfathomable. We'll try not to mention it again. This isolation thing. It doesn't make for good storytelling, see?

The Golden Summer between High School and College

It was the summer of tennis. It was the summer of being stoned EVERY DAY. It was the summer of Mick's convertible (which he once drove at 110 miles an hour down Stage Road with Neill as a thrill-seeking, yet terrified passenger...don't tell Neill's folks.) It was the summer of temp jobs and tans and sex and reveries and friendships and a heart, if not impervious to being broken, made calm by palliatives of sex and boo.

In looking back on it one would be right to ask: can you play tennis stoned? The answer is no. Though Neill and Mick and Greg and Hawker and Brack tried.

It was also the summer of Camus, Kafka and Vonnegut.

Neill, deciding he didn't really learn much about these cryptic objects called books in high school, thought he might try to self-educate. Up to this time (he is now approaching the liminal age of 18) he had no patience for books. He missed all the great classics of childhood. He spent his time watching *The Twilight Zone* and *The Dick Van Dyke Show* and *My Mother the Car*, thinking about girls and their unwhisperables. Books were for smart people. He had read some Poe and some O. Henry. You understand why these two authors. Because they wrote brief things, things that didn't take longer than a half hour to read.

In high school, it was all Shakespeare and Chaucer and Oliver Goldsmith and John Greenleaf Whittier. There was a poem in his senior English text that caught Neill's attention. It was called "Constantly risking absurdity" and it was by some hep cat named Lawrence Ferlinghetti. Mrs. Reid didn't teach this poem. Neill found it on his own and it vexed him, like a pea brain underneath his mattress brain. It turned something inside him like a small rusty key inserted into a small rusty heart.

So, to the Raleigh Library Neill went. The Raleigh Library was about the size of a Quonset hut. Neill went, by instinct, to the place where his future lay. He stood in front of the wall of Fiction (one entire wall on the west side of the squat hut) and said aloud (perhaps aloud), "Teach me." The wall said, Try these three.

Kurt Vonnegut's *Cat's Cradle*.

Kafka's *The Metamorphosis*.

Camus' *The Stanger*.

Don't say libraries don't have theurgical powers.

Um, Tennis, Tea, Sex

And so, they beat on, boats against the drift, the drift of inattention and youth, O youth. Some afternoons were for tennis. It must have been in the high 90s in Memphis those summer afternoons, but they were young and their flesh browned like Thanksgiving turkeys, and sweating and belting topspin backhands were part of the landscape of their minority.

Some afternoons were strictly for smoking tea, often with Hawker and Greg and Sly, and whoever else was around, especially someone with a new lid. New lids were held in the kind of esteem one imagines that a free pass to Cleopatra's chambers was esteemed back in that place and time called Ancient Egypt. At that time a lid was $15. Imagine.

Some afternoons were for visiting young women, sometimes just driving around looking for young women to talk to. Such chutzpah! Mick and Neill were happiest finding gaggles of gals at the mall or alongside suburban curbs or posed seductively behind gleaming counters at fast food emporia and chatting them up. They had no compunction about approaching strangers, young women who attracted them, with lines worn out from overuse, lines one would think didn't work in the first place. Sometimes they did!

Mick hooked up with one pretty girl this way. Let's call her Sizzle Aguedo. Because her name wasn't Sizzle Aguedo. She was exotic, dark like a Native American princess. Mick and Neill descended on her house like love gangsters. They spent many afternoons sitting on her couch filling her dark little princess ears with all kinds of foolishness.

Once Neill went alone to her house. Mick was working at JCPenney at the time, in the garage, and this afternoon Neill was on his own. Suddenly, he found himself locked in a loving embrace with this Sizzle Aguedo (or you pick a name), her willowy figure pressed against his, her dark hair curtaining his face, her hot young mouth all over Neill's cooler, older mouth. She was dishy. She was sexy.

So, it was with some surprise the next day when Mick announced that he had a date with Sizzle Aguedo. Neill felt a Sly feeling slip over his recalcitrant heart. Mick was nuts about Sizzle Aguedo, it seemed. They had been talking on the phone a lot.

Neill, of course, stepped aside and it was never mentioned again, that one-time cuddle on Sizzle Aguedo's couch, neither to Mick nor to Sizzle Aguedo, who Neill now saw sometimes when the boys double-dated. Luckily, Mick didn't want to double-date very often. Why? Because he was nailing his girlfriend nightly in his convertible at the drive-in. Once, they did it four times in one night. We can only imagine that it was a double or triple feature. Mick could do it four times in one night? It made Neill feel inadequate (and, forevermore, even when Neill was in his 50s, whenever he thought about Mick's 4-a-night prowess, Neill would feel that old devil in his head tell him, **you** *are not a stud*.)

More Summer, More Sex

"Flirtation is like a circulating library, in which we seldom ask twice for the same volume."
  −N. P. Willis

At this time, the summer of 1973, young people gathered at the "dam" on Lake Windermere. The dam was actually just where the road split the lake into one large piece and one small piece. That little stretch of macadam was a great place to park your car and stand around under God's Cimmerian sky, smoke a little weed, and flirt with the opposite sex.

Sly and Neill spent many summer nights there. Once they had a "burial at sea." Neill had snuck one of his father's pipes out of the house sometime earlier (the time of The Universal Fish) and the boys had used it to smoke, saving money on papers, and lending an air of Sherlockian cool to getting high. They nicknamed the pipe Maxie James, after Neill's father. Maxie James lived in the glove compartment of Sly's Pokey-orange Pinto. It served them well many purply evenings.

Until it didn't. It stopped drawing. And in trying to poke out the obstruction with a piece of stiff grass, the boys had managed to stop it up permanently. Hence, a grave ceremony took place at the dam one late night. With due pomp and circumstance, with words of hope and love and Eternal Goof, Maxie James was consigned to the bottom of Lake Windermere.

Something else happened that summer on the shore of Lake Windermere. Something small that redounded down the years like the tolling peal of a bell that Dopplers into the distance yet never quite fades away.

There was a Bartlett lass, class of 72, one year ahead of Neill, whose name was Sui LaBurrs. Sui was, quite simply, a real splendor, and desirable as the flowers of sin. She was as enchanting as beauty weeping in her weeds. She was on the Bartlett tennis team and she hit a top hand like a pro, but what brought the boys out, what made her that obscure object of desire, was her ampersand and thighs. She had thighs like oiled thunderbolts. And, tanned beneath a short white tennis skirt, they were coveted more than your neighbor's ass. She was a tasty bit of crackling.

Ok.

One evening Neill found himself in the crepuscule at the dam, near Sui LaBurrs and her body gave off heat like a stove burning seasoned logs. They chatted. Neill was a little nervous and a little high. Somehow, he charmed Ms. LaBurrs, who was home from UT-Martin for the summer.

The next thing he knew they were at her house, just across Lake Windermere, and it was about two a.m., and her darkened living room's Southern side was one enormous glass door from which you could see the moonlight ricocheting off the lake like shards of glass, and there was music on the stereo, turned low, music which might have been The Moody Blues or The Green Mountain Boys, and Neill and Sui were stretched out on a cramped davenport and their hands were doing things to each other which both esteemed.

Neill's hands were inside Sui's shorts and his fingers inside Sui's Aunt Annie. And Sui's hands were spelunking in Neill's shorts, finding Neill's root and squaring it in a matter of a few minutes. Neill came quickly. Forgive him. He was giddy. This was Sui LaBurrs! She was in college!

And they began to date, sorta. Mostly it was tennis some afternoons (one particularly memorable afternoon was spent on one of Sui's friend's backyard grass court. It was the only time Neill played tennis on grass, a fine experience, like eating escargot for the first time [and it might have been that afternoon when Neill and Sui had their best sex, Sui wearing her short white tennis skirt which allowed Neill easy access to her house under the hill and her magnificent backside—even in later years Neill was to swear that Sui had the softest poop chute he'd ever had the good fortune to caress]) and heavy petting some evenings. Good enough. It helped Neill's self-image. This was Sui LaBurrs!

Neill was happy just thinking about it.

This Happened Next

One evening Neill and Sly were doing their visiting rounds, which consisted of seeking out any young woman who was home and who would let them in to eat munchies and make jokes and use whatever wiles they conspired to make a young woman drawn. There were at least a good dozen prospects, and Neill and Sly spread their cheer around to different young women nearly every night.

This one evening they found themselves at Tessie Shremp's house. Tessie was a freshman at Sly's high school (technically, she was a sophomore or, as they later designated kids in the summer, a rising sophomore) at Raleigh Egypt. She was cute and friendly and, possibly, in love with Sly.

The trio sat in the Shremp's kitchen. Sly and Neill were riffing, possibly using song lyrics as if they were their own clever speech ("Really don't mind if you sit this one out..."), laughing at themselves more than Tessie was amused.

The conversation took a kink.

Out of the blue, without context, Sly took this opportunity, this audience of one 15 year old cutie, to say this to his best friend:

"I don't understand, really, what Sui LaBurrs is doing with you. I mean, she could have any *college* guy she wants."

Bile in Neill, rising.

"Sly, that sounds like jealousy talking," Neill managed.

"Well, you have her now but that's because I haven't tried with her."

"It wouldn't be the first time you went after one of my girlfriends, would it?"

It just came out, like a dead fish falling out of a pant cuff. The room grew frigid. Gelatinous. Dead. Tessie was dismantling a Rice-Krispies bar as if defusing a bomb.

There it was. Out in the open. Naked and for all the world to witness. (Let's let the appealing Tessie stand for the world, for now.)

"Ahem," Sly said.

"Ahem," Neill said.

(And, as these things go, Neill began to suspect that Sui LaBurrs wasn't really that keen on him, thus justifying Sly's frontal attack on his buoyancy.)

What Seems Anomalous, Especially in Retrospect

What seems anomalous, especially in retrospect, is that this did not destroy the amity between Sly and Neill. Perhaps this is further proof, as if further proof were needed, that Neill never felt worthy of anyone's friendship, not even a backstabber's.

Something cool had entered in, however. An icicle grew up the spine of their friendship and never quite liquesced.

Yet, when Sly went away to college and Neill stayed in Memphis and attended Memphis State, (and Sui LaBurrs went back to UT-Martin, without even a goodbye) the fellows wrote loving letters back and forth. (Sly wrote a very funny letter about when his school played the University of South Dakota and George McGovern was in the stands. "Damn," Sly said. "So I saw him sitting there and I thought, so this is what college football is. Then they beat us 60-6.") And, later, when Sly was kicked off his college football team and expelled for possession of marijuana, it was to Neill he went for commiseration and comfort. Folks are odd, and the connection between one and another odder still. It's made of gypsum and dryer fluff.

Meanwhile, in His Secret Cave Underneath Wayne Manor

Neill, that summer, was quietly transforming himself into something new: a reader. The three books he checked out of the Raleigh Library were working their literary sortilege on him.

The first book he chose, for its brevity, was Kafka's *The Metamorphosis*.

"Whoa," Neil said to the cobwebs in his mind. "Whoa."

Neill wondered if all books were this good. This was as cool as *The Twilight Zone*, but, somehow, somehow (and Neill wanted to understand *how*) more powerful, more interior, deeper.   Second, he chose, for its brevity, Camus' *The Stranger*.

Neill spoke aloud to the spirits in the cave: *take me now*. There are worlds within the world.

The Vonnegut novel, *Cat's Cradle*, again, hit Neill like a shot of heroin. Again, hit his private bull's-eye. Were all books this accurate, this much a true dissection of what it means to be alive? Or had he just, through some spectral means, chosen three important books his first time up at bat?

"I read," Neill said aloud. "I am a reader. I read books."

The next day, he was back at the Quonset hut, standing in front of the fiction wall, looking for more clues to the riddle of existence. Not MAN's existence, but Neill Rhymer's. Neill understood something abstruse: humans made art and Art remade humans. This was worth considering. This was worth spending a few hours away from the search for the act of ultimate androgynation.

BOOK II: CONSUMMATION

"If one is thirsty, he dreams of water; if one is cold, he will dream of a thick robe. It is my nature to dream of the pleasures of the bedchamber."
–Ikkyu

The Lottery

That was the time of The Lottery. Not Shirley Jackson's Lottery, but one equally full of Soul-death. Gather round, Folks, we're gonna put your son's birthday in a big tumbler and spin for a chance to go to that great theme park in Southeast Asia, One Big American Flag Over Vietnam!

The year before Neill was 18 his number was 16. This made him quake. This gave his stomach aches stomach aches.

For a year Neill sweated it. If drafted he would head to Canada to live with his mother's crazy Canuck family, try to learn the rules of hockey and curling, relish his peameal bacon every morning, and forget that he used to live in a country that he loved but one that had rained war down upon the Indochina Peninsula for little reason.

The next year, the year of Neill's possible drafting, the gnome in the White House called an end to the war though they held the lottery anyway, just to show young men they could. Just to flex their muscles and show Neill that his life was not within his own control. That year Neill's number was 278.

Things were looking up.

College, in Name Alone

Neill began his freshman year at Memphis State feeling somewhat good about himself despite the roller coaster summer he had undergone. A few friends from Bartlett started Memphis State at the same time and that eased the transition a bit.

But best of all, Brack, divorced and decommissioned (do they call it that in the Air Force? check) and determined, started Memphis State at the same time. It was Brack's idea to remake himself –having seen everything that was dear to him crumble, powder, liquefy and pool around his ankles—and this was what Brack was about to become: damnable smart. He was always an ok student, whereas Neill excelled with half the effort. This was only one of the changes in the tide. Brack dedicated himself to textbooks as if they were ancient holy texts and he a Spiritual Warrior. And, Neill, found it not quite as easy to toss off an hour's work at night and have the teacher pat his curly little head and say, *Good student, lovely student.* Neill, for the first time in his life struggled at school.

For instance: in high school, Neill was a math major, even passing Advance Math his senior year with an A-, a class he spent a lot of time enjoying through a druggy haze. In college, something shifted. Perhaps, it was all the dope and late nights and affairs of the heart that summer. Perhaps, it was a seismic shift in his psyche that found Neill suddenly avid about poetry and fiction and that part of his brain, which previously housed sines and cosines, now made room for Sikes and Cosette. Neill, freshman year, took what was commonly referred to as "football player math" (with apologies to football players everywhere). It was basic stuff.

Neill dropped it before two weeks had gone by. The teacher, who was Vietnamese, may have been speaking Vietnamese.

Neill went to his advisor. Neill's advisor said, "You can take logic instead of math, logic in the philosophy department."

Neill hit his advisor with a rolled-up report on bird imagery in Yeats. "Why didn't you say so?" Neill said.

Between Women

Neill was officially between women. Instead of love notes his backpack was full of poetry books: Richard Brautigan's *The Pill vs. The Springhill Mine Disaster*, Leonard Cohen's *The Energy of Slaves*, James Tate's *The Oblivion-Ha-Ha*, John Lennon's *A Spaniard in His Works*, W. S. Merwin's *The Carrier of Ladders*, Sylvia Plath's *Ariel*. They were powerful talismans. They were friends.

But, Lord, the sights and sounds of a college campus! Neill had never seen so many beautiful women in one place.

There was one young woman in his zoology lab. She was freckled like Jenny Agutter. She was short and buxom and made out of biscuits. Neill wanted very badly to touch her in places private and dark. He approached her. She laughed as if he were joking so he acted like he was. After all they had a whole semester to get through together.

They never spoke again.

Then, there was Solly Bass. She went to Raleigh Egypt with Sly. She was brunette, about 5' 7," with scenic contours. Neill made her the target of his most fervent cacoethes. He wanted Solly Bass. He had to have Solly Bass.

He contrived to bump into her as she left her class in the journalism building. He was skipping Psychology for the chance. Desperately, he watched the multi-colored students filing past. Such a crush. She wasn't there. She was out today. She knew his plan and had gone another way. She knew his plan and was ducking him. She knew his plan and was disguised. She was the short, heavy, Chinese student with the blue anorak.

Then, he saw her. She was stunning.

He quickened his step and drew alongside her like a hearse at a gravesite.

"Hi," Neill said. "Hi."

Solly Bass looked at him as if he were a hearse alongside a gravesite.

"Neill," Neill said.

Solly laughed. "Sorry," she said. "Girl has to be wary. Many predators about."

"From Bartlett," Neill said.

"I know. I've got you now."

"Right." Neill thought, you can have me. Do I have you now?

"What's up? You're out of breath."

"Right," Neill said. He willed his chest to stop panting. He willed his heart to stop beating. Ok, not to stop beating, but to stop doing it in such a rootless and irritating fashion.

"You taking a journalism class?" Solly Bass inquired.

"No," Neill shouted, as if he had been caught out. Actually, he was taking journalism 101, but not today.

"Ok," Solly Bass said. Her smile was dwindling.

"Sorry. I was just late for—for class," Neill said.

"Ok."

"You wanna go get a bit to eat?"

"It's 9 a.m.," Solly said. Her cheeks were indented with dimples as clearly cut as the tooth of time.

"Yes," Neill said. He stopped walking, so Solly Bass stopped too.

"Did you mean another time? Are you asking me out?"

Was that what Neill was doing? Oh, yes!

"Yes, I guess I was. Am. I guess I am."

Solly laughed. It was a sleigh bell.

"I'm seeing someone, Neill." Solly laughed once more quickly. "Otherwise." She stopped and suppressed one final laugh. She laid a consoling, o humanly warm, hand on Neill's chest. "How could I resist such a smooth approach?"

"Ok, bye," Neill said, but he stood still. He was fading like an old Polaroid.

"We can still talk sometime, if you'd like that. I mean, Jep and I are pretty serious, but..."

"I guess not," Neill said. "You're beautiful."

Solly smiled and walked away. Neill watched her caboose. They would never again be on the same track.

Thistle Reappears Briefly

Home from Lambuth on break Thistle called Neill one weeknight to see if he was doing anything. Neill was not, so he strolled, in heliotrope twilight, through his verdant neighborhood to Thistle's contiguous verdant neighborhood.

Thistle was going great guns at college and had much to talk about. Neill listened and joked, and they slapped at each other like children and laughed and the night came on, dark as stains of wine.

Eventually, Thistle's parents went to bed and the two college freshmen faced each other, eyes alight, on the large davenport in the living room. The TV was on but the sound was low and burbling. The late-night movie might have been *Union Pacific*.

"How come you don't have a girlfriend, Neill boy?" Thistle asked.

"Between girlfriends. I don't know. It's not happening for me."

"Me neither," Thistle said. "There was a guy. Then, there wasn't."

"I understand. I thought I liked one woman but, well, she was a little insipid. She thinks life is a romantic comedy with her as the kooky, but loveable, heroine."

Thistle snorted.

"So, we're both free," she said after a pregnant pause. A pause almost to term. A pause perhaps presaging a home birth.

"Well, yeah," Neill said, utilizing the rapacious wit of Cyrano.

Thistle (Bold, Thistle!) leaned forward and put her pouty lips on top of Neill's. It was a long drink of water for two thirsty chums. Thistle put her hand on Neill's thigh. Her hand sweated through the thin material of Neill's double-knit pants. After about 4 years they drew apart.

"Thistle Sharer! I didn't know you felt this way about your old pal."

"You knew."

"I had an inkling. A tiny inkling. I dismissed it as my own dick-driven ego."

"Kiss me some more," Thistle said.

And he did and he put his hands under Thistle's shirt and practically tore her lung-sling off. Thistle had the breasts of a small boy, but her nipples were terrific, weighty and full and hard as kernels. Soon they were prone and clothing was loosened and hands went jouncing about. They were both panting. Neill ran a hand between Thistle's thighs. Her letterbox was as dry as her palms were wet.

"I—I did not expect this," Neill said, as he slipped his hands into Thistle's panties and cupped her magnificent ass cheeks.

"You think I stopped thinking about your balls?"

"My balls?"

"I used to sneak looks at them when you wore loose shorts."

"Oh my."

"I wanted to kiss them back then."

"Thistle, my boarding house dumpling, you can do that now, please."

"I—I sorta don't know how."

"To kiss—"

"To give a handjob, to make a boy come."

She said 'boy.'

"I think you can do that. I think we can teach you that."

Neill opened his pants and his roundhead rogerry popped up.

Thistle put one sweaty palm around it. She held it too tight, as if it were a Louisville Slugger and she Rocky Colavito. Neill thought she was gonna choke up on it and point to the fences. Instead, Thistle exhaled like one afraid to go on.

"Move it up and down a bit," Neill said.

Thistle pulled a few times. It was painful. Neill thought he was being skinned. Thistle let go. She covered her sweet face with her sweet hands.

Shortly thereafter Neill hoofed it home, his balls aching, his mind whirling like a panicky midge.

And Then There Was Dew Drynow

Readers, tread lightly here. We are entering delicate ground, ground really consisting of a few bamboo poles covered with light fronds over a chasm deep as midnight's starry treasure. It is a jungle trap. It is not for lions or tigers or bears. It is for Neill's soul.

There was a lass who went to Raleigh Egypt. Her name was Dew Drynow. She was the prettiest thing Neill had ever seen and Neill had seen Mary Tyler Moore in Capri pants. She was brown like a chestnut. Her hair was chocolate brown. Her complexion was smooth café au lait. She was small and shapely, and her tanned legs did things to men which men thought they wanted done but in reality, twisted them into shapes almost indiscernible as human. Neill saw her from afar. He learned her name. And, having learned her name, he internalized it and it became a stone inside him, working its way to painful places like the heart and kidneys.

He had to talk to her. There wasn't a choice. There wasn't a "none of the above" on the questionnaire his heart had created for him.

He also found out that she had a boyfriend, but he was on his way out. Dew had already packed his bags and he was standing on the threshold with his cuffs full of rain. His name is lost to this account.

Neill saw her at McDonald's with friends. He wanted to approach her but felt foolish.

He looked up her address in the phone book. She lived with her enchanted family in a hollow tree in Scenic Hills. Neill drove by the tree. Fairy light surrounded it. Fairy rings surrounded it. Neill asked himself this question: Can I approach Drynow Castle and ask for the princess's hand? His self looked back as if Neill were a toadstool.

Nevertheless, Neill girded his loins. His loins girded. He made like a knight errant. This was a task worthy of Hercules. But Neill, lily-white Neill, tremulous Neill, awkward Neill, was going to attempt it anyway.

One night he just showed up on her doorstep. (The bold marauder, if you've been paying attention.)

He rang the bell. It played Pachelbel's Canon.

He stood on the threshold, perhaps the way the ex stood, except the ex was looking at the past and Neill was looking at the future.

A woman answered. A mother. An exquisite mother, as lovely as her daughter, even through the pentimento of age.

"Hello," Neill spoke as if he were human. "Is Dew in?"

(In? he asked himself. Did you just say *in*?)

"Yes," the mother spoke as if Neill were a human, but perhaps a dodgy human. "Who may I say is calling?"

(She spoke like that. It made Neill feel a little better about saying 'in.')

"She won't know my name but you may give it to her. It's Neill Rhymer."

"Come in, Neill. Sit in the living room here. Dew is doing her homework, so don't keep her long. I will get her from upstairs."

Neill sat on a chair that may have once belonged to Marie Antoinette. The room was built of fine things, finer things than Neill's parents had ever contemplated adding to their purlieu (or parlor). Neill sat for a long time. He tried to make his inner voices lie still. They chattered away as if Neill was not even there. They were planning an animal tea party and Neill was to be the ass.

Then she emerged from upstairs. She walked down the staircase the way angels walk down moonbeams.

"Hi," Neill said, standing. He held out his hand. "I'm Neill."

Dew approached like a doe, a doe wondering what the hell the hunter was doing outside his blind, weaponless and without camouflage.

"You don't know me," Neill said.

"I know," Dew said.

"I went to Bartlett. I know some people you know."

Silence like the inside of a clock.

"I went to Bartlett," Neill said again. Suddenly, he had no idea what to say next. It was preposterous that he had prepared nothing.

He plunged on.

"You're the prettiest woman I have ever seen," Neill said. "I am foolish, I know. Rash and reckless. But, I had to ask you out. I have been carrying your face around in my noggin for weeks and I had to meet you and ask you out. Forgive me. I am really a nice fellow and did not want to begin by making you wary, but I saw no other way. I was driven here by the simple compulsion of overwhelming admiration. I'm a freshman at Memphis State. I know this is awkward. Perhaps you would sit down and talk to me briefly, and maybe we could do that one or two more nights and then you could see whether you want me to ask you out on a real, certified date."

It was quite a speech.

"I'm in high school," Dew said.

"I know," Neill responded.

"I don't know," Dew said.

"Of course you don't," Neill responded.

"I can sit for a minute." And she sat.

Neill sat.

Then, Dew did something that was like finding the magic key inside the ball of light which arises from the middle of the bewitched lake. She laughed.

"You are bold," she said. "No one has ever approached me this way," she said. And she laughed a little more.

Neill was in.

That night, driving home, Neill's head was full of fairy light. His browed was encircled by fairy rings. Dew Drynow, the most beautiful woman he had ever seen much less spoken to, had agreed to see him again.

Concurrently...

Concurrently, Neill began his way down a road that would carry him, a drifting romantic, for the rest of his life. This is not hyperbole. It is a holy road, one made for fools and saints and true believers. Though Neill fell somewhere along the continuum between fool and saint, this was a road that seemed lit from above rather than below.

Neill had to find a part time job if he were to have dating and album money. Neill asked this poser of himself: what is your passion? And, though embryonic and still with a new car smell, he found the answer and the answer was reading books. Books. Neill wanted to do something with books.

Now, in Raleigh Springs Mall at this time, as has been aforementioned, there existed a bookstore named Waldenbooks. Neill, at this time, did not know the difference between a chain bookstore and an independent locally-owned bookstore. Indeed, in the early 1970s there was a small war a-brewing, which would continue from then to this day. Chain bookstores, backed by corporate millions, were springing up in every community big enough to warrant a mall. And, Memphis had a number of malls at this time, the newest being Raleigh Springs Mall, right in Neill's backyard.

Neill applied at Waldenbooks. He interviewed. He was asked whom he read. He answered Camus and Kafka and Vonnegut. The manager nodded. Neill could not read her responses.

"Thank you," Neill said, as he left.

"Thank you," the manager, whose name was Joy, said. That was her first name. She was pretty in a country girl sort of way.

"I'd be surrounded by all the collected knowledge of the universe," Neill told Brack. "Imagine. The wisdom of the ages would seep into me by osmosis."

"It would be a good place for you," Brack said, as Neill navigated the family's new Toyota into a parking space south of Memphis State, just across the railroad tracks from Patterson Hall, aka The English Building. (The Toyota, christened in the brothers' Canada adventure, yellow as a country egg, while not formally given to Neill as a high school graduation present, became Neill's car. It was "officially" called The Family's Second Car.) (The English Building, which had a conversation pit in the lobby (seriously!), was where Neill was studying Freshman Composition and English Literature [which meant *Beowulf* and *Sir Gawain*].)

Reader, he got the job.

His first day he showed up (50% of life according to some wit) with great unease. He imagined that he would be found out. He imagined that authors, whose books were on every tongue but his, would line up to drum him out of the profession. "It's just a job," he told himself. But secretly, he wanted it to mean more. He wanted people to think he was smart.

(One parenthetical comment at this point: also, fresh on the job at Waldenbooks in Raleigh Springs Mall, was a young lass who went to Raleigh Egypt with Sly, and who was the daughter of the Rhymer's family physician, who was also a freshman at Memphis State, who was called Victoria Lucas, and who had brown hair made of stuff finer than amber or ambrosia or Amstel, and who had a wagon that could turn any man to swine. More later.)

To Dew or Die

So here was Neill, gaga as a drunken goat. Here was Neill actually dreaming he could win the princess even while knowing he was no knight, and knowing that his day had not come. Here was Neill dreaming large.

He and Dew went to hear Steely Dan because Dew expressed admiration for them. The seats were cheap. They were in the upper frosty regions of the Auditorium North Hall. Neill wished they were sitting front and center, thinking this would please young Dew more. The concert was excellent, as near as Neill could remember. They played "Reeling in the Years" at a tempo so fast they seemed to be on horseback. This is all Neill will remember of the concert. It was more important that Dew Drynow was holding his hand.

He and Dew attended a tennis match at Memphis State because a striking Lochinvar from Bartlett, who was a friend of Neill's, was returning as part of the University of Tennessee Tennis team to play his Tiger counterpart on the concrete courts of Memphis State. All Neill could recall from this day was that his friend was beaten like a drum and the wind was as cold as Diana's Crescent. It was more important that Dew Drynow was holding his hand. She was warm. Her skin was soft as the murmur of sleeping Spring.

The wind blew in vane.

Evenings at Dew's house ended with polite necking. Dew's kiss was like dew. Neill wanted to hold that kiss forever. He wanted it to last until the end of the Mayan calendar. She was so beautiful, this Dew, that Neill dizzied gazing at her. She would not come into focus. Neill assumed her beauty could not be seen clearly by mere mortal man. She fuzzed.

Neill told Dew he loved her. He told her numerous times.

Once she said it, in return. Neill's heart crooned like a swan gone to bliss.

One bold night, on the porch swing at Castle Drynow, Neill, locked into a warm embrace and emboldened by Dew's pulpy tongue in his mouth, cupped one of Dew's breasts (outside of all her clothes, yet still Neill felt its heartbeat like that of a fallen robin). Dew drew back as if stung. She asked Neill to never do that again.

She asked Neill to never do that again.

She asked Neill to never do that again.

Reader, Neill never did.

He Said She Said

"Neill, listen."

"Oh no."

"I really like you."

"Oh, God, no."

"I just think, well, I just think I don't love you."

"God, no."

"Listen, you're a great guy. You'll have so many girlfriends."

"But, I love you."

"I'm sorry. I really want us to be friends."

"Oh, God, no."

"Neill."

"God, no."

So It Died on the Dewy Vine

You possibly assumed we were heading this way. Possibly the "relationship" carried its own death around in a watch fob pocket from the very first night Neill showed up on the castle steps.

Neill went into a tailspin. He stopped eating. He stopped sleeping. He worried his mother. Neill's mood turned dark and his mother feared for her son's interior life, if not his life entire.

One middle-of-the-night, Neill, sleepless, in the kitchen with his head in his hands, Mrs. Rhymer appeared in her robe and sat at table, too. (Lolly Rhymer was a lifelong, card-carrying insomniac, a horrible malady, which was one of the horrible maladies Neill got from his mom, which also included, as a bonus prize, a dangerous inner demon who occasionally asked if life were worth living. This demon's name is Everything Sucks. His brother is You Suck.)

"What is it?" Neill's mother asked, setting down two mugs of warm milk and honey.

"Nothing," Neill said, because this is how teenagers answered their parents.

"You're not sleeping," she persisted. "Talk to me."

"I hate my life," Neill said, not for the last time.

"What do you have to hate? You have so many friends. You have a job, you're in school, what is it that eats at you?"

"I have nothing," Neill said, not for the last time.

Mrs. Rhymer was quiet for a while. Neill's head hung precariously close to his warm mug of honeyed milk.

"Did anything specific happen?" she asked, finally.

"No," Neill said, because this is how teenagers answered their parents.

"What would make you happy, Neill? What, right now, would make you happy?"

"If Dew loved me again," Neill said.

"You don't need her," Neill's mother said, because this is what mothers say.

"I need nothing else," Neill responded.

At the Bookstore in Raleigh Springs Mall

Neill, despite his shattered heart, was fitting in at the bookstore. He was a quick learner about most things. He managed to understand the intricate truculence of a cash register for the first time in his life. He learned how to wait on customers, make change, smile sincerely and say, "Thanks, have a nice day." You, who have never done such things, laugh not. They are more difficult than they seem, and not everyone gets past the first hurdle.

The second hurdle, the one that had Neill shying, was learning about books. Having just begun the process of self-instruction Neill was lacking in a good backing in literature. Knowing the names Tolstoy, Dostoevsky, Joyce and Updike did not mean knowing which book was considered their best, which one you personally recommended, knowing how to even talk about what makes a book good. (This is, as noted, a sticking point even with the most seasoned readers.)

Neill muddled along.

This helped: Victoria Lucas, who Neill had known for years because of the melding of the two nearby high school populaces (Bartlett and Raleigh Egypt), was not only an attractive reason to make it into the office, she seemed to like Neill, and she had read more than him, and she took him under her protective wing. Victoria ran with people he ran with. They both knew Sly well. And Victoria knew the Dew Story and recognized a shaken human being when she saw one.

Also, starting at the same time Neill did, was a young fellow named Bidden Route. Bidden was hawk-nosed, thin as gold leaf, with a shudder of brown hair. He looked something like the young Samuel Beckett. Bidden came from the tough streets of Frayser, just north of Raleigh, a place of gangs and drugs and a great Whataburger. Bidden, like Victoria, had read more than Neill and Bidden was even shyer than Neill and took the customer service part of the job hard. He tended to talk into his collar. The boss, the woman who had interviewed all three new employees, Joy Johns Dun, was gentle with Bidden, but she did insist that he be more assertive. She might as well have told him to sing the aria from *Aida*. (If *Aida* has an aria; we assume it does.)

So, Neill, slightly bolder than Bidden, covered for him with customers and Bidden, in turn, covered for Neill's astonishing ignorance about literature. When a customer corrected Neill's pronunciation of Proust (it rhymes with 'roost' not 'oust,' they tell us) Bidden said, "He knows that. He was having you on." Neill was ashamed, of course (years later he could still feel the burn of this particular public humiliation), but he was also quite fond of Bidden suddenly. The two young men were forming a bond.

One afternoon, a young woman came in. She was dressed in elf clothes, greens and browns and a small, cockeyed beret. Her face, lovely as a seraph's, dark eyebrows and pillowy lips, was drawn as if she had been crying. Both Neill and Bidden noticed her and exchanged the kind of glance men exchange when beauty enters.

She shopped around for a while. When she checked out Neill rang up her purchase: *I'm Ok, Your Ok*; *Sailing Your Own RelationShip*; *What to do After you Cry*; *You're Better Off Without the Asshole.*

Neill looked at her red-rimmed eyes. She looked up and Neill gave her an understanding smile. That's what he hoped he was giving her. She let a small whimper escape. Neill quickly bagged her books and said, Thank you.

"Lost her boyfriend," Neill said.

"Oh Jesus. Who would leave her?"

"I know. It's an obscurity, the human heart."

"And sometimes, there are just assholes who complicate your life. There is something even sadder about her thinking she might comfort herself with self-help books."

"True."

"You didn't read any— "

"Because of Dew? No. I just stayed in my room with the lights out calling myself ugly names and hoping to die."

"Much healthier."

"That's what I think too."

More About Victoria Lucas

They both loved books and movies, Neill and Victoria. Victoria was better versed in both. Her knowledge of movies went all the way back to Buster Keaton and up to the latest Bergman. Her knowledge of books went all the way back to *Betsy-Tacy* and up to the latest Iris Murdoch. She was cunningly smart and funny, and just the right amount of goofy. She and Neill would meet sometimes in the student center or in the conversation pit in the English building. And at the bookstore, they made working overtime seem fun.

We Recount Further Events as Well as Divers Things Worth Knowing

At this time, Brack was living with a Nordic gentleman by the name of Freyr. Freyr was also attending Memphis State, and often Brack and Neill and Freyr met in the cafeteria for lunch, sometimes skipping classes if the conversation was lively enough, and it often was. Sometimes female companions also joined the men, Freyr's girlfriend, Loyola, Neill's friend Janet Marshall, or Brack's friend Shelly Ellie Eliot. Sometime,s new friends drifted in just to sit near their conversational campfire. It was a dynamic group. Sometimes, they laughed so hard they set off the fire alarms. Sometimes, they talked so deeply and passionately about things, carnal or literary or politic, or cinematic or historic, that professors eavesdropped and eventually modified their syllabi because of some ort of wisdom from the table.

Also, Freyr, aside from being expansive and funny and loveable, was a competitive sportsman. He liked nothing better than challenging all around to table tennis, basketball, soccer, cheese rolling, stickball, spear-throwing, or whatever. And, from this, around the middle of the first year of college, the three men and whatever fourth they could find (sometimes Janet, sometimes Freyr called in a ringer like the captain of the Memphis State women's tennis team), began their late-night tennis matches at the public courts in Bartlett, Tennessee. Because Neill often worked the terrible 1-10 shift at Walden's often these matches did not begin till 10:30 p.m.. And, all 3 men had 8 a.m. classes. How did they do it? The elixir of youth known as adrenaline. Sleep was of secondary, tertiary or quaternary importance. This was life!

It was also around this time that Brack and Neill began getting high together. Weekend nights usually meant a little weed at Brack's apartment, some cheap cheese curls and something freaky on TV. VCRs were becoming common and it was a kick to get stoned and watch old monster movies, especially those containing bugs or lizards grown large due to bad nukes. Anything with Kenneth Tobey or Jeff Morrow. (Isn't the title *The Giant Behemoth* repetitive? Neill asked.) Both Brack and Neill were single, so the stoner talk, in between maniacal breath-choking chortling, was often about this female or that. Brack had a buxom blond co-ed he was interested in. Neill had his dreams.

The stoner confab proceeded, sometimes flowing, sometimes in fits and starts. Sometimes, it resembled the garbled nonsense between Quixote and Panza.

"You really lonely now, Bro," Brack said.

"Sure, sure."

"You know, you've had some amazing girlfriends."

"I have. Where are they tonight?"

"I liked that cheerleader in high school. What was her name?"

"Cheerleader."

"I don't think that was her name."

"No," Neill spluttered around the doobie. "Akin. Akin Upspins."

"Yeah. She was a cheerleader."

"Right."

"You get there with her."

"Not quite. Close. Close but no cigar. No inserting of said cigar."

Now, Brack spluttered, which made Neill laugh harder. Soon, the conversation began again.

"Lost it to Orbit," Neill said.

"Yeah."

"Orbit of the orbs, the great mammalian orbs, the orbs of Manos, the orbs of fate."

"Her tits."

"Right."

"Were magnificent. Could see that even with her clothes on. Tits with their own zip code."

"Yeah. She and I did it. We did it. We did the. The. Consummative deed."

"Fucked."

"Yeah."

"Yeah."

"Those tits."

"I bet," Brack said. He took a long toke and the brothers were quiet.

"The cheerleader had a nice body," Neill said finally.

"Aspen."

"Akin."

"Right."

"You fuck her?"

"I don't think so. But it was close."

Moving On

In life, friends, one walks to get from one place to another. In books about life, the movement is left up to you, gentle readers. Keep turning the pages. Neill is your marionette.

At Memphis State, Neill was holding his own. He shared one class with Brack, which was both a gas and a drag. The drag was that Brack was now the better student, a turnaround from their previous school records.

In the English Department, Neill was finding his footing. Still too intimidated to talk in class he made up for it with some pretty good writing, some pretty good papers. Sometimes, Neill had to fake it. Neill was a lazy scholar and he preferred the felicitous phrase to the correct judgment or the proper analogy or semblance. His passion, he was slowly discovering, was for 20th century literature, especially American. But, he still found a serene pleasure in *Beowulf* and Shakespeare and even poets who rhymed.

The weight of a full schedule at school and working 5 nights a week at Walden's was onerous, though Neill was having a good time. He had new friends at work and school and he was *active*. Neill wasn't always *active*.

Sedentarianism suited him. Laziness. Sloth.

Still, the evenings after work playing tennis or going out for pizza with Bidden and Victoria, felt, to Neill, as if he were really participating in life rather than watching it, decoding it, pinning it to a page. (Neill was also writing little poems based on ideas cadged from his new heroes, James Tate, W. S. Merwin, Mark Strand and Sylvia Plath.) And, now a third party had joined the party. A new employee at Walden's named Pas Brunt.

Pas was short, beautifully proportioned, kind and yet fiery, and the color of a funeral scarf. Her blackness made her face, with its textbook cheekbones, shine a dark light. She became the fourth wheel and the vehicle of their new mobility was finished. They were all young, living at home still (except for Victoria who had recently moved into an apartment off campus with a willowy beauty, who does not figure heavily in this account, so we'll call her Ranee), and making pretty good money for the first time in their short lives. Money meant movies and the after-work 4th meal, pizza. Raleigh's corpus, with the mall as its heart, was made up of fast food joints and gas stations and churches and movie houses. It was the nondescript side-road to any American highway. It was Edge City. Our trio usually ate at Pizza Hut or Raleigh Pizza (The Best Pizza in the World), where they shared a large pie and cokes. Sometimes Bidden had a short beer. They became musketeers. They became convives and confidantes. They became as inseparable as nuts and bolts.

One Monday Morning

Neill and Victoria were sitting on the steps inside Patterson Hall. They were talking about the movie they had all seen Sunday night: Ingmar Bergman's *Cries and Whispers*. Neill was slightly baffled by the film, though hypnotized by its color and tone, and its beautiful actresses. Victoria loved it without reservation. (Later, when a more seasoned Neill made his list of the ten best films he'd ever seen *Cries and Whispers* came in at number 3).

They were sitting scrunched up next to each other so other students could pass them on the stairs.

"Liv Ullmann is one of the prettiest actresses alive," Victoria said.

"She is," Neill agreed. "And a powerful actress."

"And a powerful actress."

"I'm not sure Pas liked it as much as we did."

"No, I don't think so."

"Bidden loved it. He's smarter, more intuitive than I am about film. Well, about everything. He's one smart cookie, our pal."

"He is our pal."

"You're my pal, too."

"I am," Victoria said. "And, you are mine. You are one of my best pals."

Victoria was now looking intently at Neill's face. Victoria's face was puck cute, her smile just this side of goofy, her eyes sparklers. Neill was gazing intently at her, but he couldn't focus or something. Something had perfumed and befogged the air. Neill cleared his throat, looked down at the notebook in his lap.

"We're sitting awfully close to each other," Neill said. What a bonehead remark, he thought. Yet, he wondered, what is going on? Is she attracted to me? Am I to her? It's not like he hadn't thought about it. Like every male animal, he pined after every female animal, even his best friends, especially his best friends. Ask any male otter. He will say he wants to bonk every female otter. Neill had imagined Victoria naked. He wondered what that ass would look like denuded. Of course, he wondered the same thing about Pas and Freyr's girlfriend Loyola, and Brack's newest squeeze, and Judy Carne, and Supergirl, and even his boss, Joy.

"We are," Victoria smiled her kitten smile.

"I'm sorry," Neill said. His palms were as moist as the beest in the reyn. "I think I've invaded your territory, your, um, personal space. This is closer than friends sit. I don't know how this happened."

"Shut up," the You-Suck guy in his head said.

"My territory," Victoria said.

"Yes, your territory, um, yes."

"You're right about personal space, of course. Everyone has little invisible boundaries."

"Damn you," You-Suck said.

"Then again…. maybe my territory needs invading."

There it was.

Neill waited a moment to make sure he had heard correctly and, having heard correctly, he had interpreted correctly.

Then, he leaned over and placed his tongue inside Victoria's mouth. She sucked on it. She placed her tongue inside Neill's. He sucked on hers. Their mouths became suctorial, salivating. Their hungers stirred.

The You-Suck guy left in a sulk.

Later, that Same Day

After work that night, after ten p.m., two of the bookstore coworkers did not go out for pizza. Nor did any one of them repair to the Bartlett tennis courts for late-night tennis. No, on this night, these two rogue coworkers went to an apartment off-campus. They went there to test the water. They went there with equal parts trepidation and excitement mixed in their young beakers.

Victoria's apartment was small and messy. There were books and album covers and ashtrays and whatnots (food? dead flowers? a bong? a muskrat hide?) on the floor. There were two bedrooms, one to the left of the living room and one to the right. Neither would be discovered by Neill on this night. On this night, there was no roommate so the two booksellers sat together on a sprung couch with a 6-stack of albums on the stereo (some Moody Blues, Neil Young, Van Morrison, Billie Holliday). They sat and they figured, independently, that some talk was due as preface.

"Do you think Bidden caught on?" Victoria asked. Her hand rested on the velveteen between their legs.

"Just because we cancelled pizza, both of us deferring at once?"

"I guess so, then."

"I guess so."

"Not that it matters."

"No."

Was this enough talk? Should they broach the awkward subject or just dive in? There was a lot to be said for both methods. Neill, as we have drawn him, would be one for diving, even diving from a dizzying height? But, Victoria? Where lies her heart?

"Should we talk about this?" Victoria asked.

"About what?" Neill wiggled. Maybe he should go.

"This," Victoria said and she put her hand on his thigh.

"About your hand on my thigh?"

"Among other things?"

"Other things like this?" And Neill bent forward and his tongue, of its own free will, splashed into Victoria's ready mouth. She had a very wet mouth, impish in shape and sopping and soft. Victoria's hand stayed on Neill's thigh. It did not move one micro-millimeter.

After a moment, Victoria pulled her mouth to the side and rested it against Neill's cheek. Her breath was hot in his ear. "Other things?" she sighed.

"Like this," Neill said, reaching under her white t-shirt and unsnapping her bra. His hands quickly found her breasts, small like perfect apples and soft as sinner's silk.

"Oh," Victoria said. "Oh."

Neill pulled her t-shirt off. He put his tongue and lips to her nipples. He was marveling at the perfect appleness of her breasts. He was kneading one while sucking the other. Then, vice versa.

"Huh," Victoria said. "Huh."

Her hand moved, a small encroachment.

It was enough. Neill felt that delicious electric tingle in his testes. He unsnapped Victoria's jeans.

"Neill," Victoria said. "Huh huh."

"Ok?" Neill said.

"Oh, yes, faster." And she pulled her jeans off till they fell to the floor.

Neill embraced her in a frantic kiss. His hands toured her hips and thighs. She was wearing plain white panties. His hands went under them like a mole slipping into a pup tent. His hands surrounded her ass and Neill suddenly knew something for the first time, something important: *I am an ass man.* And Victoria's was the first prize in the sexual contest that was youthful dating.

He pulled her onto his lap. His hands were trapped between their thighs. He pulled hard and the panties tore with a sound like the starting of a power saw. Victoria Lucas sat naked in his lap. She was panting. Her eyes looked woppity.

Neill, by now, had explored every curve and crease and indentation to her peerless ass. His fingers had now found her hot center spot as wet, if not wetter, than her mouth. He put one stiff digit into her sweet housewife.

Now, Victoria bucked. She threw herself off Neill's fingers. Neill thought he should stop...maybe...

"Vic," he said.

"Put your finger back in me. Quick," she said.

Neill obliged. Victoria rode his finger. Neill held her upright with his other hand firmly entrenched in her soft ass cheek.

Suddenly, Victoria sat bolt upright. Her face was squinched tight. It both frightened and fascinated Neill. He wanted to make her scream. He wanted her pain and pleasure. He wanted both and, if he had time to stop and think, this would have confused our hero.

"Arnnnhhhhhh," Victoria said, stiff as a corpse for a second and then, "Ssshsssssssh," she said, like steam escaping, and she went limp like an unstrung puppet.

"Jesus," Neill said.

"Jesus had nothing to do with it," Victoria said, gasping.

Neill laughed. They held each other for a moment. Neill assumed this was the end of the evening, though, naturally, he wanted his share. He was still fully dressed. He still had his shoes on.

"You're still dressed," Victoria said. "You still have your shoes on."

They both laughed.

"I was lying in a burned-out basement," the stereo said.

"Undress, Pal," Victoria said like a gunman's moll.

Neill did. He stood and undressed and Victoria didn't take her impish eyes off him. She watched as if she had paid for this attraction.

When Neill dropped his briefs and stood next to the couch unclad his dojigger was soft and squishy. Victoria was looking at it.

"Sorry," Neill said.

"No, it's just that I've never seen one before."

"Seriously?"

"Yes," her look was almost scientific.

"You—you're a virgin?"

"Well, technically, no. My last boyfriend took me, but we didn't know what we were doing. I never saw him naked, nor he me.

"Huh," Neill said.

"Oh, sorry," Victoria said. "Come here. Lie down on the couch."

She got up and Neill lay down like a patient etherized upon a table. Victoria squatted next to the couch and began running her hands, softly, up and down Neill's body. It was like she had discovered an alien creature, a fascinating bit of zoological study.

Neill closed his eyes when he wasn't sneaking peeks at Victoria's naked body. She was resting entirely on the balls of her feet and the shape of her thigh and hip was drawn by one of the great masters.

Neill's dojigger was not soft and squishy anymore. It was at attention, a brave little soldier, ready for duty.

"Oh my," Victoria said. She enclosed it with her hand.

"Ohh," Neill moaned.

Victoria began to move her hand up and down, now down to his balls and then up to his head, squeezing there. It was clear she had done this before and enjoyed her power doing it.

Then, it was clear she was practiced at other things.

It had been Neill's brief experience that some women go down too slubberingly. There's not tease, nor foreplay. Victoria took it slow. She kissed his stomach. She kissed his thigh right next to his balls. She kissed one ball gently. She licked along his side and then onto his stomach. She pointed his pointer at her mouth, holding it firmly, and licked the delicate first pearl from its tip.

Then, Victoria got up onto her knees and lowered her seeping mouth onto him. It was like getting blown by fog. She swirled around him, the pressure just enough to keep it going. Her right hand squeezed his balls tenderly.

Neill began to make barnyard sounds. It was coming. It was all beyond calculation now. Pure animal desire was in the room.

As it rose in his dick Victoria could feel it and grabbed onto his boolies with a grip like vice and held them. Neill began to pump his rich cream into her mouth. Victoria stopped for a heartbeat—was she surprised?—then swallowed loudly, making sounds as if she had just eaten lobster for the first time. The orgasm went on for some time. Cocks crowed, took the day off, came back from vacation, and crowed again. Everyone grew older.

Then, Victoria crawled on top of Neill and covered her with her warm bare body.

They both had things to say. And then they didn't. Victoria pulled an afghan over them and they fell asleep like children in an enchanted tale.

When Neill woke in the morning he was muzzy-headed and dry-mouthed and he felt as if he had been thrown up and down on a blanket by the town roughnecks. Victoria was in the kitchen wearing only her t-shirt. She was mixing up eggs and hotdogs in a frying pan. Neill sat up and began to once again appreciate her fine bomsey.

Then Neill had the same worry he had his entire life. How could he go to the bathroom with her only a door away?

It was only a momentary worry. He did it. He went into her unfamiliar, small, messy bathroom and did his manly business. Morning shits were often problematic. They could also be inconvenient. This morning all went well.

And Neill, who did not believe in omens or fortunes, thought nevertheless that it was a good sign. A few hours later, they walked together to the campus and attended their 8 a.m. classes. It was quite an inauguration.

There are Always Complications, or, Hi Potenuse!

Never two without three, as the adage goes.

Neill was pretty sure, right away, right out of the gate, heart stuck open like a carburetor gulping air, that he had fallen in love with Victoria. She was the most absolute complement to his romantic side he had ever known. But, there was a fly in the porridge. She had a boyfriend.

For our intents and purposes, he will remain Nameless.

A typical work time conversation went something like this:

Neill: How are you, tonight?

Victoria: I'm ok. I'm making you sad, aren't I?

Neill: Well. I don't know what you're thinking. If you're thinking what I'm thinking we should—you should—do something about it.

Victoria: What are you thinking?

Neill: That we belong together.

Victoria: Oh. I know. The something I need to do then is tell Nameless that I have fallen for someone else.

Neill: That would be meet and right.

Victoria: Easier said than done. He's so nice.

Neill: Of course.

Victoria: You're nice, too.

Neill: Thanks.

Victoria: I hate that look on your face.

Neill: My heart is stuck open like a carburetor gulping air.

Victoria: Oh.

Neill: So, anyway.

Victoria: Anyway. I will do something. Soon.

Neill: You will make a decision.

Victoria: Yes. I will make a decision.

Neill: So, I could still lose out to this Nameless?

Victoria: Oh, Neill.

Neill: Don't cry.

Victoria: Let me handle it. I will.

Neill: Quickly.

Victoria: Of course.

But, it was not decided quickly. Days went by, weeks. Neill fretted. He doubted and he cursed. He was Man, a right unholy beast.

In Music Appreciation

Music Appreciation was the last class Neill had on Fridays. It was taught by an avant garde drummer who had better things to do than teach music to kids only taking the class because it was an elective and rumored to be an easy A. Neill liked his teacher. Neill wished he was an avant garde drummer.

But, the last class on the last day of the week was a time of great drowsiness and dreaminess. Neill was often either wool-gathering or nodding off. Many days he was fantasizing about sex. Sex with any of the gals in the class. The one in the poodle skirt and horn-rim glasses. The one with the pants so tight you could see her denimed vulva. The one with the turned-up nose and braless nipples. Sex with gals from the past. Sex with teachers. Sex with movie stars (though, oddly enough, for his entire life, Neill had trouble masturbating to visions of movie stars or rock singers, because to really tickle his scrotum, a fantasy had to be at least somewhat plausible).

Many days he thought about Orbit. Her tits, of course, her blowjobs, of course.

One Friday, he drove by her house. Her car was there. He parked and went to the door and knocked.

Orbit was surprised. Orbit assumed Neill hated her, street sex or no street sex.

"I'm surprised," she said, ushering him inside. "I thought you hated me…"

They sat on a sofa in the living room. Neill smiled at Orbit. She smiled a tight smile in return. (*If you smile at me, I will understand…*Neill was thinking.)

"Who's home?" Neill asked.

"Just Granny. She's in the back room. She never comes out."

Neill remembered Granny, a wizened stick-woman, going not so gently mad, mean as a snake. Neill hated her. Neill feared her.

"She never comes out," Orbit repeated.

Neill stuck his tongue in Orbit's mouth. Orbit grabbed madly at him as if he was the Titanic's last flotation device.

Neill opened her shirt and unsnapped her bra with one, hand. He wanted them.

"God, I wanted them," he told Orbit. He sucked her full nipples back and forth, back and forth. "I was fantasizing about you in Music Appreciation Class," he said, between dockyard rivets.

"Really," Orbit said, her breathing lopsided. "Wha-what were you fantasizing?"

"Suck me," Neill said.

And, readers, she did. She took Neill's aching member into its familiar cave and expertly worked it with lips and tongue and saliva until Neill shot off, a strong plosion that went straight down her gullet and into her stomach without a waystop.

"Jesus," Neill said. Then he zipped up.

Soon, this became a standard Friday date. A half-hour date. A lollygag, a breast tickle, lip service, and then home. Neill looked forward to it all week (even while loving his bookstore girlfriend, missing her, imagining her with her other man) and, readers, we think Orbit looked forward to it, too.

At the Pizza Hut After Work

Neill liked the thin crust with bacon and pepperoni. Victoria liked vegetarian. Pas liked plain cheese. Bidden would eat anything. He was passive. "I'll eat some of everyone's," he said, "If that's ok."

It was 10:30 p.m. when the pies arrived.

Only Bidden drank beer. The rest quaffed sodas full of sugar and caffeine. Later, they would nonetheless sleep.

Victoria and Neill had not been together for a while. There was a large unsaid abyss between them. Or a wall, the Wall of Jericho, made out of the undergarments of Victoria and her beau's hector protector.

The conversation flowed anyway.

"I think the fingernails on one hand are growing faster than the other," Bidden said.

"I've had that," Neill said. He was savoring the small detonation of flavor that was a scintilla of bacon.

"I'll tell you one thing," Pas said. "If I have to Liquid Gold one more piece of crappy bookstore furniture or one more square of parquet floor, I will throw the whole bottle at the Rosemary Rogers display."

"It's absurd, really. I don't think the stuff is even good for the wood," Neill said.

"I don't even think it is wood," Victoria said.

"It's make-work. You know? Like we don't have enough to do. 'There is always something to do in a bookstore,' Joy says," Pas said.

"Like masturbate in the stockroom," Bidden said.

Pas hit him with a wadded up napkin. It bounced off his young man's nose.

"I'd much rather straighten a section," Victoria said.

"Oh, easily," Neill said. "I like putting my hands on the books. Of course, Vic, if you re-do the children's section one more time Joy is going to hit you with her Nazi baton. So far, you've done it by author, age, publisher, color...what else?"

"Fuck you," Victoria said, smiling.

"Ok," Neill said.

The Pizza Hut grew quiet. Every patron in the place stopped talking. The employees put down their swabbing rags, their pizza shovels, their cold drinks. The jukebox stopped in the middle of "Seasons in the Sun."

The quartet made eating pizza a fine-tuned art like watchmaking or miniature boat building.

"Well, I guess there are no secrets among friends," Neill said, after he had regrouped. "Anyone know someone who can break kneecaps?"

"You want Victoria's boyfriends knees shattered?"

"No," Neill said, solemnly. "My own."

Other Things

In Biology Neill had a D. In Intro to Philosophy an A. In Intro to Sociology a B. In Phys. Ed. an A (tennis!). In English Literature 101 an A.

At the lunchtime table with Brack and Freyr and various friends from Bartlett and elsewhere, Neill had a troupe. He and Brack were closer than ever. They believed themselves to be a 'somewhat invincible' doubles team in tennis. This was a jolly good thing. Apart from lunch and dope nights and tennis (tennis!,) they found much to talk about. Women, of course, were heading the bill. Brack had someone he was interested in, a buxom blond named Old Lady Shoe (her first name wasn't really 'Old Lady,' but her last name really was "Shoe," and Neill never could keep it in his head what her real first name was ("On With The?" he wondered.) (We know. Is it important?) (Stop being coy: it was Other. Other Shoe.) She and Brack were palsy and spent a lot of time grinning like Italy. Neill liked her and secretly wished he was playing with those borsties. (Does it seem at times that Neill is a breast man? Mayhaps, this is only because, so far, he is just a pup. Mayhaps, breasts are more of a young man's fancy. But, truth be told: Neill was and is today an ass and legs man. Ok?)[Said this already?]

Neill, though, apart from this camaraderie and book learnin', often felt bereft. He spent too many hours wondering what Victoria and her man were doing. He tried not to picture it but Neill was a good picturer. He spent too many hours alone in his bedroom in his parent's home masturbating and reading Dostoevsky. Soon, he thought, I am going to get an apartment. It will be maturing. It will be heaven. I will have sex with a different woman every night.

In his backpack, besides his texts: *Selected Poems of Leonard Cohen*, Sylvia Plath's *The Bell Jar*, *The Beatles Illustrated Lyrics* (introduction by Richard Brautigan). *Everything You Always Wanted to Know about Sex but Were Afraid to Ask.*

Mates

Thistle was at Lambuth, aw we know.

Sly was home from playing football for a small Illinois university where his late father had played football, handed his walking papers fairly quickly, after first having his shoulder operated on for arthritis, and then being arrested on campus with a bong full of Arkansas Fulgur Weed. (His life would later consist of a series of odd jobs: bartender, welt binder, film puller, hair boiler, light bender, rodeo clown, chicken sexer, cow hoof trimmer.)

Akin was studying art at the University of Tennessee, Martin. Rita ditto. Lindsey Crouse went to Alabama and majored in Tumble Finishing.

Mick and Greg were at Martin, also, studying nothing except how to cheat the phone company on long distance calls (which later became known as The Martin Telephone Hijinks and Federal Edict Caper, both young men dismissed from school in lieu of being actually charged.)

Goffredo and Hawker were both at Memphis State, though Neill saw little of them on campus.

Sam Onides went to Harvard and was given two Fulbright Scholarships, an NEA grant, a Governor's Award and a Purple Heart.

Sweeney Waterman went up east never to be heard from again.

Does this catch us up?

And, Bidden was at Memphis State, also, majoring in Philosophy. His paper, "Hegel's Phenomenology of Spirit: Contradictory in its Contradictions or as Amusing as Rocky and Bullwinkle," is still much discussed. Late nights at the Pizza Hut, with enough beer in him, he would back football players and roughnecks against the wall, demanding to know where they stood on Empiricism.

And then This Happened at the Bookstore

A few days had passed.

It was a slow night at the bookstore, though really there were few slow nights. The mall was always crowded. This was a boom time for malls and even for bookstores in malls. And, as Joy the Overlord said, "There is never a time you can do nothing."

Nevertheless, on nights when Victoria, Neill, Bidden and Pas all worked, there was a bit of larking about, covering for each other, laughing, mall-walking (which for Bidden and Neill meant ogling the vast population of young women workers, a whole labor force made up of amazons with skin opalescent like pearl and figures made to figure out.)

This night Bidden was showing Pas how you could Liquid Gold the front bookcases in a half-ass way that still looked like they had been done well. Neill was in the stockroom breaking down boxes. Breaking down boxes was an eternal and thankless job somewhat akin to peeling potatoes in the service. There were always boxes. Once broken down they would rise again like Goethe's seas trying to swallow Mickey Mouse.

Neill, cutter in hand, turned when the door opened and Victoria came in.

"Hello, Bunky," she said.

"Hello, Pal," Neill said back. He called her Pal.

Victoria climbed up on top of a step ladder and sat on the top.

She sighed.

"I did it, Neill. I broke it off. I choose you. I choose you, Neill. Am I too late?"

Neill stared at her across the sea of broken cardboard.

"It is right on time," he said.

Victoria smiled. A smile crept across her face like a wavelet. Then, she laughed.

Neill laughed, too.

"And, I have something for you," Victoria said.

She opened her legs. She wasn't wearing underwear.

Neill was astonished. He and Victoria had coupled a few times but this boldness was a new turn, an upping of the ante.

"I'm astonished," Neill said. His todger stiffened.

"And look what else?" Victoria said. She put her fingers to her crotch and began to fiddle about. She had one finger insider herself before Neill had the strength to speak. He had never seen a woman masturbate before. It was the show of shows. He must ask every woman to do this for him from now till he wears the suit of dirt.

"Jesus," Neill managed. Ok, it wasn't Cyrano de Bergerac.

"You like watching?" Victoria said.

"I do," Neill said and he took a step toward her.

"I'll lock the door."

AJ Has Some Trouble in High School

Forgive us for giving short shrift to young, duoliteral AJ, Neill's little sister. When they were younger AJ was one of Neill's best companions. They fought like brother and sister, but they also played endless games (Monopoly, Sorry, Mousetrap, Candyland, Skooz-it, Parcheesi, Checkers, Chinese Checkers, Crazy Eights, Four Corners, Stratego, Twister, Hands Down, Carrom, Yahtzee, Othello, Feely Meely [Mrs. Rhymer made a homemade version], Dominoes, Tip-it, Life, Mystery Date, Double Solitaire [a lovely oxymoron], Aggravation, Clue, Put and Take, Milles Borne, Mastermind, Pit, Scrabble, Battleship, Boggle, and a game they devised themselves called Traffic, which was quite elaborate and pleasing in its handspun way) like brother and sister, also. Or they shared all the latest toys (Vacuform, Incredible Edibles, Easy-bake Oven, Mr. Potato Head, Play-doh, Super Balls [and their precursor, India Rubber Balls], Etch-a-sketch, Silly Putty, Spirograph, Tinker Toys, Magic 8-Ball, Creepy Crawlers, Creeple People, Wishniks, Old Maid, Erector Set, Viewmaster, Odd Ogg, Pez, Soakies, Slinky, Super Stuff to name a few. Aurora and Revell plastic model kits [as aforementioned], Tiger Joe [a tank], Lite-Brite, Lincoln Logs, Kiddles and Matchbox and Corgi cars [Neill was crazy for metal cars, as aforementioned]), Mr. Machine, The Secret Sam Briefcase [complete with a cunning little plastic camera that actually worked {Neill still has black and white shots taken at their grandmother's house in Niagara Falls, Ontario, with that crappy little camera, including one of AJ with a live baby bird on her head}]). (We should have talked about this earlier. *Edit.*)

It was also with AJ that Neill shared some of the other insuperable joys of childhood: junk food (There was the Ice Cream Man, which in Memphis, meant The Merrymobile, a round vehicle built upon a golf cart; there was Charles Chips, a real treat, the best potato chips in the world delivered to your door in umber round cans; there was even a candy truck (it must have had a name)—a van tricked out with shelves of processed and dyed sugars), vacations with backseat torture and delight, skinned knees, badminton, readings from the family library of children's books (even as an adult, so called, Neill thought *The Poky Little Puppy* was one of the great works of Western Literature), even the creation of their own line of comic books, mostly featuring the escapades of the family dog, a mongrel named, Scamp.

At the time, we are now (you with us?) at the time of the beginning of Neill's college career, bookselling career, and love affair with Victoria, AJ was a sophomore at Craigmont High School, a new, stark, cement and iron school sitting irresistibly, like a toadstool oubliette sprung up overnight, between Bartlett High and Raleigh Egypt High.

AJ was having some trouble at school. Not academic, but social. Most folks found the social part more difficult than the academic (save for Neill, who in later years would marvel when people talked about how much they hated high school, how scarred they were from it). AJ's problem was one of time and place: as aforementioned bussing occurred in the 70s in the American South and, with it, problems of adjustment.

Neill came home one afternoon to find his sister and mother in the living room. A pall hung over the room. Seriously, a serious pall.

AJ was in tears.

"Hey, what's up, Sis?" Neill said. He really did love his pretty little sister. It's not his fault we've left her out of the narrative.

"I hate my school," she said. And a new torrent of tears.

"Sure, sure," Neill said.

"You don't hate your school," Mother said.

"Well, ma—" Neill began.

"She hates the blacks."

"Niggers," AJ said, her face set in defiance, daring her brother to scold her for the vulgarism.

"Sis—" he said.

"You don't know," AJ screamed, her face a red crease from which tears dropped dramatically well onto her lap.

"I do, though," Neill said. He was trying to keep a well-modulated tone, but his hatred of racism was pulling him in a contradictory position. His heart beat with a dangerous admixture of love and hate. "We had bussing. We had some trouble."

"You were never pushed up against your locker and your breasts fondled roughly though, were you, Gandhi?"

Neill was sick. He felt sick. Jesus. Where to go with this?

He had no idea.

"I-I'm sorry," he said. He sat down next to his sister to put his arm around her, but she leapt from her seat as if he were one of her tormentors and ran from the room.

Neill looked at his mother.

"Well?" she said.

Neill was deep-down depressed and a little frightened.

"I am naught," he said. "I have no answer."

Vitoria in Bloom

In the dim light of Victoria's small gray bedroom Neill could just make out her shape and he was learning her body with his fingers, as if she were the braille edition of a girlfriend.

Victoria's small breasts, with their precise brown nipples, put Neill in mind of a line from Leonard Cohen where he compared his lover's breasts to the upturned bellies of sparrows. Neill thinks it was sparrows. Wrens? One of the breasts had a small hair in the middle of its bulge, like a single palm tree on a desert isle. Neill didn't like that hair. He wished it to hell.

Victoria's ass (we won't dwell on this too long, but it's worth talking about) was as round as Plato's year, two identical swelling mounds of desire. The surface of them was pebbled, rather than smooth, with permanent goosebumps. Neill relished rubbing them as if they were rich velvet. He wanted to strike his match on them.

And Victoria's pubic hair was another cause for a carnal carnival. It was long like the hair on a dog's back, auburn-colored and curly. Neill loved the feel of it on his fingers as he played with her.

Victoria was on the pill. The young lovers went at it like crazed squirrels. It was, up to that time, the most sustained sexual relationship either had had. Neill was fervid and Victoria seemed to be, too.

"Pals forever," Victoria whispered in Neill's ear as they lay one evening in afterglow.

"Mm," Neill said. He ran his hand down her hip and held onto her ass one more time as if he feared it would be taken from him.

"I give good head, don't I?" Victoria said. It was a statement. Did she doubt, even a little?

"You sure do," Neill said.

"I like sucking you," Victoria said.

Amazing, Neill thought. It must be love.

"Amazing," Neill said. "I love you."

"Want me to do it again?" she asked. Her eyes lit like a puppy's.

"Once a king always a king but once a night's enough," Neill said.

At Red Lobster Because of the Hushpuppies

They were drinking Cokes and eating hush puppies. It was 11 p.m. on a Friday night. Closing the bookstore had taken longer than usual. They didn't leave till 10:35, knowing they never got overtime. They did it because they were working in a bookstore, and it was exhilarating.

"Your book," Bidden said. "Your book. The one that exemplifies you."

"*The Stranger*," Neill said, without any thought.

"Alice Walker's poetry," Pas said.

"Because, like you, she is black and female and lovely," Neill said.

Pas threw a small piece of hushpuppy at Neill hitting him in the eye. He grinned like a cobbler.

"Anais Nin's diaries," Victoria said. She looked at Neill and smiled. Neill smiled, too.

"She's reading the diaries," Neill said. "All 43 of them. She wants to be fucked by Henry Miller."

"Shut up," Victoria said, leaning over and putting her plump little thumb into Neill's mouth. Neill sucked as if this was customary human behavior.

"See, I would have said *The Moviegoer* for you," Bidden said to Neill.

Neill reflected. He felt embarrassed. He would bow to Bidden's book for him. He would allow Bidden to choose his book, because Neill was that unsure of his own opinions, even about himself, even among those who love him. Bidden loved Neill and Neill loved Bidden, and still

Neill thought Bidden had the better mind. Nevertheless, sometimes Neill took his nascent attempts at poetry to Bidden's apartment and sat in tense stillness while Bidden read the poems right in front of him. Bidden was always kind, always generous.

"Yeah, you're probably right," Neill said.

"What's your book," Pas said to Bidden.

"*Everything I Always Wanted to Know About Sex but Was Afraid to Ask,*" Bidden said.

Neill Finds a Roommate

Then, one day Neill looked and decided he had a pretty good bank account to go with his pretty good job and pretty good schoolwork and pretty good gal. So, the next step, the adult step, was to move out of Max and Lolly's house.

His first thought was Bidden because they had gotten that close, but Bidden already lived in a U-Haul sized apartment in Frayser. He moved out of his parents' house as soon as he was earning steady money at the bookstore.

So, Neill went to see his old friend from Bartlett, Goffredo Crump. Goffredo was working at Seesel's Grocery Store and was also at Tiger High, majoring in something or other. Neill went by Seessel's and found Goffredo at the back of the store in front of many fruits of the sea, swabbing the scuffed linoleum floor with a mammoth mop.

"What's up, Tiger Lily?" Goffredo greeted him.

"I've got an idea. Maybe it's a good idea."

"Hit me."

"You ready to move out of your folks' house? You making enough to do that?"

Goffredo appeared to consider it for a pregnant moment.

"Yes," he said.

"Ok," Neill said.

"Ok then," Goffredo said.

The two young men began scouring Raleigh for available apartments. They calculated what they could afford and that helped narrow the field. They settled on a large city-block sized complex on Yale Road, just a half mile from the mall. It was cramped and crappy, with walls thin as the petals of flowers. You could not only hear the people living next to you or below you (their apartment was on the 2nd floor of a 2 floor block), but you could hear the apartment next to the apartment next to you. The living room had beige shag carpet.

The living room had beige shag carpet.

But, they also had tennis courts!

Neill's parents were kind and supportive about his move even if Lolly had to say, "Is it safe? Max, do you know? Is that place safe? Will the boys be alright there?"

They moved in the first of December. And, Neill's thought before falling asleep that first night in his own apartment was, "I will wake on Christmas morning in a place that is not my mother's or father's house." And, this did not comfort him. And, as he slept, he dreamed of snakes and eels and basilisks and limnetic abnormalities, the whole procession setting upon him like the curse of damnation.

Celebrating the New Apartment with a Long Night of Androgynation

All day Neill was pent up. He wasn't paying attention in Biology. He was terse at the lunch table.

"What's with you, brother?" Brack asked.

"Nothing," Neill said. "School work."

"Tennis tonight," Freyr said, dropping his backpack on the floor.

"Can't," Neill said, so quickly the entire table looked at him. He bent over his French fries with mayonnaise, like a monk over his illumination.

At work that night, he and Victoria kept giving each other sly looks. They both felt they were on the cusp of something extraordinary but it was hard to say why. It was not going to be their first time.

"New Harlequins come in?" an old woman asked Neill.

"Are you on the list?"

"What list?" the lady spat out as if she had been given Sophie's choice.

"We take advance orders and bundle them for people when they come in."

"I'm not on any list," she said definitively.

Neill walked her over to the section, a section of books that Pam handled (Pam was married, had strawberry blond hair and skin it looked like you would love to lick, skin like ice cream). Neill hated the romance section. He picked out the Harlequins, but was missing one volume.

"I'm missing one volume," he said.

The lady looked at him.

This could go either way, Neill thought.

"I don't care," she said.

Later, someone came in and asked for a poetry book recommendation. "Someone alive," the young man said. Neill sold him Mark Strand's *Darker*, and felt better about things. There was balance.

The drive to the apartment was accomplished in about 2.48 minutes.

Victoria spun around in the cramped living room as if it were the dance floor at The Hermitage.

"Wonderful!" she squealed. "Where did you get that couch?"

"Goffredo's."

"Oh."

"So you wanna?"

"See your room? Nah."

For a moment Neill was nonplussed. It was only nerves making him so insecure.

"Lead me there, Stallion. You know why we're here."

They could hear the music coming from Goffredo's room. Procol Harum.

Neill's bedroom was small, dark, incommodious, with a bed, a dresser, a stereo, a tiny closet. There was room enough for three people if two of them were on the bed. Neill had, in time-honored new apartment fashion, placed upon his wall posters: Brueghel's "Children's Games," and Jethro Tull. Debbie Harry awaited, rolled up and placed in a corner.

Between the bed and the stereo you could stand up if you had thin shins.

The bed was his single from childhood, the bed he'd slept in his whole life.

"This is the bed I've slept in my whole life," he said.

"We're gonna do more than sleep," Victoria said. She pulled her t-shirt off. She wasn't wearing a bra because her breasts were the small upturned bellies of sparrows. Neill took his own shirt off, and kicked his shoes, one, two, into a corner.

"Wait," Victoria said.

Topless she moved over to Neill and kissed him long upon his mouth. While doing so she was unbuckling his belt. His pants dropped at the same time her tongue came out of his mouth with an audible pop. Victoria ran her hand along the outside of his briefs. His erection was trying to escape.

"Mm, mm, you're so ready," she said.

"I know."

"Shall I suck you first?"

"I don't know. If you do it might be over too fast."

"Right."

Victoria took a step back and looked at her boyfriend from head to toe.

"Look," she said. She undid her jeans and let them fall. She was wearing the kind of brief underwear Neill had seen in Playboy magazine. On Victoria's wide hips they worked voodoo inside Neill. Victoria's secret?

"Jesus," he said.

They toppled onto the bed. Their ardor was strong. Eventually they were both naked.

Neill ate her pineapple until she was squirming like an eel.

She came hard against his jaw.

Afterward, after she caught her breath, she said, "Let's try something new."

"Ok," Neill said. His cock ached.

Victoria flipped onto her stomach and put her face in the pillow. She raised her ass in the air like a barnyard Cyprian.

"What do—" Neill said. Then, "Oh!"

He positioned himself behind her. Kneeling on the bed was slightly uncomfortable. He was leaning forward at an odd angle. He tried to steer his cock in but it was hitting everywhere: cheek, thigh, bunghole. Finally, he took it in his hand and pushed it into Victoria's hot cunny.

"Oof," she said. "Lordy," she said.

Neill held her hips as if they were harnesses. His view of her magnificent ass and his dick going in and out was just about the most erotic thing he'd ever seen.

"I'm coming!" Victoria screamed.

"I'm coming, too!" Neill parroted.

Afterwards they fell back into the world of men.

"Whew," Victoria said. "What do you wanna do now?"

"Dunno," Neill said, out of breath. "Make prank phone calls?"

The next morning, over a breakfast of English muffins and jam and instant coffee with heaping tablespoons of Cremora (the way Victoria always drank it), at the coffee table in the living room, Goffredo, with a smile that seemed more wink than smile said, "So, you both came."

Bidden Route Visits

Bidden and Neill and Goffredo were sitting together on the small couch in front of the small television watching a late-night science fiction movie. Someone had a Nazi's head in a petri dish. They were as stoned as Salem's housewives.

"I've seen this," Goffredo said.

"I think I have too," Neill said. "Do they have a giant chicken in this, too?"

"I think so."

"Is it possible to pull a muscle defecating?" Bidden contributed.

"And other real-life problems."

"What?"

"Sounds like an Irma Bombeck title. *Is it Possible to Pull a Muscle Defecating and Other Real Life Problems.*"

"Irma Bombeck. Ha!" Goffredo said.

"Or how about, *It's not Dirty it's Stained,*" Neill offered.

"Or—*I'm Better but I'm Not Well.*"

"Good one."

"My mom used to read Irma Bombeck," Neill said.

"Everyone's mom did. It's why she sold a gazillion copies, because everyone has a mom."

"Wasn't she married to the Family Circus cartoonist and that strip was based on their family?"

"You know. That's about the limit of time I can spend talking about Irma Bombeck."

"Tell me, Bidden," Goffredo said. (The two were only close through Neill and sometimes the simplest conversation between them became awkward, stilted.) "You got a gal yet?"

"Why do you ask?"

"Neill said you were lonely. I mean, he said that because I was talking about how lonely I am."

"No one wants an ugly, pot-bellied man working at a crap job at the mall."

"That's where you're wrong," Neill said.

"Sure, you say that. You look like Peter Frampton."

"Roger Daltrey," Goffredo said.

"Either," Bidden said. "You know, I thought if I worked in a bookstore, there was a chance I'd run into someone as sexy as Dorothy Malone in *The Big Sleep.*"

"Of course—"

"I'm not Bogart."

"Well, none of us are."

"Some of us are Roger Daltrey."

"Or Peter Frampton."

"Shut up," Neill said, just as the Nazi head began to speak. "Our strength is our quickness and our brutality," it said.

Additionally

The past is misted over, even to those who record it. Perhaps most often for those who record it. We are faced with truth that doesn't work as fiction or fiction that is implausible at every turn.

We are doing our best here. Neill's story stops and starts, because life stops and starts. Yet this is not history, pure history.

One of us wanted to put this up front: *Based on actual events.*

We think it sounds too much like a parapsychology show, like the kind of stories you see in magazines accompanied by "real photos" of ectoplasmic emanations or "ghost orbs."

Ok.

Relax. Take a deep breath.

We continue.

¼ of the Beatles

There was news. George Harrison was touring and bringing his solo work to the Mid-South Coliseum. Victoria insisted that they go.

"Of course, you want to see him, right?" she asked.

"Well, of course."

"Because you missed the Beatles the one and only time they came to Memphis?"

"Right. I was nine. They were burning Beatle LPs outside the Coliseum. The KKK, in all their ridiculous, swaggering, hooded glory, was there. Yet, I should have been more aware, right? I mean, I curse my younger self for not knowing how historic the event was. I can't forgive the nine-year-old me."

"So now you can see ¼ of them," she said, grinning. Her grin could wake up roosters.

"How are we going to get tickets?" Neill asked, ever the pessimist about his getting anything worth being excited about.

"I'll get them," Victoria said.

And, so she did. She slept outside the Coliseum box office the night before tickets were to go on sale. She was hundreds of people back.

The sun rose. Rosy-digited dawn revealed a rag-tag bunch sleeping on the concrete steps and in the parking lot of the Mid-South Coliseum.

Some folks passed around coffee. Some passed around food. Some passed around marijuana. The sixties were only dying; they were not quite expired.

Victoria rose, feeling woozy. She accepted some coffee, but it didn't have enough Cremora in it. She sipped.

Some official looking official arrived. A man in shirtsleeves and a tie walked past without acknowledging the crowd. He pulled out a ring of keys a zookeeper would envy. He went into the Coliseum. A buzz went through the crowd. Two buzzes.

There was movement. The line tightened up as if they were paratroopers about to freefall. Victoria began to feel even woozier.

And just as the door began to open, and the crowd moved like a charmed snake, Victoria went into a dead faint. She fell, readers. She fell to the concrete steps, bumping her shoulder and cheek.

A gasping few surrounded her. Someone came out of the Coliseum.

"What happened?" the man in shirtsleeves and a tie asked.

"She just dropped," a guy wearing a striped djellaba said.

"What should we do?" asked a woman wearing a t-shirt that said "Phi Krappa Zappa."

Victoria could hear the voices around her. She opened her eyes. She was in Wonderland. There was a tea party.

No, she remembered. She had to get George Harrison tickets.

"Are you ok?" the man in shirtsleeves and a tie asked.

"I think so," Victoria said.

"Come on inside," he said.

And that is how Neill saw George Harrison from the fourth row.

And during the concert someone was passing around some fine Thai stick. Victoria looked at Neill funny when he toked. Not exactly a reprimand. More of a curious *wither?*

And George sang songs from *All Things Must Pass*. And, even though he apologized for his sore throat, he tore into "While my Guitar Gently Weeps," which inexplicably he changed to "while my guitar gently smiles." Perhaps George was happy to not be a Beatle anymore. Perhaps he was full of positive energy.

And after the concert, our couple went back to Victoria's apartment because it was closer.

"That was fantastic," Neill said, once they were embedded.

"Superb," Victoria said.

"Splendiferous."

"Absolutely."

"Absofuckinglutely."

"Are you still high?" Victoria said.

"I don't know. Are you wearing a Grace Kelly mask?"

"I am," Victoria said.

And then they fucked like thunder and lightning. And then they fucked like Grace Kelly and Jimmy Stewart. And then they fucked like Tom and Jerry. And then they fucked like Sonny and

Cher. And then they fucked like bacon and eggs, like toast and hashbrowns, like a sinker and a cup of Joe with extra Cremora.

When It's Love

So, it was capital L Love for Neill and Victoria, the first time for both of them. They were learning how lives could intertwine in such a way that neither was separate from the other, how they could tie themselves to each other in a thousand ways and not feel constrained.

Dinner at Victoria's family's house became a beloved ritual. Her father, the good doctor, was eccentric and funny and soft-spoken. He played the piano and sang old Billie Holliday songs in a cracked voice. He cooked steak shish-kabobs when the occasion was special enough, and it often was. For the rest of his life Neill would love steak chunks slathered in plain ketchup, the way Victoria ate them. Victoria's mom was round like a barrel, but sharp and loving and lively, and full of good conversation. She and Neill bonded immediately.

There was also an older sister, who was like the daughter in the Munster family, beautiful, delicate, and seemingly sprung from other roots. She was the sorority type and was made of magnolia petals and Southern grace. There was also a younger brother cut from his father's tailcoat, as was Victoria. They were neurotic every other day. They were loopy and troubled and entertaining and smart as serpents. The younger brother, Peak, late at night, made frozen cheese pizzas topped by sliced hotdogs and Kraft American cheese. Hotdogs were Victoria's favorite meal. She preferred them microwaved on a bun with the same American cheese. Later in life, she lived off these and coffee and cigarettes. Later in life, Peak would come out of the closet, but not until most people stopped wondering. "He's really asexual," Victoria would often say.

Christmases together became celebrations of their bond. Victoria also started something that Neill would carry with him the rest of his life, the large, generous gift-giving for birthdays and Christmases. No longer would Neill be content with a nice new hardback novel or the latest Jethro Tull album. Presents came in stacks.

There was also the bond over movies. They were movie hungry. And this was at a time in Memphis when there were a half dozen or more venues showing old films, art films, double features. In this way they were introduced to Chaplin, Bergman, Fellini, Truffaut, Australian cinema, Ealing Studio films, Godard, etc.

When it's love there is a bond deeper than the furious activity in bed. When it's love, there is an everyday connection, every little thing somehow becoming part of a larger pledge.

There is No You in Insomnia

As mentioned earlier, Neill was a lifelong sufferer from that most debilitating of everyday (everynight) problems: insomnia. Iris Murdoch said, "There is a gulf fixed between those who can sleep and those who cannot. It is one of the great divisions of the human race."

In high school it was pretty bad but the average teen can get by on 4 or 5 hours of sleep a night. It may be the case that the average teen thrives on lack of sleep. But, in college, Neill began to see it as a real problem. A scourge even. Soon the late-night tennis, the late-night pizzas, the sex with Victoria, became untenable. Nights before exams were especially vexing, because Neill's brain began to churn with how many hours there were till the actual exam, the one he hadn't studied for. On non-exam days Neill used to pin a note to his bedroom door at his parent's house: "DO NOT wake me for school. I am still not asleep. Neill, at 4:00 a.m." Now that he lived with Goffredo the insomnia was complicated by the fact that he couldn't wander the apartment at 3 a.m. looking for relief. Because he might run into Goffredo who would talk to him and then, having engaged vocal cords, sleep would be an impossibility.

He talked it over with Bidden, another card-carrying insomniac.

"I'm feeling cursed. I seriously have forgotten how to sleep."

"I know," Bidden said, sipping his Regal Lager, which he always ordered for the palindrome of its name. "Last night: two hours."

"Two's good. I got about two, too."

"There's no you in insomnia. It has to be the most solitary of afflictions."

"Yes, alone with your own lack of devices."

"What is the world like if you're really rested?"

"I have no idea."

"When God gives you insomnia give him back poetry."

"You write at 2 a.m.?" Bidden asked.

"Some nights. I was quoting what that shrink said to me. Most nights I think if I get up to write I have completely given up on sleep."

"What shrink?"

"Oh, Jesus, I haven't talked to you about the shrink."

"You haven't."

"My mother's idea. It started when Dew dumped me. I was disconsolate. I was outside the human ken. I thought I wanted to die."

"But you didn't."

"I didn't die, true."

"You didn't really *want* to. Die."

"I guess not. You know the hopelessness, the twistedness of night logic."

"Do I."

"Anyway, this shrink, with his walls of Franklin Libraries, asked me all kinds of things like, what I feared most, what did I want from the middle of the night, what would be my ideal day, that kind of crap. I tell you I never felt so desperately at odds with the world as when I walked out of his office. Dr. Sardonicus."

"Not his real name."

"No. Dr. Savonarola."

"Stop it."

In Victoria's Room

Scene: one November school night in Victoria's room, door closed roommate in her own vestibule with her own male member to entertain.

Neill was studying for an exam in Sociology. Neill had thought the study of sociology was to be an exciting one for him. He was picturing Lukac's *The Theory of the Novel*, and got instead a textbook so densely mind-numbing that Neill lost the thread after two or three sentences. His mind wandered like a Jew.

Victoria was reading *Othello*.

They were at opposite ends of the bed. Their plantars were touching as if they were standing on a mirror and seeing their opposite sex twin.

"This is driving me nuts," Neill said.

"Our feet grope?" Victoria said, not raising her eyes from Shakespeare.

"That, too. But I meant this sociology crapola. My mind won't let it in."

"They met so near with their lips that their breaths embraced together."

"What?"

"I'm reading, my carnal pal."

"Ok."

It was quiet for a while except for soft susurrations from the roommate and guest. Their small, human gasps of pleasure seemed to be playing counterpoint to the Billy Joel album that was playing so low Billy sounded like Billie.

"Well, happiness to their sheets!"

"Ha!" Neill said.

"I'm still reading," Victoria said. But, this time, she looked up from her Signet Classic.

"That's in *Othello*?"

Victoria turned herself 180 degrees and held the paperback under Neill's nose, her short, tapered finger pointing to the line.

"Huh," Neill said.

"Can you hear them?"

"Yes. That's what I thought you were commenting upon."

"Makes one horny just to listen, doesn't it?"

Neill pulled Victoria's t-shirt over her head. Down below she wore men's pajama shorts over her lacies. She had both off in a trice. Or maybe even half a trice.

Neill looked like a drowning pelican as he pulled and threw and dragged every stitch of clothing off his own young body.

They were soon on the floor, naked as the graces.

"I love your balls," Victoria said, cupping them.

"I love the way you love my balls."

"It makes you so hard."

"Mm."

"And me so wet."

"Let's see," Neill said. He put one, two fingers inside her.

Victoria pushed against Neill's hand. She was grunting.

"You're gonna make me come," she said.

"Yes," Neill answered.

"I want to come with your dick inside me."

"Good girl," Neill said. He was smiling. "You said dick."

"I know. Heat of passion. Eskimo talk."

Victoria and Neill joined their parts.

After a while, Neill let loose inside her. His orgasm took 87 seconds. And afterwards, he jerked and spasmed as one getting Ladislas Meduna's electroconvulsive therapy.

"I love your aftershocks," Victoria said, bowing her head to rest it on Neill's chest. Their combined saps ran down Neill's front porch and legs.

Victoria fell asleep. Neill stroked her thick brown hair and looked at the ceiling and let his mind go swimmy. Inside the watery vagueness of his peaceful thoughts a poem tried to surface. Neill did not want to disturb his sleeping mermaid. The poem flowed the way of all saps.

After 31 minutes Victoria woke.

"Mm," was her waking comment.

"Let's do it again," she said, blearily.

"I don't know," Neill said. But even as he began to protest his peacemaker began to stiffen.

They did it three different ways, including doggy-style, which had them propelling their two-backed beast from one end of the carpeted bedroom to the other. They were bucking and pushing and sweating and groaning and coming.

The next morning Neill had a sore cock and sorer knees. The carpet burn stayed on him for a month, a memento of the first best sexual night of his life.

"I've got nice carpet burns," Neill said to Victoria as she was making them toast and jam for breakfast.

Victoria smiled. She turned her back on Neill. She pulled her shorts down to reveal two large moon-shaped and scarlet carpet burns, perfectly symmetrical, on each cheek. Now Neill smiled. He wanted to bite that apple-red ass.

Sunny Day, Toyota

One afternoon, Neill and Victoria were on the way to the Rhymer's for dinner. The day was as yellow bright as gamboge. It was toasty in the little foreign car, the sun coming through the windows like breakers.

They were driving north on Covington Pike toward Stage Road. Used to be, when Neill first learned how to drive, he would go north on Covington Pike and soon found himself on winding country roads, ceilinged by leafy umbrage. He drove fast, relishing the feel of the tires on the country curves. Now, Covington Pike was over-developed. It was six lanes wide and there were new businesses on every side, Target, Marshalls, an electronics store, a Taco Bell, and, across the street, a real Mexican Restaurant, Estoy de Negocios.

"Whatcha thinking about?" Victoria said. She had one arm out the window and was feeling the wind flow over it as if it were a wing.

"The Abbey Road album," Neill said.

"That's peculiar."

"It's a very good album. No, it's a great album."

"It is."

"That's what I was thinking."

"Ask me."

Neill looked at her. Her puckish face wore an inscrutable expression. Her inscrutable face wore a puckish expression.

"Say, Victoria, what are you thinking?'

"Penny for my thoughts?"

"Yes."

"Ten dollars."

"Ten dollars for your thoughts. That's kinda steep."

"Not for these thoughts."

"Ok, ten dollars."

Victoria brought her arm back inside the car. She scooted her pretty dummock sideways on the small car seat.

"I was thinking about sucking you off."

"Good times, right?"

"I mean now. I was thinking about sucking you off now. Future tense, or no, present tense"

"Ha. You wouldn't," Neill said, even as his corm stiffened.

"I would. I will."

She put her hand over the knot. The traffic on either side of them was as close as clapboards on a house.

"It's kind of a busy street," Neill said, feebly. "We're surrounded by daylight."

Victoria already had his cock out and was stroking it. She undid her seat belt. She squeezed her head, with its luscious mane, between the steering wheel and Neill's thighs. She licked his pecker's head.

Nick groaned. "This isn't gonna work," he said, trying to concentrate on when to push the gas and when to push the brake. Victoria was ignoring all protests. She was bent on making this escapade a thrilling reality. She went all the way down on it.

"Jesus," Neill said.

Victoria was now sucking loudly on him, exaggerating the slobbery sounds. She sounded like a Great Dane drinking water. They were coming to a stop light.

She did not even hesitate.

Neill looked at the car to his left. An old man and woman were having their own special time, fighting like cocks. Neill looked to his right. A young black man, muscled bicep resting on his rolled-down window, was looking right at Neill. Neill smiled weakly.

Neill came hard inside her mouth. He filled her mouth with young semen. Neill realized that he had his eyes closed. The car behind honked. The black guy hadn't moved either. He wanted to see the conclusion, too.

Victoria raised her head. She kissed Neill's cheek. Neill began to roll through the intersection. Victoria turned to the handsome black guy beside them. She smiled and wiped her mouth overdramatically, and then held her spermy hand up in salute. The fellow saluted back. He then accelerated away, off to his own quests.

And Another Time, Parking

Victoria was now becoming something other than the prim doctor's daughter from Raleigh Egypt High School. She was becoming a woman, a sexual creature. She was adventurous, she was horny. She was celebrating.

She asked Neill if he'd ever been parking.

"No," Neill lied. "I can't imagine it's much fun," he added, blandly.

"Let's do it," Victoria said.

So, even though they had apartments to go to, places where there were beds and blankets and carpeted floors, they drove one Saturday night into the snaky darkness beyond Raleigh, into a place of new streets and wooden frames, a place where no humans yet subsisted.

They parked in a cul-de-sac.

"Kiss me, Hunky Dory," Victoria said.

"I'm more Dory than Hunky."

"You're more Hunky. Smooch me."

Neill did. It was a long, thoughtful kiss, with lots of saliva and tongue.

"Look, what I bought," Neill said, leaning over and opening the glove compartment.

"Sex toy?" Victoria asked.

"Well...not exactly." It was a small penlight. A flashlight about the size of your average ballpoint.

"Ingenious little thing, isn't it?"

"What do you want to do with it?" Victoria asked.

"Lift your skirt."

Victoria was wearing a short blue-jean skirt. She pulled it up. Her white panties seemed to blaze in the absolute country dark around them.

"You thought ahead," she said.

"I'm going to examine you," Neill said.

"Ooh, Doctor."

"If you'll just take those grundies down."

Victoria kicked them off. They went over their shoulders into the back seat.

"Nice trick," Neill said.

"What now, Doctor?"

"Spread your legs, Ms. Lucas."

She did. And Neill bent down and shined the tiny light into the dark wedge between her thighs. It looked delicious. Her chocolate tangle of hair was sparkly with moisture.

"Anything wrong down there?"

"Please. Let me examine you thoroughly."

A devil took Neill's hand. It guided his next move, of which Neill was unsure. Neill began to insert the penlight into Victoria's cunnicle.

"Oh!" Victoria said.

Neill's hand stopped.

"Hurt?" he asked.

"No, Doctor. It just surprised me. I've never been to the gynecologist before. I am a little nervous."

"Relax, Ms. Lucas."

Neill inserted the penlight deeper. Victoria began to pant. Neill moved the instrument slowly in and out. Victoria was tightening up. Her legs pushed against the floorboard. The muscles in her neck stood out. Neil could only see occasional glimmers of illumination. He wished he could see the sodden Hottentot lips.

Let's say the rest lies under the protection of doctor patient privilege.

Something about Neill

Often Neill felt the victim of his own bleak worldview. It was an agony of solipsism and twisted validity. Because he found the world unfair (at 5 discovering that death ended all this and seeing how that just wouldn't do), he alternately freed himself up, morally, to act indifferently, to act abominably, even. Because every day there was a worm in his cosmic apple he found excuses for infidelity and apathy, a coolness that was either apparent or not. There was a small hard ball of ice in the middle of Neill's heart.

This is ok, right? This is humanizing.

Did it matter whether everyone felt this way? Did it matter that there were people who were good and selfless and giving, all day, every day? Not in Neill's mind.

It's not ok. It is humanizing.

Because he found things that most people took for granted difficult: sports, being able to ride a bicycle, peeing at a urinal, driving a car with confidence, loving, he also disliked himself. And, in that hot odium, he freed himself to be despicable. Perhaps that's too strong a term. Neill wasn't evil. To most people, he was as funny as Slappy White, and lovable, and great company. No one could see the black spot—the black ball of ice—but perhaps, this is belaboring the obvious. Perhaps most people—surely, not everyone, Neill knew better than that—thought themselves wanting in the morality department. Witness the Catholics. All those confessions. How long since your last confession? Neill would answer the priest in his head: only an hour or so, sir.

They Saw Every Goddamned Movie

In the 1970s, if you were a movie fan, you were in high cotton. In France, there was Godard, Truffaut, Malle, Rohmer, Bresson, Agnes Varda, and Melville. In Germany, there was Fassbinder, Wenders, Lina Wertmuller, and Werner Herzog. In Italy Fellini, Leone, Rossellini, Bertolucci, and Michelangelo Antonioni. In England, Lindsay Anderson, Ken Russell, Nicholas Roeg, Monty Python. In Australia (they went through a big Australian film craze, our protagonists did), Gillian Armstrong, Peter Weir, and Bruce Beresford. In Japan, Kurosawa, Ozu, and Teshigahara. And in America, Robert Altman, Woody Allen, Martin Scorcese, Francis Ford Coppola, Arthur Penn, and Bob Rafelson. And, reigning supreme over them all, the incomparable Ingmar Bergman.

During these halcyon days, even in a cowtown like Memphis, there were not only thriving movie theaters (Cineplexes, many of them, *but still*), there were phenomena called repertory theaters. There were "film showings." They could be anywhere. At any given night, in Memphis, there was a film showing at the Lyceum, which was held in the basement of a downtown bank, or at the University of Tennessee Health Sciences, in the Student Center at Memphis State, at the Jewish Community Center in Germantown, or in the vault of the library, or at the Overton Park Shell. And there were also second-run movie houses, places that showed old films, art films, often two in one evening. The Bristol on Summer Avenue (run by a godly innocent named Bill Kendall...Chaplin, old westerns), The Guild on Poplar (*Inserts,Bedroom Mazurka*), The Memphian on Cooper, The Balmoral on Quince (run by a son of Argos named Frank, who had a thing, an onerous, heart-quaking *thing* for Laura Antonelli), The Studio on Highland (famous for showing *The Stewardesses* and *I am Curious Yellow*.) To these virtuous emporia, our heroes went to see Chaplin, Laurel and Hardy, *My Man Godfrey*, The Marx Brothers, Bunuel, *Dr. Strangelove, Children of Paradise, If..., The Third Man, Rules of the Game, Red River, Hiroshima Mon Amour, Blow Up, The Miracle of Morgan's Creek, O Lucky Man!* It was a cinematic profusion that would never happen again.

It was the era of the auteur. It was an era when the audience applauded the names of cinematographers. Neill clapped along if Vittorio Storaro's or Sven Nykvist's name appeared on the screen. Sure, it was pretentious, but weren't we having some fun?

And our intrepid friends, Neill, Victoria, Pas, and Bidden, rarely missed a showing. Movie nights were almost all Neill and Victoria did for dates. They saw every goddamned new movie that came to town, plus attending all these lovely smaller forums. This is how they knew about foreign films. They were available! This was before VHS, even, before cable and satellite. Neill and Victoria saw every goddamned movie, so they saw some dreck (*Cross of Iron, Girl on aMotorcycle, The Towering Inferno, Heavy Traffic, Once is Not Enough*), some so-so films (*Girl from Petrovka, Harry and Walter go to New York, Hi Mom. I Will I Will...for Now*), some movies better than expected (*Rollercoaster, Three Days of the Condor, The Life and Times of Judge Roy Bean, The Silent Partner*), some rare discoveries (*They Came from Within!*). Overall, it was more joy than pain. Literally every movie. Imagine that. The openings of new films were events for our valiant troop. And popcorn and coke were de rigueur, gifts of Jambhala.

"Do you think Italy is really prettier than the United States?" Bidden asked after seeing *The Tree of Wooden Clogs*.

"I think they just have better cinematographers," Neill said.

After One Year of College

Neill did ok his first year of college. Not great, just ok. A little under a 3.0.

Bidden a bit better, Victoria a bit worse.

And Big Brother Brack rolled like the tide. Older than the rest of his class, he was on the road to wisdom. He finished his first year with a 4.0.

Good Jesus or Bad Jesus

In the early days of the summer of 1974 Neill's parents and his little sister, AJ, took a trip to the beach (Myrtle, probably). Neill did not go with them because of a wildass plan Brack had hatched. Later that summer, Neill and Brack were taking Neill's sunny little Toyota out onto the American interstate system. They were going to drive to New York City (neither had ever been) and then on into Ontario to visit the kinfolks. It was an audacious plan. More anon.

So, Neill was left to housesit his parent's home, all alone. Alone except for his girlfriend. And, they were envisioning a fuck-fest. They wanted to try new things. They studied up on new things. It wasn't like they wanted to have a threesome or work with mechanical toys. Their imaginations didn't go that far.

They settled on this: whipped cream. They had heard of other couples covering each other in whipped cream and licking it off. Affirmed oralists, it sounded like a great idea.

The day arrived for the departure.

Goodbye Dad, Goodbye Mom, Goodbye Little Sis. Yes, yes, I'll take care of everything. Feed the old cocker spaniel bitch, yes yes. Have a great trip, bring me something. Don't let the door hit you in the ass.

That night Neill and Victoria skipped dinner. They would feast on whipped cream and each other. Anthropophagi!

In the early evening light, on the wall-to-wall carpeted floor of the family home on Kenneth Street, our pair of lovers stripped naked without preamble. Neill wielded a bright new red white and blue can of Aerosol UHT Sweetened Whipped Light Cream; Ingredients: Cream, Milk, Sugar, Dextrose, Sorbitan Monostearate, Artificial Flavor, Carrageenan, Mixed Tocopherols (Vit. E) To Protect Flavor, Propellant: Nitrous Oxide.

Neill put a tiny crown, shaped like a pixie's cap, on each of Victoria's pert tan nipples. He slowly licked it off, taking time with each nipple, until cream-cleared.

Then, a line down her sweet, flat stomach (presaging a later scar), stopped just above the inverted pyramid of her curly brunette pubic hair. He licked that off also (the cream not the pubic hair), though he felt he was hurrying these steps in anticipation of the main attraction.

Victoria was squirmy and giggling.

Neill put the aerosol can into the pube tangle and let go a blast.

"Oo," Victoria said

Neill put the nipple of the can just outside The Pink Palace's door. He let go a quick blast.

"Jesus!" Victoria said.

Neill looked up from his lab work. "Is that a good Jesus or a bad Jesus?"

"A surprised Jesus."

"Pleasured?"

"I don't know. But don't stop."

Neill grinned. Victoria lay back and closed her eyes. Her vulva was now whippy-topped.

Neill licked around the edges first, the way one eats a hot fudge cake sundae, saving the best for last. Soon, he had his face pressed into the sweet white mound under which was his lover's sweet white mound. Covered in sugary stickiness, he found the *membrum muliebre* after enough exploration. He sucked it as if it were honeysuckle.

"Oh Jesus," Victoria said. "Good Jesus."

Neill worked up and down. He had the whipped cream gone (leaving behind a tacky overlay) and was running his tongue from clit to slit and employing it like a small, nimble prick. Soon Victoria's speech was gibberish, and then one long exhalation, an invocation for the coming of the coming.

Neill rested his head and tired lingam on Victoria's belly.

Soon, Victoria popped upwards and expostulated: My turn!

Neill lay back. His cock was at half-mast.

"Do you want me to do your nipples?" she asked.

"Um, no," Neill decided.

Vic sprayed some around his naval. She was treating it as if it were an art project. She used her fingers to create "Starry Starry Night" around the little swirl of hair on Neill's belly. She did "The Fall of Icarus" and "Guernica." She bent and licked the sugary, foamy objets d'art away.

"Yum," she said. "I forgot how good whippy top tastes."

"More," Neill said.

Victoria sprayed a healthy amount all over his Fort Bushy, all over his Abraham, all over his chumblies. Neill was now properly attired. His body would now only rate a PG.

Victoria ate the cream greedily, quickly. Neill's cock bobbed around the outskirts of her mouth. Soon it was the only thing with sugary whiteness obscuring it. Victoria fixed her eyes on Neill's (he had been watching the procedure with profound interest), and then leaned slowly over and licked the head clean, keeping her rascally eyes on Neill's.

"Good Jesus," Neill moaned.

Then, she licked the whole thing clean, possibly too quickly. Neill was eager to come, but he was also aware of how sticky he was. He was simultaneously wishing that it would go on forever and that he could wash his gluey privates.

Victoria now had the semi-clean pintle in her funnel. She was extracting in earnest now, her hand juggling Neill's gummy balls. It didn't take long. Neill squeezed himself up tight and then the quick release was like a rubber band popping inside his chest, like the liftoff of a rocket. He came in copious amounts. He came a rainstorm. He came a flood. He came a 4 hour movie

(1900, say). He came a stretch limousine. He came *Thick as a Brick*, both sides. He came *The Sot-weed Factor*. He came and came.

Victoria finally lifted her head. It was difficult to see which was spunk which syrupy goo. Come ran out of her little monkey mouth, her dimples each holding small gibbous moons of semen.

"Good Holy Jesus," she said. "That was the great flood."

"I know," Neill said.

"Was it the whipped cream?"

"No. I think you've just gotten that good at oral sex."

It was true. Victoria smiled smugly, the big head about good head.

Later that night, in Neill's parents' bed, they managed a weak erection that barely entered Victoria's secret chamber. It didn't matter.

Then someone tried to break into the house through the back door.

The rest of the evening was spent first quivering and frightened, and then talking to cops, who were smirking about two young people alone in the parents' house, then lying awake and talking.

The next morning, Neill woke to find a hickey on his shoulder. It was as big as a silver dollar and shaped like Brazil. How did this happen? When did this happen? Neill spent the next few days self-conscious about it. He thought hickeys tacky.

When Neill's family returned from their trip Neill said, half-jokingly, "What did you bring me?"

His mother whipped a paper bag out of her suitcase. Inside the bag was Neill's present. Drumroll. A paisley tank top!

"Try it on," Lolly said.

"Yeah, try it on," A J said.

"Later," Neill said. "I—"

"Come on. I wanna make sure it fits. I wanna see how it looks on you. You love paisley, right?" Lolly said.

Neill went to the room that used to be his. He put the tank top on. (It was an era when tank tops were sorta popular for both men and women, strange as that might sound to you now, ed.) The hickey shone on his shoulder like a second head. It looked like Ray Milland.

The family looked at Neill in his new shirt.

"It fits," Neill said weakly.

The hickey was speaking. It said, Ha ha! Look at Neill, kinfolks! Except for the hickey, the room was silent. The audience was restless.

"We better unpack," Neill's dad said. He smiled a straight-line smile.

They were soon all busy.

"Thanks for watching the house," Neill's dad said as he wandered back down the hallway to his room.

Neill was 19 years old, yet he felt like a child who had just written a dirty word on the living room wall. Like Gregor Samsa with an apple rupturing his carapace, he scuttled back into his former room.

Another Night in the Korova Milkbar

"Bidden, is what I'm hearing true?" Neill said around a partially masticated piece of pizza. "You're seeing someone?"

"I don't know."

"You don't know?" Victoria said with a kittenish smile. (It was always Victoria's self-imposed duty to make all her friends happy, and she took the matchmaking thing with Bidden quite seriously. His self-deprecating stance that no woman would be interested in him was like a challenge to her.) "This must be some woman."

"I think there is a compatibility problem."

"She doesn't like *Streets of San Francisco*?"

"She has no sense of humor?" Pas asked.

"She lives by WWKGD," said Bidden. He drank a meditative sip of beer. "I can't see it working out?"

"Who—"

"What would Khalil Gibran do?"

"I was thinking Kevin Garnett," Neill said.

Neill was never really a true believer when it came to pop-sacred texts like *The Desiderata*, *The Prophet*, *Jonathan Livingston Seagull*, *The Joy of Sex*, or *The Poky Little Puppy*, though he did like the line in the Desiderata, "Avoid loud people because they are vexations of the spirit."

"I want to date a lesbian," Bidden said.

"Because?"

"I don't know. Less pressure."

"Seems like it would be more to me," Victoria said. "A woman who prefers women, you know, prefers women."

"You're right," Bidden said. "I don't want to date anyone. Except I'm, you know, wretchedly lonely."

"I have a cousin," Neill said.

"Seriously?" Pas put in. "You have a cousin for Bidden? What are you waiting for?"

"I was making a joke. Actually, I have a cousin named Bed, who is 17 ways beautiful. Unfortunately, she lives in Canada."

"I can't do beautiful," Bidden said. "I need a homely Eskimo. Or a homely alien, who doesn't recognize what is attractive in humans."

"That's the route I went," Neill said.

Victoria snorted. "In your dreams. I recognize what is attractive about the human male. And I know what to do about it."

"Yes. Yes, you do," Neill agreed.

"You guys make it hard for the rest of us, you know? We see you and that's what we want," Bidden said, somewhere between sadness and pride.

"Well...." Neill started, but abruptly he realized he had nothing to say.

The Opera, The Symphony, Mark Twain

Victoria liked the arts. She liked opera and the symphony orchestra. Neill went along to numerous longhair performances at the Auditorium North Hall (the same place, later, he and Brack would see Steve Martin open for The Nitty Gritty Dirt Band). Often, it was painful. Operas last 5 hours! Neill couldn't get over this. He kept repeating it for weeks, after their first. Operas last 5 hours!

Throughout each opera (name them here? it seems pointless since they all seemed the same to Neill's ignorant ears), Neill had the impulse to shout: "Edit! Edit!" When he said this afterward to Victoria he expected her to laugh.

Instead she said: "You're just used to movies."

"That would only be American movies," Neill said. "Because they move quickly and are a thrill a minute. I get you. But, keep in mind, I also love the slower European films."

Even to Neill this sounded pedantic and phony.

Hearing the Memphis Symphony play was a little better. Sometimes, he recognized a piece of music (though never "Peaches en Regalia" or "The Horse" [Neill was not the nudnik in the balcony, however, who yelled out "Free Bird!"]) and, at least initially, he was overwhelmed by the clarity, the thickness, the color of a live orchestra. But, this frisson didn't endure through the whole evening and, by the end of the program, Neill was naming the characters on "Green Acres" in his head.

(There will later be another chapter about opera. Probably.)

Once, Victoria and Neill went to see Hal Holbrook do his one-man, live stage show about Mark Twain. This was more like it. During the continually entertaining two hour show, Neill was laughing, engaged, and full of fellow-feeling. He also made a mental note to read more Mark Twain. He put his hand on Victoria's thigh and she moved it to her crotch, which felt hot and wet even through her jeans. After the show, the lovers joined the crowd outside the auditorium's backdoor, and when Hal Holbrook came out, he signed Victoria's program, giving her his famous squinty smile.

Back at Victoria's apartment after the show, they fucked like minks. Victoria ground down hard upon him, and when she came she said, "Fucking hell! We need Mark Twain every night!"

Then: "Sorry for the Eskimo talk."

This Happened during the Reign of Victoria

Neill had his first poem accepted for publication. It was just a little, now long forgotten, literary zine out of Chicago called *Scapegrace*. Neill's poem, "Possession," began like this:

"I am the presence of
something we thought
forgotten. I am the man
alone in the dawn, inviolate."

It was self-conscious and wobbly and in imitation of Mark Strand, who Neill was enraptured by at the moment, the topmost book in his backpack being Strand's *Darker*.

Victoria made a cake with the word "Possession" written on it in yellow sugar script. Neill felt ten feet tall. Well, not really. What does that mean? Tall and hence formidable? Neill felt—well, in a sense, nervous and excited, and absolutely sure that the editor had made a mistake, or was at best a buffoon and all would soon be revealed, cake or no cake.

Yet, he ate the white cake with white icing and yellow lettering, and kissed his girlfriend, and he acted as though he was on the road to *prajna*. He felt writerly, feebly writerly.

He also felt like a damn *luftmensch* for even thinking he was a poet.

And, finally, he felt exceedingly horny and took Victoria's sweet, baker's paw and put it over the protrusion in his trousers.

"You horny poet," Victoria said.

"Baby, I am. I am 100% tusky. I want you to sit on me and rock me like a cradle."

And Victoria did. She stripped naked and lowered herself onto Neill's tentpole and, for a while, Neill was untroubled about whether or not his poetry stunk, or whether one publication in a no-name journal constituted the beginning of a career, or whether, indeed, he even cared about whether he would attempt one single more line of poesy. Instead, he held her flaring hips and felt her pubic bone grind against his mid-self and saw her small breasts glowing with sweat until he closed his eyes and let his protracted, sweet cream exit himself and enter his aficionada.

A Question and Answer Chapter

How are we doing so far?

Some things are limpid and some things remain murky.

Like life?

No, like reading a book held underwater.

Do we have a clear picture of Neill, since he is the protagonist and in every scene?

There is a picture emerging.

Should we say more about his physical appearance?

No, one gets the idea. Young, cute, slight, almost pretty. Hair like Angel Clare.

Do we need to have more or fewer conversations?

Always more.

Because?

Character is revealed through speech. Perhaps even more so than through action.

Is there enough action? Enough sex?

One equates the two?

We're asking the questions?

More sex.

Seriously?

Action. Sex. Romance. Friendship. Conversations. Rising and falling. Rising again. Love in sex. Sex without love. Friends who are not great friends. Relationships that matter. Relationships no more important than changing fashions. *Conflict.*

Ok. Should we ask questions to catch up on things? Should we insert more question and answer chapters?

It seems a cheap way to get away with not being good at explication, at psychological depth.

Yes. We will have more question and answer chapters.

This is the Best Part of the Trip, This is the Trip, the Best Part

One sere summer day, the Brothers Rhymer planned a trip Northward in Neill's lemon-yellow Toyota, just the two of them, though they both had girlfriends, Memphis gals made of marzipan. Neither, today, can remember the genesis for such an impetuous expedition, but the memory of it is as ripe as a mellow little pippin.

The strategy: drive to New York City (neither of them had been) and then on to Niagara Falls, Ontario, where their roots were still embedded in the frozen Canadian tundra. On Max and Lolly Rhymer's kitchen table (their parents' home was neutral ground as if they needed that home base for their ambitious strategy), they spread out the service station map which, utilizing two sides, showed the highway system that ran between Memphis and New York City, home of all the writers Neill worshipped, home of Real Adult Life, home of Art and Commerce and Literature and Music and Fucking and Bohemia and Dancing in the Starlight Balanced on the Edge of the World.

It was the summer of 1975.

The first side of the map showed the route to Roanoke, Virginia. Memphis sat like a blackhead in the lower left corner of the map's face and Roanoke sat like an Algonquian headdress across the face tangentially in the upper right hand corner. Flip the map and its colorful mishmash took you from Roanoke (now down in the corner where on the other side Memphis sat like a blackhead, etc.) upward and to the right straight into New York City itself.

The brothers nodded. It was clear that one day's drive would take them to Roanoke and another day's drive would deliver them to God's feet, as represented by the gray and silver skyscrapers and the scuffed, contaminated sidewalks of Big City Nirvana.

Provisions

The brothers packed habiliments and necessaries and foodstuffs and balms and creams and body soaps, blacksmithing supplies, and cartography equipment. They also carried flags, gift fardels, lincti, and other items they would need for their journey, outward and inward. Much time went into ensuring a sufficient supply of these objects, and more.

Horse feathers.

Most important of all: they packed eleven perfectly rolled joints. Eleven droogs, eleven blunts, eleven cannabinoids, eleven tickets for Wavy's Gravy Train.

The Morning of the Trip

The morning of the trip rose earlier than usual; the sun hauled upward on rusting chains.

The morning of the trip was rosy-fingered like that gal from the tennis courts. The morning of the trip found our plucky explorers wide-tailed and bushy-eyed. They were set to go. They were pilgrims.

Goodbye, Mother. Goodbye, Father. Goodbye, AJ. Goodbye, Lovers and friends and Memphis Soul. Goodbye, Barbecue. Goodbye, Elvis. If we do not return, sell our stuff and give the proceeds to The Diggers.

The Road Itself

The boys drove to Roanoke, stoked on brotherly energy and the open world of possibility. The road was a dance, a song, a TV series seemingly without end, like *Gilligan's Island* or *As the World Turns*. It took them about 13 hours to reach Roanoke. So, poor igmos, they assumed they had another 13 hours the next day to NYC.

That night in their Days Inn room, they shared some mojo smoke and took fatuous photos with a Polaroid. Photos that seemed hilarious at the time. Sitting on the TV. Torso-less head coming out of their luggage. Sitting on the commode. Ha ha.

It was soon dinner time. The bell was mostly internal. Yet, its ringing was a vespertine song. They were hungry as hell. I want a pound of flesh, Neill said. They decided to eat at the Days Inn restaurant. Why not? Why drive around high when they were that famished and did not care a whit about Roanoke, Virginia. (Sorry Roanoke, nothing personal.)

On their way across the sizzling asphalt parking lot Brack feigned agog and spoke these words to his younger brother, the hero of our saga (consider calling the book *The Neilliad?*): "Neill, you forgot your pants!"

And, in that marijuana brain-flash, that cracked *presque vu*, Neill believed it and his heart beat like a winged virtuoso, and the expression on his young heroic face was one, briefly, of abject terror. It was the kind of face that could bring a wild braying laugh from the perpetrator of the jape, who understood, as he said it, that being this well-oiled, it was possible Neill would believe it—for the microbial slice of time it took him to lower his gaze from the aforementioned eatery to inspect his privates. And, it did. It brought that kind of laugh to Brack's stoned comportment. He brayed, he guffawed, he cackled, he teared up and spit a sizzling gob onto the tarmac.

And, Neill, though the brunt of the joke, joined the laughter after a moment. It took the brothers some time to calm down enough to enter the restaurant and eat their chicken fried steak and mashed potatoes plus gravy and good Southern vegetables. Eventually, they did and the food was consumed and so was the evening, and before sleep the brother lit up one more doobie and their dreams were made of silver and the flashes of color from the kind of wheel their parents used to illuminate the aluminum Christmas tree way back in their childhood home in the land of the Lotus Eaters and the Time of the Clan.

Anyway…you're way ahead of us. You know that the next day they did not have another 13 hours to drive to reach the City that Never Slips. They had about 6 or 7.

Why? they wondered.

They took out their map and studied it. One side went from Memphis to Roanoke. The other side went from Roanoke to NYC.

Did you study map scales (a ratio which compares a measurement on a map to the actual distance between locations identified on the map) in school? Yeah, so did we. The latter side of said map was double-sized. Live and learn and live again.

Newark (Cerberus at the Ready)

So, our intrepid highwaymen steered their gingko-yellow Corolla through the Garden State. They could almost smell the rotting Apple ahead of them. But their thoughts were full of efflorescence and fogbows and the City as seen in Martin Scorsese's *Mean Streets*. They could have been driving on a yellow brick road. They could have been driving on air.

Suddenly—a shot rang out. No, suddenly, there was a police cruiser behind them with its warning light appearing to be the chimes of freedom flashing. What the hell? the brothers thought as one. Briefly, it flickered through their young minds that somewhere in the darkened recesses of their trunk, along with their soiled undergarments, suitcases, and comic books, were 3 perfectly rolled joints, all that was left of their stash. Neill knew not where. Brack had secreted them and, Neill hoped, secreted them well.

They pulled onto the breakdown lane. The cruiser parked behind them and the police officer did the slow, oh so casual, saunter up to the car. Neill rolled down his window. His palms were not desert palms: they were as wet as fish.

"Where ya goin;?" the officer asked in a New Jersey voice, so clichéd, it was as if they had hired him from Central Casting for just such pull-overs. Perhaps that is what New Jersey does, or did back then, in the golden, halcyon days of the 1970s.

"New York City," Neill said. "Sir." He may not have said 'sir.' He may have only thought it. His heart was a bird battered by storm.

"Ya eva been there?" the kind policeman asked.

"No, sir," Neill said. He definitely said sir this time.

"It's a shithole."

The brothers sat in stunned silence. What was going on?

"I pulled ya ova because I saw your Tennessee tags and I thought you were lost."

"No, sir," Neill said, still slightly dazed. "We know where we're going." In the Corolla. In life. But not afterwards.

"Where ya gonna stay?"

"Um, don't really know."

"In tha city?"

"I guess so."

"Ya won't find anything in tha city."

"Ok."

"Where ya gonna stay if ya don't stay in tha city?"

"Dunno. Sir."

"Ya didn't think it through."

"No, sir. We're just gonna drive into New York City and hope for the best."

The peace officer looked at the boys, long-haired, youthful, nervous, the way Thomas looked at the Lord's stigmata. (Give him a break. It was the First Stigmata. Who knew?)

"Ya won't find anything in tha city."

"I guess we'll stay in Newark, then," Neill managed.

"Ya eva been there?

"No, sir."

A Pinter Pause.

"It's a shithole."

There was a silence. The silence was inside Brack. The silence was inside the police officer, who was really thinking about getting home and talking to his wife about dinner; he didn't want that vegetable casserole again, the one that gave him such heartburn he was up half the night. And the silence was inside Neill like a stone that covers the exit to his Cave of Thought.

"Ok then," the policeman finally said. "You guys be safe."

"Yes, sir," Neill said.

The cruiser waited for them to return to the slab, to the highway of dreams. Then, he passed them and hit his horn a couple times. The brothers waved but the policeman wasn't even looking. He was thinking about roast pork.

The Wanderers See The City for the First Time and Are Agog Almost Exactly as if They are Walk-ons from Hooterville

There is an entrance into New York City across some bridge (look this up) that— unexpectedly —there it is, BAM!, the city you've dreamed about, the city you've seen in so many movies. You can already pick out landmarks. You have watched that much TV. The city glistens in the sun (on this day anyway) and looks, for the entire world, like Atlantis, surrounded by amethyst, wavering, watery light.

The brothers' jaws went slack. Brack was now driving, having taken over at a rest stop right outside Newark.

"Oh my," Neill said.

In response Brack picked up the map, whose wise counsel brought them from backwater Tennessee to the brink of one of the world's greatest metropolises, and hit himself numerous times, smartly, in the face. Neill looked at him and smiled like a troll. He understood. They were brothers. When Brack put the map down, still wearing a grin as goofy as Goofy's, Neill picked it up and aped Brack's facial flagellation.

"Effing NYC," Brack said.

"I sorta thought we'd never make it."

"I know what you mean. What do you mean?"

"I don't know. It's just. I always feel like great things can't happen for me, that something will sour them, compromise them. When the cop pulled us over I just assumed we'd be busted, arrested, imprisoned in Newark, New Jersey, and then sent home with our hillbilly tails between our legs."

"Yeah. I get that. But have faith, little brother. We did indeed do it. We are about to enter Oz."

"The Emerald City."

"Wherever."

"I feel giddy. Do you feel giddy?"

"I do. I feel downright giddy."

The Boys Drive In and Out and End up at a Howard Johnson's in Newark

Does that chapter heading tell it all? Should we even write this part? Swift did that in *Gulliver's Travels*, remember? At the beginning of every chapter were 3 or 4 sentences about what is about to happen. Theoretically, you could just read those chapter headings and finish up the novel in about 15 minutes. Seriously.

Yet: There is stuff to tell about that drive into New York City, as brief as it was. The brothers goggled and aw-shucked and gaped and pinched themselves and rubbernecked and acted like yokel tourists and found everything around them, including the street person whose sign said, "*See my Dick. $1*," enchanting. They were in a new world. It might as well have been Katmandu.

They drove around. They found a parking place near Central Park. They walked a few blocks. The sun was setting. They were tired, adrenalin leaking out of their ears like yellow matter custard. They decided to go back to Newark (see, you already knew), and they slept in a Howard Johnson without even breaking into the grass. Presumably they ate dinner that night, probably in the Motel restaurant, but we have no record of that. They vowed that the next day they would not only arrive, but conquer.

They slept like bantlings. The next day crept into their dreams in ways surprising and mundane and when they woke, they were bleary, and happy and ready to hunt for the Snark.

New York Fucking City

It's said that fifty percent of the people who live and/or work in New York City have never been to the top of the Empire State Building, or visited the Statue of Liberty, or dropped into the New Yorker offices to talk to their editors.

Scratch that last one.

All the brothers knew was that they were tourists and they were not going to act like natives. They wore cameras. They wore spoony smiles. They eyed every woman on the sidewalk: they all looked like either Diane Keaton or Tuesday Weld. They gave pocket change to beggars. They stopped giving pocket change to beggars. They walked and walked and saw things, wondrous things.

They did go to the top of The Empire State building. They did have an egg cream whenever they wanted one. They did go to The Strand and Gotham Books. They did not take the ferry to the Statue of Liberty, but they stood at the railing and, across the choppy river, waved to her. She waved back and then waggled her finger to warn the travelers about getting too big for their Tennessee breeches. Or at least Brack said she did. Neill thought she gave them the one-finger salute.

Central Park! And St. John, still alive!

Times Square! MOMA!

So, on and on, boats against the tired, they walked those gray and grimy streets. They capped the evening off with dinner in a Russian deli where the Reuben sandwiches they consumed tasted of paradise, lost or regained. They had more egg creams. Neill said egg creams were the second best thing he'd ever put in his mouth, naming the nipples of Orbit's supernally rounded tits as the first.

Neill said to the waitress, who was cute-sexy in an Ann Beattie way, "This is the best egg cream I've ever had," as if he'd been drinking them his whole life.

The crusty guy behind the counter, possibly the cook, shouted out a little too loudly though none of the patrons turned their heads, "It's made with shark's eggs. Put liquor in your picker." He said 'picker' so it would rhyme.

Neill and Brack laughed and toasted him with their glasses.

They returned to Newark and bedded down and dreamed about what they saw and didn't see and what they imagined they saw and didn't see and in the morning they still had big city stars in their puerile little crania and they prepared for a drive that would take them out of the United States of America and into Canada, the world's second largest country, a land founded by Norsemen and minor gods, like Sandy the Goddess of Publicly Funded Health Care. The land of Marshall McLuhan and Anne Murray and Leonard Cohen and Frank Gehry and Alice Munro and Slumach Katzie and Molson's and Neil Young and Dudley Do-right.

Expatriates

So, they crossed the border the same way they had done dozens of times in their youth.

Anything to declare? Purpose of visit? Length of stay? It took about 45 seconds. They left the U. S. of A.

They had planned ahead and booked a room in their Aunt July's house on Coach Drive. Aunt July was close to their mother's age (did the brothers know their mother's age? they did not), both of them right in the middle of the 16 children pack their mother and father birthed out of the Canadian wilderness. Aunt July was very close to Neill when Neill was young. Was she his godmother? (Check this.) She was overjoyed to see them.

Also, living at Aunt July's and Uncle Tulip's was their cousin Stretch. Stretch would go on later to have a successful baseball career. He was a helluva pitcher. Uncle Tulip called him "Ragarm." Stretch and Neill were about the same age and had been good friends for most of their young lives.

Postcards from the Ledge

Neill wrote his friends back home. He'd bought a small stack of postcards in each of the five boroughs of the city that never sleeps.

He sent Bidden a card from Gotham Books: "Wise men fish here. I have no bait yet fish for air. Is that Zen?"

He sent one to his parents, a generic of the Empire State Building: "Brack and I are about to leave the United States. All the Canadians await us. We may take up curling and stay. Love, son #2."

He sent one, a picture of Woody Allen, to Victoria: "Pal, wish you could see this stuff with me. Love the bookstores in NYC. Love you."

Peameal Bacon

Sure, the brothers wanted to see their large Canuck family, the overabundance of aunts and uncles, the zillion cousins. But, if pressed, they would tell you that there was an overwhelming reason to return to *A Mari Usque ad Mare*: Canadian Bacon.

Here in the states what is called Canadian Bacon is a poor substitute, a form of cured ham that is ok when put on a pizza or simmered in spaghetti sauce (to go one rung further down the evolutionary scare, McDonalds has something called an Egg McMuffin. It's a blend of egg-like substances pressed into circular form that looks like a small slimy white puck and an "English" muffin, and "Canadian Bacon." God knows what is really in it).

Real Canadian Bacon is Peameal bacon: boneless pork loins, short cut from the leaner portions of the loin, to ensure a more uniform product. External fat is generally trimmed to within 3 mm. Smokeless and tender, sweet pickle-cured and rolled in a traditional golden peameal coating. It is the signature dish of Toronto and in Niagara Falls, across the Niagara

River, across The Peace Bridge, from where the lads were born in Niagara Falls, NY, it was standard breakfast fare.

The boys spent much of their lives explaining what REAL Canadian bacon is. Every pizza ordered rankled. Every McDonalds commercial made them rend their garments.

And, and, later in life, the brothers were heartbroken to discover they would never again eat peameal bacon unless they cross that Peace Bridge.

The Falls, the Tourist Traps, Their Most Minky Cousin

The Brothers Rhymer had one pre-stated purpose in visiting the Falls of their Youth: they were going to do all the tourist stuff their family eschewed. They were shocked that most of their cousins and aunts and uncles had never ridden The Maid of the Mist. This was the small boat service that took holidaymakers on a trip to the base of each of the three parts that make up The Great Niagara Falls: The American Falls, The Horseshoe (or Canadian) Falls, and the Bridle Falls, seemingly a tired God's afterthought, a mere giant's shower stall compared to its roaring and overachieving siblings.

They dressed nicely in sharp, casual summer wear. Neill, a paisley short-sleeve and blue jean shorts. He splashed on Hai Karate ("Be careful how you use it!"). Brack was an English Leather man. It had the cooler bottle.

So, Stretch took his cousins down to the noisy, bright, hyperactive, colorful shops, and museums that lined the beautiful brick walkway on the Ontario side of The Falls, down along Clifton Hill, where, during the summer, the beautiful Canuck teens made their mad money.

And, it was among these shops that a cousin of the cousins worked, and not just any cousin, but the Page Three Girl of the multitudes of cousins created by the Rhymers' mother's enthusiastic parents, the heavily rutting grandparents all the kids loved with a mix of awe and curiosity. Bed Jarones was the beautiful daughter of the prettiest of their aunts, Aunt Queue and her husband, the witty, baronial Ron "Da Doo Ron Ron" Jarones. Aunt Queue, even to the eleven and twelve-year-old male cousins was a dish. She looked a bit like the actress Jo Ann Pflug, but Aunt Queue was sexier. And, she passed those sexy genes on to her two daughters, Bed, who was a couple years younger than Neill, and Merry, who was a couple years younger than Bed. Bed had her mother's easy grace and her perfect cheekbones. Neill had been in love with Bed his whole life. He wasn't alone. All the male cousins wanted to see the back of her dress cut away and her white panties revealed.

Bed worked along Clifton Hill, at the bottom of the hill, in an information booth where she dispensed wisdom to the naked mob along with tickets to Viewmobile Tram, which was run by the Niagara Parks Commission, as were a number of businesses in this humming area. Neill was nervous about seeing Bed again. Surely, his lifelong crush had dissipated with his maturity (yeah, right), and, surely, he could now be cool around her.

He saw her from about 25 yards away, talking to some kids on bicycles. She shone like ambergris. She was a goddess. She was stunning. She shone like sunlight through honey. She was Bed, the Invincible, Bed, the Eternal.

"Hi," she shouted as Neill and Stretch and Brack approached. "My mom told me you were visiting. How are you?" Her smile was a hummy streak of lightning.

She may have said some more introductory comments, but Neill had gone deaf. He also had stopped walking.

Brack looked back at him. He slowed and whispered in his brother's ear.

"Surely, your lifelong crush on Bed has dissipated with your maturity," he said.

"Gurg," Neill said.

"Good to see you, Bed," Brack said, leaving his brother stuck in the mire.

"You guys get in last night?" Bed asked. She smiled. O, how she smiled!

"Yes," Brack said. He reached back and grabbed his brother by the collar, dragging him closer.

"Hey, Neill," Bed said. "Great to see you again. It's been like ten years or so, ay? Remember that time down in Uncle Finn's basement. You were so funny!"

"Gurg," Neill said. "Urg."

"Neill's a little tongue-tied," Brack said. "Bad mix of cough syrup and sitcoms last night."

"You have a cough?" Bed asked. Her voice was the tinkling of chimes.

"Nurk," Neill said.

Eventually, the brothers moved away, telling Bed they were about to do all the tourist things they could pack into their days here.

"Gonna do the Maid of the Mist?" Bed asked.

"We are," Brack said.

More about the Cousin because Neill would Want it That Way

She had a head of sloppy butterscotch curls, a sneeze of freckles laid across her bobbed nose by a master artisan. Her lips were ample and seemed moist, even from a distance. *They gleamed.* Bed (short for Beddie, we think) turned men into gomers, yet she was as sweet as the apple in their mouths. Sweet and funny and talented. There are women like this in the world. Why? Because no one promised an even distribution of pluses or minuses. At least, we don't think anyone promised this. Perhaps, there is something in the ancient writings of Mesopotamia about such a guarantee, or carved among the still untranslated bits of hieroglyphics. Or in the expurgated books of The Holy Bible, the so-called Apocrypha, or Deuterocanonical books.

Perhaps, in the same place we would find a rose garden promised.

When she was young, and they were all young, she could make the lights come on. If boys tried to talk to Bed, it came out jabberwocky. Boys became jabbering monkeys within ten feet of her.

In short, she was as lovely as the first green in the wood.

On this day, returning a more mature version of himself to his hotbed past, Neill walked away frustrated and kicking himself. He wanted to say things to her. He, perhaps, didn't know until he saw her that he wanted to say things to her, but now the missed opportunity stung like a slap. He also knew that before sleep that night he was going to pine for his dishy Canadian cousin.

It was to be and not to be.

This May Not Have Happened

The songs you punched are dreaming
  Listen, they sing of love so sweet
  –Joni Mitchell

All biography is tinged with myth, even for so unknown and indefinite a personage as Neill Rhymer. This part of the story is, well, shaky. Its undercarriage is weak.

Stretch had gone on to work, leaving the Rhymer boys without a cicerone. The brothers were doing the sightseer thing in their near-homeland. They visited Madame Tussaud's Wax Museum and Ripley's Believe it or Not Museum. Ripley's brought back to mind the Rhymer Family car trips. Each child got his or her choice of 2 comic books and one paperback book. The comics were Spiderman, Batman, Superman, Archie, Green Lantern, The Avengers, Caspar the Friendly Ghost, or Thor.

The paperbacks were usually *Mad* collections or *Ripley's Believe it or Not.* Neill, at age ten or eleven, delighted in reading aloud the descriptions of the man with the longest fingernails, or the man who was struck by lightning 14 times and lived underground, or the Confederate soldier who was shot in the face but lived and 58 years later coughed up the slug.

Good times.

After lunch, drowsy and jostled by the colorful crowds, the brothers were sleepily strolling toward the railing around the Great Falls itself. They were hailed from behind.

"Neill," an unmistakably feminine voice called.

They turned.

It was her.

It was their cousin Bed.

Neill coughed into his fist.

"Steady, Brother," Brack said.

"Hey, hey," Bed said, catching up. "I was looking for you guys. I got off unexpectedly early."

"Wonderful," Brack said.

"Wonderful," Neill said. "Dammit," he thought.

"Can I tag along? Where are you going?"

"Anywhere," Neill said. This was a little better.

"I love anywhere," Bed said.

So, the three cousins strolled slowly around the glittering landscape, half carnival and half paradise. Half hucksterism and half God's munificent wonder. The roar of the falls was like some drum in their blood. One could feel it at all times, as if a second heart beat within you.

"You get used to this, I guess," Brack said.

"I don't really," Bed answered. She looked thoughtful. "No, I don't really."

"If you could see it with our eyes," Neill said.

Bed looked at him, squinted one eye, and took his measure.

"I will," she said. She slipped her arm under Neill's.

They walked and walked and that arm stayed there. And, consequently, Neill began to feel more like a functioning human male. Eventually, his wit and his loosened tongue made the whole day shimmery and bright.

He made Bed laugh and making Bed laugh was like re-creating the sun.

Toward evening, sitting in Victoria Park, which lay alongside the roar of the great cataract, the trio felt friendly and happy, and the talk was lively and loving. Bed kept touching Neill here and there, on the shoulder, on the thigh, once on his cheek, a caress as soft as the breath of even.

"I'm getting hungry," Brack said.

"A bit peckish myself," Neill said.

Bed laughed and playfully slapped Neill's bicep as if he were up to some kind of devilish shenanigans. Maybe she thought peckish meant something else. Maybe that day it did.

"I think Aunt July is cooking pot roast," Neill said.

"That's tomorrow night," Brack said.

It wasn't.

"Listen," Brack continued. "I think I am gonna go to Uncle Bart's and drink beer and shoot pool. You two go on without me."

God bless Brack.

After he left, Neill hoped the concrete would not return to his tongue.

It didn't.

"What do you want to eat?" Bed asked, re-slipping her arm under his. Even though they sat on a stone bench Neill felt as if they were about to make out on their parents' couch.

"Peameal bacon," Neill said.

Bed's laugh tinkled like the green bells of Cardiff. "Of course you do," she said. "I think there's a good steakhouse near." She was smiling like a shark.

"Or, I could take you to my apartment and cook you peameal bacon."

"You have an apartment?"

"I do. Just like a grownup."

"You have a roommate?"

Bed gave Neill another one-eyed squint. "I do not," she said, and pulled him to his feet.

Bed's apartment was small but neat. Its walls were hung with tasteful art and her album crates were full of Joni Mitchell, James Taylor, The Moody Blues, and Leonard Cohen.

They ate fried eggs and peameal bacon and warm buttery toast and for dessert a lime sorbet.

Afterwards they sat on her over-stuffed couch.

"TV?" Bed asked, settling very close.

"Or not TV," Neill said.

"Not," Bed said.

"I. Well, I don't know what to say. Do you know how long?" He lost the thread.

"What?" Bed feinted left.

"How long," Neill said.

"When we first met today, what was all the nervousness about, ay? I thought perhaps you didn't have fond memories of me, or you were disappointed in how I had grown up."

"Oh, Bed," Neill said. His throat caught. "Just the opposite."

They were silent for a few moments. Bed took Neill's hand and they were silent for a few more moments.

"I've wanted you my whole goddamn life," Neill finally said.

"Ah," Bed said.

"But, impossible, right? I mean, first cousins and all."

Bed seemed to think this over.

"It's not like we're gonna procreate," she said.

"True," Neill said. Then: "Wait, what? What do you mean? You mean, we can, um, fool around?"

"You're a beautiful man, did you know that, Cuz? You look like Roger Daltrey, ay?"

"Ha."

"And you smell good. Is that English Leather?"

"Hai Karate."

"Be careful how you use it, right? Fool around, yeah. I think we could do that, ay? After you walked away this morning, I was kicking myself for not making you more comfortable. Plus, well, hell, I wanted to kiss you."

"Jesus," Neill said.

"Now," Bed said.

She leaned in slowly. Her face, like an ancient visage on a coin, moved toward him out of dimness into clarity, and then into dimness again. Neill forgot to close his eyes.

Her lips were soft and, yes, really that moist. Her mouth was like a freshet. Her tongue was firm and as erotic as electrical phenomena.

Neill kissed Bed's butterscotch neck and shoulder. Bed ran a finger down Neill's shirt front.

Soon, their hands were all over each other. The hands moved of their own volition. Neill tried not to think who this was, yet he wanted, simultaneously, to never forget for one second the who and how and why this was. After Bed had removed her shirt and bra, and Neill his shirt and pants, they sat back and looked at each other.

Bed's breasts were small and perfect, fruits no mortal man should miss. Her nipples, against the lighter coloring of her fawn skin, were like sunburned stones.

"My God, you're beautiful," Neill said.

"Neill, Neill, Sweet man," Bed said. "Let's go."

"Bed to bed?" Neill said.

Bed chuckled as if it were the first time she had heard it.

After they rose, Bed let her skirt fall and Neill watched her walk away from him clad only in panties, a shade of pink only slightly different from her magnificent flesh.

Bed turned. "Come on, Cuz, quit staring and follow. That's a flattering mass."

Neill looked at the front of his skivvies. They tented outward as if Neill had secreted there a billy club. Ah, the erections of youth!

Bed lay down. Neill took another moment to look at her body, its perfection, its curves. Bed slipped her panties off and there was a delicious snarl of pubic hair like a smaller

version of Bed's head. Blond, helical and drizzly.

"My God, you're beautiful," Neill said.

"You said that. So are you. Take those off."

Neill did. Have I ever been called beautiful, Neill wondered. Neil was rapt. "I could stand to look at that for a long time."

"Come here, Sweet Man. Jesus, Cuz. Is that for me?" Bed asked, nodding at Neill's verga.

"Only two decades worth."

"Ha. Like we knew how to do this when we were kids."

Neill slid next to her. As their bodies came together Neill gasped. His erection against her silky skin felt like bliss.

"All I knew back then was that I wanted to do *something* with you," Neill said.

"Like this, ay?" Bed said, simultaneously covering his mouth with hers and taking his bobbed toy in her supple palm.

"God," Neill said, when the intense kiss ended.

Bed expertly moved Neill's nether-stone erection around in her hand. She was doing something to the head that seemed unprecedented in Neill's short life. She knew magic tricks.

"I want to suck your dick," Bed said.

Neill groaned.

"Wait," he said.

"Ok."

"No, I mean, if you did *that* it would be over so soon. I desire you so much, really a lifetime's worth of whitewash is behind that barker. Lemme go down on your first."

"By all means," Bed said.

Then, Neill did. When he put his lips to the moist center of his cousin's body and tasted the honey there and began to lick and suck, the conversation, the witty repartee disappeared. It was replaced by intimate sounds and passionate squeezes and animal noises as the gloaming fell over the apartment and transformed the room's browns and golds into grayer shades. At one point, Bed turned on the bedside lamp so that she could see what her cousin was doing. What she saw was the Roger Daltrey top of his head moving like a sun-kissed stoper between her legs. When Neill began to work on her clit with his lips, while moving two fingers in and out of her, Bed gritted her teeth, grabbed the sheets in frantic fistfuls. She tensed her body upwards, not unlike Linda Blair. And then, Bed released a sweet-sounding bray as her orgasm took her over.

Neill put his cheek against her stomach. His mouth was slick. She tasted like fruit punch.

Bed ran her fingers through his hair as she gathered herself.

"Now, may I suck your dick?" she asked.

They both laughed.

Until she took it all the way into her mouth and manipulated his testicles the way a gambler caresses the dice before his final throw for the night. Neill felt the sea rise within him.

"Bed," he panted. "Do. You. Want. To. Fuck? Because. If. You. Do. You. Better. Climb. Aboard. Quick."

She did.

"Birth. Control."

"No. Worries."

She sat on him and Neill saw her perfect, puckered, honey-pink body, lit by the small lamp by his head and by the light of Eden's perfection before the, you know, Fall. She really was the most beautiful woman Neill had ever seen. (We know. Neill thought this a lot.)

Bed came one more time. She sang like a silver-voiced thrush. Then, Neill came and he came hard. It almost knocked Bed ass over teakettle.

Afterward they collapsed together, their sweat and other bodily humors, made them adhere even if their passion would not have.

They both dozed a bit. Still tickling each other. Still caressing.

"Neill," Bed said, somewhere in the dim early morning hours.

"Bed," Neill said.

"I am on the pill."

"Oh. Good. Thank you. I thought that was what you meant."

"We're safe. We don't need a pregnancy."

"No. Thank you. Especially since our kids might have four irises or something."

"Something else we possibly should have asked beforehand: do you have a girlfriend?"

Neill's impulse was to lie.

"I do," he said. "She's very special."

"I'm glad. You deserve someone special."

They circled each other's private parts with damp fingers some more. Neill knew he had to ask too.

"Do you have a boyfriend?"

"Yes."

"I would think you would."

"Woof."

"Don't bark at me, Woman."

"His name is Jeff Woof. Everyone calls him Woof. I love him."

"I'm glad," Neill said. He wasn't.

"Where is he?"

"Toronto."

"Oh good."

"He's visiting friends."

"Oh."

"He comes back tomorrow, ay. I mean today. In about six hours."

"Fuck."

"I'm sorry."

More silence, but still loving, still tender, still erotic.

"Was I wrong to take you this way when I knew it could only be once?"

Neill thought about it. He really wanted to have the right answer ready. So much seemed, in the moment, to hang by a precise response.

"I have no idea," he said.

The Matriarch

Neill's mom, Lolly Rhymer nee Graves, came from good German stock. Her parents both came from the old country in the early part of the 20th century, settling in rural Ontario where Opel "Open" Graves worked as a lumberjack and carpenter. Even into his 70s the man could walk a two-by-four on the 3rd story of a house frame the way you and I walk a smooth sidewalk. He was almost superhuman to the grandchildren and, in return, he loved their audience.

But, his wife Ema, was closer to the children. She was as big around as she was tall and she was only as tall as a small icebox. She could cook for droves, out of necessity, having birthed 16 children, and after most of the children were gone, she worked her culinary skills for area restaurants. Her kitchen, which seemed so small it was a wonder it could accommodate her and another person, was constantly in use, hot and full of cooking odors that could curl the cilia in your digestive tract(if there is cilia in the digestive track [?]). It was a gathering place despite its size. There was a small, silver-legged kitchen table four could squeeze around. There was a red three-tiered stool, which could fold out into a small step-ladder or, unfolded, do well for one more seat. Neill, when younger, was fascinated by the maid's staircase which was only as wide as his young sylph's body, and whose door was right next to the kitchen table, hidden in plain sight. It led to the upstairs (there was also a grandiose, dark-wood staircase off the living room) where Gramma rented rooms, always to Mounties. Neill, when younger, was also fascinated by the Mounties in their bright red costumes, just like Dudley Do-Right. He was also a bit afraid of them in the same way he was afraid of all figures of authority, especially those wearing uniforms.

But, from this German heritage came some warm childhood memories. Anything hot on the dinner table brought this warning: 'poost on it first.' This meant blow on it. And cloot soup, which Neill spent most of his life believing everyone ate, was made from Campbell's Chicken Noodle Soup with flour/egg dumplings added. It was a staple at the Rhymer's. These odd phrases, Neill thought later in life, came from some form of bastardized German. The oft-repeated expression, "Isn't that a kick in the schwantz?" Neill had wrongly translated as a 'kick in the ass.' It was instead a kick in a more important part of the male anatomy. In fact, these idioms may be more vernacularized family speech than any official language.

The boys made a pilgrimage to Gramma Graves' house their second full day in the Falls. They sat at their grandfathers' feet (metaphorically) and listened to his tales of walking to school in the Canadian wilderness, where he would occasionally come face to face with wolves in the deep winter snows of the forestland surrounding them. One morning, he had to pull the pistol (what kind? Luger?) he carried to school and shoot a particularly stubborn wolf (what kind? timber?) right between the eyes. The Rhymer boys listened like good wedding guests, Neill fiddling the whole time with the family coconut, which sat in the Graves' dining room for as long as anyone could remember. No one knew from whence it came.

They also sat in the sweaty kitchen and listened to Gramma tell, while making knodel and

German potato salad and Schwartzbrot pudding, about her days in the German Bund and how unpopular they were after WWII. (Well, yeah, Brack thought.)

Footloose in the Falls

So, the wanderers wandered. The landlopers landloped.

And they rode The Maid of the Mist, as they said they would. Their relatives scoffed at their rubes' outing but the brothers left the gorge agape. Boarding the boat on a becalmed (relatively) part of the Niagara River, near the Rainbow Bridge, they were soon sailing into a tumult as intense as the segues in a maniac's dreams. They stood below one of the truly majestic grandeurs of nature and looked upward into God's wet face. They were exhilarated.

At the foot of Clifton Hill they were joined by their cousin Stretch. He was on lunch break. (Where did he work? at his dad's car lot?) He laughed a bit at Brack and Neill's enthusiasm for The Maid.

"You've taken it then?" Brack asked.

"Well, no, not actually," Stretch said.

"Virtually?'

"Ha. No, not at all."

"Well then."

"You're right."

They passed a hotdog stand and Stretch said the dogs and burgers here were first rate. The brothers decided, yes, a Canadian hot dog to remind them of home.

Stretch knew the young woman who waited on them, a chocolate-colored beauty, slim and graceful, and with a smile that could dim the sun. Her short afro surrounded a lovely face like an ornate frame. She caught Neill's eye. He was feeling a tad bereft after his incredible night with Cousin Bed. A tad bereft and sad, already heart-broken nostalgic for the night before.

And this bonbon beauty was smiling at Neill.

Stretch looked at the young woman, and then at Neill, and then at the young woman, and then at Neill again.

"Hay, Neill. Neill, Hay," Stretch said.

"Hey," Neill said. He put on his Belial smile. "What's jumpin' off, Babe?" (Where did that come from?)

"Hey you," Hay returned.

"You're prettier than seven cats," Neill said. His smile widened.

Brack looked at Neill as if his little brother had just flirted in Cherokee. He was impressed.

"My cousin," Stretch finished.

"Your cousin is a flirt," Hay said.

"Only when it matters," Neill said. "What's the rest of your name, Hay?"

She eyed him with caution, with curiosity.

"Hay Watts Tempt," the beauty answered.

"Tempt," Neill said, and then rolled the word around in his mouth as if it were a fine wine. "Yes," he said.

"Where you guys live?" Hay Watts Tempt asked.

"Memphis," Neill said. "Home of the Tigers. Home of the King-killers."

"You guys eating?" she now said. Perhaps she was deflecting.

But no, as soon as the three cousins had their lunches Hay returned her attention to Neill. "You in college?"

"I am," Neill said. "African-American Studies."

Hay laughed.

"What time are you through here?" Neill ventured.

Hay took a moment to decide. She looked at Brack. Brack shrugged. She looked at Stretch. He smiled like he was about to strike someone out with a sinuous slider. She looked back at Neill. Neill's eyes glowed like torch flames.

"Five," Hay said.

Hay Maker

"So, why'd you agree to come out with me?"

"Did you really say 'what's jumping off, babe?'

"Jesus. I did. I might have Tourette's."

"I don't know what Tourette's is but you have something."

"Something that made you come out with me?"

"Yes. Other than that, you are as cute as that guy on *Great American Hero*."

"You're saying I am that cute?'

"Do you always begin dates with so many questions?'

"Do I?"

"You're funny."

"Thank you. I'd rather be funny than cute, though, if cute brought us here together than I relish cute."

"Where should we go? We're walking aimlessly."

"Your town, babe."

"You called me babe again."

"Shit. Hit me with your handbag."

"I don't have a handbag."

"Hit me with your open hand, right in the kisser."

"We'll save the kisser for later."

Neill found himself in that age-old place of Terror and Wonder. He was suddenly the luckiest man in Niagara Falls, Ontario. He was walking next to a young black woman with a face like Diahann Carroll and legs as long as the Mississippi, and the same color. Hay put her hand in his.

"There's a great fish and chips place up here."

"I can do fish and chips."

In Canada, because it's, you know, a constitutional monarchy, with a goodly Queen as its head of state, there are many British amenities, not the least of which is genuine English fish and chips, served with malt vinegar. Accept no substitutes. Like Canadian bacon, this is the real thing and a treat for the senses.

Hay smiled throughout the meal even when Neill wasn't trying to keep up the witty banter. She seemed to know something Neill did not.

"So, you're a Confederate," she said.

"Ha," Neill said, around a half-masticated piece of fried dough and steaming hot cod. "I'm from up here, you know. But I have lived in the South almost my entire life."

"You like black women anyway?" She said it with a cockeyed smile that tore a hole in Neill.

"Oh, yes'm. I like you," he said. And, he returned the frisky smile.

"I'm only half black," Hay said. "My father is white."

"Then, I only half like you."

Hay laughed. "Which half?'

"The sexy one," Neill said. Then, to himself, shit, that's too fast.

But, it wasn't.

"So, you wanna go walk in the park, help this heavy dinner settle?"

"I do," Neill said. He paid the bill and they left hand in hand.

Victoria (ironically) Park

There is a park adjacent to the Horseshoe Falls. It is called Victoria Park and it is maintained by the Niagara Parks Commission (God bless them), who own much of the area our two beautiful young people now traversed.

As they entered the park, replete with shady trees and large patches of nothing but grass, the gloaming was just moving in. Things were becoming shadowy and muted. The park was suddenly Ichabod Crane dusky.

And Neill felt as addle-pated as Ichabod, though he was obviously doing ok. He didn't know what to expect. He did know that this long-legged, bewitching, mulatto, 17-year-old track star at Stamford Collegiate High School liked him. She was holding his hand as if he was a prize at the fair. She seemed happy.

They found an area where there were few other couples and lay down in the grass. It was Tuesday night. Neill and Brack were leaving for home Saturday morning. Time was flying. Neill was dancing as fast as he could.

They lay down. Side by side, as Mr. Sondheim would say.

The rumble of the Falls was palpable. It palped them. They felt it underneath them as if it were the workings of the Eternal Forge. It moved in their blood and their blood moved in it. They were one with nature. Or three with nature, the Falls occasionally as turned-on as was Neill. Its crash sporadically seemed like the susurration of passion.

The first kiss was easily accomplished and comfortable and soft as polite poetry. Hay's lips were spongy and fit Neill's lips like a kidskin glove. Her tongue was tentative until Neill's tongue was not. She was trying to match him, calm for calm, intensity for intensity.

Yet, when Neill's hands traveled the length of her long body, from shoulder to hip to thigh, she squirmed a bit. Neill did not know if this was a good squirm, an encouraging squirm, or an uncomfortable squirm. He moved one palm slowly over her muscular achers. She stopped moving.

Ok, Neill said to himself.

They kissed intensely for about an hour, in between murmurings of mutual affection and tidbits of information about their lives. She spoke of track meets and scholarships. Neill spoke of Memphis State's need for female runners (what a bullshitter), and not once of his girl back home. Who was that again?

They reluctantly rose from the green sward, with tender kisses and light caresses, and Neill drove her home in his Toyota Corolla. They kissed at the door and made another date for the next night.

It was still Tuesday night.

Making Hay

Brack and Neill did some things during the day on Wednesday. Who cares?

They visited some aunts and uncles. Cousin Stretch asked Neill how his date went.

"You've been here a couple days and you already have a date?" one of Neill's aunts asked.

"I did. Sorta. I think we have another tonight. Sorta."

"Who with?" the aunt pressed.

"You know," Stretch said. "Hay Watts Tempt."

Silence.

"From school," Stretch clarified.

"The jig?!" the aunt said.

Neill shuffled out. How terrible. *Comment embarrassant affreux.*

That night Neill and Brack were both waiting for Hay when she got off work. Brack wanted to use the car to see some of the family. On the way to their 2nd date, Brack punched Neill and shook his head, and did the things men have learned to do to imitate their apish approval of each other's heterosexuality.

Brack greeted Hay and Hay introduced her little sister, Ivy Tan. Ivy Tan was shorter than Hay and, perhaps, more beautiful. She was fifteen. She had the refined features of a face model. (See notes.)

Ivy Tan skipped off with Skip and Biff and Juicy and Stinky to go do whatever Canadian teens do summer evenings. Brack left and Neill only briefly wondered how he would get back to Aunt July's.

Neill and Hay did some date-like things. They ate dinner. They watched a performance of *I am Curious Yellow* by a local puppet troupe. They walked all over the area maintained by the Niagara Parks Commission. They both knew where they were heading. They held hands and moved parkward as Old Sol began his diurnal dip. They wanted that grass again. They wanted to feel that surge underneath them and inside them.

Soon it was all happening again.

And, as these things go (surely there is a Scientific Principle at work here), there was more intensity. How much more, Neill would have paused to ask if he was not so headlong crazy for how this beautiful young woman felt in his arms.

This time, hands underneath shirts were as readily agreed upon as the Camp David Accords. Hay's hands were remarkably smooth (she was so young!), and as they ran over Neill's chest and stomach his marrow bone was awakened and how.

Neill's hand, meanwhile, had unhooked Hay's bra and his hands were roving her small breasts. She had bristly little hairs around her nipples. The nipples were as hard as olive pits. Hay panted as Neill pulled on them. So, he ran his hand down her smooth and well-developed stomach. His fingers hit the waistband of her jeans. She stopped breathing. Neill stopped moving. Neither knew what to do, what they wanted, what to say, where to go, whom to love, what movies were playing, where they were, where they would never be, where the center of the earth was, when summer changed to fall, who was drummer for The Rascals, what happened to Ambrose Bierce, how The Prisoner got to the island, who was president (or prime minister), who wrote and who ran track, what their names were...or what day it was.

It was Wednesday.

Thursday

Cut to the chase. (That's an awful expression. Find an alternative).

Thursday evening, Victoria Park.

Making out for ten minutes max, before hands began submerging, willow wands looking for water.

This time Hay's bra was removed and laid gently next to them in the grass like a tool they might have to use later to repair the car. The car's motor, however, was revving. Her shirt was open to the night air. And her skin, the color of the night air, was exposed and her boyish breasts a gift for the Heavenly Overseers.

Her hard nipples felt good in Neill's mouth, like an all-day gumdrop. Hay's breathing was a beautiful musical counter beat to the percussion of the megatons of water spilling into Niagara Gorge. Sometimes the Falls tripped and had to catch up. Mostly, they were in sync. It was a music that was turning Neill into an ass. His horselike pizzle was straining the front of his blue jean shorts.

This time, his hand traveled southward with no stoppage of play. No whistle blown.

He moved his fingers over the top of her jeans (she could rock some jeans) and cupped her crotch, which she tentatively displayed by moving her knees apart. Neill kneaded her through the denim, now growing damp. Hay put her mouth to Neill's ear and panted and licked and said his name softly, the way the wind says it when the wind is thoroughly horny.

"May I unsnap your jeans?" Neill said, in the same kind of windy, panting breath.

"Um," Hay said.

Neill unsnapped the jeans.

"Um," Hay said.

Neill pulled his hand back.

Everything grew still, like in the Garden right before Eve plucked her knowledge (it's not really *knowledge*, you know? that's a bad translation) from the forbidden tree.

Then, Hay reached down and lowered her zipper.

"Just this," she said.

Neill thought he understood. He thought she meant, don't take them down any further.

It was good enough.

Neill's fingers found her bristly public hair. He gently pushed his fingertips further. He could feel the beginning of her damp center. She opened her legs further, saying "oof," as she did it, but the tightness of the pants still prevented Neill from complete access.

By small incremental skulking his fingertips found her hot bearded leisure center. He was able to diddle her clit and get a finger partly in.

Hay tensed her whole body. It was a strange rigor mortis. You could have skated on her.

"NEILLLLL," she said. And bucked a few times, and then fell back to earth.

Neill was delighted. Was she that easily orgasmic?

Hay lay in the grass, head in clover, eyes to the stars, open and uncomprehending.

"That was something," Neill whispered, as if he didn't want to wake Snow White.

"Oof," Hay said again.

"Orgasm?"

"Oof," Hay maintained.

"A real Hay maker," Neill said now.

Hay looked at Neill's young face in the moonlight. She began to laugh, at first a chuckle and soon a cascade. She threw her arms around Neill's neck and pulled him on top of herself.

"You're a nutty nut and I am bonkers for you," Hay said.

"Oh, Hay," Neill returned. "Me too. I don't want this to end."

Hay pouted. "I know."

They lay still for a long time, like an old married couple after one of the children had sleepwalked into the wall.

Hay scooted onto her side and propped her head on an elbow. The moon made a rainbow of her short afro. Her shirt was still open and her skin glistened like obsidian.

"Neill Rhymer, what am I gonna do with you?" she said. Her oboe voice was wistful, playful, *sweet.*

"Anything," Neill said.

"Oh!" Hay answered. She sat back and looked at him. "Look at that," she said.

Neill was still a pony in heat.

"Yeah," he said.

"Let's take care of you, too," Hay said.

Hay unzipped Neill's shorts and pulled them down. She ran her hand over his stiffy through his underwear. She pulled the underwear down, too. There it was.

Hay handled it as if it were a hash pipe or a magic crystal.

"It's so pretty," she said.

"Oh, Jesus," Neill said as her hand moved awkwardly up and down on it. "Have you ever seen a white man's?"

Hay was quiet but she was still trying to get her hand movement to work smoothly.

"Sorry," Neill said. "You don't have to answer."

"I've never seen anyone's," Hay said.

Neill thought about this. Neill put his hand over hers.

"Here, like this."

Soon, she was doing just fine. Her hand, so smooth and humid, found the necessary progression. Soon Neill was tensing. He wriggled so that his shorts fell below his knees so he could spread his legs.

Hay began to pump harder. Her concentration was admirable.

"Should I touch your balls too?"

"Ughh," Neill answered.

She moved so that she could use both hands. Her other hand began to roll his balls around as if they were Queeg's marbles. And, her pumping hand was going sevens and nines. She was staring at her own work, her face expressionless.

"Uh," Neill said. "Uh uh."

Hay stopped pumping.

"I feel it," she said.

"Unh."

"Oh, right. Don't stop."

And, she pulled and pulled, and when Neill's jiffy popped, it sent a thin white stream up into the air where it mixed with the mizzle of the American, Horseshoe and Bridal Veil Falls, and it rained back down on the two lovers like a blessing. They were naked forest creatures covered now in the tears of the moon.

"Holy cats," Hay said.

This was Thursday evening.

Friday

The brothers spent the day Friday going from home to home to make sure they saw the lion's share of their enormous family before they left. They even drove over the Peace Bridge into Lewiston, NY, home to their father, to visit their great Uncle Frank, who spoke exactly like Jimmy Stewart at his stammering best. (So, boys, I went to, uh, see, uh, a game at the, uh, old....uh Cincinnati stadium....)

Neill went by Cousin Bed's. A Viking answered the door in a bathrobe. Bed may or may not have been within. Neill asked the Viking if he had accepted Flip Wilson as his savoir and the Viking closed the door.

The evening finally came. When Neill arrived at the food stand Hay was already outside. She was dressed in a short, flippy skirt, which almost knocked Neill's heart out of its gilded cage.

Her legs were long and smoky. He remembered a passage from James Baldwin's *Blues for Mr. Charlie* where the young negress's legs were described as coffee-colored. This had stuck in Neill's mind and now it became unstuck and drifted onto his tongue. It tasted tart. She had long, coffee-colored legs. She was, in a word, radiant. His heart broke, picked itself up and broke again.

They ate their last meal together at an upscale Italian restaurant. Neill didn't taste his food. That is, he ate it, but it might as well have been refined cardboard. He couldn't keep his gaze from Hay's tarny eyes, nor keep his hand off her smooth, brown thigh.

Would nightfall never descend? the young lovers asked of The Fates. (The Canadian Fates were busy at a go-cart track in London, Ontario, where there was a kid with Down syndrome who was just about to win the first race of his life.)

Night came because it had to.

Hello darkness my old friend, Neill said to himself. Beside him, her hand warm as a pocket clutching his, Hay seemed as nervous and/or as excited as Neill.

They found their obscure patch of grass. They kicked their shoes off. They lay.

Kissing commenced anon and the heat that previously took a while to kindle began in earnest without delay. Hay's tongue was especially bouncy in Neill's wanting mouth.

Both lovers used their hands to explore each other's entire frame. The short skirt allowed Neill to immediately probe Hay's sweet panties—scant and made of a soft material as comforting as a throw —and soon his hand was caressing her bare track-star ass. Hay did her part, too. She had Neill's shorts unbuckled and pulled aside enough to caress his roggery through his underwear.

Neill could almost not concentrate on how lovely her ass felt as his surge began. He ran a finger down her crack and found her cunnicle already wet.

"Oh," Hay said as Neill's finger ran over her dripping lips.

She let go of Neill's dick and threw her arms around him, grinding herself against him, while his fingers continued to explore the edges of her mysterious cave.

"Take your panties off," he whispered.

Hay hesitated. But, she wanted her orgasm. She wanted Neill to continue his exploration, to go further. She pulled her panties off and laid them carefully next to Neill.

Neill put a finger inside her and had only waggled it for a moment or two when Hay's breathing became deep and serious. She was whispering in his ear, "Neill, Neill, Neill," then, "Neilllllll," as she pressed her pussy against his hand and secured her first orgasm of the night.

She fell against his chest, wrapped her runner's legs around Neill's less athletic legs.

"Oh, Neill," she said. "I—I—don't know what to say." Her sexy voice was now even sexier, practically an animal's huff.

"You don't have to talk," Neill said, as if gallant.

"Can I play with your—" Hay stopped. They both waited. "Cock?"

"Ha, my little vixen. You'd better."

"I don't know what a vixen is but I guess she would do this."

She pulled Neill's pizzle, still adamantine, from his underwear and brought it out into the misty air.

"Oh, baby, baby, baby love," she said as she began to work it, already an improvement over last night's experiments. (Was she channeling Diana Ross?) She gently fingered the drop of semen on its tip.

"Hey, Hay," Neill said. "You're doing it wonderfully well."

"Neill," Hay said, her eyes on her new toy, "I, um. I don't know how to give a blowjob."

"That's ok," Neill said. Then, almost foolishly passing up the opportunity: "Oh, would you like to try? I can lead you."

"I think so, yes," Hay said.

Neill shrugged his shorts and underwear off. They were both naked from the waist down.

"Just be careful with your teeth. Make your mouth an O. Use your tongue and lips. Enthusiasm helps, of course. And, you know, from there it's almost impossible to do it badly. Like with a grenade close enough counts. And produces a similar detonation."

Hay glanced at her proctor and smiled. She scooted her sweet ass around on the grass and her face began a slow descent toward its goal.

As her gabber began to cover his dick Neill could feel nothing. She had it in her mouth, but her mouth was not touching it, a good enough trick, but not very satisfying.

Then, she started swirling her tongue around and closed her lips around him. Her mouth was *hot.*

"Oh, Sweet Jesus," Neill said.

Hay lifted her head. "Am I doing ok?"

"God, yes, don't stop."

She returned to her providential undertaking. Neill felt his gorge rise.

"Hey," he huffed. "God, that's good. Hay, I want to make love with you."

Hay stopped moving. Her mouth stayed around Neill's coot, but it was as still as the night. The Falls stopped falling.

"I'm sorry," Neill said, quickly. "Carried away."

Hay lifted her mouth off but put her hand around the thick stem as if to mark her place.

"I'm not technically a virgin," she said.

"Ok," Neill answered. He was trying to visualize what she meant.

"I want to do it with you, Neill."

"Ok then," Neill said. "That makes me very happy."

"We only have tonight," she said. Her voice choked briefly.

"I know."

"I want to do it with you so you'll remember me."

"I'll always remember you." (Neill couldn't possibly know that he wasn't lying. He carried that torch, like an Olympic competitor, the rest of his life.)

"Ok," she said.

"Ok," he said.

"What should I do?"

"Do you want to climb on top of me? Then, just put it in and you're basically in control. You get to drive."

Hay laughed.

They both waited again.

Then, slowly, like a parade float inflating, she began to move over him.

She gingerly placed herself over his pointer. Its head was on the welcome mat of paradise.

"Here goes," she said.

Neill almost laughed. Almost. But her cunt was even hotter than her mouth. It was a pleasant burn, like hot pudding. Hay was sitting very still. It was clear she was unsure how to move. Neill gently moved his hips. He did a modified Elvis wriggle.

"Oh, Fuck!" Hay said. She had come again. Just like that.

Neill let the tremors subside. Hay was shaking. Her whole body was shaking. Neill looked at her, framed by the old goose moon, a dark figure against the sky. He pulled her shirt off. She was naked. Her skin was rich mahogany with her nipples, in the dim night, so black they were purple, and sticking out so far he had to thumb them.

"You are so beautiful," he said.

"Oh, Neill. Can we keep going?"

"Yes," he said, solemnly.

Now she began to move her hips. Now she found a dance that she liked. Her ass was wonderfully silky against Neill's bannocks.

Neill gripped her hips. Now he did a little driving himself. They were working together. Her strong brown thighs were engines of pure joy. Neill moved his hands to her ass and helped steer her to a new rhythm.

"Ggggggod," Hay said, and her thighs tightened around him like a winding sheet.

"Good God, you're orgasmic," Neill said.

"Am I?" Hay gasped. "More than usual?"

"I don't know what's usual."

"Me neither."

"This seems pretty unusual. I mean all this. You're so beautiful," Neill said again.

"Neill, honey, I'm not on the pill or anything. Is that bad?"

Neill cursed himself.

"Oh, Sweet, I'm sorry. Of course, you're not. I should not be inside you." Yet, he held her there.

"Even if you don't, you know, squirt?"

"Hm. Even if I don't. It's safer if we stop." Yet, he held her there.

"If I move my hips a little bit more..." she teased, moving against him.

"Sweet Hay...stop."

"I will." Instead she came one more time.

Then, she removed herself from her precarious perch. Neill's pong felt her absence and it hurt like an awareness of death.

"Oh, oh," Hay said.

They looked at the sky together.

"Oh," Hay said, as if she just remembered her chores.

She got on her knees and returned her mouth to his cock, now wet with her own juices. She tasted herself for the first time. It was not unpleasant. Neill had a beautiful view of her moonstruck darkish fundament.

She got right to it. And, instinctually, she began to play with his balls at the same time. Her lips took a firmer grasp now. Her tongue seemed more muscular.

Neill could feel it rising. Should he come in her mouth? Surely she is expecting it. What to do? But he couldn't fret long.

Hay felt his dick fill. It thrilled her. She planted her knees firmer in the earth and squeezed his balls hard. Her mouth, just at the right moment, took the head firmly between her lips.

Neill began to come so hard he worried he would blow her head off him. He came and came. And then he heard her. She was saying, "Mm mm mm mm," as if savoring a custard tart.

When she raised her head Neill could just make out in the moonlight the glimmer of semen on her sheeny brown chin.

"Come here," Neill said, and he opened his arms.

Hay fell against him.

"I drank your come," she said.

"I know," Neill answered, petting her soft afro.

"I liked it."

"I'm glad, Sweet, Beautiful Hay," Neill said. "Sweet dusky butterfly."

And then, she began to cry. Softly at first, but gaining in timber and intensity. Soon she was sobbing against his chest.

"I don't want you to go," she said. "Neill, I don't want you to go. I don't want you to go."

"I know. I don't want to," Neill said.

After a while her sobbing subsided into a soft murmur. "I don't want you to go," she whispered.

"I know, Baby. Hey, have you thought about Memphis State as a college destination?"

Neill was not forgetting that he had a girlfriend back home. At that moment though it seemed real. It seemed possible. She could move to Memphis. They could do this every night.

"I have actually. I thought about it last night. I am pretty sure I could get a track scholarship somewhere. I wasn't sure you wanted me to turn up in Memphis."

"Nothing would make me happier," Neill said. He meant it, really. How complex, how contradictory, is man.

"I have this for you," Hay now said.

She handed him a small envelope. Inside was a pink card with a clover pressed inside it and big x's and o's written with a silver pen. Also, her senior high school picture and her phone number and address.

"Oh, Baby," Neill said. "We will stay in touch. It's going to be beautiful."

Don't Touch my Bags if You Please, Mr. Customs Man

The boys left the Falls full of themselves. They bid fond adieu to their aunts and cousins, all those awake and gathered for peameal bacon in Aunt July's small, bright kitchen. The light outside was the color of tiger fur. The brothers felt like Young Gods of Babylon.

They nosed the little car Southward, back across the Peace Bridge, apropos rainbow in the mist of the cascade and rapids. When had they ever felt better? More alive?

They reached the border, the same border, about as demarcated as a fading scar, which they had crossed hundreds of times in their short lives. "What is the purpose of your visit? How long do you intend on staying? Anything to declare? Did you put on fresh deodorant this morning? Masturbating much?"

This time the guard, the American Guard, looked inside the car. It was a fifteen second glance. He said, "Drive your car over into that garage area."

Brack was driving, thank God. Neill would have put it in reverse and tried to erase the previous half hour's drive by going backwards.

Neill took an objective look at himself and his handsome brother. Neill's mane was shoulder length, his shirt a Zappa Crappa design. Brack's hair was not quite as long but held off his face by a thin leather band. They looked like hippies. It was the early 70s. Cops were nervous and nervous cops made bad judgment calls.

Brack calmly parked the little yellow nugget in a garage area that differed little from the service stations back home. Back home. What if they never got back there? Oh, the shame their mother would feel! Hanged upside down in a border prison and beaten on the soles of their feet daily.

The agents opened every door and the trunk and engine hood. They put the luggage on a nearby bench and opened every bag. They ran their hands through the brothers' cheap clothing. T-shirts, jeans, white socks, white briefs, English Leather.

Neil was so nervous his anus was biting quarter-sized pieces out of the cheap plasticized cover of his seat. How much chillums did they have left? Three joints, he thought. Would they arrest them for three joints? Surely not. This was not Russia. This was not Turkey. This was not Bumfistan. They were American citizens, never before arrested, never subjected to this kind of treatment. Neill was sweating. His stomach was playing "Louie, Louie" on 78 speed.

The agents were about 2/3 through. The benches were piled with clothing. The bags were empty and they were running their fingers around the walls inside the suitcases.

Brack leaned over and whispered in Neill's ear, red with shame: "They've already passed them."

Neill was flooded with relief. Suddenly these kindly civil servicemen were his friends, caring, benevolent souls who were only there for the public good. How could he have doubted them? They were good people, Christian people, only doing their difficult jobs. Neill stood.

"Need any help?" he called in his best Beaver Cleaver voice.

"Nope," one stone-faced Cheka copper said, without looking up. He was stacking clothing back in the bags. "Bout through," he added.

After they neatly put all clothing back in their proper places and secured the bags in the trunk of the car they all turned to go except one kindly soul. He had a face pitted from childhood acne. He was probably teased his whole life, the butt of school bullies, the play toy of capricious and teasing girls. He probably was the kind of kid neither brother had as a friend.

The officer put one finger to his cap and said, "You boys have a good trip now."

That was it. Thirty minutes was all it took. It felt like 5 to 10. Years.

It wasn't until they were about 45 minutes back inside the United States before either spoke.

"Were you scared?" Brack said.

"As Macbeth before the ghost of Banquo," Neill said.

"Me, too."

"Jesus, where did you put the joints?"

"Inside my cufflink box, under the little cardboard piece."

"Fuck."

"I know."

"Would they have arrested us for three joints?"

"I have no idea. I'm glad they didn't find them."

"Me, too."

"They probably wouldn't have arrested us."

"Fuck."

"I know."

"Who wears cufflinks anymore?"

The Long Road Home

Neill and Brack are in the Toyota now, pointed southward.

"You did alright Little Brother," Brack said.

"I know. I dunno. It was, you know, wrong, with a girl back home and all."

"Yet, you are grinning."

"I know. She is something. I mean she is something to think about, this Hay Watts Tempt."

"She's gorgeous."

"I know. And sweet.

At the next road stop, an exit ramp leading to about 200 yards of green grass with 3 heavy-duty picnic tables and a lot of garbage. Neill took out the small packet of paper orts that spoke the name Hay Watts Tempt to his boiling heart and he placed it in a large, smelly, bee-loud trash barrel. Adieu, he whispered. He felt as if he were scattering a dear one's ashes. And in a way, readers, he was.

Back in the Bluff City

Neill wedged himself back into his life. He started another semester at Memphis State, by this time dropping the practical major of journalism for the whipped-cream impracticality of the English Department.

("What can one do with a degree in literature?" Professor Nail asked the class and then answered himself because he knew no one else would, "Get a job in a bank and think interesting thoughts.")

He and Victoria re-engaged. If she ever suspected Neill was a tomcat she did not let on. He told Bidden the whole story because that is the kind of friend Bidden had become. Also, at this important juncture in the lives of the Waldenites, a new man came aboard. He was a freshman at Memphis College of Art. He was red-haired and freckled and tall, and had a smile that was the kind of smile one imagined Neal Cassidy shone on Jack and Allen. It was wry. He was also funny, friendly, warm and open, and smart as the light of Heaven. His name was Crow Mitred. He was soon a contributory part of the after work confabulations.

And said confabulations had shifted from Pizza Hut or Shakey's or Red Lobster. There was a bar in Midtown Memphis called the P&H (most folks assumed it stood for Poor and Hungry, though some wags said it was Parlous and Heady, and the more crude called it Pussy and Head) and here gathered the bohemian congeries of Memphis: artists, writers, actors, singer/songwriters, lubbers, polyglots, rotters, lickspittles, Poo Bahs, madmen, and English dogs. For three guys and a couple gals from Raleigh this was a step toward enlightenment. This felt heady and a little parlous, and they liked it. The talk became more intimate. The talk became rowdier, funnier, hornier, richer and crazier. The friends fell in love with each other and these bonds, could, would, should last a lifetime.

(We are not here to throw water on such naïve views. Love fades is how Woody said it. We say who knows? Every situation is different. Maybe these folks will remain true to each other for the rest of their time on Spaceship Earth. Maybe not, but, sorry to say, we may not know by the time this narrative ends.)

A Phone Call from Crescent City

Sometime during that school year Neill received a puzzling phone call. It was from Orbit Unborn, who had relocated to New Orleans, where she was pursuing her passion for acting (or at least drama) and her quest for Paradise on Earth.

The purpose of this call: she wanted Neill to fly down and stay with her in her apartment over the weekend. Flights were cheap and she was dying to see him.

She said this: you've spoiled me for other men.

Neill didn't have to think very hard about it. Sex with Victoria was going just fine, perhaps more desperate from his side than hers but, still, after a few years together it wasn't bad. But, in his mind, Neill saw those globes of pleasure, those sempiternal tits. Oh God, yes, he wanted to suck them again. He wanted to see Orbit naked again. He wanted her wonderful Hoover of a mouth to take in his member and welcome it back to her club.

"Yes," Neill said.

He told Victoria he was going to visit his old friend who needed him. "And besides," he opined, "The flights are really cheap right now."

He packed a couple novels—E. L. Doctorow's *Ragtime* and Iris Murdoch's *Flight from the Enchanter*—and hopped aboard an airplane one Friday afternoon heading for good food and sure sex. Neill was a happy viator. How many men have boarded planes on missions which, they were sure, were to lead inevitably to sexual abandonment? Hopeful bulls all.

Orbit met him at the airport. She looked the same, maybe a little thinner. Her hug was warm and the buss quick, but friendly. She was in a cab. Why was she in a cab? Perhaps to impress Neill with her big city adulthood. It worked. It was the first time Neill had ever been in a cab. He would never forget it.

"Back seat ok?" the cabbie asked. He was a wizened little puppet with a Don Knotts Adam's apple.

Orbit smiled at Neill. Neill imagined he was supposed to answer.

"Sure," Neill said.

"Just got it back. Had to take it in and clean the blood off the seat. Last fare, guy and his woman. Argued like a Jew and Arab. Suddenly the guy calls out, 'Lemme out here.' I pull over. He throws me a twenty and takes to his feet. I say to the gal, 'You still want to—" and I see she's got a knife sticking out of her side, bleeding like a stuck pig all over my seats. 'Fuck me,' I said. And, I had to drive her to the hospital. Wild, huh?"

Neill's throat was too tight for speech. He squeaked.

"Fucking Arabs, right?"

Neill was confused about whether the guy was really an Arab. Had he listened to the story carefully? He didn't care. He wanted out. He didn't want to take cabs. He didn't want to live in the Big Dangerous City. He was only a child, a wee bairn!

Tennessee Williams and the Not-so-Sweet Bird of Youth

Orbit took Neill on a walking tour of the Quarter near where her small, but light-filled, apartment was situated. They held hands but something was awry. Orbit had no illumination behind her eyes. It was the old Orbit and then again it wasn't. (Body snatchers, Neill thought. *Don't go to sleep.*)

She showed him the restaurant/inn where she worked.

"Tennessee Williams wrote Streetcar right here in this room," she said.

"Huh," Neill said.

They ate raw oysters at Acme Oyster House. This was a first for Neill, also, raw oysters. They felt like sex. A lot of this trip was a first for Neill.

He only wanted to get back to the apartment. He had espied the large white bed in the large white bedroom and he only wanted to be in there, pelvic girdle to pelvic girdle.

Eventually, they returned to the apartment. It was a long, nice stroll. The air was as thick as porridge.

They watched a movie in the VCR. It might have been *Viva Zapata!* or it might have been *The Three Stooges in Orbit.* "Let this night end," Neill prayed.

"Ready for bed?" Orbit said. She said it the way you might ask a child if he wanted a Snickers in his lunch.

"Uh, sure," Neill said. He couldn't help but sense that something was skewwhiff.

Neill stripped to his t-shirt and briefs. He got under the white bedspread.

Orbit emerged from the bathroom. She was wearing tangerine-colored panties as sheer as a moonbeam and a top that was scant and perhaps even sheerer. Her great borsties were right there, still as round as grapefruits and still capped with large, succulent nipples.

She slid under the covers.

Neill put his arms around her. They kissed.

The caloric level remained steady. Orbit was kissing like a backstop.

Neill persevered.

He took those blesséd spheres out of their ridiculous diaphanous container.

They felt wonderful.

Orbit's expression never changed. She looked like She Came from Outer Space. Something had entered in, a coldness. Neill was not aroused. What a horrible feeling. What a horrible, unsettling, stilted, half-life feeling.

Neill didn't even get hard. It didn't matter. He wasn't there for sex. Why was he there?

She didn't ask him there for sex either. What did she want?

He stayed next to Orbit all night. He did not sleep.

In the morning, she took him for chicory coffee and beignets.

In the afternoon, they ate soft crab po-boys.

That night she made them what she called homemade nachos, which were really Triscuits with melted cheddar cheese from the microwave, topped with a slice of jalapeno pepper. They were tasty enough. Later, Neill read *Ragtime* from cover to cover while he was supposed to be sleeping on her undersized, hard, bumpy couch. The next day he flew home, bleary and ireful.

What just happened? he asked himself.

And you might be asking, why didn't he ask Orbit what was going on?

He would say: because she was no longer human. He would say: *They're already here. You're next. You're next. Love, desire, ambition, faith – without them, life's so simple, believe me. You're next!*

Fidelity Loans

Now, back in his life, Neill began to ponder something unpleasant about himself. Introspection was his bane and he spent much of his life trapped in his own head. Now, he had a pea underneath the mattress of his wellbeing: he recognized that he was a philanderer.

He and Victoria were still viewed as the ideal couple. This was from the outside looking in, of course, and based, mostly, on the fact that they were both cute, funny, and book readers. This seemed enough to most people. "If only I could find a relationship like yours…" was a refrain Neill heard often. One of its chief proponents was his roommate Goffredo, who, Neill suspected, had loved Victoria from the first day he met her.

This ideal relationship misnomer also came from both sets of parents. Victoria's mother, for one, thought Neill the perfect young man, especially for her eccentric, intelligent, daughter.

But Neill's eyed traveled hither and yon. Sometimes it went so far hither, he lost sight of yon. Or so far yon, he lost sight of hither.

One such occasion stands out and its reverberations were to affect the rest of Neill's life.

It came, not inappropriately, and ideally plot-wise, from Sly.

Sly and Neill loved to visit their old high schools. They still had friends there. They still had young women whom they admired, and who may or may not have admired them. One afternoon, at Raleigh-Egypt they happened to be walking the waxy, concrete halls when cheerleader practice was in session.

The cheerleaders all looked like cake. They all looked *physically* sexy.

But one stood out.

She had a face as cute as Carole Lombard's and a David Bowie haircut that accentuated her large nose and prominent cheeks.

Then, only a week later, the gang went to see the Bartlett/Raleigh-Egypt football game. Sly and Neill, Thistle, Sadie, Lindsey, Gulley, Sam Onides, and various Pharaohs. They took turns sitting on the Bartlett side and on the Raleigh Egypt side. They played "25 or 6 to 4" and "The Horse" on kazoos. A good time was had by all.

Then Neill spotted that cheerleader again. She was effulgent. Her smile could kill or light a candle in the darkness.

"Hey, who's that?" Neill nudged Sly.

"Which?"

"The one with the Bowie haircut."

"Neill, there are four Bowie haircuts."

"Oh, yeah. That one," he gestured with his program.

"Ah. Yes. Thought you meant her. Her name is Dinah Mist. She's only a junior."

"Uh huh," Neill said. Only a junior like that was a bad thing, like there really were statutory rape laws.

Neill tried to catch her eye. He thought he did. He thought one of her extended, "Go-o-o-os," was directed at him. Go and beat your crazy head against the sky? Go away? Or, go ahead, make eyes at me?

Neill assumed the latter.

A few nights later, he did the Dew Drynow gambit all over again. He showed up on a girl's doorstep with no plan, no preamble, and no good sense.

You Know I Heard Some Dinah Mist Hum

Lord, she was cute close-up. This was Neill's first thought.

And then, he was unmanned.

"I know you," she said.

"Do you?" Neill said. His strut was wobbly.

"You're Sly's friend. You're the guy from the football game."

"Yes. Neill."

"Neill Rhymer."

"You're good."

"I do my research, too. You found out where I lived and I found out some things about you. Some good, some bad. And, no..."

"No?" Neill asked.

"No, I am not that good." And then, that smile. It was like a cut in a jack-o-lantern. And, it shone outward in that way.

"Want to ask me in."

"Nah, my brother's inside. He's a cop."

"I promise I am not wanted."

"Somebody wants you."

"Ha. Somebody does."

"Your girlfriend?"

"Oh. Aha!"

"Yes, aha. But, listen, let's sit out here on the porch."

"Thanks. I am. Unmanned or something."

"I doubt that, Neill Rhymer."

"I think I'd like you Dinah Mist. I know I like your face. No, I think I love your face."

And there was the beam again, teeth like jewels.

"It's ok," she said, after a minute.

"What is?"

"Your being here. I approve."

"Oh, thanks. Because, well, I couldn't resist. You're about the cutest thing I've ever seen."

"It's the Bowie haircut."

"No, there were too many Bowie haircuts," Neill said. Then quickly, "But you wear it best."

"Thank you. I think you're awfully cute, too."

"Really? You know, cute is all I get. Someday I hope to be handsome."

"When you grow up."

"When I grow up, exactly."

Meanwhile Back at the Ranch

Now, Neill discovered something else unsavory about himself. He could dissemble. He lied to Victoria as easily as if he thought it ok. And, damn, part of him did think it was ok. He reasoned this way, faultily or not: I am not married. I am awfully young. Too young to be married, too young to be tied down. Life is long. And death is longer and stronger.

What Neill did not realize was that this was the standard rationalization that every young man and woman used to make rogueing ok in their cheating heart of hearts.

Add this: Neill loved Victoria. He really did. She answered something in him that perhaps no one else answered. Perhaps she answered something that no one else ever would. This scared Neill. Yet...yet....he was drawn to this new planet, this new Dinah Mist. He began to go to her house every afternoon between school and work. And he told Victoria a variety of stories, some plausible, some ridiculous. Did he believe Victoria believed him? We think he did.

Authors Visit

One of the pleasanter aspects of bookselling is meeting authors. Books are written by people, most of them. Later in life, when speaking of the author signings he had hosted, Neill would say that most authors were fine people, good, pleasant, smart, kind people, with the exception of one Rolling Stone, one pompous fiction teacher from Iowa City, and one new-agey squit who spoke unintelligible, purply bafflegab, in between trips to the head to coke up.

Even at Waldenbooks in Raleigh Springs Mall authors occasionally visited, though the store was not set up for such things, and the Home Office did not really care about hosting poetry readings or such. To the Home Office, books were like cans of fruits and vegetables. No one asked to meet the canners.

Rosemary Rogers came once. At the time she was the bestselling author in the world. She wrote romantic potboilers. Only six people showed up. Neill began to question the decision to host a signing. She probably would have done better elsewhere. But, Ms. Rogers herself, was, how to put this delicately?—*a babe*. And, sweet as sin. Somewhere there is a picture of Neill and Rosemary Rogers, and Neill is leaning toward her as if the irony in him were being drawn by a magnet. Ms. Rogers also showed Neill a picture of her daughter—like mother like gorgeous progeny—and hinted that she and Neill would make a lovely couple.

Later, another author visited. This came about because of Neill's new friendship with David Spicer, a local poet and editor of the esteemed Memphis small literary journal and press, raccoon books. Neill had admired David to the point that he was a mite cowed by him. And, raccoon books was a first rate press. First rate.

Neill had just discovered a wild-man poet named Terry Stokes. Neill had been reading Stokes' firecracker book, *Crimes of Passion*, and he was taken with the funny, drunken, madcap lines that Stokes wrote. His wasn't like any of the other poetry Neill was reading.

And, here is a coincidence to keep even Jung up at night, it turned out that David was publishing a chapbook by Terry Stokes. David called Walden's and asked Neill if he wanted to host a signing/reading for this new poet. "His name is Terry Stokes," David said. Neill jumped through the receiver and hugged David's neck. David didn't know what prompted such a show of emotion but he was happy Neill was enthusiastic.

And, lo, the signing/reading came about. Neill had strong-armed all his friends into coming. It was quite a showing. Terry and Neill hit it off and Terry remained Neill's friend for many years to come. Terry signed at the front of the store, facing outward toward the department store and the cheese and pickle store. He read to the standing audience. He then repaired to the stockroom to read some more, where, packed in the overly heated, crowded space, Crow's girlfriend fainted. Later, Neill told everyone it was because of Terry's poems.

"He has uncanny powers," Neill said. "Poetry is juju."

One Night: A Surprise

One night Neill took his compact car and picked up Dinah. It was the first time they went anywhere. Neill told Victoria that he was taking his sister to the movies.

Neill and Dinah went to McDonald's for burgers and fries. They held hands in public for the first time. Neill, God help him, thought it made it ultra-amatory because it was *verboten*.

They drove to Audubon Park in East Memphis. It was a nice autumnal night. Neill wore corduroys and a jean jacket. Dinah wore a short skirt (those cheerleader thighs!) and a girly sweater and shirt. They parked because that is what you do.

They kissed and kissed. The kisses were electric.

Neill put his palm over Dinah's crotch. Dinah liked it.

Dinah put her hand on Neill's crotch. Neill unbuckled his belt.

Neill put a finger inside Dinah.

Neill spoke: "You're wet."

Dinah unzipped Neill's corduroys and took his thingy out.

Dinah spoke: "Your stomach is warm and soft. You have a little hair trail from your bellybutton to your crotch as if a guiding path. But, I already knew the way."

"Just don't push my bellybutton because my legs will fall off."

"Funny man. Your—um—penis is warm and hard and the skin is so silky."

Dinah started moving her hand up and down. She was trying to match Neill's rhythm when he fingered her. She was trying to match the rhythm of their kissing. It was a tango.

"Not quite so hard. Don't grip so tight," Neill said, and placed a loving hand to the back of her neck.

Dinah improved.

Neill leaned back. He said, "Jesus."

Then, he shuddered into her young cheerleader's palm.

Dinah finished and looked at her hand.

"I made you come."

"Ha, yes," Neill said.

"I've never jacked off anyone before. It's quite lovely."

"You are," Neill said, gallantly. And, gallantly, he handed her his handkerchief.

They drove home quiet but beamish. Dinah kept a hand on Neill's thigh. Neill kept a hand on hers.

Dinah Mist Uncovered

Most visits to Dinah's house on Kerwin Street took place on her front porch. The neighborhood, just a little Northwest of Neill's, was very similar. Small, comfortable houses on a street full of bikes and dogs and kids and games and noise. It was cozy sitting on her porch. It was also exciting.

Neill wanted to look at her face for a long time.

As these visits accumulated, they kissed long and hard. Dinah Mist could kiss. Her solid tongue played in every corner of Neill's wanting mouth. And she sucked on his as if it was a treat.

Once Dinah had just come from cheerleader practice.

Neill was a goner.

That cheerleading uniform. What is it about that cheerleading uniform? (Neill was, really, to ask this question the rest of his life and never find a satisfactory answer.)

They began making out as soon as they sat down. Dinah swung her sweet, muscular cheerleader's legs over Neill's lap. Neill put a hand to Dinah's waist where the top did not quite meet the skirt.

"Dinah, something is stirring," Neill said.

"I can feel it," she said and laughed. Her left thigh was against his erection.

"You're so, so, damn cheerleaderly lovely," Neill said.

"Wanna go inside?"

"Really?"

"No one is home."

"Why didn't you tell me that right away?"

They went inside. They did not go to a bedroom. Perhaps this had to do with Dinah's age. They practically leapt onto the couch, which was the color of tarnished gold and long enough to seat eight comfortably. If Neill noticed the room, which he wouldn't for a few more weeks, he would have seen a small, modest living room, not unlike his parents.' The TV was already on, the only light in the room. The sound was turned down. A game show was on. A woman was jumping up and down, not unlike a cheerleader.

Neither of them saw her.

Neill's hands were under that skirt within seconds. Dinah opened her thighs and Neill kneaded her through two layers of underpants.

Two layers of underpants?

"Cheerleader spankies," Dinah said and clumsily removed them. Her underpants were white, thin, wet.

Neill began to finger her. This is what the young people called it. "Did you finger her yet?" as if she was a mob informant.

Dinah clung to his neck. Her grip was firm, more assured and Neill would not stop now. He had a finger inside her and another playing with her clit. And his other hand was holding her ass underneath her panties.

Soon Dinah was rocking as if to an erratic beat. Then, she stiffened. She was stiff as a poker face for a good sixty seconds. She was stiff for a great sixty seconds. Neill's neck ached.

Afterward Dinah kissed Neill really hard. Her lips crushed against his.

"Hoo," she said.

"Now you," she said.

Ah, female generosity. Neill counted on it his whole life.

Dinah unzipped Neill's jeans. Neill helped her tug them free. His erection was straining against his kecks and had made a nice wet circle at the top of the mound.

"Hmmmm," Dinah said, picking up the hem of his underpants like a scientist opening the dorsal sac of an alien species.

"What do we have here?" she said.

She took it out. It was as stiff as Mrs. Gaines' spine in 11th grade English.

Dinah put her hand around it. She seemed to have fallen in love with it.

Then, with a grin, she lowered her mouth to Neill's urgency.

Friends, we may have overstated this throughout this biography. We may have exaggerated here and there, praised some who didn't deserve praise, gave short shrift to those who deserved better, but Dinah Mist gave the best head—perhaps the French word *gamarouche* is more apropos—of any woman Neill was ever with—for his entire life. Others came close. Certainly Orbit. And later, someone else. But Dinah, well, Jehoshaphat. She knew what she was doing.

And working Neill's joint as sweetly, as expertly as she did, it wasn't long before Neill felt himself fill.

Did she want to drink his come? (Man's question since the Dawn of Time.) He hardly knew her. What if she was put off and that ended things?

She was not put off. She felt the gorge rise and knew what it meant. And, as Neill began to spurt a bountiful amount of whitewash into her so the top of Neill's head came off. After a moment, he put it back on, long enough to observe Dinah straighten up, her cheerleading top still on but askew, and open her mouth to show what was gathered there right before she drank it as if at an oasis.

This, Continued

This continued. It became their routine. They liked, as all young lovers do, to think of things as *theirs*, even if routine.

Neill would arrive every afternoon he was free just as Dinah got home from school. If he was lucky, she would be in her cheerleader uniform. If he was unlucky, he was still lucky because she looked good in anything.

Inexplicably many of these afternoons they were all alone. Think of the freedom. Think of what this means to young lovers.

Dinah always had a game show on, The Match Game or The Newlywed Game, unless there was a good Million Dollar Movie (for the rest of his life the theme for the Million Dollar Movie would make Neill's prick prickle.) They turned the sound down (so they could hear anyone pull into the driveway) and made out like their plane was going down.

One afternoon Dinah was eating frozen semi-sweet chocolate drops. Soon, they were passing them mouth to mouth.

While their hands found every dark corner of the other's young tabernacles.

While they raised each other to orgasmic frenzy.

While they learned how to make the other come and come well.

Some days Neill brought his spiral notebook and read Dinah his latest, poor attempts at poetry. Dinah hummed as if they were Anthems of Great Nations. Once he read a poem to her called, "Dinah, Can I Weigh." Dinah thought it had to do with her weight and immediately vowed to diet.

It went on because love entered in. Because they were so compatible. Because they made each other laugh. Remember this about Dinah if nothing else: she was as funny as throwing a hardboiled egg into an electric fan.

The End (Sorta) of the Victorian Age

Neill and Victoria at Taco Bell (Neill's fast food of choice for decades. At this point in his life Neill's ambitions are [1] screw Nastassja Kinski, [2] be published by Atheneum, and [3] own a Taco Bell).

Victoria is about to place her order. Neill knows what's coming.

"Do not make a fuss," she tells Neill.

"Two tacos, hold the meat, extra cheese," she says to the Taco Distributor.

"Hold the meat?" she asks, this placid young woman with her afro in a hairnet, because he or she always does.

"Yes."

"But extra cheese."

"Yes, that's right."

"I'll have to charge you for the extra cheese."

"I know," Victoria says and she cuts her eyes at Neill, a look that says, I know it's corporate bullshit but on a small scale and not worth bitching about, ok?

They sit. Neill is having his usual Burrito Supreme and Tostada.

"Where were you last night?" Victoria asks around a mouthful of cheese and taco shell.

"I went out for a bit but mostly came home early and read. I started the new John Barth."

"Where out?"

"Out," Neill says. His insouciance is not cool. He can't do confrontations. It's like he's already read ahead in the script and he sees the end and it's ok with him if they just get there.

"With a Raleigh-Egypt cheerleader?" Victoria asks. Now, the half-eaten veggie taco is lying in a pool of dark red sauce. It looks like blood.

"Yes," Neill says.

"And this is ok with me?'

Neill is stopped.

"I don't know," he finally says. By the time he says it, tears the size of pendants are running down Victoria's lovely cheeks.

"Pal," Neill says. "It's not like that." It is, of course.

"What is it like?" Victoria asks.

"I don't know. Sometimes I think I thrive on finding new people to like me, new people to impress if I can. I admit that it's low."

Now, Victoria places her hands on Neill's cheeks.

"Pal, what are we doing?"

"Life," Neill says. His stomach lurches. He hates himself.

"No more pals forever?'

"Always pals forever," Neill says.

In the car outside Victoria's apartment Neill kisses Victoria for a long time, a kiss to last through the dismal Time to Come. Neither expects him to get out and spend the night at Victoria's. A sea change has occurred. The toothpaste is out of the tube. The vultures are making dinner reservations.

The Death of Elvis

The Death of Elvis does not in any way serve as a symbol for the death of Neill and Vitoria. One person changed music forever, sold a million records, made a gazillion dollars, took too many drugs, shot TVs with a handgun, and ended on the commode full of junk.

The other muddled through first love and watched it end like a trickle of dirty water into the great gutter of impermanence. (Edit?)

They were not immune to feeling bad about The Death of Elvis, Neill, Victoria and the gang. They understood that he once captured the Sun in the palm of his hand and redirected its energies into the calcified soul of America and beyond.

But, honestly, they were Beatles kids. Yeah, yeah, yeah.

Late Night at the P&H (One of Many)

Often the late-night klatches now were Neill, Victoria (when she was speaking to Neill), Bidden, Pas, Crow Mitred (the new kid at the bookstore), and on rare occasions, Gulley Jewel, Sly's older brother, who was at the College of Art with Crow. The watering hole of choice was the P&H, which some said stood for Poor and Hungry. Bidden said it was Pissed and Horny.

Much of the conversation was about books. Some about art. Some about women (Pas and Victoria either giving with the rolling eyes or snorts of derision). Bidden was convinced he'd never have another lover (he told them he'd only had one and that an ignominious affair begun at a drunken high school party where several Frayser pals "rode the train"). Gulley was sympathetic. If Victoria was absent Neill was allowed to join in, though the boys grew tired of his bellyaching since he was having fairly regular sexual congress with female humans.

"I'm a waste of harvestable organs," Bidden said.

"Stop it," Pas said.

"Let him go," Neill said, laughing.

"What's the Brautigan line about the fly?" Bidden asked.

"If I were a piece of shit I couldn't attract a female fly. Something like that," Neill offered.

"Right," Bidden said, as if Neill had confirmed his position in the God-forsaken universe.

"Change the subject," Crow said.

"Yes," Neill agreed. "Poetry. Let's talk poetry."

"As in writing of?"

"Yes. Or reading."

"You're writing much?"

Neill made a squinchy face. "Sad bastard 2 a.m. poetry. I write and write and write and it all sucks."

"Doubtful," Bidden said. Bidden was one of Neill's best (only) readers and encouragers and the secret, never spoken, was that Bidden was the superior poet. But, easily discouraged, he did not follow through. How many writers have we lost this way?

"Victoria says she's memorized the entire book 101 *Poems.*" Victoria is not there this night, claiming headache, could be heart.

"Doubtful," Bidden chimes in again.

A group snickering.

"When I read someone like Rilke I get a little intimidated, you know?" Neill asks with too much earnestness, too much earnestness not prized in group-think. "Such crystalline sentences, such attention to his craft, such dedication to a life of art."

"Well, Rilke didn't have Cinemax porn to distract him."

Back on the Tarnished Gold Couch

"Anything kicky fun at school today?" Neill asked.

"You're making sport of me, aren't you? Like did you have a pop quiz, my teeny bopper?'

"No. Seriously. What did you do at school today?"

"Dope in the locker. Wet lesbo parties in the locker room. Rubbing Spazz's dingie under the bleachers."

"Sounds like high school to me."

"You rubbed Spazz's dingie under the bleachers?"

"Once a week."

"Funny man."

"Funny teeny bopper."

"Really? You think I'm funny?"

"I do. You are."

"Is that why you like coming here?"

"Well—"

"Sense of humor is ok, but fellatio is a real welcome mat."

"Something like that. Fellatio, then funny."

"Fellatio then gag."

Neill snorted a loud laugh. "You don't gag. You swallow as the night does sound."

"Sounds good to me."

"It does, little schoolgirl?"

"Yes, Mr. Principal, sir."

"You've been bad again, haven't you?"

"Yes, sir."

"Ok. I must paddle you again."

"I know, sir. I'll lie across your lap. Like this, sir?'

"Yes. Now lift that cheerleader skirt."

"Like this sir?'

"Yes, have you been spanking through the underwear bad or bare-assed bad?"

"The latter, sir."

"[Sigh]. I don't know what gets into your kids. I'm taking *both* your panties off. That's it all the way off, kick them off your feet."

"Yes, sir. I deserve this, sir."

"You do."

"Ow. I mean, ouch, sir. That hurts."

"Of course it does."

"Do the other cheek."

"Speaking of cheek. You have a little too much. You enjoy having your bare ass spanked?"

"I do, sir. Am I really bad?"

"You are."

"I can feel your hard dick underneath me."

"Jesus, you are bad. You better start coming to the office once a week."

Now the serpent was more subtle than any other wild creature that the Lord God had made.

The treachery of one's friends: this is a theme larger than a parson's barn. Whole books could be written on the subject. This is not one of those books.

Neill was working at Walden's the night Dinah came by with a bomb. Specifically, he was applying copious amounts of Liquid Gold to the small patch of parquet flooring at the entrance to the store. He was, appropriately, on his hands and knees.

"Hey, Soldier," Dinah said.

Neill looked up at her lovely legs. His eyes traveled upwards and there she was, as pretty as a haystack sleeper and just as delicate.

"Dinah Mo Hum," Neill said, rising. "I'm so glad to see you."

When he stood he realized Dinah's smile was false. Her real feelings were somewhere in a murky bog beneath that dazzling show of dentition.

"Can we talk?" she asked. Now, the smile fell like a Macy's float on Friday.

"Of course." Neill looked back at Bidden. He was ringing up one the Harlequin customers, all twelve pinkish paperbacks stacked as neatly as dinner plates. Bidden smiled a wry smile and waved Neill away.

Neill and Dinah took a seat in the mall's concourse on one of the many marble benches.

Next to them was the White House done in Legos. Kids were gathered around it as if it was the communal fire, while their parents looked bored or restless or homicidal.

"What's up, Baby?" Neill said.

Now, the smile was as disappeared as Amelia Earhart.

"I had a visitor this afternoon," Dinah said. Her tone was somewhere between despair and anger. In his confusion, Neill was thinking this was female code for pregnancy, though later he would recall that, if it were code, it would be code for *not being pregnant*.

"Who?" he rightly queried.

"Your pal Sly."

Neill's stomach missed a button.

"What did he want?'

"I'm not sure."

"But you think—"

"I think he was making a pass at me."

"Fuck," Neill said. "Fuck."

"It might not have been," Dinah quickly added. Neill's paroxysmal anger frightened her.

"It was. It's his pattern. Tell me what he said…or did."

"He didn't do anything. You know me better than that."

"Of course."

"He told me you would never leave Victoria and that I was wasting my time."

"Fuck."

"I'm sorry. It made me very sad."

"It's not true, Dinah. We've talked about this. Victoria and I are fading. We're running on fumes."

"I thought so."

"But he convinced you otherwise."

"Yes. And he put his hands on me."

"What?"

"To comfort me. You know. He rubbed my thigh. Squeezed my shoulder."

"Right. That sounds right."

"I told him to go to hell."

Neill looked at his heroic inamorata. Neill was well-pleased with her.

"I am well-pleased with you," he said. "I'm sorry about Sly. He's batting 1000. He's hit on every single one of my girlfriends, all the way back to my first high school girlfriend. He's unbelievable."

"Fuck," Dinah said. She said it in Neill's voice.

Dinah made Neill smile. Neill loved Dinah.

After work that night he called Sly.

"You suck, man," Neill said.

"What? What for?"

"You talked to Dinah today?"

"Oh. What did she say I said?"

"You know what you said. You know what your intentions were, because I know what your intentions were."

"I'm sure she misunderstood. Neill...it's Sly, man. C'mon."

"We're through."

"What do you mean? You—"

"You and me. We're through."

Neill hung up. He did not sleep that night, not even the sleep of the just. Instead, he smoldered with the insomnia of the betrayed.

And So, Inevitably....

Victoria also wanted to talk. This was two days later. It was in the car. Neill was picking up Victoria because they were going to see *Bobby Deerfield* at the Plaza. They didn't make it out of the driveway.

Victoria was crying. Neill hadn't even turned the engine on yet.

"What's up, Pal?" Neill said.

"You and your fucking cheerleader."

"Been talking to Sly?"

"Of course. What did you think? He was my friend before he was yours."

"Ok."

"Ok? You think it's ok?"

"No. I don't." He did, though.

"You tell her you love her?"

"No," Neill said. He looked out the other side window. The night was full of cicada song and watery streetlight glow. His mind was wandering.

"I guess we're finished."

"If you say so," Neill said, not unkindly.

"I say so. Yes. That is what I am saying."

Now, Neill felt tears welling up. Could he really walk away from Victoria? She was everything to him for a long time, his strongest ally, his best friend, his most constant lover. Could he give up her family who loved him the way he loved them? Could he give up crossword puzzles together? Steak shishkabob nights? Their laughter, their shared tastes, their special love patois. Their shared books. Neill had been with Victoria longer than any previous girlfriend. All their friends thought them the perfect couple. Bidden would be hurt. Neill felt like shit suddenly. He felt like something on the sole of life's jackboot.

"I'm sorry," Neill said now. "Do we really have to end it all?"

Victoria screwed up her face. Her red-hot anger and hurt were becoming the ash beneath Jean d'Arc's pyre.

"I made out with Goffredo," she said.

Of course

Of course Neill did not go home and confront his roommate. Too much confrontation, he thought. Instead he and Bidden went out after work a few nights later and, over beer at the P&H, they talked of loves lost and wayward.

"It is painful to overestimate your importance to someone," Neill said.

"Always."

"The heart is made of something sticky and foul."

"I wouldn't go that far."

"You're right."

"Who are you mourning? The loss of Victoria? Or Sly? Or Goffredo?"

"I don't know. No one. Maybe Sly. No, not mourning. He deserves to be eviscerated, but I deserve it too, for recognizing what he was doing all those years and still wanting to be his friend. How did I get to be so needy?"

"Bad breast feeding."

"I wasn't breastfed."

"There you go."

"I believe you, you know. I always believe you. I think you're wiser than the rest of us? Does that bother you?

"You're deluded. That bothers me."

"I am deluded. But not about this."

"Ok."

"What about you? Seeing anyone? It occurs to me we never talk about your love affairs."

"Short subject. Nothing there. A short story. A poem, a haiku."

"This is your guise."

"No, really. I slept with my cousin once."

"You did not."

"I might have. I can't remember."

"Look around, Bidden. There are women. They want to go out with you."

"No."

"Yes, there are. Look around the P&H."

"Uh huh."

"Ok, bad example."

"These burgers though. They're better than sex."

"They are good."

"It's the buns I think. They get them from across the street, fresh from the bakery. The bakery guys just hand them out the windows to the cook here. I've seen them do it."

"They really are exceptional burgers."

It was in this mode that Neill and Bidden worked long and hard over what could revolutionize courting rituals in the US and beyond. In their laboratory, using only their wits and wit, their cunning, desperation, and wobbly experience, they worked long into the white nights on what would become The Route/Rhymer Perfect Pick-up Line. Men and women around the world would later express their gratitude.

So, after weeks, months, years, they had winnowed it down to this simple formula. Upon sighting of a member of the opposite sex one wished to woo here is your opening line:

"Hello, are you drunk enough to consider me attractive?"

It was flawless and here is why. No matter the answer, there was a comeback that would assure that the prey would be naked and in your arms sooner than soon.

If he or she said, yes, of course, you were in. Just like that.

If he or she said, no, your simple retort...wait for it...is, "Let me buy you a drink."

Go ahead. Pay your tributes. It's genius.

Of course

"You do love me a little, right? It isn't just sex?" Dinah was asking, post-gamming.

"Of course," Neill said. "This wouldn't work for me if I didn't."

Neill was to use this line of reasoning for much of his life. He believed it himself, despite later one-night couplings, and sex with strangers.

"And Victoria?"

"I don't know. Some tatters remain, tatters that cling."

"Uh huh."

Books or Academia

Now a life-changing event happened for our hero. He was offered the position of manager at Waldenbooks. He had already been working 40+ hours a week, but this meant an even larger commitment. At the same time, he had just been accepted into the Honors Program in the English Department at Memphis State.

Neill decided he could not do both.

Neill was not a ditherer. He could make a decision. He could even make a decision without asking anyone else. As a matter of fact, he preferred to do it that way.

He chose the bookstore and, in so doing, chose his life's path. He did not know he was doing that. He thought he was choosing the easier path because he was lazy and schoolwork weighed on him like an albatross around his landlubber's neck.

He asked Bidden to be his assistant manager.

Victoria took exception to this.

She quit.

And, she started on her own path. She began waitressing at a club in Overton Square called Solomon Alfred's. Overton Square was the place the young and hip went to drink and dance like adults. Drink like adults and dance like subscribers to The St. Vitus Review.

Neill saw it as a repudiation of their lifestyles. She was now smoking cigarettes and drinking like Otis Campbell.

Neill worried about her.

"I'm worried about her," he told Bidden.

And he felt guilty as if breaking it off with her had done irreparable damage to their beloved Victoria.

"I feel guilty, too," he added.

"Not your fault," Bidden said. Perhaps he even believed that. Bidden was a good friend. He was support, succor, and unwavering devotion.

So, our hero (perhaps protagonist is a better word, though Neill was the youngest manager in the entire Waldenbooks chain of over 600 stores, which is, *mildly*, heroic) took upon himself the yoke of leadership. (Most Ambitious?)

His parents were both proud and concerned. "I hate that you have to quit college," Mr. Rhymer said. "You're so smart. I really thought you'd go far, academically speaking."

"Thanks, Dad. But, you know, I am a very good bookseller. I think it might be my calling."

He said *calling*. How pretentious, Neill castigated himself.

Around this same time a reporter for the daily newspaper, The Commercial Appeal, wrote an article about bookstores in Memphis. At this time, in the world of bookselling, a war was being waged between independents and the mall bookstore chains, of which Waldenbooks was the biggest. Memphis had a smattering of independent, locally-owned bookstores, of which two stood out: The Book Shelf in Poplar Plaza, and The Roundtable, whose slogan was "Where better books are sold." Neill and Victoria knew all the Memphis bookstores intimately, including the second-hand paperback stores, The Book Cottage in Overton Square, and the Grandfather and Grandmother of all Memphis bookstores, Burke's Book Store, established in 1875 and, at this time, housed in an ugly brick building on Poplar Avenue, near downtown, nestled in amongst liquor stores and pawn shops.

Anyway. In the article the reporter wrote he had the audacity to rank the Memphis bookstores. It turned out to be a minor bombshell (one doesn't want to deal too heavily in hyperbole....it couldn't compare to, say, the Christmas Day bombings in Vietnam, or the George Putt killings), and the waves in the small community of book buyers, and sellers lasted longer than one might have anticipated.

The crux of it was: Mike, the reporter, named Waldenbooks in Raleigh Springs Mall the best bookstore in Memphis. He even couched his statement in apologetic terms. He knew the independents would be incredulous, if not fit to be tied.

Mike had applied a somewhat systematic method to help him determine this. He picked five representative literary authors and counted the number of titles by each author each bookstore had in stock. He chose William Faulkner, F. Scott Fitzgerald, James Joyce, Virginia Woolf, and John Barth. Neill's mall store won hands down. Later, Neill would say it was John Barth who tipped the scales. Neill was passionate about the self-reflexive, experimental works of the immortal Barth. Neill also knew that it was because of Bidden, Victoria, and Pas that the store stacked up. Mike further asserted that even before he had made his official tally he knew the Walden's store in Raleigh Springs Mall was special. It carried things the rest of the bookstore chains did not: small press poetry, obscure East European novelists, feminist essayists, avant garde playwrights, the neoteric jottings of madmen and lyrists.

Victoria Redux

Like many young lovers Victoria and Neill found their passions waxing and waning. Neill still loved her with a young swain's fervency, and, we think, Victoria may have taken the break badly. She changed.

Quitting the bookstore was a blow. It was a thumbing of the proverbial nose.

The drinking ditto. She knew Neill hated drunks, hated drinking.

Yet, they found themselves in each other's beds off and on during these days of flux.

Neill's heart (and, let's be honest, his dangling participle) was as focused as sparks off an anvil. He wanted Dinah, too. He wanted her—in many ways, some honorable, some dis. Forgive him?

He also met a sexy young woman in the bookstore who wore her hair Twiggy-short and her clothes even briefer. She stood about 5'2" and weighed about as much as a Virginia ham, and her flesh was brown, and her eyes were wide as an open book, and she was digging on Neill, obviously. She was like sex on two pleasing legs. Her name was Harness Myers. Neill was aware of her the way the earth is aware of the sun, even in the tangle of DinahVictoria. VictoriaDinah.

Then Came This Afternoon at Dinah's

Neill waited outside Dinah's house. He sat in his car. It was a balmy autumn afternoon. The radio was playing "Riders on the Storm." Then it was playing "Aqualung."

Minutes pandiculated like old dogs.

Neill was getting anxious. He was sure Dinah's mother kept parting the drapes. She hated Neill. Or, at least, she hated a college fella seeing her cheerleading, junior-in-high-school daughter.

Dinah was late. Neill was sure cheerleading practice had been over for a long time. He was about to start the car and drive home in a huff when a car of teens pulled alongside him and a giggling, gangly Dinah spilled out one door like a gift delivered via Cosa Nostra.

"Neill, babykins, widdershins, pumpkin skins," Dinah crooned.

She was chewing gum.

"The gum doesn't hide much, you know," Neill said in childish pique.

"Hide?" Dinah said. She leaned on Neill the way a cat would if the cat thought Neill was about to put it in a bag and deliver it to the shores of Big Muddy.

"You're stoned," Neill said. Why was he on his high horse? Did he care if she got stoned? Perhaps he did. The way jealousy can moth-eat young love is mysterious and multifarious. Neill was jealous that Dinah was having fun elsewhere while he waited? It's hard to pin down.

"Come in, come in," Dinah said.

Dinah popped some popcorn while Neill sat and fumed and tried to make sense of himself. Neill did not understand Neill. At times, Neill did not like Neill.

Dinah returned with a bowl of popcorn the size of a horse trough. Her hand was already into it as she walked and she was stuffing her mouth full of needed munchies.

"Were you stoned at cheerleader practice?"

Dinah tittered.

"I dunno. I hate being a cheerleader."

"You've told me that before."

"I'm not the cheerleader type."

Neill let that go by.

"Except, I have these great legs and you love me in a cheerleader's uniform, dontcha?" And she slung her legs coltishly across Neill's lap.

"*Imitation of Life* is on," Dinah said, opening the television.

"Never seen it. That was our afternoon date. Remember?"

"I know! And here we are! And there is Lana Turner!"

"We missed the beginning."

"Oh."

The air went out of her.

"You're upset with me," she mewed.

"I am," Neill said. He wouldn't meet her gaze.

Dinah pouted.

Neill pretended to watch Lana Turner. Then he did a spot-on imitation of John Gavin.

Dinah laughed. Then she laughed some more. Then her laughter turned into something else, a form of hilarity convulsion.

"It's not that funny," Neill said.

"I know," Dinah said. And suddenly, her face fell.

"You're a mess," Neill said. (Where did he get off?)

"I know."

"I better go."

"To see Victoria?"

"No," Neill said though, who knows, he might have ended up there.

"Go ahead. Sly was right."

"Sly is never right."

"He pegged you though. You're never gonna leave her. Not for some silly high school cheerleader."

"Stop it, Dinah."

"It's true, isn't it?"

"Just stop."

And now it came out like a scream, like the scream at the heart of the makeshift world.

"IT'S TRUE. YOU ONLY LOVE HER. AND YOURSELF!"

And Neill left.

And Dinah cried.

And, for a good many years, that was the end of their chapter.

The Accident

Sometimes the boys, Neill, Bidden, Crow, and Gulley, visited Victoria at Solomon Alfred's. It wasn't really their *scene* (as was said in those winsome days) but they were clinging to an older version of themselves, of their group, a version where Victoria was their rock, their confidant, the shoulder on which they cried.

The sea change in Victoria was remarked upon. She seemed to be unraveling, something in her rotting the way youth does, fruit in the gutter.

She was drinking. She was smoking. She may have been taking her male co-workers into her narrow bed.

Neill liked being at Solomon Alfred's some nights, even though guilt could sidetrack him. Neill being (somewhat) single, he liked to watch the young women dance. There was one, Stephanie, who moved like the ocean under the enchantment of the moon. She made Neill's insides whirr.

One night the Mark-Almond Band played the bar and even Goffredo attended. (Though Neill and Goffredo were close, they tended to run with different crowds when out and about.) Nothing was said of the kiss (or possibly more kisses, or possibly more than kisses) between him and Victoria. What did it matter?

That night Victoria seemed particularly high-strung, and that's saying something. She was bouncing from moonbeam to moonbeam. Her eyes were the glass on your grandmother's knickknack shelf.

They left late. They bid Victoria a fond farewell. Neill bussed her cheek, tried to make close-up eye contact. Goffredo stood by, uncertainly.

"She doesn't look good," Bidden said on the drive home.

"That's an understatement," Crow said. "She looks like Judy Garland."

"Is it just booze, do you think?" Neill asked the group.

"I think it's more than that," Goffredo said. A silence descended. A silence as awkward as the negligence of woe.

Later still, as the boys were in the arms of Morpheus dreaming of Godknowswhat (in Neill's case perhaps that coryphée named Stephanie), Victoria fell asleep at the wheel of her car and wrapped it around a light pole on Hollywood Street. The car was bent into a U. Victoria was impaled on the steering wheel. Her face, her impish face, was beaten black and blue, eggplant and lemon.

The boys gathered again at the hospital in the early morning hours. They were all sick. They were as quiet as saints.

She would live. The doctors said so.

And, she did. Victoria survived the first accident. She had a scar from sternum to pubes that was the shape of the Yangtze River. Her face looked like the losing pug. Her smile, her glimmer, was MIA.

Once she returned home it was to her parent's house in Scenic Hills. Set the scene: she camped in her childhood bed and fed from a tray in her lap. Next to her bed a cup of tea, cold and with a thin scrim of milk scum. The bedside lamp was girly, perhaps the only girly touch in the very adult bedroom. The TV was on, a grey Dorothy Lamour movie, volume low, its burble something Stygian.

Neill visited often. As Victoria got better Neill's heart began to pine for her. Was it guilt, desire, or simply pure love? (Nothing pure is ever simple; nothing simple is ever pure.) Who can say?

"I brought you the last volume of Nin's memoirs," he said, one sunny afternoon.

"Frank you," Victoria said through fat lips.

"How are you feeling?"

Victoria lifted her dressing gown. There were her sparrow-sized breasts and beneath them the Asian river, painted in angry purple. She fixed Neill with a fixing gaze.

Neill put his hand gently over the scar. Her skin was hot.

There was a medicinal smell, adhesive tape, and wound ooze.

He rubbed her belly lightly. She closed her eyes.

He moved his hand downward into her pubic hair. He was suddenly filled with a young man's quantity of spunk. His needle pointed toward True North. This is true north, he thought, Victoria, my love, pals forever, the woman made for me.

"Don't," Victoria said. Her eyes snapped open like the Bride of Frankenstein's.

"You have no right. You are not welcome there anymore."

And that was that.

Harness Myer

Minute Harness Myers was becoming a frequent bookstore visitor. She didn't buy many books, the occasional mystery mass market paperback. It was obvious she was making moony eyes at Neill.

They chatted occasionally. ("Why are you in the mall so much?" "I used to date Lysander the Pharmacist at Walgreens next door." "Used to, but you keep stopping by." "He won't let it go." "Sometimes men won't." "Oh, I don't know." "You're irresistible, is what I am thinking." "Flatterer." "Well, you do have the cutest Greek side." "What's that?" "Butt." "Mr. Bookseller. I thought you were too high-minded for such observations." "No red-blooded male is above looking at a great corybungus." "Words, words, such big words." "All the better to flirt with." "Are you flirting?" "I guess I am." "Neill...what?" "Neill Armstrong, first man on your moon." "What? No, Mr. Bookseller, Mr. Rhymer, what was that word again?" Etc.)

So, they went out.

The first date was the movies. What else? Neill was not a creative first-dater. They saw *The Haunting of Julia*. Neill thought it chin-dribble. Harness Myers ventured no opinion. She hung on Neill's words as if he were an oracle.

Dropping her off at her house, way out in Frayser, on Highway 51, they lingered in the dark car, parked in the Myers' driveway. The night was muggy and inside the car it was warm like the womb. They were cozy.

They kissed and one thing was apparent. Harness Myers was a masterful kisser. The caloric reading inside the car rose like the garden of Hesperides.

When they broke from the clutch, Harness Myers spoke:

"Whew. That was some kiss."

"You're very good, Ms. Myers."

"You, too. I think I know something."

"You think you know something?"

"You know what I mean."

"I don't."

"I know something that's gonna happen."

"Gypsy. Seer. Nostradamus."

"Speak English, Mr. Bookseller."

"You can see the future?"

"Sometimes. Right now I can. Wait and see."

"Till?"

"Wanna go out again tomorrow night?"

"I do." Neill was supposed to go out with Bidden and Crow and Pas and, possibly, Victoria. Bergman's *Face to Face* was playing at the Malco Quartet. It would be easy to wiggle out of it. He didn't really want to see Victoria right then.

"Yes," he said. "Get a bite to eat? I don't work at all tomorrow."

They went to get a bite to eat. They went to The Half Shell and feasted on oysters and onion rings and shrimp. After dinner, since they were out east, they went and parked in Audubon Park. Harness wore a halter top (her nipples looked like tiny buttes) and the briefest shorts Neill had ever seen. They fit her small, tight body the way Barbie's clothes fit. There wasn't enough material on Harness to cover two Barbie dolls.

The kissing began straightaway. The previous night was not a fluke. She was one fantastic osculator. Soon their shirts were catawampus and bunched about their limbs and upper torso. Hands found flesh. Harness had breasts even smaller than Victoria's, a boyish chest with hard nipples like buckeyes. Her bright Hawaiian-hued shorts were made of some elasticky material which stretched as easily as a cat in heat and Neill's hands, seeking her pussy, found, quickly enough, her smooth, perfectly rounded ass.

Harness was not only a great kisser, she was bold. She grabbed Neill's central knot through his jeans.

"Mm, Mr. Bookseller," she cooed in his ear.

"Tell me, little pigsney. What is making you hum?"

"You're funny."

"Ok, but don't stop doing that."

"This is what I meant. This is the future I could see."

"Audubon Park groping."

"No. This." She unzipped his pants and his touch-trap sprang upward.

She ran a thumb around the eggplant-colored head. She smiled like Jean Genie and ducked her head downward.

She began to circle it with her tongue. She pushed more trouser and underwear aside so she could really work. She was an artist. She warmed the head with her tongue, ran it down all sides, then slowly descended on it. Her mouth was foamy and soft and she moaned as if the blowjob were being done to her. The sounds she made enlivened Neill more than her ministrations, though her ministrations were adept.

"Mm, mm, nnngg," she said. "Oh," when she caught her breath.

She loved sucking cock. This was, perhaps, the biggest turn-on Neill had encountered in his short life. A woman who loved oral sex and was good at it. Neill had found nirvana. If anyone asks this may serve as one definition of nirvana: a lover who loves oral sex and is good at it.

Soon, she could feel the surge. She grabbed Neill's balls firmly as if readying for the launch. She squeezed with just the right amount of cogency, like knowing just how much to turn the hot water tap. She was willing the spunk upward. Like a snake charmer, she was luring it toward her tonsils.

Soon, this magic act was rewarded. Neill came amply into her yapper. He came for something like fifteen minutes. He came some more, a half-hour, an hour. It was as if he was coming for every boy out that night with blue balls and a recalcitrant date, for every lonely boy stuck at home with only his imagination and a jar of Vaseline. (But, boys, not Vaporub.)

Afterward, he fell forward onto the steering wheel in mock stupor. The horn sounded, "*Honk!*" And, they both laughed.

"Jesus, Harness."

"Good, right?"

"Better than that."

"Great?"

"Supernal."

"I don't know what that means."

"Better than great. You're amazing."

"See. I knew we were heading that way. I knew the future."

"Tell me more about the future. Any more of it as good as that?"

"More and better. More and better."

And she was right. Neill began to crave her blowjobs more than he craved the toothsome fare at Taco Bell. It's all he thought about when away from her and when he was with her; everything was designed for that final moment when she would once again play him like Coltrane played his dazing sax. Normally, they closed her thin bedroom door on the other side of which her family watched television while their daughter owned her new boyfriend's wang-tang.

Harness cut hair for a living. She worked at a place in Bartlett called Head Down. Forgive Neill for being enthused by the very name: Head Down.

A Pattern Develops

And this was the pattern that developed. They would go to a movie or grab some dinner and then adjourn to her small bedroom, on her small bed (usually unmade, often replete with old stuffed dragons and beasties, and satiny pillows), and there they would fondle and finger and grope and lick and gyrate until the moment when Harness did her amazing solo performance on Neill's eager instrument.

It was as if their relationship was marked "Strictly Blowjob." (More on this theme to come.)

Was Harness fulfilled? It's hard to say. Neill was not exactly a selfish lover. He did make her come with his fingers—and she came easily and often, slick with her own lubricants—and he wanted to fuck her. She was on the pill. Why did it never happen? It's difficult to say.

One evening, when the Myers were out and Harness's lovely, blond, younger sister, Moan was out on a date, they spread blankets and pillows on the living room floor in front of some inane television show and both removed all of their clothing.

Harness's wee body was strong and smooth, like an unsullied creature, an otter or sea lion. Neill had not seen her naked before and it was quite a sight. She was pretty as a honeybee.

And Neill went down on her, not for the first time, but intensely, with the freedom of an expanded stage and the relaxation that came with their being alone. Harness came once and still Neill sought more. He owed her. He owed her many oral orgasms.

Then, while searching for number two orgasm, Harness let go with a shuddering queef.

Neill had never seen, felt or heard such a thing before. Harness was so embarrassed she cussed and covered her face and began to cry.

Neill pulled her close.

"What? What happened?" he said. Poor noodle.

"Forget it. Forget it," Harness said from behind her hands.

"Baby, baby, it's ok. Kiss me."

Slowly Harness lowered her hands. Her koala eyes were moist and the TV light bounced off her tears.

"Will you fuck me now, Neill?"

Neill's heart began to beat fast. Why not, Neill? Why would you not penetrate young, beautiful Harness Myers? Suddenly, it occurred to him that it was the same pattern he had fallen into with Dinah. Why? Was Neill uptight about intercourse? Did it have to be love before he could mount his girlfriends? It was a puzzler. He loved Victoria. Did he still? And was that the only difference? He had loved Victoria and hence he fucked her. He hadn't loved anyone else since.

All this pondering, which really only took a second or two, disconcerted Harness.

"Never mind," she said.

She bent over Neill and took him into her mouth. Her slim back was a beautiful arc in the bluish light. And she was experimenting with her oral artistry, soloing bebop style, or so it seemed.

And when Neill came, it was full of electricity and thunder and songs of innocence and experience, animalia and ghosts, cattle lowing and poor babes waking, dogs barking and cats cooking, verbs atrembling and gerunds genuflecting, ministers and tradesmen, gods and monkeys. He came as if for the last time, emptying his body into the asthenic flesh of the lovely, light, tiny, perfectly formed Harness Myers.

As Manager

Neill tried his darnedest to be a good manager, though, in truth, he didn't know what that meant. He liked the hiring part and the turnover of part-time help meant he and Bidden were interviewing constantly.

Neill favored beautiful young female employees. No surprise there. He did appreciate a well-read young person, too. They had a shifting staff, sometimes strong, sometimes filled with kooks and layabouts. Sometimes the wise, sometimes the foolish. Sometimes, the cracked.

There was one young woman named Michelle about whom, for the rest of his life, Neill would say: she was the most beautiful woman I've ever stood next to. (He says this too often, ed.) She had the face of a Madonna and the body of a Monroe. She was dark and smart and athletic and mysterious. And, like all angels according to Rilke, dangerous. Neill was in love with her, that goes without saying.

One of the more interesting occurrences during Neill's captaincy was the Great Gay Conspiracy.

Some local pinhead churchgoer spotted *The Joy of Gay Sex* on the shelves at Waldenbooks, Raleigh Springs Mall, and made it his or her (they never did discover the progenitor of this project) mission to have the book removed (and burned! it was implied). He or she began a campaign, first in her own church, Raleigh Baptist, then spreading to all the Raleigh churches run by pinheads (mostly Baptist but also Church of Christ and one Presbyterian), the goal being to harass the store into removing the offending text.

It began as something almost comical, the makings of good after work chitchat. Neill told the first few callers that he was sorry but they did not remove books from their shelves because someone objected to them.

Then, the police arrived. Neill, having read too much Kafka, was as paranoid as Alfred Hitchcock about authority figures. He was a smitch shaken but the officers were nice and explained the law to Neill this way: any adult material had to be five feet off the floor. This seemed reasonable (even to anarchic and combative Neill) and the book was placed on the top shelf.

Then, the harassment began in earnest. Calls every hour. Visits every few hours. It was a well-organized crusade and it rapidly became quite irksome. The saddest calls or visits were from children who had been coached into what to say. Some forgot the script. One girl, perhaps 14, asked to speak to the manager. Neill presented himself.

"Are you selling that book about how to be gay?" she asked. Her little squirrely face seemed ready to cry.

"That's not what the book is," Neill said, as if were talking to a reasonable adult.

"You will go to perdition if you keep—keep—" her courage failed her and she fled.

The sheer length of the crusade began to wear on everyone at the store, especially Neill. He was the one who had to personally confront each and every pinhead.

Joy Dun, now district manager, had a talk with Neill.

"How are you feeling about this harassment?" she asked Neill in the stockroom where they had gone to deliberate.

"It's tiring," he answered.

"Do you think we should remove the book till this blows over?"

"Absolutely not." Neill set his jaw. Sometimes he could do that.

"Ok. I'm gonna rely on your smarts."

This was ok with Neill. He had a few smarts. And Bidden and Pas and Crow were there behind him. An emergent Memphis group, The Gay and Lesbian Alliance, called to voice support and instructed all their members to frequent Neill's store.

Then, Neill received The Call.

The head of Waldenbooks, the head of the whole damn company, Harry Somebody (look it up) called Neill.

"Hello, sir," Neill said.

"I have received numerous letters from your local church community about the book, *The Joy of Gay Sex*."

"Yes sir, there is quite a local campaign against us right now."

"What has been your response?"

"I told them we did not stop carrying books simply because someone objected to them."

"I see."

"We have talked to the police and we are within the law," Neill said. He almost added, even here in the South, intuiting that perhaps this rich Northerner would consider them all a bunch of hillbillies.

"What if I asked you to remove the book? Not from the store but from the shelves. Just keep it under the counter."

Neill's throat constricted. Whenever really incensed Neill usually became a sputtering nincompoop. And, for a painful moment, Neill could not speak.

"Neill?"

"Yes, sir. I would tell you no, sir. I would t-tell you we can't do that. Next a group of rednecks will object to James Baldwin, or a mis-guided group of women would want Hemingway removed."

Harry was silent.

"Ok, Neill," he said. "I am not going to make you remove it. I am only going to suggest that you do."

After the phone call, Neill felt all alone in the world. The company he worked for was wrong. They were plain wrong and Neill was left to face the music himself. There was writing on the wall. The writing was written by pinheads.

Unharnessed

During the Gay Crusade, Harness had spent a weekend out of town. She told Neill she and her sister Moan were visiting their cousins in Hot Springs, Arkansas.

That weekend Neill was left alone, and he and Bidden and Crow went to the P&H for a beer on Saturday night. Bidden was pining after one of the bookstore's employees, a round-cheeked lovely named Pandora. Bidden had only had one girlfriend in his short life (if you could believe his version of his own story) and Pandora had a boyfriend, a guitar-playing actor who sported one earring, quite an exotic touch for that time and that place. And Crow was having trouble with his girlfriend but he would not spell it out. He was not as free-flowing as the other two men when it came to personal problems.

The jukebox was playing "Mack the Knife," the Bobby Darrin version, for the 4th time that night.

"The problem is that anything, which attracts, any random piece of morphology, curly hair, round breasts, cleft chin, can be artificially produced," Bidden said. "One never wants to be duped, especially in romance."

"But, there is still actual physical beauty, untouched, seemingly by cynicism or worship, beauty beyond thinking."

"You're speaking of Michelle, of course," Crow said.

"Fuck," Neill said.

"I know."

There was more commiseration. The night spiraled downward.

"Where are our other convives tonight?" Bidden asked.

"Who knows? Do we have other friends?"

"I like smaller gatherings," Neill said.

"Sure," Bidden responded. "Fewer people to judge us."

Unharnessed, Part Two

Monday night Neill went to Harness's house to have dinner with her parents. It was a big step. They were wonderfully kind (and seemingly incurious and trusting since they never knocked on their daughter's bedroom door), and Neill liked them, and they liked Neill.

Neill was looking forward to seeing Harness again. It wasn't love but it sure was Adult Playtime, with extra Pleasure and Attachment.

Before dinner, Neill and Harness went for a walk in a field near the Myers' home.

"I missed you this weekend," Neill said.

"You did, Neill?" Harness said, increasing the pressure on Neill's arm which she was clutching like a lifeline.

"Surprised?"

"I don't know. I don't know how you feel."

"You do," Neill said. He put his arms around her and kissed her. Her wet little bow of a mouth was delicious.

"I missed you, too."

They strolled back to the house and it was still 30 minutes before dinner. They went to Harness's room. They made out on the bed. Neill pulled Harness against him, holding her imperial ass with both hands.

Harness grabbed Neill's pecker through his pants.

"I missed this," she said.

"It missed you."

"After dinner. For my dessert," Harness said. She smiled a half-mast smile. Something was going on behind her baby blues that Neill had never seen before.

Just then Mrs. Myers knocked on the door.

"Come help me set the table," she called.

Harness pressed her mouth hard against Neill's and gave his cock another squeeze. Neither of them could know it would be their last intimacy.

While Harness was out of the room Neill idly picked up the book sitting on her nightstand. It was an innocent move. Neill always picked up a book to see what it was. Occupational habit.

It was Harness's diary.

He couldn't resist. He should have resisted. He wanted to know what Harness thought about him—in her most private thoughts.

He found the early days of their courtship. He was touched. She wrote effusive, flowery prose about how crazy about Neill she was. She wrote about the sex. She wrote about Neill's Long John, which she called "a straight and lively pinkie."

Then, the worm turned.

The pages about the previous two days, the Saturday and Sunday she was away (the ink was barely dry) were all about Lysander the Pharmacist and their "passionate" weekend in Hot Springs.

Neill felt sick to his stomach.

When Harness came back into the room she espied the diary in Neill's hand.

"Oh no," she said.

"You cheater," Neill said. "You little slut."

"Neill," Harness cried, tears springing forth. She ran toward him.

"Don't touch me," he said.

"Neill, Neill, it was the last time. Neill!" she wept.

"I don't care," Neill said.

"Neill, don't. Neill, please don't."

"Kids, dinner is on the table," Mr. Myer's called.

Neill brushed past Harness and took a seat at the table. His face was as grim as a mug shot. Harness sat and wept silently into her dinner. The beautiful steaks, which Mr. Myers had grilled to "welcome Neill unofficially" to their home, went untouched on both Neill's and Harness's plate.

"I'm sorry," Neill said, rising. "I don't feel too good. I hate to waste this beautiful food. Mr. Myers, Mrs. Myers, thank you."

And, he walked out.

There were painful phone calls for the next few days (Neill spoke about honor and truth and steadfastness as if he were an Old Testament prophet, Neill who had cheated on his girlfriends often, got up on his righteous hind legs. Harness took it all. She cursed herself. Neill let her. It was a way to end it. It was a painful way to end what was, really, a dead-end relationship, though Neill would later think of her often and wonder if he had been too hasty, had made a bloomer. Neill lived in regret.)

Now Began a New Phase

Now began a new phase, a sequential monogamy phase. Neill dated and it was exciting and dispiriting and restless and thrilling and lonely. Neill needed love. More than sex? It's hard to say. (*So much is hard to say. ed.?*)

There will be other such phases in Neill's life. We shall enumerate one lengthy period later. Later. Because his life goes on.

The anti-gay crusade died down. They went back to torturing their own parishioners.

Work was work. It involved books. That was all Neill cared about. He knew the corporate side of things would eventually drive him crazy, drive him elsewhere, but for now he relished the time learning about literature, and the time with Bidden and Pas and Crow.

Until Crow had a drama of his own.

The night shift at the bookstore required 3 employees. Nights were busy. Plus there was the clean-up every night between 9:30 closing and 10, when they were off the clock.

One night Crow didn't show up. No phone call. Neill and Pas worked the shift alone, which would have been fine had Joy not popped in that night.

"How are things?" she asked Neill. (Still, sometimes Neill wishes he could take his boss into the stockroom and see what her slovenly but willowy body looked like naked. This even occurred to him now.)

"Ok," Neill said. He grinned (I will not picture you unclothed, he tried to vow.)

"Did you do the 420 sheets?" This was Waldenbooks arcane inventory code.

"Pas is working on them. It's been really busy."

"Who else is here?"

And, there it was. This is how it happened.

"Uh, Crow's not here. I think he's sick."

"He called in sick?"

Neill shrugged. It wasn't exactly a lie, that shrug.

But, the next day Crow didn't show up again. This time Joy called him at home. Crow answered after 8 rings. He sounded like he had seen the netherworld and it was not pretty.

"You sick?" Joy asked.

"No, not exactly," Crow cawed.

"What happened?" Joy's voice showed genuine concern.

"My dad had a heart attack," Crow choked out.

"Oh, Crow," Joy began, but Crow had already replaced the receiver in its cradle.

Joy called all the hospitals. She was intent on sending flowers. No hospital had admitted a patient named Mitred.

This was because Mr. Mitred was at home doing fine. As a matter of fact, he was playing snooker with his wife when Joy called him.

"Sorry?" Mr. Mitred said.

"I heard you were ill," Joy said.

Long and short of it is this: Crow got his ass fired.

A Crow with No Mouth

Neill visited Crow at his parents' house where he was still living.

Crow's face looked like a black stone under a mazarine sea.

Neill knew Crow was a private man, not given to bouts of confession or self-revelation. Gradually, he got the real story.

Crow's girlfriend, whom Neill had only met once, a slim little brunette doll with a crooked smile and a lisp, had gotten pregnant. Crow was both terrified and ecstatic. He knew what to do. Marry her and start life young.

But, she had other plans. She did not want the baby.

Apparently, they fought long and hard about it.

Then, she had it aborted without Crow's consent. (Yes, yes, it was her decision, of course, of course.)

To Crow, this was betrayal on a cosmic level. It sent an arrow through his heart, through his very moral core. Who knew he felt this way?

Crow was a man of principles and strong moral fiber. He believed what he believed, and his acceptance of himself was as solid as a cactus stem. Neill wanted to be like Crow. He wanted that kind of inner gyroscope.

At any rate, Crow broke things off with this girlfriend.

Some Family Matters Best Enumerated

Whenever Neill was between lovers, he declared himself the loneliest man in the world.

"I am Bobo, the Unmateable Gorilla," he told his sister, AJ.

AJ had recently gotten engaged to a fine young fellow named Dan Johnson, with a sense of humor as rich as Delta soil. Their wedding was upcoming with a reception afterward at the Moose Lodge. Mr. Rhymer had been a Moose his entire adult life. He pulled Neill aside one day and said, "Neill, this isn't going to sit well with you, but please, if you bring a date to your sister's wedding, don't make it Pas." Neill had to think about this for a moment.

"Because…?" he said.

"The Moose Lodge. They don't allow blacks."

"Except as kitchen help."

"Yes."

"And yet, you are still a member there."

"That discussion is for another day. I am not proud of the policy."

Neill had never planned on bringing a date to AJ's wedding. Now, he wanted more than anything to invite Pas. Or perhaps one of the gay fellows he had met during the Anti-Gay Crusade at the bookstore. He would have loved to walk into that dance hall holding hands with a beautiful young man. And to his astonished father's cronies, he would say: "This is Punky. He is as white as you and me."

Of course, he didn't. Why? Because he was chickenshit. And because he didn't want to spoil AJ's happy day.

Meanwhile, their older brother, Brack, was living with a gorgeous Scandinavian woman, with a mane of blond hair down the middle of her back, in Storrs, Connecticut, where they both taught at The University Connecticut. Brack had gotten his Ph.D. in Medical Sociology at Memphis State, graduating Summa Cum Laude. His nickname among his and Neill's friends was "Dr. Death." He left his parents, siblings, ex-wife, and children behind him. Was this an emotional scorched earth policy? Hard to say. Brack was always a bit of an enigma and he wanted to be thought of that way.

Neill and AJ were having lunch at Taco Bell.

"So, you're not seeing anyone?" she asked.

Neill wiped red sauce from his lips.

"Not really."

"Not really means?"

"Some dates. Nothing sticks."

"You'll meet someone."

"Well, you know, my theory has always been that if I am to meet my heart's desire, it's gonna be in the bookstore. She would have to be a reader."

"Yes, that makes sense."

"So, all I have to do is wait. Just sit and wait."

"Which you find impossible to do."

"Yes."

"What then?"

"How about that friend of yours? The one with the electric blond-red hair? She works in the mall."

"Sandy."

"Yes, Sandy. Of the Hair."

"She's seeing someone, I think. And, besides, I don't think she is much of a reader. And she is painfully shy."

"I'll be gentle."

"I'll see what her situation is."

AJ never got back to Neill on that one.

Crow Weds

Crow, who was working on becoming a formidable artist, first with photography and then with oil, had gotten his girlfriend, a new girlfriend of course, pregnant again. This time things went better, which is like saying that the ocean liner which followed the Lusitania was a lot more fun. Crow and Sarah had known each other at Raleigh-Egypt High School. They became pals in the art room.

So, after the debacle of his last relationship, Crow looked for a steadying hand, a sweeter, calmer presence in his life. Sarah was that.

Then, she got pregnant. Oops.

Then, they got married. The ceremony was held at The Church by the River (Unitarian), and a party afterwards at one of the riverside parks was attended by Neill and Pas and Bidden, and a lot of strangers.

Crow and Sarah went to Santa Fe for their honeymoon. When they returned they rented a small apartment near Memphis State. Their son was born six months later.

They named him Neill. (Crow's choice was Boy. Sarah nixed it. Crow loved Tarzan as much as Neill.)

(Hence forward, Little Neill, which led to Big Neill being more careful about what he called his willy.)

Neill was as proud of that kid as if he were one of his own.

The Coming of the Sun

And lo, it came to pass, that, after many one date situations, Neill met someone who twisted him around and sent him into paroxysms of delight and frustration.

Neill often visited Crow and Sarah and their infant. He was happy around this small, makeshift family. He thought dandling Little Neill on his knee was as satisfying as reading a good book. Crow was working for an art supply store (appropriate that) and Sarah had been working part-time at a grocery store while their child grew inside her, a mustard seed.

And Sarah had a lifelong friend whom Neill met at their apartment one night when he and Crow were breaking in a new bong. Her name was Clorinda Sun.

She and Sarah had been out to a movie and when they returned Neill and Crow were riding a good buzz and watching *Attack of the Crab Monster*.

"You look productive," Sarah said with an edge like a dull razor blade.

"Dreams, Love," Crow said. "We are producing dreams."

The new woman laughed. Her laugh was like a Labrador puppy wagging its tail. For a split second (called *presque vu*), Neill thought she was a Labrador puppy. She had chocolate brown hair and dimples cut with an angel's scalpel, and a sylph-like body, that Neill found himself staring at, mouth agape.

"Neill, this is my friend Clorinda. Clorinda, Crow's friend Neill, from the bookstore."

"Ah, the bookstore Neill," she said. "The Big Neill."

"Clorinda, Clorinda, where you been so long?" Neill sang. (Or approximated a singing voice since Neill was completely tone deaf, as tone deaf as Little Stevie was blind.)

"That's Corrina," Sarah said. Was the edge still there?

Neill was confused.

"What's Corrina?" he asked.

"Her name is Clorinda," Crow said.

"Corrina's name is Clorinda?"

"There is no Corrina."

"I didn't think so. That's why I was singing to your friend."

"With the wrong name."

"She has the wrong name."

Eventually, it was straightened out.

The women went upstairs to watch something that wasn't *Attack of the Crab Monster*.

"Give me her phone number right now," Neill said.

Crow laughed. "I think she's seeing someone."

"Doesn't matter. I am a steamroller heading straight for her unpaved roads."

"You're stoned."

"Completely. But tomorrow I will remember Corrina, and I will call her and my life will be changed for the better."

"Clorinda," Crow said, around an inhale.

"What?"

And So the Sun Days Began

Neill did indeed call her the next day and Clorinda was indeed seeing someone else, Danny or David, or maybe another Lysander. It didn't matter.

She agreed to meet Neill for coffee and pie at Steak 'n' Egg that very night.

"Joe and pie," Neill said, looking into Clorinda's pallid blue eyes. "Almost as good as joe and sinkers."

"Meaning?"

"Coffee and donuts."

"Ah."

"So, you're already fixed in the romance department."

"Yes, I am," Clorinda said to Neill. To the waitress she said, "Chocolate Cream."

"I'm fixed, too," Neill said to Clorinda. "Same," he said to the waitress. "But, it didn't stop my sex drive."

"Wha—" Clorinda began and then she got it. She snuffled into her napkin.

"Sarah said you were funny."

"I'm a laugh riot."

"And a writer. Is that true?"

"No, not really," Neill said, though he wanted nothing more than to be thought of as a writer.

"I thought she said—"

"Yes, I write some poems now and then."

"Published?"

"In a couple rags with readerships in the single digits."

"Still—"

"And you?"

"I don't write."

"No, I meant—"

"Oh. Yes, I have a job at Pier One. Temporary. I want to finish school."

"What was your major?"

"I don't know. That's why I quit. I wanted to paint but once I got into the art department everyone was so much better than me. Then I tried journalism."

"I tried journalism, too. Did you have Sanders?"

"I went to Tennessee Knoxville."

"Oh. Continue."

"No, that's about it. I quit school and started working and got a brand new adult apartment."

"As opposed to the kiddie apartments," Neill said.

She laughed again. Neill's heart turned to treacle again.

"I mean, just like an adult. I am pretending to be an adult."

"Me, too," Neill said.

"So, I got this apartment but I don't have furniture. I am sleeping on a mattress on the floor. I have a mattress. And some pots and pans. A good start, eh?"

"Sure," Neill said. "Where is it?"

"The apartment?"

"No, the Ark of the Covenant. Yes, the apartment."

She laughed again.

They couldn't get into their cars fast enough.

Sure enough it was one bleak apartment. Wood floors and paneled walls and absolutely nothing there but a mattress in the middle of the floor.

This is where they sat. The electricity between them, just like that, could have turned on a lamp if there were a lamp in the apartment.

Clorinda lit a cigarette and sat next to Neill on the mattress.

"You smoke?"

"How did you find out?" Clorinda said with a milky smile.

"It's ok."

"Thanks, I appreciate that. You don't like smokers?"

"Raised by two of them but still, no, I don't like to be around smoke too much."

"I'll put it out."

"No," Neill said, but Clorinda was already grounding it out on a small saucer that sat by her "bed."

"Ever kissed a woman who smoked?" she asked.

Neill was charmed, excited. It was happening.

"No, actually," he said.

"That is a wolf's smile," Clorinda said.

"You're not Little Red Riding Hood," Neill said.

"Shut up," Clorinda said. "Kiss me."

And he did. Her mouth tasted of smoke (Neill was to remember the taste of Clorinda Sun's mouth for the rest of his life) and it was somehow delicious. Clorinda was wearing a white t-shirt with no bra and shorts and panties and flip-flops. It was not much to remove, and once accomplished, Neill discovered that her sylph-like body was soft like the inside of soft. Neill's erection ran across her stomach like a skater. Her ass in his hands was so soft he thought perhaps she did not have a skeleton. She was like sensual silk. It was like making love with a sea creature.

And they did make love.

Neill brought her off with his mouth (O! her furze was a patch of flowers!) and she, in turn, went down on Neill's eager cock. Her mouth was—oh, fuck. SOFT! Ok?

He came into her cheeks. She lit another cigarette. Their next kiss tasted like bleached tobacco.

"You're beautiful," Neill said.

"You are too," Clorinda said.

Neill almost asked about Danny (or Manny, or Lysander) but it didn't really matter to him. This moment mattered. And, tomorrow, he would want it repeated again and again, and for a long time.

Ah, Neill. Ah, life.

You Can Call me Clory

Clory and Neill had a passionate fling. It didn't last long, but it stuck inside Neill like a memory of Christmas morning.

Many (three? Five? 17?) nights they lay denuded in Clory's denuded apartment, on her thin mattress on the floor, and brought each other off with mouths and hands.

The curious (randy) reader will ask: did they not jig-a-gig? That is, did Neill not insert his Tab A in Clorinda's Slot B?

They did not.

And here is why, though it is a delicate subject: for the first time in his young life Neill experienced that age-old problem, the Erection Fade. Everything was fine—better than fine, it was erotica as hell—until Neill tried to enter her Cave of Wonders. His dick balked. The EF.

"Is it me?" Sweet Clory asked.

"I don't know. I mean, no. No, it isn't you. I am not sure what it is. I can't seem to fuck you."

"Well, we could call what we've been doing fucking?"

"Yes. Thank you. That is kind."

"But your horse shies at the stable door."

"I don't understand it. It's never happened before. And God knows I want to be inside you. You have such a soft and inviting pussy."

"It's inviting you in."

Neill felt close to tears. Clorinda lit a cigarette.

It Never Got Better

It never got better.

Damn the EF.

Neill sought Brack's advice, popping for the long-distance call.

"I don't know what's wrong but now I feel like I wanna die."

"That's a little strong," Strong Brack said.

"It's just so important to me, you know? I think intercourse is just about the best thing on this ersatz planet."

"You put that much importance on it?"

"I do. Don't you? Doesn't everyone? Is it not the life force?"

"I don't think so," Brack said. "Because you think it's so important you're failing."

"Important equals impotent?"

"Isn't that possible?"

"I don't know." Neill was close to tears. "I want her so bad. And, I'm Mr. Softy."

"You know, Bro, sex is not like in the movies, right? The back scratching, howling, animalistic frenzy that goes on for hours is not the norm."

"I don't expect that. Just a nice intravaginal eruption."

"I see. You know what I am going to say?"

"Relax and you'll be alright."

"Yes."

But it never got alright and Clorinda, guilt-ridden anyway, went back to her Larry or Manny or Lysander, and Neill was thrust once more onto the open seas of lonely bachelorhood. Though a new important chapter in Neill's life was about to open, a chapter that would reverberate profoundly for the rest of his life.

The Mall at the Heart of the World

There was a curious period in this history when 4/5ths of the Rhymer clan worked at Raleigh Springs Mall. Neill at the bookstore, of course. AJ at Spencer Gifts, a young innocent seadog in a sea of catchpenny plastic sex. Brack, briefly, was selling suits at Goldsmith's (this was just before he fled to the north). And, Mother Rhymer working at Hancock Fabrics, the first and only job in her long life.

Neill found this a comforting thing. He loved taking long breaks from work and walking the mall, stopping to see family members, making his little capgun heart spark with pleasure. (Is this akin to Neill, in first grade, morose and needy, imagining every time the classroom door opened that it was his mother come to rescue him?) (When he visited Brack he made an extra effort to pass through Goldsmith's women's section where there was a perfume counter behind which stood, occasionally, a Nordic princess, a woman carved from white light. Neill never talked to her because he was a mere mortal, a serf, a bug.) Even without family there Neill loved to walk the mall. It was the world. It had everything. Food, music, books, a movie theater, and scores of attractive young women who, like Neill, saw Raleigh Springs Mall as a great magic kingdom of employment opportunities.

In the center of the mall, facing eastward with its back to the western entrance and the movie theater (or movie complex as we learned to call it), was the Information Booth. Now, what the Information Booth was for was to greet consumers with joy and titillation, with comfort and joy, with sweetness and light, not really with any depth of information. The Information Booth was not the Library of Congress. Stop and ask any of the young people in the booth who the Visigoths were, or who played bass in The Jimi Hendrix Experience, or how many tablespoons in an ounce, or what the second book in Proust's *Remembrance of Things Past* is, or if they knew the way to Santa Fe, or if there is balm in Gilead, or if anybody really knows what time it is, you would have been met with a radiant smile and a shake of a lovely head.

The Information Booth was the Tree of Knowledge, with fresh apples but little knowledge, if you can accept the conceit that the mall is an Eden.

Because the Information Booth was always manned (womaned) by attractive young females, usually still in high school, girls who could turn your heart to tapioca with said radiant smile and a shake of glistering hair. Neill knew some of them. He wanted to know all of them. It was Flirtation Central. There was one he called Angel Eyes. He sang (sorta) "Pretty Little Angel Eyes" to her, but she was not hungry enough to eat the dish Neill was preparing.

Then, there came into this booth, this small oasis in the desert of the mall (that metaphor doesn't work, because we have shown that the mall is anything but a desert, ed.), a young woman, so finely put together, Neill thought he was dreaming her. She was the embodiment of everything Neill found attractive. She had big eyes, prominent cheekbones, a sweet and slightly lascivious smile, lovely cup-sized breasts, an ass like the one upon which the world sits in somebody or other's mythology, tanned limbs... and a head of hair that needed an address of its own. A head of hair that deserves a book of poems, a hymn of praise, a statue made of matchsticks. It was full and lustrous (slightly Farrahesque because that was the era), and mahogany and chocolate and auburn, with amazing copper highlights that shown as if sewn there by empyrean hands. She was, with the possible exception of You-Know-Who, the most beautiful woman Neill had ever seen. (Except for Michelle at the bookstore? ed.) He knew she was out of his class. He knew any foray would be repelled. He knew that if he tried talking to her his voice would come out a bray similar to the asses in Pinocchio.

And yet.

And yet. He had to try.

He had to try because of his credo (have we mentioned Neill's credo before?): Someday we will all be worm food so it is important that we try to mix it up as much as possible while we are still walking around in our heavenly human forms.

Neill Tries

So, Neill began more frequent absences from the job (he was the manager, after all), and sometimes he visited his family, and sometimes he walked back and forth in front of the booth because she was there.

He ate more giant pretzels than was good for him.

He drank more sodas and slushy drinks.

He sat at the fountain with giant pretzels and slushy drinks because the fountain and its benches sat right in front of The Information Booth.

Finally, Neill approached. He approached her the way Jim approached the alligator right after Marlon Perkins said, "Jim, will now wade in and attempt to tag the beast."

She lit up a smile as bright as Phoebus' sphere.

Perhaps, she expected Neill to ask her if there was a religious bookstore in the mall. (There was, named Zondervan, at the far Northern corner, a strange, otherworldly place manned by robots.)

Perhaps, she was used to being hit on. It wasn't exactly the most original thing Neill had ever thought of approaching this Booth of Beautiful Women.

"Hi," Neill said.

"Hi," the angel spoke, but with human voice.

"Bite?" Neill said, proffering a doughy, salty pretzel, slathered in yellow mustard. Immediately, he realized he had no opening gambit. This was weak. This was pitiful. Why hadn't Neill prepared?

"Yes," the angel said, surprising Neill.

She took a small bite from the pretzel but her eyes stayed on Neill. Eating, she was as sexy as Goldie Hawn dancing tattooed with one-liners.

"So," Neill continued his charming approach.

"You work at the bookstore?" she spoke. Her eyes glittered. Her hair sparked, arced, its copper wires crossing.

"I do," Neill said.

"I thought I had seen you walking past a lot on your way there."

Jesus. Spotted. Caught. Apprehended.

"Yes," Neill said.

There was a pause while two hearts looked for a beat they both could dance to.

"Because I can't get enough of looking at you." He said it.

The angel's smile blew a few overhead lights. Her neck and chest reddened.

"I'm Neill," Neill said. "Sorry."

"Sorry you're Neill?"

"Sorry if I embarrassed you."

"You did."

"Sorry. Embarrassed you so badly it borders on sexual harassment? So badly you will now never reveal your name to me."

"Syrie Hardwood."

Impossible, Neill thought, but luckily did not say.

"Go ahead and say it," Syrie Hardwood said.

"Will you go out with me?" Neill said.

Readers, She Said Yes

Yes, and with no small amount of enthusiasm.

Neill walked on air (look for something less clichéd) all the way back to the bookstore. He felt a citizen of the world. He was allowed admittance into the Guild of the Ecstatic.

There are few times in life as sweet as the blossoming of new romance. Why should that be? Shouldn't there be such pleasures more easily attained? Say, the first time you try schnitzel? Or, the first time you see a Bergman film?

These things are nice but they are not as deeply soul-enriching as new romance.

And, Neill's new romance was with the woman who was the prettiest woman he had ever seen (with the possible exception of You-Know-Who).

Syrie Hardwood and Neill Rhymer were about to change each other's lives for all time.

First There was Mr. Hardwood

There was a catch. Initially a catch.

Syrie Hardwood was 16 years old and Neill was 22 about to be 23.

So, first there was Mr. Hardwood.

Syrie had forewarned Neill that her father wanted to speak to him before she was allowed to go out with him. Neill approached the Hardwood residence with a catch in his throat and a drum solo played by a monkey in his heart. The Hardwoods lived just off Stage Road on Orangewood Road. They had a nice two-story home that spoke of a slightly higher economic bracket than the Rhymer's. They were a beautiful family, also. Syrie, the baby, had two older brothers, an older sister who seemed to be always away at college, and a mother who looked only slightly older than Neill.

Mr. Hardwood, an amateur handball enthusiast, who was tanned like a kangaroo hide, met Neill at the door.

"Neill," he said. It seemed to Neill the severe intonation was uncalled for and a little phony. He was *acting* like a father.

"Hi," Neill said, softly.

They entered a fussy living room and Neill sat on the hot seat (a flowery couch) while Mr. Hardwood sat in a wingback chair a few yards away.

"I admit that the age difference bothers me," he began. He continued with a voice like a TV dad.

"Yes sir," Neill said.

"You can't understand why that would cause a father worry."

"No sir."

"Tell me a bit about yourself."

Neill, give him this much credit, knew it was not time for a joke, jocularity being his wonted shield.

"Well, sir, I went to college some."

"Why did you quit?"

"Um, well, sir, I quit because I was made manager of the bookstore—that's Walden's in the mall—(Mr. Hardwood nodded) and I found I could not do both."

"How long have you worked at the bookstore?"

"Since I was 19."

"And you are how old now?" He knew, the bastard.

"22, sir."

"My daughter is 16."

"Yes sir, I know. But she is a very poised 16."

This made some kind of impression. What kind?

Mr. Hardwood put his hand to his chin. He rubbed imaginary whiskers. Really, he should stop acting like an actor.

"Here's what we will do, Neill. I will let you go out tonight and, if you and Syrie continue to see each other, it will be on a trial basis. The first note of wrong-feeling and I cut you off. Good enough for you?"

Neill didn't know what 'wrong-feeling' entailed but he said, heartily, "Yes sir."

Mr. Hardwood rose, so Neill rose. He stuck out his hand because Mr. Hardwood stuck out his. They shook as if Neill had just purchased the man's TV daughter.

Did We Mention that it was Summer?

And it was hot.

On their first date Syrie wore a sleeveless dress, short enough to show her tanned thighs and turn Neill into an instantaneous lecher. Jesus God, she was pretty.

He opened the passenger side door on his fading yellow Toyota and she smiled as she swung her delicious body into the seat.

Neill drove. He was nervous.

"Where we going?" Syrie said, pleasantly.

Straight to bed, Neill wanted to say. If I don't see you naked in the next 15 minutes I will pull my own head off, Neill wanted to say.

"Oh, right, how about the movies?"

"I love the movies," she tinkled.

"Me too," Neill said. "Second only to books."

"Which movie?"

This is going well, Neill thought.

"Have you seen *Equus*?"

"No," Syrie said. "I don't even know what it is."

"I've heard good things about it."

"I hope it's not playing at the mall. I've had enough of the mall today."

"Malco Quartet," Neill said.

With popcorn and cokes, they sat in the darkened theater and watched a movie about a young man who blinds horses. Neill could barely concentrate on the story. He almost forgot to appreciate the ungodly lovely sight of Jennie Agutter nude. At one point in the darkened theater, Neill squeezed Syrie's hand. She squeezed back. Her palms were sweaty. He wanted her.

After the movie Neill asked Syrie if she wanted to go to Shoney's for strawberry pie or hot fudge cake Sundays?

"Sure," Syrie said.

"Did you like the movie?" Neill asked as they drove.

"Yes," she said. There was hesitation. "I am not sure I followed it all."

"Well," Neill began, but he stopped. He fought a pedagogical urge. "I couldn't quite either," he said.

"Oh."

"Because sitting next to you was all I could think about."

He chanced a look at Syrie Hardwood.

She beamed.

"The feeling was mutual," she said.

"Do you really want dessert?" Neill asked.

"No," Syrie said. "What else could we do?"

The angel smiled a smile they don't impart in heaven.

In the Bedroom (We Starve-Look at One Another Short of Breath)

At Neill's apartment they entered to find Goffredo in front of the TV.

"Hi," Syrie said. Was she flushing again?

"Hi," Goffredo said.

"Syrie Goffredo, Goffredo Syrie," Neill said.

"They're showing *The Duelists* on Channel 10," Goffredo said.

"Wish I could watch it," Neill said, grinning like a scalawag.

The new couple breezed past and into the bedroom. Neill put *Music from Big Pink* on the stereo.

There was only a dresser, a stereo, and a bed in the room. Obviously, the bed was the destination.

They lay down together and it was not to keep warm.

The first kiss was deep and wet and involved a lot of tongue. Neill pressed Syrie's small, dark body against his own. She was made of finer stuff. Her smooth chestnut thighs pressed Neill's jeaned thigh in a warm flesh vice.

Neill kissed her nuddle and chest and shoulders. She was mottled with a deep flush.

Neill wanted to take her dress off. (She's only 16!) A *drunkard's dream if I ever did see one.* As if through pure thought her dress was taken off. Later, Neill was pretty sure she had done it without his bidding. Her unnecessary bra was thrown aside and caught Garth Hudson's bellowing organ in mid-passage, and Garth skipped once and continued.

She only had snowy panties on.

Her small breasts were so white against her dark skin they seemed to glow. Her nipples were fudge-colored. Neill ate them.

Syrie Hardwood gasped and sighed a lot. Was she a virgin? (Friends, she was not, but prior to Neill we can imagine her sex had been of the backseat variety with Skippy and Jimmy-Joe.)

Neill took his own shirt off and their skin adhered as if they had been doing this all their life. They seemed to fit together like a key in a lock.

"T-take your pants off too," Syrie gasped as Neill started to put his hands down the back of her panties. Her ass was the ass Leonardo sketched, the archetype.

Syrie undid Neill's belt and unsnapped his jeans and unzipped them, too.

Bold teenager! Neill thought.

They lay together in their underwear and Neill's hands soon found her ass, her bumhole, and the hot wet pit between her legs. He put his finger inside her.

"Rggggg," Syrie said.

Neill thought it was a good sound, so he continued.

Syrie Hardwood was bucking and rolling like one in a fit of ecstasy. Neill didn't know it could be this way. Brack was wrong. Sex can be like in the movies. (Neill did not allow the thought to enter his cranium that Syrie might be as good an actor as her dad. We're sorry really for even mentioning it here).

She pulled her own panties off and threw them aside.

There she was. The most beautiful woman (well, teen at this point) he had ever seen naked before. The white marks, which showed that Syrie favored very brief bikinis, were islands of erotic pyrotechnics. Neill had never seen anything prettier than her pubic patch in the middle of that field of bleached young skin.

Syrie fumbled at Neill's crotch. She pulled the tool out of its cloth sling but seemed stymied about what to do next. Her approximated handjob was clumsy, even a bit rough.

Neill, to stop her and to keep moving forward, pushed her gently down onto the pillow. He spread her legs and bent to her pussy the way a horse bends to a trough. Her intense blood-mottling was also evident here, each thigh like a chocolate swirl ice cream. He began to lick slowly around the black central cave, circling the hair, licking thigh and stomach.

"Uh uh uh," Syrie said.

Neill slowly lowered his tongue into her steamy jungle. He tongue-fucked her while his finger played with her clit.

"OH MY GOD!" Syrie said. And, apparently, came. She shook like loosened music.

She panted. Her flush spread over her entire chest. She lay back as if pole-axed.

Neill nestled next to her again and kissed her cheeks and neck.

Finally, she spoke.

"That was a first," she said.

"The oral sex?"

"That. And what happened next."

"You came?"

"Yes. For the first time in my life. My God. My God."

"Well, good then," Neill said. He was trying not to bring up his straining erection, which was knocking on Syrie's right thigh as if it were the door in the tree that leads to the elves' kingdom.

"Do you want to, um, make love to me now? I mean, put yourself inside me?"

"I do. Really badly."

"Let's do that and make you come."

"Are you on the pill?"

"Oh, um, no."

"Diaphragm or anything like that?"

"No, no. Sorry. That's bad, right?"

"Well, we must not have intercourse then, young lady."

Syrie seemed about to cry until Neill smiled. They both laughed nervous laughs. They were naked and beautiful, and young as dawn.

"Would you let me take you to the Reproductive Health Center and get fitted for a diaphragm?" Neill asked, as gallant as the Cid.

"I guess so," Syrie said. She now sounded as childish as her years.

"We'll do that."

"What should we do with—*that*?" Syrie asked and another nervous laugh emerged.

"Do you want to suck me?" Neill asked. Suddenly, he felt a bit guilty. She was a babe and he was Aqualung.

"I don't know how to do that," she said.

"Ok," Neill said. And lay back. His pointer was aimed at the dog star.

Syrie sat up on one elbow. She looked deeply into Neill's eyes. Her own were rimmed with happy tears.

Neill smiled and kissed her deeply.

Syrie wrapped her hand around Neill's pointer and began to jerk it around a bit.

"Here," Neill said, gently.

He took her hand and guided it into a steadier progression. Soon, she was pumping it better if not quite expertly. On her own she gave the head some light attention between pumps.

"Yes," Neill said, breathing heavily.

Pleased with her success, she began to experiment more and, guided by Neill's pleasurable grunts and sighs, passed her first lesson in handjob.

As he began to bung up Neill tensed his body. Syrie stopped.

"No, keep going, keep going—"

She renewed her efforts and then she could feel the difference, the way it felt like a surging hose. And then, Neill came. And he came and came. His fountain was one of the most copious of his life. It formed a glassy lake over Neill's stomach and thighs and Syrie's own thighs. It was quite an oil slick. Syrie's eyes grew wide. She kept pumping him expecting it to go on for 15 minutes or so.

"Ok, ok," Neill said. "That hurts a bit after I've come."

"Jesus," Syrie said, unlike the little Catholic schoolgirl she was. "Is it always like that?"

"What?"

"That—much?"

"I guess so," Neill said. "Are you a virgin?"

Syrie's pretty face crumpled.

"No," she whispered.

"Sorry—sorry—I didn't mean it that way. It's fine. You're fine. You're better than fine. You are magnificent. And you're the prettiest thing I've ever seen. Ever. In my long life. Look at you. You're effing Grace Kelly."

And Neill slowly swiped a hand the entire length of her delicious body.

"I love you," Syrie said.

The Next Night

Guess what the two young lovers did the next night?

The same things, save the movie and small talk.

They went to bed. They built fires within each other. They stoked those flames and eventually extinguished them with their hands (both lovers) and mouth (Neill alone so far.)

Neill marveled again at how beautiful this young woman was naked. She dazzled.

Neill was dizzy. His headstrong heart began to follow his dick like the little dog beside Spike.

An Update: Victoria's Secret

After recovering from her accident, Victoria continued to work at Solomon Alfred's. She continued to drink and smoke, and act as if self-destruction had been penciled into her date book.

Neill worried about her (guilt). Bidden worried about her (love). Goffredo worried about her (romantic love). Victoria's parents worried about her (such anguish, such debilitating anguish).

But Victoria had a secret and, if Neill had known, it would have assuaged his guilt somewhat. The secret was this: she and Gulley Jawell were engaged to be married.

When announced, it surprised everyone.

Our Heroes Buy a Diaphragm

Good Neill. Conscientious Neill. Steady and mature Neill.

He took Syrie to the Memphis Reproductive Health Center on Poplar Ave. Neill was comfortable with the Center, having visited on a number of occasions, some gynecological, some friendly because Brack's love, who moved to Connecticut with him, had once been the head of the place. Neill still knew a couple of the women on staff there.

None were present when Neill and Syrie arrived.

Syrie was nervous. She was still so young.

Neill was nervous. Syrie was still so young.

But, they were treated with respect and consideration and gratitude. Neill felt puffed up and important. They took Syrie inside.

At the desk, they asked Neill who would be paying and Neill stepped up like the grown-up he suddenly dressed as.

"I will," he said. His jaw jutted. It might have been the first time Neill's jaw jutted.

After a long time, Syrie emerged. She was flushed but smiling.

Neill took her hand.

They said their goodbyes and left, hand in hand, like a mature (X-rated) Pyramus and Thisbe.

"Everything all right?" Neill asked.

Syrie was hard to read. She was keeping her own counsel. She was quiet, gathering her thoughts.

"Let's go to your apartment," she said finally.

They Do It

"Hi Goffredo," Syrie said.

"Bye, Goffredo," Neill said.

"Tonight on—" Goffredo said.

In the bedroom, they could not discase fast enough.

Was it Neill's imagination or had Syrie's artistically divided (dark and light) young body gotten more exquisite? The brown parts seemed browner. The white parts like meringue. The nipples like nuts. The pubic patch like rich loam.

They lay face to face, legs entangled in a Gordian knot.

Syrie's wet rosebud pressed against Neill's left thigh. Neill's hard dingle tingled against Syrie's soft, smooth middle.

They kissed one long deep kiss just to signal to the body that this was the commencement of something new and that it was about—should we call it love?—-and not just penetration.

Neill pulled Syrie tight against him, wrapping both hands around her ample ass. He spread the cheeks in his tension. He put a finger into her hole.

"Oh Neill," Syrie said.

Neill began to move his erection against her sealskin. He could have almost come because her breadbasket was so supple, so downy.

He fingered her harder, two in and a third seeking that little elusive bud, the one that sent Magellan around the world.

Syrie came.

She shook against Neill.

"OH! My goodness," she said. She was nervous and her flush made her skin, in the dim light, look like a zebra's.

"I'm just getting started," Neill joked.

"Whew," Syrie managed.

"Still excited enough to continue? Want to wait a bit?"

"I don't need a day between orgasms," Syrie said and ducked her face into Neill's shoulder.

"Pull on me," Neill said.

Syrie's silky hand went immediately to the demanding dingle. Her handjobs had gone from D pluses to A minuses in just days.

"You feel so good, Neill," she gushed.

"You want me in you now?"

"I do."

Syrie flopped onto her back and spread her legs as if she were at the gynecologist. Neill thought, "Ok, missionary to start."

He rose above her. He looked at her face. Her loveliness made Neill's heart go ka-chunk one more time.

He fumbled with his erection. Syrie lay stock still.

Finally, its head, that sensitive little envoi, found Syrie's wide, wet opening.

"Mmp," Syrie said.

Neill slowly put it all the way in. Syrie was so wet, so large. She could have fit Neill's tool and a hoe and a rake besides. Neill slowly pulled it out.

Syrie lay still as if waiting. Was this how it's done? she asked herself.

Now Neill began to move it in and out a little quicker. A new cadence began. Neill found he could move around in circles, so copious was her dark cave. He put a hand under her ass to help him find some friction and to help her find some movement.

Now she joined him. And she was breathing little words that may have made sense to someone, somewhere, at some time, in fairy tales perhaps. Little kitten sounds.

Syrie shifted slightly, opening her legs wider and moving her ass more under Neill. It helped.

Neill could not close his eyes. He wanted to watch this beautiful woman (girl) [stop that] find her pleasure. She closed her eyes tight and another orgasm shook her.

And as she came again, she found her vaginal muscles and tightened them around Neill.

"Yes! Jesus!" Neill shouted.

Somewhere, in a den far away, Goffredo turned the TV up.

Now Syrie knew something new. She squeezed with her inner muscles again.

"Do that," Neill said. "Keep doing that."

His movements became more frantic. He danced like a lubber in a net. He was flopping like a weak defender. The ecstatic experience was upon him.

Then Syrie grabbed his ass. That was the kicker.

Neill came.

Afterward they lay entangled, with Syrie's juices flowing down Neill's thighs. This night began a new routine for the young lovers. They would make love and then they would wrap themselves around each other and nap. It was sweet. It was as grand as The World's Plan.

In Attendance at the P&H

There was Neill. There was Bidden. There was Crow.

Bidden speaks: "So this is going well, you and this—"

"Bairn?" Neill said.

Bidden laughed. "I was going to say copper-haired beauty."

"It's going well. It really is."

"She's about the prettiest thing I've ever seen," Bidden said.

"I know," Neill says, shakes his head and sips his diet Pepsi.

"When do I get to meet her?" Crow asked. "I like pretty things."

"Fourth of July?" Neill said.

It was an annual event at Crow's house, the Fourth of July gathering. At this point it was only 2 years old (this would be #3) but it would extend long past this telling, into the dotage of all involved.

"Yes!" Crow said. "That'll liven things up."

Neill was nervous about testing a new love at the party. The folks there, while welcoming, even loving, could also intimidate, simply with their intelligence and wit.

"Why aren't you with her tonight?" Bidden asked. "If it were me. I."

"Something her dad is making her do."

"Still under the trial basis thing?"

"Yeah."

"What is that?" Crow asked.

"Father thinks I might be a child molester and is allowing me to see his prize daughter only until he decides whether I am a real human being or not."

"Reasonable," Crow said, taking a long swallow of beer. "Reasonable."

"Oh, he's nothing if not reasonable. He's also a bit of a phony but forget I said that. I don't want anything to jinx this. This is the best—ahem—sex I've maybe ever had."

"What's the best sex you've ever had?" Suddenly Gulley Jawell was standing by the booth.

"Scoot over," he said, and Crow did. "Who you talking about?"

Neill was stymied. This was awkward, right? They hadn't really even talked about the whole upcoming wedding thing though Neill and Gulley had seen each other out a couple times and everything seemed cordial.

"New gal," Neill said. "You know, a new lover is always the best lover."

Nice catch?

"Who is it?" Gulley asked. The normally tight-lipped Gulley was being especially effusive.

"Her name is Syrie Hardwood."

"Seriously?"

"I know. Yes, seriously."

"She's prettier than Candice Bergen," Bidden said.

Neill smiled at him. "Prettier than Tuesday Weld."

"Prettier than Liv Ullmann."

"Prettier than Ali McGraw," Crow said.

It didn't matter that he'd never seen her. The game was afoot.

"Prettier than Julie Christie."

"Prettier than Catherine Deneuve."

"Prettier than Nancy Walker."

"Prettier than the girl from UNCLE."

"I get it," Gulley said, signaling for the waitress. "Prettier than Doris Day?"

Crow laughed.

"He's serious," Bidden said. "He lusts after Doris Day."

"She's got a great pooper," Gulley said.

"So does your fiancé," Neill chanced.

Gulley let a smile develop slowly around his lips. The air was gelid.

"She does indeed," he said.

At the Movies

At the University of Tennessee Medical Units, a new film series sprung up. This made Neill and his compatriots giddy. Their first offering was Godard's *Weekend*.

Neill took Syrie.

Afterward they walked out along Union Avenue. A fine mist was falling, making halos around the streetlights. They held hands and Neill felt on top of the world. The Godard film lit a fire in Neill, the way art can, the way it should.

Godard's blazing vision of life as a traffic jam seemed to fill Neill with the infinite possibilities of creation.

"Ah, life," Neill said. (Or something similar, a sound like a sigh that welcomes in the variegated universe.)

"You're feeling happy?" Syrie asked.

"I am." Neill stopped. The warm mist around Syrie framed her mignon face, a work by a besotted Seurat. Neill leaned down and kissed her softly.

"I love you, Syrie," he said.

Neill tried to walk on but Syrie was suddenly as still as a statue. As immovable.

"Neill," she said, softly.

"What is it, Beautiful?"

"You love me?"

"As if you didn't know."

"You've never said it."

"Of course I have."

"You haven't."

"You mean, in bed, even in the throes of passion, I have not uttered the magic words? "

"You haven't. You've spoken to God and Jesus and Buddha a lot, but you've never said—that."

"I love you. I love you. I love you, Syrie Hardwood."

"I love you, Neill. You have no idea."

"I might have a little idea."

"You don't. You're—I don't know—I'm not good at words like you. You're—everything."

"Sweet."

"Babe, I love you."

"You called me *Babe*?"

"Ok?"

"I like it."

"Ok, Babe. I love you, Babe."

"Syrie." They kissed some more. They had wandered near where they had parked.

"Neill," Syrie said. "Babe?"

"Yes, Love?"

"I didn't understand one minute of that movie."

Neill's reptile brain sprayed some reptile juice onto its reptile casing. Neill felt a rift in his happiness. Am I this petty? he asked himself.

"It's ok, Love," Neill said.

"Explain it to me?"

Neill thought for a moment. "You know," he said. "I don't think I can."

Relief spread over Syrie's face and she laughed a girlish laugh.

They drove homeward, which meant, naturally, toward the fusty twin bed in Neill's apartment.

The T-t-t-t-trip

Once during these halcyon days, Neill and Crow, leaving behind girlfriends and wives and child, took the little yellow Toyota on a tour of the Southwest, specifically New Mexico and Texas. They drove and drove and drove and, at the end of two days of driving, they stopped in Albuquerque, New Mexico.

There wasn't much point in the trip. It was a questing after questing.

Crow missed his son. Neill missed Syrie, sending her a postcard from Albuquerque with a jackalope on it. On the back he wrote,

"I lie down in the heart

of the conversation, wanting

to be steamrolled, right into your

arms, baby, right into your middle distance."

In a second-floor motel room in Albuquerque, with the door open and a nice breeze breezing, with the snow-capped Sandia mountains as background, Neill read "Howl" aloud, in its entirety. It seemed like the right thing to do.

Then, they drove home across Godforsaken Texas, swung into New Orleans, broke down coming back up through Mississippi, and finally made it home, tired and sweaty.

Did they feel like Odysseus and his foreign cater-cousin Ulysses? They did not.

They left and they returned. What else do you want to know?

Meanwhile at the Bookstore

The job at Waldenbooks was beginning to weigh on Neill. He found himself dreading the 8-10 hour shifts, the constant flow of humanity, the piles of Harlequin Romances, the bad bestsellers that far outweighed the one or two Updike or Virginia Woolf fans who stood before the altar of the bookstore with their hands full of pennies.

Neill, though happy in almost every other corner of his life, was becoming disenchanted in one large center room (it might as well be the living room): his job.

After the attempted gay purge Neill felt less and less at home in the bookstore. He had talked it over with Bidden and Pas. They understood.

Then Pas got a job working for the city in the food stamp bureau. The old gang of four was down to two and Neill was wavering.

Poetry and Pokery

As the weeks passed, Neill and Syrie spent more and more time together. Her father loosened the constraints.

They went to the movies often (more exoteric fare usually) and they ate a lot of Taco Bell, Neill's, and now Syrie's, cuisine of choice. Neill could wax poetic about the complex depths of Nachos Supreme or the simple vividness of the Bean Tostada.

Speaking of poetry, Neill, who had been writing steadily, began to read poems aloud to Syrie. Bless her generous little heart: she thought every word burned and illuminated. She was smitten with Neill's brain (such as it was, or such as she perceived it was) and, increasingly, with his body (such as it was) (*stop that*).

Many nights Neill read to her as they lay side by side on the bed, Syrie's head on Neill's chest, the bedside clamp-on light the bon-fire by whose side they warmed.

After a few poems, after Syrie gasped a few times, and after she looked into Neill's eyes with the longing and pleasure of a (now) 17-year-old nymph, they unclothed.

Now that bread and butter (intercourse) were on the menu, the young couple began to experiment enthusiastically. Syrie liked to be on top. She could really snuggle that perfect ass down on Neill's central heating. She had learned to move it in such a way that Neill would groan with carnality. She also discovered that dandling Neill's balls while she was thus impaled brought about fomenting orgasms.

One night when Neill was particularly drawn to the white patches of Syrie's sylph-like body, he invited her off the bed.

"Stand up for a minute," he said.

She hopped off the bed naked as 'a corowne with out stones' (Chaucer). She was largely at his command (readers will recognize the pedagogical impulse in this, Neill the older proctor, Syrie the willing student, and, we hope, will forgive Neill this indulgence. We won't mention it again).

"Turn slowly so I can look at you." Neill marveled anew at the flawlessness of her. She was an Ur-bride.

Syrie giggled and turned around a full 360.

"More slowly."

She did.

"Now just turn round."

"Like this?" Syrie asked as she turned and looked back at her paramour over her little teenage shoulder, her look as smoky as any 30-year-old temptress.

"Oh my," Neill said. "Have I mentioned that your ass is the World Ass? The one upon which Eternity sits."

"Not in those words," Syrie said. She was charmed. She was turned on.

"Move over to the dresser," Neill said.

Syrie looked quizzical but stood next to the dresser, which had a large mirror attached to the top.

"Now turn toward the mirror and lean your elbows on the dresser."

She did. Her white ass shown like a swan upon a lake. In the mirror, she could see the pleasure this was giving Neill. She moved her ass around a bit.

Neill took his erection in his hand and, humming with the desire of the observer, stroked himself as he watched Syrie's ass rolling in the darkness like the Cheshire Cat's left-behind smile.

"I want that," Syrie said with a mock pout.

Neill got off the bed. Syrie began to turn toward him.

"No, stay that way."

He moved up behind her and put his hands gently on each side of her hips. He ran his hands over her impossibly slender waist and then down her smooth thighs. He let the tip of his cock slide down the crack of her ass.

Syrie put her head down on the dresser.

Neill took his implement in hand and ran it up and down her crack and then, oh so slowly, slipped it into her cunny hole from behind.

He sank it deep and pulled her ass tight against him.

"Jesus," Neill said.

"Oh!" Syrie said. She lifted her face.

As they began to fuck Neill was able to watch, in the mirror, Syrie's flawless features crinkle with gratification.

Neill, though a bit clumsy with the angle off by about 2-3 degrees (he could stand on tiptoe to correct the entry position but it was very enervating), rocked behind her, drawing himself all the way out and then diving all the way back down. Syrie began to pant heavily. Neill could feel her walls tightening and he tensed as her orgasm flowed over him.

But Syrie did not rest. She did not miss a beat. She came and then she began to move more, dancing a bit, working for her lover's orgasm.

Then, recalling one of her better instincts, she reached around and cupped Neill's scrotum. She squeezed. They came.

"Didn't know you could do that," she said.

Neill's heart exploded. It left his insides a field of shrapnel and debris. This was Love. He was sure.

The Second Meeting with Mr. Hardwood

They sat in the same places. Neill half-expected an amanuensis sitting nearby, transcribing on her steno pad, Meeting Number Two, Neill Rhymer and Mr. Hardwood.

Neill was only slightly nervous. If this blustering grownup man, sitting across from him, wearing a gubernatorial smile, were to bar Neill from seeing his prize daughter, a Romeo and Juliet romance would result. There would be deaths by sword. There was no way he was going to stop seeing Syrie.

"So," Mr. Hardwood said. He put his hands on his knees. He let out a puff of air and expanded his chest.

"You and Syrie are pretty serious?" he posited.

"Yes, sir," Neill said. He smiled a sitcom smile.

"I think we can declare the trial period over," Mr. Hardwood said. He was Judge Hardy now.

Neill sensed it was going well. He was about to get the Big Ok and not the Big Kibosh.

"I just want to say...welcome to the Hardwood home, Neill."

Neill rose as if the judge had risen.

He took a step toward Mr. Hardwood. The judge rose.

"Thank you, sir," Neill said. "I won't let you down."

Later, in bed with Mr. Hardwood's 17-year-old daughter, Neill recounted the conversation.

"You said, 'I won't let you down'?"

Neill chuckled.

"I have no idea where that came from," he said.

And then, he entered her.

And What Have We Learned Today?

Summer became autumn and Syrie returned to school to finish her high school years at St. Agnes Academy, a tony Catholic private school on Walnut Grove. Sometimes, on his days off, Neill would pick her up from school. He never got arrested. (These concerns about older lovers and teenagers were not in the news so much back in the more-innocent seventies. [How say this?])

The first time Neill picked her up, it was a sunny fall afternoon, and, suddenly, emerging from a gaggle of young women, all in uniform, was his lover. She looked like a kid. She looked like a woman. She looked like the sexiest thing he'd ever seen and, for this, he felt guilt. (*Who turned on the guilt complex?*)

And this occurred to Neill for the first time: She was wearing a Catholic School Girl uniform. It might as well have been pasties and a G-string.

A little background: On Kenneth Street where Neill grew up, all the kids were public school kids. They rode the same buses. They wore the same t-shirts and shorts. They were white-bread Middle America.

But, from perpendicularizing Stage Road, the Southern end of that particular block of Kenneth Street, there emanated, every weekday afternoon, swarms of Catholic schoolgirls in uniform. The bus, apparently, rather than delivering the kids closer to their homes, made one catch-all stop at the base of Kenneth Street.

These girls, walking by, would disrupt street football, or driveway corkball, or curbside bullshit sessions. Everything would grow still. Neill and his friends would stop talking and their arms turned weedy and fell to their sides, balls dribbling onto the asphalt and down the sewer drains. These girls were as exotic as Tutsis.

Those uniforms! Simple blue and gray plaids, stopping just above the knee, revealing slender thighs and calves which ended in white socks and saddle oxfords. The whole neighborhood lusted for them. To take them in like communion would be the ultimate sexual thrill. Neill and his cohorts dreamed about them. They were earthy divinities and they created visions similar to those suffered by the saints of lore in their self-flagellations.

Back to the present (or the present past of the narrative, right?) Neill was agog as Syrie approached him.

"Shut your mouth," Syrie said.

She lunged at Neill and put her yapper against his, an obvious demonstration for her less mature classmates. Neill, odd duck, was slightly aghast.

"Kiss me," Syrie said, putting her books on the hood of the car and throwing her arms (clad in virginal white dress shirt) around Neill's neck.

"We'll get you into trouble," Neill said.

"Pfft," Syrie answered, but backed off. "This school."

Once on the road Neill could not help but look at that glistening brown thigh under the hem of that infernal uniform.

"What is it?" Syrie asked.

Neill smiled broadly.

"That uniform."

"What? I look stupid, right?"

"No, no."

"Like a child?"

"No indeed. It's—I can't explain it. It's such a *turn-on*."

"Really?" Syrie giggled. She pulled her hem higher.

"I'm gonna wreck," Neill said.

"Take me to the bed."

"You don't have to be any place?"

"Take me," Syrie said.

At the apartment complex, they scampered up the stairs to Neill's second-floor apartment, practically tripping over each other. Neill thought he was going to come in his shorts.

Once in the bedroom Syrie pushed Neill onto the bed.

Neill laughed. "You minx," he said.

"I don't know what that means," Syrie said, "But if it has to do with this schoolgirl thing turning you on, let's get to it."

"Oh my Syrie," Neill said in overflowing admiration.

"Lay back, Babe," Syrie said, a saucy minor.

Neill almost corrected her grammar (oaf, ox, simpleton) but bit his tongue.

"You like it because I am like the bad schoolgirl and you are the adult?"

"I can't explain it."

"Do you want me to leave it on? Do you want me to twirl in it, like this?"

Neill groaned.

"Do you want me to slowly strip it off?"

"I don't know," Neill said. "Lemme think."

Syrie stood before him, in the lemonade afternoon light coming through the dusty drapes, shifting her delectable body from saddle shoe to saddle shoe.

"Take off the white shirt," Neill said, thinking hard.

Syrie did. The bra looked silly under the straps of the skirt.

"And the bra," Neill said, almost impatiently.

Syrie did.

"Ah!" Neill said, as if he had just discovered gravity. "Shoes off, socks on. Panties removed."

Syrie kicked one shoe into the northwest corner of the room. It landed on a stack of Mothers of Invention LPs. She kicked the other shoe off and it careened off the wall next to Neill's head.

She put her hand to her mouth. "Oops."

"Careful. Minx," Neill said.

"And the panties?" Syrie said, now fully in character.

"Uh huh," Neill said like a mooncalf.

"My white, white panties?" Syrie said, raising the hem of her skirt slowly.

Neill was a mute celebrant.

"Shall I just take these nasty things off?" Syrie, skirt hiked up, put her thumbs in the waistband of her white, white panties and slowly lowered them. She now stood before Neill in checkered straps and skirt (and white socks) alone.

"I think I might swoon," Neill said.

His Syrie.

The Lawsuit

Most small businesses have a revolving door of employees (it's hard to get good help; it's hard to keep good help) and bookstores seem especially subject to this malady. Perhaps, it's because readers, that is folks who read books and then want to sell them, are dreamy, moony, unworldly, sensitive flibbertigibbets.

Waldenbooks in Raleigh Springs Mall was no exception.

Some wide-eyed gommies lasted a week or two until they found out that it wasn't all about Jack Kerouac and Charles Bukowski. One woman quit after the first night because she was asked to vacuum. So it went.

And then, there was the woman who lasted a few months, witnessed how much overtime Neill, Bidden and Pas worked without comment or compensation, and called in the Feds.

Word came down from HO. Federal agents were coming to interview everyone.

When it came Neill's time to confer with the gray eminences in the store's stockroom, he had worked himself up into a smug lather. His decision, based on his scant readings of the accounts of the House Un-American Activities Committee, was to say nothing. The agent interviewing him was perplexed.

"You won't tell us anything about anyone else?"

"That is correct."

"I don't understand."

"Look. Lemme be honest with you: you guys scare the piss out of me. I don't understand what this is about completely and I am a real idiot when it comes to law. So, I would rather you get answers from everyone else and just give me a pass."

"I am not the enemy's interrogator. You are the manager."

"That is correct."

"You don't really have to understand anything to answer our questions."

"That's what they told K."

"Who is K?"

"It's not important. Can I go now?"

"Neill, you are the manager. However this goes down, it won't involve your getting extra money because you are on salary. And these infractions happened before you became manager. You are in the clear."

"Thank you," Neill said, shook hands and walked out.

The Federal Agent looked as if Neill had just kicked their favorite toy to the curb.

Then the suits from The Home Office came.

Two men, dressed well, hair combed thoroughly. One regular joe, one surly bastard. Good cop, bad cop.

"I don't understand," Bastard said.

"I didn't talk to the Feds. I don't want to answer you either."

"That was good, Neill, you're not opening up to the feds. That was good," said Joe.

"Thank you."

"So, we're right pleased with you. Can't you talk about the charges a bit?" (Joe)

"And, we mean right now. You won't be given another chance to tell your part of the story." (Bastard)

"Good then," Neill said and rose to shake hands. Joe shook hands and looked at Neill with the face of his nicest uncle. It was almost admiration; it was almost pity. Bastard pretended to look at the papers in his hands.

Exit Neill.

Then: nothing else happened. Neill never found out who the disgruntled employee was (though Neill, Victoria, and Pas had fun speculating over after-work pies).

"Are you now or have you ever been a running dog lackey of the bourgeoisie?" Bidden said.

.

One Wedding and a Funeral

It was in this sere September that Neill got an invitation in the mail to the wedding of Thistle Sharer. Neill naturally had mixed emotions. One always hates when one's old mates find someone new, someone who makes them happier. Still, Neill loved Thistle and was, as much as he could goad himself to be, happy she was happy.

It was also going to be an opportunity to reconnect with some of Neill's old Bartlett High School friends. He loved his high school friends. Whenever he told people about how happy he was at BHS, they were often incredulous. No one else seemed to have enjoyed high school.

Then, the unthinkable happened.

On the way to her sister's bridesmaid dinner Thistle's sister Sadie was killed in a car accident, hit by a drunk driver on the curviest part of James Road. This was terrible. The telephone brigade began in earnest. Neill talked to people he hadn't talked to in years. Everyone was speechless in the face of it, yet the calls went on, round and round.

Sexy Sadie gone. It was unbearable.

Saturday morning a funeral was held. Neill made small talk with Akin, Jeff, Lindsey, Hawker, Sam Onides (who flew in from Harvard), Mick, and Greg. Weak, terrible jokes were made. No one knew what to do.

And that night, Thistle was married. Everyone attended. At the reception afterward, a band played songs from their high school dances: "Joy to the World," "I'm Your Captain," "Sunshine of your Love," "Stairway to Heaven," "Light my Fire," "Lucy in the Sky with Diamonds." Some people danced. They danced like tatterdemalions, detached from their brains. Brave Thistle danced with her new husband. Mr. and Mrs. Sharer danced stoically.

Some people danced and cried on each other's shoulders. Old lovers danced for the first time in a decade and wept from grief and wept from despair and wept because the world moves on indifferently. The world does not care for the spores that inhabit its surface.

And that day, the world wobbled on its axis. The old world was as agley as a pig full of rocks.

Look What Else I've Learned

"her mouth played with my cock
  the way a cloud plays with the sky."
  –15th c. zen poet, Ikkyu

One afternoon, after Neill picked up Syrie, she said she had to go straight home. This was dispiriting. Neill was, as usual, horny and had painted pictures in his head that would be banned in all fifty states.

"You have homework? Your dad punishing you?"

"No, nothing like that, Silly," Syrie said. She made as if she were primly tugging the hem of her uniform down. The drive back to Raleigh was a quiet one.

Neill pulled up to the curb at the Hardwood's. He let the engine run. He was sulking.

"What is it, Babe?" Syrie said.

"Nothing. I guess I'll talk to you tonight."

"Ok," Syrie said. She still sat in the car. A smile was spreading across her cheeks like a blood smear.

"What?"

"Come in with me," Syrie said.

"Why?"

Syrie waited a beat. She seemed temporarily flummoxed.

"No one is home," she said finally. "It was a surprise."

"Oh," Neill said. "You mean—like not at home for a while?"

"Like they all went to a handball tournament in Hot Springs."

The car engine died, the key was removed, and Neill was on the sidewalk in one motion. Syrie laughed.

Inside the house Neill grabbed her and held her in his arms.

"Oh my packet of joy," Neill said.

"Wait," Syrie said. "Sit here and I'll be right back."

Neill sat on Mr. Hardwood's couch. He felt his pulse to make sure he wasn't in danger of having to call the Harvey unit.

Soon Syrie said, "Psst."

She was standing in the kitchen, just off the living room behind Neill and off to his left. Only her face was showing.

"Hi," Neill said. "What are you up to?"

Syrie slipped into the room, still standing behind the arm of the couch. She was only wearing a pair of ridiculously brief panties. Lavender panties.

"Jesus God," Neill said. "You did have a good idea."

"That's not all," Syrie said and she took a deep breath.

"What?"

"Swing your legs over the arm of the sofa," Syrie said.

"What?" Neill said again.

Syrie put her hands to Neill's calves and began to lift them.

"Oh," Neill said. He was now on his back—or resting on his elbows—his legs dangling over the end of the couch. Syrie took off his shoes. Syrie took off his socks. Was she going to wash his feet? The religious overtones added titillation.

She stood up. Holy cats she looked good. Her flush was a Pollock canvas.

She unbuckled Neill's pants and, with his help, managed to pull them off. Then Neill's briefs.

She smiled a tight little smile. Then she insinuated herself between Neill's knees.

"Oh!" Neill said.

"I don't know how good I will be but I wanna learn," she said.

"This is a dynamite surprise," Neill said, suddenly full of positive-thinking coaching.

Syrie took Neill by the member. He was as hard as a cricket-ball. She put the whole thing in her mouth without preamble. She stuck it all the way down and gagged slightly.

"Sorry," she said.

"Relax, Love," Neill said.

She did. She relaxed into it. The sight of her, nearly naked, bending over, her coppery hair falling over his stomach so that he had to part it to see his cock going in and out of her gob, was just about the spiciest thing Neill had ever seen.

"Am I doing ok?" she asked.

"Oh yes," Neill said.

"Is this called deep throating?"

"If I were bigger perhaps."

"Bigger?" Syrie made with the wide, disbelieving eyes. "Bigger than *this*? Woof."

She added vigor. She took his balls in one hand and the bottom of his shaft in the other and began to alternately suck and pump. Like many novices before her she misunderstood the expression "suck me." Her vacuum was a tad tight, a tad abrasive. It didn't matter.

Neill siphoned a full cup of jism into his teen lover's cake-hole.

When he was through Syrie raised her head. She smiled with a little ort of come at the side of her mouth. She smiled proudly.

"I swallowed it all," she said.

"Wow," Neill said.

"I wanted to learn how to do that for you."

"How did you—learn it?"

"Oh, I just asked one of the cheerleaders," Syrie said.

Months Passed

And the lovers became even closer. They were both happier than the kine in the fields. Some nights, Syrie was made to stay home to do homework and Neill either went out with Bidden or Crow, or stayed home with Goffredo and watched a movie (VCRs became popular around this time in our story, so that Neill would never have to watch a bad movie again), or he stayed home and read. He read *Giles, Goat Boy* that fall and his passion for Mr. Barth increased ten-fold. He was also writing a lot of poetry, mostly love poems, mostly love + sex poems.

Some nights, he even ate at the Hardwoods.

Neill found it hard to talk to the family, but he did his best Boy Scout impersonation. The brothers never addressed him directly. Mr. Hardwood was all bluff and bluster and a false kindness that said, see how liberated I am that I have let you into our lives.

Mrs. Hardwood, so far only mentioned once, was an odd duck. She was about the same height as Syrie (5'4") but with raven hair and a perpetual tan (a blackening) that made her look

Hispanic, or mulatto. It was a spend-all-summer-at-the pool tan that whispered *skin cancer to come.* She was darker than Neill's Canadian lover Hay Watts Tempt.

Also living with the Hardwoods was Mrs. Hardwood's identical twin sister, Canter. They were identical right down to the darkness of their overly tanned flesh. Why Canter was living there was a family secret Neill never did discover. Canter took an immediate dislike to Neill and the Hardwoods loved to have the two of them together in one room.

"This is little Syrie's boyfriend?" she would say. "Not much meat there, is there? Not for such an older man."

Or she would say, "They tell me you're a poet, Neill baby. That's groovy. You write about twats? Your poems ever touch on the mystery of twats?"

Mrs. Hardwood did sometimes talk to Neill, in more natural ways than anyone else in the family, though not often. It seemed as if, long ago, she had ceded to her husband the role of Dominant Personality. She was quiet (desperation or depth or calm?). One evening, she left Neill and Canter alone in the living room. "I'm going to bed now, kids," she said.

They were watching *Saturday Night Live.* Where was everyone else? Mr. was out for the night. The brothers were out for the night. And Syrie was upstairs in her room on a long-distance call with a cousin who was recently released from jail and someone Syrie hadn't spoken to in donkey years.

Canter was already in her pajamas, which was strange enough. They were brief pajamas but she was wearing a robe.

The guest host was Sissy Spacek. She was twirling a baton. It was quite lovely.

"Do you think she's pretty?" Canter asked.

"I do," Neill said. "Well, maybe not pretty. She's fine. Like porcelain. She's also, somehow, really sexy."

"My, you can wax poetic. No wonder Syrie is so taken with you."

Neill was embarrassed.

"She's awfully pale," Canter said.

It took Neill a moment to realize she meant Sissy Spacek.

"Yes. That strawberry and cream look. She really is lovely."

"You said that."

"Yes."

"Do you like white skin or dark skin?"

It had vague racist tones the way it came out. And racism was certainly possible in the Hardwood household. But racism was not the intent.

"I don't know," Neill said. "Depends on who's wearing it, I guess."

"Do you think I am too dark?" And she opened the sash of her robe.

Her pajama bottoms were very brief. Her thighs were as dark as sloe. Or gunpowder.

"Ah," Neill said. He was so taken aback that he thought he might faint. Yet, his eyes went to her thighs and he did not lift them.

"Someone at the club, that damn Billy Waddell, told me I looked like a pickaninny."   And there it was. Maybe racism wasn't the intent but its poison was present.

"He said my skin was probably tough as leather—just like a pickaninny!"

And there it was again.

Neill was sick. He was also erect. He was looking at his girlfriend's aunt's thighs and crotch. The aunt that hated him, and baited him. That crotch was a mere millimeter out of sight. He imagined it was hell, pitch, and eternal feverishness.

"Feel it," Canter said.

"Ah," Neill said again.

"Does that scare you? Jesus, Neill. It's not like I'm asking for a fuck. I can get a fuck anytime, you know. Any. Time."

"Yes, ma'am," Neill said.

"Ha!," Aunt Canter said. "That's right. Yes ma'am. Now, my young friend. Touch my thigh."

A dangerous minute passed. Neill looked from the thighs to Canter's hard, dark face. Her eyes flashed. Was it anger? Need? Was she drunk? The Hardwood parents did seem to drink a lot.

But, reader, he touched them.

He first put his pointer fingertip on her left thigh.

"No, that's not rough," he said, quaveringly.

"Rub them, Neill."

Neill hesitated only one second.

The devil entered in. Neill was fed by fiendish ire. How dare she?

He ran his hand up and down that black thigh from knee to the edge of her ridiculous pajama bottoms. He did it twice. Dammit, she felt good. He moved his hand to the other thigh and repeated the movement. He looked into Canter's black eyes. It was as if they were hypnotized. And, now Neill was choleric. He squeezed her thigh. He pushed down hard and ran his hand, using more pressure, down to her knee and this time he went right to the hem and stopped. His eyes looked into his girlfriend's mad aunt's eyes. He quickly covered the terry cloth over her pussy with his hand and squeezed there. He squeezed it a number of times while their eyes were locked. Finally, Canter blinked. She blinked and an involuntary gasp came from her mouth. She put her head back in wanton invitation.

"Mom," Syrie called from upstairs.

"Mom! Sugar wants to talk to you!"

"Yeah, coming," they could hear Mrs. Hardwood reply.

Neill kept his hand there. Canter reluctantly opened her eyes and put a hand to Neill's cheek just before Syrie re-entered. Neill's hand was damp.

Syrie came and plopped down next to Neill.

"What have you two been up to?" she said, in innocence.

"Talking about Sissy Spacek."

"Do you think she's pretty?" Syrie asked.

The Position that Was All Theirs

Somewhat like the post-coital nap with their legs entwined and Syrie's hot wet box on Neill's thigh, the young lovers found an odd position that they employed almost every single night.

After Syrie became a past whiz at giving head, during their preliminaries, she would almost always kneel at Neill's outstretched feet, lean over and suck him while he inserted his big toe into her pussy. She sometimes brought herself off on the toe, and sometimes she held the orgasm until she could mount his wet, pre-hardened lingum.

Syrie as in Serious: Months Passed (Again)

Christmas passed, and birthdays (Syrie is 18!), and Neill and Syrie saw a lot of each other. The Hardwoods had relaxed the strictures on their only daughter and Syrie spent almost every night in Neill's bed, in Neill's arms. The after-intercourse nap was a particularly sweet part of their relationship (years later Neill was able to recall exactly how Syrie's muggy crotch felt against his thigh as he drifted out of the conscious world).

Neill went to Syrie's prom. He was embarrassed. He felt like an ass. The photo taken that night has, Neill hopes, disappeared, never to be seen again by the eyes of Adam's broods.

For Syrie's graduation Neill took her to The Four Flames restaurant on Poplar Avenue. It was quite a way from Raleigh and they both felt very adult. They ate filet mignon and baked Alaska. They held hands and kissed and romance was as ripe to them as the first prismatic days of spring.

The next summer Syrie and Neill spent more time talking to each other at the mall than they did working. Their respective bosses were nonplussed but both Syrie and Neill had job security. Neill, though the youngest manager in the store chain, was one of its most dynamic. His profitability was at the high end of the scale (most ambitious?). Lazy by nature he still managed to do enough creative things to win the approval of his immediate boss, District Manager Joy, and even some of the nabobs at the Home Office, despite Neill's on-record queerness about the Great Overtime Probe, and the Gay Pride Incident.

And Syrie, so attractive that men came from five surrounding states just to ask inane questions (How much is that doggie in the window? Do you like Journey or Rush better? Have you heard about these new laser disc movies? Are they a good investment?). Neill, sometimes insecure in the face of her popularity, mostly tolerated it. After all, Syrie was Neill's. Her devotion to him was as secure as the orchard turf.

Polaroids

And their sex! My God, their sex!

Syrie was game for anything. Neill had to be more creative than he ever thought he would need to be.

They tried candy underwear. (Yuck)

Body paints, which turned to soap in the tub (seemed like a sexy idea and Syrie with bright blue swirls around her exquisite little cupcakes did look a sight as exotic as a jungle priestess...and it was nice rubbing her purple crotch into a lather), were a little disappointing.

They ate honey off each other. Chocolate syrup. Taco Bell sauce.

Then Neill had a wonderful idea. One evening he took a break from the bookstore and went down to Penney's and bought a Polaroid camera. Would Syrie balk at a permanent pictorial record of their escapades? It was worth a gamble.

That night he produced his secret from its paper bag. He held the camera out in front of him as if it were myrrh.

"What for?" Syrie asked, and then, quickly, "Oh! I see."

"Sex on camera. What do you think?"

Syrie acted like she had to think it over.

"I imagine you have some poses in mind," she said, in her huskiest voice.

"You know me," her paramour answered.

"Let's go," she said.

First, Neill left the room after instructing Syrie to take off everything and put on his bathrobe. She called him when she was ready.

He re-entered with a book in hand and gave the book to her. *Lolita.*

Her face was quizzical. It was a visible joke slightly over her copper-trussed head.

"Get on the bed. Hold the book like you're reading it."

"Naked?"

"Not yet. Just in the robe. You can show a little cheesecake if you want."

Syrie tittered.

She assumed the pose. Neill adjusted her slightly. She sat against the bed pillows, her legs canted under her, the robe pulled up high to expose her dynamite thighs. One could imagine that there, the darkness under the robe, was the Cave of Seven Delights. One could only *imagine* it.

"Now a come-hither look," he said, stepping back with camera in hand.

She knew how to give a come-hither look. She smoked.

Neill popped a shot and the bright flash surprised them both, like a spotlight from the guard tower catching their escape.

They sat together while it developed. It was beautiful.

"It's beautiful!" Neill said. "You're beautiful."

"What next?" Syrie asked. She was like a happy puppy.

"Lean back and open the robe."

She did as Neill resumed his position at the foot of the bed. Her body looked great under the reading light, shadowy as the river Styx, with highlights of gold. Sunset on the Styx.

"Um...touch yourself," Neill said.

Syrie did not even hesitate. She began to rub her little kitten.

"Mm," she said.

"Jesus," Neill said.

Syrie had a finger inside herself when Neill took the next shot. His hand shook.

They scampered together to wait for it to develop. It took four hours.

Finally—there it was.

"Damn," Neill said. "Damn."

"You like?"

"I like a lot."

"Lemme do you."

"Well, ok. But men, you know, they're not, you know, works of art like women are."

"Get naked, Bub," Syrie said, taking the camera and pushing Neill toward the bed.

The picture she got of him showed his dingle at half-mast.

"Hm," Neill said.

"Hm," Syrie said. "What to do?"

"Suck it," Neill said.

Syrie kneeled on the floor and put the half-dingle in her maw. It grew. It was stiff as a dry Quaker. Neill snapped a shot of his cock halfway inside Syrie's mouth. The picture was mackled—he was too close—but you could tell what was happening.

Syrie leaned over the dresser, fully naked now, one hand reaching behind her to spread her cheeks.

Syrie kneeled on the bed and fingered herself from behind.

Neill jerked himself while watching Syrie finger herself and simultaneously took a picture. This time his cock looked like a serviceable contrivance. It stood straight and tall.

Syrie returned to the dresser and Neill entered her from behind. He took a picture straight down his still slim young body at his erection being swallowed, seemingly, by Syrie's perfect, cordate ass.

Then he dropped the camera.

At the Rhymers

Often, on Saturday nights, Syrie and Neill went to the Rhymers house for games: Uno, Put and Take, Boggle, Tripoley.

Neill's sister AJ and Syrie had gotten very tight. Sometimes, when Neill worked and Syrie didn't, AJ and Syrie hung out together, sometimes just driving around talking about their respective loves (AJ was wild about her husband) (better than the lunkhead AJ dated for a while who once Neill found pushing his sister against a wall. Neill said, "Hey, dipshit," but with a rapid heartbeat. The lunkhead was twice as big as Neill and, if he wished to, he could have popped Neill's head open like a grape.)

These family gatherings only reinforced Syrie's and Neill's love affair. She was being groomed to be Mrs. Neill Rhymer, wasn't she?

We're Gonna Skip Ahead

Lovers' bliss, when not our own, can become cloying, repetitious, tiresome. One wants to be on the side of love (and sex) but, really, something gets in the way of celebrating another person's happiness. Nu?

Much time passed and Neill and Syrie stayed sexual and committed, and they grew together like two trees, trunks like conjoined twins. (Did we already use that phrase "conjoined twins?"—check).

They saw a lot of movies.

They ate a lot of Taco Bell.

They visited Bidden and Pas.

They visited Crow and his wife and their infant son.

Neill spoke lovingly of Syrie whenever given the chance. All his friends thought him the luckiest swab onboard the liner Romance. Goffredo was especially effusive in his praise of Syrie (mentioning as often as possible her extraordinary caboose.)

"She's as pretty as children's thoughts," Neill romantically described her.

This also happened: Neill published a few poems in a few rags. Some people in Fargo, or Oakland, or Truth or Consequences, perhaps, who knows? might have read a poem of Neill's. This, to Neill at this time, felt like lagniappe. Life was rich. Life was placentious. Life was a shivaree.

And Who is This New Woman?

Here is one thing we believe: happiness in a relationship, experienced simultaneously by both parties, even when both parties are sexually satisfied, even rapturous, is not proof against cheating. How come? The human machine is poorly planned, perhaps, poorly constructed, with a brain made of unnecessarily powerful chemicals.

There is a moment (it might be the penultimate moment) in Truffaut's *The Man Who Loved Women*, where the protagonist, a Lothario, leaves his lover's bed and walks out onto the street. The camera follows as he eyes a pretty woman approaching. The camera, now *his* gaze, follows the woman walking away. He loves women. Even satisfied, sated, full of (love?) for the woman whose bed he just left, he eyes a new skirt. Forgive him?

Is Neill a Lothario? He is certainly mulierose, and profligate in the ways of the heart. (Theme? ed.)

So, who is this new woman?

Why is she often at Waldenbooks in Raleigh Springs Mall?

What is she saying to Neill over by the science fiction paperbacks?

Is she really that tall? Her hair that black? Her breasts that full and round?

What is her name? What is her story?

Where is Syrie?

O Syrie!

Here we paste her name for the record: Mercedes "Abby" Twa. Called Abby. Sometimes called Twa. Rarely called Mercedes.

She is from Lucy, Tennessee. She is a country gal but smarter than the secret life-force within seashells. She reads books. She has refined tastes. She is vegetarian. (She told Neill to get on the 'branwagon.') She is agnostic. She is a free-thinker, a woman's libber, a socialist.

She loves Godard, Truffaut, and Bertolucci.

She thinks American Cinema, with the exception of Robert Altman, is bushwa.

There is plenty of fuel here for conversation. Neill finds her opinionated, fascinating, infuriating, extremely attractive, and, ultimately, irresistible.

There Were in Those Days Also Many Nights at the P&H

Neill, Bidden, Crow, Pas, and Gulley spent many nights at the P&H. It's hard to parse them, to figure how weighted they should be in the final telling.

It was just palaver, neither astute nor asinine.

It was just talk.

Sometimes when Gulley was there Neill didn't talk as much.

Sometimes this was due to the whole awkward Victoria thing. Sometimes it was because Gulley intimidated Neill. Gulley was the smartest person Neill knew until he later met the Jewish writer, Shlomo Einstein (who, we think, will spring fully to life in the 3rd and 4th part of this formulation, now entitled *Cock-a-Hoop*).

Neill: "I have to see the Jeopardy final tomorrow. My gal Rose is going for it all."

Bidden: "I thought this was teen week."

Neill: "It is"

Bidden: "So, that would make Rose about 17?"

Neill: "Or so."

Bidden: "That's—well—"

Neill: "Syrie's age. No, wait, she's 18, my Syrie."

Bidden: "Yeah that's better."

They laughed.

Gulley said, "I want to be one of those guys who call Benjamin Ben, Thomas Tom, and Richard Dick."

Bidden: "Really, Gull?"

Neill: "I want to be one of those guys whose name gets shortened. From now on call me Ne."

Bidden: Or N.

Gulley: Or.

One Night At the Bookstore Late

Right before closing she came in. Her hair, if it was possible, was even blacker. She was a hex, a shapeshifter. She even seemed taller. (She was actually nose to nose with Neill...and being nose to nose with him enflamed him, because Abby Twa released a musk that was intoxicating and also, being nose to nose also meant her large turtledoves were practically touching his chest.)

"We're about to close," Neill said, but he was smiling.

"Did you say too close?" Aby Twa batted back.

"Is there too close?"

"Why I'm here," Abby Twa said.

"You want to help us close?"

"I want to help you open."

Neill's smile turned into a chuckle, which turned into a guffaw.

He went to the stockroom and called Syrie and told her that Bidden was having woman troubles (this was true, lending some verisimilitude to Neill's swinish lie) and that they were going to a Raleigh bar and talk it over. (*Aw, Babe, she whispered...I bought new panties...*)

After Neill shut down the cash register and put the money away and bid his co-workers adieu, he was half-hoping that this raven-haired temptress had absconded and that he could go home a guilt-free man.

But, no, she was waiting for him, leaning on a red, convertible Mustang.

"Not really?" Neill said.

"What?" Abby Twa said.

"This is not really your car?'

"You approve or disapprove?"

"It's the—coolest (Neill tried to stop the word 'coolest' from emerging from his nervous mouth) car known to man."

"What you nasty boys call a pussy machine."

There was Neill's laugh again.

"You have a charming laugh," Abby said.

"Thanks," Neill said, not quite through laughing.

"As a matter of fact, you have a great mouth." And here she grabbed the front of his shirt (surely she had seen this in some made-for-TV movie) and pulled his mouth against hers. Her mouth was plush and wet and her tongue large and lively.

When Neill came up for air, Abby ran that same tongue up his cheek.

Neill laughed one more time and said, "So what do you wanna do?"

They went to her place. She lived in Scenic Hills in a house that her parents had given her. Neill twigged to this: Abby Twa's family was loaded. Besides the obligatory backyard swimming pool, there was a grass tennis court. A GRASS tennis court.

"You play?" Neill said, looking out the sliding glass doors into Abby Twa's backyard, lit by poolside lights.

"And how," she answered.

"You're a panther, aren't you? Like in *Cat People*? You have a lot of animal in you."

"Scare you?"

"Not particularly," Neill knew to say, though he was about to piss himself.

"Wanna go for a swim?"

"I guess here is where I say I have no suit and you say, you don't need one."

It was Abby Twa's turn to laugh.

She threw her shirt on a chair. She threw her short skirt onto the floor. She kicked off her shoes and undid her bra. As it fell, Neill thought his heart would stop.

"I'm not a breast man," he said to himself, "But Jesus God those are delicious."

The "But Jesus God those are delicious," he said out loud.

"Thanks, Sailor," Abby said and skipped out the door.

Neill clumsily got out of his work clothes. He was just brave enough to strip down to his underwear.

"Helloooo," Abby said, looking at Neill's poker.

She put her arms around him and kissed him long and hard again and, at the end, leaned sideways enough to send them both into the pool.

Wet, her breasts felt like unearthly bliss against Neill's boyish chest. In the shallow end they kissed again. Neill was pushing Little Neill against Abby Twa as hard as he could. She was humming into his mouth.

Neill, to counter her aggressiveness, reached down and pulled her wet panties off. He grabbed both her cheeks and pulled her hard against him. Then, he put a finger in her anus.

"Ah ah," Abby Twa said, breaking the kiss.

Neill thought it was a good sound but he wasn't sure. He wiggled the embedded finger.

"Oh ah ah."

It was a good sound. "I'm wearing nothing but a diaphragm," she said into Neill's ear.

It wasn't long before Neill was also naked and Abby Twa was pulling on him (a soupçon tad too enthusiastically, perhaps, for it was almost painful. To stop her, he spun her around and stuck his cock inside her. In the pool the coming together was so easy.

Neill had only one prayer. Don't come too early.

He didn't.

They made it to Abby Twa's bedchamber, which was enormous, with 15-foot ceilings and a stereo system slightly smaller than The Who's. On her bedside table: Hannah Arendt's *Eichmann in Jerusalem*, and Pauline Kael's *I Lost it at the Movies*. The walls were black, blacker than deep black. The bedclothes, right down to the satin sheets, were black.

In bed, she favored being on top. This didn't surprise Neill.

The sight of those breasts and their erotic rumba sent Neill into rapture. As he came he hoped she had already or was about to. After he collapsed next to her, he didn't care. He fell asleep as if poleaxed.

In the morning he woke to that unsettling feeling of *where the hell am I?*

Then he saw the hair, an ink stain on pale well-rounded shoulders.

Neill sat up slowly. His young body hurt, especially his dingle.

Abby Twa stirred. She opened one eye and beheld him.

"Sneaking off?" she said, her voice throaty with sleep.

"No," Neill said. He had no idea what his intentions were. "Gotta pee." Yeah, that was it.

When he returned, he realized they were both still naked.

Abby was sitting up. Her breasts.

"Whatcha wanna do?" Abby said. She hugged her own drawn-up knees.

"Breakfast?" Neill said.

"I don't do breakfast, but I can make us up some coffee and if you want something you're free to use the kitchen."

"Ok," Neill said, though he wasn't sure what he was agreeing to.

Abby jumped from bed. Abby's body.

She started grinding coffee beans and signing over the din, "*Woke up, it was a Chelsea morning...*"

She came back. Neill was about to pull his underwear up.

"Oh," Abby said, a phony pout added for emphasis.

Neill stopped as if he were doing something wrong.

"No clothes yet, Bunky."

"Ok," Neill said. He was a little worried about coming again so soon since last night he had, what we will call, *a good one.*

"Wait," Abby said, and, for the first time, her smile and bouncy step seemed girlish. She came back with tennis rackets.

"Ah," Neill said.

"One quick set then breakfast and a swim!" Abby said. Abby's body.

Her girlishness went straight through Neill's heart.

"Ok...I don't have shorts."

"Naked tennis!" Abby said and marched out the door before Neill could respond.

They played tennis. It was ridiculous. It was surprising and erotic.

Abby's body. Abby's breasts. Reaching for a forehand. Hitting an overhead smash. Serving. Approaching the net.

God forgive me, Neill said, but not out loud. I want to do this every day.

Afterwards, dripping sweat, they had coffee and bagels.

Then they took a shower in Mercedes Abby Twa's spacious shower stall (as big as a cage at the zoo). The lubricity of a woman's soft, soapy palm on your pistol is worth thinking about. Neill needn't have worried about his ability to perform again.

Abby Twa.

If They Saw *The Shining* This Must be 1980.

1980 was a liminal year in the story of Neill. 1980 changed him forever and, unfortunately, for some around him, it changed them as well.

1980 was a Year of Transformation. Someone told Neill once that humans replace their entire cell structure every seven years, in a sense creating a whole new person, with new opportunities, with new blood.

That would have made Neill's years 1962, 1969, 1977, 1984.

Yet 1980 is one of the signposts on the Neill Rhymer Interstate.

1980 will bridge the 2nd and 3rd Books Of Neill.

At the Bookstore: Raw Mammoth

Corporations run on committees and files and computerized data. They do not run on people and they do not care about a wee poet in Memphis Tennessee who is the youngest manager in the chain or one whose store rating remained consistently high.

Neill felt the indifference like a chill down his sacroiliac.

A memo was handed down from Parnassus, an edict from The Home Office. All cash register systems would be upgraded to something called a Point of Sale system (POS for short). Neill hated change. Even worse, he hated change that made him feel like a nincompoop.

The tech guys showed up with the new registers. They looked like small space ships. (The registers, not the tech guys. The tech guys looked like Republicans.)

Neill was cowed.

There were training sessions in the stockroom before the new systems would be installed. "The beauty of this system," the tech training guy said, "is that all the info you plug in, rooted by the code of the product, in most cases the ISBN numbers, will be immediately read by someone at Stamford (Connecticut, the home of The Home Office) and printouts and other documents to help you maintain the desired inventory (in other words the bestselling books that were not only sold at every other of the 600+ Waldenbooks stores, but at Every Bookstore in America)."

Neill asked, kindly not pointing out that 'ISBN number' is redundant: "What about books not in the system? Small press things. Stuff we like to hand sell."

"There will be a 2% leeway."

"So 2 % of our stock can be stuff we really want to sell."

He smiled a tight-lipped smile to note that he got the sarcasm.

"Believe me," he said. "In two weeks you're gonna love this. It is going to make your job much easier."

(After two weeks, Neill still hated the POS [or the POS system as Neill and Bidden chose to call it to mock the tech guy]. After two months, Neill still hated the POS. And he felt inadequate every time he had to use the cash register. The rest of the staff seemed to pick it up quickly enough. Neill was a Neanderthal. He didn't want fire invented. He wanted to eat his mammoth raw.)

At the Bookstore, One Night

At the end of the 1-10 shift Neill and Bidden and Pas were all knackered.

"I've worked 6 days straight," Pas said.

"I thought Rick was going to work for you tonight," Neill said, as he was alphabetizing a cartload of mass market paperbacks from Bantam.

"He had something at Kathy's parents' house, a bar mitzvah or something."

"Even though Kathy is a Lutheran."

"Whatever it was. A religious something. *Something* something. I don't know," Pas said. She wasn't in a good mood.

"Not in a good mood," Sensitive Neill asked.

"Not," Pas said.

"Why don't we all go for a pizza," Bidden said.

"I'm in," Pas said. "But not that meat lovers you men ordered last time. I could feel my aorta clogging afterward."

"You guys go ahead," Neill said. "I'm picking up Syrie."

"Ten o'clock on a school night?" Bidden asked.

"Parents out of town."

Bidden made with the Groucho eyebrows.

"Yeah. That's happening. And somewhere that is not my bedroom."

"I envy," Bidden said.

In the parking lot Neill waved to Bidden and Pas as they drove off in Bidden's crappy Ford. Neill unlocked his car and, wearily, dropped into the driver's seat.

"Tough day at the store?" Abby said.

She was in the passenger seat. Neill jumped like a Calaveras frog.

"Jesus Fuck, you scared the hell out of me."

"Hey, Lover," Abby said.

They hadn't seen each other in over two months. Neill had called a couple times but was almost thankful the phone wasn't answered.

"How did you get in my car?"

Abby smiled her mouser smile.

"You're a woman of ugly talents."

"Is that from *Who's Afraid of Virginia Woolf*" Abby Twa asked.

"I think so," Neill said.

"Let's go. I want to swim in Lake Windermere," Abby said. She did up her seatbelt.

Neill shook his head.

"I have other plans," he said. "Swim Lake Windermere? In the dark? It's full of snakes."

"I'm full of snakes."

"I know," Neill said, but he had to laugh.

"So let's go. Naked in the moonlight. Could be fun."

"I really have to be someplace else."

"Girlfriend?" Abby Twa asked.

Neill gave her a one-eyed squint. "Girlfriend," he said. It didn't matter to her.

"Ok, we'll go by my place first. You can call her from there."

"Abby..." Neill began.

Abby swiftly placed her hand over Neill's crotch.

"Abby...." Neill continued.

Abby began to massage the creature to life.

"I really."

"I can do it here or in Lake Windermere. Or both. Doesn't matter to me."

"I know," Neill said. He was sad. He was disappointed in himself.

Abby unzipped his pants. Friends, Neill could have resisted. Obviously. He did not.

Abby pulled Little Neill out.

"There's my chum," Abby said.

"Ok," Neill said. He started the car.

"Yay," Abby squealed like a teen.

Neill drove. His meat was still on the counter. He was a mixed bag of emotions and desires.

"Want me to put the trickster away?" Abby said, all triumph and with the mansuetude of the victor.

"No," Neill said.

Abby put her hand on it but did not move. Her hand lay over Little Neill like an antimacassar.

"At least show me your tits while I drive," Neill said.

He wanted a small, inane victory of his own perhaps.

Abby readily pulled off her top, negotiating around the seatbelt. The bra looked like something from Victoria's Secret, made of lace and breath. She removed it also and laid it over Neill's cock.

Abby's tits. (Sing a song of.)

That night they swived on the banks of Lake Windermere after swimming across it. They lay in someone's backyard, on a gently sloping hill, and did it three ways before Abby came twice and Neill once. Afterward, they lay on their backs and looked at the sky. It was a soapy black. The moonlight shown on Abby's mons, as if consecrating it.

"You don't have the biggest dick I've ever had," Abby said.

Neill thought he was going to cry.

"Thanks," he said.

"But it's so nice. It's.... *responsive.*"

"Ok," Neill said.

"And you talk during sex. I like that a lot."

"Ok," Neill said.

"Tell me what you like and don't like about me."

Neill thought a minute.

"Your pussy is like a vise."

Neither of them spoke again for a while.

"That's something you like," Abby said, as if deciding it.

He Lies to Syrie Again

The phone rang at 6 a.m. Neill had just walked in.

"What happened?" Syrie said. She sounded like she was twelve.

"I'm so sorry, Babe."

"Where were you?"

"Oh, it was awful," Neill said. He was a pretty good actor. He sounded angry, upset, and exhausted. Perhaps, it didn't take that much acting. Those feelings predominated.

"What happened, Babe? I waited up all night."

"Oh shit. I'm sorry. Can I grab a nap and meet you at Taco Bell for lunch?"

"It's a school day," Syrie said. She was crying.

"Fuck. Sorry. Um, ok. Pick you up afterward and we'll have an early dinner or late lunch."

"Can we make it Taco Bell?" Syrie sniffed.

"Of course," Neill said.

At Taco Bell

"You need more taco sauce?" Neill was solicitous.

"No," Syrie said. Her eyes shone. With love, with tears.

"Why you crying, Babe?"

"I'm scared you're gonna tell me something bad."

Neill stopped. He looked intensely at his beautiful girlfriend. He put his tostada down.

"I love you, Syrie. Don't be scared."

"Are you seeing someone—" her voice caught.

"No," Neill said, quickly, adamantly.

"Where were you?"

"I was with a woman but she's a friend of my brother's. It's nothing. I just went to her place. We listened to the new Jethro Tull album. We had some wine. I came home."

"Why didn't you just tell me?"

"I thought you would get upset."

"I got upset because I didn't know."

"I see that now," Neill said. He felt a little nauseated.

"You do love me," Syrie said. Her smile was brave.

"I do. Forever. Forever and a day." And Neill meant it. (And, decades later there was much lingering truth in this simple pronouncement.)

"Oh, Babe, I'm so glad you do."

"It's solid as beechwood in a blast."

Syrie let a small giggle out.

"What does that mean?"

"I read it somewhere, I think."

"Are you finished eating?" Syrie was feeling light-hearted again.

"Not quite," Neill said, but he did not pick up his tostada.

"Ok." Syrie put her hands in her lap. She hadn't eaten much.

"Do you think you can get everything from one person?" Neill said then.

Syrie's face crinkled.

"Do you mean—me? Do I think I can get everything from you?"

"No—I meant in general. But, *you*, can you?"

"From you, yes."

Neill thought. He picked up the tostada and set it back down.

"I don't think that. I think you can get love and sex from one person and companionship from another and intellectual stimulation from another. I wonder if people are ever 100% invested in one mate."

"You're not with me." The tears were ready offstage.

"No—I mean—Syrie—You know. You and I are lovely together. We fit."

"I think so."

"I do too."

"What do you mean then?"

"Forget it. It just occurred to me."

"I'm not smart enough for you," Syrie said. There was no anger in her voice. She had never said one angry thing to Neill. She was like a saint.

"Of course you are," Neill said. Because that's what you do. You fudge to protect the vulnerable heart of your closest love.

Something Terrible Happens

Neill was seated at the Hardwood's kitchen table. They were playing cards. It wasn't very much fun. The Hardwoods played as if to lose meant they were weak, prey. Neill, not proud of his own competitive streak, was showing off what a good loser he was.

Aunt Canter, dressed completely in a black leotard thing, so that she looked like some cracked ninja, was alternately ribbing Neill ("poet-boy") and rubbing her bare foot on his shin.

One of the brothers was watching TV in the next room.

"Oh no!" he said.

"Wow," he said again.

"Damn," he said.

"Son," Mr. Hardwood said, "What? Just tell us *what*, so we can go on with our game."

"Someone just shot John Lennon," he called back.

Neill suddenly felt bilious. It couldn't be true.

He sprang from his seat.

"He's not dead, though," Neill said to the screen.

"I think he's dead," the brother said.

"No," Neill said. "Oh no."

"Pfft," came Canter's voice from the kitchen. "He's not bigger than Jesus now."

Syrie came up behind him.

"I'm sorry, Babe," she said. Then to the room she added, "Neill is a big Beatles fan."

Neill asked if he could use the phone.

He called Bidden.

"It's true," Bidden said. "I'm watching the TV right now."

"Can you meet me at P&H?" Neill said. He was choking on desperation, the kind of foulness when something happens that is too awful to be true.

"Right now," Bidden said.

"I've gotta go," Neill said to everyone. "Sorry."

Mr. Hardwood put the pack of cards down with exaggerated calm. Aunt Canter lit a cigarette and blew out a noxious blue cloud.

"Where are you going?" Syrie asked.

"I've got to meet Bidden," Neill said. He wasn't thinking. He was stumbling, mentally stumbling.

"I'll go with you."

"No," he shot it out too quickly. "That is, lemme go talk to Bidden. I feel the need to talk to Bidden alone."

Syrie's face showed that crease again. But, she never complained.

"I understand," she said.

She didn't.

On the drive to P&H (the bar that night was as quiet as Eden ere the birth of man, the drinkers all wore eye patches on *both eyes*, the jukebox refused to play no matter how many quarters were inserted, Wanda was transparent, a spectral owner only) and the next day when he woke and hoped that somehow, during the night, reality had changed, he contemplated what it meant that he could not be with Syrie, that he could not share his grief with her. She wouldn't understand, he told himself. It's not her fault, she can't understand what this means. It's just the age difference.

But, it was more than that and he knew it.

It was years before Neill could hear "Imagine." If it came on the car radio he not only turned the radio off, he stopped the car. Then when he decided to listen to it again, he played it straight through forty-seven times and found a new word each time to cry over. Forty-seven tear-worthy words.

The Next Few Weeks

During the next few weeks Neill tried to call Abby Twa numerous times. He got her machine. It said, "This is Abby Twa. I don't care what you do next."

Neill left this simple message, uninflected: "Call Neill back."

Neill and Syrie still saw each other as much as possible. Their nights were still filled with fireworks and laughs and a closeness that was more than flesh hunger.

Neill called Abby Twa one more time and she had a new message: "This is Abby. To let go is to lose your foothold temporarily. Not to let go is to lose your foothold forever."

If she had changed her message, she had gotten all of Neill's.

Neill was being dumped. The phenomenal hoyden, Mercedes Abby Twa, had moved on. It was for the best.

(Neill did see her one more time: he was in Target desultorily looking through their poor selection of CDs while Syrie was elsewhere in the store buying sexy underwear. Abby's voice behind him said, "Looking for Tommy Roe's greatest hits?" Neill turned slowly. Abby Twa looked different. She had cut her hair into Bettie Page bangs and she was wearing a shirt so low cut that a sliver of aureole shown above each edge. It hurt Neill's heart to look at her. "How are you?" he asked in his calmest actor's voice. "Moving to Los Angeles," she said. "Good," Neill said and turned back to the CDs. Syrie came up just then and said, "Babe, who was the babe?" "Someone from high school," Neill answered. "I think she's a hooker now.")

Restless without Rest

Still, Neill was restless most nights.

He would leave Syrie early and, instead of driving to his shithole apartment and seeing what Goffredo was doing, or calling Bidden or Crow, he would drive around his old haunts, by the homes of his high school girlfriends, the same route he and Sly used to make when they were high and horny and youth was a different country.

Sometimes, he would stop at his parent's house and sit in the living room and watch *Gunsmoke* with them. If they wondered why their adult son was visiting alone late at night, they never said.

Sometimes, he sat and fantasized about Orbit, of all people.

"You want popcorn?" his mother would ask.

Neill did want popcorn. But he also wanted something else...something, dammit, that wasn't Syrie.

Distracted

So, Neill felt as if he were being pulled in many directions. He began to fear a return of the demon in whose grips he fell after the Dew Drynow debacle.

He loved his Syrie. He also loved the heady feeling of talking books and movies and, well, there is no delicate way of saying it, Syrie just wasn't up for that. Give her a few years, Neill thought.

But, he was also distracted by these wily, oomphy women, these Abbys and Orbits. He didn't want to be tied down. He was too young. He wanted to sow the axiomatic oats, even the unaxiomatic oats.

And working for the corporate chain was wearing on him, too. It was a ponderous chain. Neill felt as if he had forged every link. (*He saw a beach of sand beside the sea. And there before him he saw every grain and he wondered has every man his chain...*)

Despite all this swirling in his crepitating brain (and no, he had not gotten over the death of John Lennon), he still managed to love his lover and keep company with his friends, his dear friends, on whom he counted heavily for steadying reassurance.

So, there were still late-night conversations at the P&H.

There was still Tripoley at the Rhymers.

There were still awkward dinners at the Hardwoods.

And, yes Virginia, there was still the bedchamber with Syrie, beautiful, beddable Syrie who could make the angels weep. Lovely, loving Syrie, whom Neill did not deserve.

These are the Times that Try Men's Souls

A memo from The Home Office had arrived at Waldenbooks store #466 earlier in the month. They were going to re-carpet the store. How would this be accomplished? In an all-night session of heavy-lifting with friends invited along to help. They were literally going to take every book off every table, and then move the tables into the mall concourse, so that the carpenters could lay down new fitted carpeting. Then, everything was to be moved back in and set up in the exact same place. They assured the staff that this could be done in one night.

This ticked Neill off, but perhaps Neill was ready to be ticked off. He did not want to work all night. He hated the middle of the night. As a dues-paying insomniac, the witching hours spooked him like no one's business. Even that pugnacious Norman Mailer said, "I can handle anything except the middle of the night."

Nevertheless, the time came like all heavy-handed times must.

That day Neill was in a funk. He hated the world. Occasionally, Neill got into funks and hated the world. He sneered. He grunted instead of spoke. Neill didn't really, in his walking around hours, hate the world. There were some things he hated: big business, licorice, Republicans, but, overall, Neill thought that life was a wild ride. Sometimes, you just hang on and let it spin you around by the feet. Sometimes, you even manage to say, Wheeeee....

With the store closed and the workers there with their new flooring, Neill felt an uncomfortable thrum in his guts. It was building up like a squall in his liver. A liver squall.

It was not funny. Neill felt like he was going down. He was afraid of the night. It spread out before his inner vision like the road to Perdition. Where was his Virgil? Bidden was there. He seemed unafraid. That didn't help. Gulley and Victoria were there to help, Gulley because he was more powerful than a locomotive, and Victoria because she was a child of the night and did not sleep.

He was not listening to the working men. He was cowed by their middle-of-the-night ability to transform an entire bookstore. He couldn't hear them and he couldn't understand what he heard. He could never learn to use the new computerized system (POS) and he didn't want to. And, he couldn't move every book in the store into the mall concourse and back again. He could not.

He stopped. He held up a patrolman's palm.

"Stop," he said. "I'm not feeling well."

Bidden moved toward him. Pas moved toward him. The new girl, who was built like Raquel Welch, did not move toward him and, inwardly, Neill cursed her.

"No, I can't. I can't go on tonight." And Neill was gone.

Where did Neill go? It was 1:15 in the morning.

He went home. Of course, Goffredo was asleep.

He started to take his clothes off but he knew sleep would be an impossibility.

A swelling of anxiety had begun inside Neill and it threatened to burst forth from him, a torrent of terribleness and weakness and pain. His hands were numb. His ears rang.

Neill ran out into the Negro streets. Or was it Negro dawn?

Outside he fumbled into his car and drove. Without thinking about it he drove to his parents' house. He parked the car, got out, and sat down on the driveway. He didn't want to wake anyone.

Kenneth Street was as still as a stopped clock.

He would wait outside till dawn.

They would understand, Neill was thinking. They would see that Neill was in such pain that all he could think to do was sit outside all night on the concrete driveway.

The seat was hard. Neill's eyes were vacant and a sadness the color and breadth of evening welled up in him.

Neill felt alien. He felt *other*. He did not fit into the world.

It was the same feeling he had as a child starting first grade, and, hence, it felt foolish and immature and improper and embarrassing.

The sun rose behind Neill. Its querulous rays hit the back of his head and murmured to him, *What the fuck, Neill?* The newspaper came flying out of the window of a passing car and landed beside Neill as if he were invisible. Neill wished he were invisible.

Around 6:30 a.m. Neill stood and walked to the carport door.

He used his key. His mother was in the kitchen. She was always in the kitchen.

"Neill!" she said. "What have you done?"

"I haven't done anything," Neill answered, irritably.

"Why are you here?"

"I think—"

Neill's father came in.

"What's up, son," he said in his affable way, his eyes bleared, his red checked housecoat a theme of deep comfort.

"I think I quit the bookstore."

His mother expressed a disdainful snort. His father stood by in stoic adoration.

Lolly: "So, you did do something. You quit the job that you kept so that you could quit school."

"What now?" his father asked.

"I don't know. I just walked out. I've been wandering the streets all night."

"Wandering the streets?" his mother asked. "This isn't New York City. You've been walking the neighborhood?"

"Have it your way."

His dad put a strong, soft hand on his shoulder. "Tell us what happened."

Neill sat. His parents sat.

He tried to explain the ineffable, the inexplicable. He tried to describe human angst but, he knew, he was learning, that one's human angst is so personal, so private, that its language only exists, if it exists at all, in the sufferer's consciousness. It was a tough lesson.

"What are you going to do now?" his empirical father said. If there is a problem, there is a solution. This was Max Rhymer's leitmotif. (Max was wise and steady, where Lolly was hot and wavering. It was Max who said, "This too shall pass." It was Max who said, "My habits are established; yours occasionally need adjustments." It was Max who said, "Let us reason together." And, "The universe is neither stacked for nor against you." These pronouncements became known as, in the family idiolect, Maxims.)

"I'll find another job," Neill said as he squared his shoulders. "I will. I might work in a bank."

This just occurred to him. He gave his father a grim smile. He tried the same grim smile on his mother.

Then Neill, like Jesus before him, wept.

BOOK III: CONCEPTION

"It may begin as devotional, your lovemaking, but the brain goes dark, as a city blacks out, and some antediluvian pre-brain kicks in that all it knows to do is move the hips."
  −E. L Doctorow

Unemployment

Neill gave Waldenbooks his two-week notice. His boss Joy expressed regret. Neill thanked her for everything and blamed his departure on his own lunacy.

On his last night he shook Bidden's hand. He didn't want to take Neill's place as manager. "I'm not good enough to be manager," he said. And, he took Pas into the stockroom and kissed her shining black face on the lips. "I've always wanted to do that," he said. She smiled tolerantly.

Neill didn't let the grass grow under his feet.

He decided—God knows why—that he would work in a bank. Perhaps it went back to Mr. Nail's class at Memphis State. He asked, rhetorically, what one could do with a degree in English. His pause expected no response. And, he answered himself: work in a bank and think interesting thoughts.

Neill found getting an interview at a bank was challenging enough. He got two, one a smaller bank, the other a Big Bank.

The latter was a waste of an hour. The smaller bank was very kind but admitted, at the end of the conversation, that most banks only hired clerks with experience.

The obvious question Neill asked anyway: how does one then get experience?

The woman smiled indulgently.

"It's a real Catch-22," Neill said.

The woman smiled blankly. She was thinking Neill was cute, but a pumpkinhead.

During all this time, Neill had also applied for unemployment. This was one of the most dispiriting exercises in absurdity and debasement Neill have ever experienced. The office itself was straight out of Kafka, colorless and spy-flecked walls, scuffed and sagging linoleum, and the sourest faces ever collected in one public space. Not just the other poor jobless hopefuls and hopeless but the clerks, straight out of Dickens, who loved being the dogs you had to get past.

Everything was designed to dissuade you from signing up for unemployment.

Neill ran the gauntlet and took his paperwork home. He had to prove he had been looking for work and every time he asked a prospective employer, who had no intention of hiring him, to sign his little form Neill felt like the butt-end of nothing.

At home, he sat sunken in self-pity and despair.

Goffredo tried to get him out. Neill preferred staying home and reading.

Syrie called.

"Babe, I'm sorry," she inevitably said. "Lemme come over."

"I'm not up for it, Syrie. Sorry," Neill said. Neill felt a lethargy move through him and take residency in his heart.

"It's been a week since I've seen you."

"I'm having a hard time here," Neill spoke more sharply than he intended. Sweet Syrie, she deserved better.

"Ok, Babe," she said. Sadness trickled through the receiver.

After hanging up, Neill felt worse than ever. And he realized that he could not accept Syrie's succor. He realized he was through with Syrie and that made him dumpish and rounded by self-hatred.

He would have to tell her. Could he be honest with her?

Hurt Syrie Hardwood? He's rather cut off his own paw.

But in the end, he kept his paw and broke her everlasting heart.

And, heartbroken, smashed like a fine porcelain figure, Syrie cut off all her beautiful copper mane. She wore a bob and, bobbed, she floated on the surface of her tears, though she felt as if she were sinking.

It was the first time Neill thought about The Breakup Haircut.

Beautiful and Great in Bed and Still Not Enough

"She wept like a walrus o'er the waning moon."

"I can't believe you broke up with Syrie and quit your job," Bidden said.

"I know. It seems self-destructive, doesn't it? I'm a shitheel."

"I don't know. It's not that, is it? You're not just sweeping everything aside to start anew."

"No. I needed out of the corporate bookstore. I needed out."

"I understand that."

"And Syrie. What can I say? I love the fool out of her...but, she just didn't take me all the way. She wrote me a love letter once. It strained so hard at the English language that the language broke the leash and skipped away. Her attempt at being poetic was painful. *Painful.*"

"She's so beautiful."

"Not enough, right? Beautiful, loving, true, kind, listens to me when I read my poetry. And, it's not enough."

"I don't understand relationships, of course. I have no track record."

"Beautiful and great in bed and still not enough."

"She was great in bed, too?"

"Oh, Lord, Bid. She looked like a wet dream. And game for anything."

"Then you are crazy."

"I know. But—well, hell, I have a restless heart, I think. A restless cock, too."

"You didn't cheat on Syrie, did you?"

"Sure."

"Wow."

"I know. It's just that one starts thinking about the decline of the body, the putrefaction of what was once so vital and—well, it just seems ok to get the most out of things."

"You are in your 20s."

"I know. I started the death-worry early."

"I did, too. I wish I had your reckless sexual fantasy life as recompense."

"You really don't."

"Because it's not making you happy. Maybe there is something to the 'live in the moment' idea. Maybe you are looking forward too much, too quickly."

"I do that. When I am at a concert I can't wait for it to end so I can start remembering it. When I am reading a book I am thinking about the next book I can read."

"Live in the now, the new agers say."

"I have a problem with 'live each moment' and 'one day at a time,'" which are essentially the same thing except one is a little more humane. The problem is what if it's a bad moment or a bad day? And, similarly, there is the frightening corrective, every moment is new. There is no preparation for even *one damn moment.*"

Unemployment, More of It

The unemployment rigmarole was telling on Neill. His stress level was high.

He was jumping through all the hoops. He was turning in his paperwork. He was applying for jobs.

And every time he had to go to that Government Office of the Damned (GOD) another little piece of him died.

But the days were winding down. A clock was in Neill's chest and about to cuckoo. He had bent but did not break, and he was about to get his first unemployment check.

Apostles of The Word

In Memphis at this time, there was a plethora of small independent bookstores, all run by smart, well-meaning, literary folks: The Book Cottage in Germantown, its Midtown counterpart, The Book Cottage on the Square, Pinocchio's (a children's bookstore), The Roundtable, and The Book Shelf in Poplar Plaza.

Neill suspected that seeking employment at one of these lovely small bookstores was probably foolish. He suspected they were already staffed, low-paying and, he admitted to himself, sharper and more literary than he.

Nevertheless, he applied at The Roundtable and The Book Shelf.

At The Book Shelf, he met the two owners, rich, attractive women who loved books and were dedicated to selling them. They were apostles of the word, backed with their husbands' wealth.

Neill dutifully filled out the application, thanked each woman for her time, and was headed for the doorway.

"Wait!" he heard behind him.

He turned with a querulous expression.

"Can we talk for a minute?"

It was one of the owners, a woman named Ianthe Smith.

"You're Neill Rhymer?"

"I am," Neill said. This was making him nervous.

"Wait here for a moment. Please." Ianthe dragged her partner and another woman to the rear of the store where they disappeared into the stockroom. A confab was taking place.

Perhaps Neill was about to be arrested. Surely, he had committed a crime somewhere, sometime. He was trying to remember when and how.

Moments later they came back out.

"Sorry," Ianthe said. "This is my partner Maude. And our manager Heidi. You ran the mall store that won best bookstore."

"Oh. Yes, I did."

"Listen, can we talk for a few minutes."

"Sure."

They all went to the stockroom. They chatted for a few inconsequential minutes.

"When can you start?" Ianthe asked.

"Today," Neill said.

The ladies, oh the ladies laughed.

"Tomorrow? Nine-thirty?"

"I'll be here," Neill said, and he shook all their hands.

"There goes my job," he heard Heidi say to her bosses as he walked out of the store on the last day of his unemployment.

How to Celebrate

Neill went home and sat on the sofa and smiled while flipping through a copy of *Poets and Writers Magazine*. He felt good. A tad nervous, but pumped up by this new opportunity.

Neill called his parents and told them.

"How much is the pay?" his mother asked.

"That's great son," his father said.

Goffredo was working. Neill called Bidden.

"You off tonight?" Neill asked.

"Yeah, what's up?"

"I got a job. The Book Shelf in Poplar Plaza. I wanna celebrate."

"Oh, damn. I mean, that's great, Buddy. I've got a date with Gretel."

"Who's Gretel?"

"New employee. I want you to meet her. Third date."

"Meaning sex."

"Yes. Meaning something really closely approximating sex."

"Good for you, Man."

"I'll cancel though if—"

"The hell you will."

Now Neill wanted sex, too. He was the suggestible sort. And, of course, he was never far from thinking about sex. But he had no partner and no possibility. He had not even looked around much after dumping Syrie and being dumped in turn by Abby.

Neill called Syrie.

"Hi," Syrie said. "Surprise."

"You have a cold?"

"No, I'm ok."

"What are you doing tonight?"

A pause so pregnant, it might have been triplets.

"I'm supposed to work." She practically whispered it.

"I got a job today. Looking for someone to celebrate with."

"That's great, Neill. Where?"

"Bookstore. In Poplar Plaza."

"That's wonderful. Good for you."

"The unemployment thing was really weighing on me. "

"I know. Lemme call in sick. I can be there by six."

"Really?" Now Neill was overjoyed at the prospect of seeing Syrie again. (Consider the human animal. [Have we said this before?])

"Yeah, I'll even bring dinner."

"Wonderful."

After talking to Syrie Neill felt even better. He took a quick shower. It was 4:10. He was leaping about inside his own head. He could not settle into his book (John Fowles' *The Ebony Tower*). The TV was babbling flumadiddle. He was nervous. About seeing Syrie again? He couldn't figure it out.

At 6:03 Syrie knocked on the apartment door.

"Hi. I'm so glad you could come," Neill said. He put his arms around her.

"Oop," Syrie said, holding her casserole dish in one hand.

Neill kissed her quickly on the mouth.

"And you brought food!"

"Well, you know I'm not that great in the kitchen." (This was sadly true.)

"Anything will be gravy."

"Gravy? Did you expect something with gravy?" Her lovely face creased.

"No, no, I meant gravy, extra special. The real treat is seeing you."

"Oh." Syrie smiled. "Mac and cheese with hotdogs mixed in." She uncovered the dish with the flourish of Vanna White.

"I love that!" Neill said. He meant it. Not quite as good as beanies and weenies, but close.

Syrie prepared two bowls and microwaved them. Neill fixed ice tea. They sat in the living room on the couch and watched *Sanford and Son*, which Neill hated. They ate mostly in silence.

"This is good," Neill said. "Soul food."

"Soul food," Syrie echoed.

"And *Sanford and Son*," Neill said.

"Tell me about the job."

Neill related concisely his brief interview at The Book Shelf.

After they ate, they sat face to face. Neill took Syrie's fingers in his fingers. Conversation was coming hard.

"Dessert?" Syrie asked.

"I want you," Neill said.

Syrie jerked her head as if she had a twitch.

"You want me?"

"For dessert," Neill said, and then felt bad, as if he were saying only as dessert.

"Oh."

"Sorry—I—"

"Don't be sorry. You want to have sex with me?"

"I really do," Neill said.

"You can. Anytime. I mean that. Any time. I will come any time day or night and do anything you want. Maybe that is pitiful."

"Syrie, you're too good for me."

"Don't say that, Neill. Don't tell me I deserve someone better."

"Ok," Neill said.

Syrie leaned forward. She put her mouth over Neill's. It shut him up and it was balm, an answer to the chaos and doubt in his mind. Neill stopped thinking (as much as Neill ever stopped thinking).

Soon, they were in the bedroom.

Soon, they were naked except Syrie had on a pair of panties so sheer and brief they looked like they were made of fog. They were new.

Soon, she didn't have those on either.

Soon, Syrie was atop Neill like a Bridge Over Troubled Waters. She had his cock in her mouth and her ass was in his face and he was licking her hot pussy.

But before he came he whispered to her, "Get on me. I want to come inside you."

Syrie climbed onto him. Neill watched her intense, beautiful face as she rode him hard. She was after her own orgasm and soon she had gotten there, eyes clenched tightly closed.

"Now you," she said, with the same husky intensity.

She grabbed Neill's balls and lovingly bobbled them, briefly pushing them against her own ass. This caused the surge in Neill he had been craving.

Right before he let loose, he opened his eyes to find Syrie staring at him with wide, wet eyes. Neill put his hands over her wee breasts and came hard.

Afterward, they found their old position and lay in afterglow like beached seals.

"God, Syrie, you are so good in bed," Neill said.

Syrie began to cry.

"I'm sorry. Don't. Don't cry."

"Neill," she managed.

"Don't cry, Syrie. I will always love you."

She raised her eyes. "Really, Neill?"

"Absolutely." Neill could not add a qualifier. Not now.

"My mother asked me where I was going and I didn't lie."

"Hm," Neill said.

"And Aunt Canter said something mean about you. She's a shriveled up old thing and frustrated and a liar."

"Hey, did you have your diaphragm in? I forgot to ask I was so carried away." Neill was happy to steer the conversation away from Syrie's family.

"I do."

They thought about that for a minute.

"So, you anticipated that we would have sex."

"We always have sex," Syrie said, now suddenly shy. "Did you notice the new panties?"

"For me?"

"Neill, only for you."

"I love you, Syrie Hardwood."

"I love you, Neill Rhymer. Forever. I love you forever."

Day One, The Book Shelf in Poplar Plaza

It didn't take Neill long to learn the simple clerking duties at the new bookstore. Both owners were there and the manager, Heidi. They were all so nice Neill thought he had landed in Paradise. There was no underlying stress to the place. The customers were a motley lot and many of them came in for Literature. Capital L. Neill had some old doubts return: *Am I brainy enough for the customers here? Well-read enough?*

There was one other clerk on duty. An elderly woman named Betty. The Book Shelf did a great business in cards and stationery, handling wedding invitations, and the like. Betty was in charge of this. Betty was kind also, and Neill was to learn later, had a dry wit worthy of her namesake Betty White. A Betty White wit.

When it was lunch time Neill asked what was good in the Poplar Plaza. He was told the Kroger deli was pretty good and the Britling's Cafeteria a few stores down. Neill, a big fan of the Southern fare cooked up in cafeterias, headed there. He lunched on fried chicken livers, green beans, corn bread, and whipped potatoes. It was as satisfying as his new job.

When he got home that night he called his folks and told them how well it went.

"That's great son," they said.

Then, he called Syrie.

"The first day was so much fun. I think I'm gonna love it there."

"I'm so happy, Neill."

"Wanna come over?"

"I started my period today."

"Meaning no?"

"I'll come. I'll come right now."

And she did and it was delightful.

The Love Tattoo

Readers, even we don't want to leave Syrie behind. This account, like life itself, is subject to the whims of the winds of change. We love Syrie, perhaps even more than Neill does (or did). She will pop up now and then because love does that: it leaves a gluey residue that one never quite cleanses. In this way, love is like a tattoo. You can take it off but it leaves a scar.

(Think about metaphors and how appropriate they are in talking about the human heart. Perhaps re-edit.)

She may pop up again. She may have to.

A New Phase of Flesh-Loneliness

Now, Neill entered a phase in his life where he spent many evenings alone or with Bidden, Crow, and Gulley. He did not want another girlfriend, and he did not want to be without sex, and he was as mixed-up and conflicted as any relatively happy adult in the world at that particular time.

He loved his job and, as the months passed, he found that he was quite good at it. He did not know if the grounding he received at Walden's would help him in this new, headier environment, but it did, and he flourished. He was reading and writing constantly, and he was meeting new people. The clientele at The Book Shelf was an inspiration to him and he found himself quickly enamored of many new men and women. Customers became friends.

He was thrilled one afternoon when Shelby Foote dropped in and Neill nervously conversed with him. Mr. Foote was an imposing gentleman, wise as Time and Silence, and kindly, too. He seemed genuinely pleased to talk books with a young, wet-behind-the-ears bookseller. Neill had just finished reading Joyce's *Ulysses* and he, on a whim, brought this up in their conversation. It turned out that Shelby Foote was an expert on Joyce and his statements about *Ulysses* opened Neill's head the way a can opener opens a can of beanie-weenies.

After he left, Neill said to Betty: "I just talked to Shelby Foote." There were little cartoon whirlies in Neill's eyes.

"He comes in often," Betty said.

"You know him?"

"I've known Shelby since we were both teenagers," modest, funny Betty said. "He was a wild one."

The other staff at The Book Shelf consisted of a kindly middle-aged woman named Esther, who was a Christian Scientist, and who was one of the nicest humans Neill ever encountered, and an uncooperative scallywag named Iago. Neill initially warmed to Iago but eventually learned that he was lazy, self-important, and, well, as strange as a warlock's dream.

Still, Neill relished his job and soon would openly declare that working in a small independent literary bookstore was about as good as life got.

Neill was happy.

And flesh-lonely, oh so flesh-lonely.

Nights

Neill spent a lot of time at home with Goffredo. They had discovered that a VCR made for some extremely gratifying evenings of staying at home. Suddenly, there were new businesses everywhere, sprung to life overnight like mushrooms: video stores. They were everywhere!

There was a small store in Raleigh, not too far from their apartment. One could also rent movies at almost every other business.

Kroger, groceries and Video Rental.

Big Cat Records and Video Rental.

Patterson's lingerie and Video Rental.

Burton Tires and Video Rental.

New World Flooring and Video Rental.

Egg Candling and Video Rental.

Vookles Moving Service and Video Rental.

Alley's Exterminating Company and Video Rental.

Minette's Escort Service and Video Rental.

Reynold's Sunrooms and Windows and Video Rental.

When they weren't watching movies, they were reading books or going to the P&H, or going to any of the movie emporia around the city. It was around this time that The Memphian turned itself into a second-run movie house. They showed two movies a night (Antonioni and Altman, Bergman and Bertolucci, Huston and Hawks, Godard and Guest, Sturges and Scorcese), and with a big Coke and some popcorn, it was a thrilling evening out. Sometimes, Neill and his cronies went 3 times a week. Neill's cinematic tutelage was enhanced.

(Neill would have stuck with The Memphian forever, enjoying double features 3 or 4 times a week but, eventually, like the USSR, something this grand could not last. Dwindling audiences created grumbling. Then, the heating went out and the bill to fix it was too onerous for them to continue. Neill was there that last week, in bitter, icy January, like in the USSR, watching a double feature of *Death in Venice* and *Lolita*, shivering in his pea coat, feet numb, date [who was it?] impatient and then outright angry.)

Sometimes, it didn't matter if he didn't have a woman in his life.

Sometimes, it hurt like all get-out.

He and Bidden talked over their broken hearts. Gretel had dumped Bidden for a lumberjack who quoted Kipling.

"She had a voice you could use to grate cheese," Bidden said. "But I still wasn't through seeing her naked."

"I feel for you, Buddy. I need some canoodling and soon."

"You're not seeing Syrie anymore? I thought y'all occasionally got together."

Neill was shamed.

"We do. I'm terrible. I'm stringing her along and I don't mean to."

"How often?"

"Once a week at the most. I sincerely try not to. But she calls and I go all mushy."

"You go all horny."

"Yes. But, you know, it's hard to get her off the phone when she calls. I feel like I am walking on eggshells, trying to say the right thing, the honest thing. Talking to her on the phone is like talking to Marvin K. Mooney. She doesn't hear the conversational cues that mean I am wrapping this up now. And I end up inviting her over."

"That's rough."

"You're being sarcastic. I know I am lucky to still have her young beautiful body without strings but it's tearing me up. I feel guilty all the time."

"I feel guilty all the time but without the sexual element."

"What if doing something horrible makes you happy?"

"I guess you stop doing it. I don't know."

"I don't know either."

Enter Shlomo Einstein

Along with more literary customers came more book signings and more hero worship from Neill. Writer after writer graced The Book Shelf touting their newest releases. Among writers Neill felt simultaneously infatuated, cowed, and thrilled.

There were also authors Neill did not warm to, nor even speak to: the snooty chick who wrote *The YuppieSourcebook*, the jerky head-shrinker, who wrote the religious self-help book, *The Road Unrivaled*. There was the peculiar medico who penned the unforgettable *Rear Wind: A Book about Farting*. The great folklorist and religious philosopher Eliade came for his autobiography, *Mircea, Mircea Me*. Etc.

There was also Richard Ford and Rosellen Brown, Willie Morris and Eskimo Sidebottom, Alane Rollings and Budd Insky. Ellen Gilchrist and Euphonious Moniker.

And there was a Jewish writer who lived in Memphis whose name was Shlomo Einstein. Shlomo wore wire rim glasses, sported a Gene Shalit mustache and had a tangled skein of black curls he sometimes let grow long, ala Harpo Marx. He had published a collection of short stories called *The Legend of the Tabletops*, with a small Arkansas Press, Illegitimate Editions. He and Neill had talked a bit back at Walden's when that little tome came out and Neill immediately liked him, even if overawed by his obvious smarts.

When Stately Mansion Books was set to publish Shlomo's first novel, *Mooning When the Sun Don't Shine*, Shlomo paid a call on The Book Shelf to see if they would host a signing for him. He and Neill ended up going out to lunch at Britling's. Over plates of fried food, they began a friendship that would last the rest of their lives, even after Shlomo went on to the fame we are all familiar with.

"You know I've already read *Mooning*. Your publisher sent it to me in manuscript form. It's quite splendid." ('Quite splendid' sounded ridiculous to Neill, but he found himself questioning his every sentence, such was his insecurity.) "It deserves to be published by a bigger house."

"Every writer has his 'coming close' story. Mine was when Gordon Lish asked me to come to New York and have lunch with him. At the time, he was editing for Random House. We had the lunch. He sang my praises. Random House paid for everything, including my air fare, and I left New York City feeling puffed up and full of myself."

"Random House," Neill parroted.

"So, a few phone calls and I find out that Lish doesn't have the kind of power he thought he had, or I thought he had, and his bosses were unconvinced when he declared me the next great Jewish American writer, to follow in the footsteps of Bellow, Roth, and Ozick."

"Damn. Still. How many writers come that close? You'll break out, if that's the right expression. Meantime, you have that confidence booster to keep you going back to the typewriter."

"Oh, you know....as a writer my confidence waxes and wanes. And when it waxes, it leaves me hairless."

They scheduled a signing. Neill fell in love with Shlomo Einstein. Life was becoming more interesting.

Do You Think We'll Always be Like This?

"Where do you see us, five years from now?" Bidden asked as Wanda set a burger in front of him.

"You're asking, can we see beyond this? Beyond our lifeless lives, lives without commitment or hope?" Neill said.

"Jesus, was I asking that?"

"You're asking, will we always be like this?"

"In five years, ten?"

"In a lifetime? What else is there for us, for all of us?"

Crow, Bidden, Neill, Pas. Holding pattern?

Show Me the Way to the Next Little Girl

Neill was still spending many hours alone or with Goffredo watching sometimes two movies in one night. (*Panic in Needle Park* and *Demon Bug!*) Goffredo had just gotten a new job with an office supply store in East Memphis. The roommates talked about looking for a small house inside the city limits rather than out on the gray barnacle called Raleigh. Neill began to scout houses to rent.

Around this time, Neill had an unexpected visitor at The Book Shelf.

He was on the floor opening a carton of books from the book distributor, Ingram, when he heard a female voice above him.

"Buy a girl a paperback?"

His eyes found a pair of tennis shoes at the bottom of a long pair of bare, shapely legs. His eye traveled upward as slowly as he felt allowed, past the dress hem, over the slim waist, pausing upon the shapely bosom, until he finally found a dollbaby face from his past. Standing over him was Helen Guru. The Guru family had lived in Scenic Hills near Victoria's parents' home, and Victoria and Neill had babysat for Helen when she was a wee one. Here she was grown up. Or nearly.

Neill rose and shook Helen's hand. Helen kept Neill's hand in hers. Her teenage face aimed at sauciness and came damn close.

"Helen! What brings you here?"

"I wanted to see you, Neillo," she breezed.

"Well, what a happy thing. It's good to see you. You've (how to say this without inappropriate ogling)…grown up."

"You like?"

Now, she was giving out with the sauce. It was all over her. Neill wanted to lick it off. Little Helen Guru had grown up to be beautiful.

"I do," he said.

"Take me out?"

"What—what do you mean? Now?"

"No, tonight?"

"I can't tonight," Neill said. It was a kneejerk reaction.

"Ok. Soon?"

"Sure," Neill said.

"Walk me to my car?"

"You're driving?"

"Neillo, I'm 16, not 12."

"Right. Betty, gonna step outside for just a moment," Neill shouted back. Betty gave him the fisheye.

Helen was driving a little convertible sports car. Neill knew the Gurus had money but not enough to buy their 16-year-old daughter a sports car.

"Like my car?"

"I do, Helen. I like the car. I like you. I am in a liking mood."

Helen laughed as if Neill were Mort Sahl.

"Can we do something soon? Really, Neillo?"

"I guess so," Neill said, hesitantly, but he could not stop smiling.

"I've had a crush on you ever since you brought me McDonald's French fries when I was 6."

"Ha! Helen. Were you 6? Were you ever 6?"

And here, Helen leaned forward and kissed Neill on the mouth, letting her little teenage tongue slip inside.

"My day off is tomorrow," Neill said, realizing there was no turning back. There was no cavalry coming, no *deus ex machina*. He had spoken the words that broke the Seventh Seal. "What time does school let out?"

So, the next day Neill found himself on the campus of Central High School waiting for a child he babysat once upon a time to emerge—and—then what? Neill was often amused by his own absurdity. He was also often appalled.

Helen Guru came running out the rear school door into the parking lot. She looked ten years old—if you didn't look at her body.

"Neillo!" she screamed. "You're here!"

"Did you think I'd renege?"

"No, no. I know you are true blue."

She hopped into the passenger side of the faded yellow Toyota and threw her books into the back seat. Her dress was so short Neill was surprised Central High School hadn't had her arrested.

"Where we going?" Helen said. She was nervous. She was also cocky. It was an incongruous combination and at the same time very endearing.

"You want some ice cream?"

"Neillo, I am not the kid you babysat anymore."

Neill chuckled. "Ok, where to, Captain?"

"How far away is your place?"

Neill squinted. "Helen, do you know what you are doing?"

"I'm trying to seduce you. Am I not doing it right?"

"You're doing it better than right. There is the little problem—"

"I won't tell anyone," Helen Guru said. And she put her palm on Neill's thigh.

The drive back to Raleigh was awkward, long, bizarre, and titillating. Frankly, Neill had fantasized the night before about what Helen's almost grown-up body would look like. Now he was balking. Had he not learned his lesson with Syrie?

In the apartment Helen ran around looking at every piece of bad art, at every poster, at every bookshelf.

"Your room?" she asked, leading Neill into it.

"Yes," Neill said. Helen flopped down on the bed. Her dress rode up even further. Her panties were pink. "Music?"

"Yes. You have any Joni Mitchell?"

"Of course."

Neill put on *Blue* and lay down next to Helen Guru.

They began kissing. She really knew how to kiss and her mouth was minty.

Though a dash faint-hearted, he sent his hands scouting. His right hand found her bare thigh and it was as smooth as a cherub's cheeks. He reached under the tight dress and under the pink panties and found her sweet spherical ass a delightful delight.

Now Neill took his own shirt, shoes, socks, and pants off. He was only wearing his briefs.

Helen sat up and pulled the dress over her head. She was not wearing a bra, which was amazing since her breasts were so ample. They stood up by themselves, he marveled. Ah, youth!

Now, he lay back down and pressed his body against hers. What gratifying pliable flesh!

Neill sucked on those breasts. They were obscenely rounded and firm. The nipples were the size of pips.

Now, in his heat, Neill pulled Helen's pink panties off. And then removed his own underwear. He lay next to her and began to kiss her as if she were his best love.

Helen, now, was hesitating. She had lost some of her swagger.

Neill stopped his roaming hands. He waited. Something was coming and he did not know what it was and he doubted it was gonna be good.

"Do you love me?" Helen asked.

Neill stopped. His heart fell out onto the counterpane. His bagpipes deflated. He pulled Helen Guru against himself, sorrier than he'd ever been seeing a woman naked and holding her.

"Helen, we will stop now," he said.

Helen let a tear or two fall.

"I can bring you off if you want," she said. Her dollhouse was crumbling.

"I do love you, Helen Guru," Neill said. "So, get dressed, and let's go get some ice cream."

Our House is a Very Fine House

It came to pass that Neill found a wonderful house to rent near Memphis State for a price he and Goffredo could afford. It was on Holmes Circle, just west of the campus and just east of The Memphis Country Club. It was small and ecru-colored and had a tiny kitchen, a nice dining room and living room (with working fireplace) and two bedrooms, one off the hall and one at the end of it. Neill took the one at the end and was happy to do so because it was quieter. The house was warmed in the winter by floor furnaces and cooled in the summer by window units. It had a long, narrow, smallish backyard with an old shed that, at one time, had been a carport. The shed looked like it might be concealing Jimmy Hoffa's corpse.

Neill and Goffredo moved in during a balmy Spring morning. Neill's dad, Bidden, Gulley (he of the quarterback build, who could lift the heavier items by himself), and Crow helped the move. Crow had a small pickup truck in which they hauled the furniture. Around noon they took a break, ordered some pizzas, and sat around the new front yard (shaded by a walnut tree) and talked of things to come.

They finished the move in late afternoon and, though Neill hated the clutter, the dusty items moved with their dust intact, and the unpacked boxes (72 just for the books!), he went to bed that night pleased with his new home, pleased with his new life. Poplar Plaza, where Neill worked, was a 3-minute drive. On nice days, he could walk.

Though it was balmy Spring, one of the first purchases Neill made for the new house was a cord of wood, delivered and stacked for a mere $45, in the yard beside Jimmy Hoffa's tool shed. Neill later taught himself how to make a good fire in that fireplace. It was an entity of deep pride and comfort.

Wednesday Night Basketball

Wednesday night basketball. It became important to Neill.

Goffredo, Hawker, and that winsome Coach Elaine. A couple more guys from Bartlett, Ted, Jerry, sometimes Lafayette Porch, and sometimes Mick, making it a foursome from Kenneth Street, stretching the childhood tether.

Full court. Five on five. It was the only way to play.

Neill liked being on Elaine's team because she was kind to him and, both playing guard, she would feed him sweet passes and he would try to return the favor. He liked playing against her also because he could mask his desire to touch her slim, graceful body, with his desire to play good defense.

Here's Neill as a player: he's got a nice jump shot from 20 feet or so, occasionally on good nights, from 3-point range; he can't handle the ball well to save his life (this was somewhat hidden in half-court ball, or driveway ball) and hence was a spot-up shooter (though he had a running one-hander that was somewhat indefensible, a shot honed on his backyard court due to the court's narrow confines—Neill literally shot it falling out of bounds); he feared being hurt and physical contact, so he was a lousy rebounder; he feared making an ass out of himself against some of the more athletic, more gifted players.

And there were some Wednesday Night guys who played high school ball, one guy who played for a junior college. They daunted our Neill.

Nevertheless, how glorious it was to do something so strenuous, so competitive, so fun, a couple hours each week.

And they were a hardy and loyal lot. They rarely missed a Wednesday (even playing when the unairconditioned gym's temperature was literally 100+ degrees) and, when they did, they were surly as bulls among bumblebees. They sat around their bar of choice and cussed and talked about nookie and bitched about their jobs.

Neill normally didn't attend the bar get-togethers, which were also a part of the tradition after every game, sweaty and full of testosterone, drinking beer, munching on bar nuts.

Neill didn't drink. And many Wednesday nights he had an after-game date, or a novel waiting. And, let's remind ourselves: Neill was not that social.

A Discussion, Late Night, a New Place called Antenna

Bidden: So how long have you been coming here?

Neill: Just a couple weekends.

Bidden: It's loud.

Neill: That's just the videos on the TVs. Wait till you hear the band.

Bidden: Music videos. Who came up with that?

Neill: A genius.

Bidden: Should we sit at one of the tables?

Neill: I don't know. I don't think so. I've never seen anyone do it.

Bidden: We just stand in the back here?

Neill: And watch the beautiful women dance.

Bidden: They are beautiful. The one in the leather jumpsuit.

Neill: I think that's the drummer's girlfriend.

Bidden: How do you know?

Neill: I asked last weekend.

Bidden: You asked her to dance?

Neill: Right. Like I would do that. Dance. With the drummer's girlfriend.

Bidden:

Neill:

Bidden: I don't know.

Neill: Is it horny in here or is it just me?

Bidden: Huh. I am feeling whatever the opposite of sexual is.

Neill: Dead?

Bidden: Not quite that.

Neill: Asexual?

Bidden: Ok.

Neill: Ask the drummer's girlfriend to dance.

Bidden: Right.

Neill: Sorry, you wanna go to P&H. It's only a hundred yards away.

Bidden: I don't know.

Neill: Wait, here comes the band.

Bidden:

Neill:

Bidden:

Neill: OK. YEAH. LET'S GO NEXT DOOR.

There Were Dates, There was Some Concubitus

Neill, though often lonely, though there were many evenings at home with his books and his fireplace and his VCR and Goffredo or Crow or Bidden, still managed to have a few dates. He complained to anyone who would listen if he went a few weeks with no female contact. Neill was a kvetcher, a bitcher, a man who believed, if he wasn't promised a rose garden, he was at least promised a little loam once in a while in which to bury his seed.

So, sometimes people fixed him up. Sometimes he approached women at the P&H or at the bookstore, and sometimes he was charming enough to get a date or two. There were many misfires, of course. Put two strangers together in the Skinner Box of a date and you often get a scuppered experiment, an inert coupling, a stink.

Sometimes though there was sweet sex, even with strangers. This was still a while before AIDs became the prevailing proctor for promiscuous single folks. This was still when only pregnancy was the real scare.

So, women were sometimes as loose as Neill, sometimes more so. Sometimes, they did not want second dates and this hurt Neill if he thought he had made a good impression and had liked the woman. Just as often they fell a little for Neill and Neill did not fall in return.

There was the woman, a friend of Victoria's, a beautiful buxom blond waitress named Malty Shag, who liked books and who liked sex even more. She also had a boyfriend.

Neill pursued her. Eventually, he wore her down. She agreed to a low-pressure, one-time date. They went out to eat. Then they found a leafy bower next to a man-made lake in Chickasaw Gardens (a gated community), which was less than a mile from Neill's house but, within that bower, time and distance were malleable, and the place seemed as if it were Tarzan's jungle. It was a Lost World in the middle of posh Chickasaw Gardens. Sometimes, there were dinosaurs.

They sat on a hard stone bench and watched the ducks. And tried to talk. Neill tried to find his witty banter. It had departed with the milk money and without so much as a note.

The woman, banana-blond hair cut in a hip style that stirred Neill, wide pale blue eyes and lips like strawberry wine, batted some of Neill's weak attempts back. Neill thought: this is awkward, I am going to kiss her.

He slowly found his way to her mouth and her lips were as soft as pap and she welcomed Neill's tongue and offered hers in return. Neill pulled her close. Her breasts rumbled across Neill's chest like thunderclouds.

"Jesus, I've wanted to do that for a while," Neill said when they broke.

"We haven't known each other that long," she said back, but her smile was devilish.

Neill kissed her again. There was heat. He was starting to relax.

"Well, what say?" Neill said when they broke again.

"What say what?"

"My place. A stone's throw from here."

"Not a glass house then."

"Funny, you're funny. You wanna go back there and leg wrestle?"

She laughed. They went to the car.

Once inside Neill's dusty, fuscy room, Neill felt this woman's presence as if a carnal spirit was perfuming the air. He wanted her so badly.

After some vigorous necking, they were down to underpants. She wouldn't take hers off. Her breasts were so large, they were almost too large. Bigger even than Orbit's but not as firm. When she leaned forward, they elongated like water balloons. Neill was as hard as a miner's life.

"We can't fuck," this blond goddess said. "But I want to suck your dick."

Her language surprised him.

She stood up. She pulled Neill's briefs off. He was at full attention. She stood above him and bent from the waist.

"Mm," she said. "I love giving head."

And she did. She loved it and was effing good at it. Neill was watching her dangling breasts, hearing her slurping sounds, thrusting in and out of her watery mouth, and he began to fear that something was wrong.

She looked up from her work.

"Do you want to come on my face? Would you like that? Shoot off all over my face, yeah?"

Then something happened that was unprecedented for our hero. His tool began to buck and jitter and pump and nothing—nil—nada—emptiness—no damn thing came out. It was an orgasm without jism! What the hell? Neill asked the gods. He was shooting blanks! He wanted to give this incredibly sexy creature his best goop. Dammit!

For her part, she sensed it was over and quickly got under the covers. Apparently, she was going to spend the night. Neill's heart was trying to get out of its cage.

"Do you mind if I masturbate?" she asked as Neill turned the light out.

"Jesus," Neill said.

"What?"

"That makes me feel—" But Neill didn't know how it made him feel.

"I thought it might turn you on," she said, simply.

"Let me go down on you," Neill now offered.

"No. The panties stay on." This was, evidently, the rubrics she had established for herself for the evening. She had a boyfriend, you know?

So, Neill slept not at all and the next morning this woman kissed him as she leapt from bed and said, "Bye, Neill, sorry I got to fly."

And Neill was left alone with his terrible feeling. He had stepped onto the adult stage and been embarrassed. He couldn't cut it in the big leagues.

By coincidence, a week later, this bombshell moved into Neill's neighborhood. Neill had called her a couple times during the week but she told Neill she felt too guilty to get together with him again. One Sunday morning, he walked down to her new house and she was awake but still in her pajamas, soft cotton patterned blouse and pants, her breasts barely tamed.

Neill went in. They sat on her futon. Neill pulled her to him and kissed her. It was like kissing the hem of her garment. She was through with Neill.

Later, to make it worse, it wasn't the boyfriend that was the stumbling block. He was out and someone from one of the touring metal bands was in. And Neill was so far out he was invisible.

There Were Dates, There was Some Concubitus 2

Then, there was the petite brunette who was a friend of a friend. She had come into the bookstore and asked Neill out. He was taken aback. How lovely, he thought. And she was too, lovely, like a fawn.

She cooked him dinner, pasta that was quite filling and expanded in Neill's gut after consuming it. Post dessert they went straight to bed, which was just off the kitchen in her small apartment.

She rode Neill, and she was small and yellowish-brown and her breasts were pleasant small roundnessess and she came and Neill came inside her (she was wearing a diaphragm, ok?), and Neill kissed her goodnight.

Then, he never called her again. And, she didn't come into the bookstore again.

Years later, Neill thought she returned to buy books and Neill not only couldn't remember her name but he couldn't remember exactly what they had done together. Or if it really was her. For her part she asked Neill for a book as if he were Sylvia Beach, or some other bookselling stranger.

And there was the daughter of one of the city's richest families. Neill spotted her in P&H one night and knew her vaguely from mutual friends. He asked her out and she was enthusiastic with her assent.

Their first date was a double date with Bidden and his new lover, Clementine (we think that was her name—*check this.*). They went to the Mid-South Fair and were having a hellishly good time. Neill bought a turkey drumstick as big as a car axle for his dinner and Bidden said, "This is the Mid-South Fair we will remember as the year Neill got the pterodactyl leg for dinner." The two couples strolled languidly, played a few games, skee-ball and target shooting. The women wanted to ride rides and they did a few. Neill was not high on rides, especially high rides. I don't like any activity where my feet aren't on the ground, he said. His date smiled and leaned against him in a friendly way.

At one of the booths—the one where you shoot a water pistol into a clown's mouth—Neill's date leaned forward to aim and, maybe it was the pistol-to-mouth image, Neill boldly leaned against her, pressing his half-stiffy into the pronounced crack of her ass. She turned and smiled. She filled her clown.

Neill took her hand as they walked away. She whispered in his ear, "That tribute to me?"

"It is," Neill said.

At Neill's house, they couldn't wait to strip each other completely naked. It was raucous good fun.

"Oh my," Neill said. "Your breasts."

"Approve?" she simpered. She knew he approved. They were Ann-Margaret breasts.

Neill lapped there avidly.

He kissed down her stomach.

She was panting.

Neill ran a tongue down her navel and into her pubic hair.

She panted his name.

Then he slowly circled the thickly-haired whizzer. Abruptly, he was caught up short. He almost stopped but he was too much of a gentleman. Her fish pond smelled like all the fish had died and no one thought to haul them away. It was overpoweringly malodorous.

Still Neill dove. He tried not breathing while he licked and sucked. It went on forever. He thought he might faint. Finally, she gave with the arching back and the dirty string of syllables and fell back, sweaty and flushed.

Neill sheepishly crawled next to her. He put a hand over her stomach. He could taste the bad odor on his lips.

"Wow, no wonder you're popular," she said. "You give great head."

Neill thought, *Am I popular?*

Then, she reciprocated and it was good. Blowjobs are always good. Always.

Neill tried a 2nd date with her and even a 3rd. He was praying that she was only having a bad night on their first date. But it was not to be. She stank.

They did manage an ok fuck on the 3rd date but, then Neill stopped calling her. She called once or twice then stopped. Neill wasn't that popular.

More Tales from The Book Shelf

Meanwhile Neill continued to grow in stature at his small independent bookstore. And, again it came to pass, that indeed, he did take over the manager's position and the old manager, Heidi, moved on to other things.

It was the time in Neill's life when he began to hone his reading skills. He was in search of more and better writers. He wanted to read them all, the Victorians, the modernists, the postmodernists, the prosaic and the wild, the ludic and the loony. It was the era of the Rise of South American Authors (on the great coattails of Garcia Marquez, came Jorge Amado, Julio Cortazar, Jose Donozo, Mario Vargas Llosa, etc., suddenly spreading magic realism [a new term at the time] like Nutella across the fat belly of America) and this rise was boosted by

Avon's shiny paperbacks, all designed in a similar and recognizable style. Neill devoured them like marzipan.

(Neill hates marzipan? Check this. ed.)

It was also the era of James Herriot and Lee Iacocca, whose books sold like water. It was the era of *Bright Lights, Big City*, and its concomitant launch of Vintage Contemporaries. It was the era of John Jakes, John Irving, and Leo Buscaglia. Of Stephen King and Pat Conroy, Danielle Steel and Umberto Eco. Of *The Silver Palate Cookbook*.

And Neill began to love, in earnest, some of the clientele at his new place of work. How to say this? A better class of people?

No, but richer. Decidedly richer. The owners were rich and their friends were rich, and this was a beautiful time in human development when rich people bought hardback books and almost exclusively from neighborhood bookstores. What a life! What a way of life!

And, because money makes people prettier, the customers were prettier.

Ok, that's absurd.

But—Jesus—there were a lot of pretty women. Pretty women. Like Richard Cory they glittered.

There was one gaggle of beautiful women who were part of a book club and they all ordered their books from The Book Shelf. Neill dubbed them The Gorgeous Young Housewives Book Club. When they found out their 'secret' moniker, they tittered and glowed and flirted with Neill. Neill wanted to fuck them all. One by one, of course.

There was one in particular. Let's call her Luna. (Because Luna Wildfowl was her name.)

She was about ten years older than Neill and married to a guy in his 70s, a rich guy, of course, a filthy rich guy, a guy who bought her a home in Chickasaw Gardens and sired upon her beautiful twin girls.

One winter day, Luna came in and she was wearing a fur hat that surrounded her flushed-from-the-cold face like a nimbus and Neill had to steady himself on the counter. She was Zhivago's Lara.

"Gorgeous Young Housewives Book Club," she said and her smile was a slice of cheesecake.

"Heh heh," Neill said.

Behind him, Iago wrung his chapped-raw hands and cursed Neill. His jealousy burned like Tophet's fire.

"How are you today, Neill," Luna tweeted. Her eyes caught the glint off every reflective surface. She was too bonny to look at directly. Neill thought he should be punching a hole in a piece of cardboard.

"Ok," Neill croaked. "Anne Tyler?"

"Yes, we're doing *Earthly Possessions*. Do you like Anne Tyler?"

Neill immediately vowed to begin reading Anne Tyler that night.

"I adore her," Neill said.

"What's your favorite?" Luna stood in front of Neill with the eyes of Laura Mars.

"Uh, the one, the one with the housewife..."

"Hm. I don't know. There are a lot of housewives in Anne Tyler."

"I know. I love that."

An awkward silence sat upon them like the shade of a black umbrella.

"Well, ok. Good to see you," Luna tinkled. And turned to go.

"Be careful out there," Neill said, with too much heat.

Luna turned, smiled, and re-ascended.

Book Signings at The Book Shelf during Neill's First Year and a Half

Barry Hannah for *Ray*

Jean Fritz for *Champion Dog, Prince Tom*

Creole Myers for *I Had a Good Time and Nothing Made Me Sick*

Rosellen Brown for *Cora Fry*

Norm du Plume for *What we Talk About when We Talk about Books Beginning with What we Talk About*

Carla Binnage for *The Gentle Art of Fetch*

Bird Hurt for *When You Wish Upon a Tsar*

Burned out Memphis Rock Star Ginger (of Ginger and the Minnow Crew) for *Doobie or Not Doobie*

Choo Choo Everingham for her picture book *Hey Bajiba!*

Elizabeth Spencer for *The Stories of Elizabeth Spencer*

Frank Sheen for *Share Jesus without Fear: A Guide to Holding Your Own Last Suppers*

Rob Elyas for *De modo cacendi*

Nudist/health nut Ann Wee for *Yoga Bare*

Bernard Malamute for *Orts for Fido: A Poor Man's Dog*

Bill Page for *Clutch Plates*

Clarence Hightower for *The World According to AARP*

Also, at this time, the novelist and short story write, Peter Taylor was teaching for a semester at Memphis State. He made frequent visits to The Book Shelf and Neill found himself enamored of the gentleman who would win the Pulitzer Prize for his next novel *Summons to Memphis*.

Like Shelby Foote, Peter Taylor was a great conversationalist and, though nervous, Neill enjoyed their brief friendship, if he could call it that.

Neill told Mr. Taylor that he had just read Eileen Simpson's account of Taylor's peer group (Berryman, Lowell, Schwartz, etc.) entitled *Poets in their Youth*.

"That's one of my favorite accounts of that time," Peter Taylor said.

"It seemed to me that you came off as the hero of the group, the steady hand, the one always ready with the generous loan, the necessary bail. You really seemed a hero," Neill gushed.

"Perhaps that is why that book seemed so good to me," Peter Taylor said.

Enter the Goorile Family

They were like Russian matryoshka dolls. Mrs. Goorile, a beautiful woman in her 50s, and three daughters, eldest, middle, and child. They came in. They chatted. They bought good books and could talk good books.

Mrs. Goorile's favorite book was André Schwarz-Bart's *The Last of the Just*.

Neill loved their visits, so full of bright chatter and feminine scent. They brightened his day with their twinkly good looks and their senses of humor and their innate smarts. Sometimes the smallest Goorile would come behind the counter and stand by Neill. Neill was lousy at guessing ages but imagined the child to be nine or ten.

And Then There was the Redhead from the William Stafford Reading

At this time, in the cultural history of Memphis, Tennessee, there was a program at Memphis State called The River City Writers Series. Begun by the visionary poet Gordon Osing, it brought fiction writers, poets, essayists, literary critics, and rogues to the university for a 3-day stay, culminating in a Friday night reading.

Neill loved them and went to all of them, even when he didn't know much about the poet.

One week they brought William Stafford. Neill had not read a lot of Stafford (he was not in Donald Allen's *The New American Poetry*, one of Neill's bibles) but the few poems he had been shown he admired. He and Goffredo attended.

The reading was memorable. William Stafford was a remarkable reader of his own work. Neill was stirred by him and vowed to read more of his poetry (Neill did this after every single reader he heard). And, after the reading, there was a small reception for the poet in a lounge off the main ballroom in the University Center. There was the clichéd bowl of punch, nearly flavorless, and some Oreos and shortbread.

Neill and Goffredo stood around uncertainly, and mostly just talked to each other.

Until, she walked in.

She was tall, solidly built with thighs like cannons, and a rear end like a red velvet cake. And, she had light red hair (like sunshine through a grapefruit), which made Neill fret and sweat the same way a red cape turns on a bull. She had red hair. (Have we mentioned Neill's enthrallment to the redhead before? An oversight on our part perhaps.)

"Who is that?" Neill said. The glass of punch in his hand had begun to boil like the 3 witches' cauldron.

"How the hell should I know?" Goffredo said. "I don't go to school here anymore."

"It was meant, you know, rhetorically."

"Uh huh." Goffredo watched his roommate with a bemused expression. "Do I sense another of your headlong, ballsy assaults?"

Neill handed his glass to Goffredo, who then stood holding two as he watched Neill move like a laser beam toward the red-haired beauty.

"William Stafford," Neill said to the stranger's face, which now wore a bewildered expression.

"No," the red-haired stranger said. "That's not me."

Neill laughed.

"I'm Neill," Neill said.

The redhead looked into his face. Then, she ducked her head (shyness, dismay?) and scanned the room. She was nearly speechless.

"You also have a name," Neill said.

"Sissy," she said.

"They used to call me that," Neill said.

Now she laughed.

"Are you a student here?" Sissy asked.

"Used to be. Back in the Taft administration."

"What do you do now?"

"Bookstore. I work in a bookstore."

"English major."

"Right," Neill said. He was impressed with this Sissy. "What do you do?"

"Student," Sissy said.

"Studying?"

"Sometimes."

"You banter."

"English."

"Ah."

The long and short of it was that they then exchanged patronymics and Neill had the full name (Sissy Chastain) and phone number of this intriguing redhead.

Neill called her the next day. She lived in a dorm. They made a date for the following Tuesday night. They were showing *Band of Outsiders* at the Memphian.

All that day and night Neill tried to remember Sissy's face up close. It was difficult. Neill would have made a lousy witness to a crime. But he did remember her clear blue eyes and her delicate albescent skin with its appropriate sprinkling of freckles. And that ass. He had watched her walk away. She moved like a dresser with the drawers pulled out.

Neill Buys

Neill, the manager, now discovered something new in what became his lifelong career as a bookseller: the position which holds the most power and the most pleasure is that of buyer. When Neill became the buyer for The Book Shelf he felt as if he had discovered his niche. He was a good buyer. He knew what books to stock, what books his customers would want.

This meant that he met with sales reps (as colorful a lot as a box of 64) from publishers (this was back in the days of yore when there was still something called a traveling salesman and even the book business had them) and went through their colorful catalogs and got to say yay or nay about which wares would be sold through his beloved outlet.

Most of the sales reps were good folks, as moony as Neill, some of them, and most of them in love with books qua books. Some brought old salesman's ways into the gentle trade and their brow-beating, strong-arming tactics (no doubt to meet some numbers imposed upon them by their superiors) made Neill quail and quiver and dread those visits. Later, once Neill had developed his instincts as a buyer and his confidence soared, he was able to tell these chowderheads, "Look, I'm gonna buy what I think best so just throttle back on the hard sell."

Neill Travels

And, concurrent with this new power, this new glory, Neill was offered the opportunity to travel by airplane for the first time in his life.

Every year the American Booksellers Association put on a convention, which brought together publishers, sales people, celebrities, drunks, CEOs, everymen and everywomen, Poo Bahs, polyhistors, coxcombs, autodidacts, writers and readers from around the globe for a three-day book-fest. They were held in convention halls the size of Valhalla and the atmosphere there was heady, dizzying, frightening, occasionally dispiriting and occasionally inspiring.

The first one to which his lovely bosses sent him was held in Washington, DC. Neill flew and found he liked flying. There was little trepidation. And when the jet first left the ground and Neill was tenderly pushed back against his seat he thought, it was almost sexual in its body-altering alchemy.

And Washington DC was glorious. So many museums! Naïf Neill wandered around like Mr. Smith, gawking at every famous face, statue, painting, building, street, and taxicab. He was agog.

And, in the convention itself, the same thing. Neill was in dreamland.

If he had been excited by authors visiting the bookstore, he was awestricken with the number of great writers, whose books were given to Neill free of charge, so that he could wait in their queue and get their signature. This was tempered a bit when Neill discovered that the line to meet Mr. T was 5 times as long as the line to meet T. C. Boyle.

When Neill reached Tom Robbins, whose first novel Neill loved, Neill was a bit star struck. He had been handed a galley of Robbins' new novel and he placed it under the author's signing hand and his tongue grew thick in his mouth. But Tom Robbins looked up, smiled his wry mustachioed smile, and said, "You're from Memphis?"

Neill thought he was not only a fine writer but a clairvoyant. Then, he remembered it was on his bookseller's badge.

"Oh, yes," Neill the Wit, said.

"What's Graceland like?"

And then it came back, his brain, and Neill said, "It's just another roadside attraction."

And Tom Robbins hesitated, and then Tom Robbins laughed a round, genuine laugh, and he thanked young Neill.

(Aside: anyone a Memphian meets, the great and the insignificant, will ask that Memphian the same question Neill was asked by the droll Mr. Robbins. What is Graceland like? Kings and streetwalkers, novelists and generals, stateswomen and yeggs. Everyone is curious about Mr. Presley's final abode.)

The convention went pretty much like this. He met Umberto Eco. He met John Irving.

He walked around in a daze. He ate alone in nice restaurants, all on the store's tab, and he returned to his very own hotel room each night, happy and tired.

After he returned home and reflected on what had happened, he believed he had been tried and had come through. He could travel. By himself. He could negotiate a new city by himself. He could talk to authors. Neill, briefly, liked himself.

The Brief Return and Final Concluding Finishing and Absolute Demise of the Relationship with Syrie Hardwood

And, when Neill got back, he found he wanted to see a woman and soon. He wanted to try out his new manhood, the man who could travel, as if it were a cape and super powers.

He called Sissy Chastain. She wasn't home. Their first date had been quite pleasant. The Godard film knocked Neill's socks off and, on the walk back to the car, Sissy took his hand. They kissed goodnight outside her dorm room. She was shy. She said, "Call me?"

When Neill couldn't get Sissy on the phone after the convention, he did it again. He called Syrie.

She came over. She visited his new house for the first and last time.

She and Neill fucked in Neill's new bedroom for the first and last time.

They kissed goodbye on Neill's new front porch, ditto.

And the next day, Neill had an unexpected visitor at the bookstore.

He looked up and there was Mr. Hardwood. Mr. Hardwood did not look happy.

"Neill, I only want to say one thing to you," Mr. Hardwood said.

Neill tried a smile but it was false courage.

"You know, I didn't trust you initially because of the age difference, but I thought we had gotten past that because you loved my daughter. Now, in your egotism and selfishness, you are making her extremely unhappy. You will not see her again," Mr. Hardwood said. And, after a beat, while Neill tried to get his heart out of his throat, he added, "Or else."

Neill thought about this for a moment.

"Mr. Hardwood," Neill said. "Are you threatening me?"

Now, it was Mr. Hardwood's turn to pause.

"Yes," he said, and turned on his heel, mounted his steed and was gone.

Neill was guilty and heartsick. Neill hated himself.

Neill's Championship Season: Neill is Popular

Neill always believed he would find his soulmate—when he would admit to the term—just by working in the bookstore. His reasoning was sound. His soulmate would have to be a reader and, hence, would have to shop in bookstores. [This has already been made clear.] And because Neill believed The Book Shelf was the best bookstore in Memphis, he reasoned that she would come in and her presence would light him up like a pinball machine.

In the meantime, Neill wanted to date, to court and be courted.

This is a theme. Throughout Neill's life he was torn between plenty and singularity. He wanted to know—in every sense—a wide variety of women. He wanted to kiss the girls and make them smile. Concurrently, he also wanted Love, capitalized. He wanted the one woman who would end his roaming. He would find her.

Many times.

For whatever reason or reasons, an admixture of youthful good looks, sense of humor, and an emergent maturity, Neill found himself popular. Almost like high school. He was getting attention from women and he relished it as much as one can, as much as one can recognize it in the moment. Toward the end of Neill's life, he was to look back at this period and discover just how pleasurable and enlivening it was. And he gave thanks that once upon a time he had a championship season.

Is there also some suggestion that Sweet Syrie was left behind partly because there was Raleigh Neill and there was Midtown Neill and ne'er the Mark Twain shall meet?

Sissy Chastain

Neill and Sissy finally did manage a second date.

They went out. Sissy was nervous and deflected anything approximating heat. It was ok. He really liked her. She was shy and funny and smart. And, oh so pretty.

They went out again and again there was deflection. Perhaps, she did not really like Neill *that way*. Sometimes it's hard to figure.

Then she called Neill and asked him out. This was new. They went—that's right—to the movies. This time they saw something at the regular theater, the Malco Quartet, at Highland and Poplar, which was a stoner's throw from Neill's new house. They saw *Tootsie* because Neill refused to see E. T.

"Why not E. T.?" Sissy asked in the car on the way there.

"Spielberg. I don't know. He makes movies for kids, doesn't he?"

"Or for the child in all of us."

"That's the way he probably sees it."

He didn't want to diss Spielberg to one of his fans. He didn't want to explain that he wanted to be one of few people who could say they'd never seen E. T. Neill was creating awkward tension. He tried to defuse it.

"I like your top," he said, gallant.

"Thanks," Sissy said. "You can kinda see through it."

"Yes," Neill said and noticed for the first time that it was true. It was almost like a net and he could see her brassiere and the small hummocks of her cleavage.

"I like your bottom, too," Neill said, and he smiled like Peck's Bad Boy.

"Ok, mister," Sissy said. But she smiled widely and took Neill's hand.

The movie was pretty good, though Neill was mostly thinking about what might happen afterward. Plus, they were seated behind an entire row of sorority girls who had seen the movie a dozen times and all sang along with the insipid theme song at the tops of their voices. It was a bit of a mood breaker.

Afterward, they went to Neill's house and to Neill's bedroom (after he asked if she wanted to have a drink and watch TV or go to his room and listen to music, though the way he said it made it clear he wanted to go to the bedroom more and, perhaps, she did too). They sat on the bed and sipped lemonade.

"This is good," Sissy said.

"It's Crystal Light," Neill said.

"Oh."

Neill set his glass down. In nervousness Sissy said, "You've got a lot of books. Have you read them all?"

Neill smiled. "No," he said, quietly.

"Dumb question," Sissy said.

"It's ok. Are you nervous?"

"I guess so."

"Me, too. We're gonna kiss though, right?"

Sissy set her glass down and squared her shoulders as if preparing to recite. Neill watched in amusement, not sure what was happening.

"Yes," Sissy said.

So they did. They kissed and sucked tongues and their hands touched here and there, but not *there*. Sissy was a little edgy still. Was she unplucked? Was she a virgin?

Nevertheless, things proceeded. Soon, her net shirt was removed and her bra. Her breasts were pink like roses. Neill kissed them and sucked their pale nipples. Sissy sighed. She was enjoying herself. That was important.

She ran her hands up Neill's thighs. He was wearing jeans, which, as any lover knows, are too thick for enough sensation to be generated in the skin beneath. She reached for Neill's belt. It was the next thing, the next step. They were doing fine.

Neill stood and bade Sissy stand with him. Simultaneously, they undid each other's pants and the pants fell. They were both only a thin layer of underwear away from naked. Sissy was thick—large-boned—but not fat. Though she might have outweighed Neill, it was beautifully distributed.

Neill held her and kissed her a long, warm kiss. His hands went down the back of her panties. He found there something firm and smooth and sensuous.

"God, I love your ass," he said.

"I've got a bongo butt," she responded.

Neill was to think about that later. At the time, it seemed like acceptable sexual chitchat.

Sissy tightened up when Neill's hand traveled the crack of her ass and found the warm pool between her legs.

"Ah," she said. "Ah ah."

Pleasure or warning?

Neill slowly removed her panties. Even in the dim light of his room he could see the beautiful orange patch of pubic hair. They fell backward onto the bed.

Neill began to play with her patch and finger her gently.

"Ah," she repeated.

Then she pulled Neill's dick out. She was a bit clumsy with it but it still felt grand. There was an increase in zeal.

"Sissy," Neill whispered. "Are you on the pill?"

"No," Sissy said and buried her face in Neill's neck.

"It's ok," Neill said.

"I can't. We can't."

"Ok," Neill said.

"Are you sure it's ok?"

"Of course, why wouldn't it be?"

"I don't know. I thought you were expecting us to, to, you know, and now you'd be disappointed in me and maybe not call again."

Neill held her for a moment.

"Sissy," Neill said. "It's not like that."

"Ok," Sissy said. And she reached for him again and began to pump him good.

"Ohohoh," Neill said. "Before you do that can I lick you?"

Sissy froze. She did not speak.

"It's ok," Neill said. "Next time."

And Sissy's hand began again as if switched back on. Soon the sap rose and soon it was all over Sissy's pale, pink, flat stomach.

"Wow," Sissy said.

"Yeah, that was fun," Neill said.

"It's all over me," Sissy said.

"I'll get a washcloth."

"No," she said. "I want to wear it home."

More About the Gooriles

This must have been during Spring break because the middle Goorile daughter, whom Neill now knew was called Sue, was home from school. Sue was so blond and pale she was almost invisible. She had a funny nose and her white-blond hair was cut like a little boy's and she was as slender as a cat's elbow. She looked like she was twelve years old. She had skin the color of milk straight from the bovine.

When the four beautiful Gooriles visited and bought books they always took time to chat with Neill. Neill liked them very much.

On this day, they seemed to be full of some secret mirth because they giggled every time they walked past or spoke to Neill.

"Something is funny," Neill said. "Am I wearing a woman's shirt by mistake again?"

They laughed some more.

"No," Mrs. Goorile said between snorts. "We have to tell you what Patsy said."

Now Patsy stomped out the way kids do when peeved.

"Mom was talking about leaving Patsy home alone because we all have to be in Little Rock,"

Sue said. She chuckled a bit more and looked Neill in the eye the way young gals do when they are seeking sparks. Neill was a tad nonplussed by the look. "And Patsy said, 'Maybe Neill will stay with me.'"

"'Neill'?" Goneril, the oldest sister said, picking up the joke. And Patsy said, 'From the bookstore.'"

Now Neill laughed.

"That is funny. I am flattered."

"You should be," Sue said, and again the look, this time with an extra smoky tang.

"Ok," Neill said, checking them out the way Sue had been him. "*Speak Memory*. I love Nabokov."

"*Speak Memory* is a book I give to all my friends," Mrs. Goorile said, and her eye twinkled, too. Maybe all the twinkling was in Neill's mind.

"Bye, Neill," Sue said and spun, and when she spun her little skirt flipped up a bit and Neill saw for the first time the best pair of legs he'd seen since Schnorrer's Day.

Another Date with Sissy Chastain

"You can't see my dorm room" Sissy said, opening it a crack. "I'll be right out."

Neill waited in the corridor which looked like a corridor.

"Ok," Sissy said, stepping out and shutting the door behind her.

She was dressed in a light blue blouse and tennis dress.

"You play tennis?" Neill asked.

"Yes," Sissy said. Then came the embarrassed tucking of the head.

"What?"

"I thought you were being snarky about my apparel."

"Jesus, no. You look great. You have beautiful legs."

"You've seen them before."

"Right. But tennis dresses make them look about 48% better. Kinda like cowboy boots. Put a woman with average legs in a short dress and cowboy boots and suddenly her legs look like Elle MacPherson's."

"I see."

They dined at Pete and Sam's, a Memphis tradition, a small Italian restaurant on Park Avenue, famous for its atmosphere, spaghetti and thin-crust pizza.

"Been here before?" Sissy asked him.

"Yes. Many times. I had an old girlfriend always called it Peter and Samuel's. Do you like it?"

"It's very nice. Your dish looks better than mine. Is that spinach?"

"Italian spinach. It's great here. Here, have some."

"That is good," Sissy said. "Garlicky."

"Yes. But as long as we both eat it."

"Of course."

After dinner, they took a walk down Park Avenue, holding hands. It was a pleasant spring vespertide. The sky was the color of a gutted salmon and the light was quite exquisite on Sissy's pale, freckled skin.

"Where we going?" Sissy asked. "Not that it matters. I am happy just to walk with you."

"That's all. Just for a walk. We could go to Peaches and look for the new Elvis Costello album. Peaches is right there."

"No, I like just walking."

"Me, too. It settles the dinner."

They walked a bit further.

"Settles the dinner before any other, um, physical activity," Neill chanced.

Sissy cast a sidelong glance at Neill.

"That's what you think is gonna happen huh?"

"I am. I hope, I mean. Not that, you know. I just. Hoped."

"Me too," Sissy said, and she ducked her head one more time.

Back in Neill's bedroom they took an exceedingly long time to undress each other. They had decades ahead of them. Why festinate, except that they had their hands over each other's crotches on the car ride home?

Once they were naked, Neill began to lightly knead Sissy's treasure.

"Oh Neill," Sissy said within her panting.

Neill fingered her a bit and then began to kiss her stomach, traveling toward his goal slowly. Perhaps tonight she would allow us to go this far, he was thinking.

There was no hesitation. She gave herself up to Neill's practiced tonguing. She came once very hard. Neill held his mouth there and gently sucked as if it were a sponge.

"Whew," Sissy said.

"Yum," Neill countered. "My Blue."

"Blue, like a porn movie?"

"It's an old nickname for redheads. I think."

"Want me to do you now?"

"I guess I do."

"Mr. Reluctance."

Sissy tried to mimic Neill's slow descent. She spent a goodly amount of time trapped in the still waters right above Neill's schlong. Her ship's sails had lost their wind. She was thinking too hard about it.

Then she put just the head in her mouth.

"Ahh," Neill said. "My head has a very sensitive on button."

Sissy slid it in a little further. She seemed to be having a hard time taking it all, though Neill was of modest size.

In truth, she didn't know what she was doing.

"Neill," she said, with the head resting on her lower lip. "I put in a diaphragm."

"Oh," Neill said.

"If you want to."

"Come here."

They kissed deeply.

Then Neill lowered himself over her, pointer pointing the way. Sissy's mouth was a tight slit and her eyes were squinched tightly shut.

Neill almost laughed. He put himself right outside her door.

He hesitated on the stoop. He knocked once. Twice.

As his cock began to slide in Sissy bucked and almost through Neill off. Neill's mister slid out.

"Sorry," she said. She seemed on the verge of tears.

"Do you?"

"Yes, yes. I do, Neill."

Neill remounted and, this time, as he slid in she again bumped upwards. Neill persevered and discovered he was breaking in a virgin. It was a surprise. Neill didn't know whether to go ahead or not.

Sissy now pushed her hips upwards, effectively impaling herself on Neill. The roadblock gave way. Neill drove in. Sissy held herself still. Her hands clutched bouquets of bedspread.

Neill slowly pumped in case he should have to stop at any time. Gradually, he forgot all caution, and spurred on by the sight of her pink breasts and the feel of her ass in one hand, Neill began to drive her more amain.

Then Neill felt his pistol load and, as it filled, her walls clamped around him tightly. It was good instinct. Neill began to come inside her.

Sissy Chastain's eyes opened wide.

"I can feel it," she said.

"I hope so," Neill said, with a gruff chuckle.

"I can feel you coming inside me. It's like..."

Sissy closed her eyes again. Neill thought she might be going to sleep.

Then she said, "pudding."

More Late Night Confabs

"I had a bully in high school. Hated me for some reason. He reminded me of Randy on *Peewee's Playhouse*," Neill said.

"High school is hell for most people," Bidden said. "But not for you despite the bully."

"Yeah, that's true. I was good in high school. I had friends. Though, I also was full of self-doubt."

"Sure."

"I had girlfriends. Nice girlfriends."

"You're seeing someone now, right?"

"I don't know. I think so."

"She's invisible?" Crow asked.

"She's really lovely. And, she reads books."

"That's a nice thing."

"It is."

"The woman I went out with, one date, was not quite a reader. She colored. She colors. With crayons."

"She's an artist?"

"No, I mean she colors in coloring books. Right now, she's working her way through a *Huckleberry Hound.* She says she never got over the thrill of the 64-count box."

"Huh."

"Yeah."

"Well, she—"

"Hey, sometimes she doesn't use the right colors. Like Huckleberry Hound is, I think it's cerise."

"That's something."

"It is, isn't it? Maybe I'll call her again."

All three men laughed.

"You can't laugh. You're married," Neill said to Crow.

"The end of laughter."

"No, I mean, you know. It's ugly, dating."

"I didn't do much of it, you're right," Crow said. "And now, I have a kid so dating is really out."

"Heh. You and the wife still ok?"

"Sure. When you have children you find yourself praying for odd things like, 'please let Neill's bowel movements occur naturally and with very little stress.'"

"I pray that way about myself," Bidden said.

"Me, too," Neill chimed in. "I hate defecating. That's another bone I have to pick with God. Why make shit smell so abhorrent? I mean, it's something you're gonna do once a day, usually, so why have it be unpleasant? Why not make it come out easy and smell like, I don't know, fresh vanilla? Or citrus? Or the soft crease in a baby's neck? Or a woman's crotch, or even the aroma of sautéed onions and garlic? If it smelled like eucalyptus, I'm telling you, there would be fewer neurotics in the world."

"Like his testing Noah in the desert."

"Was it Noah in the desert? I thought he had a boat."

"This was before the boat. The ark."

"I think it was Moses in the desert."

"How about like his testing Job?"

"I think that's right."

The Signing for Shlomo's first novel, *Mooning When the Sun Don't Shine*

Shlomo Einstein's signing was well-attended. It was the largest, hippest crowd The Book Shelf had hosted, and, when Shlomo treated Neill like a friend among this heady throng, Neill was proud as a government mule.

Afterward a bunch of folks, including Shlomo's woman Daisy and Neill, went to the Rendezvous for ribs. There was a table of twenty. Neill ate ribs and tried to only speak when spoken to, like the child he felt he was. The conversation was fast and mean and witty and intimidating. But, damn, the ribs were good.

As the party broke up Shlomo pulled Neill aside.

"Thanks for this, man," he said, putting a tight squeeze on Neill's shoulder.

"Hey, it was all for you and because of you," Neill said.

"You threw me a nice signing. I won't forget that."

"You brought the cool," Neill said. It sounded somewhere between immature fawning and wit.

Shlomo smiled at him, hooked arms with Daisy, and a smaller crowd went on to drink and dance. Neill went home and lay awake. He wanted his life to be more like this evening. He wanted friends and books and women like Daisy, who used to be a ballet dancer and had the legs to prove it.

Neill lay awake and felt lonely. Why am I lonely after such an invigorating night? he asked himself.

I don't know, he answered. Because you want a woman?

The Coming of Sue Goorile

Sue Goorile called Neill at The Book Shelf.

"Hi," Neill said. "Need a book."

There was a pause.

"No, not really."

"Oh." Now Neill felt tongue-tied. "What's up?" he ventured.

"I was wondering if you'd like to have lunch with me?"

Lunch. Safe. A start. Neill understood lunch.

"Yes," Neill said, with enthusiasm that surprised him.

"You do know which sister I am?" Sue Goorile asked.

"I do," Neill said. "You are as white as the paper of Syria."

Sue Goorile laughed.

"Ok, Sweetcakes," she said.

She called him Sweetcakes. She had him hooked already.

The next day was Thursday, Neill's day off.

They met at a vegetarian restaurant that had just opened and was currently very in. When Neill entered the crowd was a din and a disturbance to his field of vision. He felt momentarily like Mr. Magoo, adrift in a big cacophonic city.

Sue Goorile was seated at the counter near the back of the restaurant, zealously guarding the stool next to her. She was wearing another short skirt and there were the ur-legs, the legs from the original mold, Eve's legs.

"Hey," Neill said, sliding into place. "This place is manic."

"It's too busy. Do you want to go someplace quieter?"

"No, no," Neill said. Was he avoiding someplace quieter? Was he avoiding thinking of this very young woman as a possible O and O? How old was she?

Sue ordered a fake BLT so Neill did, too.

"Add avocado," Sue said, as if it was an insider's secret.

While they ate the conversation was convivial, and Sue was smart and funny, and Neill had a good time. She's not thinking of boyfriend material, Neill thought. She just wants an older guy to talk books and stuff.

After they ate Sue said, "Watch this." She held one hand in the air and made an invisible squiggle with it.

"What was that?"

"The international sign that you are ready for the check."

The waitress came over. Neill laughed.

In the parking lot Sue walked over to a well-used BMW.

"Nice car," Neill said.

"The Beemer," Sue said.

"Well, ok. This was nice."

"What else are you doing today?"

Neill hesitated. So he told her literally what he had planned.

"I just bought a new bookcase and I was going to go home and see if somehow I had turned into a man who can read instructions and put it together."

"I'll give you a hand if you want. I am really good at those kinds of things."

"Ok," Neill said. "Follow me?"

Neill drove his little Toyota which now felt like a second-hand toaster compared to Sue's Beemer.

Once inside Neill's house he fixed them both a glass of ice tea. They spread the bookcase parts out on the dining room floor. Neill looked at the instructions. Neill hated instructions. He couldn't read from point A to point B.

And, it became immediately obvious that Sue had no idea how to help. If anything, she was less competent than Neill.

Still, they persevered, and with cussing and laughter, they cobbled the damn thing together. Neill stood it up. It listed slightly to one side.

"Good enough," Sue said.

"You were a big help. Thanks for telling me how handy you are with tools. My dad used to say, 'You're handier than a shirt pocket.'"

"It was just a ruse. I thought you were fixing to dismiss me for the day."

"Oh," Neill said. He looked at Sue Goorile. Her funny little face had a beauty to it that was like something pure and untrammeled. It was a beauty waiting to be born. Her skin glistened.

"How old are you?" Neill said.

"How old are you?" Sue countered.

"I'm 27."

"I'm, um, ten years younger than that."

"Whew," Neill said.

"Problem?"

"I don't know, Sue. You know, it's illegal or immoral or something."

"You're not attracted to me?"

"I am," Neill said. "I am. I need to act like an adult. Sorta."

"Sorta, Sweetcakes?"

That was it. She leaned toward Neill and Neill leaned toward her. The kiss was soft and tender and a tad awkward on Sue's part, an inexperienced kiss so that Neill recalibrated and dialed his back a bit, but it still had enough heat, a burble on a back burner neither knew was there, that they ended up in the bedroom with the hook on the door.

"We can only kiss," Neill said. "Seriously. I have to think about this."

"I understand," Sue said.

They made out and it was quite steamy. Neill could not NOT run his hands over her. Her sweet little ass was as tight as a peach, and he went so far as to run a hand under the skirt so he could feel those thighs. They were as marvelous as Neill had anticipated. Of course, she feels brand new, Neill thought. She's a child! But, really, she was not any younger than Syrie was...except Neill was older still.

They broke their clasp for a moment and looked into each other's eyes. Sue's were slate blue. Neill thought perhaps a dove's eyes were that color blue.

Fuck, Neill thought. She really is beautiful. Could I not see immediately how beautiful she is?

"We can at least take our shirts off," Sue Goorile now said.

"I'm helpless," Neill said.

Sue Goorile removed her shirt, underneath which she was not wearing a bra. Her breasts were small, white as lambs, and had pink nipples like a child's. Except they were standing up like a grownup's.

"You too," Sue said. She helped Neill pull his shirt off.

Back together Neill knew he had failed to keep a handle on the situation. There was no way that ethics was still in play. Morality, principles. standards, scruples, mores, goodness, decency, godliness, integrity, probity, rules, laws, they all caught the last train out. Neill was left alone with an almost nude seventeen-year old, who was as beautiful as Adam's first wife.

She was the First Woman, before, you know.

Soon Neill's shorts and Sue's skirt were also on the floor.

Neill ran his hand inside her panties and felt the cool, sweetness of her ass. She had a death grip on his neck. And her hands would stroke his belly but would not go further. But Neill, now in the service of Satan, pulled Sue's panties off. She was pristine in her nakedness, like something fresh out of the package. She had small, tight buttocks, which sat up high on her shapely legs. Neill was dazzleded by seeing a small mole that sat like an island in the silvered sea near her pale, white-yellow pubic hair, almost gossamer against her alabastrine skin. Sue's crotch was the prettiest thing Neill had ever seen, a little pussy like a moonflower. He put his hand over it.

And he began to softly stroke it, the way one absentmindedly pets an old cherished cat. This cat had a moist little tongue.

Suddenly, Sue began to shake a little. Neill thought he had scared her and pulled his hand away.

"No...no, more," Sue said. She sounded like a cartoon, an adult cartoon.

Neill returned his attention to her white muff and this time slid a finger in. Her little clit was sticking its head above water. And Sue began to shake again and hold Neill tight. She was having an orgasm!

Afterward, they were still for a moment.

"You want to stop now?" Sue said.

"Are you always that easily orgasmic?"

"I guess so."

Neill squinched up his face.

"I'm not a virgin," Sue said, quickly. "If you're worried about that."

"No, no," Neill said. And he fit himself behind her, spooning up against her naked ass with his cotton-covered johnnie.

They were lying in repose and Neill was lazily tracing a hand down her body, over her demitasse breasts, down the beginner's slope of her hip. Neill's erection was finding its way, on its own, into the crack of her little buttery butt.

She still had not touched him.

"That feels good," she said.

Neill thought no more. He unsheathed his pointer and put it in her crack.

"Oh," Sue said.

"We should stop," Neill said.

"Yes," Sue said. "Stop. That's what we should do." Her deadpan was so funny, so twee, so right on. It hit Neill where he lived because he lived in The Land of Irony.

Instead, Neill took his cock in his hand and ran it down her crack and found the hot, wet spot that he had visited earlier with his fingers. He slipped in.

Her young body fit against his like a pit in a peach.

Neill was fucking her slowly from behind. He kept sneaking looks at her ass and his pood going in and out of her. It was a dream.

"I'm on the pill," she said, as she started to pant again.

And then, she had another orgasm.

And then Neill, safe, mature Neill, let himself fill the delicious niveous nubile honeyed body of delightful Sue Goorile with his mature, yet intemperate, whitewash.

By Phone

"Another teenager," Bidden said. His voice was patient, non-judgmental. He sincerely wanted to hear what came next.

"I know, I know. It's foolish. I know it appears as if I am clinging to a rapidly receding youth through these extremely young women."

"Well, not *extremely*. I mean it's not kiddie porn."

"It feels wrong."

"Nah," Bidden said. "What about the other woman, the redhead?'

"Oh Lord. She's so wonderful. I mean, she is really someone you'd want to be with for a long time."

"But..."

"But, dammit. This Sue fit into me like a shell on a crab. It was like we were made to join together. Two puzzle pieces."

"Yin and Yang."

"Yes, I actually said that to her. What a goop I've become."

"So, it's really just about sex with Sue? I mean, that's good, that's fine. Sex with a beautiful young woman is not to be taken lightly. It is surely one of God's gifts to mankind."

"Well, it's not really just sex. She's funny, bright, great company. She reads."

"That's good then. There is a real connection."

"She did say the Beatles were overrated."

Neill listened while Bidden snorted and guffawed.

"You ok?" Neill asked then.

"Sorry. I spit out my Dr. Pepper."

"I know. The opinions of youth, right? To have an adult-level opinion one should trash someone monumental."

"What did you say when she said that."

"The Dr. Pepper came out of my nose."

Bidden laughed again.

"No, really," Neill said. He was trying to use his grown-up voice. "Sue is—I don't want to say *everything*—but she and I are extremely compatible."

"And Sissy?"

"I don't know. I'm crazy about Sissy. Why, after months of loneliness and masturbation, am I suddenly plagued by too many girlfriends?"

"I should suffer so."

"Are you seeing someone?"

"I had a date."

"Good, good. Who is she? How did it go?"

"My brother fixed us up. You don't know her. She's from Frayser like me."

"Ok. Good. How was it?"

"She used the n word."

There was a stunned silence.

"Right. How were her tits?"

Bidden laughed. "I imagine they were as good as white supremacist tits get."

"You ended the date and took her home."

"I did."

"You're my hero."

"I hate talking on the phone."

"I know. So do—-"

Rhymer, the Scrivener

Neill was writing a lot. Perhaps this period of inexplicable popularity also stirred Neill's creative juices. He wrote a lot of bad to mediocre poetry. Much of it had to do with love, and the lack of sex and the lack of understanding, and the lack of intelligence, and the lack of.

He also was trying to stretch his middling gift into prose. He had recently read a little short story collection called *What We Talk about When We Talk About Love*, by Raymond Carver. They were small clocks, each tale. Short and yet they turned on perfect moments, perfect phrasings.

It gave Neill the idea that he could approximate that kind of story. He was a mooncalf, of course. What looks simple in art is often the most complex, webby, incorporeal fairy cake, magic that looks like nature.

Still he persevered.

The first story he wrote was about his childhood. It was called: "The Bigger Boys Laughed." It wasn't very good but it gave Neill pleasure.

He also wrote a story about Sue Goorile, called "Your Heart is a Thurible," changing the names of the two lovers who were setting sexual records while spinning a cocoon only big enough for two young souls. It wasn't very good either but it gave Neill even more pleasure.

And then, he knew somewhere deep in his squamata brain that if he were to really become a writer he would have to leave the autobiographical shit behind. What nudnik said 'Write what you know?' Neill didn't want to write what he knew. He knew nothing. He wanted to take lead and make gold. And the lead of his life was too base, too grimy, too uninspiring, too anserine, and too damn puerile.

He wanted to invent worlds.

He wanted to write like Shlomo Einstein.

More Sissy

Sissy called Neill.

Neill felt guilty.

She asked if he wanted to get together and Neill said, yes, very much so, because it was true. And it was easy to say.

They went to an art exhibit at the Turner Clark Gallery, in the main branch of the library. The artist was Gulley Jawel and it made Neill joyful to see his friend Gulley happy and to show off for Sissy. The work was very abstract and Sissy spent a long time over each painting as if she could absorb from them their meaning by standing close, by stubbornly staying still. Neill admired her impulse.

She was wearing a short skirt and boots (see above). Neill was enjoying watching her as he stood next to Gulley and listened to Gulley get praise from strangers. Gulley, naturally, said little. Both men were happily watching Sissy.

When she shifted her weight, unconsciously cocking one hip out as she leaned toward a painting Gulley caught Neill's eye.

"I know," Neill said.

"That's a pooper," Gulley said.

"One of God's best works."

"My art pales in comparison."

"Pfft. Great stuff," Neill said to Gulley, though Neill knew absolutely no reason why it was good or bad or in between. They were *pretty*, he thought.

"Eh," Gulley said. He was taciturn, as usual.

To Sissy Gulley said, "Nice to meet you. Neill says nice things about you."

This was a glib, social lie, unlike Gulley really, but Neill appreciated it.

Sissy and Neill left the opening with a sort of static electricity between them. They held hands walking to the car and it was as if the shared public art event was tickling their small hairs.

In the car Sissy began kneading Neill's thigh, while looking straight ahead, as if her hand was acting of its own accord. Bad hand. (Good hand.)

"I'm gonna wreck," Neill said. "You're really turning me on."

Sissy did her little incomprehensible hums and hems as if singing to herself. She was smiling.

"I like turning you on," she said, ducking her chin.

Neill reached over and placed his hand on her thigh in return. Her short skirt was showing a lot of pinkish-orange skin and her flesh was cool under his palm.

Sissy moved her hand closer to Neill's baubles. Neill pushed the hem of her skirt up with the side of his hand. They were both staring ahead with tight smiles. It was a game, and a good one.

Sissy wiped gently over Neill's bluejeaned crotch.

Neill slipped his hand under her skirt and found her panties and the thighs around them damp.

"Oof," Sissy said.

"Damn," Neill said.

They were driving in a deserted part of town just south of Midtown. Neill pulled the Toyota into an alley, gravel flying, as if he were Jim Rockford pursuing a miscreant. He stopped the car between two dark tall buildings, pulled the parking brake up, unhooked his seatbelt, and turned off the car. They were in an alley, garbage bins to each side. It didn't seem safe. Neill wasn't thinking about safety.

"Is this safe?" Sissy said. She spread her legs wider and squeezed Neill with added vigor.

"I'm not thinking about safety," Neill said.

He pulled her panties off in one powerful and deft motion.

"My God," Sissy Chastain said.

Neill wasn't listening. He put his fingers inside her. She let go of his Balzac and pulled the lever that dropped her seat backwards. She closed her eyes to take her own pleasure.

Now Neill lifted her skirt and dove face-first into her lap. Sissy opened her window and hung her right leg outside the car.

The angle was crazy and Neill could barely get his mouth on her, but with the work of fingers and lips and tongue he had Sissy splayed wide open. And, in this way, he brought her off.

She said this: "Gaa, gaa, gaa."

Neill brought his sodden hand up and touched Sissy's cheek with her own liquor.

Sissy sucked a soaked finger.

"Hooo," Sissy said. "That was intense."

"Diaphragm in?" Neill asked.

"In the car?"

"We can but try."

Neill undid his own pants and pushed them down around the accelerator and brake. His little man was delighted.

Sissy awkwardly attempted to climb aboard. (Remember Sissy was not willowy.) Her skirt was hiked up around her waist though she still had her shoes on.

"Open the door," she said.

God, I love her, Neill said to himself.

He opened the driver's side door and quickly fumbled the dome light off.

By placing one leg outside the car and by leaning Neill's seat back they were able to slide Neill's taut cock into her extremely wet tarn. It was not the most graceful copulation and it took Sissy opening her shirt and showing Neill her rose-colored breasts for Neill to achieve his orgasm, but it was an adventure and young lovers love adventures.

They parted and both gathered themselves and then their clothing. After their flight, they put their seats back into their upright positions. Then they kissed a long wet kiss. Neill started the car and began to back slowly out of the alley. His crotch was dripping. He relished the grubbiness of it.

"Can I sleep at your house?" Sissy said, again with the chin duck.

This was new. Would Neill like it? He was a bad sleeper but he thought about waking next to the rosy naked wonder of Sissy Chastain, and he said, "Oh, yes, great idea."

When they got home Goffredo was out somewhere so they were not embarrassed walking down the hall to Neill's room, clothes all askew, slick with each other's extracts. The telephone sat in a little nook in the middle of the hall wall, the nook an old-fashioned embellishment. Its petite message button was blinking. Green for go.

Stupidly, Neill hit the button.

"Hey, Sweetcakes," Sue's voice sang out, with crystal clear zeal and youthfulness. "I want to see you. I want to see if I can have more than four orgasms this time. And I want to try to fellate you. (Fellate?) Ok, I guess you're out. Where are you? I hope Goffredo doesn't get this message. Call me when you get home."

Neill couldn't believe they stood there and listened to the whole damn thing. It was as if they were frozen by the voice of Oz.

"Who's that?" Sissy said. And then, she began to cry.

By Phone Again

Neill called Sissy the next day. She hung up.

Neill was heartsick. He never wanted to hurt Sissy, sweet woman. That night she had cried in the car all the way back to the dorm. Every time Neill tried to get her to talk to him she kept saying, "It's all right. I'm all right."

Neill tried to walk her to the dorm but she was out the door quickly and shouting behind her, "I'm all right."

Neill tried many times to call Sissy from the bookstore. She stopped answering.

He did not know what to do.

Parallel Universes

Crow believed in parallel universes. By his reckoning, there is another place where Neill chose Sissy over Sue. In that place Sissy and Neill stay together for decades and raise three erythrismal children, Peter, Paul and Mary, and they make enough money to tithe the charities of their choice and still have rooms of floor-to-ceiling bookcases, overflowing with their favorite authors, all in alphabetical order (even to the point of clarifying the Mac- Mc- dilemma), and they play tennis and swim, and their lovemaking only improves and deepens, and sometimes, alone at night, when the kids are in bed, they hold each other in front of the fire, and sing the entire Beatles catalog from "I Wanna Hold Your Hand" to "Why Don't We Do it in the Road?" softly to each other, their voices harmonizing like two strands entwining.

As Ernest Hemingway said, "Isn't it pretty to think so?"

The End of the Rites of Spring

They both knew the day was coming when Sue would return to her boarding school in Dobbs Ferry, NY. They crowded a lot of activity into the last week she was home, much of it in bed.

The night before she was to return, Neill took her out to eat at Pappy and Jimmy's. Afterward, they went next door to Paulette's for the dessert that was known to turn people inside out with pleasure, Kahlua Pie called, affectionately, K-pie.

Then, they went back to Neill's. Goffredo was watching MTV when they breezed through.

"Hey, Sue," he called back over his shoulder, spellbound by The Bangles.

Neill played Leonard Cohen's *New Skin for the Old Ceremony*, an LP he had recently purchased and one that he was living inside. He thought it was the music his brain made scraping against its skull walls. In other words, it spoke to him *personally*.

"Suicide music," Sue said. She seemed a tad petulant.

"Why is it that, sometimes, listening to the saddest music in the world can make you happy?" Neill asked.

"Can you get me a soda?"

Neill went to the kitchen and returned with a Mountain Dew.

"Is this all you have? I'll be up all night."

"Sorry."

Sue swallowed a large draught.

"What's wrong, Sue?" Neill sat next to her. She was distant. (Humans did that. Turned distant at the wrong times. No one knows why.)

"Nothing, Sweetcakes," Sue said. "Let's get naked."

They did and it was balm. Holding her Neill knew a peace that had eluded him with so many other women. Yet...in many ways, Sue was impossible. She wanted something more than Neill. She wanted travel, adventure, success.

Neill did not want any of those things. He wanted—*what?* And, if he were honest with himself, he knew he was only an educationalist along Sue Goorile's highway. She was young, so young. At times, Neill thought her youth a fine thing because he, himself, was immature.

A few dates back, Sue had proved herself a willing student in the ways of the boudoir. After not being able to even touch Neill's willy, at first, she had become quite good with hand and mouth. And, now, this was forcing the atrabilious thoughts from Neill's tiny brain. While they were kissing, Sue pulled his head around and put her mouth up against his ear. She said, "I want to go down on your cock." It was feigned maturity, but it didn't matter.

She was drawing Neill in and out like a lollypop. If she wasn't the world-class suckstress that Dinah Mist or Harness Myers was, she did ok.

And, in returning the favor, Neill bent over that little honey pot, with its soft white fur like a kitten's, and Neill made Sue come four times.

And then a fifth and sixth when she climbed on top of him and rode his gearshift like a bronco buster. This was their record. 6 orgasms in one night.

Only one other woman in Neill's life came as readily or as eagerly or as many times. (We'll get to her later.)

Then Neill had his one, squirting so much into Sue that it dripped down her thighs all night and into the morning, and was still trickling ankleward on her flight back north.

"You only come once. It's hardly fair," Sue said, in repose.

"You know. Once a king always a king, but once a night's enough."

"Heard it."

"Ok."

The petulance had returned.

Neill drove her home that night, back to Charon Hall off Lamar, a near-castle secluded in a deeply wooded lawn, off Lamar Avenue. The family home was called Charon Hall. ("I used to date a girl named Karen Hall," Neill the wag said.) They both cried. Neill thought Sue was feigning her sadness a bit, trying to match the intensity of his own agony. They vowed to write and/or call every day.

Excerpts from an Epistolary Romance

Dear Sue Goo,

I miss you as if a limb has been lopped off. Every night I am not holding your white body against me is a wasted night. We are given only a finite number of days and a lonely one is a chit for the devil's side. I can only dream of the summer when the angels will, once again, be victorious, and I will kiss you from stem to stern, especially to your downy stern.

Bidden and Crow and I went to see a movie called Risky Business. It was pretty good. Some young stud is the star but, for me, for all of us, the real revelation (if that's not putting it too strongly) is this new actress named Rebecca DeSomething. My God is she sexy!

Not as sexy as you, my little snotty lover. Not near.

I'm reading Ann Beattie's Chilly Scenes of Winter. I may have discovered a new favorite writer. I think she is writing about me. I guess that's what books can do, right?

But, I wanted to share this quote from Little, Big, with you. (I keep a notebook of collected quotes—is that anal?)

"...and so because he had no choice, Smoky sat down to make love through the mails with a thoroughness just about vanished from the world."

This is what I want to do, converse with you thoroughly. I will probably call you tonight but I am writing anyway. It helps me think. It helps me remember.

And right now, I am remembering your little mole, the one that points the way to the entranceway of your hot place.

I love you, Sue Goo.

xoxo

Neill

Dear Sweetcakes,

It was so lovely to talk to you on the phone last night. It got pretty heated. My dorm mates think you are 45 years old and a greying, distinguished writer of verse. I guess I sorta let them think that.

I miss you. I miss the sweet things you say. I miss your hands and your mouth and your...um, you know: little Neill.

Classwork is so onerous. I am always tired.

Some of us go into town for beers. This is forbidden, of course. Aren't we dangerous and unmanageable?

love forever,

Sue

Dear Sue Goo,

How many more days do I have to wait? Talking to you on the phone last night was unsatisfactory. Were you preoccupied? I'm sorry if I turned the conversation too quickly to sex. The truth is I crave you. I can't stop thinking about your body, which I think is perfect, from the top of your sun-white head to the bottom of your pink toes. Not to mention that sweet spot in the middle.

Ok. Instead of sex, this. I enclose a poem I wrote about you. I am writing a lot. I've had a few small rags accept some work, giving me just enough confidence to continue.

I also am working on some short fiction. I was talking to one of my old English teachers at Tiger High (he's teaching a free class on poetry once a week at Charlotte's bookstore—I'm learning good stuff, Robert Lowell, Emily Dickinson, Yeats) and he said he was writing a novel. How I envied him! I will never be able to write a novel. Imagine working on something for over a year. It is too daunting. I am too chickenshit and too scattered to pull it off. But—well, just imagine saying, in earnest, I am working on a novel.

With these things I try to distract myself while you are gone.

I miss you like a kitten away from its mother. I am lonely as this finger (Turgenev).

Talk soon. I love you.

Neill

Dear Sweetcakes,

I am sorry I missed your call the other night. A group of us went to a party in the city. Sorry, in New York City. It was at this restaurant under the Brooklyn Bridge. Wild. We had such a good time, though some of us, not yours truly, drank too much.

I do miss you sexually. You can go right into sex mode whenever we talk. I like it.

Gotta run now. Got a botany exam. Ugh.

love you,

your Sue Goo

And on it went. Sometimes thrilling, sometimes frustrating. Neill caved in and felt bereft often and doubted Sue's love. She was so young. Of course, she should be going into the city for parties, meeting new people, having the time of her life. But, let's be honest, it hurt like hell and Neill was jealous. Jealous and horny. Epitaph for Neill's stone had he died of missing Sue: He was jealous and horny.

Merciless Phone News

Neill called Sissy. He didn't think it was wrong. He told himself he was just checking on her. Truth be told, he might have fucked her had she not flushed him from her life. Maybe he would have. He missed Sue something awful. And he vowed to be true to her.

Yet, a part of him could already see his life down the line, the part after Sue moves on to more practical lovers, richer, talented, whip-smart, and ambitious lovers. He could already see that part of the road and himself standing alone in the middle of it. The sun was setting. Neill was alone on the road.

But, Sissy did finally answer the phone.

"Hi," Neill said. He used the voice he imagines they use in the Funny Farm when talking to someone who has just taken a warm bath with a sharp object.

"Hi, Neill," Sissy said. "What's up?"

Was it boredom? Weariness? Pain?

"I just wondered how you were. Are."

"Uh huh."

"That's not why I called?"

"Who knows?"

"Sissy, look, you wanna go get some dessert or something."

There was a pause like a hiccup in a storm.

"Neill, I know your little high school honey is back at school and you're thinking, I don't know, any port in a storm."

This stung. Did it sting because there was an element of truth to it? Will Neill's inner voice continue asking itself questions?

"Sissy, it's not like that. I want to be." Neill stopped. He hated himself.

"Right. Bye, Neill."

"Sissy."

But there was only a hiss, the kind you get for a bad performance.

And at the P&H

"Is Crow coming?" Bidden asked with popcorn in his mouth. Wanda had installed a Jiffy Pop hotplate. The thrill of watching the silver balloon inflate was almost better than the popcorn, except that Neill and Bidden loved popcorn. When microwave popcorn came into their lives they both vowed to leave all their money to whoever invented it.

"He said he was."

"Meaning probably no."

"Meaning probably no."

Hamburgers were placed in front of our goslings.

"What about Gulley? Or Shlomo?"

"Gulley is doing something with his wife. He has a wife."

"I know that."

"I just mean. He has a wife. He has a life. Crow has a wife. What are we doing?"

"Right."

"And Shlomo is fixing to get married. Can you believe that?"

"To the dancer."

"Daisy, right. Is this hamburger particularly good tonight?"

"I was just thinking the same thing. I think the difference is the freshness of the buns. They must have just gone across the street for a hot case."

"Yeah, that's it. Did you get an invitation to Shlomo's wedding?"

Bidden put his hamburger down. He looked toward the jukebox, which was playing "Mack the Knife."

"Sorry," Neill said. "I just thought, if he invited me, he invited you."

"You and he are a lot closer."

"I don't know."

"Where is he getting married?"

"Wolf River Society. That club downtown on Madison, I think, where the lawyers meet. 2nd floor, walkup from the street."

"Don't know it."

"Marriage though. We should be closer to it, don't you think?"

"Who says? You're closer than I am."

"Naw. Not with my teen lover."

"You want to get married?"

"Not right now. Not tonight. Not this year. I don't know. Sometime. Though I am bothered by the idea that marriage is like a meal with the dessert at the beginning."

"That's a tired joke."

"All my jokes are tired. They've been up all night trying to come to grips with self-irony. You're Captain Blithe."

"Steal from forgotten writers. That's my advice," Bidden said, licking a last daub of mustard from his lip.

The End of Spring

Neill thought the summer would never arrive. Sue's latest letters had been perfunctory and he couldn't get her on the phone the whole final week before she graduated. He assumed she was busy with parties and outings circling around the graduation festivities.

Parties. Yes, this concerned him.

The day she arrived home Neill was invited to dinner at the Goorile's manse, Charon Hall. He was happy to go. He liked it at the Goorile's. The sisters were beautiful and funny and Mrs. Goorile's new husband, a man richer than Croesus, was bland and cool, and accepted Neill as only the latest of too many young people traipsing in and out of the manse.

Sue was beautiful. She seemed older, better put together. She was dressed in a short cotton dress that showed off her nonpareil legs, which ended in ballet slippers. She threw her arms around Neill and kissed him long and hard on the mouth, in front of God and the Gooriles.

Dinner was prepared by their long-time maid and cook. This was still the South. Though she was a beloved part of the family—and Neill loved her immediately and whole-heartedly because she seemed placid and as if she contained the wisdom of the ages—it still made Neill a little uncomfortable. The word 'domestic' kept sticking to the roof of his mouth.

After the meal—the best fried chicken Neill had ever tasted, specifically requested by Sue for her homecoming meal, and mostly pleasurable and heady conversation except when Mrs. Goorile said something amiss, something about her new stepson who was absent, that made Sue blush with anger and go quiet for a spell—the family gathered in their sunken den, a room of dark woods and an entire wall bookcase, stuffed with great fiction. Sue sat in Neill's lap in an old overstuffed chair.

The announced entertainment for the night was that Neill was going to initiate the Goorile family into the cult of Leonard Cohen. Sue had mentioned Neill's passion for the gloomy Canadian scop and songwriter to her parents and, being the intellectually curious smart folks they were, they asked Neill to bring an LP and play it for them.

He chose the first album, *Songs of Leonard Cohen*.

As it played Neill's stomach was beginning to knot. The fried chicken was attempting to stir-fry Neill's gut. They hated Leonard Cohen. They saw how puerile and insipid Neill's tastes were. He had not read Proust (there was a *hardback* box set in the middle of the book wall) and he was a pretender, a con man, a phony. He didn't know big wood from brush.

Then, the LP was over. The room grew quiet. The new husband puffed away on his pipe as if he were Professor Jacob Barnhardt from *The Day the Earth Stood Still*.

"That was beautiful," beautiful Mrs. Goorile said.

"He really is so great," Sue said.

"He is," Goneril added, smiling at Neill. Neill loved Goneril.

"I love him," Patsy piped up.

The new husband puffed up his pipe. "Those songs are quite well-written. I am not sure you can call it poetry, but it has a certain *something*. I am not crazy about the fussy arrangements though. I could have done without those female singers."

All Neill was concerned about now was taking Sue Goorile back to his lair to do all the things he had been saving since Spring Break.

"Sweetcakes," Sue said, as they moved away from the family into her bedroom, where her suitcase lay on the bed, its contents spilled as if it were gore from a wound. "Would you be terribly hurt if I pleaded fatigue and just went to bed here? We can get together first thing tomorrow."

Neill was terribly hurt. He thought his life was over. He thought he would never be happy again.

"Ok," he said. "I'm tired, too." (He wasn't.)

And he drove home and all night clawed at his own flesh coating, attempting, seriously, to remove it from his skeleton.

To See the World in a Drop of Semen

The next morning, Neill exited his bedroom, having slept fitfully. He had those wild ass middle-of-night illogical fantods. He was tanked-up on sleepless anxiety.

Still, he was looking forward to seeing Sue alone this morning. It was a Sunday and so he did not work. Iago always took the Sunday shifts so he could sit on his ass at the register and eat pork rinds and read his Civil War histories and, reluctantly, point customers toward approximately where they could find the book they were looking for.

Should Neill call Sue first thing? Was that too needy? Needy is such a turn-off. He at least understood that.

But to not call seemed silly.

He waited till 10:30. Not ten because that seemed too early. And not eleven because that would seem as if he were waiting for an exact right time to call.

"Hi, Mrs. Goorile," Neill said. "Sue up yet?"

"Hi Neill. She's up and you can have her."

"Ha ha," Neill laughed. "I'll take her."

There was that hissy silence again. It wasn't a joke?

Sue came on the line.

"Hey, Sue Goo, everything ok?"

"Get me out of here."

"Gladly," Neill said and gladly he jumped in his car and went to fetch. He found her standing under the portico as if waiting for a bus. She ran out to the car and jumped in.

"Not a good morning?"

"My mother," Sue said. She had her arms crossed. Neill wanted to feign concern, but more than that, he wanted to fuck Sue Goorile.

Sue sighed. She uncrossed her arms. She leaned over and kissed Neill.

"Everything is alright now," she said.

So, at eleven on a Sabbath morning, Neill and Sue were lying in his bedroom, listening to Thunderclap Newman's *Hollywood Dream*, completely naked, holding each other like conjoined twins.

Sue was more sexually confident. This would have worried worrisome Neill had he not been so intent on touching, kissing, sucking, and licking every square inch of his nubile lie-a-side.

Neill was pulling apart the cheeks of Sue's ass, a hand on each side, hoisting her off the bed. He kneaded her fresh cheeks and relished their young pliability. He slipped a finger over her anus and into her already sweltering box. In a few moments, she had her first orgasm.

Neill was happy. He was also so aroused he feared he would detonate.

"Hey, Sweetcakes," Sue said after the first orgasm. "Lie still."

She gently pushed him onto his back. "Close your eyes," she said.

Neill did and Sue, kneeling next to him, began to run both hands lightly over his chest and arms and stomach. Neill groaned. Sue ran her smooth little hands down over Neill's hips and down each leg. She massaged his calves and feet. Then her hands made a slow, light ascent toward their ultimate goal.

"Neill," Sue whispered, as if it were a séance. "Look."

Neill opened his eyes. He did not know what she wanted him to see but he liked what he saw, her marble-white body, naked as the wind, kneeling beside his manhood, hovering like a saint at her altar. She looked like a statue entitled *Morning Figura Veneris Prima*.

"You're beautiful, Sue. God, I missed your body."

"No, look," Sue said, nodding her head toward Neill's dick. Neill had seen it before.

"That little bit of sunlight coming in the window is shining inside the drop of sperm on the head of your penis."

Neill saw it now. Sue was rapt.

"It's beautiful," she said.

"Take it," Neill said.

And she did. She licked it off, slowly, circulating his engorged head the way a mother cat cleans its kittens.

"It tastes like sunshine," Sue said.

Then, she stuck his whole dibble in her mouth and began to suck on it, expertly, as if she had been practicing. It was a delicious blowjob.

But instead of coming in her mouth, just at the right time, Sue leapt atop him and buried his overfilled dick inside herself. She came one more time just as Neill let it go.

It was the Summer of Sue Goorile

It was the summer of Sue Goorile.

Neill was besotted. Sue was fun, funny, sexy, and as pretty as sunlight. The petulance only made an occasional appearance. When it did, it was like a cloud over the picnic. Neill would hold his breath and wait for it to pass and pray it didn't ruin the day or night. Or, most especially, the chance for one more time in the sack.

Sex with Sue Goorile was to Neill what Spring was to Planet Earth.

Did we mention that Neill had never felt another female body interlock with his in quite this way? He really believed (was he foolish to believe this? was he goopy with love and desire?) that their bodies were made to fit together like puzzle pieces. When her young vaginal muscles gripped him, and he held her slim, boyish body close, and when they would number three together, Neill thought it had cosmic significance.

In many ways, Sue Goorile was the first woman Neill fell completely in love with, the kind of reckless love that cannot be held back by wall or moat. He decided, or the Fates decided for him, depending on your religion, that he and Sue were to stay together forever, till dust do them part. Did he think about the term 'marriage?' He did. For the first time.

Once, driving in Midtown Memphis in the Beemer, with the heat index around 100, they stopped at a red-light and Neill leaned over and kissed Sue deeply. When he righted himself he noticed a trio of young black women sitting on a low brick wall waiting for the bus, just to the left of the driver's side. They were beside themselves (in truth and in mirth) and it was such a curious thing that Neill rolled his window down, and with a smile, said, "What?"

They all looked at each other. They guffawed again. The light changed. Neill sat still.

One of them, a beauty with skin like Mississippi River water said, pointing beyond Neill, "Is that a boy?"

Neill burst out laughing. Sue laughed too, bless her. She knew it was the short hair, the boyish shoulders.

"I assure you," Neill said, "she is not a boy. She is, I tell you with all sincerity, the most exquisite woman I have ever fucked."

This brought about another gale of laughter and Neill rolled on, satisfied.

Another afternoon, late in summer, when Neill had already begun to dread Sue's going to college (of course she was going away to college, to Bryn Mawr no less, she was a Goorile, she was brilliant, she came from money), they took a long drive to the country home of Sue's grandmother. Riding along the almost deserted country blacktop, Talking Heads booming from the tape player (*Burning down the house, dooga dooga doog doog*) (forever and anon after this day Talking Heads would cause Neill a twinge of sadness and regret), Neill could not keep his eyes off Sue's funny/comely face, nor his hand off her rounded thigh, soft as a sigh in a dream.

They arrived at a mansion in the woods, home to Mrs. Goorile's mother, ancient but full of character and still appointed with priceless antiques and severe-looking paintings, slightly dusty, with long rooms where a football game could be played comfortably, with 22 players per side and a grandstand. Sue's grandmother was away so they were greeted by the maid.

"Hey, Priddy," Sue said. "This is Neill. We're gonna go for a swim."

"Yes, ma'am," Priddy said, nodding a greeting to Neill. "Mrs. Webster told me you were coming. I've laid out some lunch and ice tea in the kitchen."

"Wonderful," Neill said, and gave Priddy his grownup smile.

"Thanks, Priddy. We might swim first."

"Ok," Priddy said, and then drifted away.

The swimming pool was down a walkway, a good distance from the house, and secreted beneath overhanging trees. It was dark like a tarn and the water seemed more like lake water than a backyard swimming pool. The air was cool and scented with a leafy-chlorophyll perfume.

Sue pulled her shirt and shorts off, underneath which she was wearing a light beige two-piece. She almost looked naked; the suit was so close to her skin color. Neill stripped down too, and before they got in the pool, Sue came close to him and put her hand over the tuft of hair that ran between Neill's boys and his navel.

"Have I ever told you how much I like this patch of hair?" Sue said and slipped Neill a kiss before jumping into the pool, gracelessly, a half cannonball, half belly flop. Neill calmly descended the mildewed steps.

He dove under. The water was warm and slightly brackish. When he surfaced Sue was still in the shallow end.

"Come on," Neill said.

"Neill, *Sweetcakes*," Sue groaned. "I can't swim."

Neill laughed.

"Then why are we in a swimming pool? Why did we come this far?"

"To get away, Knucklehead." Neill swam over to her. "And so we can do this."

Sue leapt into Neill's arms. Weightless in the water, Neill was able to hold her up and press his mouth against hers. His watery willy was pressed against her belly.

"And this," Sue said.

She reached down and pulled him out of his bathing suit. Neill's suit drifted to the bottom of the pool. She was using Neill's dick like a magic marker, writing secret codes on her bare belly. Neill was in a reverie.

He pulled her bottoms off and she readjusted herself. Neill sank slowly into her.

"Oh, you feel so good," Neill said.

Their lubricated bodies slid together like a sausage and its thin skin. Soon they established a sculduddery rhythm. And sooner than later, Neill began to come inside her. Sue pressed her mouth against his.

"This was a good idea," Neill said.

"Mm hm," Sue added.

The little cloud appeared.

What had gone wrong?

"I didn't come for some reason," Neill's multi-orgasmic girlfriend said. And then she was up the steps, out of the pool, naked as a Scotchman's knee, and running toward the house. "Come on," she called. "I'm famished."

Neill awkwardly pulled his swimming suit back on. The cloud was inside him now.

Meanwhile in Retail

A sea change occurred in Memphis around this time. The book business, traditionally dominated by mall bookstores, especially Waldenbooks and Brentano's, had recently seen the growth of something called Superstores, free-standing bookstores that were large, well-moneyed, and diverse. Barnes and Noble was the ugly pimple on the face of what was a gentle business, but there was also a new chain called Borders, originating in Ann Arbor, Michigan, of all places. Their edge was their size and their smarts. They were, even at gargantuan magnitude, decidedly literary. To use a basketball metaphor, it was like having a big man who can shoot threes.

And, in response to this explosion, Waldens began to fade. And in further response, there sprung up a small, Southern, homemade version of the Superstore, called Pluto and

Persephone's. Started by two female social workers in Nashville, Tennessee, just down the road, as we continue to call Interstate 40. They were sharp women who saw the development before many did and their two-story Nashville store became a powerful force in Southern bookselling.

So, it was inevitable, as Mark follows Matthew, as Springsteen follows Dylan, that Memphis would soon have their own Pluto and Persephone's. Or, put more correctly, that the mini-chain would see Memphis as its next step.

They opened a semi-large store, right between the two best small independent stores in Memphis, Neill's The Book Shelf and Charlotte's The Roundtable. Deliberate? Of course. Even with social workers, this is how business is done.

And Bidden, who had bounced around since he left Waldens, found his calling there. And, following him, as Luke follows Matthew, as Tennille follows the Captain, Victoria was also part of the opening staff at the new store.

And, further AND, Neill's delightful bosses could not foresee what would happen (who did?...more later) and sent a basket of fruit to the Grand Opening of Memphis' Pluto and Persephone's store.

Neill was happy for Bidden. Bidden deserved any success he could find.

And, So

Sue started Bryn Mawr. Neill started pining. The letter writing continued, steadily, if not with the same starved ardor. If Neill were mature enough he would say to himself, she deserves to grow up among her peers, to wring from her college years every bit of education, experience, and adventure it could present. Life was just beginning for Sue!

But Neill was not that adult. How many of us are, regardless of age? Instead, Neill fretted that Sue was moving beyond him (he perhaps got used to the idea of the older man and the younger woman and had begun to count on it for its pedagogic tilt), and that Sue was having affairs with new men, younger men, smarter men, stronger men.

Of course, she was but we only know that from the perch of The Omniscient Narrator. Neill could not be sure and so he lived with hope, hope that Love was so strong between them that Sue would prefer him to experience.

Neill spent his time selling books, reading books, writing lovesick verse. There were a few minor flirtations abrewing also and he tried one more time to talk to Sissy. She hung up.

His nights involved either lonely reading or lonely outings with Goffredo, or Bidden, or Shlomo Einstein, who was fast becoming one of his best friends.

The fall passed. The autumn passed. Winter was a cumin in. Sue was returning from her first semester to spend Christmas with Neill.

Have You Talked to Gulley Lately?

"Have you talked to Gulley lately?" Neill asked.

"I have," Bidden said. He was looking at one of his French fries with a surgeon's concentration.

"What's wrong?"

"With Gulley? Same old thing. You know."

"With the French fry. And with Gulley, too."

"This fry has a black spot. Is that good?"

"I don't think it's bad."

"I thought black spots were bad."

"On your skin. You think your fry has cancer?"

"I guess it's ok." He swiped it through the ketchup as if he were adding disinfectant.

"What's wrong with Gulley?"

"Victoria. What else?"

"Not getting any better?'

"I have to work with her," Bidden said. Now he was digging in one of his teeth with his pinkie fingernail.

"How is she as an employee? You know she came to work for me briefly at The Book Shelf. Disaster."

"Same here. She's gonna get fired and I'm gonna feel like shit."

"What's her problem?"

"Well, when she shows up, which is about 50% of the time, she is usually so drugged up and sleepless that she is like a zombie. Customers don't like zombies waiting on them."

"Except at Halloween."

"Even then I would think not."

"Well, she's not your concern out there, I mean, professionally."

"No. But I spoke up for her."

"Jesus. It doesn't get better."

"Gulley says she lives on microwaved hotdogs, cigarettes, and Darvon. She weighs about as much as Little Neill."

"I haven't seen her in months. Where is Gulley tonight? And—wait—why are you digging in your tooth?"

"I think that cancer spot is stuck between my teeth."

"It will surely become a cavity."

"That's what I was thinking."

"You want me to look."

"He's on the boat."

"What?"

"Gulley. He shipped out."

"Oh, yeah. The tug. What an awful job."

"Gulley kinda likes it. Solitude, basketball. When he's not in discussion with redneck whites about General Forrest, or buffed up blacks about Larry Bird."

"I guess it's an escape for him. Six months gone, six months away. For me, anathema."

"They have an inhaler for that."

"Ha! Anyway, I couldn't do it, be gone and on a floating jail for six months."

"Well, me neither. I need to stay close to my home bathroom."

"Exactly."

"Got it." Bidden brandished something on the tip of his finger.

"That's not black."

"It's not, is it? What do you think it is?"

"Something orangish. When did you eat something orangish?"

"I don't know. What food is orange?

"Oranges."

"I hate oranges."

"Something from a potpie?"

"Yes! Of course. It's potpie crust."

"Orange crust?"

"I thought it looked funny but I ate it anyway."

Winter and Other Challenges

First off, Neill could not drive on ice or snow. Though he had Canadian genes, he got a bad dose apparently, and he was terrified of being out of control behind the wheel of a car. He had nightmares about it. Bidden suffered from the same phobia. They let it color half their year. About September Neill began to worry about icy days. The fact that Memphis had one, maybe two icy days each winter did not comfort our hero, nor his compatriot, Bidden.

Neill had been counting the days (well, hell, we need something better than this cliché) until Sue was to return from her first semester of college. Their correspondence had been sweet, even sexually longing in places, but not as constant or as fervid as Neill would have wished (Neill thought it a lifelong plague that he was more passionate, in too many of his relationships, than his mates). Neill had marked the December date of Sue's return on the calendar in his head and, at night, he would conjure wild sexual escapades that he hoped would be his during this festive season. Noel!

December 18th. That was the date.

Of course, Memphis got a rare early snowstorm, dumping two inches on the Bluff City and coating the streets with a rink-like glaze. Fuck it all to hell, Neill said to himself. He called Bidden. Fuck it all to hell, he said to Bidden. Bidden was supportive.

Sue called. She was home. Her plane had arrived safely, though late and she was waiting at her mother's ancestral home for Neill's return to her.

"The streets are icy," Neill said.

"I know," Sue said. "I just rode on them from the airport."

"Who picked you up?"

"Roy."

"Does he have a crush on you?"

"What? No."

"Ok. Can he bring you to me?"

"Neill. Come over here. The whole family is gathered to celebrate the return of their now grown college-attending daughter. "

"But the streets are icy," Neill whined like a tea kettle.

"Just come over. Or don't."

Sue hung up.

Neill freaked. He walked around and around his small house. He was seeking peace and finding only disquiet and cowardice. He also sought his balls. They were missing as well.

What trumps fear? he asked himself. Sexual Desire. That could be true. Sexual Desire that has been building for five months.

Neill bundled himself in cheap layers of old clothing and put the car keys in his pocket. His Toyota moved about as well on ice as a shoebox would.

Neill made it down his street and to the corner of Central Avenue. Central would lead him straight to Sue. He sat at the light and craned his neck westward. It looked like the Ice Capades in Gehenna. It was densely packed hoar, with glimmers of silvery ice. It was pretty if you had a death wish.

"If my life ends here know that I loved you," Neill said.

He steered onto the field of play. The car moved lightly as if it were riding on air. Neill managed about 15 miles per hour. The car slid a little this way, a little that way. What was it his father said? Steer toward the skid? Could that be right? Why are counterintuitive things often the right way?

Lucky for Neill, the street was all but deserted.

He made his slow progress toward his sooterkin. Finally, he made it to Lamar. It was a little better. Traffic had made tire paths. Neill's confidence grew. Soon Sue Goorile would be leaping into his arms and pressing her perfect white mouth against his, and he would greet the family as if he had just flown across the Pacific, and he would swoop his ladylove into his arms, carry her back to the Death Machine, and take her back to his house, where he would show her the 43 new positions he had been studying. He even allowed himself the fantasy that Sue's mother would let her spend the night at Neill's rather than chance the roads one more time.

At the door, Sue did indeed kiss Neill. A light kiss, a sweet kiss.

"Whew," Neill said. He wanted a badge, or something.

"Come in, we're all down here."

They were in the sunken, book-lined den. They were watching *The Bells of St. Mary's* on TV. Neill had never seen it.

"Hello," Neill said, unwinding a checkered scarf, unbuttoning his heavy coat.

"Neill!" many in the room said. "Hot chocolate?"

"Well," Neill hesitated. "I don't know."

He was waiting for Sue to say they couldn't stay long.

"Sit down, Goofball. Take off your coat and I'll get you a cup."

Neill reluctantly took off his coat. And sat in the chair that was where he was served his cocoa and his girlfriend took a seat on his lap.

Neill sipped. They watched a little of the movie. Bing Crosby is a priest? Who's the kid with the angelic voice?

"I've never seen this," Neill whispered.

Sue whispered back. "Me neither. It doesn't look that compelling."

"Do you want to go now then?"

"Go?"

"Back to my place."

"Neill," Sue said, as if her patience with him was paper thin. "I just got home. I don't want to go out on the icy streets."

Neill's heart sank. His temper rose.

"I know," he rasped in Sue's ear. "I didn't want to come out in it either. But I wanted to come get you."

"Here I am," Sue said. And she turned her face to the screen.

Neill sat a while longer. Then he rose and grabbed his coat and scarf.

"Thanks for the cocoa," Neill said. He had a catch in his throat, a small catch that he wanted to throw back.

He headed for the door. Sue padded obediently behind.

"Goddamn it," Neill said at the door.

"I'll talk to you tomorrow," Sue said, gently closing the heavy door.

Neill returned to his car. He prayed that God would spin him off the road and into a heaven where beautiful young lovers always got together, every day, every night.

Neill Slept Little

Of course he slept little.

He was full of anguish. Neill was faced with a beautiful young woman's indifference. A young woman he *loved*,really loved. He would rather have faced a firing squad or a pack of hungry weasels. He wanted to face weasels. He wanted to bleed, to show some kind of physical difference that limned the pain inside.

The next day the bookstore was closed because the roads were still too icy.

Neill had instant coffee and a honey bun about 8 a.m. Then, he got sick to his stomach.

Then, he tried to read (Thomas McGuane's *Ninety-two in the Shade*) but his concentration was shot through with starlight. There were holes in the ceiling of his mind. He turned on the TV, found MTV immediately. Music videos. Who thought of them? They made Neill happy, mostly. (Who was that cute VJ, as we learned to call them...Martha Something? And the Toni Basil video made him horny.) Not this morning. Somebody called Laura Brannigan doing a song called "Solitaire."

The thing about being horny, about carrying that erection around with you, all alone in your home, is that it is so insistent, so overpowering, so *human*, that you can't imagine that everyone wouldn't want to feel that way, RIGHT NOW. It just made sense that you could call *anyone* and tell her, 'Listen I am really thinking about sex right now," and they would drop what they were doing and join you for some great, fleshly yoni yoga.

It rarely happened this way and it caused Neill no small amount of wonder and disappointment with the universe.

Goffredo had a new girlfriend. He slept at her place a lot. He was there now. This made Neill feel even more isolated.

Around 11 a.m.—how did he get there?—Sue called.

"Good morning, Sweetcakes."

How to play it?

"Hi, Sue," Neill said.

"You pissed?"

`   "No, no." Of course, he was. At her? At the world? At himself?

"Roy is going out in about an hour. He offered to drive me to your house."

"He spent the night there?"

"Of course. The roads were icy."

When had Neill landed in Wonderland?

"Yes. I mean, yes, that's nice of him. Come over, please."

"Ok, Sweetcakes, see you soon."

Neill paced. Then, he showered. Then, he paced some more. He dressed as nicely as he could. (Neill and clothes, not such a good match really.)

When Sue knocked on the door, Neill was standing too close to it. He couldn't jerk it open as if he had waited at the door the whole time. He walked backwards silently. Then, he walked forwards and opened the door.

"Lemme in. It's goddamn cold out here."

Neill put his arms around her. She had on a bulky winter coat so it was like hugging a soft redwood.

"Lemme get my winter things off."

"Yes. Great. Put them on the couch."

"Coat," Sue said, and coquettishly tossed it onto the couch. "Scarf. Hat. Galoshes." It was a funny striptease, except Neill left his sense of humor in the bathroom.

"Throw them by the door. Do you know what the singular of galoshes is?"

"Galosh."

"You knew."

"No! Is it really?"

"It is. You stripped enough?"

"I don't know," Sue said, putting a finger on Neill's chest. "You want to put this freezing body under some covers?"

"I do. I honestly do. "

"Let's go, Sweetcakes. I've missed your dick."

They went to bed.

Under the covers, they undressed each other. It was like playing inside a pup tent. They both kept their socks on. Somehow, this turned Neill on even more.

Sue's body. There it was again. Those hips like snowy hills. The equally smooth snowy hills of her fanoir. Those pale, ghostly breasts with their delicate pastel nipples. That mole. That delightful, blond sweetgrass. And her frothy, ever-ready harbor of hope.

And her hand pulling on him as if she really did miss him after five months. Everything was ok, he thought, for now, for now.

Conception | 293

"Do you remember the first time we went to bed together?"

"Of course. The book shelf day."

"Yes."

"And you said, 'maybe we can just take off our shirts.'"

"Ha. I did. I was so bold, right?"

"You were."

"Do you also remember entering me that afternoon, the first time?"

"Yes. I cherish that memory. I will take it to my grave." (This is true. Neill did.)

"I want you to do it to me that way again."

"From behind?"

"Yes, please." And here, she turned and made an S out of her young body and her white fundament was there for the taking. Neill took it.

Afterwards, as the semen reversed course and began to flow down Sue's legs, they held each other and kissed like the lovers they were meant to be.

My yin, Neill thought. Or is it yang?

A Tangled Colloquy at P&H

In attendance: Neill, Bidden, Pas, Crow, Gulley.

Bidden: Here's something interesting: there was a racecar driver named Dick Trickle.

Neill: Did you know racecar is a palindrome?

Pas: You're a palindrome.

Gulley: What have you got there?

Bidden: World Almanac, um, 1968.

Neill: You brought that with you?

Bidden: No, it was here on the seat.

Crow: When someone tells you that they are just honest or sincere, duck. It means they feel free to put you down in any manner possible.

Gulley: In the same way that preparing for a difficult journal helps you become able to accomplish the journey.

Pas: You still with the ghost-child?

Neill: Yes.

Crow: Ghost-child.

Neill: She's—paley.

Crow: She's like a pal?

Neill: Paley, long A, as in Grace.

Gulley: You're thinking of Grace Kelly.

Neill: Always. But I meant Grace Paley, the writer.

Bidden: She does not look like Grace Paley.

Gulley: Nor Kelly.

Crow: Who?

Neill: Who what?

Crow: Looks like Grace Kelly.
Bidden: Only Grace Kelly.
Gulley: That's the god's truth.

Happy Holidays from Neill Rhymer and Sue Goorile

Those were golden days. Neill tried to put any doubts he had about Sue's enthusiasm for their pairing out of his head and just pay attention to what was in front of him, namely Sue's sweet, meringue-white, naked torso. As beautiful as Syrie was Neill was more drawn to the almost boyish unmitigated sexuality of Sue Goorile.

They went out. They ate lunch together on Neill's lunch breaks. Some nights, they went to the movies. Some nights they stayed home and rented something on VHS and then did it like bed-lamites.

It was a good time, yet Neill was aware how it was precariously balanced on the unreal and on the tip of the temporal pyramid. They were about to slide down the other side. Sue was about to return to college.

As the date approached Neill became more frantic about pounding every pleasure out of every minute they were together. He overcompensated, overheated, overindulged, overall over-acted like a madman.

Three days before Sue's departure, they went out to eat at Pete and Sam's. Sue was full of smart talk and enthusiasm and wit. Her bright chatter was scraping against Neill's jittery cupidity. With every joke and anecdote, he felt her moving away from him. He smiled grimly. Sue prattled on. She was either unaware of her lover's attenuated state or she was standing outside it.

Apparently, the latter.

After dinner they went to bed. Their rutting was hot (the floor furnace was up too high but adjusting it required a high degree of ability, something like a nuclear physicist might enjoy) and sweaty. When Sue was sitting on him, in the dim glow from the small bedside light draped with a handkerchief, her glistening alabastrine body seemed unearthly. She had departed the earthly plane. She was a putto.

A sweaty, orgasmic putto.

She came three times in that upright position, each time her midi, exquisite breasts bobbing in ungodly sexiness. Neill almost blew her off the bed when he came. He came long and hard. Afterward, his balls ached.

Afterward, they lay entwined in their customary position, the one Neill was convinced was heaven-sent, or at least influenced by the minor minions of a just God. They clicked like closing a pocket-watch.

"Sweetcakes," Sue began, running a finger around in the sweat on Neill's sternum. "I'm gonna miss you."

"Oh, Jesus, Sue Goo, I don't want you to leave. I love you more than ever. It is hurting my heart. Literally."

"Neillcakes, you're an exaggerator. But I love you."

"I love you," Neill said back, stupidly.

"I'm leaving a little earlier than I told you."

Fuck.

"How much earlier? I can still get off work and drive you to the airport."

"Well...I am leaving tomorrow morning early."

Fuck.

"Fuck," Neill said, with unnecessary vehemence. "Why?"

"Oh, it's gonna be better this way."

"Better? How better? Less time together? How is that better?"

Sue hesitated, yet she had the poise of the young, who feel little that is lasting because they have centuries ahead of them.

"Better that I leave and go to this party."

There was more. Neill was holding his breath. Sue had stopped writing in his perspiration.

"There's a group of us, well, we got close last semester and we are gonna meet upstate for some skiing."

"You don't ski," Neill said. It was almost a supplication.

"That's not the point. I think it's better." Fuck. "If we." Fuck. "Break it." FUCK! "Off clean."

FUCK!

"Clean? What the—" But Neill knew *what the.*

"I'm sorry, Sweetcakes."

Neill was speechless. His throat was tight. Tears were gathering like a posse in search of a madman.

"This is it. It's over?"

"Sweetcakes—"

"Don't—"

"It's better. I am too young for you. You can do better than me."

Neill, rightly, hated this kind of crap faux-reasoning, this kind of affected breakup blather.

"I've got a lot of time away from you ahead of me. It's not fair to you to ask you to wait."

More of the same. Fuck.

"I will never forget you. You've been such a beautiful part of my youth."

She had grown beyond him. He was ten years older than her, but she had passed him by on the road as if he were a cretin hitchhiking with a sign that read "Rapist Needs a Ride."

Sue kissed him. She pushed the blankets aside. Neill grabbed her arm. She gently shook him off. She was dressed before Neill could think of anything pithy or nocuous or ingenious or vicious or self-destructive to say. Something to stay the execution. The governor was asleep. He didn't care about one more poor lovesick swain dying. Pull the fucking switch.

"I'll call you when I get back to school."

Sue walked out of the bedroom. Neill couldn't move.

Sue came back.

"I forgot. I need you to drive me home."

Neill did. They kissed good night. They kissed goodbye. One dry kiss to kiss it all off.

You know the rest. Sue never did call Neill. Neill wrote some poor poetry, some weak missives, some rattle-brained pleas to reconsider. They all went unanswered.

Neill's whole life was now a PS. Post Sue.

The hours he wept over her, the length of time he wept over her, the perfect ass he was about her, went on and on, unspooling like some great film never to be shown or shared again. It was some kind of record, this lengthy longing. Some kind of sad perfect inane annal of pining.

Neill Calls Bidden Because He Can't Think of Anything Else to Do

"I'm really sorry, Buddy. Do you want me to come over?"

"No."

"Do you want to go to P&H?"

"No."

"What can I do? How can I help you?"

"You can't."

"Neill, you'll get through. That's not much but you know it's true."

"Meaning only that I won't die. That I *probably* won't die."

"I'm coming over."

"Ok."

"Stay right there."

"Where would I go?"

"Ok. I'm coming over."

"Thanks, Bid. I love you, man."

"Ok." Neill had never said this to a man before. Bidden did not know how to respond.

"And hey, Bidden. Can you bring me a hooker?"

"You really want a hooker?'

"No. Wait. You could get one?"

"No."

"Ok then."

"Want some Taco Bell?"

"No. I'd throw it up."

"Ok. I'm on the way."

"I could try a tostada."

There Were Dates, There was Some Concubitus 3

So, having no choice, Neill went back to the dating scene. After he cratered, after he fell apart emotionally, for a while, of course, wobbling crookedly through his days of bookselling and his nights of either masturbation and dark verse or weak conversations with Bidden, Crow, Gulle,y and Shlomo.

The boys were all supportive because boys are. And they had all been there. Sometimes one wants the company of one's gender, especially in those weeks after the opposite and opposing gender has turned your heart into an inedible puree.

The bookstore continued to feed Neill's need for other people and his appetite for literature.

Eventually, he felt good enough about himself to chance some private facetime with a woman. Or, as Shlomo put it, he needed to get his wick wet again.

And so he met a woman through an ad in *The New York Review of Books*. Seriously. Bidden brought it to him: a personals ad in that august paper from a single woman in Memphis. He did the thing required to get in touch with her. (Bidden brought it to Neill, though Bidden could have as easily answered the ad except that Bidden had even less heterosexual buoyancy than Neill.)

On the phone, she was very nice. She said she was frustrated by the dating scene (she did say 'dating scene,' which made Neill's cheek twitch) and figured that if there were a man in Memphis for her he would read *The New York Review of Books*.

Neill did not read *The New York Review of Books*, though he was *aware* of it, but he didn't not fess up to this. They made a date.

She worked in the lab at The University of Tennessee Health Sciences. She was very nice. She was attractive in the plain American smart woman mode, glasses, bangs, nice hips. Neill was attracted. She also had fingers that were as rough as quoits, burned by the chemicals she worked with every day.

They saw a movie. They went back to Neill's house. They made out on the couch.

Neill never called her again and she never called Neill again. Why? Who knows? Because the world's axis tilts one way and not another.

Then came Kat Dix (Yeah, her real cognomen...), a beautiful redhead with a body like Lisa Lyons. As it turned out Kat worshiped Lisa Lyons, and her sculpted, muscular physique was modeled after the Robert Mapplethorpe photographs of the striking bodybuilder.

Kat Dix was muscular and she had breasts that were so perfect Neill thought they were counterfeit, done up in Russ Meyer's lab.

But, we're getting ahead of ourselves. Let's say he hasn't seen them yet, but only dreamed of seeing them. Ok.

Kat was a friend to many of Neill's friends. Midtown Memphis is incestuous and a city within the city where everyone has dated everyone else at least once. Initially, Neill wasn't that attracted to Kat. She was certainly pretty and her red hair was like a flower for Neill's stinger. But she was also a tad graceless (big-boned is how politely his mother would have put it) for all her impressive physical attributes. She was heavy of step, a bit like Alice the Goon, if Alice the Goon were a fine-looking redhead.

When Neill called to ask her out she was taken aback.

"Really?" she said. "Really?"

"Is it so surprising?"

"I don't know. I know some of the women you've dated."

"They've spoken ill of me." It wasn't a question.

"No, no. I don't mean that. They are all just, well, *gorgeous*."

"No," Neill said. (Were they really? he thought) "None prettier than you."

Needless to say, he was in.

They made a plan to see a production of A *Streetcar Named Desire* that was playing at Playhouse on the Square.

Kat and Neill

So, they began seeing each other. Not every night, but steadily.

After the play, the first date, they went back to her place, a second story of an old duplex near Overton Park (being up high it seemed almost a treehouse) and they sat and talked about books and movies.

On her walls were many photographs. One in particular caught Neill's attention. It was a nude, black and white, the woman bent forward so that her hair covered her face. Her body was shapely, large-breasted, strapping. Neill suspected he was looking at the naked body of his date.

"Presents," Kat Dix said, waving her hand at all the photos. "From an ex-boyfriend."

Was there any embarrassment in her pronouncement? Neill couldn't tell.

At the end of the evening they kissed and it was a good kiss, a kindling kiss, the kind of first kiss that was like rubbing a stick in dry leaves. Only a little smoke was created. But Neill went home thinking about a second date.

The second date occurred only a few nights later.

After a movie (*The Dresser*) they returned to Kat's apartment. This time, with little glasses of wine in their hands, they went straight to the couch and straight to some rather expert osculation. Neill never did drink his wine (he really didn't drink alcohol anyway—have we already made this clear?)

This time the kiss took flame. Neill's hand under her shirt, over her bra, could only marvel at the shapeliness of what it was caressing. Neill's hand was full of wonder and desire. It sent a message to Neill's animal brain. "Let's see these," the message said.

As if intercepting the message and decoding it the way THRUSH might have, Kit Dix reached inside her shirt and removed her bra. What spilled into Neill's hands was a quantity of soft, yet firm mammary that rivaled his high school sweetheart's. In short, Kat Dix's breasts were perfect on a grand scale. *The Last Supper* of breasts. The Joyce's *Ulysses* of breasts. The "Peaches en Regalia." So, when Kat pulled her shirt off Neill was virtually blinded by gorgeousness and pulchritude. But, what his eyes saw, his hands ate hungrily. Jesus God, Kat Dix felt great.

Hands volitant, bodies arching, crotches ablaze. Soon Neill's shirt was also off and Kat Dix was pressing her palms against the sides of his thighs, leaving no doubt that she wanted to do more. Neill swept in and began to knead her Y through her denim shorts. Kat began to pant.

Kat Dix liked sex. This was a remarkable turn-on. (Remarkable because not every woman liked sex? Or were confident enough to act on liking it? Here, we venture into sociology and we'd rather stick with narrative. This is narrative.)

She began to rub Neill's dingum through his pants. Neill fell backwards in delight, throwing his arms out, panting himself. In mock abandonment he said, "Oh, just take me!"

Kat Dix laughed. She swung up and kissed his mouth quickly and just as quickly, like a *pharmakeus*, she popped Neill's pants open and pulled his bunny up into her strong hands. Jesus, her hands were strong.

If her handjob was a little too robust, her blowjob was as tender as a kitten licking milk.

"Holy Moses, Kat," Neill said, holding her red head in his lap as she licked and sucked.

She looked up.

"Are you smiling, Neill Rhymer? Are you having a good time?"

"Jesus," Neill repeated, stupidly.

"Come in my mouth?"

"Phhtt, Kat. I'd love to."

"Ok then," she said, tickling his scrotum as she conversed.

"I should make you come first," gallant Neill said, between gasps.

"Because afterwards your desire will have gone the way of all flesh?"

"Yessss," Neill said, as her fingertips were running around on his balls, like bugs skittering across a toy left outside.

"Next time me," she said. "Well, and you too."

And she went back to work.

When Neill came he pulled the red curtain of her hair aside so he could watch her digesting his sperm. She seemed to be gargling it in her cheeks as he pumped more into her. Kat Dix loved giving blowjobs! She loved come in her mouth!

Neill wanted to run out into the night and shout it.

Instead, they lay in repose for a while. The sight of Kat Dix naked, lying across his lap, filled Neill with tenderness.

Next time, she had said.

Neill thought about that going home. He wanted a next time, yessir.

Was this the start of a relationship? It was too tricky to tell. Neill was confused and Neill confused is problematical. Have we already demonstrated this?

Kat and the Gang

Kat called Neill the next day and asked if he was free that night. It was a Saturday night, traditionally the time for the gathering of the tribe at P&H. Should Neill invite her to join them? This was always a minor sticky-wicket. Bidden had brought a date once. But Gulley always came without Victoria. Pas was a welcome feminine addition to the gang but she was an insider, a progenitor of the entire series.

"I'm meeting friends at P&H," Neill said.

"Oh," Kat Dix said, her voice dropping slightly.

"I'm sorry—I—"

"It's ok. I wanted to cook for you."

"Sunday night?" Neill asked.

"I can't," Kat Dix said a little too quickly.

"Why don't you come to P&H? We could eat at your place first?"

"Dynamite," Kat Dix said.

"Ok then. I'll show up—when?"

"Soon!" Kat Dix said. Her enthusiasm was lovely and child-like.

"Immediately after work. Say 5:30?"

"Yes," Kat said. "I'm gonna give you something good to put in your mouth."

Neill laughed. "Well," he said.

"Not as good as what you have for me," Kat Dix said and hung up.

All that day at work Neill's head was full of this brawny redhead. He wondered about what she was doing Sunday night though it was way too early for jealousy. Wasn't it? The old boyfriend, the photographer, perhaps?

"You're jumpy," Iago said.

"Gotta date," Neill said.

Iago slumped off. Iago never had a date. He hated that Neill did.

Neill showed up at Kat Dix's door at 5:20. He was usually neurotically early.

Kat Dix opened the door. Her hair was wet. She was only wearing a robe.

"I'm sorry, I know I am early."

"Come in," Kat said. "I'm naked but come in." She scooted off.

"We could skip dinner and P&H," Neill said and laughed at himself.

Kat turned back. She let the robe drop. "Really?" she said.

Neill stopped as if turned to a pillar of brackish sludge.

"Egads, you're beautiful," Neill said.

Her long, sinewy body was perfectly proportioned. Her arms were things of beauty. Her legs looked like they could crush you and Neill wanted to be crushed by them. And her gingery pubic hair was a shimmering invitation.

"Egads?' Kat laughed and skipped off again. The robe lay pooled on the floor like a bloodstain. Neill caught a glimpse of her rootus as she rounded the corner. It was, of course, powerfully built.

"I'd rather eat you than the dinner," Neill called after her.

Her voice came back from the hallway. "You don't even know what we're having."

Neill let the joke drop. She was dressing anyway.

She returned in a white blouse and jeans. They almost hid that exemplary body.

Dinner was simple pasta with a lemon/parmesan topping and fresh broccoli on the side. It was delicious. Occasionally during the meal, Kat took Neill's left hand and played with his fingers while they both made shy conversation between bites of pasta.

"Are your friends going to accept me horning in?" Kat asked in the car on the way.

"Of course. Everyone brings friends or lovers. It's a loose gathering."

"I guess I fall under the 'lover' designation."

"I guess you do," Neill said and squeezed her hand.

"If not now certainly by the time the night is over."

Neill got stiff. He couldn't believe the body next to him would be naked in his arms before the night ended. Life, friends, is occasionally not boring.

Pas and Bidden and Gulley were already there.

As they walked toward them their conversation stopped and they were opening staring. It was disconcerting for Neill. He imagined it made Kat frantic.

But no. She stepped forward, extending her hand to each person in the booth.

"Hi, I'm Neill's friend Kat. Thanks so much for letting me join the festivities."

"Neill, you told her there would be festivities?" Pas said.

The talk was congenial. Kat had a beer. Neill had a diet Pepsi.

"What do you do, Kat?" Pas asked.

"I'm finishing up med school."

"Ahh," Bidden said.

Kat laughed. Things were going well.

At some point, Shlomo slunk in and the booth became a boisterous and crowded party.

"Oh, someone new to dislike me," Shlomo said, when introduced to Kat.

"I've read your new novel," Kat said, surprising Neill.

"I'm sorry," Shlomo said.

"I think you're a genius," Kat said. Was she laying it on too thick? Out of nervousness? She didn't seem the shy type.

"I used to be a genius," Shlomo said. "But I didn't like the hours."

A general chuckling and eye-rolling arose. Everything was going so well!

"Gotta go pee this beer away," Kat said, rising and walking, heavily of foot, toward the darkened and smoky recesses of P&H.

"She's lovely," Pas said.

"Great tits," Shlomo said.

"You're in rare form tonight," Neill said.

"Sorry. Getting married. Eh."

"I know you're happier than you let on," Neill said.

"You know no such thing. But tell me about this feline."

"Kat's great. This is only our 2nd date. She's sexy as hell." Neill bit his tongue. He wanted to boast about what they were going to do later.

"But she dresses like a gym coach," Shlomo said.

"She does. She undermines her sexiness with a sort of plain-Jane act. I don't get it. There's something..."

The booth grew quiet. Neill didn't finish the thought.

On the drive back to Kat's apartment, Kat was ebullient.

"I love your friends," she said.

"I'm pretty sure they loved you, too."

"Shlomo Einstein. He's a trip. And a great writer."

Neill let a small boil of jealousy pass.

As soon as they were inside the door, Neill pulled her close. Standing they kissed long and with strong sucking and tongue wrestling.

"I've wanted you so badly all night."

"Me too," Kat said. "Get in bed."

Neill found the bed in the poorly lit apartment and Kat disappeared into the bathroom. He undressed down to his skivvies. And waited. It took hours, days, weeks.

Finally, the bathroom door opened and a sword-blade of light fell across the floor. It was quickly extinguished and Neill could only vaguely see Kat's approach.

She slipped under the covers. They embraced and restarted the French kiss.

"Mm," she said, as Neill moved his mouth to her neck. "What are you wearing?"

"Underwear," he said into her neck, which smelled of bath soap.

"Let me see," Kat said. She snaked a hand down his belly and over the bulge in his briefs. "Uh huh," she said. "I have this terrible worry that during the time I put in my diaphragm the man is going to lose interest. I am glad you didn't."

"Diaphragm. Other men," Neill said. He meant to only speak to himself.

"Bad? Bad? Sorry. Did I say something wrong? I hate to say the wrong thing."

She was genuinely worried.

"It's ok," Neill said. He just wanted to get to it.

"It's that diaphragm comment? My assumption of intercourse?"

"No. Nothing is wrong." But Neill had deflated. He hoped she couldn't tell.

"You've deflated," she said. She seemed on the verge of tears.

"Temporarily."

"I can't sustain it. The sexy thing. I can't sustain it."

"You can. You do. Come here."

She pressed up against him.

"Let's start this game over. What are you wearing?" Neill said. He assumed it was a game.

"Bra. Panties," she said. "Very brief panties."

Neill groaned. "I wanted to see them when you got through undressing. You skittered toward me in darkness."

"I'm a little shy, I guess."

"I saw you totally nude just hours ago."

"Oh yeah. I guess I was feigning boldness."

"It worked."

Neill removed Kat's bra. Her nildi. My God. He spent an inordinate amount of time kissing, sucking, pulling on them. Their fullness was potent. Everything about them was large, as if on another scale: tall, thick nipples, and aureoles like shadowy saucers, their heft was outsized, as was their power and their power to incite.

After they had reached inside each other's underwear and then stripped them off, Kat started to go down on Neill.

"Nope," he said. "You. We must do you."

Kat flopped back down on the pillow. She hit the bed like a sack of concrete.

`   Neill pulled the covers aside. There was just enough light that he could see the celestial shape of her. He kissed down her belly, around her navel, down her thighs, down her calves, licked her toes.

"Ooh," Kat said. She had thrown her head back in delight.

Neill put the vehicle in reverse and worked back northwards. Kat was opening her thighs as he did so. She wanted to be eaten.

Neill obliged. Her orangey crotch tasted vaguely of spermicide but her lips were soft and wide. He used his tongue and his fingers. He licked her clit. He lifted her buttocks and sucked deeper. He returned to the clit and began to give it some intense pressure. He felt good about himself. He was doing very well.

Kat grabbed him under the arms and pulled him onto her. She was so strong. And with such good aim. Neill's dick, only at half-mast, landed just over her sodden pussy.

"You're not hard," Kat said. That little ring of worry returned.

"Almost," Neill said, weakly.

And as he spoke, it did return. (Thank you, Neill silently invoked.) And soon they were finding a pleasing pace. She was so strong. And when she reached down and grabbed his scrotum as if to steer the ship home, Neill began to come and come.

Kat grabbed his ass and held him in place over her. She continued to grind against him.

After a while she slowed, slowed, and then stopped. Neill rested upon her.

They were both sweaty and Neill was relishing the damp, ticklish feel of the full length of her against him. He was luxuriating in afterglow. Great one, he was telling himself.

He kissed Kat. She kissed him but something was wrong.

"Something wrong?" Neill asked. (See, direct, that's the best method.)

"No. I just didn't come."

"Oh fuck," Neill said. "I was selfish again. Let me go down on you some more."

He moved downward again. He could smell his own sperm.

And just as he started to lick her, she began to cry.

"Never mind," she said.

The rest of the night was confusing and all lines of communication seemed to have blown down in a storm Neill didn't even remember witnessing. By the time he got dressed and made to leave, Kat had shut down completely.

"You're leaving," she said.

"I can stay," Neill said.

"No."

"Ok. I don't know what to do. I'll leave. I'll call you tomorrow."

"You won't," she said, and turned away from him.

He let himself out.

What?

What was going wrong with Kat Dix?

Neill was hung up on this question. Did she sense that he wasn't fully engaged? Did she sense he was holding that little something back? Wasn't it too early for such suppositions? Was she still thinking about her 'gorgeous' predecessors? It bothered Neill.

He did call her the next day. He needed a pretext so that it wasn't him calling simply because she doubted he would.

"Hey, Beautiful," Neill said into the plastic mouth of the devil.

"Neill, you did call," she said, sleepily.

"You were asleep."

"No, I wasn't. That's ok. I stayed up studying."

"After I left?'

"What day is this?'

Neill switched gears.

"You heard Jim Carroll?"

"Jim Carroll? I don't think so.

"He's dynamite. Can I bring his new album over and we'll listen to it together?"

This was weak. It was all he had.

"That would be great. Tonight? You want me to cook?"

"Let's get a pizza delivered."

And so they did. They ate their vegetarian Pizza Hut pizza and Neill expatiated a bit about Jim Carroll. The song "People Who Died" brought a wide-eyed look from Kat.

"I know this song. I heard it on WEVL. Had no idea who it was but I wanted to find out. I think I called the station. I don't remember."

"Shh," Neill said, smiling. He held up a teacherly finger.

Kat smiled and listened harder. They went through the entire album and the entire pizza. During the song "Catholic Boy," Kat was as still as a prostrate column.

"Wow," she said. "I was raised Catholic. He hit it all."

Then, they began to make out. Kat was wearing the loosest of shirts. Any looser and it would have been a scarf. Her bullish and superlative breasts were held in check with a black bra. Neill was so turned on, he got daring. He forgot they had so little history.

He took her hand and led her into her own bedroom. He stood her against a wall and he took a seat on the end of the bed facing her. He was the audience.

"Strip," he said.

"What?" Kat said. She looked genuinely confused.

"Strip," Neill repeated with a smile.

"Like dance?"

"No. I just want to watch you undress."

Kat was still uncertain. She began to take her clothes off quickly.

"Slower," Neill said. "I want to savor the sight."

She moved slower. She unhooked her bra and it fell away.

Neill sighed.

Kat began to slide the pants down her legs slowly, but she clearly was not into this. She stood back up. Her pants were still around her shins. Her face started to crinkle again.

"Forget it," Neill said, standing. "I'm sorry."

He held her. She put her head on his shoulder. Her body was full of sighs. Then, they made love slowly, reverently.

They never got together again.

Wanda: Class is in Session

"Kat coming tonight?" Bidden asked. "I'm thinking popcorn."

"Kat, no," Neill said. "That's over."

"Sorry. What happened?"

"Nothing."

"I know that feeling."

"She's great. I mean really great. And her body—I can't tell you. Ann-Margaret."

"And her hair."

"Right. She's Ann-Margaret."

"But."

"Right. But. I don't know."

"Sorry."

"Popcorn?

"Yeah, I like it. It's Jiffy-Pop. Let's watch it rise right over there."

"Let's live."

"Exactly."

"Kat. Damn. Now what?"

"What's that?" Bidden asks, gesturing toward a manila folder Neill has in front of him"

"Oh, new short story."

"Short story? You're doing fiction now?"

"I told you."

"You didn't. I would remember. I love your poetry, as you know."

"So can you tell me what's wrong with this?"

"Probably not. I can read it though. I want to read it."

"Thanks."

Wanda, the owner of P&H, and a local legend (actress, activist, raconteur, bon vivant), appeared beside them.

"Hey boys. You wanna order?"

"You waiting tables tonight?" Bidden and Wanda went way back to when the P&H was at Madison and Morrison.

"Sue's got a sick kid."

"Sorry. Listen. We want popcorn."

"Sure."

"And two diet Pepsis."

"You boys are maniacs. What's that?"

"Oh, nothing," Neill said. He tried to will the folder to disappear.

"New short story," Bidden said. "Neill's a wonderful writer."

"Can I read it?"

"Oh. I."

"Let her read it."

"Sure. Thanks."

Wanda took the story and walked away.

"Jesus."

"I'm sorry. Did I do something wrong? You didn't want her to read it?"

"I don't know. I have no confidence in my prose. Not to suggest I have a whole lot in my poetry."

"Pfft," Bidden said.

Wanda returned with popcorn and Pepsis. "I'm reading. Have it back in a minute."

"Damn," Bidden said.

"What?"

"I forgot to watch the Jiffy Pop."

"It was quite a show."

"You saw it?"

"I did. Not since the Niagara Falls..."

"Ok. Stop."

"It's about Victoria."

"What?"

"The story. I tried writing about Victoria. It's almost impossible to get her down on paper. I should have started with something easier. The story of a boy and his dog."

"Like *Champion Dog, Prince Tom*?"

"You know *Champion Dog, Prince Tom*?" Neill's eyes actually lit up.

"Only from hearing you talk about it."

"Oh, right. Right."

They ate popcorn. The jukebox was playing "Mack the Knife."

"Dead tonight."

"Thursday night. Gonna be lousy with thespians in about an hour."

"Right."

Wanda returned. She placed the folder gently down in front of Neill as if it were made of ash.

"That's pretty good," she said.

Neill let a smile commence its creep.

"You used *lay* where it should have been *lie*."

Neill's ears burned. His face flushed. His stomach lurched. He was outed. He was a phony.

Bidden picked up the story. Wanda pointed to the place with a long coral-colored nail.

"She's right," Bidden said.

Now Neill was more ashamed. Bidden, his best friend, could see his tenderness, his absurdity. Neill vowed to give up writing.

"I think we both want burgers now," Bidden said. He was trying to hustle Wanda away.

"I'm sorry," he said.

"I can't write."

"Oh, fuck that. I'm sorry. It's one mistake. Lemme read it and I'll call you."

"Ok."

Neill went home that night feeling like the south end of a goat trotting northward. He was without female companionship due to his own—what? –intractability? complexity? phony search for perfection? Who was he to seek perfection? Only the nonesuch would do? He was nobody. He didn't know the difference between lay and lie.

The phone rang.

Neill thought it might be Kat, or Sue, or even Syrie. Then the demon inside his head told him how pitiful that was, that momentary soaring of his heart based upon pure fantasy.

It was Bidden.

"This is great," Bidden said.

"Oh. No. Thanks."

"It really is. I think you did get Victoria. I think you've written something here that is highly publishable. Like Raymond Carver with more heart."

"Damn. Thanks, Bidden. You're—"

"I mean it."

"Thanks. Thanks, really."

"Ok. Good night, Neill."

"Good night, Bidden. I am going to go lay down now."

At The Book Shelf

Neill was explaining the Bidden Route Rule to Esther and Iago.

"It's simple. If you have to work on one section of books, say science fiction, and there is one customer in the store, that customer will be in the science fiction section, hence thwarting your intentions."

"That's good. It's good it has a name," Esther said.

"And it can be shortened to 'I've been Routed.'"

'That is good," Iago said. "I've been Routed."

Customer comes in. It's the middle of the week. Neill's seen her before, attractive brunette, hair parted on the side, stylish short cut that flatters her round cheeks and bright eyes. Her name is Marcane Fry but right now, Neill doesn't know that.

Neill is at the counter. He is working on STOP orders, a system set up to order one book at a time, pre-paid, from just about any publisher. Neill loves STOP orders. It's hard to say why. Something about sending them off, hopeful as the doves from the Ark, and a few weeks later getting a book back, a new book, shiny as a bike.

Marcane Fry approaches the counter.

"Neill, right?" she says.

Neill looks up into her bright eyes.

"I'm sorry I can't remember your name."

"You don't know my name. It's ok. It's Marcane Fry. I am a friend of Ianthe's. We go way back. Way way way way way back."

"Ok," Neill said. He's smiling, but he is not sure why. This woman is...funny. It occurs to him. She's just funny and Neill loves funny.

"I need a present for my daughter. She's about to graduate high school."

"She a reader?'

"Nope."

"So you've come to the bookstore to get her a present."

"That's kinda crazy isn't' it? I guess I could be here for stationary."

"If so you need to talk to Betty."

"I don't want stationary."

"A book then? For someone who doesn't read?"

"Do you know Trish Turner?"

"I don't think so. I know a Page Turner."

It was one of life's perfect jokes. Suddenly, it was just there like The Brandenburg Concertos. Or the Hanging Gardens.

Still a beat passed. Then Marcane Fry laughed. And in her laugh there was bamboo music, there was wind chimes.

Neill laughed, too.

"So you're funny," Marcane Fry said.

Neill shrugged.

"I think maybe I should give my daughter you."

"What's your daughter look like?"

"You are superficial for a bookstore employee."

"Manager."

"Forgive me. Manager. Then, very superficial for a bookstore manager."

"Beauty is important. In literature as well as flesh."

Marcane Fry looked Neill Rhymer over. She reached into her pocketbook and pulled out a wallet. She put a picture under Neill's nose. By this time they had migrated back toward the fiction section, on the off chance that Marcane Fry really wanted a book recommendation.

Neill took the picture and held it directly under one of the neon ceiling fixtures.

"Wow," he said, without irony. Marcane Fry's daughter was stunning.

"She's pretty," Marcane Fry said.

"She's more than pretty. She's wow. Yes, I think you should fix us up. I think you should go home right now and call her. Hurry. I have little vitality left."

"I will," Marcane Fry said. "Now a book."

"Do you really want to buy her a book?"

"I thought I did when I came in. I think you've dissuaded me."

"That's my job. To unsell books."

Marcane Fry laughed again.

"Recommend something for me then," she said.

"Ok. There's this first novel I am high on right now. Henry Bean is the author's name." Neill walked along the fiction wall. "Here," he said. "*False Match.*"

"Never heard of him."

"I know. I can't remember why I picked it up. It's great."

"Ok, Neill, thanks," Marcane Fry said.

"You're welcome Mrs. Turner."

"What?" Marcane Fry said.

"Isn't your daughter named Trish Turner? Or, are you divorced and you have a different name from your child."

"My daughter's name is not Trish nor is my name Turner. Trish Turner is a mutual friend of Ianthe's and mine. I thought—well, never mind. My name is Marcane Fry." She held her hand out.

Neill took her soft hand and said, "Nice to meet you. I want your daughter."

"I'm gonna fix it right up," she said.

As she was walking out the door she turned back. "My daughter's last name is her father's by the way. And we are divorced. Fry is my maiden name."

"Ok," Neill said.

"Ok," Marcane said. "I thought you should know because." She stopped and looked around as if one of the novels would finish her thought for her. "Because my daughter is damaged goods, coming from a broken home and all."

"She in a gang?"

Marcane Fry laughed for the last time that day and left.

Neill felt happy though he had no idea why.

At the ABA

It was May again and May meant the ABA Convention and Neill's kind bosses sent him alone to enjoy the frantic, stimulating climate of international booksellers, authors, and publishers. This year's event was held in New Orleans. Neill had not been back to New Orleans since that debacle with Orbit.

Neill took a cab from the airport to his hotel which was in the heart of the French Quarter. Neill felt like an adult as he paid the cabbie. He felt sophisticated like Cary Grant or Clark Gable, tipping his cabbie, asking for restaurant recommendations, remarking on the reason he was in town.

That night Neill had turtle soup at a restaurant in the Quarter, sitting alone, reading a Thomas Berger novel. Afterward, he strolled around the Quarter by himself. He saw many booksellers and publishing folks with their ABA badges. Neill had purposely left his in his room. He found some nice used bookstores. Musty and full of the arcana and lore of the centuries. He found a voodoo shop but was afraid to go in by himself. Was Neill superstitious? Perhaps.

The next day, on the convention floor, Neill felt that same heady rush he felt at the first convention. There were authors everywhere! He passed by George Plimpton who nodded at Neill's recognition. He passed Rich Hall, from Saturday Night Live, whose book, *Sniglets*, was a huge bestseller. Rich Hall was on crutches. Neill stopped him as if they were old drinking buddies.

"What happened?" Neill asked.

Rich Hall paused as if they were equals.

"You probably won't believe this but I fell off the stage."

Neill laughed.

"And I was sober," Rich Hall added.

Neill had a great time visiting publishers' booths. Every time he discovered a new publisher he was a literary Magellan. And, he had been given a blank check for whatever he saw fit to buy for the bookstore. He spent a nice hour ordering Fotofolio postcards. He visited the Chronicle Books booth because he loved their colorful coffee table books and idiosyncratic children's line. There was a willowy young woman in the booth, posy of freckles across her nose like a dusting of cinnamon, dark brown hair, who was wearing a nametag that said, "Sharilyn."

Sharilyn? Neill thought. That's an odd name. And, he longed to introduce himself but he suddenly had a crisis of confidence. Where was the ballsy young man who showed up on Dew Drynow's doorstep? Gone with the wind. He walked on.

There were a lot of grown people in enormous animal costumes. They tried to catch everyone's eye and they spoke to everyone as if they were all at a child's birthday party. Neill gave them a wide berth.

At the Klutz Books booth, Neill looked over the gimmicky children's toy/book packages. This was a company which had made a fortune with *Juggling for the Complete Klutz*, a book which could, purportedly, teach one to juggle, served up with a net bag and three beanbags. With the success of that one item, an entire publishing empire was born. Now they had kits for everything: sewing, puppet making, bubble making, shrinky dinks, turning lead into gold, etc. Neill found their stuff charming and the juggling book was a big seller even for The Book Shelf, whose strength was not children's books.

Also, at this booth, another woman made Neill's heart go pitty-pat. Tall, long red hair (egads! the red hair again), freckled naturally, gentle blue eyes, small breasts, long torso, small puckery mouth. Neill studied her. She was out of his league, he thought, out of his league.

He passed on with regret.

That night there was a party at Tipitina's, thrown by one of the hipper sales rep groups. Neill's rep had gotten him a ticket and told him it was *the* party to attend if he only attended one. The Neville Brothers were playing. Neill knew nothing about Tipitina's and a little about The Neville Brothers. So he went with modest anticipation, except that he, again, was relishing this faux adulthood. Look at me, Neill's little inner demon said, alone on the surface of the planet, gliding across this Earth-y space, moving around as if welcome anywhere.

Tipitina's was rocking. It was dark and crowded and hot and everyone was dancing. The Neville Brothers were doing "Iko Iko," a song Neill knew from other versions. He stood at the back near the bar with a coke in his hand.

Suddenly, there was a woman approximately 9 ½ inches from his face. Neill was jolted and almost took a step backwards, except that he was staring into the loveliest pair of purple eyes he'd ever seen.

"I picked you," she said.

"What?" Neill said, rightly so.

"I have been here an hour and I have surveyed everyone, and I have picked you."

Is this a New Orleans thing Neill was not hip to?

"Am I now King of a Krewe or something?" he asked.

"Screw. Not Krewe," and this purple-eyed woman laughed at her own joke.

"I'm sorry," Neill said. "I'm not getting it. My name is Neill," he said and held out his hand.

"Lizbeth," Lizbeth said, and took Neill's hand. She was still approximately 9 ½ inches from Neill.

"What did you pick me for? What do I win?"

"Me," Lizbeth said. "I came here tonight determined to hook up with a guy and I want you to be that guy."

"My, my," Neill said.

"My my? You're not married are you?"

"No," Neill said. "As single as a slice of cheese."

The purple-eyed Lizbeth laughed.

"Then what do you say?"

"I don't know what I am volunteering for but count me in."

"Great," Lizbeth said and put her arm through Neill's. She waved at a woman across the dance floor and gave her the 'ok' sign. "She didn't think I would be successful."

"Really? I would have thought that approach would work every time."

"Well, you gotta be careful you know. And some men don't like aggressive women."

"I see. So now that we're a couple, what do we do?"

"Seen enough here?"

"Yes," Neill said.

Lizbeth dragged him outdoors where it was only 1% cooler and 1% less humid.

They found a dark spot under a tree a half-block from the club.

"Ah ha," Neill said.

"You getting it now?"

"I think so. I hope I am getting it or about to. You're not a hooker, are you?"

"Neill. Buddy. I picked you!"

"Ok."

Now, Lizbeth ran her hand down Neill's chest and let it rest over his belly. She gently kneaded the skin there through Neill's sweaty shirt.

"Calming me?" Neill asked.

"I thought I would try to excite you instead"

"Sorry. Something I read in Carlos Castaneda. You put your hand over someone's navel to calm their spirit or something. Something emanates from the human navel. I am not really clear on it."

"I must not be doing it right." She rubbed a little harder, in larger circles. "You have such a nice flat stomach," Lizbeth said.

"I think it's working now," Neill said, as his little man asked him if the game were afoot.

Lizbeth slipped her arms around Neill and pressed her mouth against his. Her grip on him was fierce and her mouth was hurting Neill's gums. Still, he liked her tongue in his mouth and her hands on his butt. He returned the favor and put his hands on hers. They made out for a long time.

"Whew," Neill said, at one point.

"Yeah, that's pretty good for a couple of strangers."

"So, what now?"

"I don't know," purple-eyed Lizbeth said.

"I thought you were in charge."

"Oh, right, I am. Um, I think I better go find my roomie and head back to the hotel."

"Ok," Neill said. "You're at the convention. What's your publisher?"

"Not a publisher, per se. We make hang-gliders."

"What?'

"Well, we make hang-gliders and we have a book about how to be a hang-glider."

She handed Neill one of her cards. "Find me tomorrow first thing."

Neill was turning the card over in his hand.

"Will you?"

"Oh, yes, of course. First thing."

"Good job, Neill. You've won another date with Lizbeth." And she kissed him too hard again, his puss numb.

Papa's Got a Brand New Bag

Neill did indeed make a beeline for Lizbeth the next morning. (Wouldn't you?) He had trouble finding her booth, which was in an annex to the main floor where there were many calendar publishers and other booths of non-book items.

"Neill!" Lizbeth said. "I thought you wouldn't show."

"Seriously?"

"Well, I was counting the minutes."

"The floor has only been open fifteen minutes."

"I know. I counted to fifteen. What took you so long?"

"So, this is your life, eh?"

"For now. This is my boss, Ken."

A guy wearing some kind of skin-tight athletic gear turned and gripped Neill's hand as if he wanted to wring it for its pulp. He turned back without waiting for Neill's name.

"Do lunch later?" Lizbeth asked.

"Yes, let's," Neill said. He liked this woman who took charge, who left no doubt.

At lunch, on a rickety wooden table, they ate bland sandwiches and sipped watery soft drinks. Neill couldn't stop looking into her eyes. Now that they were under bright lights, he saw the rest of her. She was compact and had wide shoulders and a gait that was built upon two sturdy and shapely legs. Her bim, which he had felt the night before, was prominent and firm. All in all, a lovely woman.

"So, Neill at my Feet," Lizbeth said, her purple eyes sending off purply twinkles. "What say you?"

"This is our last night."

"It is," Lizbeth said, and put a hand on Neill's thigh.

"Are you going to James Brown tonight?"

Every ABA convention ended with a free concert by a big-name entertainer. Neill was excited about seeing The Godfather of Soul.

"I have tickets. I told my roomie I'd go with her."

"How's about we all meet there?"

"That would be great," Lizbeth said. "We can meet outside the door. At what time? Should we eat first?"

"It's my understanding that we get free grub AND music."

"Whoa. Ok. Let's meet around 7 at the door. I'll be with my roomie."

“You said that. I’ll be with my God.”

Lizbeth laughed too hard. She put a hand behind Neill’s neck and pulled his face close to hers. Her tongue went deep into his mouth. It might have tickled his uvula. It sure felt like his uvula had been tickled. This was cataglottism for which the word was invented.

Neill dressed nicely for the evening.

His hotel was walking distance from the place where the concert was held. It was a nice evening. The humidity had dropped. The sun was using all 64 colors, even flesh.

Neill spotted Lizbeth and her somewhat statuesque roomie standing on the sidewalk outside the hall.

“Neill!” Lizbeth hollered.

He greeted her with a kiss which she returned though with perhaps less heat than at lunch.

“You know Becky? Becky Sharp. Neill. Oh Fuck.”

“O’fuck?” Sharp Becky Sharp said.

“From Donegal,” Neill said.

“I don’t know your last name.”

“Rhymer.”

“You a poet?” Becky Sharp asked.

“No,” Neill said. “Merry-Mobile driver.”

“I don’t know what that is,” Becky Sharp said.

“He’s pulling your leg. He’s a bookseller.”

“I would never pull such a shapely leg,” Neill said.

“Slow down, Bub. You won the Lizbeth Lottery, remember. The Becky Sharp Lottery has yet to be played.”

They found a table and a fourth joined them, someone Becky worked with at her place of business, which Neill never found out. His name was Jeff. Or Jim. Or Jocko. The table seated four and was covered with a white cloth and cloth napkins and real silverware.

There was a warm-up act. Jazz combo, New Orleans style. Everyone was polite. Everyone was there for James Brown. During the warm-up act they served—surprise!—chicken breast and sauce, rice and mixed veggies. It was fairly toothsome. Neill liked institutional food: cafeterias, airplanes, hospitals.

Around 9 pm., the lights went down on the audience and up on the stage. James Brown’s MC, Danny Ray took the stage. The band was already set. Danny went into his shtick. Perfervid energy was passing through the crowd like Legionnaires’ Disease.

And then, there he was. He looked like he looked on The Ed Sullivan Show when Neill was a pup. He was looking at James Brown.

“Wow,” Neill said.

Lizbeth squeezed his thigh under the table.

“If he plays ‘Papa’s Got a Brand New Bag,’ I’m gonna come,” Neill whispered in Lizbeth’s surprisingly delicate ear.

She laughed.

James Brown and his band whipped through the night like a cyclonic storm. “Please, Please, Please,” Neill sang along softly under his breath. It was electrifying. He did about six numbers, complete with breakdowns and that inimitable dancing that was his alone, and then he leapt into "Papa's Got a Brand New Bag."

Neill threw his head back as if he could see stars through the roof of the ballroom. Lizbeth squeezed his thigh again, a little closer to the scrotum. After the song was over, she leaned close to him and said, "Well?"

Neill nodded.

"Damn," she said. "I hope you have more."

Jeez Louise. This was on. This assertive, bouncy, funny, smart, purple-eyed beauty wants to have sex with me, with little Neill Rhymer. He could almost not concentrate on the rest of the concert.

They bade goodbye to Becky and Jeff. (Jip?)

On the walk back to Neill's hotel they held hands like Hansel and Gretel on the way to rob the old witch. As they reached the hotel Lizbeth pushed Neill against the coarse concrete side of the building and went spelunking in his mouth again. And her hand stroked his thigh forcefully.

"We're really gonna do this?" Neill said aloud as they unhitched.

"What's that, Neill Baby," Lizbeth said, as she licked the length of his neck. "A one night-stand?"

"That's what the sophistos call it," Neill said.

"Scare you?" Lizbeth said.

"Not really," Neill answered, as they walked into the hotel, arms around each other's waist. Were women always asking of men if they were frightened, or was it just Neill and his women?

Inside the room Lizbeth wasted no time. She grasped Neill tight and the kiss lasted a fortnight and during that fortnight it was established that they were going to undress. This they did, practically scratching each other's duds off.

Down to panties they fell upon the bed. And something terrifically engaging dawned on Neill. Lizbeth's body was so muscular it was cut like a professional athlete's.

"Whoa," Neill said.

"See what I was hiding?" Lizbeth said. She was enjoying his pause and his apparent approval.

"You're what, like a club bouncer? Mob enforcer?"

"Ha. Body-builder, dopey. You like?"

"I do," Neill said. "I've never seen a professional body-builder naked."

(This was only technically a fudge. Kat was not a professional though her body was almost this muscular.)

"Frightened?" she asked again.

Neill didn't like the question and ignored it.

Lizbeth's bare breasts sat high on her toned chest. They were small, like little tumuli of muscle, with small nipples as hard as rubber erasers.

The lover-strangers lay side by side. The kissing was outrageously passionate. Lizbeth ripped Neill's underwear off. It was part of her routine apparently. She threw them aside with practiced aplomb. Her grip on his low neck was firm but her palms were soft as jelly. And she knew how to give a handjob. Then she hopped up onto her knees, like a gymnast, gave Neill a smug look and went down on him.

There is a saying, perhaps you've heard it, that any blowjob is a good blowjob. Neill ascribed to this opinion. Nevertheless, the blowjob Lizbeth was offering was the worst part of her hamming. It was too...toothy or something.

Neill pulled her head gently upwards. She lay back down on her pillow and now Neill moved onto his knees. He put a hand lightly on her sturdy, flat belly. He rubbed her there for a moment. Lizbeth closed her eyes. Now, Neill ran a hand slowly over her brief, see-through panties. He could tickle her pubic mound through the material. He bent over and blew against her panties, slow, moderate breaths. Lizbeth sighed.

He pulled the panties down slowly. Lizbeth's thighs were granite, but smooth. (Perhaps *marble* is better.)

She was naked. Neill took a moment to look at her body. It was unlike any female body he'd ever seen. Muscular but with soft curves and hills. And her pubic hair was like shining moss. Neill bent there and began to lick around those curves and hills, circling the moss.

When he finally found her slit with his tongue, she gasped. Neill knew his way around a clitoris and he found that way and with flicks and licks and teasing he was making Lizbeth gasp and squirm. So, after a while, he dove right in. He did his best mouth work in a long time. Lizbeth came twice. Neill did not want to stop. Finally, he looked up and Lizbeth's skin was mottled with blushes and she was practically swooning.

"I, I," she said.

"Mm hm?" Neill asked.

"I, I," she repeated. "Wow. I. I guess I am glad you won."

Lizbeth had ceded control to Neill. It was subtle but she was now the one cowed by the intensity of the sexual experience. Neill bringing her off twice with his mouth had tamed her. The tamer, more subdued Lizbeth was still sexy as a black pudding. Neill entered her missionary style after he had found the diaphragm with his fingers.

The final hump was not quite as dramatic as eating her had been. They both had a good time and when Neill came Lizbeth pulled his ass cheeks apart with the vigor of her enjoyment. Perhaps she was trying to regain the upper hand, though no hand, upper or lower or middle management was needed now. They were now officially lovers, sated and covered with each other's juices.

Lizbeth slept. Neill never did. He lay awake until he sensed the morning sun behind the heavy curtains of the hotel room. His flight was early, so he slipped out of bed.

He started the shower and Lizbeth a few minutes later slinked in beside him, gloriously naked still.

"Join you," she said, sleepily.

"Please," Neill said, because he was a gentleman.

In the cramped stall they played soap-each-other's-privates and Neill thought he, perhaps, had come close to giving Lizbeth another orgasm. She pulled gamely at Neill's cock, still raw from the night before, and managed to fashion a simulacrum of an erection out of it; it was as if the clay was stubborn and wanted to remain formless.

They fell back onto the bed and this time Lizbeth sat astride Neill and attempted to re-insert his johnny. It was not to be. Neill was tired, his dick was sore, and he was worried about catching his flight.

They kissed instead and lay in each other's arms.

"What time is your flight?" Lizbeth asked.

"About an hour," Neill said.

"Oh, you gotta go."

"I do. What time is your flight?"

"Afternoon. Two, I think."

"Where do you live?"

"Colorado," Lizbeth said. There was a pause. Lizbeth was circling Neill's flaccid penis-tip with one finger. "Neill. Can I give you my number and address? Do you write letters?"

"I love writing letters," Neill said because he really did.

Lizbeth hopped up and found another business card. She turned on the lamp on the table and bent over it to write her particulars on the reverse side of the card. Neill studied her beautifully designed backside.

Downstairs, as the cab sat waiting for Neill to enter, a shier, gentler Lizbeth held Neill's hand and shifted from foot to foot.

"Call me," she said, in time-honored fashion.

"I will," Neill said in same.

They kissed and then Neill was on his way to the airport, tired, bleary eyed and full of wonder. He looked back and saw Lizbeth enter a taxi of her own. It would be his last glimpse of her on this bardo.

"A one-night stand," Neill said to himself, snuggling back against the taxi seat. "Fancy that."

Back to Memphis

Back to Memphis. Back to his doss house. Back to the bookstore. Neill alit.

Dating Neill. Carbon-dating Neill.

He once had a get-together that almost didn't make it to the end of the night. The young woman, attractive enough, talked during the movie. People shushed her. Neill burned. He wanted to be far away. She was oblivious. She kept talking.

"Is that Robert Mitchum?" she asked. "Are those his real teeth?" She spoke as if they were alone in her living room in front of the TV.

"Have you ever been to Maui?"

Even Neill's silence did not deter her.

Neill wanted to see her naked but a part of his desire had dissipated. At the door, he shook her hand. She was nonplussed.

"Have a good time?" she asked, even as Neill was sliding his hand out of hers, and moving backwards.

"Fine," Neill said. "I'll call you."

He ran to his car.

Years later, he was at a movie with another woman. Someone nearby was talking in conversational tones during the movie. It was her. Neill smiled and to his date shrugged. She asked, "Aren't you going to do something about that?"

"Who am I, Zorro?" Neill answered.

Neill didn't see *her* naked either.

She Returns

One afternoon Neill looked up at the jingle of the door's bell as if he were Pavlov's dog. He wanted a treat.

And, he got one. It was Marcane Fry.

"Hello, Neill," she said. She looked even better than last time.

"Hello, Mrs. Fry," Neill said.

"Marcane."

"Marcane."

"What's new?"

"Your world. I'm just living in it" (Neill picked up this particular breezy conversational meme from his postman, who was as cool as Miles Davis and as handsome as Billy Dee Williams. Neill had an innocent, asexual [perhaps only asexual] crush on him. He also gave Neill this expression, which Neill tried to shoehorn into the least appropriate places, "Even Stevie could see that.")

[Later, Neill tried to fix him up with Pas. It fell just short of being a disaster.]

"That's quaint," Marcane Fry said, but she was smiling.

"Looking for another book for your daughter who doesn't read?"

"Smartass," Marcane Fry said, but she was smiling. "I came to tell you that the book you recommended to me kicks ass. I want another like it."

"What did I recommend? Oh, wait—*False Match*. You liked?"

"I liked it a lot. Feed me more."

"I can do that," Neill said. He began to walk to his personal Western Wall: Fiction. "Hmm," he said as if he were Pooh.

"Have you read Robertson Davies?"

"No. Tell me more."

"Canadian novelist. *The Deptford Trilogy*—it's about as good as fiction gets."

"Can I commit to a trilogy?"

"You need only buy the first volume and, if it fails, that's the end of Robertson Davies for you."

"Good deal."

"Great. And a bargain at only $3.95"

"Thanks, Neill."

"You're welcome."

She remained standing there.

"Since you feed me, maybe you'd let me feed you."

"You have books in your purse?"

"No, but I make a mean linguine with clams."

"Oh! Real food."

"Can you come?

"I think I have an opening in my hectic social life. When?"

"Thursday night?"

"Good for me."

"Great. See you around 6 or so?"

"Okey doke. Your daughter gonna be there?"

"No, but I told her about you. She's interested. Right now she is on a rafting trip."

"Of course, she is," Neill said. He didn't know what he meant.

"Why of course?" Marcane Fry said but she was smiling.

Neill shrugged.

"Goodbye, Neill. See you Thursday."

"Goodbye, Marcane with the imaginary daughter."

Marcane exited laughing.

Dinner

And so Neill went to Marcane Fry's house for dinner. The ostensible reason was to discuss his getting together with her daughter. That was so, right? Neill thought it was true, but he was also attracted to this older woman, this Marcane Fry. She was funny and classy and quite lovely. How old must she be to have a daughter in college?

"Hello," Marcane said, opening her door. Her bungalow (her word for it) was 3 blocks from Neill and Goffredo's, on Alexander. A modest house on an immaculate street.

"Hi," Neill said, entering.

"My you're punctual."

"Neurotically so. I always assume if I am one minute late the person will cancel the plan, spit in my face and talk bad about me to every mutual friend."

Marcane Fry laughed her wry laugh. Her laugh was wry.

"I should have brought something," Neill said because he suddenly realized it. "Wine or something. I don't know anything about wine. I don't really know how to go to someone's house for a grown-up dinner."

"Relax. I have wine. Would you like some?"

"No," Neill said. Then he shook his head. "I don't like wine."

"Ok, mind if I have a glass before dinner?"

"Of course not. Dinner smells good."

"I haven't started cooking yet."

"Oh."

They sat in the living room. It was tastefully decorated in shades of off-white and tan, everything clean, orderly and placed just so. Feng shui modern.

Except for the chair Marcane took. It looked to be about 150 years old, was a faded mustard yellow, and its sagging cushions had room enough for three rumps. Neill sat across the small room on the off-white couch.

"So, your daughter," Neill said because he had nothing else.

"Nora," Marcane said. "As in Joyce."

"Good golly, Joyce," Neill said with a smile. "You read Joyce?"

"Thank you, no. What do you want to know about her?"

"Nora Joyce?"

"Nora, Marcane's daughter."

"Does she put out on the first date?"

There was no good reason to explain why Neill thought this appropriate or funny or acceptable in any way. An innate sense that Marcane Fry knew a joke was always appropriate? Like David Letterman said, "99% of the time, go for the joke?"

Marcane Fry laughed.

Neill laughed. "Sorry," he added.

"It's ok. On the first date, probably not. Actually, I have no idea. I am only the mother."

"Of course."

Dinner was linguine with a clam sauce and a fresh baguette with unsalted butter. Neill thought it was the best meal anyone had ever cooked for him.

"That was really good," Neill said. "I love baguettes. How did you know?"

"I didn't make the baguette."

"Oh. You made the pasta? It was even better."

They had a coconut sorbet for dessert and then returned to the living room.

"What can I tell you about Nora to get you interested?" Marcane Fry said, and then held up a policeman's hand. "Besides the putting-out thing."

"Does she read?"

"Oh. No. I mean, she can read. She doesn't. Read. Good books."

"Hm. I don't know. She sure is pretty."

"She is that. My other daughter is pretty also."

"Wait. What? You have another?"

"Vin. Yes. She's in high school. She might be even prettier than Nora."

"I should probably stay away from high-schoolers."

"You should. Hey, look. I've got pictures."

She left the room and returned a minute later with a photo album. She sat next to Neill on the couch. She smelled like something fresh, vanilla or cream.

"Look, here are my girls when they were little."

She flipped through the album telling the story of her small family and the husband who left ("mingy bastard"). Neill was frankly bored with most of it. What did he care about her little girls? He didn't even know her very well.

"Here are the girls older. There's Nora."

"Oh yes," Neill said, politely.

"Oh, look! Nora in a bikini!"

Neill looked closer. She did look a bit of alright. Neill moved his face closer to the album and closer to Marcane Fry's face. He breathed in deeply.

"You can't smell her from there," Marcane said, and laughed.

"She has a." Neill stopped.

"Bitching body."

"Yes. She does. Look, so does Vin. Little Vin."

"It was a picture of a surly dark-haired teenager on some Florida beach. She was curvy like a dangerous road. Neill didn't want to look, nor did he want to look away. He had to say something.

"What if?"

"What?"

"What if, well, I was losing interest in dating your daughter?"

"Ok. Was it something I said? I admit, she is probably not your type and, honestly, she wouldn't go for you. Probably. But, Neill, wouldn't you want to see her naked?"

Neill laughed a gruff little laugh. Marcane was clairvoyant?

"It's not that," he said. "What if I were more interested in Nora's mother?"

"Oh. Well. Um."

"I'm sorry. That's totally—"

"No, it's ok. It's well, flattering. I don't know."

"I know it's absurd. You probably have a million successful grown men suitors."

"Not quite a million. But the line is long."

"Yes."

"I'm joking, Neill. I'm joking because it made me a little nervous."

"I'm sorry."

"Neill. Would you want to kiss me?"

"I would."

They leaned toward each other. It was not hunger. It was the stealth of the bomb expert trying to decide which wire to cut.

The kiss was nice. Marcane Fry had a soft mouth. Her cheeks were soft, too. Neill put his hand to one while they held the kiss. There was a little tongue action, still tentative.

They broke.

"Well," Marcane Fry said. "That was unexpected."

"For me, too. I didn't come over here to."

"I know. But you thought about it?"

"Well." He hadn't.

"I admit I did a little, too."

"Really?" Neill said. He leaned back in. They kissed harder. The photo album slid to the floor like a family going downhill. Marcane leaned back against the couch pillows. Neill's body followed hers. They were almost prone but each kept a foot on the floor as if in some kind of Victorian drama.

Neill pressed his erection against Marcane Fry's thighs. His hands felt her all over. Her body was soft and pliant through her clothes. Neill had no clue how far he should go, but he was getting carried away.

Marcane began to pant. So, Neill put his hands under her shirt and found her bra. His hand tunneled under the wire like an escapee. Her breasts were small and soft from childbirth. Her nipples, though, were youthfully enthusiastic.

Now Neill put a hand down the back of her pants, which were loose like Barbara Eden's. And it was to her garden of earthly delights that Neill's hand went. He found her already dripping wet and his fingers explored the entrance to the cave.

"Huh, Neill," Marcane said in his ear.

"Jesus," Neill answered.

"To think I almost gave you to my daughter."

Neill's heart was going like Hellzapoppin.

He fingered her some more. She panted and then suddenly put her arms around Neill's neck and hugged him close, pulling him hard against her own face.

"Eh eh eh," she said.

She was coming! Neill was amazed.

He slowed down his digital action and let his finger rest in the warm pool outside her opening. They were quiet for a while, but now they both moved their whole bodies to the couch. The precluding feet were relocated upward.

Now Marcane Fry's hand began a downward slide. Neill held his breath. Was she really going to take care of him, too? For some reason it seemed absurd. Yet the hand, a furry animal, moved inexorably toward Neill's crotch.

And then she was cupping his scrotum through his jeans. Though the denim was thick, she was pressing hard enough and expertly enough to move his jackhammer toward a high rev. And then she was unbuckling Neill's belt. Neill was more nervous than he had ever been with any previous lover. Was it the age thing? Possibly. Neill pondered how much more experienced than him she must be. That is, he thought about it in the back closet of his brain and more about it later. At this time, he was more interested in the fact that she had his johnny in her velvety hand.

She did know what she was doing. She was jerking him off as well as he could do himself. Well, almost. No one ever does anyone else's genital manipulation better than the owner.

Neill fell back against the pillows and Marcane scooted up onto her elbow. She was watching herself. This was a big turn on. She wanted to look at Neill's dick. She wanted to watch it shoot off.

Neill did not disappoint the audience. As Marcane felt the tube fill up she became even more vigilant. She moved her face closer and, just as she did, Neill's load blew out into the air. It soaked his belly and shirt. It was quite an orgasm, quite a copious detonation.

"Jesus," Marcane Fry said. "You come like ack-ack." She turned toward Neill. There was a small spot of jism on her lip. She wanted Neill to see her lick it off.

Then, they fell together again and were silent. Neill's open pants and cooling ejaculate did not concern him greatly.

"You came, too?" he asked, trying not to sound like a 13-year-old.

"Right away," she said. "It's been a long time for me."

"Seriously?"

"A long dry spell. I was worried about whether I would ever do it again. I thought, well, I am old and have had my pleasures."

Neill fought the impulse to ask how old she was.

"It's been so long," she continued. "I wanted to watch you come. I hope that didn't embarrass you. I haven't seen a dick in years."

"What's wrong with the male population of Memphis?" Neill asked.

"Well, there are men. There just aren't the right men."

Now, Neill felt puffed up. Now, Neill felt terrified.

"You have a nice dick, Neill," Marcane Fry said. "I'd like to see it again sometime."

So, as Neill later rose and did up his clothing, damp from his orgasm, he was entertaining future trysts in his always fervent imagination. Neill stood. He was unsteady.

At the door, he took her in his arms and kissed her again.

"Goodnight, Neill," Marcane said.

"Ggg-god," Neill said. He was shaking all over.

"Are you ok?" she asked.

"Yes," he said. He thought he was going to faint or throw up. He'd never felt this way before. Maybe it was love. Maybe it was terror. How old is she?

That night sleep didn't come until an hour before the alarm and the next day at work Neill was practically worthless. A zombie.

"You ok?" Ianthe asked, just like Marcane had asked the night before.

"I don't think I've ever felt better," Neill said in the tone of the body-snatched. "I think this is me extremely happy."

Shlomo on the Line

"You can't seem to find a happy medium," Shlomo laughed.

"Is there such a thing?"

"How would I know? I'm married and don't wanna be."

"Seriously?"

"I don't know."

"I want you happy, you know."

"In a sexless marriage, would you rather be the one desired but without desire of your own or the one who desires and faces a prophylactic brick wall?

"Either way it's a sexless marriage."

"How old is this woman?'

"I don't know. Should I?"

"It certainly doesn't matter to me. Is there a future here?"

"Future. Pfft."

"Right. You gonna see her again?"

"I hope so. Should I call her?"

"I don't know."

"Right."

"What are you doing?"

"Working on a little poot of a short story to avoid working on a large bowel movement of a novel."

"Wanna talk about it?"

"No."

"Right."

"You wanna go to Earl's Hot Biscuits for breakfast?'

"You read my mind. Oh, wait, I gotta work. Can we drive to West Memphis and be back by 10?"

"We can sure try. Would it matter if you were late?"

"No."

"Right. You driving?"

"I'll pick you up."

"Your clunker will make it?"

"I don't know."

"Right."

Neill Does Call Her

After biscuits and a breakfast heavy as an opiate, Neill was dropped off at The Book Shelf at 10:05. He hustled in. Iago was there.

"You're late," Iago said.

"I recognize that," Neill said. Despite the wax in his stomach he felt like a million dollars, less taxes. Neill loved Shlomo and the sad sack Jewish writer never ceased to make Neill laugh or, incongruously, feel good about life.

"Doesn't matter to me," Iago said from his seat behind the cash register. He already had a book open and a bag of Funyuns next to him. Neill smiled and went to the stockroom. From the phone there, he made the call.

"Hi," Neill said.

"Hello?" Marcane Fry said.

"Marcane."

"Yes?"

"It's Neill."

"Neill."

"From the bookstore."

There was an ugly scratch of a pause.

"I know, Neill. I was having you on."

"Having me on."

"Like an ill-fitting suit."

"You think it's a bad fit?"

Pause. "Wait, let's start over."

"Hi," Neill said.

"Neill! Neill Rhymer! As I live and breathe!"

"You're overdoing it."

"I do that."

"Overdo things?"

"Yes. Constantly. Like painting. I put on too many coats."

"It's warm out."

"Exactly."

"So, I waited two days to call," Neill said, hesitantly.

"You did. I hadn't thought of that."

"Really? Well, I was wondering if you wanted to. That is. What? What did I wonder if you wanted to do?"

"Cook you dinner again?"

"Yes, that's it."

"I do. When?"

"I'm sure you have plans tonight."

"Come straight from work?"

"Really? Yes, I'd love to."

"Ok. See you then. I must grocery shop."

"Oh. If it's too much—"

"Come after work, Neill."

"Yes."

"And, Neill?"

"Yes, Marcane?"

"I was actually hoping you would have waited only one day."

The Second Dinner

The second dinner should have been a little easier. They at least knew vaguely what emotional territory they now occupied, however embryonic. Didn't they?

Neill had doubts because Neill always had doubts. Surely, he kept saying to himself, she has better things to do. Better *men* to do.

The dinner was another pasta dish, this time with vegetables (zucchini, eggplant), and some kind of lemony sauce, and parmesan. It was delicious and there was a fresh baguette again.

"My baguette," Neill said.

"Of course."

"This is delicious. You're a cook."

"Not really. I have a limited palate."

"I have a whore for a palate. I like almost everything I eat."

"Foodwise."

"Other things, too."

"Well, this conversation got there fast."

"Sorry, I."

"No sorry. I've been thinking about it."

"About food?"

"About your eating me."

"I was going to suggest I take you out for dessert after dinner," Neill said, a piece of baguette in his mouth swelling like a snakebite.

"There's a new Haagen-Dazs on Poplar."

"Mm. Ice cream. Want to go?"

"Yes."

"Ok then. Ice cream."

"Or we could stay here and eat each other."

They tumbled into the bedroom. The dishes were left on the dining room table to coagulate. This time they stripped each other bare. Marcane's body was hippy and soft and her thighs were like thistledown. Her breasts were small and softened like rising dough, with nipples like dark chocolate. Neill relished the feel of her under the gentle service of his hands.

When she wrapped her hand around Neill's johnny, it felt like being kissed by deathless lips.

"There's a tidy little dick," Marcane said.

Instead of questioning the possessive, Neill questioned the qualifier.

"Too little?" he said, puffing.

"Don't huff. I only meant it as an affectionate term."

"I wasn't huffing, I was puffing," Neill said.

Then Marcane spit a couple times into her own palm and returned her hand to Neill's now iron penis. No woman had ever done that before and Neill thought it a most cunning jiggery-pokery.

"Not so little now," Marcane said. "You're expanding."

"Wait—" Neill said. Marcane slowed but didn't let go. "I'm gonna come if you keep at it. Let me." He shuffled out from under her hand and arranged her fine thighs the way he wanted them. He kneeled between her knees admiring her body. She smiled her wry smile. She always had a wry smile at the ready.

He moved with confidence toward her pussy. Her pubic hair was dark and wispy. It made for a pretty tableau as he saw it on the way down. He circled its landing pad for a little while. Marcane's sighs drew him on. She was as wet as a dewy lawn.

When he found her clit with his tongue and put a finger inside her, she bent her back upwards and spread her legs as wide as they would go. Neill went at it. Her pussy was sweet—tasted sweet—was it vanilla, or cream? Neill lapped it up. And when Marcane came, it was as if electricity was passing through her. It took her five minutes to calm herself after thrashing. Neill stayed kneeling between her legs, watching her. He ran a finger around in the wet area he had created.

"Whew," Marcane Fry said. "I should call Nora."

Neill looked at her with his own wry smile.

"It's only fair. She would want some of that."

"I think we should forget the Nora plan."

"Yes."

They were still while Marcane struggled to regain her breath.

"I guess it's your turn now, Bucko."

"Want me to bring it to you?"

"Bring it to me? I can see it from here."

Neill slithered upward until he was kneeling over her chest. He ran his pointer over her nipples.

"Oh," she said.

"You don't even have to get up."

"Gimme," Marcane said. She was leaning against piled pillows. She grabbed his scrotum and tenderly pulled him toward her mouth. Neill put his dick slowly between her lips. He let her guide how far and how fast. Soon, they had established a nice fox-trot and Neill liked how Marcane used her left hand to control her intake while she used her right hand alternately between his balls and asshole. Soon, he was filling and Marcane could sense it. It turned her on.

Neill pressed further into her mouth. He was almost all the way in and she held still so as not to gag and so she could feel the swell. Neill, even in his near frenzy, sensed her right hand leaving his balls and moving downward. He turned to see her fingering her snatch. He thought perhaps his dick had excited her that much and that, in turn, excited him. He shot off down her throat.

Bless her. She took it all. Even with Neill in her up to his root. He coated the back of her throat, her uvula and her trachea, her lungs, her esophagus, and her stomach. It was that much come.

Afterward they went for Haagen-Dazs. Marcane got coffee and Neill honey.

While they sat on the curb outside the ice cream parlor, Neill suddenly thought of something.

"Where is your other daughter?"

"Vin?" Marcane asked around her cone. "I guess she was in her room."

"What?" Neill said. "You're kidding."

"Yes, I'm kidding. She is at a camp for the weekend. You can meet her on Sunday night if you want to come to dinner again."

"I shouldn't wait two days?" Neill asked.

"You should not," Marcane Fry said.

Meeting Vin

"Mom, you've got the unsalted butter again," Vin said, after taking a bite off her baguette.

"Yeah, that's the best kind, *darling*," Marcane said. Was she nervous?

"It's not. It's tasteless," Vin elaborated.

"No, listen. Neill, back me up here," Marcane said. She was almost laughing.

Neill looked at Vin and smiled, and then back at Marcane.

"I'm afraid I'm with Vin on this one," Neill said.

"Oh no. All these years I've been serving tasteless butter."

Neill looked at Vin as she ate. She ate like some of the football players he knew in high school. She tore the baguette with her teeth like a dog.

Vin was not delicately made. She was almost mannish—broad shoulders and strong arms. This was balanced by a near perfect figure, breasts like coconuts, slim waist, shapely and sturdy legs. Her face, delicate if she smiled, which was rare, dimpled, surrounded by dark hair, almost blue-black. She was undeniably beautiful, but there was something forbidding about her.

Neill imagined her naked because he could, because there was no law against it, unlike acting upon such fantasies. He imagined her pinioning his arms behind his back, slapping him, and grabbing his root in a painful grip. He imagined her contorting her perfect, athletic body into ways which enabled Neill to enter her from various angles. Yet, in all these fantasies, he also was a bit afraid of her.

Because in real life, he was a bit afraid of her. She had a teenager's disgust with the world, a ready sneer, and an acid tongue, which spent a large amount of time berating her mother about almost anything: food, clothes, money, what she did with her time, why she invited younger men to dinner. There was anger in Vin that was inexplicable. It went beyond the divorced child's grudge.

And Marcane took it all. Not just on this first night but always. Her child held her by the short hairs.

After dinner Vin went off with friends. Neill assumed they were smoking gunney, drinking, getting into trouble. He did at that age but he lacked the courage Vin displayed at every turn. Perhaps she and her cronies were out hot-wiring cars.

"How'd you like my little Vin?" Marcane said as they loaded the dishwasher together.

"She's lovely," Neill said.

"You mean she has a killer bod."

"No. Yes. I mean, not just that. She seems to be a lovely young woman."

"She's mean as hell."

"I see."

"Sorry. I mean, sometimes. She was showing out a bit tonight. She'll be nicer once she gets to know you."

After cleaning up they took cups of tea into the living room. This was an after-dinner tradition, apparently. Neill sat on the couch and Marcane sat in her sprung throne. She made tea with a little sugar and a heavy dose of sweetened condensed milk, so that it tasted like baby food. It tasted like breast's milk, Neill fancied.

"Tea good?"

"It is," Neill said. "I've never had it like this."

"Condensed milk. It's so yummy."

"Mm."

"Neill, listen. I didn't mean to presume that you were going to be around for a while so that Vin would get to know you better. I didn't mean—well, I mean, you will want to start banging girls your own age again rather than waste your time on this old broad."

"Marcane, that's absurd. I love your body."

"Do you really, Neill? That quite amazes me. I assumed my days of sexual attractiveness were behind me."

"They are not. I want to fuck you right now."

"Well, ok then. Wanna do it in the kitchen? For variety, I mean?"

"Sure," Neill said. He was trying to not sound like an excited kid. "Not that we need variety but variety is well...nice. Will Vin walk in?"

"I doubt it."

"Would it bother you if she caught us?"

"I guess it would."

"Would it bother you if people found out about us?"

Marcane thought about that for a minute.

"I'm not sure. It's so—*unexpected*. I think there are some people who would think I look ridiculous with you on my arm."

"So, we can't go out."

"Oh, we can. We will. Do you like the symphony? My brother is a music nut and always has tickets."

"The symphony? Sure. Or the Antenna Club."

"Funny. We can go out." Then she thought a moment. "Perhaps, at first, it would be best if we acted like mentor and pupil, until we see where this—relationship—is going."

"Mentor pupil?"

"No good?"

"How about coach and student?"

"Hmm. I like that. Coach. Yeah, I'm your coach. Speaking of which, I haven't introduced you to an important part of my life."

"You have another secret child?"

"No. An avocation. Running."

"Oh. Really? Running?"

"Yes, usually every night between work and dinner. About 3-4 miles, around the neighborhood, down into Chickasaw Gardens, through the rich folks' winding ways so I can look in their windows, and back home."

"Wow. I'm impressed."

"Don't be until you see me run. It might turn you off so much that you have to move."

"I doubt it. I'll try to keep up with you."

"I gotta do something to keep this body somewhat toned if I am going to have a young lover."

"All you have to do is sit on the kitchen counter naked," Neill said.

"Ok then."

And Marcane did. They both let their clothes fall to the kitchen floor and Marcane hoisted herself onto the counter and spread her legs. She looked damn toothsome and Neill's prick agreed.

When he squatted on the kitchen floor in front of her and ate her, he had a small eureka moment. The previously elusive flavor of her crotch was sweetened condensed milk.

Running

"You don't need to lift your feet as much. You can kinda shuffle," Coach Fry said, the next night on their first run together. "Don't hit the pavement so hard with your feet."

"I'll look like Tim Conway's old man character."

"I don't know what that is but are you saying I look old?'

"You look wonderful. Can I jog slightly behind you so I can watch your ass."

"Keep your focus on your breathing, my only student."

"I am trying to focus on trying to breathe. Is that the same thing?"

"No. Concentrate."

"Or—"

"You want to be paddled, don't you?"

"Maybe. I like games."

"You're bad."

"I know. Can we walk a minute? I'm dying."

They slowed to a walk. It was humid out but in Chickasaw Gardens, among the homes of the very wealthy, they were shaded by old trees.

"Are you ok?"

"Yes, Coach. Stitch in my side."

"Saves time?"

"I think we can save time by driving the rest of the way."

When they resumed, Marcane said, "One of the many advantages of running—and please don't call it jogging—is that it shakes the gas down and you can experience really vivid farting." And she demonstrated.

"It's carminative," Neill said.

Marcane looked at him askance and rolled her pretty eyes. "Right," she said.

Having survived their first run they dined on salad and poached fish and, of course, baguette with unsalted butter.

"You like a big fancy salad, I see," Marcane said. She was looking at Neill's lips.

"I do. I like all the toys."

"What?"

"The toys, the croutons, the celery, the hearts of palm, whatever these little cunning things are—"

"Bits of watercress."

"Yes, you make it with lots of toys. I like it when you have to scoop around the bottom of the bowl and gather all the cunning little objects among the vinaigrette."

"You're a fascinating man, Neill."

"Where is Vin tonight?"

"I should have gotten the salted butter."

"What? No. Well, I mean, yes, for flavor. But, where is Vin?"

"I don't know. Maybe volleyball practice."

"She's an athlete?"

"And how. I don't know where she got it. Her dad was only mildly athletic, and then only because he had to justify his membership in the Country Club."

They moved to the living room with cups of tea and sweetened condensed milk. Neill thought about Marcane's silky pussy.

"Can we go see a game sometime?"

"Really? You want to? We could but it necessitates a real commitment on your part."

"How so?"

"Oh, I don't know. Another future date means we are expecting some kind of future."

"Some kind, yes. Aren't we?"

"I guess I keep waiting for you to return to your young cuties."

"You don't know my young cuties."

"You were fucking Sue Goorile. She was about 13, right?"

"Oh."

"Yes, Neill, this is a small town. Especially if one is a real estate agent. All the old families are connected, incestuously, historically, socially. There are really only six families in Memphis. The rest is done with mirrors."

"You know the Gooriles."

"Not so much. I know who they are. And I have heard stories."

"Tell me."

"Oh, you can guess. Old money. All hers. A few husbands who have to move into her family manse. She's a tough old bird. I wouldn't cross her."

"The mother, I assume you mean. She was always very nice to me."

"She probably wanted to fuck you."

"Oh stop."

"No, it's not that I think everyone wants to fuck you—well, sometimes I think that, yes—it's that I know her."

"Fascinating. I should have been fucking her instead of her youngest daughter. Like here."

"Not funny."

"Sorry."

"Ok, a little funny. Don't you hate people who, instead of laughing at your jokes say, that's funny? Or, *you're bad*?"

"You said that to me on our run."

"I recognize that I did. I didn't catch myself in time."

"So, you know about Sue. That doesn't make a checkered past, you know."

"And Fred Hardwood's beautiful young daughter."

"Wait—really? I thought the separation between Raleigh, the poor part of town which suckled me, and where we now sit, was as wide a gulf as that between waking and sleeping."

"No. Well, somewhat. Fred Hardwood used to fancy himself an up-and-coming handball star when he was young. He went to Central, while I was at East, but my boyfriend at the time knew him from the handball circuit. He was pretty good."

"But not good enough apparently to go pro. Perhaps this is the root of his frustration and his bullying attitude."

"He bullied you?"

"Well, not at first. He *allowed* me to date his underage daughter. Then when it all went pear-shaped, he threatened me."

"With violence?"

"Implied violence."

"That's Fred Hardwood. He was hated in the locker rooms, so the story goes, for being a blowhard and a bigot."

"A bigot?"

"He notably refused to shower if there were any n-words in there."

"At the Country Club?"

"No, of course not. N-words weren't allowed in the Country Club except to serve canapés and martinis. In the locker rooms of the handball circuit."

"I would assume that that kind of prejudice would have met with some approval back then."

"It did. Somewhat. But, coupled with his arrogance, he was not well-liked."

"Huh. His daughter sure is beautiful."

"Isn't one of her brothers in prison?"

"Yes. I think so. That is, I think he is still in."

"And a mysterious older sister who went to college and was never heard from again."

"How do you know that?!"

"You want me to keep on about your past loves."

"No. Not really. Surely you can't know too many more."

And here Marcane Fry mentioned the name of the young woman with the malodorous crotch. And Neill debated about whether to talk about the malodorous crotch and decided he would not. He didn't kiss and tell. Or at least he didn't perform cunnilingus, gag, and talk.

"Ok. That didn't work out."

"But what a dynamite body."

"Yes."

"Hence my hesitation in showing you mine."

"I haven't noticed much hesitation."

"That's pure lust. I want you. And, I want you to want me."

"I want you right now. Look at this prominence."

"Oh, my good student! Is that for your coach?"

"Mom!" Vin called from outside the door. "Open the damn door. I can't find my fucking key."

The Ascent Beckons

Friends, this time with Marcane Fry, this February-September romance (Neill was 25 at the time, Marcane 38), was perhaps the most important relationship of his life, certainly up to that point. Having never graduated college or tasted the kind of writing success that comes from genius plus heavy work, Marcane Fry opened the door onto a world of sophistication, art, music (opera, symphony orchestras), dinner parties (with the wealthy and the influential, including an ex-pro football player and a mayoral candidate), and more mature ways of looking at the world.

The fact that Neill felt he held his own, sometimes, and that he was loved by this older, wiser woman, gave to Neill a gift that lasted the rest of his life. He was—*launched* is a word from a different era—set upon a path, even if the path was mostly interior. Perhaps most paths are.

And the sex was magnificent, too. Another plank of confidence added to the bridge Neill was building that went—*forward*.

After the first six months of furtive rutting, and Marcane's embarrassment at escorting a much younger man, an inevitability about the whole affair took over. They were seen out so often in each other's presence that they became a couple without having to make a public declaration, or some kind of peace within themselves. For Neill, he was proud to be out with this sophisticated and pretty older woman, who knew everyone and was beloved by almost all.

There were older men, men closer in age to Marcane, even if older than her, who continued to try and court the sought-after divorcee, confused by her refusal to date, men who could not imagine that their longed-for place was occupied by a goofy bookseller with a passion for The Monkees and Frank Zappa, Richard Brautigan and James Tate, Stanley Kubrick and Ingmar Bergman, Leonard Cohen and John Lennon.

One such older man—and here we shall omit his name, since he came from one of the better families—who was a jogger like Coach Fry—once showed up on Marcane's doorstep before breakfast. The sun was just rising. Marcane was getting dressed when the doorbell rang. She pulled the curtains aside to espy this sweaty middle-aged jogger strip out of his sweaty running clothes. There, he now stood on her porch dressed only in high-priced running shoes.

Marcane was aghast. She was also trying not to laugh.

"P–," she called through the door. "What the fuck are you doing?"

"Let me in, won't you," the dangling man hissed. "I'm naked."

"I know you're naked," Marcane said. "This is why I am not opening the door. Do you understand that?"

This flustered P. He hesitated, gave his balls a shake with one hand and with the other stooped to retrieve his running shorts and shirt. They were reluctantly re-donned and the man proceeded on his jogging way.

Marcane told Neill the story that night while they ran. Neill tried to fight his green streak.

"He was completely naked?" Neill said, puffing alongside his ladylove.

"He kept his running shoes on," Marcane said. "You know that's crazy."

"He wanted you. I can imagine lonely hours contemplating your shapely backside with such intensity that, in his mind, you two were already lovers."

The jogging (sorry, running) sweethearts were quiet for a few minutes. Marcane was thinking.

"That's pretty wise," she said at last. "You've been around."

Neill let the compliment flow over him like a warm shower.

"How big was his dick?"

Marcane laughed. "Let's race this last half mile. When I say—"

"Cheater!" Neill shouted.

"Go!" She burst ahead of him.

Neill watched her ass for a few moments, and the odd lump on one hip where she was once hit by a car, and her legs in their runner's shuffle, and his heart was full of tenderness. He accelerated and, in the final 100 yards, managed to pass his older lover.

Dinner Parties and Such

And now Neill, intrepid Neill, was cast upon society. In the company of his older lover he found himself at elegant dinner parties with international guests, moneyed folks who were, mostly, kind and funny and well-read, if occasionally pretentious. Neill was sometimes uncomfortable and sometimes lively and charming.

There was a beautiful Swedish couple named Eric and Pia. Marcane had found them a condominium in which to live while they were in Memphis for six months doing some kind of cabalistic banking thing that Neill didn't understand. Neill didn't even try to understand.

Sometimes Neill and Marcane dined out with Marcane's brother and his girlfriend. The brother was a doctor and, of course, well-off. His red-haired girlfriend was younger and sweet, and possessed of a giantess's bosom. They were tits you could live inside. Neill squirmed. Also, the brother had two daughters by his recently divorced wife and one of the daughters, Melanie, was so pretty Neill squirmed and fantasized. Melanie, Neill realized, was one of the dark, hip chicks he had watched dance at The Antenna Club. She had black hair and freckles and Neill, knowing it was wrong to even think about her, thought about her.

But, mostly, it was a grand education for Neill.

And the sex, well, there was the life-enhancing sex. Marcane Fry knew some things and she was an enthusiastic bedmate.

Once she came up with a sly plan. There was a mansion on Belvedere in Midtown that was up for sale while they renovated it. Marcane had the listing and, hence, the keys to the house. She asked Neill what he thought about fucking in a stranger's bed, a rich couple who were out of the country. Neill thought it was a capital idea.

So, in the middle of the day, Marcane drove Neill to this mansion and they walked in as if it were their business to do so. The house was sparkling and like something out of a movie or glossy magazine. There was a lot of metal, a lot of white. The kitchen looked like a kitchen in an upscale restaurant. The house seemed to shimmer of itself, as if it needed no electricity.

On the second floor, they scouted out the bedrooms. It was enjoyable picking one. It was forbidden and, hence, extremely exciting. Neill favored what appeared to be the teenage daughter's room. There were Ramones and Television posters on the wall, and the bed had black satin sheets. (Abby Twa call home.) In the dresser drawer Neill found panties of various hues, including a wine-red, crotchless pair. There was also a glass dildo.

Marcane preferred the master bedroom. It was the size of the north forty and the bed was copious and covered in fine white linens.

They settled there.

They took each other's clothes off fast. They were like children showing their peepees in a tree house. There was an enormous glass window, almost the entire west wall, that was uncurtained and sunlight poured in as if Steven Spielberg were outside manipulating the illumination. Marcane assured Neill no one could see them but Neill was secretly wishing for a voyeur or two, someone a block away with field glasses.

They rolled around on the bed, licking and pulling and kissing. Neill had a large illicit boner. He wanted to fuck like Jesse James.

But something was wrong. Marcane was dry, impenetrably dry. No matter how much Neill licked her clit, she wasn't responding.

"Neill," Marcane said. "Sorry."

"What is it? Am I not doing well?"

"I think I'm nervous. I think I have overstepped my bounds. This is my job and, well…"

"Because the house is in your care, so to speak."

"I guess so."

"That's ok," Neill said, but he was disappointed. He loved to transgress. And transgression in the sexual realm was like candy to him.

"Do you want to come up here for a visit?" Marcane asked.

"A visit?" Neill asked. There was the old twinkle in Marcane's eyes.

"That's what I've been calling it to myself."

"What—"

"When you straddle me and put your cock in my mouth."

"A visit."

"Yes. Like you're visiting the upstairs."

"Hm. I like it. I like the name and I like the action. And it's doubled, because we are upstairs. I am liking this phrase."

"I think your willie does too."

"Oh yes,"

Neill climbed over her, a knee on either side of her chest. His aforementioned willie waggled near her mouth. His balls were resting on her clavicle.

"You like this?" Neill asked, partly teasing, partly sincerely curious.

"I do. It turns me on. I like to touch myself while you—""

"Fuck your mouth."

"Ooh."

"Too coarse?"

"No, I don't think so. Say it again."

"Fuck your mouth. Marcane, do you want me to fuck your mouth?"

"Neill. Give me that dick. Fuck my mouth."

Neill almost came from the language alone. He was word-oriented that way.

He slid his hard baton into her wanting mouth. She put a hand on each of his buttocks as if to steer him. Then a finger down his crack, lingering on his anus, tap tap, tap and then around to his scrotum. Meanwhile, she was mouthing him as if he were a dog's toy.

One of her hands disappeared. Neill craned his neck because he suspected she was fingering herself, turned on by her own talent at fellatio. And she was. She was playing her clit as if it were a banjo and the song was "Foggy Mountain Breakdown."

Now Neill felt his power swell. He began to move his hips more, to take the power of the thrusting and sucking away from her, just a bit. He poked himself in and out. She relaxed her mouth, aware of the slight change. Neill now began to bump her mouth more vigorously. He was afraid of choking her but he was wild, abandoned to their forbidden game in their forbidden bed. He thrust harder. She opened her mouth wider. He began to really push it into her mouth. She opened her eyes and looked into Neill's. She moved her head slightly up and down. Her eyes sparked: they said, Do it, do it harder. Choke me.

Neill pressed down as far as he could. She took it all with a slight gag. He pulled out and pushed it back in even further. She gagged but the hand at her crotch was going crazy.

Then Neill held still for a moment, his dick deep in Marcane's throat. She sucked hard once, twice, and Neill flooded her throat with jism.

As he did, pulling out slightly so she could drink him, savor his seed in her mouth, and spraying the last drops onto her lips, Marcane gritted her teeth and through them said, "Fuuucccckkkkk."

She came, too.

Opera

Neill's first experience with opera was as Marcane's escort. They went twice. Neill couldn't tell you which operas. But he knew this: he hated opera. Ignorant about it, yes, but also, there was a fatigue factor. Being a fan of cinema, Neill had to fight the impulse, at numerous junctures, to stand and shout, "*Edit, edit.*" When he could follow the action, which was rare, he understood that it took them 30 minutes for every small gesture, incident, and interaction.

(This would turn out to be a lifelong aversion. Even in movies, if there was an opera scene [say, in Scorsese's *Age of Innocence*], Neill would feel the familiar squirm beginning in his squirmer.)

There were also concerts of classical music with the doctor-brother and his girlfriend, the buxom redhead who looked like a rich dessert. After the concerts there was discussion. "The Scarlatti was played too fast," the doctor would say. "I was surprised there were not hotdog vendors," Neill would say.

Nevertheless, it was around this time via an employee at The Book Shelf that Neill found himself, on three separate occasions, actually IN the opera.

Let's explain how this worked. This was during a period when the Metropolitan Opera sent a traveling squad to various cities to perform first-rate operas in hick venues like Memphis, Tennessee. The theater of choice was The Orpheum, still one of the grand palaces from the days when movies were sent from God. And, when they did, as extras (supers, or locals they were called) were recruited through Southwestern University. The temp employee at the bookstore (let her remain nameless, though Neill was very fond of her) was dating a Falstaffian fellow named Logan who taught English and Medieval Studies at the university. Logan and Neill hit it off pretty well and often talked books when he came to pick up his gal. Logan asked Neill if he wanted to be a super for The Met (as Neill grew to call it) during the current season.

Did Neill? Of course, he did. He was curious. He was adventurous. He was a ham.

So, the first time Neill was draped in a drab kaftan and his job was to pull a tumbril on stage, where he stood at the very back, all but invisible, during the final scene. Neill thought it was a gas. And, as a jape, he opened his mouth wide and made fantastic facial expressions as if he were part of the chorus. The rush of music and voices swirling around him was dizzying. It was like standing *inside* music. Neill tingled in his tingly places.

Did this convert Neill to opera? As mentioned above (are you paying attention?), it did not. He couldn't even tell you which operas he was in. [Reference?] One of them had the anvil chorus. Neill got to stand in the wings, a mere ten yards or so from the stage. It was quite thrilling.

But, the best part was the final opera. Placido Domingo was the star. And, when Neill and Logan arrived, they were asked to get the full makeup and costume treatment. What did this portend? Neill asked himself, as he was joking and tripping with the professional dressers and makeup artists. He soon found out.

He was called to be part of the opening scene. And backstage, a cramped, chaotic place that stood in stark contrast to the beauty and poise onstage, Neill was smushed between an attractive milkmaid (to his aft) and Mr. Domingo himself (to his fore). Neill's nose was literally pushed against the imposing back of the great soprano. In Neill's hands was a box of myrrh. As it turned out, he was to be part of Placido Domingo's entourage. His character (who knows who he was playing? Romeo? Don Carlos? Barney Google?) was bringing gifts, ala the magi. Neill floated onto the stage right behind his buddy Placy and was onstage the entire first act (which lasted something like 3 days). It was exhilarating. Neill tried to act, tried to live up to the responsibility he had been given. He wanted to be the best myrrh carrier in super history.

And, one of the best parts of all this, Neill thought, was that Marcane was in the audience every night.

Yet...yet...after the 3rd opera, starring Neill and Placy, Marcane began acting oddly. Neill couldn't figure it out. When they went back to her house—it was late and Neill had to get up for work—Marcane was distant. Neill was ginned up and wanted to jump her bones. He was full of operatic muckle spit. But Marcane said she was tired and had a bit of a back ache. Neill nodded, kissed her and left.

Afterward, it occurred to him that he had upset the Coach/Novice balance. Marcane, who had taught Neill about opera, had to sit and observe his actually partaking in it, sans her, sans her influence. Could Neill be ready to enter the adult world without her? These were Neill's dark, confused thoughts afterward.

The next night, Marcane was fine and the previous night's abnormality forgotten (*mostly*—Neill was to remember that night later).

Poor

Sometimes Marcane was sunk in funk. This usually had to do with the real estate market, a turbulent roller coaster and one which, right now, was stalled at the bottom of the tracks. Marcane worried, literally, about her ability to pay her bills. Vin was at a well-heeled private school, the most expensive one in Memphis. Her father was supposed to be paying but often didn't out of spite or cheapness or just a black spot on his soul.

One night, Neill arrived to find Marcane sitting in the dark.

"I can still cook," she said from the eclipse of her sunken chair. "The stove is gas."

Why There is Sex

One evening, after the run and after the dinner (where Vin sat in silent sulk, her sports bra and sweaty gym shorts a sparkle in periphery), Neill showed Marcane the movie *Stop Making Sense*. Marcane had never heard of Talking Heads and she was duly impressed.

Vin went out.

Neill and Marcane took a shower together in her small stall. The soap had them both lubed and aroused, and they tumbled out of the loo and into bed still wet.

They did it all. It was hot and healing, and the kind of harmony only lovers who have been together for a while know how to make. Marcane wanted it on a visit, then from behind, then with her on top, and at the last minute (really, the last 30 seconds because Neill was about to burst) she stopped moving against his pole and moved his hand around to her backside.

"Feel this," she said.

"Damn," Neill said. "This is why the interruptus is extinct."

"Sorry, just feel this." She placed Neill's hand at the base of her spine.

"There's a knob there," Neill said, now interested though his pole lost the fish.

"I have a prehensile tail."

"What?"

"It's true. Some people have them. A residual trait, I think it's called."

"Huh," Neill said, taking his hand away as if it were a snakehead.

"Sorry," Marcane said. "I just thought of that. I wanted to show you my imperfections."

"Ok," Neill said.

"Don't get in a huff."

"I'm not in a huff. Maybe half a huff."

Marcane laughed so Neill smiled.

"I'll make it up to you."

"Ok," Neill said.

"You wanna come on my face?"

"What? Really?"

"You ever done that before?"

"No," Neill said quickly. He couldn't remember doing it.

"Does it intrigue you?"

"I think so," Neill said, not wanting to sound overly enthusiastic in case this was some kind of feminist trap.

"Come here," Marcane said, wiggling off him and flopping down next to him. "Come up for a visit."

"Ok," Neill said. The fish was nibbling.

"Come here, big boy," Marcane said, like Mae West.

She gently rubbed her fingers over his willy. She tickled his balls lightly. She ran a finger over the flesh bridge and gently into his backeye.

"There we go," she said as Neill rose to the task. "Pull out right before you come."

"You sure?"

"Yes. I want to see how it feels. They do it in porn movies."

"Do they?" Neill said, putting his cock in her mouth.

It didn't take long. The pent-up spray came back to its proper place quickly. The fish started to jerk. (These mixed metaphors are awful.)

"Now," Neill said.

Marcane pulled her mouth away and Neill took his own personal, private, well-loved-by-him tool in his own personal hand and jerked it three times before he started to flow over her cheeks and nose and lips. Some hit her left eyebrow. It took a bit and Neill began to feel the aftershocks coming on. He was doing a jimmy dance over her as every last drop spilled.

"Hmm," Marcane said.

Neill scooted back a few inches.

"Ok? You like or not like?"

Marcane licked it off her lips.

"It's warm. It feels ok. It was sexy while you were spewing."

"Not so much now."

"Not so much now."

"I'll get a washcloth."

Neill warmed a washcloth under the bathroom sink and returned and gently washed her come-covered face.

Subsequently, they lay next to each other and talked.

"Whew," Marcane said. "You come a lot."

"Do I?"

"Not like older men. They put out a little dribble if they are lucky."

There it was. Neill flattered at the praise (was it praise?) but jealous of all the older men she had had, the bankers and lawyers and real estate developers, dictators and financiers.

It was right then when they heard Vin try her key in the lock. They had bolted the inside door again. She began to kick and pound on the door.

"Open up, fuck!" she screeched.

Neill leapt from bed and pulled his clothing on. Marcane was freshly ashamed and began to look for her clothes in the sheets. They were in the bathroom still and she made her way there, practically stumbling in a nude, bear-like dance.

Neill was dressed first and reached the door.

"Sorry," he said, and he began a lame reason why they had locked the inner door.

"Hey Neill," Vin said. "You're shirt's on inside out."

Pillow Talk 1

"Do you have sex dreams a lot?" Marcane asked, stirring the homebrew on Neill's belly the way a child plays with finger paints.

"Yes. Yes, I do."

"I don't have many. I don't have many dreams, period."

"I'm a dreamer, a big dreamer."

"Favorite kinds of dreams?"

"Well, celebrity dreams are fun. I have dreamt numerous times that Paul McCartney was my friend."

"He's not even your favorite Beatle."

"I know. Dreams are bizarre that way. Of course, I like sex dreams better than celebrity dreams. There were dry periods in my sexual life when I prayed for a sex dream. I guess the best would be sex dreams with a celebrity."

"You want to fuck Paul McCartney."

"Well, he is the cute Beatle."

"Yeah, I'd like to fuck Paul McCartney. But only if you weren't around."

"Ok."

"Who do you dream about sexually?"

"Oh now. I don't know."

"You do. Tell me."

"This gal from high school. I've known her since fourth grade. Rita Houston."

"Rita Houston, the real estate agent?"

"Jesus. I forgot how long your tendrils are."

"It's real estate. A close community. Who else?"

"I don't know."

"You ever dream about either of my daughters?"

"No," Neill lied.

"It's ok if you did. It's like you say. You can't control whom you dream about."

"Never your daughters," Neill lied. "Yet."

"Bastard."

"Once about my boss Ianthe."

"Ianthe! My old running buddy Ianthe!"

"Well."

"Oh, she would love that."

"Don't tell her for Godsake."

"But she'd be so flattered. I don't mean she'd love that you dreamed about her. She'd love to fuck you."

"I didn't dream we fucked."

"What then?"

"69."

"Your favorite."

"I know."

"I guess I better keep an eye on you and Ianthe. There is that large stockroom after hours."

"The Goorile sisters."

"All at once?"

"Yeah. Wish I could have that one again."

"Weren't there too many—orifices?"

"Not in dreamland. I was up to the challenge. How about you?"

"I've never dreamed about Ianthe or the Goorile sisters, as attractive as I find them."

"Funny."

"I don't have sex dreams. Well, I had one once that I remember but I won't tell you."

"C'mon, that's not fair. Someone I know?"

"No. Not even someone I know."

"Sex with a dark stranger. That could be exciting."

"Dark ha, yes. I'll tell you but you better not tell anyone. I'd die of mortification."

"Someone unpleasant?"

"Once I dreamed." She hesitated, smiled a weak smile. "Once I dreamed a dog was licking my pussy and I orgasmed."

"A dog!"

"Neill."

"Sorry. You orgasmed in the dream?"

"No, in reality. I woke up from an orgasm and felt grand for a second. Then I realized I'd been dreaming about a German Shepherd."

"A Nazi dog, no less."

"Does that count as a celebrity dream?"

"I don't think so. I guess I'm gonna have to watch you around pets."

"Very funny. Of course, if you ever tell, I'll kill you."

"Ok. Once I dreamed about the Pointer sisters. That's sort of in your ballpark."

"I'll kill you, you know."

Poetry Talk

"Are you sure you don't mind me showing you my poem?" Marcane looked suddenly ten years Neill's junior as she held a single sheet of typed paper in her hands.

"Of course not. But I have no cachet, no authority. I would make a lousy teacher and probably can't tell you if something is wrong with the poem even if I were brave enough to tell you something is wrong."

"That's a lot of disclaimer."

"Just saying—I don't know."

"You told me a lot when you explained one of your own poems. You were quite—authoritative."

"Ok. Well, I know less about poetry than you know about mortgages."

"Granted. I went to school for that."

"I went to school, too."

"Poetry school?"

"Well."

"Never mind. Read it. Take it home and read it." Marcane handed him the poem.

"Not here?"

"You mind?"

"No. Just be quiet."

They sat across from each other. Neill sipped his heavy tea, its sweet milky taste of Marcane's pussy.

Marcane sipped. A few more moments passed and Marcane made a childish slurping sound.

"Ok," Neill said.

"Sorry."

"No, I mean ok. I've read it through twice."

"Embarrassing, isn't it? I'm sorry. I shouldn't have—"

"It's quite good."

"Really?" Marcane sounded positively girlish.

"Yes. It's quite good. As far as I can tell."

"False modesty."

"No, not really. It's just—well, I don't know the technical stuff that well, grammar, scansion—I don't even know what some of the terms mean. I'm better at the instinctual stuff."

"And your instincts."

"My instincts like this very much."

"It's about my sister-in-law. She had that happen to her."

"Hm."

"Anyway. I won't write anymore."

"Why not?"

"I guess what I mean is I won't write anymore and show you."

"Ahh."

"You know that's crazy, right? You know that's crazy?"

"It's not too late to become a poet, you know?"

"Perhaps I should write fiction. You know, real estate agents find out a lot of secrets, what's in people's closets, the things they put away in drawers, whether they have books and what kind of books if they do. It's really a sociological wonderland. You've inspired me. You really think I could be good?"

"I do," Neill said.

His soul stank. He was lying.

Things Said

"Do you get tired of coming here every night," Marcane said once. They were having their tea.

"No. Or I wouldn't be here."

"I just thought—you know, there are all those young women who come into the bookstore and fuss over you. You must want to—"

"No," Neill said.

"It's just my idea of being in love is that you want to be with that person all the time. All day, every day and night."

"I see it that way, too," Neill said. And, he did.

So, Neill had professed love and Marcane had professed it back. They were in love. (This was earlier. We should re-position this in the manuscript.)

And, what with the dinner parties and concerts and brunches they attended, Neill had found a peer group he savored, even if, at times, he felt out of his depth, the young nipper among the wise graybeards.

"I mean this idea of personal *space*," Marcane said.

"I hate that phrase. It's right up there with 'we better talk.'"

"Exactly. No one wants space. No one who is in love."

It sounded right at the time.

"It's not right till it's right," Neill said, apropos of nothing.

Luckily, Marcane didn't follow up on that. She was off on her own path.

"Anytime a man told me he wanted space I gave it to him. I gave him wide open vistas. I gave him veldts. I gave him savannas and deserts."

"Ha!" Neill said. "Also, whenever someone tells you they don't want a relationship right now what they mean is they don't want a relationship *with you*."

"So I monopolize you."

"Monopolize me, Baby. Take me walking on the Boardwalk. French kiss me during Free Parking. Put me in Jail."

"Electrocute me."

"What? Oh, because of the utilities. Good. You turn on my tap, baby."

"I love you, Neill."

"I love you too, Marcane."

Sometimes There were Conversations like This

"This pasta is especially good."

"It's the same shit I always make. You've had it a hundred times."

"Really? I thought there was a new spice perhaps."

"There's never a new spice."

"You mean in food, in our lives?"

"Either. Neither. Whichever."

"You ok, Coach?"

"Why wouldn't I be ok?"

"Money problems?"

"You're eating, aren't you?"

"_"

"_"

"Well, it certainly is tasty."

"If you say so. I am sure you could be fed better elsewhere."

One of Those Every Nights

"What time do these dancing sugarplums start?"

"Neill, it's *Cinderella* not *The Nutcracker*."

"Right. *Cinderella.* I saw the Jerry Lewis movie."

"I don't get the reference."

"Never mind."

"Eight o'clock," Marcane said.

"So, we need to leave when?"

"I don't know. Seven thirty at the latest, I guess. Why all the questions? I'm trying to get ready."

"What do you call those?"

"What?" Marcane turned away from the mirror where she was putting on eye makeup. Neill was sprawled on her bed, leafing through a New Yorker.

"Those sheeny things."

"I thought sheeny was the un-PC term."

"Ha ha. Those—knickers?"

"Knickers? Neill, what are you looking at?"

"I'm looking at your ass in those tight shiny things."

"Oh, yes?"

"I've never seen them before."

"You have too."

"You bought them new."

"I did not."

"You bought them so I would look at your ass in them and want to make us miss the ballet."

"Ha. We can't miss the ballet. My brother got us the tickets. They're very expensive."

"Oh."

Marcane stopped the ministrations with the tiny black brush.

"What time is it now?" Marcane asked.

Neill looked at his watch. "Ten after."

"How quick are you?"

"Seriously?"

"Yes, now I can't concentrate on Prokofiev."

"I love it when you talk dirty."

"Make it fast, buster."

Neill kicked off his shoes. He shoved his slacks down. (Slacks, ugh, thought Neill when Marcane picked them out for him to wear on these occasions.)

"You were ready."

"Bring that sheeny ass over here."

Marcane did. She walked backwards toward him.

Neill put his hands on her shining ass.

"Ooh, these are so—silky."

"You better get in them fast. We now have six minutes."

Neill pulled them roughly down and bit one side of Marcane's ass.

"Ouch," she said. "I mean—keep going."

Neill put a hand up between her legs where she stood, back to him. She was already wet.

"Over the bureau," Neill said.

Marcane leaned against her makeup table. Neill hustled up behind her and, without any further foreplay, stuck his pole inside her.

"Oh. Oh God," Marcane said. "Yes."

Neill went at it. He loved the look of her ass. He loved watching his own swack going in and out. Marcane began to finger her own clit."

"Jesus, Neill, hold it for one more minute. Heh—half a minute."

Then, she came and as she did she clenched her vaginal muscles around Neill. He let go inside her.

They dressed quickly, both breathing heavily.

"What's our time?" Marcane said, once they were dressed.

"Thirty seconds to spare."

"Go again?" Marcane said, laughing.

In the car, Marcane put a proprietary hand on Neill's knee.

"You're something, kid. You know that?"

Neill grinned a wolfy grin.

"You can pull it off in little time. That's a good trick. You're quick when you need to be."

"The situation called for it," Neill said. He leaned over, almost stopped by the shoulder-belt, and kissed her cheek.

"You're quick like a bunny. My little Bunny."

And a sobriquet was born.

Pillow Talk 2

Neill said, "Have you ever noticed that after a break-up one of the ex-coupled alters his or her appearance in some way? Usually with a haircut, or if the man growing a mustache or beard, or shaving a mustache or beard. It's like a thumbing of the nose to the ex. Saying 'See, I don't need you to feel good about myself.' Or, perhaps, 'I changed and I am not the person you loved and let go.'"

"The Breakup Haircut."

"Yeah, exactly. It is a known thing, already studied and labeled?"

"No, I don't think so. I'd never thought of it before. I think you're onto something."

"Where did you say Vin is this weekend?"

"Camp Something."

"I think I went to Camp Something."

"You never went to camp."

"No, of course not. Because I am an indoor person."

"And a good one."

"Thanks, Coach."

"You're welcome, Bunny."

"Did you really like what we did?"

"Most of it, yes."

"What didn't you?"

"I'm ragging you. I loved it. Did you not hear me squeal?"

"I think my mother in Raleigh heard you squeal. I think my sister in Bartlett heard you squeal. I think my brother in Connecticut heard you squeal. I think Vice President Bush heard you squeal. I–"

"I get it."

"Wait. I had one more. It's a good one."

"Ok."

"Never mind. It's not that good."

"You have to say it now."

"I think Phil Ochs, moldering in his grave, heard you."

"I don't know Phil Ochs."

"I told you it wasn't that good."

"Ok, Bunny."

"Kiss me, Coach."

"Gladly I shall, Bunny."

....

"That was a good kiss, Coach."

"Thank you, Bunny. Let me rub your little bunny fur belly."

"Ok. Here it is."

"I love that line of hair from your navel to your dick."

"Say it again."

"Navel."

Out with the Boys

Neill went out with the boys one night. It didn't seem to be that big a deal. No, that's not true. He knew he was transgressing. He knew Coach would not be happy about it. On the phone, she was all false cheer.

"Of course, you should go out. You haven't seen Bidden or Crow in ages."

"That's it exactly."

"I'll just sit here and work on my scrapbook."

"You don't have a scrapbook. I don't have to go."

"No scrapbook. Damn. I'll just macramé."

"Stop. Want me to come over now?"

"What time are you supposed to meet them?"

"Now."

"Go then. Go. I do have a new book to read."

"What book?"

"Now you're just making phatic conversation. You sold it to me."

"I know. But the repetition of book titles is an arcane spellbinding."

"*Dinner at the Homesick Restaurant.*"

"I love that book."

"Goodbye, Neill."

Later, he would run this conversation by Bidden and Crow and Shlomo. He tried to reproduce it verbatim. He tried to make Marcane not sound clingy while at the same time resentment sat on his brow like a ring of sweat.

"I'd never miss a night of clicket," Shlomo said. "But that's just me."

"You're out. You could be home with the wife."

"Neill."

"Right. Marriage. The boundless badlands as far as rantum-scantum goes."

"How many different terms do you know for copulation?"

"Copulation?" Neill said. "Is that like fucking? Wait, I'm writing that down."

"Do you know why the bride is smiling walking down the aisle?" Bidden said, swallowing his beer. "Because she knows she's given her last blowjob."

The boys laughed. But a stillness settled down upon them like a fog. They were contemplative eating their burgers and fries and drinking their bottled beer. The silence lasted a good long time. It was about the length of "Inna-gadda-da-Vida" (the album version), and were it not for the comfort these men felt in each other's presence, it would have been awkward and, hence, hard to break.

"I should hump housewives," Bidden said, finally, as if that was what they were all thinking about.

"Because they are not screwing their husbands and hence need screwing."

"The logic falls apart?"

"No, it's a good plan. Whom to start with?"

Bidden looked around the table. His smile was sly, neat.

"Don't look at me," Crow said.

"You're still having sex?"

"Holidays."

"Holidays, sure."

"You can have Daisy," Shlomo said.

The Collapsing of the Infrastructure

Neill and Marcane were together for a year. It was an important year for Neill. He learned how to jog (run). He learned how to talk to rich people at sit-down dinners. He learned that he was no longer a child, that he could have a lover (whom he loved) who is sophisticated, smart, and funny. These were important teachings.

But, cracks began to show. Marcane grew impatient with Neill. She seemed to pick on anything he said that did not concern her. She seemed even *angry* with him at times, as if he wasn't living up to expectations.

They began to squabble like an old married couple.

She did not like his going to P&H with his old friends. He knew she didn't approve. It went against her tenet (which Neill also endorsed so what did his transgression mean?) that when you loved someone you simply wanted to be with them always, every night.

Neill grew tired of it. It was the undermining of all the confidence and maturity he felt he had earned in recent months. If Marcane disapproved of him, if she thought he was insipid or off beam in some way, then the little guy in Neill's head, the "You Suck" guy, would sharpen his sticky things and start back doing the evil grind and graft.

Neill began to think it was time he told Marcane about his doubts, about his misgivings, about his sensitivity to her criticism. He figured he would sit down with her and just be honest. He would say, "If I can't be honest with you, it can't be love."

This was horseshit.

Neill hated people who said, "I've got to be honest with you." It always meant, ""I'm gonna take this right foot and I'm gonna whop you on that side of your face and you wanna know something? There's not a damn thing you're gonna be able to do about it."

An Unpleasant Parlay

"You seem to be angry with me."

"What would I be angry about?"

"I don't know. I mean, it's like a dark river running underneath our conversation. I don't feel—*loved*."

"I love you, Bunny." This was said with a kind of weary resolution. As in, well, I *love* you…

They were still at the dinner table. Their dishes of olive oil and pasta were half-eaten.

"What is it? You're not as pleased with me as before?"

"Before what?"

"You know what I mean. You're not happy, I guess is what I am saying."

"I'm not happy. That's true."

"I've stopped making you happy."

Marcane sat a long time looking at Neill. Something was formulating and Neill feared what it might be.

"I think you don't love me," she said at last.

"I do though. I've not stopped showing you."

"Have you really not?"

"What's missing? I'm here every night. We have great sex."

"You're bored with me sexually."

"Absurd."

"Why wouldn't you be? Look at the young women out there. Their brown limbs, their nimble steps, their saturating pussies."

"I'm sure I don't know what you're talking about. I find you incredibly sexy. Did I not just buy you lingerie from Victoria's Secret."

"I can't wear that."

"Oh."

"I mean, really, Bunny. Can you see me in that?"

"I wanted to."

"It's ridiculous. It's like an unconscious taunt on your part."

"Oh—for God sake—"

"Maybe even conscious. Maybe you're making fun of me."

"Marcane. Coach. Where is this coming from?"

"I've lived long enough to sense these things."

"Your sensors are off."

"Rarely. You can't wait to get to the next woman on your list, a younger version, a sleek new model with tits and ass, and as horny as an Irishman."

"Stop it."

"No. Fuck you, Neill. Fuck you. You want to leave."

"I do, right now."

"Go. What's to keep you here? Not this saggy body."

"Enough. We'll talk later when you're not so—crazy."

"Crazy? Ha. Get out of here. You can't wait."

"Later then."

Neill rose. He started to pick up his plate and rinse it in the sink. The gesture seemed inane. He put the plate back on the table with studied deliberation and headed instead for the front door.

"Neill. If you go out the door don't come back. I mean it. I don't need this humiliation."

Anger was rising in Neill. He was bristling at the injustice, the unreasonable injustice of this. She was right. He didn't want to come back.

"Go ahead, Asshole!" Marcane was shouting now. "Leave. You're gutless, Neill. You can't follow through on anything. You're a failure. Go on. You've got no courage."

Neill turned just briefly at the door. Marcane settled back in her chair. Her face seemed to be expecting a blow—or a reprieve. There was anger there—red-eyed anger—and yet still hope.

"I never said I was brave," Neill said, and he walked away.

"Go, Fucker. Runaway. Weakling," Marcane rained on him. "And believe me: I am NOT CUTTING MY HAIR!"

Though later, much later, a nervy peace was brokered and they occasionally had dinner together, Neill never again went to bed with Marcane Fry, nor kissed her, nor sought her approval.

BOOK IV: BIRTH (AND DEATH)

"He must have her. He must have her, or someone else. He needed contact, skin to skin, muscle to muscle. Above all, he needed the oblivious moment of penetration when, for a second, he could stop thinking about himself. Unless, as too often happened, the appearance of intimacy unleashed a further disembodiment and a deeper privacy."
  –Edward St Aubyn

You Cannot Petition the Lord with Prayer

So, another new phase in Neill's life. He was once again 'dating.' What an antediluvian word. If Neill were in charge of the world, he would have stayed home with his Hellers and Murdochs and Roths and Vonneguts and watched his VCR, and the women of the world would have shown up, one by one, on his doorstep, offering food and the sustenance of their young, fertile bodies. What a world that would be.

And yet: Overall a new confidence was busy being born in our protagonist, Neill Rhymer. If you want a rational explanation (and really, such connections are spurious), one could say that Neill reckoned that if a woman as attractive, urbane, and bright as Marcane Fry loved Neill...well then, he might just be loveable.

We could run through a series of these dates but let a few stand for many (if such a thing is preferable or indeed possible).

Neill went to Hollywood Video near Goldsmith's in East Memphis because Video Magic on Union, which was some kind of nirvana for serious film buffs, had closed, sold to the Blockbuster across the street, so they could shutter it and dispense with the competition. Ugh, Neill said. Another beautiful thing perishing too soon.

Hollywood had a decent selection of foreign films (not nearly what Video Magic had had, of course, and now Blockbuster was deep-sixing the variety that had threatened their gargantuan business) and kept numerous copies of the hot flicks. Neill liked to browse, to go with no movie in mind, to let the experience bequeath him the movie he deserved. Neill was full of such hooey.

This one night Neill wanted something simple, something like a British caper film perhaps, or an American action film. He was returning Bergman's *Virgin Spring*, a luminous enchantment, so perhaps balance was what Neill was seeking.

What he found instead was a lovely pair of wide-open eyes, a fringe of dark hair over them like a canopy, cheeks as cute as cheese, and a roly-poly body that looked, to Neill's flesh-lonely state, like fresh dough.

Her name tag read SPICE. Seriously.

The approach was easy enough. Neill was as sure that she got asked about her name by every horny male in Hollywood Video as he was sure that it didn't matter a damn about his own approach.

"Seriously?" Neill said. His smile was the one with the diamond-hard glint in it. Sometimes it worked.

She smiled back and pretended to straighten a row of film boxes.

"My parents," she said.

"I get it. You have a sibling named Sugar. Or perhaps Tang. Or Rosemary, or Mace."

"Please stop," Spice said. But, she laughed.

Neill introduced himself and they chatted a bit. It was going well. She declared herself a French film fanatic, but she did not know Godard. That didn't matter. Neill could talk about

Malle and Truffaut and Rohmer all day. They talked a bit about books, too, but this path was squishier and Spice seemed to want it to end quickly.

"Listen," Neill said. She listened.

"After work..."

"I can't," Spice shot out. "Sorry."

"Oh," Neill said. His confidence leaked from him like a tune in a dream.

"I mean, tonight," Spice added, and did some more faux shuffling of film boxes.

"Tomorrow night?" Neill asked.

"I'm off!" Spice said with a spritely grin.

"Let's go out to the movies, what say?"

"Yes," Spice said. "I live in Mississippi."

"Ah," Neill said. This seemed like another dodge.

"Just over the state line. Do you know where Southwestern Community College is?"

"Vaguely."

"Right by there. I'll draw a map."

She did. And the next night Neill set out for Mississippi to pick up this odd creature, this Spice, who loved movies and who had a great face and eyes like dark gems.

"Hi," Spice said. "Neill this is my mom."

"Hi," Neill said. He wanted to add Mrs. Something but he didn't even know Spice's last name.

"You kids be careful," the mother said as they went out the door.

Something about that statement prickled Neill's sensitive gloom radar.

They went to see something (it's not important, is it?) and afterward went to Shoney's for strawberry pie. Yes, it was a classic Neill First Date.

(Ok, dammit, the film was *Romancing the Stone* because *Amadeus* seemed like a bad choice for a first date.)

Over pie, they found a rapport. At least, Neill thought so.

The drive home was pleasant. Neill reached over and took her hand and she clasped it right away and covered it with her other hand. Her face had a rascally element to it.

In Spice's driveway, in Southaven, Mississippi, Neill and Spice began to make-out. It was real teenagery making-out. Lots of tongue and, very quickly, lots of wandering, grasping hands.

"Damnation," Neill thought. "She is so hot!"

When Neill unbuttoned her blouse and was presented with a fine swelling of young white mammaries, Spice seemed eager to show them. She helped him unhook the bra. They were perfect. Neill felt their heft, even at the terrible angle a car offers. He sucked on their soft but firm nipples. Spice began to make little puffy sounds. Neill thought, oh boy, a woman as orgasmic as Sue Goorile. This was one enthusiastic petting session.

When Neill raised his mouth from sucking those supple nipples, Spice took Neill's hand and leisurely raised it to her mouth. Looking Neill in the eye, she slowly sucked his index finger into her ample and sopping wet mouth. She ran it in and out slowly. The message couldn't be clearer.

Neill dove down the back of her skirt, the hem of which was elastic, blessed elastic, and was quickly playing with her baby-smooth ass. He ran a finger down her crack and suddenly found himself on the edge of a hot pudding pool.

"Ah, ah," Spice said. Neill hesitated. Spice shook her young black hair.

Neill put a finger in, played around the rim, tickled her clit, put two fingers in. Spice bucked so hard Neill was afraid she would shake the car into neutral.

There was nothing neutral about how excited she was.

She came. Once. Maybe twice.

She looked Neill in the eye. She was a bold vixen, or good at playing one.

She began to rub the bulge behind Neill's zipper.

Mm hm," she said. She seemed to be measuring him.

"Mm hm," she said again. And unbuckled his belt.

Her hand found the pit-digger's tool, wrapping it in cool, soft fingers.

"Mm hm," she said again and then, "Mm hm hm."

She took it out.

It was then that Neill did something inexplicable, something unprecedented in his life and something he was never to repeat.

He removed that young woman's hand from his erect penis. And spoke:

"Spice," he said. "I want to do this right. I want you to come back to my house tomorrow night and let's do this right. Let's do it in a bed."

Spice looked at him as if he were The Last Gentleman. She looked at him as if he were Spartacus. She looked at him as if he were Robert the Bruce.

They kissed goodnight passionately.

"Mm, baby," Neill said. "I can't wait till tomorrow night."

The next morning, as early as he thought practical, he called Spice Clonanger's phone number (he did get her last name and forgot it quickly). Her mother answered.

"Wait just a moment," she said.

"Hi," Spice said.

"Hey. I've been thinking about you," Neill said.

"My mom says I can't go out with you again."

Neill shrank. Suddenly, he was wee. He was Scott Carey with a sewing needle for a weapon. He was so small he was afraid of Goffredo stepping on him when he awoke. How could he get big again?

"I don't understand," Neill said. But he did.

"You're too old for me," Spice said, as if it were her idea. There was no disappointment in her tone.

"But—can't we—you know, sneak out? Can't we do the Capulet thing?"

"No. I'm sorry, Neill."

\   And that was that.

It was one night and it was over.

Except, for the rest of his restless life, Neill regretted that night out of all proportion. He never saw Spice Clonanger again. But, for eternity, he would remember that mouth pulling his finger in and he would petition God to let him go back to that night for just long enough to finish it properly.

"Good Lord," Neill prayed. "My Shepherd, King of Kings, Prime Mover, First Cause, Light of the World, please give me just long enough, ten minutes is all I ask. I WANT THAT BLOW JOB!!"

More Conversations Among Men

"The first time I was invited to do a reading I thought, this is an easy gig," Shlomo said.

"When I got there I realized they meant aloud."

"You do it well, nevertheless," Neill said. "And you're really good at the Q&A part. Because you know from whence literature sprang."

"You flatter me. Sometimes I think I am the stupidest writer published today. For instance someone asked me something about Lichtenstein once. I fumbled around. I don't know anything about Lichtenstein. I don't even know where it is."

"You know your subject," Bidden put in. "A writer's subject is his or her home country. You have that."

"My little Jewish Memphis."

"At least."

"Once a girlfriend asked me if I had really done something that was in a poem of mine," Neill said, though he felt foolish making writer talk with Shlomo Einstein, perhaps the finest writer Memphis had ever produced.

"It was an outré sexual position?" Crow said.

"You think you know me so well."

"Sorry," Crow said. He drank some beer. "What was it then?"

"An outré sexual position. But, it could have been anything. That's the point."

"I get it. I'm sorry."

"So I said to her, 'It's the poetic voice but not necessarily the poet's.' 'But you say "I" she said.' And I told her, 'Listen, you don't think the guy who wrote "I've Been Working on the Railroad" really had been, do you?"

"Good one," Shlomo said.

The gang laughed, because that's what gangs are for.

"I don't know about live poetry readings," Crow said. "I have a hard time following them. My mind goes in a million directions."

"I do that, too," Neill said. "Sometimes a poet catches fire for me though. Robert Bly did."

"Poetry readings," Bidden said. "You either love them or you hate them."

"You know, whenever someone says to me, 'You'll either love it or hate it,' I always find that it's simply not true, "Neill said now. "Almost every time someone says that it concerns something about which I am totally ambivalent."

"Sometimes, my ideas are better than my executions. And sometimes, my execution seems the best idea," Shlomo said.

Noted here: the gang laughed again.

"What does that have to do with what we were saying," Neill said after the laughter rolled away.

"Nothing," Shlomo admitted.

"I let the wrong word slip while kissing persuasive lips," Neill said.

"Because you're really Secret Agent Man," Bidden said.

"Yes," Neill said and finished his beer.

And Then There was This Gypsy Lass

When Neill worked in Raleigh Springs Mall there used to be "Gypsy Warnings." What this meant was that the phone brigade—a quaint security system where stores called each other in a long chain of forewarning —would announce that Irish Travelers were in the mall.

Neill was fascinated—and somewhat afraid of the Travelers. All the men, in their ragtag clothing, look like river bottom roughs and all the women looked deadly, even when sexy. They would come into the bookstore, 3 or 4 at a time, easy to spot because each of them were just so *singular*. They would pretend to be interested in the stacks of remaindered books or the Doc Savage paperbacks, but they were really scouting. It was the job of the bookstore staff to keep an eye on them and we did, moving as close as we dared, play-acting like them, mirror-images of their actions, here straightening a stack of books, here kneeling to dust a lower shelf. Once one of the gals, a young woman with dark-red hair and creamy skin marked with a snug black beauty mark high on one bloodless cheek, walked up close to Neill and stuck her little puppy nose close to his face and smelled down the length of his cheek and neck. Neill stood stock still. He was shocked. When she pulled away, with a hiss of colored fabric, she left Neill with an enigmatic wink.

So, when some Travelers descended on Poplar Plaza one afternoon, Neill already knew the situation and its luster was somewhat diminished by familiarity. An older couple and a young woman came into the bookstore. They smiled at Neill as they passed him at the register. The younger woman stared at Neill as if he were something peculiar. Neill returned her quizzical look with one of his own.

Iago came rushing up from the back, his fingers still greasy from the pork rinds he was eating while shelving books. He pushed his oleaginous mouth up next to Neill's ear and whispered with a porky odor, "Gypshies."

"I'm not blind," Neill said.

Iago looked at them and back at Neill. Then he nodded as if something had been decided.

Neill went back to the microfiche reader, to his job of ordering new books from the distributor.

He did not hear her approach.

"Hi," she said.

Neill looked up. Her hair was so black it had blue highlights and her skin was as white as molten glass so that her angled eyebrows and faint moustache looked as if they had worked into her skin by a calligrapher's ebony ink.

"Hi," Neill said. And now he was looking into her eyes, a pale beryl like the top of cresting waves. "Can I help you find a book?"

"No, I don't want a book," she said. And then, she did the damnedest thing. She laughed, and her laugh was like china falling.

Neill laughed too. "This is a bookstore," he said, smiling.

Now she seemed almost shy, except her eyes flared.

"You're on television," she said.

Neill was confused.

"No, not me," Neill said. "Post office wall maybe. No late-night news stories."

She didn't understand the jape but moved ahead anyway.

"You are the American hero," she said. She said Ay-meer-ican heero.

Neill laughed. "I get that a lot. It's really just the hair."

"No, it's not," she pressed on. "You are beautiful."

Now Neill was abashed. "I've never been called beautiful before," he said.

"Shame on everyone who has ever known you."

"Thank you," Neill said.

"Deirdre," she said, and stuck out her hand. Neill expected bangles and bracelets but the wrist was bare save for a braided string. He took her hand in his. Her fingers were slim and capped with long nails painted midnight blue. She used her thumb to rub the back of Neill's hand the way one tests fabric.

"Neill."

And she did. She knelt below him without relinquishing his hand. Neill was suddenly horrified until she looked up with a sly grin. She could jest as well.

"Funny," Neill said, relieved. "You're funny. Please get up."

And still, she held his hand.

"I like you, Neill," Deirdre said. "Will you take me out tonight?"

"Oh, well," Neill began, suddenly afraid.

"Oh! You are married."

"No, no," Neill said. "Not even close."

"Then how about it?"

"Yes," Neill said, his decision a lightning bolt. "Yes, let's do that."

He was still a bit afraid as Deirdre drew him a map on the back of a paperback cover that Neill had stripped to return.

"Eight?" she said.

When Neill told Goffredo his plans for the evening, Goffredo was incredulous. "A gypsy?" he kept saying. "Really? a Gypsy?"

"Am I crazy?" Neill sincerely wanted to know.

"I'd say you're the luckiest son-on-a-bitch I know."

Neill followed the crooked line Deirdre had drawn. It took him out East past the fashionable suburbs, along the Nonconnah Creek to an area in the county that was farmland and some industrial plants. It was foreign soil to Neill. This part of Memphis, if it was still Memphis, if it was still Tennessee, if it was still the Sublunary World, was new to him.

The end of the treasure map—where Deirdre had drawn a star—was a dirt road that led into a semi-tree-sheltered area. Where there was a star on the map there was, in reality if it was such, a Volkswagen van painted a dull house-paint navy, an almost miserable modernized vardo. There were no other vehicles around. The sun was setting and the deep ochre glow of the field added mystique to an otherwise pedestrian pitch.

Neill sheepishly knocked on the side of the van. He heard some movement inside but could not imagine what it was. It sounded—animalistic and mechanical at the same time. Then suddenly, the door slid open revealing Deirdre amid a cluttered background of clothing, rugs, silverware, pots and pans, realia and unrealia, stiver and gold, and a small neat stack of knives of all sizes and shapes.

"Neill!" she exclaimed as if surprised. "You want to come in?"

"Is there room?"

"I hope so since this is where I live with my parents."

Neill stuck his head inside. He had expected Madame Ouspenskaya's wagon. It was bigger than it looked from the outside, almost like an optical illusion. There were three beds and a kitchen area. There were no other humans.

"Where are your folks?" Neill asked, hopping awkwardly inside, landing half on one thigh and his shoulder.

"They went with the Murphys to Southland Mall and then, I can't remember where. They might be gone all night."

Neill looked into those hypnotic eyes.

"They *will* be gone all night," Deirdre amended.

"Well," Neill began, trying to pull his eyes away from hers, "Did you want to go get something to eat?"

"Not really," Deirdre said. "Are you hungry?"

"Oh, no," Neill lied.

"Drink this," she said, offering Neill a small clear glass of clear fluid.

"What is it?" Neill said. He brought it up to his nose. It smelled like dry cleaning chemicals.

"Moosemilk," Deirdre said.

"Seriously? Moose milk?"

Neill set his tongue inside the glass. His tongue recoiled.

"Drink," she said.

Neill tossed it back. It hit the back of his brain like a neutercane. His eyes popped. His heart was burned with a fiery stick.

"Want to swim in the creek? I haven't bathed yet today."

"Oh, ah, sure," Neill said. He shook his bobble head.

Deirdre immediately shrugged off her blouse. Underneath were glowing white breasts the size of softballs. Their nipples were almost as charcoal as her hair, a deep eggplant purple. Her underarms wore small black tufts like chia pets and the odor off her body was visceral and creaturely.

"Whoa," Neill said.

"Swim naked?"

"I just wasn't ready."

Deirdre kept her eyes on Neill's stunned face as she wriggled out of her faded, skin-tight jeans. Again, no undergarment. And her pubic hair was a black hole into which your vision could tunnel and never return to the surface. The smell was intensified. Deirdre was enjoying Neill's discombobulation. She scooted a couple feet away and let him look.

As Neill could not lift his eyes from the thickest, blackest belly whickers he had ever seen, Deirdre slowly parted her thighs so he could gaze all he wanted at her yoni entire, tunneling into its singularity like Space Lab on a suicide mission.

"Jesus," Neill said. "You are..." And he was fishing for a word beyond beautiful. He fished in vain. "Beautiful," he said.

"You are beautiful, Neill," Deirdre said, and scooted closer again. She put her long-nailed fingers on his cheek.

"Let's skip swimming, Neill," she said. "You are shy."

"I'm not really. I mean, if you want to bathe."

"Swim," he quickly added.

"I need bathing, yes," she said. She smelled her own armpit. "Perhaps you will wash me?"

"Sure," Neill said. Little Neill was knocking on the door of his coop. "With what?" Neill glanced around the van but he did not want to take his eyes off Deirdre's body.

"Your tongue," Deirdre said. Then, she laughed. "No. Look here."

She moved to a small water basin. It was trimmed in gold and looked to be fine porcelain. In it was about three inches of tepid water. Deirdre added a small stream of a musky perfume to the bowl from a vial that was tucked under her pillow and then she pulled a handkerchief from under a different pillow and dipped it in the water. "Here," she said, presenting it to Neill as if he were a shaman about to free her trapped spirit.

"Where first?" Neill said, and his voice caught.

Deirdre laughed. "Anywhere you like, Flyboy." She spread out her arms and opened her legs again.

Neill dipped the cloth in the bowl, wrung it out, and lifted it to one of Deirdre's hirsute arms. He wiped unhurriedly down it, intent on doing a good job. He did the other arm and both pits, relishing how her hair caught minute water droplets and held them. Her body hair almost repelled water the way certain gundog's fir will.

He dipped the cloth back into the basin and wrung it out again. He began to delicately wipe one breast. He placed his free hand under it as if it were a baby bird.

"Mmm," Deirdre said. Her nipple seemed to expand and contract at his contact. It was a living thing.

He did the other breast and down her stomach with its little ant-line of hair, rinsed and wrung, and began to wash her legs. He took a long time over each. They both knew where he wanted to go—and where Deirdre wanted him to go—and they were both content to prolong it.

With a freshly rinsed cloth, he began to gently wash her vulva, which she presented to him by spreading her legs like a gymnast.

"Oh, Neill," Deirdre said, and let herself fall backward onto the bed. Neill continued to wash her pubic area, adding pressure. He was spreading her lips with the perfumed cloth and she began to chirr like a cat. Neill was intent on doing the best job of bathing her she had ever experienced. It was sexual but there was an aberrant pride at work also. The funk of her body and the musk of the cloth were enchanting Neill.

"Neill, Neill," she panted. "Heero."

"Turn over," Neill said.

"What?" she asked, raising her head slightly.

"Turn over. Your ass is dirty."

Deirdre did as she was told, the tangle of her legs with Neill's making the turn clumsy. Her fundament was as perfect as an astronomical chart, each cheek stippled with tiny stars of goosebumps. Neill wiped her round cheeks, delicately hirsute, and then down her crack, which indeed was slightly soiled. He then used his index finger inside the thin damp cloth to enter her anus.

"Oof," she said.

Neill pushed in further. It was hard to say why.

"N–Neill," Deirdre whispered. "My heero. What are you doing?"

Neill moved his index finger around inside her. While doing so, he bent over and licked one ass cheek. It tasted tangy, salty. Then, he bit it.

"Yikes!" Deirdre said. "Yikes, Neill!"

Neill removed his finger from her tight asshole. And fell back.

"I'm sorry," he said. "I don't know what came over me." He was bewitched. Bothered. Bewildered.

Deirdre righted herself and now, on her knees next to him, whispered. "Do not be sorry. You are drunk on Deirdre."

"Sorry," he said again.

"Neill, Deirdre liked it," Deirdre said. "You still have all your clothes on."

When Neill had undressed, Deirdre took a good look.

"You are very thin," she said.

"Not really Great American Hero stuff," Neill said.

"What about here?" Deirdre said and grabbed Neill's pecker. "What about this *heero thing*?"

And then, they kissed for the first time. Deirdre did not let go of the pecker but managed nevertheless to snake her tongue deep into his mouth. She then licked down his cheek, down his neck, his chest, his belly. She looked up. "You smell like flowers," she said.

Neill didn't have time to regret his choice of cologne. Deirdre put his cock into her mouth and began to suck on it with zest. Then she did an astounding thing. Slowly working her mouth over his entire cock she managed to go even further and gently placed his balls inside also. It was quite a stunt.

"Jesus!" Neill said and he lay back.

Deirdre did some more oral monkeyshines that Neill could not imagine but it felt like nothing he had ever experienced before.

Then she stopped and Neill looked up.

"What?" he said. Deirdre was kneeling between his legs and pondering something.

"Neill, where would you like to put that?" she asked.

"God, Deirdre. In your hot pussy, I'm thinking."

"I was thinking that too. But then I thought, 'I bet Neill has never fucked a woman in the ass before'. Am I right about that, Neill?"

"You are," Neill said. It seemed true to him.

"Here," Deirdre said, and she squatted over Neill as if she meant to pee on him. "Let's get you good and lubricated." She lowered her cunt down onto his prick and slowly took him in.

She was unnaturally hot. Like a sulfur bath.

"Deirdre," Neill began to breathe heavily. "Just fuck me."

"Mm, tempting, Neill," she said, and moved her ass around on top of him. "But I want to be your first real piece of ass."

So, she moved next to him, turned 180 degrees, leaned over the open door of the van (Neill had only one brief moment of panic when he realized the door had been open this entire time) and knelt so that her ass was up in the air, like a dog waiting to be scratched.

And Neill scratched her.

It was so tight going in, he thought he was hurting her. She was quiet and then a slow moan came from her and he knew he was alright. Once in it became easier to move and, wet from her nectar, he found the right speed and angle. When he came, it felt strange as if he were surrounding his own dick with warm cream. Deirdre let out one long feline keen.

Afterward, they lay in each other's arms. They kissed and snuggled, and Neill thought he would remember forever the musk of her body and the way she moved against him like a dancer, or a feral quadruped.

When the sun began to rise it woke the two naked lovers. The air was cool on their rosy fingered skin.

"You two awake?"

There was Deirdre's father standing about a yard from the open door.

"Oh my God," Neill said. He grabbed for clothing but did not find any. He covered his piss-hard with the scented handkerchief he had used to wash Deirdre.

"Yes Father," Deirdre said.

The old man stood in the doorway. He did not seem to be bothered in the least by his daughter and a stranger naked on the floor of the family van.

"Best get dressed, Deirdre. We need to move quickly."

"Get netted?" Deirdre said.

"Not exactly," the old man said.

When Neill and Deirdre were both dressed they stood outside the van. There was another van about ten yards away, presumably the Murphy's. The sun was climbing a hazy sky but the surrounding fields were shrouded in mist. It appeared as if the small group and their three vehicles were a Hollywood set of a film called One Illusory Heaven. The entire world was about an acre square and beyond it only miasma.

"Kiss your man goodbye, Daughter."

"Father, this is the Great American Hero."

The old man nodded and walked away.

Deirdre kissed Neill for a long time. Neill's head was a turbid stew. She was leaving? She did this all the time? Do I even care?

"I—I'll miss you," Neill said.

"Naw, Neill. Tomorrow you won't even remember my name," Deirdre said. And then, she leaned in close. "But my batti you will never forget."

Fog

Neill stood in the field and watched their vans drive away. He did not think Deirdre was waving from the rear window of their van, but he imagined she was. He waved the way a polite audience claps for a poor performance.

His crotch itched and he had a momentary fear that he had picked up some exotic Gypsy Sexual Disease. A GSD.

The vans vanished into the fog. It was otherworldly and, after they could no longer be seen, Neill believed that they had never been there. He believed that he was still asleep somewhere far away, in a bed in another town, a bed piled high with pillows, a fairy tale bed.

Neill stood for a long time in that hazy, blushing dawn light. He felt as if he were between worlds and he wondered if, when he returned to Memphis, if it would still be the same Memphis, if it would still be his home. Would he be the same Neill? Reluctantly, feeling almost shaken with hangover, he fished his keys out of his jeans pocket. And he found, festooned and tied tightly around his key chain, Deirdre's dainty, braided bracelet. Neill raised it to his nose.

Heart: Set to Oscillate

Readers, if you are out there and have stuck with us this far (and have read between our many lines), you realize this about our man, Neill. His heart oscillated between the excited fervor of new conquest (how many naked women can I see in one lifetime?) and the search for stability and love. Neill needed to be loved, and not just by beautiful women. Can we blame the mother? The stoic father? Who knows? Not even Freud, not even your omniscient narrator(s).

Sometimes, Neill wanted to drift on the calm surface of a lake. Sometimes, he longed for the rushing relationship rapids one negotiated when Love was in attendance.

It was always exciting to Neill to spend most of his days in the small halidom of The Book Shelf. He got to talk about books to bright, colorful strangers, or to kith, or to familiar customers whom he loved. He got to read on the job (don't tell) and he got to witness a parade of members of the opposite sex, many of whom loved books almost as much as Neill.

The Gorgeous Young Housewives Book Club. How Neill burned for each member! How he longed to visit their get-togethers, and after ingesting cucumber sandwiches and the prose of Anne Tyler, he envisaged them all stripping him down and touching him like the sensual angels he fancied they were.

And there, in the middle of his GYHBC fantasies, was Luna. Remember Luna? Married to the rich old man? Face like a Renaissance painting? Cheeks flushed with winter? She still could tie Neill's tongue simply by smiling—and she knew it. Once Neill wrote a poem about her, a poem that used a Guess Who lyric ("*What good is it if I can't even sing it to you?*") as its epigraph. She refused to take it, though she let Neill walk her to her car and once there planted a chaste kiss on his cheek.

This was exciting, in its way, and its way was One Way.

There were other young women, too. Midtown Memphis was a small community and Neill, having come to it via the Goorile family and then Marcane Fry, was becoming one of its known denizens. He knew some hip folks. He dated some hip women.

There were more Spices, more Vivs (or Ivys). There were more one date wonders. There was a lot of pining, down time, many evenings spent at home with Goffredo and a rented movie and some microwave popcorn (a major discovery for Neill and his gang; Bidden declared it the best thing to happen to food since tin foil). There was masturbation. And poetry. Sometimes simultaneously. Sometimes, the masturbation was between the lines. Sometimes the lines were written between masturbations.

One Evening at Home

Neill planned his evening around the Memphis State Tigers basketball program. He had loved them fervently since the 70s and the team with Finch, Kenon, and Robinson. He stuck with them through thin times and thick. The local PBS station, WKNO, aired the Tigers' games at 10 p.m., tape delayed. At that time, it was the only way to see Neill's beloved Tigers, except to go to the game.

One night, lonely as a cloud, Neill popped some corn, re-watched *Stop Making Sense*, and settled into the couch in preparation for the game. Goffredo was watching the game live at the Mid-South Coliseum on a date (a new gal who does not figure in the story except in these parentheses) and Neill relished the solitude, even as his flesh longed for the touch of a feathery hand and his heart ached for being loveless. (And those damn cheerleaders with their newfangled dance routines made of Neill a quivery clabber.)

The game began. The Tigers looked good but it was tight.

At 10:20 Goffredo walked through the door.

"Don't tell me anything about the game! I've spent the whole night dodging the news broadcast." Neill shouted in greeting.

"Ok," Goffredo said, holding up a reassuring hand. "But you're gonna like the outcome."

Neill thought about various kitchen utensils that could be used to dismember roommates.

And So There Came a New Love

Remember Neill's credo that he did not have to seek love because any woman he would be interested in would come through the door of the bookstore where he worked? This, however, required great patience, especially during those long, lonely months when he was convinced he was Bobo, the Unmateable Gorilla.

This part of the story began with a book signing.

There was a curious fellow in Memphis at that time named Stanley Booth. Neill thought he was kind of a loveable nut. He would come in and chatter at Neill in a manic manner, his thoughts pinballing around inside his head before they pinballed around the space between him and Neill. He talked of many things, Walker Evans, Shelby Foote, grizzly bears, Sam Phillips, Neal Cassady, Abbie Hoffman, bread pudding, and James Joyce, all as if everything is connected. And, perhaps it is, dreamers, perhaps it is.

But, gradually, Neill noticed, over a couple visits, Stanley's talk began to swirl around one subject: The Rolling Stones. He began to tell stories about the Stones and Neill always felt as if he had entered the listening *in media res*. Stanley seemed to think Neill knew things that he did not, and his rambles about the rock world were more immediate and impassioned than his talk about anything else.

From this manic swirl Neill began to piece together the idea that Stanley was an intimate of the Rolling Stones, that he had indeed palled around with them, had even been at Altamount on that fateful, dark day that placed an ugly mole as a period at the end of the 1960s. And, in these Stones stories, another theme began to emerge: Stanley was a writer. And his book about the Stones was going to be published by Random House. Neill wrote it off as the ravings of a Big Dreamer (Memphis Style), albeit an amiable one.

But it was not the ravings of a Big Dreamer (Memphis Style). Stanley Booth was the real thing. And yes, he is in the documentary about the Stones, *Gimme Shelter*. Imagine that.

And his book, entitled *Dance with the Devil, was* published by Random House. The Book Shelf hosted a well-attended signing for the book. Stanley was an eccentric but gracious and charming star, dressed in a white suit, his handsome face alight with mischief and arcana.

During this event, there came through the door of the bookstore a woman of witchy beauty, with wild café-de-leche hair, and hips upon which the world could move. Neill could not take his eyes off her. She bought Stanley's book, got him to sign it and was on her way out when Neill chased her down.

"Hey, I should know you," he said.

"I don't think so," the wild one said.

"Yes, yes," Neill said. "We should know each other."

The woman stopped and looked Neill over. She smiled with half a lip.

"Who are you?" she challenged.

"Richard Farina," Neill said.

"Richard. As in Dick."

Neill was amused, aroused, antagonized, agog.

"Not really Richard Farina," Neill said.

"Who then?"

"Neill," Neill said. "Neill Rhymer."

"Like a bad poet."

How did she know?

"Like Thomas the Rhymer, Scottish laird and prophet."

Now both lips smiled.

"And what do you want Mr. Prophet?"

"I think for you to go out with me."

"Hm, hm. I don't know."

They faced each other, guns holstered but at the ready.

"Here. Let's do this. I'll give you my phone number and if you think about it and want to try a date, gimme a call."

She was amused. "Ok," she said.

Neill scribbled his name and phone number on the back of a Book Shelf business card.

After she had gone, Neill realized he didn't ask her name.

But, when he returned home from work that day his message signal (O blessed little pinpoint of green light!) was blinking.

"Neill, this is Chara Winsky, the woman from the book signing. I'll chance that date. Call me back." And she left a number.

Neill called and they set a date for the forthcoming Friday night.

Later, Chara admitted that she was immediately attracted to Neill and loved how brash he was and how openly admiring. She also admitted that she had come to the signing to gawk at Stanley Booth, on whom she had a groupie crush.

Thank you, Stanley Booth

They went to The Half Shell on Mendenhall, a comfortable, dark, time-honored Memphis restaurant. Oysters were, of course, their specialty, but they had great soups, sandwiches, and one of Neill's favorite finger foods, fried mushrooms.

Neill picked Chara up at her apartment, which was downtown in the old Shrine Building, a beautiful 1923 pile of bricks built by Al Chymia and the gang. It had recently been renovated into apartments on the upper floors. There were rumors that ghosts of ex-Shriners wandered the upper floors naked, except for their fezzes. Neill had been told to double park at the curb and ring her bell to save himself the price of parking in the building's official lot. Chara came down dressed in browns and darker shades, a showy cloak around her shoulders, her crazy hair full of obscure electricity.

"Hello again," she said and shook Neill's hand. Her fingers were so slim they seemed like candy.

"It's good to see you," Neill said, ushering her into his car.

The drive to the restaurant was all small talk. Got any siblings? Where did you go to college? Do you like your job? (Chara worked for the city, doling out food stamps to the needy and desperate.)

Once seated in their nook at The Half Shell, Neill could look at her full in the face. She didn't look like the woman he chased into the parking lot to ask for a date. She was— *duskier* perhaps, almost foreign looking. Or maybe, it was just the shadows.

Twice, men walked past the booth and nodded to her. The second time Neill had to ask.

"Do you know these men?"

"The first one I did," Chara said. "The second one no."

So, the first man was an ex-lover (this was the absurd leap Neill's mind made though, in this case, it was correct) and the other man was simply attracted to her, so attracted he chanced a hello even when she was on a date. Was this Chara that attractive? She was, though she was not pretty. She had wide eyes and chiaroscuro eyebrows, a potato-shaped nose, and full lips like an exotic film star. She looked like Sandrine Bonnaire. She also had that hair. It first drew Neill and it, obviously, was not through with its business of drawing men.

The dinner was pleasant. The talk minimal, but friendly. They laughed some and used some inane banter to get through the night.

When Neill dropped her off at her apartment she did not invite him inside.

"Thank you, Neill," Chara said. She was an actress playing a role she was fond of. Chara Winsky had her own agenda, her own set of rules, her own *geography*.

"Shall we chance a second date?" Neill said. He was smiling like it was wit on display, but he was secretly terrified of her saying no.

"Yes, that would be nice. You must let me pay next time."

"Even better," Neill said.

Chara laughed. Maybe it was the laugh that halted her exit from the car. She took her hand off the handle, turned toward Neill, and kissed him on the mouth. It was of the thirty-second variety, some tongue, some experimentation, but also limited in its promise.

"Goodnight, Neill," Chara Winsky said, stepping out onto the sidewalk.

Neill watched her walk into the lobby. It was a good exit. She did not turn. Neill never did know if that was a good sign or not. But Chara fascinated him. And he, like many men before him faced with a challenge, wanted to make her drop the act and bare herself in more ways than one.

On the Horn with Bidden

"So you like her?"

"I guess so. She's—sexy, I suppose is the word."

"Sexy is good."

"Sexy is good if sex is involved."

"Not that that is all you're interested in."

"Right. Because that would be shallow."

"Exactly."

"We agree."

"Still."

"It would be great to see her naked."

"Without a doubt."

She Had Apparently Decided that a Second Date Proved Something Formerly Unproven

After the second date, a showing of *Places in the Heart* at the Plaza Theater, which was walking distance from Neill's home, Chara was warmer, more open, laughed readily, flirted, touched Neill's shoulder, etc. The Rubicon had been crossed.

Neill asked if she wanted to go back to his house, only a few blocks away.

"You got any wine?" Chara asked with a grin that showed her wide, splashy mouth to good avail.

"Wine? No. I have some Funny Face. Injun Orange, I think. No, wait, Goffredo drank all that. I think we only have Rootin' Tootin' Raspberry."

"I didn't understand any of that, but you wanna go to my place and have some wine?"

"Sure," Neill said. He didn't drink wine. We knew that, right? "You have a nice view of the river?"

"Not on my side. I have a nice view of Greater Memphis."

After they parked in the Shrine Building's official lot and entered the lobby and made it up to her apartment on the tenth floor, Neill felt good, excited even. It felt like a Thin Man movie, this old-fashioned way to live. A keypad with a code to get in! A lobby! An elevator! He was like Eb come to the Big City.

"This feels like a Thin Man movie," Neill said.

"You like white ok?" Chara said, bending to a lower cabinet door. Her ass was, well, *impressive.*

"I don't really like wine," Neill said with a sheepish grin.

"You're funny," Chara said.

"Bad potty training," Neill said.

"I don't understand a lot of what you say but I like the way you say it. Keep talking."

And talk they did. The two-room apartment was sparsely furnished. That's understating it. Chara had a bed (a mattress on the floor), a TV, one dim floor lamp, and a footstool. The footstool seemed totally out of place. It had a rustic country scene done in worn needlepoint on top.

"That was my grandmother's," Chara said, noticing Neill's attention to the stool.

"Nice. It fits the rest of your décor. In a sense, it pulls the whole room together."

"Funny. I can't afford furniture yet."

"How long have you lived here?"

"In Memphis?"

"Start there."

"I went to Rhodes for four years so—I guess, five years."

"When did you move in here?"

"Two months ago."

"I see."

They settled on the mattress, Chara with a glass of wine and Neill with a jelly jar of flat club soda. There were ample pillows and blankets so that it seemed a restful nest.

Neill kissed her. It was a brief kiss, like the first brush stroke of a painting. Her wide mouth was entirely kissable.

Chara put down her nearly empty glass of wine (which Neill promptly knocked over with his elbow) and lay back. The next kiss had some fire in it. Chara Winsky felt as soft as a silkie and her loose garments were slimsy enough to make any contact erotic.

As Neill moved his grasping hand to her ass, pulling her against his erection, Chara put a hand on Neill's chest.

"Wait," she said.

"Shit," Neill said, but not out loud.

"This is heading someplace and I have to tell you something."

"Ok."

"I was in a car accident when I was a teenager."

"I'm sorry."

"I have a scar."

"Oh," Neill said. And then, "Oh, I see. You think I am fixing to remove your clothes." Neill smiled.

"No—I mean, I guess. I just."

"Sorry. Joking. Scars are not off-putting is what I meant to say."

"This is from my sternum to my pubes."

"Ah."

"If we ever get to the point where you want to take off my clothes."

"We are at that point."

"Oh. You were kidding. You do want to take my clothes off."

"If you want me to."

"Such a gentleman. I do. And I want to take yours off, too."

"Sure. Because it would be damn silly if you were naked and I was clothed. Unless, I was a masseur or painter."

"Shut up."

"Right."

When Chara Winsky was stripped to her panties the scar was indeed a large one. Thick and knotty and with symmetrical stitch marks down each side, a long O scale railroad track. Neill ran a finger down it. (Did Neill think of Victoria? He didn't. That's odd.)

"Ugly, right?" she said. Her voice, for the first time in their brief acquaintanceship, sounded vulnerable.

"No," Neill said. "You're quite beautiful. Your nipples are so big."

"They are, aren't they? Is that good?"

"In this case, it's better than good. They're a turn-on."

"I'm glad," Chara said.

"Are you on birth control?" Neill said.

"I'm on the pill. Talk more about my nipples. Are you still turned on? Neill?"

"I am, Chara. Kiss me hard."

They kissed hard. Neill's hand went into the back of her panties. Chara's hand went down Neill's and grasped his Wigga-wagga. Her slender fingers were soft but worked with assurance. This was not her first clambake.

Naked then. Neill kissed her chest, a few chakras down the scar, and then her belly, which was flat and soft. Neill nuzzled her pubes with his nose. Chara sighed a loud sigh. It was a sigh a foghorn would have been proud of. Neill licked South. Chara gave with the grunts and squeals, the heavy breathing. Neill ate her to a dramatic orgasm. (Was she acting?) Then, Chara sucked him in an expert fashion. She used a lot of tongue, a lot of saliva. That splashy mouth was the perfect contrivance for the task and Chara Winsky was practiced in talking turkey.

Before he came in her mouth he pushed her gently aside and entered her, missionary style. She groaned and moaned and made a pother. She was very noisy and vocal. It spurred Neill on.

"Fuck me," she said, as if he hadn't been up to that point. "Do everything."

"Oh, oh," was all Neill managed.

"God, you've got a good dick," she said.

Neill liked the dirty talk.

"Oh—oh, I'm gonna come again," she said, and then did, her vaginal muscles contracting around Neill like the hand of a gorilla tightening.

"Jesus," Neill said.

Then Chara, quickly recovered from her 2nd orgasm, grabbed both of Neill's ass cheeks, one in each slim but powerful hand, and spread his cheeks while pulling him against her.

"Right to the root. Sink it in right to the root," she said.

"Gggod, Chara," Neill's teeth were grit. His eyes squeezed shut.

"Look at me," Chara said. Her voice was a strict proctor's. "Look at me, Neill., Goddamit."

Neill opened his eyes. Chara pulled harder on each ass cheek.

"Give me your full load," she said, her fiery eyes burning into Neill's.

And Neill did as he was told.

Afterward there was tender talk, as tender as two strangers can accomplish. It was clear, quite quickly, that Neill was expected to stay the night. He was a tad afraid to not. Chara was ferocious in her feelings. Did Neill like that?

Neill slept but not well. When the dawn came through the tenth floor windows of Chara's tiny apartment, Neill kissed her sleeping shoulder and rose to get dressed.

He had everything but his shoes on when Chara spoke.

"When are you going?" she asked.

"What?" Neill said. "Now. I have to."

"Where I meant."

"Home then—"

"Work."

"Right."

"I have to work too."

"You can sleep a little longer. I gotta go home, shit, shower and shave."

"Neill?" Chara said, her wee voice had returned.

"What is it, beautiful Chara?"

"You will come back sometime, won't you?"

"Is tonight good?" Neill asked.

This Was Already Some Kind of Commitment, Wasn't It?

The next night Neill went to see Chara in her apartment. She was cooking dinner for him. Some kind of pasta. (Why always pasta?)

When Neill arrived the apartment smelled like the basement of Umberto's Clam House in Little Italy. Chara was at the stove and her face was pinched with anger barely held in check. Choler colored her cheeks in the places heat had not.

"Smells delicious," Neill said.

"I don't know. I suck at this. Did you bring wine?"

"Oh no. Was I supposed to?"

"It would have been nice."

"I'll go get some. Tell me what to buy."

"Forget it."

"I'll go really."

"You don't even drink." Was her tone accusative?

"I like Kahlua and cream."

"Good to know." Now she moved closer and bussed Neill quickly on the mouth. "Go sit down. It's ready, though I didn't mean for it to be ready right when you walked in the door."

Neill found their settings next to the mattress. Two napkins on the floor with a fork and knife on each. He smiled.

Chara brought the dishes in, plates piled high with linguine and some kind of white sauce. And a piece of white bread resting on the edge of each plate like a cigarette on an ashtray.

"Mm," Neill said.

"Taste it before you say that."

"Sit. Relax. You seem frazzled."

To this Chara answered only with a twisted grimace.

Neill patted her thigh. "Should we see what's on TV?"

"I rented a movie," Chara said.

"Oh, grand. I didn't even notice the VCR. What did you get?"

"The second Indiana Jones film."

"Spielberg," Neill said. He tasted bile.

"Didn't you love the first one?"

Neill had not. Neill hated Spielberg, all light and no heat. Neill had seen the first Indiana Jones film when he visited his brother in Connecticut. Brack was gaga over it and Neill was gagged. In Neill's cinematic cosmography, Spielberg made one great movie, *Duel*, and then Hollywood turned him into its own Childlike Monstrosity, like the Billy Mumy character in that *Twilight Zone* episode.

The movie began.

Ugh, Neill thought from the very first image.

He took a bite of pasta.

It rolled around on his tongue like an overly spiced sea monster.

Chara had a mouthful, too, and was staring at her plate as if there she could divine what all was wrong with her life.

"Fuck," she said.

"It's good," Neill tried.

"Fuck, Neill. It's—what? Too—what? It's inedible."

"I don't know. I can't cook either."

"Thanks."

"Not what I meant."

Chara rose and took her plate into the kitchen. Neill heard the plate hit the sink. From the sound of it it might have shattered. Neill was picturing sauce on the wall. Chara was gone a long time. Meanwhile, Neill tried one more bite. It was—inedible.

Chara came back into the room. She was holding a single sheet of foolscap in her hand.

"Here's the recipe. Kate said it was foolproof." She threw the sheet onto the bed next to Neill.

Neill read it.

"Sounds straightforward. What could have gone wrong?"

"I did it exactly as it said. I thought it was a lot of garlic, but it said 4 cloves of garlic."

"Hm. I don't know."

Chara exited and came back. "Look at this. That's a lot of garlic. It took me a half hour just to press that much."

"Wait," Neill said, tentatively. "This is a clove, right? This little part. This big part is, I think it's called the bulb, and it's made up of cloves. I think that's right."

"Fuck," Chara said. Her brow was beaded with perspiration. She shut her eyes and squinched them tightly as if in horrible pain. "I suck."

"Anyone could make that mistake."

"At least we have a good movie. You want your ice cream now?"

Almost Cut my Hair

Remember Harness Myers, Neill's crazy sexual fling, the woman who cut hair? He wanted her to cut his hair. Neill called her and he was surprised that it obviously twitterpated her.

"Y-yes, sure, I'll make an appointment," she said.

"You ok?"

"No. I mean. I don't know. I never expected to hear from you again."

"I'm sorry. Is it a bad thing, my reappearing?"

There was a long pause. Neill could hear faint radio music, empty chatter.

"Harness?"

"I'm here."

"You're peeved."

"I'm busy. Thursday still your day off?"

"Yes."

"How about Thursday at 2 p.m.?"

"Fine, thanks. It was good—"

She had hung up.

Keeping the appointment Neill felt a small twang of nervousness in his chest. Perhaps, Harness hated him. Perhaps, this was a truly rotten idea.

"Hi, Neill," Harness greeted him. Her face was carved from a croquette ball. But she was still pretty with her little bowl of hair.

"Harness," Neill leaned in. He got an awkward one-armed hug in return.

"I'm ready for you." Did she mean that in any other way than the obvious? Probably not. She was not given to metaphor though life makes metaphors whether you are given to them or not.

"How short do you want it? I am not sure I can cut these golden curls without some regret."

A nicety. It was going to be ok.

"Of course, I should shave you bald and kick your ass on the way out the door."

"Ow. Sorry. Harness, you hate me now?"

She seemed to think it over. "No. I don't hate you, Neill. You broke my fucking heart."

A lady in the next chair looked over.

"I didn't," Neill said, weakly.

"I can barely talk. When you phoned, it was like a voice from the grave."

"Thanks."

"I know. I was the one who did wrong. I'm sorry, Neill. I had a long hard time getting over you. Maybe I didn't."

"Sweet Harness."

"Don't."

So, she cut his hair, just a trim really. ("I still want my freak flag to fly," Neill said.) She mentioned split-ends but Neill didn't know what she meant. After it was over, the curls were still mostly present and it did have a nice precise contour to it. Neill looked at himself in the mirror. He detected, underneath his visage, a shadow visage of an older man with darker, straighter hair. It bled through like pentimento. It was a little disconcerting.

"I think I'll call it Arthur," Neill said.

Harness didn't laugh.

Neill paid and right before he left Harness said, "Call me if you want your haircut again."

It was something, a crust of bread.

The Return to the Shrine Building

"I made you a treat," Chara said, as Neill entered.

God help me, Neill thought. "Wonderful! What is it? Do I smell dinner?"

"I thought you were taking me out to eat," Chara said. Just like that indignation flashed across her pretty face. Her eyebrows were *fierce*.

"I am, yes, I am," Neill said, quickly. "I just thought I smelled something good."

"Me?" Chara said. It was almost a command.

"You do smell good. Always."

"I made crockpot Kahlua!" Chara sang out.

"Wow. Really. I didn't know you could make Kahlua at home."

"You can and I did."

"Let's try some," Neill said, slipping his hand around Chara's hip.

"It's for after dinner. It's a dessert drink."

"Ok," Neill said, with an apologetic tenor.

"It has to cook for 8 hours, I think."

"How long has it been in there?"

"Well, I *had* to work," Chara said.

They ate dinner at the Bon Ton Café. Neill had crab cakes and broccoli. Chara a veggie plate. "Do you want dessert," the indifferent waitress asked.

"We have dessert at home," Neill said and smiled what he thought was a charming smile.

Back in the apartment Neill's belly rumbled with a punitive threnody.

"Drinks first?" Neill asked and wished he hadn't but Chara's sweet side emerged.

"Before what cowpoke?" she said.

"Before poke the cow?" Neill said, and Chara laughed a clash of cymbals.

"Let's drink," she said.

She mixed two good sized Kahlua and creams, with lots of ice. Neill took a small sip, rolled it around in his mouth as if he were an oenophile tasting the purest vintage. Chara watched him with a cheerful beam.

"This is fantastic," Neill said because it really was. "How did you learn to do this?"

"Kate told me," Chara said. Then, she took a big swallow. "Hey, that is good. Let's get drunk."

Neill hadn't been drunk since he was a teenager and the memory of that was enough to keep him sober even now. He smiled and took a bigger swallow.

"Won't get drunk that way," Chara said.

"You get drunk. I'll watch you and then take advantage of you."

This could have gone either way. Tranquility settled around them like the moment right before the deer gets shot through the neck.

"Ok," Chara said.

But she didn't get fully drunk. A little tipsy, perhaps. Neill didn't really want to watch her get bombed. He wanted to take her clothes off.

"I gotta great idea now, Neeeeeeeeeel."

"I'm listening," Neill said.

Chara wiped some Kahlua off her lip. "I'm a stripper!"

"Well ok then," Neill said. This *was* good, Chara drunk.

"You watching?" Chara said now. Her voice had a pleasantly reckless tint.

"I am," Neill said. He settled himself on the mattress. Chara was standing with a half-filled glass. She threw it back.

"Music," she said. She turned on the radio. A Bachman-Turner Overdrive song came on.

"Oo, I love this," Chara said, and began swaying to the music.

"Watch closer now, Cowpoke," she said.

She was dancing like a cobra and she began to unbutton her shirt. She began to hum along, eyes closed, and threw her shirt to the corner of the room. She unhooked her bra and tossed it aside. It landed on the television. Next, she shimmied out of her skirt and was revealed in her nearly naked Salome disguise. Her panties were lavender and had little flowers on them. They looked like the underwear of a child.

She slid those down her legs. Now, her eyes were open. They found Neill. Her look was made of fire and taunt.

She danced naked, spinning, so Neill could see her lovely hindquarters. And facing him, she put her hand on her lower stomach right above her dark pubic patch. Her scar caught the faint light coming in the window, streetlamp and neon from the night, which seemed far away. The scar was a river leading downward. It was the Styx.

Chara slid a couple fingers into her pubic hair. She watched Neill watch her.

Then she laughed and fell like a plastered statue onto the bed next to him.

"Did you like that?" she asked.

"Very much," Neill said. His stomach played "Why Don't We Do It in the Road?"

"Did Little Neill like it?" Chara simpered.

"Little?" Neill said, putting his arms around her.

"Not so much," Chara said. "Give him to me right now."

Neill was out of his clothing in a trice. Maybe a trice and a half.

"There he is," Chara said and put her cool fingers around him.

"Ah ah," Neill said. "Ah."

Chara snuggled her face into Neill's neck. She began to hum, then coo, then speak.

"I love your dick," she said. "It's my dick, Neill. It's all mine. You get so fucking hard, did you know that? You get so fucking hard. It's like a stone, or a—what, Neill? Hard as what?"

Neill was not in the mood to finish her poem, though his lizard brain leapt to the word 'petrous.' He wanted her to keep talking. Chara's dirty talk was such a turn-on for Neill. (Years later this was what he remembered most about her, when he thought about the good times, her earthiness, her reckless sex palaver.)

"Can I suck you, Neill? Huh? You like the way I suck, don't you? You moan so sweet when I am deep throating your hard hard hard dick. I get wet thinking about blowing you, feeling that hard head in the back of my throat. Did you know it turns me on to have it in my mouth? Huh, baby? I love to fill my mouth with you."

Now, Neill did moan. It was involuntary.

"Yes, like that. I'm gonna suck you now. I'm gonna put that whole dick into my mouth and while I do I am going to straddle you, ok? I'm gonna put my ass in your face. Do you know what to do then, Neill?"

Neill did not feel he had to answer. It was not a multiple choice question.

And as Chara moved over his body like a shadow, her large fundament spread itself right above Neill's mouth. Chara had one hand on Neill's bobbles and began to suck him with loud, wet sounds, like a dog drinking water. What else could Neill do, reader? He put a hand on each cool cheek and spread her. Her little brown backeye winked at him. He stuck his nose inside her already sopping pussy and began to suck on her clit.

Later, they fucked with Neill behind her holding that saddle as if he might get thrown. And Chara, keeping up her chorus of dirty verbiage.

"Just like that, Stud. Stick it in and out. Do it, Neill. Fuck my hot box. Fuck me, Neill. Slap my big ass and fuck me, fuck me."

Etc.

They both came and they both fell asleep in an embrace that was soothing and loving. Neill told Chara he loved her right after she said it to him. He was beginning to believe it was true.

The Trip to Alabama

The trip to meet the parents is an onerous task at times, part of the weft of owning up to having a 'serious' relationship. So, it came to pass that Chara invited Neill to take a weekend trip to Birmingham, Alabama, to meet Mr. and Mrs. Winsky and Chara's, purportedly more beautiful younger sister, Windy.

They went.

The day was hot and bright, and Neill's relatively new car, a Honda Civic without air conditioning (yes, Neill insisted to the car salesman who was astonished, superior and peeved, that they take the AC out of the car because he didn't want to pay for it. It was the first car he bought with his own money and began a pattern of stubborn cheapness [kindly, we can call it thrift] which lasted his whole life. The reason for this cheapness [or thrift, if reason need be given] was his mother's eternal carping about money. They were always two steps from the poorhouse in her estimate, a self-destructive part of her self-destructive monologues that scared the pee out of her children. At Christmas, it was, 'I hope you enjoy all these gifts because I don't know how we're gonna pay for them. We'll probably be in the poorhouse before the year turns.' [Never mind that there were no more poorhouses—this phrase entered Neill's permanent dark closet of bugaboos and bogymen.])

"The sun sure is hot," Chara said when they were 1.75 miles outside Memphis.

"The sun is always hot," Neill said with a smirk and a thigh-squeeze.

Chara turned away as if something alongside the highway was in need of scolding.

"How long a drive?" Neill said, to change the already over-ripe subject.

"About 5 hours. 5 ½ if we die of heatstroke."

"Ok. Should be there by lunch, right?"

"I hope so. Mom is fixing us up a lunch. She's a good cook."

"Can't wait," Neill said.

Later, down the highway a bit, Chara turned toward Neill and smiled. It was her sloppy smile, the one that just got out of bed, the one that comes and goes like swamp gas. It made Neill's heart go pittypat.

They pulled into the modern subdivision driveway of the Winsky's at five after twelve.

"Nice house," Neill said.

"I hope we haven't missed lunch," Chara said.

"Would they throw the food out if we were a few minutes late?" Neill asked, seriously.

Chara gave him a look. The look said, "I am one hundred and forty-nine years old and I am tired of this old world and its insipid relationships and meaningless chin dribble."

As near as Neill could translate.

Once inside the Winskys, the day opened like a flower. Not only were the Winskys the nicest girlfriend's parents imaginable, Windy, yes the prettier sister, was immediately easy to talk to and the lunch was a smashing success. There was southern fried-chicken and potato salad and devilled eggs and corn on the cob and sweet tea. It was quite a spread.

Along with the friendly Winskys there was a fella there, presumably Windy's fella, who was smart and handsome and funny and Neill took to him immediately. His name was Rip.

After lunch everyone sat on the back porch where a nice cross breeze was blowing and the scenery to the west was the backyards of all the other suburban homes and to the east a dark patch off which seemed to be a deeply wooded area. There was a large sloping patch of well-tended Bermuda. Just below the raised deck porch there was a brick barbecue unit, elaborate and solid, about the size of a Volkswagen. It was an enticing kaleidoscope of light and shadow as if Neill were looking through a crystal.

"That's Algernon Woods," Chara said, putting her arm through Neill's, with affection, forgiveness and proprietorship.

"It's haunted," Windy said.

"Oh, Windy," Mrs. Winsky said. "Don't tell Neill that hogwash his very first visit."

"Save the scary stuff till he is one of us," Windy said. The smile she gave Neill was a curious affair, saucy, challenging, but openly welcoming.

"Can we explore it?" Neill asked, just to say something, because nature, to Neill, was just what you had to cut through sometimes to get to the 7/11.

"Sure," Chara said. Her half-frown, half-smile meant she was joshing the new guy. "And later tonight, we'll visit Vulcan."

"Chara tells us you're a poet," Mr. Winsky said. "Another beer?"

"He's not drinking beer, Daddy," Chara said.

"No, sir. That is, no sir, thanks about the beer, and, no sir, I am really just a lowly bookseller."

"He's the manager of the best independent bookstore in Memphis," Chara said. Her pride surprised Neill.

"Isn't that nice?" Mrs. Winsky said.

"You do write poetry," Windy said. "I know you do."

"Seen any?" Neill said, trying to match her saucy style.

"I have."

"Then you know I'm really just a bookseller," Neill said, allowing his smile to spread.

A good round of affable laughter rippled over the lawn.

Algernon Woods

"You sure you want to do this, Mate?" Rip said, clasping a friendly hand on Neill's shoulder. Neill bet himself that Rip was a hugger.

The sisters had run ahead, down the long slope of lawn, which led like a helter-skelter into the Manson's lair of Algernon Woods. Chara had changed into a long, flowing skirt the color of dusky plums. Windy wore a short skirt that lifted as she ran and showed off her panties, which seemed to be patterned like a child's pajamas.

"What is this about it being haunted?" Neill asked.

"Little girl, Naomi somebody, I think, got lost in the woods and never came back. This was in the 1930s, maybe earlier. They say now that occasionally she shows herself to interlopers and newbies. She's dressed in a little pinafore of white and blue."

"You believe it?"

"I believe everything, Neill. I am a pantheist."

"Ok," Neill said. And Rip laughed a man-sized laugh. They caught up with the girls at the edge of the woods.

'The forest primeval," Neill said. "It's nighttime inside."

"The Cedar Forest," Rip said.

"What's that?"

"Mesopotamian home of the gods," Rip said. And then, to leaven the showoffiness, "I think."

They walked slowly in. It was dark and cool.

"Jesus," Neill said. "It's vast!"

"Big as your imagination,' Windy said.

"Really. It goes on forever. What are those rocks?"

"The rocks are as old as the earth itself. They go on forever, cropping up here and there like the giants of the earth pushing their brows through the soil," Rip said.

"They're part of the Red Mountain Range," Chara added. "They do go on for miles and are practically unmapped, so wild is this area. I think there are supposed to be caves further in but we never got that far."

"Never in your whole life living here?"

Windy and Chara exchanged a smile which turned into a conspiratorial laugh.

"Come on, Rip," Windy said, grabbing his hand. "Let's go find some caves."

They scampered up the gray, uneven face of the rocks and were quickly out of sight.

"What do we do? Do you want to follow them?" Neill asked.

"I don't care," Chara said. "They won't find a cave. I like being here alone with you."

"I like it, too," Neill said. He pulled her close and their kiss had some temperature to it.

"What's up ahead? Someone obviously made this trail."

"Oh yeah, the woods have been explored for centuries, but some parts are still wild and really obscure. Let's go this way."

Neill took her hand and they skipped, not unlike fairy tale children, deeper into the dark green interior of the woods. After a while, they reached a small clearing just off to one side of the path.

"Step through here," Chara said, pulling some branches aside.

Neill followed her as if she were the white rabbit.

It was a small clearing, about the size of a pantry, shadowy and cool. Around its edges were more gray stones, almost as tall as them.

"It's like we're invisible here," Chara said. "The city could be miles away. Civilization miles away."

"You're a wild child," Neill said.

"You have no idea," Chara said.

She looked at Neill with her strange challenging eyes flashing.

"What idea do I not have? You have deep secrets? You're really the child of a spirit woman and a wild mustang? Or muskrat? Or...skunk?"

"Funny man," Chara said. "Watch this."

She twirled a bit so that her gypsy skirts rose around her. She was dancing to the music of the spheres. Her pretty brown legs were revealed and her thighs seemed to glister with calefaction. Neill watched her dance as if under a spell.

She stopped in front of one of the rocks. "See anything you like?"

"Lots," Neill said. "Pretty nutbrown thighs."

"Is that all?" Chara said. She was breathing heavy, possibly from the dance.

"Did I miss something?"

"I didn't spin hard enough." She put her hands to her skirt and grabbed two handfuls. She pulled it up slowly.

As the hem reached the top of her thighs, Chara looked down to see how close she was to Act I. Then the curtain went up on the show. She wasn't wearing underwear and Neill was staring at her hairy pussy. He loved how hairy she was.

"Oh Lord," Neill said.

"You like?"

"You know I do. I love your hairy pussy." (See?)

"Come taste it," Chara said. She bunched the dress some more and pulled it up over her stomach.

Neill walked toward her. He tried to match the fervor in her eyes. He walked straight up to her until their noses practically touched. And, very deliberately, he put his hand in her fur. She was already as wet as a freshet.

"Mm," Chara said. "Taste it. I mean it."

Neill slid his body down hers until he was kneeling on the leaf-rot and loam.

He gave her whole hairy pussy one long slow lick. His face came away slick with liquor.

"Oh God, Neill," Chara said, losing some of her Forest Queen domination.

Neill gave her some of his best skulling. He was a gorilla in the jungle.

"Neill, fuck me, please fuck me."

Neill stood and Chara tore at the front of his shorts. After much fumbling, they dropped to the ground and Chara grabbed the gorilla pizzle, and turning, stuck it quickly into her hot quim. She bent over the rocks as old as the world, her wide white bottom spreading.

Neill, at first, caught up in her frenzy, began to pound away at her while she made noises that were animalistic and sometimes human. The words dick and pound and pussy could be picked out of her beastly warble.

Then, Neill began to slow down. A peace entered him. The forest was bewitching, leading him to dream. It was beautiful here, Neill thought, keeping up a steady, stately rhythm with his peacemaker, so that Chara kept up her deep-woods ballad. Neill began to drift away. It was the most erotic, powerful thing that had ever happened to him. He was not just Neill clicketing Chara; he was the forest itself bent on renewal and grace. His rhythm was the earth's rhythm. His head was floating above it all and below he could see Neill behind the she-panther, Chara, and he could watch his steaming, red pizzle go in and out of her cunt, which was the ur-cunt, the Mother of the World.

As Neill was lost in this reverie, his more mundane mind began to sense the rush of jism rising in him the way sap rises in the skyscraper trees all around him. He swung his head leisurely downward until his sight began to focus more on his immediate surroundings. Chara was grunting and making wild sounds of ecstasy. They were very loud. Neill suddenly realized where he was and just how loud his mate was. Surely, Mr. and Mrs. Winsky had by now called the Park Rangers.

Then, off to his right, in a small copse, dappled with viridescent sunlight, dark green and yellow-green, in the center of the dappled bushes there seemed to be a human face. It was the face of a small girl. It was Naomi, the lost little girl. Neill knew it was her as surely as he knew he was Neill Rhymer. And Naomi, her little pinafore still as bright and clean as the day it was bought, slowly raised a single finger to her lips, a shushing gesture. She did not want Neill to give her away. She wanted to watch. She was part of the forest and the forest wanted to watch.

Neill shook his head, right about the time that Chara reached behind herself and roughly grabbed Neill's balls and said, "I can feel it. Give it to me, Neill, give me your hot jism."

And then, clarity returned. The face in the bushes did not disappear. Instead, it became an actual living human face. It changed like a photograph coming into focus. It was the face of Windy Winsky. And as Neill emptied himself into the rear-entry passage of her sister's pussy, Windy slowly ran a tongue around her lips.

Afterward, the two couples found each other and walked slowly back to the house. They were all very tired and very quiet. The sisters had analogous smiles on their sexy, kittenish faces. Were they thinking the same thing? Chara was holding Neill around the waist.

"I love you," she whispered to him, her breath hot in his ear.

"I love you, too," Neill said, as Chara skipped ahead and grabbed her sister's hand. They ran ahead toward the house.

And Neill was profoundly changed that day. Something opened inside him, the lotus at the center of the heart. He loved Chara Winsky. He was cocksure of his love. He committed himself to her. He wanted Chara Winsky forever and for all time.

In the Flames

Neill returned to his cottage on Holmes Circle with his heart full of glop. After a few hours back among his books and music and dust bunnies the size of soccer balls, he was ready to pooh-pooh the cosmic transformation he had experienced in Birmingham. Yet, his heart engaged when he thought of Chara's face, her sexuality, her wildness, her unpredictability. She was fiery. That was what Neill had decided. He asked himself if he liked fiery and was unable to give a definitive answer.

So, fire called to him.

Remember the Polaroids of lovely Syrie Hardwood? Neill had kept them all these years and had used them often to stir his embers and get his poker stiff. They were prized possessions, Syrie's naked beauty preserved for all time (or however long Polaroids stick around, longer than a gallon of milk, shorter than the Standing Stones of Ireland).

Neill decided, at the same time that he decided Chara was as fiery as a clowder of cats, that Neill himself was an adult and in an adult relationship and heading, O great perhaps, toward marriage. So, with gut-wrenching rue, he built a fire in his fireplace, despite it being a balmy 75 degrees outside, and therein he sent the remains of his passionate and life-changing love and sexlife with Syrie Hardwood. He watched as each picture puckered, split, bubbled. In one bubble he could see the darky hairy vee of Syrie's beloved bazoo. Neill wept.

Neill wept and then he called Chara and told her he loved her with a love as strong as the love that binds the peopled universe.

Chara answered this way: "Get your skinny ass over here and scratch my itch."

Neill flew.

Neill, Bidden, Crow, Shlomo

"Yeah, why don't you ever dream that you were prepared for the test and the teacher loves you and you make all A's?" Bidden said.

"Or why not dream a wet dream about a woman who is actually a possible mate," Shlomo added.

"I still dream about Syrie," Neill said.

"Well sure, I still dream about Syrie," Crow said.

"You really liked her?" Neill asked. His burger was undercooked and he kept opening it up after every bit to look at the meat one more time. After the 7th time he did this he was asked what the hell he was doing.

"It's a little underdone."

"Send it back."

"I wouldn't do that to Wanda."

"Then leave it alone."

"You're right. It's not like it's going to be any better cooked after I've eaten it for a while."

Nevertheless, though he skipped doing so after his 8th bite, after the 9th he looked one more time.

"I dream about anyone but my wife," Shlomo said. "Anyone. Ruth Roman. Ruth Buzzi."

"Babe Ruth," Bidden said.

"Exactly."

"I dream about Chara even if we've just done it five nights in a row."

"You like her? You really like her," Crow said.

"Yes, I do. I think I am in love. You guys like her, right?"

"Of course," Shlomo said. But there seemed a dangerous undercurrent in the tight cadre of old male friends.

"She's the right stuff," Bidden said, after too long a pause.

"She's a hellcat in bed," Neill said. "She talks dirty."

"Ahh," Bidden, Shlomo and Crow said.

"Not that that is the only reason I love her."

"Because that would be shallow," Bidden said.

Chara Delivers

One Friday night when Goffredo was staying at his girlfriend's, Chara and Neill made plans to have dinner at his house. Chara said she would cook and bring it with her, and Neill said he would rent them a movie.

Neill got home at 6:15 and Chara pulled up shortly after that. Neill opened the door to find her face a grim visage straight out of a Hammer horror film.

Chara stood there with a crockpot in her hands, her eyes flashing anger like a police siren and the left leg of her loose-fitting pants showing what looked like an oil spill.

"Take the fucking crockpot, Neill," she said in greeting.

Neill took the half-filled aromatic pot from her hands.

"What happened?" he rightly asked as she barreled past him.

"I fixed the fucking dinner, that's what happened. Everything I touch turns to shit. Didn't you want shit for dinner, Neill?" Her angry boom dopplered away as she went down the hall to the bathroom. She slammed the door shut.

Neill stood in his living room holding the pot of hot *something* feeling foolish and inept and inappropriate. He was sure this was his fault somehow.

Chara came out of the bathroom without her pants. Her pretty legs were still pretty but her pretty face was the face of a harpy.

"What happened?" Neill had put the pot in the kitchen. Inside was something which smelled heavily of curry.

"I made us an Indian stew. Which I placed on the floor of the car on the passenger side. It decided to tip over as I rounded the corner off Central. I stuck my leg out to stop it and it scalded my leg. I also ran up the curb because I couldn't brake quick enough with my left foot. Good enough? Is that a good story, Neill?"

"Honey, I'm sorry," Neill said. He put his arms around her. She accepted the hug the way a flagpole accepts the wind.

"I'm sure there is still enough for dinner," Neill tried, backing away a bit.

"Fuck dinner," Chara said. She threw herself onto the couch.

"Want me to order a pizza?"

Chara looked at Neill as if he were suggesting they were right to kill Christ instead of Barabbas.

Neill sat next to her and they were quiet for a long time. Even in his distress, Neill could not take his eyes or mind off Chara's exposed thighs.

Tentatively he put his palm against one. Chara did not say anything or attempt to cut off Neill's hand with a cleaver. Of course, there was not a cleaver handy.

Neill stroked the thigh lightly. Perhaps everything could be saved by one of their high-powered fucks. Neill was getting stiff.

Chara turned toward him. Some of the hateful spite had drained from her face but there was still enough to warrant tiptoeing.

Neill's hand stopped moving.

Chara took a deep breath. "Did you get the movie?" she asked. She was thinking the night might be saved by cinema instead of tikka masala.

Now Neill panicked. He suddenly was regretting his movie choice. It was embarrassing enough renting it but now what was he to do? Perhaps suggest a classic black and white film from his personal collection of VHS tapes?

"You did rent something, didn't you?" The storm was returning to Chara's brow.

"I did," Neill said. Perhaps honesty would be the best policy. (Honesty isn't really always the best policy.)

"It's called *Crocodile Blondey*," Neill said. He grinned like Uriah Heep.

"You mean Dundee?"

"Uh, no, not the original."

The light went on in Chara's attic.

"You rented a porno film." She said it so flatly it was two-dimensional.

"Heh, yeah, I guess. I thought—"

"You're fucking crazy, Neill. Is that all you think about? You only want to fuck me or have me suck you off. You like that don't you, Neill?"

How could he answer that one truthfully?

"Shit. You're an asshole. You're objectifying me, you know, asshole?"

"Wanting sex is not ob—"

"Shut up, Neill. You won't get any tonight. No sir."

Neill sat in stunned silence but his gorge was rising.

"I guess if I am not going to fuck you you'd just as soon I leave, right?"

Neill didn't answer.

Chara rose, walked slowly to the kitchen where she made some indistinguishable noises. Then, she calmly walked past Neill and out the front door. It was a few moments after the sound of her car faded that Neill rose from his stupor, from his shock that the night had ended that quickly and badly.

Neill went into the kitchen and found the rest of the masala. Chara had opened up the silverware drawer and poured it inside.

Shlomo on the Horn

"She dumped the dinner in your drawer?"

"Every last greasy drop of it."

"She's a tigress, alright."

"Yeah."

"What are you gonna do, right?"

"I guess wait for her to apologize."

"How likely is that?"

"I don't know. She's been pretty mean before and apologized. I imagine she is already formulating her justification now."

"Um, Neill, Buddy. You really need someone mean in your life?"

"No. I really don't."

"There are balancing good times, I imagine."

"I thought so. Jesus, I love her. I think."

"It's a complicated business, love."

"It is. It's a cat's cradle."

"But no one needs, you know, cruelty. No one needs stroppy."

"You're right, of course."

"No matter how good the sex is."

"It's not just the sex. She reads books. She's smart and, occasionally, funny."

"Ok."

"I know."

Canary in a Coal Mine

Neill was just locking the bookstore door when Chara spoke.

"Hey, Cowpoke," she said.

Neill turned to find her sitting on the hood of her car.

"Hi, Chara," Neill said. A small nervous knock like an engine in need of a tune-up began in his rib cage.

"You're still pissed," she said. It was neither question nor statement. It was a canary sent into the coal mine.

"Forget it," Neill said. He couldn't say exactly what he meant by that.

"Look, come here. I'm really sorry." She slid off the car.

Neill didn't want to be churlish. He stepped closer.

She closed the difference and put her arms around him.

"Come on, lover, I said I was sorry."

"I know Chara."

"You don't love me anymore?"

"Chara."

"I know. I was crazy. It was just that I was trying so hard to please you with the dinner and it all went south. Forgive me. Let's go down to the cafeteria here and I'll buy you some chicken-fried livers. You love their livers."

"I do," Neill said.

"Come on. Forgive me, yeah? I was only trying to please you and I fucked it up."

They went to the cafeteria. The livers were as good as ever. Over the table Chara reached her hand and took Neill's. They ate companionably and afterward Neill was stuffed.

"Let's walk this off a bit," he said.

They strolled around the plaza stopping in front of the new home furnishings place.

"Hey, come in here," Chara said. "Lemme show you this couch."

A lovely brunette saleswoman greeted them.

"Hey, you folks looking for anything in particular?"

"I want to show him this couch."

The three of them stood in front of an off-white couch.

"Isn't it beautiful?" Chara said.

"Sure," Neill answered.

"It's a bargain at $200, lemme tell you," the lovely brunette saleswoman said. "That's before the protective coating, which is an extra $40."

"Protective coating?" Neill asked. "Is that like the undercoating in cars?"

"Well, you really need it for a white couch," she said, chipper, with a smile like a slice of orange.

"If you really needed it, it would be part of the cost."

The saleswoman smiled and shrugged her pretty shoulders.

After they left Chara said, "Why were you needling the salesperson?"

"I didn't think I was needling her. I was just being—what? miserly."

Chara laughed. They walked back to her car.

"Now we have two cars here," Chara said.

"Yes," Neill said. He was acting like he didn't give in easily, but we know he does, over and over. It's a pattern by now.

"Is Goffredo home tonight?"

"Yes. And his girlfriend is there."

"Follow me to my place then, ok?"

"Chara," Neill said. He had no completion to that thought.

"I really want to suck your dick, you know. I've been missing your dick."

Neill had almost forgotten her dirty mouth and how much he liked it.

"How much?" he said, and smiled a devil's smile.

"This much," she said, and grabbed a handful of his toys right out in front of God and Poplar Plaza shoppers. She held it tight. "I'm gonna stick it so far down my mouth..."

And, readers, she did.

Afterward, in afterglow, they lay and talked about this and that. The TV was on but the sound was down. They were using it as indirect illumination.

"Mm, mm, don't get mad at me anymore, ok?" Chara said.

That was an opening gambit Neill could not follow.

"Hey, you know what," Chara said, rising naked from the mattress on the floor. "Wouldn't that couch look great against the wall. See? Right here so we could watch TV?"

Neill Does What Neill Does

The next night, after work, Neill returned to the new furniture place in Poplar Plaza.

The same lovely brunette saleswoman was there.

"You've come back for the couch?"

"I have," Neill said.

"No coating."

"Right. Just the plain couch. And delivered, please."

"Yessir."

Neill handled the sale, writing a check for the full amount.

"I'm Eula," the saleswoman said, shaking Neill's hand.

"Neill," Neill said because that was his name. "I work at the bookstore."

"Right down the way? The Book Stone?"

"Book Shelf, yes."

"Good to meet you, Neill. Maybe I'll need a book someday."

"Everyone needs a book every day," Neill said, and he laughed at himself.

"Right," Eula said.

"When will that be delivered?"

"Back to business. I'll see that it's delivered first thing tomorrow."

The Poem Discovered

One evening at Neill's, while Neill was in the euphemism, Chara started flipping through a spiral notebook she found on the bedside table. It was Neill's workspace. It was where he wrote his poems in longhand before polishing them at the typewriter.

When Neill came back into the bedroom, Chara had her finger marking one poem. She wore an expression akin to Judge Hoffman's.

"This new," she said, her face a smirk, her mouth an umlaut.

Neill took the proffered notebook and looked at the page. He saw in his own scrawl these words:

Blues for Dew Drynow
After 20 years I find a picture
of you inside a book of art.
Your smile is patient:
you were waiting for what life
would bring you after me.

"Relatively new, yes," Neill said.

"Take me home," Chara said.

"Wait, what? I don't understand." (He did have an inkling.)

"You're writing poems about other women. How do you think that makes me feel?"

"Chara, it's a poem. Poems. I don't know where they come from. This could just as easily be about the corndogs they had at high school football games."

"Except you didn't fuck the corndogs. At least, I don't think you did."

"I didn't fuck Dew either."

"But you loved her."

"I was 21."

"Take me home."

Another Dinner at Marcane's

Neill and Marcane embarked on a new relationship: trust friends.

Neill had dinner at Marcane's and briefly sketched out his and Chara's sinking relationship.

"What are you going to do?" Marcane said. "That's the only question."

"I know. It's not a very good thing, our being together. She's so—volatile."

"You deserve better," Marcane said.

"Thanks, Marcane."

"Of course, there is the sex."

"Tell me about it."

"It's hard to turn away great sex."

"I know."

"I miss ours."

"Oh, Marcane. I do, too. But we—you know."

"I know."

"Thanks, Marcane. The dinner was delicious."

"I went back to unsalted butter since, you know, I am eating alone most nights."

"I love you, Marcane."

Chara by Phone

"I can't believe you bought me that couch."

"Well, you know, your place is a tad...austere."

"How bout you steer your pretty ass over here right now and we'll christen the thing?"

"I'm at work."

"Spoiler."

"Why aren't you at work?"

"I don't know. I was getting ready and this thing came up the stairs and now all I want to do is lie on it and think about you taking me from the rear with my head down in these plush cushions."

"Groan."

"Did you just say groan instead of actually groaning?"

"That's her new one."

"What? Neill?"

"No, it's not on sale. It's brand new. Yes ma'am."

"Did you hear me, Neill?"

"Yes. Wait. Yes, ma'am. Lemme see it. Here. 15.95. What were you saying?"

"Are you talking to me?"

"Yes."

"I was saying."

"Yes, that's right. Backlist fiction is the right-hand wall."

"Neill!"

"Ann. What? I'm sorry. Chara—"

"Who's Ann?"

"Beattie. I was showing the customer the new Ann Beattie. What were we?"

"I'm talking about how lonely I am on this couch. Here, listen to this. Can you hear that? You know what that was. That was the zipper of my pants. I took them off. Now I only have panties on, the deep blue silk pair you really like. Weird that I put them on this morning not even suspecting that I was fixing to get this fantastic gift from you and that it would make me want you like a horny pony. Hear that? That's my hand slapping my tight naked belly. I wanna really push it down into the panties but I might need for you to do it. Can you help me with that? I'll meet you at the door naked if you want. Or, wait, just in these panties and my nipples painted red with lipstick. Does that turn you on, Neill?"

"*Chilly Scenes of Winter.*"

"What? What the fuck, Neill?"

"It's her best book."

"Are you even listening to me? Who are you talking to, one of those gorgeous young housewife bookclubbers you're so hot for?"

"No. Yes, Chara. I do want to."

"What? You want to?"

"I want to stick my hand down those panties."

"Ok, then."

"Oh, Jeez, I am sorry. Ma'am. No I wasn't talking to you. It's—"

"Fuck," Chara said.

Nevertheless There is a Christening

Neill approached Chara's apartment that night with his newly acquired admixture of fear and excitement. On good nights, he thought of Chara's precarious side as part of the excitement. Am I really attracted to dangerous women? he asked himself. He honestly didn't think so...but the sex was wild! Who wouldn't opt for wild sex? In place of security and peace? Yet another of life's delicate balances.

He knocked. She answered.

Her face was inscrutable. Was she going to tear his dick off, or was she going to coax it into acts previously only dreamed of?

Then, she smiled. Her smile was like the smile a hooker uses when she thinks her john wants a little girl.

"Come in here, you big generous hunk of man," she said and grabbed the front of Neill's t-shirt and tugged him inward.

She covered his mouth with a long, hard kiss.

"Mmm," Neill said.

"What?" Chara said, breaking her slobbery half-nelson.

"Yummy, your kiss," Neill said, slightly dizzy. "And whatever is cooking."

"Pot roast," Chara said. She looked out of the corners of her eyes the way she had seen screen sirens do.

"Wow, pot roast," Neill said.

"Oh, but, hey, look at the couch," Chara said, pulling Neill out of the kitchen and into the living room. There, in her dimly lit, austere living room there was a new white couch. It looked smaller and slightly less white in the room. Perhaps, it was the poor lighting.

"Nice," Neill said. "Are you pleased with it?"

"I am," Chara said. "So pleased I am thinking the pot roast can wait."

"Now I am thinking that, too," Neill said.

Chara pulled her t-shirt off over her head. She wasn't wearing a bra and her cherry-stone nipples looked like precise details. Then she let her skirt fall and she was wearing new panties, if you could call the butterfly wings she had on panties. Neill thought if he blew on them they would disappear like dandelion fluff. He wanted to try.

Chara lay back on the couch, like Goya's Naked Maja.

Neill undressed, standing over her. When he got down to his briefs Chara said, "It looks like Mr. Winky likes my new panties."

"If he doesn't I do," Neill said.

"How should we christen this?" Chara said. "I was thinking of something outré."

"Outré, eh?" Neill said.

"Look," Chara said. She turned herself nearly upside down, her legs up the back of the couch, her head hanging off the edge.

"Nice," Neill said. "Now what?"

"Drop you shorts. Bring your balls over here."

Neill did and stepped closer. Chara rearranged him so that his sack hung over her mouth like grapes. Chara took one scrot gently into her mouth. With her hand she stroked Neill's ass. Then, she did the other ball as if she were bathing him and had to do a thorough job. Then, her tongue ran down under his balls and her hand moved to his zizi, which was pulsing from the attention.

Then suddenly, she stopped, swung her legs around and sat up.

"Good, right?"

"Hoo," Neill said.

"I found it in a book," Chara said. Her lusty smile was childlike.

"Which book?" Neill asked. "I'd like to read that book."

Then Chara knitted her brows and seemed about to rain. She was thinking.

"I lied. I called Kate and asked her if she knew of a new sex thing I could try to thank you for the couch and to, you know, apologize for other things." Her slightly vulpine face was hopeful.

"Who is Kate? She knows everything!" Neill said, with a laugh.

"I'd introduce you to Kate but she'd steal you from me."

"Ha, I don't think so."

"She's everything I'm not. She's sweet and kind, and she has tits like Marilyn Monroe."

"What's her number?" Neill tried.

"That's not funny, Neill."

"I'm sorry. Did Kate tell you about pot roast?"

"No, not the pot roast. My sister told me how to make that."

"Well, what do Kate and your sister have planned for us next?"

"Kate said. Kate, she said..."

"What?"

"Have you ever tried anal sex?"

"No," Neill lied quickly.

"Kate said sometimes if you give a man that he knows he can't go anywhere else for such enticements."

"Chara, that's not necessary, you know. What I like best about us is the closeness, the intimacy."

"Nice speech."

"Ok, and I really dig how dirty you talk."

"Really? Other lovers didn't?"

"No. Not like you."

Chara seemed to think this over for a moment.

"Let's do anal and I'll give you some really hot talk, too. Won't that be a special treat?"

"If you want, Love."

"I love it when you call me Love. Look, look what I got."

Chara pulled a small jar out from under the couch. She balanced it on her palm as if it were a precious stone.

"Kiss Small Honey Hole," Neill read. "Ha. Ok. Sounds like a bad translation from Japanese but who am I to argue with this special plan?"

"That's the spirit," Chara said. "And look how well this arm rest helps the position." She pulled her ethereal panties off and knelt on the couch facing away from an intrigued Neill. "Cream my ass," she said.

"Don't think anyone has ever said that to me before," Neill said with a barking laugh.

"See! See! It's special!"

Neill opened the jar and put a tentative finger into the gel. It was sensually lubricious.

"This is good stuff. Smells good, too."

In answer Chara waggled her ass. Neill spread some ointment down her darkened crack and gently applied a bit around her buckeye.

"Oo, that feels nice," Chara said.

Neill dipped another two fingers worth and spread it with more force around her nether opening. He then put a finger against the opening and pushed it slowly in.

"Mm, I like that. Is that your dick?"

She turned around. "You're still using your fingers. I see your stiffy there dying to get in. Do it, Baby. Your first asshole. Isn't it exciting?"

Neill put the cream on the floor and positioned himself behind Chara. She did look like heaven's gate from behind.

Neill put his hard little head against her greased up asshole and began to insert it, increment by increment.

"Oof," Chara said.

Neill did not stop. He pushed a little harder.

"Oof," Chara said again. She tightened her sphincter.

"Ow," Neill said. "Do you want me to stop?"

"No, no, sorry, I'll relax. This is good, eh? This is nice—eh—uh—this—uh—is *different*."

Neill was about halfway in when he decided a quick final push was perhaps the best method. He gave it a good shove and sunk its entire shaft in.

"Erg," Chara said. "That's really—uh—tight."

Neill moved slowly. It did indeed feel good. Neill thought of his gypsy lover.

"Oh oh, that—that, ok, that's feeling a little better. Yes, that's it."

"Does it feel good to you?" Neill asked. It was his last moment of gentlemanly concern. He began to fuck her ass harder.

"Oh, oh yeah. Now I'm getting it. Took—eh—a minute. Yeah. Ooh, you're so big. You're filling me."

Here came the dirty talk, the talk that unwound Neill like a kite running off its spool.

"Yes, baby, fuck my tight ass. Yes, do it. Harder, Neill. Hurt me, fuck my ass so hard. Hit it so hard."

Neill slapped one cheek.

"Harder than that. Hit me hard."

Neill slapped the cheek again harder. Then the other cheek.

"That's it Neill. Slap it so hard it glows! Who else would give you this, huh? Huh, stud? Who else would give you such a sweet asshole to fuck? No one, that's who. Uh uh. God, that's really starting to feel good. My nipp—nipples are so hard."

Chara reached a hand down to her own clit and began to slap it in frenzy. Neill's tightly-encased sausage filled.

"Oh God, this is going to make me come. Don't. Stop. Hit it hard, Neill. Hit my fucking asshole hard. Your dick is so long—eh—so hard. Do it! Hit me hard, Neilllll!"

And Chara came with a shudder that shook both the conjoined lovers. And, right behind that (all puns intended) Neill emptied himself inside her. The tremors shook them both.

Afterward, they lay face to face, talking little, kissing each other tenderly.

"No one else would do that for you, Neill," Chara said, softly.

"I know, Baby."

"I'm really yours, aren't I? You couldn't find a better lover."

"That's right, Love."

"Mm, Love."

"That's right. I love it when you talk. I love the dirty talk."

"I can feel you trickling out of me. A ticklish little feeling in a weird place."

"But you liked it."

"You liked it. Butt."

"Funny," Neill said.

They held each other for a while longer.

"You hungry?" Chara said softly into his cheek.

"Starved. What time is it?"

"Eight thirty-five."

They did not put clothes on as they fetched big plates of roast meat and potatoes and carrots. They sat cross-legged on the couch, naked as Adam and Lilith. Chara put *My Man Godfrey* in the VCR. She knew it was one of Neill's favorites.

"This has been a lovely evening," Chara said. "I planned it just right."

"You did," Neill said. "Love."

"Who is that actor?"

"Misha Auer."

"He's funny in this."

"He is. But Carole Lombard, ooh la la."

"Is that why you like this movie so much?"

Neill checked himself for a moment. He seemed to be on solid ground.

"Well, no, William Powell. He's magnificent."

"He is," Chara said. And then, "She was pretty, wasn't she?"

"Yes, quite."

"I got dessert," Chara said. "Pause the movie."

After a few moments she returned with two strawberry shortcakes.

"How did you make these?" Neill asked.

Chara hesitated. "Kate made them."

"Oh. Well, nice Kate. Let's eat them naked and watch this funny movie and be finished with saluting Kate."

Chara scooted her pretty unclothed butt next to Neill's average but equally unclothed male butt. She bent to kiss his cheek. There was only a brief moment of precarious loss of balance. Just enough to tip Neill's plate onto the couch.

"Fuck!" Chara said, leaping up. "Look at that! Fuck! Move it, Neill. Move the fucking cake off the new couch!"

Neill scraped it, as best he could, using the side of his palm like a blade, back onto the plate.

"Get some salt or something," Neill said.

"That's not going to help!" Chara was screaming now. Someone on the North side rapped on the wall. Chara did not stop.

"You fucked up the new couch! You ruined it! Goddamn it. What Can't I Have One Nice Thing, Huh? Why can't I?"

Neill was using a dampened corner of napkin now to wipe the couch.

"Answer me, Neill, Goddamn you. Answer me! You're making it worse. Get out of there! Get away from the fucking couch! Fuck! Fuck! Fuck!"

Neill stepped back. Chara, now moving frantically, was attempting to wipe the stain off the white couch using the same corner of napkin Neill was using.

"I don't think that's working," Neill said. His heart was racing.

"What do you know? Huh? What do you know about anything? It all turns to shit. And you—you—TOO FUCKING CHEAP TO BUY THE PROTECTIVE COATING!"

Neill dressed and left without Chara ever turning around. Once home he lay awake the whole night, his heart a crazed ferret. There is a tendency in certain people, Neill posited, who, when they love intensely, try to diminish the loved one, hence reducing the power they have ceded to the adored. He had to rid himself of Chara Winsky. The woman he thought he could marry was as crazy as Clytemnestra.

One More Time, Please

Neill, the next day, was still reeling from Chara's frontal assault. He was also cured of loving her. How can one be so sure that another person is 'the one' and be so hideously, ridiculously, humorously, fundamentally, completely wrong? It was a mystery.

After a few days, days Neill spent both rattled and relieved, the phone rang one morning as Neill was getting ready for work. Goffredo answered it.

He held the receiver away from his head as if it contained an earwig and mouthed, "It's her."

Neill made his voice sepulchral. "Hello," he said, weary of the world.

"Hi, Love," Chara said. She sounded like a child.

"   ," Neill said.

"I guess you're still mad."

"   ."

"You can't stay mad at me, Lover. I give you the good stuff, remember?"

Neill suddenly had a vision. Chara thought her sex was a calling card, was a hook, was a universally attractant.

"I'm not mad, Chara. It's over, that's all."

There was silence. Chara was either stunned or conniving.

"Look, lemme come over and we'll talk about it."

"No," Neill said.

"Just like that," Chara said. She was fighting the edge of her hatchet voice, because she was trying to rebuild instead of hew. Neill could almost hear her teeth grinding, she wanted to lash out so badly.

"It's not good, Chara. You're not good. You're mean."

"Neill," Chara said. And she began to cry.

"I've got to go to work," Neill said. He hung up.

The day at work was uneventful except that Neill got in a new shipment of Algonquin books, his new favorite publisher. Their small volumes were ergonomic and lovely and seemingly all little gems of Southern Literature.

When Neill got off work that night Chara's little beat-up car sat at the curb in front of his house. She got out of the car as Neill pulled into his gravel driveway. The wheels on the rocks were a perfect representation for the sound of the rocks in Neill's head.

"Neill," Chara said, skipping over. Her eyes were red-rimmed. Her face sunken. She wore no makeup and her wild hair was even wilder. It was its own Vatican.

She put her arms around Neill who remained stiff.

"May I come in?" Chara said, holding Neill at arm's length and looking into his eyes. She was searching for a magic that had stopped working.

"Ok," Neill said. 'But I'm going out soon so this must be fast."

"You have a date?" Chara said with heat. Then she smiled a weak and broken smile as Neill looked at her over his shoulder. His front door opened onto the living room. Neill closed the door and motioned for Chara to sit on the couch.

She did, folding her legs under her. She looked like hell.

"Neill, this can't be over," was her opening gambit.

"Yet, it is," Neill said.

"Why are you being so mean?" Chara asked, her voice breaking.

"Me mean?" Now Neill's gorge was rising. "Me mean?" he repeated.

"I know, I know," Chara said and began to sob quietly. "It's just that I love you so much it makes me crazy. I do, Neill. I love you that much. I might be losing my mind."

Neill doubted this. He pitied Chara but where pity is, love shrinks, withers.

"I'm sorry, Chara," Neill said, and he started to rise.

"Wait, Neill. Please. Remember the trip to Alabama? Remember that, Neill? My family welcomed you. My mother told me you were the perfect man for me. My mother knows stuff like that. I think you're my—*destiny*." She almost choked on the last word.

"No, Chara," Neill said. "I am not your destiny. You'll find someone better."

"I won't, Neill," Chara said, and Neill believed that might be true if Chara stayed nasty.

"I'm sorry, Chara. It's not gonna work. I told you before you can't be mean to me. I begged you to stop, but that side of you emerges almost without will."

"That's it, Neill. I can't help myself." The tears were running now. "Can't you see? Maybe I could get some help...and—I don't know. You and I."

Neill cut her off. "No. Not you and I." Neill had already moved on in his heart, in his head. This surprised him.

"Neill, Neill," Chara grabbed at his hand and held it. She stroked it as if it were a bad kitten. "Gimme one more chance."

"No," Neill said and started to rise again.

"Ok, ok. It's over. I get it. It's over now. Just do this one favor for me. Fuck me again. Please Neill. I love us in bed. Please fuck me one more time and then it can be over. I want to suck you and fuck you so bad."

Friends, Neill was sorely tempted. After all, he was a man. How many women in a man's life are going to beg for a goodbye fuck. Next to nil.

"No, I'm gonna be late, Chara."

He rose and, this time, Chara rose also.

"You'll miss me," she said as Neill opened the door for her.

"You will, Neill. You'll think about me a lot."

"Goodbye, Chara," Neill said.

"You're an asshole," Chara said.

"Ok," Neill said as he backed away. "Ok, Chara. I'm an asshole. One more thing. You owe me $200 for that couch."

Perhaps that was an unpleasant way to say goodbye, but Neill felt so good at having Chara in his rearview mirror that now he did want to make plans to go out. Was there a woman he could call for a simple dinner and movie? He was certainly going to try and find one.

The Snake in the Hallway

Neill, single man again, lone survivor, saw more of his friends, read more books, watched more movies, did more nice things for people around him, relished selling books to smart men and women (especially TGYHBC, of course), tried to teach himself how to cook better and healthier meals for himself, did jigsaw puzzles in the shape of his heart, made a model airplane, stayed up late with Goffredo watching Letterman or Saturday Night Live, and, eventually, felt like clawing his own chest open such was his desire to be with a woman.

It was during this rich and fallow (does this contradiction work?) period that one day Neill came home from work early and, as he was throwing the new Robertson Davies book on the couch where he planned on starting it that very day, saw a movement on the hazy perimeter of his peripheral vision. He slowly moved his head toward the hallway and saw an image right out of his nightmares. There was a small, slim, brownish snake moving down the hall toward him. Neill hated snakes. He had dreams that he was trying to squeeze their demonic little heads while they were trying to inject his body with sickness serum. (Neill watched too much Tarzan as a child, perhaps). And, of course, he had no way of knowing if this was a simple, friendly snake like Kaa, or whether it was the most vile, evil, deadly asp this side of Cleopatra's. And he did not want to get close enough to find out.

What to do?

Neill espied his *Webster's Third International Unabridged Dictionary*. It weighed about as much as a Karman Ghia. He hefted it, walked quickly toward the snake, which looked at him with an expression that said, "Neill, what's up, man?"

Neill dropped the tome upon the snake.

"That's for Eve," he said.

He had not thought ahead. Now he had to pick up his beloved Third and find snake guts on its cover. Mad at himself, he lifted it from on top of the serpent's head. There was little blood but the snake was still twitching. Neill set the dictionary on the living room table and found a broom. With more effort than this task should have required, he swept the still twitching snake out the back door and down the concrete steps, and left it there on the sidewalk at the foot of the stairs. (A few days later, he found it there still, desiccated, exterminated, an ex-nightmare.)

"A snake. In your house?" Bidden said.

"Yes. A snake. It means something. It means something bad, something Freudianly bad."

"Neill. A snake?"

"Yes! I'm telling you. It was slithering down the hall toward me like something out of Indiana Jones."

"You hate Indiana Jones."

"I know! And I hate snakes!"

"You sure it was a snake?"

"Bidden. Please. I know I am overly dramatic in my phobias. What do you think it could have been if not a snake? A very large and shapely earthworm?"

"I like the use of the word 'shapely' there."

"Thank you."

"Actually, I think this snake would be more of a Jungian motif than Freudian."

"You know the Jung man ain't got nothing in the world these days."

Later, he told Goffredo.

"Yeah, they come up out of the floor furnaces sometimes."

"So it's not a portent. It's not evil incarnate come to remind me who's in charge."

"Well, it still might be that," Goffredo said.

What Comes After the End

The idea of infinity bothered Neill his whole life. The fact that simple, human brains could not posit what comes after the end of the universe upset Neill to the point that if the idea flashed across his simple, human brain screen, it depressed him for the rest of the day.

"It's a loop," someone explained to him.

"What's outside the loop?" Neill said.

"Black holes. Negative something or other. Anti-matter."

"Ahhhhh," Neill often replied.

The Visitation of the Aunts

Around this time, the Maves daughters (7 of the 8, you remember) began annual get-togethers, and the first gathering was in Memphis, at Max and Lolly's. And by this time, Neill's parents had bought their large new home in white-flight Cordova. Neill was eager to visit this Cordovan home, at this time, because his Aunt Lane, Aunt July, and his Aunt Queue (Bed's mother, if you remember further), his favorites, were there visiting with the whole gaggle from Canada. After a toothsome meal of ham and scalloped potatoes and baby peas, everyone assembled in the high-ceilinged living room.

The talk was general. How's the book business? Did you bring any peameal bacon and, if not, why not? Do the Memphis Chicks have a team this year? Is wash rinse repeat necessary?

Then, Aunt July dropped the bomb, the A-bomb (A for Aunt).

"So, your girlfriend's sister did alright for herself."

"Sorry," Neill said, making his eyes sparkle with incomprehension.

"Your girlfriend, Hay Tempt. You know who her little sister is now?"

Neill squirmed a bit. He still felt a little guilty (and, of course a lot thrilled) about this dalliance in the Falls fifteen years ago, with the beautiful mulatto, Hay Watts Temp. (Is mulatto an acceptable term now? Check.)

"Ahem," Neil ahemmed. "I do not."

"You remember her little sister?"

"Yes." Neill's mind flashed on the beautiful younger sister of Hay Tempt. What was her name?

"She changed her name. She is Z—."

And, here, Neill was told the name of a female rock star/movie star, who was, perhaps, more famous for dating and inspiring one of the biggest rock stars in the crowded pantheon of rock stars, a name we will leave out. Think big. It was not Michael Jackson or Smoky Robinson or Bill Cosby, but in that area of the galaxy.

"Holy cow," Neill said, because his parents and aunts were there.

"Yeah. She made it big, didn't she?"

"I guess so," Neill said. "Gosh."

"And, I think, Hay has done some modeling and film work, too."

Neill's mind boggled. When he got back on his own turf, after he bussed his aunts goodbye, he called his friend and co-worker, Pas Brunt. Pas was this rock star's biggest fan.

"You're kidding!" Pas said. "Of course I know who you're talking about. The older sister did some movies and I think she is dating M— (and here she named a black film star of the first magnitude—not Billy Dee Williams or Richard Pryor or Samuel Jackson but in that galaxy) because I saw Z—on Arsenio Hall and she called her sister out of the audience. Beautiful woman."

"She was. Jesus. I don't know what to do."

"What *could* you do?" Pas correctly asked.

But, Neill never was content to let these types of things lie. Perhaps you already know that about Neill. He's impatient and restless at the best of times. His pinball mind began working on a half-assed strategy. His strategy only had one cheek. This was pre-internet. But he had an idea.

Neill got the address of the Z—Fan Club. He wrote a letter addressed to Hay Watts Tempt, c/o The Z—Fan Club. A longshot, right? A bottle in the ocean. What star really has any connection to his or her fan club?

About two weeks later, he got a call at the bookstore. It was Hay Watts Tempt.

"Hi," Neill said. "Wow. I never thought I'd talk to you again. And what a wild way to reconnect, right?"

"Neill," Hay said. There was a pause. "I don't want to hurt your feelings, but I don't remember you."

This went through Neill like an unnecessary operation. One where they leave one of their tools behind inside the body cavity.

"I have a picture of us together."

"I'd like to see that."

"Ok, gimme your address and phone number. I'll send it to you."

And Neill did. He Xeroxed the picture and wrote a witty note (which has been lost to time, though time is screwballed right now since we are operating in fiction, right, where time doesn't exist). He sent it.

By return mail he got a brief note saying, "Jeez, I still don't remember you." And, along for the ride, Hay had sent one of her 8 x 10 glossies, signed, "To Neil (sic), xoxoxoxo, Hay!!!"

Neill tossed the picture. He was saddened and ashamed, for some reason. (Why ashamed?) But he did get one good joke out of it and he told this for the rest of the life as the conclusion to this madcap tale.

"Now, there is only one person on the planet who knows who has a bigger dick. Me or (and here Neill inserted the name of the black film star of the first magnitude.)

Dinah Mist Redux and Redux

We have not spoken of this in hopes of maintaining forward momentum and trim as much fat off the story's bones as possible. But, here, we interject:

Dinah Mist had never really gotten Neill out of her system and, in a different way, Neill had never gotten Dinah out of his. They often got together, clandestinely (if Dinah was in one of her periodic short marriages) habitually for the purpose of fast sex and of keeping, ahem, in touch.

Once Dinah asked Neill to her home because her husband was away for the weekend. They ate dinner on the couple's massive bed and watched *The Discreet Charm of the Bourgeoisie*. Afterwards they disrobed and went at it. On this particular evening Dinah insisted on vaginal penetration. Thinking about it afterwards Neill decided that Dinah must think Neill only wanted a quick blowjob (this is foreshadowing, we warn you now) and Neill felt bad that perhaps he was solipsistic and, in effect, 'using' Dinah, though the phrase is as hackneyed and worn as a welcome mat. Also, on this particular evening, Dinah's husband's cousin showed up unexpectedly just as Neill was preparing to leave. As if in a Feydeau farce, Neill hid in the bathroom with the door locked while Dinah tried to hurry her in-laws away. Neill listened to the whole frantic conversation through the door while he prayed to gods known and unknown that no one had to pee.

So, it was not surprising what happened one mid-morning at the bookstore. Neill was having a desultory morning, moping around, feeling lonely, glad to be shed of Chara Winsky but already tiring of masturbating and dreaming and writing sad poems.

And enter Dinah Mist.

"What are you doing here, Sweet?" Neill asked, moving close to her.

"Came to see you, of course."

"Not books but boys."

"Something like that. But you can sell me a book if it makes you feel better."

"I always want to sell books."

"What else?"

"Husband out of town?"

"Ha. Actually, we've split up."

"Ah. Again."

"Yes. I have a discount card now at the Justice of the Peace."

"Is there really still such a thing as a Justice of the Peace? I thought that was only in Andy Griffith or Preston Sturges movies."

"They still have em."

Now Neill moved closer to Dinah. He was more than hovering. The store was empty except that Iago had just trundled in and was in the stockroom doing whatever it was that he did back there, grafting stoat heads onto lizards perhaps.

"Hello," Dinah said into Neill's neck. "Am I standing too close?"

Neill brought his body up against hers. He had a boner the size and shape of a banana, bent behind his Levi's zipper. He placed the protuberance against the rear of Dinah's delectable ex-cheerleader body. It fit in the groove like a phonograph needle.

"Oh. Oh my!" Dinah said. Her smile was gold.

"Iago!" Neill yelled. The Heepish clerk emerged from the back. He had some kind of sauce on his chin. "Taking an early lunch!"

They hustled into Dinah's car, a second-hand Cougar. "My house, fast," Neill said.

"I love your need," Dinah said. She gripped his dick through his pants.

Once inside they practically ran down the hall and slung the bedroom door closed behind them. They fell together and kissed with eager lips. It wasn't long before Dinah unbuckled, unsnapped and unzipped and Neill's wang sprang to life. Neill helped her pull his pants down to his ankles. His shoes were still on.

Dinah moved to the foot of the bed and knelt between Neill's bare calves.

"Jesus, Neill, how long has it been? You could hang a winter coat on that."

Neill couldn't believe how hard and big he was either. And, as if freshly emboldened and challenged by its puissance, Dinah used *both* hands, her lips, her tongue, and large quantities of drool to bring the monster to its apex. She appeared a mad ceramicist at her wheel, taking the human clay of Neill's extraordinary erection into and out of her mouth with such relish and abandon that, when Neill came, it knocked her backwards off the bed. The monster spit a few more arcs into the air and onto her sprawled body.

"I gotta go back to work," Neill said. "Reluctantly," he added after they had held each other for only a moment.

"In his room, Neill comes and goes," Dinah said.

They both laughed. "Sorry," Neill said.

"It's ok. That was a force of nature. We were only pawns. It was like being caught in a twister."

"You're wonderful, you know?" Neill said in the car.

"I've been trying to tell you that," Dinah said as they parted.

Breakfast with Shlomo

The Barksdale Restaurant, a Memphis tradition of long-standing, was housed in a white clapboard house on the corner of (not Barksdale, which was a few blocks west) Cooper and Courtland Place. Sometimes, Neill could not eat there because there was a house three doors away on Courtland where a former mayoral candidate and his lovely bride lived. Neill had house-sat there once with Sue Goorile and sometimes still, thoughts of Sue Goorile filled Neill with such painful longing that he was barely able to make human speech.

One of the specialties at The Barksdale was grease. They made one of the best greasy breakfasts in Memphis, perhaps in the entire world. Neill's eggs over easy and bacon were both sustained by a sheen of grease that The Barksdale's biscuits went a long way in absorbing. Shlomo had eggs, too, sunny side up (belying his lifeview), with sausage and orange juice. Both men were drinking coffee the color of cassocks.

"If I am not the least-read, published author in America, I don't know who is," Shlomo said around a masticated biscuit.

"You've got an audience," Neill said. Neill tried to be the kind of smart, neutral observer friend that he imagined great writers needed, but, mostly, he was so proud of having Shlomo as a friend and so cowed by his intelligence that he mouthed the party line. Never would he offer Shlomo anything short of pure enthusiasm. "And it's growing."

"Like mold."

"Viking, for fuck's sake," Neill said. "You're being published by Viking."

"They hate me."

"They do not."

"It's possible my editor is a Nazi."

"Ha," Neill said, almost snorting a bulbous mass of egg onto the tabletop.

"So, I am trying to be a good Jew so he'll feel superior to me and leave me alone."

"You're not a political writer," Neill ventured.

"Every writer is a political writer," Shlomo said. Neill reddened. "Sometimes the politics like min, is muddled and sometimes it's too overt. I don't write out of any sense of outrage or injustice."

"Don't you think every novel is a work of Socialism?"

Shlomo thought this over. Neill sipped coffee, sweating the silence.

"Yes," Shlomo said. 'Yes, I see it that way. Neill, you're a fucking genius."

"I might not be," said Neill, and they both laughed.

They ate and looked at the other patrons, which seemed to be a mix of Midtown hipsters and hillbillies. Once, Marcane told Neill that you could always go to The Barksdale on a Saturday or Sunday morning and see who slept with whom the night before. It was an act of sociological study for her to visit the restaurant. Its walls boasted a deer head, a U. S. flag the size of Indonesia, a framed picture of Elvis with someone in a t-shirt and apron (presumably Bob the owner of The Barksdale), an orange suit coat, and numerous pictures of hunters and Memphis politicians.

"So, tell me the story you were going to tell me," Shlomo said. "Before I went off on my solipsistic whining about my own so-called writer's life."

"Remember the black woman I had sex with in Niagara Falls, a decade ago when my brother and I visited there?"

"Um, no not really."

"Ok, lemme back up and make this a longer anecdote."

"Is a long anecdote an oxymoron?"

"I have no idea."

"Ok, so tell."

Neill told the whole story, embellishing it a bit with the part about the brothers' harrowing crossing of the border with mary jane in the trunk. When he was finished Shlomo sat back and smiled.

"You mean ___ of the *Dying to Kill Again* movies?"

And here Neill inserted the joke about there being one person on the planet who knew whose dick was bigger.

Shlomo laughed. He said, "You've had the most exciting sex life of anyone I've ever known. And, despite that, you have the most deluded self-knowledge about how attractive you are. How many women have you slept with?"

"Gad, I don't know."

"Add them up for me sometime, would you, my coxcomb friend?"

"Sure," Neill said. "Sure."

"You really ought to write a book about them. Put them all in. It would be the raunchiest novel since St. Miller."

"Then *I* would be the least read writer in America."

The Flame-haired Nautch at The New Dais

Some lonely weeks passed. Neill began to mope. He began to think that sex was a myth, like how one does not believe in heat when one is cold. There was no new woman on the horizon, perhaps not even on the planet.

He sold books. He flirted with the Gorgeous Young Housewives Book Club members. He walked down to the furniture story and chatted up the young lass there, on whom he could not get a fix. She seemed attracted to him and yet there was a nearly impermeable wall between them.

Around this time, Helen Guru returned from New York City, where she had gone like so many before her to prove her maturity. Or to test it. She returned with news of two abortions, several love affairs with writers, known and unknown, and a new womanly attitude that was as sexy as a cloud of thunder. Neill was not immune, though he did not partake of her immediate heat.

She was seeing a local guy, nice as can be, if a bit too dull to hang onto Helen. One evening Helen and this guy decided that they had heard enough of Neill's desolate grumbles and they practically dragged him downtown to The New Daisy on the recently renovated Beale Street. John Doe of the group X was playing, and both Neill and Helen's current lover were fans of X's sideways, new age punk.

"You're going with us, right Neillo?" Helen said.

"You know me," Neill replied. "I like the night life. I like to boogie."

It was a grand show. At one point during the warm-up act, a one-man band who played guitar, harmonica and top-hat cymbal all at once, punctuating his raucous music with witty lyrics, ala Tom Waits, John Doe appeared next to Neill, taking in the humorous singer from the audience's point of view. Neill could have spoken to him. He did not.

Helen and her beau were off dancing.

During the intermission, Helen appeared next to Neill, who was standing a few yards from the stage, sweaty in her sheer shirt and tiny shiny skirt. "See anyone," she asked, hip-bumping Neill.

"I saw John Doe. He stood right where you are standing."

"That's nice, Neill. Any *women*?"

"Oh, sure. You and….well, just you so far. But you look great." Neill gave with a leer that tried to balance friendship and desire. It ended up lopsided as if Neill had Bell's palsy.

"Gotta go find—" And she was off.

John Doe and his outfit took the stage and tore the roof off the place. Above, the stars crowded round to see who was making such heavenly racket, the cantankerous music perhaps of the spheres who were their very neighbors.

Near the end of the show, during a particularly beat-heavy song, Neill became aware of a presence near his shoulder. Someone was standing so close Neill could feel breath on his neck. He turned his head slowly because he feared if he did it too quickly he might bang noses.

It was a woman with wild combustions of rufescent hair which corkscrewed out from her freckled pixie face like gorgons of lust. Her blue eyes were nearly translucent. Neill was literally nose to nose with her.

"Wanna dance?" the angel spoke.

"I. I don't really dance," Neill said.

"I noticed. You're barely tapping your foot."

"I'm extremely inhibited due to a bad breastfeeding accident as a child."

The angel didn't laugh. Instead she held his gaze.

"You're cuter than cute. Dance with me."

"I don't know how, really," Neill said, though he was starting to rethink his position re: dancing.

"If you dance with me I'll fuck you." Now, her eyes were full of fire. She grinned a grin that was cut out of a witch's pumpkin. Her hair was the kind of red that looks unnatural, with orange highlights like electric yams.

"I—don't," Neill said.

"Just move with me. I'll show you. And then—you can *have me*."

Neill grinned at her. He just stood there and grinned at her like a looby. But just when he had screwed up his courage to say to her, "You're so pretty I just might—" she moved away with a look back over her shoulder that said, "You lose, asshole."

At the end of the night, on the ride home, in the backseat of Helen's beau's Chevy Cobra, Neill related the story of the dancing redhead, an undeveloped version of a story he would polish later and relate often.

"Goddamn," Helen's beau said.

"She was so fucking sexy," Neill said as if he had just woken from a dream.

"I told you women were attracted to him like bees to flowers," Helen said.

"Actually, I think in that analogy I should be the bee."

"Oh no," Helen said. "You're a flower. You're a big, showy pansy."

After Basketball

The nights were as muggy as the days as the days grew longer and twilight became a lustrous ridotto of heat and pink light. Goffredo and Neill were leaning against their cars in the St. Mary's parking lot, having just played 2 hours of full-court basketball in the un-air-conditioned gym. They dripped. Off to one side Hawker, and some of the rougher boys were laughing at some obscure joke, which involved the repetition of the inelegant phrase, 'hairy pussy.' Their laughter, as the dark came on, seemed to be conspiring with the coming night.

"Come on, join us for once," Goffredo said, wiping his forehead with an unclean towel. It was part of the 'boys' Wednesday night out to meet at Poor Red's (aka "The Hidey Hole") on Park Avenue for beers and male bonding.

"Ach, I'm beat," Neill said.

"You never come. Some of the guys tell me they wish they knew you better."

"They don't want to know me better. But I appreciate the sentiment."

"Don says so."

Don was one of the nicer Wednesday Night Boys. He was the tallest in the group (at 6'3") and hence played center, especially needed when the WNB decided a couple years later to try the city league tournaments.

"Don's a mensch," Neill said.

"You've been hanging around Shlomo too much," Goffredo laughed.

"Ha."

"It's so hot. It must be the heat."

Goffredo laughed. "Roger Ramjet."

"It's so heavy. It must be the weight."

"Ok."

"Roger Ramjet, he's our man. Hero of our nation."

"Your shot was falling tonight."

"In the first game. Because you got every rebound and kept feeding me the elbow jumper. You know I love the elbow jumper."

"You were on fire tonight. What did you shoot?"

"Oh, I don't know."

"You do. In the first game, what did you shoot."

"Well," Neill said. Then into his shoulder as he wiped the sweat from his chin, "7 for 7."

"Seriously? You didn't miss?"

"Not in the first game."

"We won the 2nd, too."

"Because of you and Hawk inside. Where I shall not go."

"Did you get peeved at the new punk?"

"Yeah, a bit. Who was he?"

"Some guy Don works with. Young pup."

"Young cur."

"What did he say to you?"

"He rightly said that I stay on the perimeter because I am afraid to mix it up inside."

"Asshole. If I had known I'd have made that elbow count double."

"You caught him a good one."

"Asshole. So, what do you say, come this time?"

"No, thanks, I gotta...."

"What you gotta? You got a date?"

"Maybe. I am not sure."

When he got home Neill took a hot shower and felt much better. Then, he found the Book Shelf business card on the back of which he had written Eula's phone number. Eula was the furniture store woman. The last time in, she was a little warmer than usual and Neill felt emboldened enough to ask her for her number.

"Who is this again?" Eula answered the phone.

Strictly Blowjob

The first date with Eula wasn't much of a date. They met for coffee and chatted. It turned out that apart from selling furniture she was also a cheerleader for The Memphis Showboats. She was flippant without being funny, but she laughed at Neill's self-deprecation and this led to further dates. Sometimes, she simply went home with Neill right after they both left work at 6.

A pattern was soon established. They went directly to bed.

While there, they began with some satisfying making out. Eula's body was fit and she was almost as strong as Neill's one-night-stand bodybuilder. He was also haunted by shades of Akin Spins, though Eula was older, stouter, more filled out. After the 2nd time they groped and felt each other up and cooed and gurgled in each other's ears, there came the unbuckling of the clothing. Eula's breasts were small and tight, and she liked to have her nipples sucked. Her ass was as tight as a melon's rind.

And that second time, with her pants around her own ankles and her shirt open and bra cast aside, she gave Neill some well-practiced penilingus. She was good at it and even seemed to like licking up Neill's hot fat. Almost immediately after sucking it up and kissing Neill's mouth she dressed and left, saying she had someplace to be.

Neill was quite taken with the athletic Eula and began to anticipate further 6 p.m. get-togethers. He also felt a little guilty for orgasming without reciprocating. So, the 4th 'date,' wherein they marched down the hall and into the bedroom and undid clothing without preamble, Neill was determined to show her his own oral skills.

This time they stripped naked. Eula's compact and strong body was quite glorious. Neill found it a lively playground. However, when he went to put his hand around her vulva she managed to flick his attention aside with an efficient body twist. And immediately, she bent her gorgeous naked body over Neill's and sucked him long and hard again.

The next time, Neill was adamant about wanting to eat her. They did not have a practiced lingo and this nearly silent afternoon rite took on a spooky rhythm. Neill playfully shoved the denuded cheerleader onto her back and, again playfully, made as if to hold her arms down while his mouth traveled down toward her navel. She rolled free.

So, on her side, Neill put his dingum against the hard mounds of her ass, preparing to enter her from behind. Eula gracefully leapt from the bed. Neill would have been offended or guilty had Eula not laughed a girlish laugh.

And she jumped back on the bed and put her face onto Neill's flat stomach. She began tapping and patting and pulling his penis, giggling until she got serious and took him full into her mouth again. And then, she was gone like an eidolon.

Here is one sweet memory of Eula, before we move on: she did a lovely version of Springsteen's 'Pink Cadillac,' complete with Pip-like moves. It never failed to charm Neill.

Later, after this little affair had died like flowers in the shade, Neill understood that she wanted him only to show off her skills with the male organ. And, a few months later, he read in the paper about her coming nuptials to one of the Showboats.

Neill was her little thing on the side while she waited to tie herself to a man for life.

Later, he wrote this poem about it...called "Strictly Blowjob.'

The Summer of Helen Guru

The heat came on, the lung-scarring heat, weeks in the high 90s, days over 100, nights as muggy as a Louisiana quagmire. And Neill was lonely, lonely.

Enter his old friend Helen Guru, now shed of the new beau, now sporting a newer beau, a writer for the newspaper. And though she was herself hitched, she gave Neill much of her time. She was true and kind, and she recognized that Neill was often lonelier than his simple situation seemed to warrant. Helen got Neill in a way no one else did. Perhaps because they were so similar. She alone sensed the depth of his aloneness, his *otherness*. Neill, since his childhood dealings with bullies and his own physical awkwardness and his inability to do simple things that others seemed to handle so easily, often felt as if he were a child, a babe in the woods, a, there was no other word for it, *failure*. I am he who fails, Neill said.

So, they spent much time together that long-ago summer, playing Trivial Pursuit, going to movies, flirting with the same beautiful young women. They rode around town in Helen's ragtop sports car, going daily to Dairy Queen for Blizzards, both young and slim enough not to worry about the calories. Ah, youth. Helen Guru got Neill through that difficult summer. And never once did they so much as kiss though Helen Guru's body, a work of precision and masterful sensuality, sat as near to Neill as doves to a dovecote. And Neill could draw her tits from memory, having uncovered them when Helen was only 16. Ah, youth.

The Book Shelf by Day and Night

We don't talk much about Neill's nights at home alone. As often as he went out with friends or had a date twice or thrice as many nights he spent watching TV or a movie, reading books and more books, writing little poems that sometimes worked like little timepieces and sometimes wriggled off the pad onto the floor and disappeared into the mystical land of the creatures of dust and hair under bed or couch.

The reason is simple: it's too boring. We're in the service of Story.

Neill, when not with Helen or at P&H, sometimes went out with women. These dates, sometimes one-night stands, or just as often the aborted beginnings of something more: two or three dates which only served to make a body wonder at the rapidity with which the human heart makes decisions, especially renunciations.

Every Angel is Dangerous

Friends, as we approach the contemplation of the end of the saga of Neill Rhymer we enter this sphere with the caveat that this is not the happiest part of the tale. (Or, as Little Alex says, "This is the real weepy and like tragic part of the story beginning, O my brothers and only friends.") Starting now Neill will be put through the wringer. Stick with us. It is not as if heartbreak began with Neill's next paramour but it was certainly intensified, refined, and reconstituted to a force nearly deadly in its poisons. Why is this so? Why are there parts of one's life that grow horns? Who knows? Why is there evil? Why is there air? And, is there such a thing as a real aphrodisiac?

And, what comes after the end of the universe? (Ahhhhh.)

There is also joy here, of course. As Rilke said, "Every angel is dangerous." Or, conversely, every hell has its popsicle stand. Rilke didn't say that last bit.

Leaving work one day, Neill felt good about himself. This was rare enough. He had a shirt on that was flattering and he felt thin and young and full of snake's hiss and alkali. And as he exited the rear of The Book Shelf, emerging from the darkened trash bin area into the bright sunshine of Old Sol sinking, Neill knew, into Old Muddy Herself, who should appear in her ragtop sports car with a friend by her side but Helen Guru?

This friend: Neill had seen her before. She was as freckled as a Norma Rockwell depiction of Tom Sawyer. She had cascading rings of russet hair that caught and held sunlight the way certain plush fabrics do. She had large bush-baby eyes, blue like robin's eggs, and her cheeks were sculpted round and full, upon which sat two dimples cut with precision and divine finesse. They were the parentheses around her nearly plump lips, which, when she smiled, made the parentheses seem like God's best work.

She was an artist, Neill thought. A photographer, perhaps?

Her name was Misso Anthill.

They stopped. They were beautiful young women out for a toot. They were high, either on natural vim and vigor, or something more secret. They were giggly in camaraderie. They hailed Neill, or Helen did, while Misso Anthill smiled and made circus animals out of the clouds.

"Neill, my Neill," Helen called. "We did catch you."

"You were trying to catch me?" Neill said, approaching the bug. "Not too difficult. If I were a rabbit, I would already be part of someone's stew. If I were a fly, I would already be hanging from a pest strip. If I were a badger, I would be tamed and declawed. If I were a pelican—"

"We get it," Helen said.

"Lemme just finish the pelican one."

"Go," Helen said. Misso was looking elsewhere, her cornflower blue eyes seeking an infinite and similarly hued piece of sky, but listening, listening.

"If I were a snipe, I'd be sniper shot."

"Good one."

"Thanks."

"Neill, you know Misso?"

"I don't think so," Neill said. He moved closer. Her face, animated by youth and budding joy, was as lovely as an iceberg calving.

"Hi," Misso said and, seemingly for the first time, turned her adolescent blues toward Neill. "I've seen you around."

"I haven't been around," Neill said, coming around the car to take Misso's tanned and slim fingers in his own.

"You're funny," Misso said.

"Laugh when you say that," Neill said.

"We're off to the Shell right now, Neillo. Wish I could invite you along but Misso has a blind date," Helen said, giving Neill one of her knowing, insider smirks.

"I hope he isn't too blind to see how lovely you both are," Neill said, backing away and tipping an imaginary hat on his imaginary head.

"Bye, Neillo," Helen said. Misso Anthill went back to chasing suncats with her cerulean eyes.

That night Helen Guru called Neill at home. This was not usual. Everyone knew Neill hated talking on the phone.

"What's up, Tiger Lily?" Helen sounded like the preacher's daughter who just found out about boys' dingly parts.

"Hello, Helen Wheels. Reading Graham Greene and wondering why I even try to write."

"Good," Helen said. It was obvious she wasn't listening. "Wanna hear a kicker?"

"Sure," Neill said.

"Misso Anthill talked about you this afternoon."

"She doesn't know me."

"She said, 'Yes, I think he could be my boyfriend.'"

"Wait, what?" Neill said. "Why did she say that?"

"Jeez, genius, I have no idea."

"I mean, really? Her boyfriend just like that?"

"I imagine there is an interview and essay to complete first, but it's at least an invitation."

"Ok," Neill said.

"Do you want her phone number?"

"Sure."

Helen gave Neill the phone number. Neill wrote it down on the back of the bookmark in his Graham Greene.

"Why does that number sound familiar?" Neill asked.

"Because it's mine, too," Helen said. "We're roommates. Housemates."

"Oh! Where is this house of infamy?"

Helen gave Neill the address.

"Why does that address sound so familiar?" Neill asked.

"Because it's 3 doors down and across the street from Shlomo and Daisy."

This is What We Know about Misso Anthill

She is the daughter of revered Memphis artist Doddy Anthill, known for decades for his stark black and white photographs (the Chiaroscuro Eggleston, he was called) of a fading countryside culture, battered barns, roadside fruit stands, state fairs, and later for his glass-blowing and his mechanical constructions, 'The Talking and Dancing Cataleptic' and 'Jeff, the Unreceptive Robot;' and Sister Anthill (nee James), a woman of great soul and empathy, who made her life and her family her art, a noble enough calling. She was once a Dominican Nun, though Sister is the name her parents gave her. Now, she works part-time as a hospice nurse. She is Gaia.

Also: Doddy was once a Catholic priest and made the papers when he declared that the only god worth one's four score and ten was Art.

Also: at this time, the Anthills had an exchange student living with them. Her name was Mehrnoosh and she was from Saudi Arabia. She was a Muslim and spoke Arabic. Her English was as broken as a day-old biscuit. She also dressed in short skirts and had legs as tan as wood and as pretty as the surface of a pond.

She (Misso) is a student at Memphis College of Art (MCA) where her father is assistant dean.

She is studying photography.

She is studying papermaking.

She is pretty in a Miou-Miou way.

She does not shave her armpits.

She does not shave her legs except when she does. Her legs are as shapely as an astronomical chart.

She doesn't have a lot of friends.

She has two brothers, the eldest, Ram, a manly fellow and a hot-air balloon enthusiast and circus hooper; the younger, though still a year older than Misso, Nibs, a more sensitive man, a wannabe baker and patissier, who is working toward studying at the August Zang Die Presse School of Nourishments and Tarts in Vienna.

She is coddled by her parents and siblings. They think she, as the only girl-child, is a princess from a lost civilization or from a dream-state. She may well be.

She sleeps. A lot.

She does not know how to drive a car.

She once took a photograph of a fairy and, having discovered what she had discovered, she destroyed the photograph and never told anyone about the hole-and-corner part of Shelby County where she had taken the picture.

She is passive except when she's mad.

She sleeps. A lot.

Her legs are as shapely as an astronomical chart.

She is sexually inexperienced at the point where she enters our narrative.

The Street with Two Houses

Shlomo and Daisy had a little cottage on Linden Street in Midtown. There they lived with their books and LPs, and a dog the size of a brontosaurus. Neill had visited many times, mostly to pick up Shlomo for one of their outings—lunch at The Cottage or Buntyn Café, dinner and a movie, talks by visiting writers at Memphis State. Neill didn't know Daisy well. She seemed not to like Neill, but Neill always thought the lovers or spouses of his friends abhorred him.

Neill's first date with Misso was to hear Adrienne Rich read at Memphis State. Misso didn't talk much on the car ride there and it was difficult to gauge her appreciation of Ms. Rich. Misso sat stock still and smiled politely whenever Neill looked in her direction. In her lap, she was turning a flyer advertising the reading into a Hawker Hurricane.

The ride back to the house on Linden Street was a bit livelier since the strangers had something to talk about: Adrienne Rich. Nothing of great import was said.

Neill followed Misso inside where there seemed to be more people housed than he had previously imagined. Helen was around but her bedroom door was closed. There was another woman who might have been one of the housemates because she came and went from a different bedroom door, dressed only in a short bathrobe and with a towel turban on her head. She smiled at Neill, but no one introduced them.

Misso's room was also the den of the house and on its floor, coloring in Tom Terrific coloring books, was a long-legged black woman named Chella and a nerdy young man with jet black hair, freckles and Mel Cooley glasses, who seemed to abhor Neill the moment he laid eyes on him.

Misso sat down next to Chella and so Neill found a seat on a rolled-up futon, presumably Misso's bed.

"Can I?" Misso asked and began to color next to Chella. Perhaps, she was nervous having Neill there in her world. Perhaps, she had forgotten him altogether.

"Who are you?" the Mel Cooley guy said. He was sitting on the floor with his legs in lotus posture.

"Michael Nesmith," Neill said.

The fellow squinted at Neill. His mouth was a disapproving vee.

"Who are you?" Neill said to be polite.

"I live here," the fellow said.

Neill had had enough.

"Well, I gotta go, Misso. Thanks for a nice night," he said, rising.

Misso looked up. She, actually, seemed to not know what to do. Then, she remembered. She stood up and walked Neill outside.

"I had a good time," she said.

Neill looked closely at her china-doll eyes and his smile was half-smirk.

"Really," she added.

"Who's the nudnik?" Neill asked.

"Um, oh, Richie. He doesn't really live here."

"Ok," Neill said. He waited for her to finish. Finally, he said, "Who is he?"

"He's well—he's kinda been my boyfriend but not really anymore."

"So—" Neill prompted.

"He continues to hang around. I'm sorry he was staring daggers at you."

"Swords," Neill said. "Snickersnees. Bowie knives. Barlows." He was showing off.

"I don't know what you just said but I am sorry."

"It's ok."

They stood there for a few more moments. The night was made of sandstone and ghostlights.

"Ok," Neill said.

"Ok," Misso Anthill said.

"Listen," Neill sucked in a breath. Maybe the effort would be worth it. She certainly was an attractive woman and Neill was drawn to her in a seemingly necromantic way. "You wanna get together again?"

"Yes," Misso said.

She said it quickly enough. Neill touched his lips to hers.

The lights were off at Shlomo's house.

Driving home he was perplexed more than pleased but—still—there was something there, something inchoate, perhaps beautiful, perhaps dangerous, perhaps both. A pea under the mattress of his emotions.

More Time with Misso Anthill

The very next day Neill called Misso Anthill and invited her out to dinner. There was something about the diffident, arty Ms. Anthill that was worming its way into Neill's liver, if not his heart. He couldn't stop thinking about her lovely lentiginous face and her callipygian body, and those legs that seemed to stretch from Memphis to New Jerusalem.

They went out to eat at Fantasia, a hip bar/restaurant where one of the bartenders was Memphis musician Rob Jungklas. The talk at dinner was still small talk but it was increasing in size. Now, you could see it with the naked eye.

Afterward Neill invited Misso to visit his humble abode on Holmes Circle. She demurred and instead invited Neill back to her place. Neill didn't really want to revisit the hostel and its hostile Richie. But, when they entered the unkempt house, it seemed to be deserted. Its silence was like the silence of space in 2001.

"Guess no one is here," Misso said.

"Good," Neill answered and tried to offer Misso a leer.

She ignored the leer or didn't understand it. Still, they went to her room. The futon was rolled out on the floor and Misso threw herself upon it and turned on a small portable television. She found a movie channel which was showing *Jaws II*.

Neill hesitated but, with little other option, lay down next to her. She lay on her stomach with her head resting in her cupped hands and her elbows akimbo. Neill found this posture uncomfortable so he rested on his side, one eye on the TV and one on Misso's sweet backside. She was wearing men's striped pajama pants, an affectation of hers that nevertheless came off as almost stylish and certainly sexy.

Neill put a tentative hand on her back between her shoulder blades. He rubbed her there for a few moments, moments pregnant with an unsure future. Then Misso turned her dazzling face toward Neill and accepted his lips onto hers and his tongue into her mouth. She was a poor kisser, docile and irresolute, but her mouth was as fresh as the dews of our prime. Neill chanced to move his hand down her back and then under her shirt. Her skin was so smooth Neill became aroused quickly.

They deepened the kiss. Or Neill deepened the kiss and Misso assumed the deepening.

Neill found her small round breasts and was pleased that her nipples were erect.

"Your nipples are erect," he whispered to her.

"They always are," she said back.

Undaunted, Neill pulled her shirt off and she helped only by lifting her lithesome arms. She was, in a word, beautiful. Her long brown body was shaped by a fine maker. You could use her nipples for golf tees.

Soon some heat was generated. Neill pressed his erection against her midsection. And his right hand explored beneath her pajamas where he found an ass that was tight and curvaceous. Between her legs, she was damp.

When they broke the kiss, Misso turned back onto her stomach and put her cheek on her folded arms. She closed her eyes.

Neill lowered the pajama bottoms and then her small light blue panties. She was presented to him in all her naked glory. And that ass, white against the rest of her nut-brown body, turned that key in Neill. Neill began to knead her buttocks and gently separated her thighs.

He pulled off his own shirt and then his pants and underwear. They were equals.

"Is this alright?" he whispered. He feared she was asleep.

"Mm," she said.

Neill wanted it to mean yes so it meant yes. He moved himself behind her and after feigning a massage for a few moments, as if she had come to him for some obscure discomfort, he began to play with her butt and thighs. She really was exquisite.

Then, Neill moved behind her and began to use his Old Blind Bob to rub her thighs. Gradually, he moved it upward, drawing on her buttocks with his erect stylus. He put a finger between her legs and she was surprisingly wet. So he ventured in.

There was some resistance at the opening (surely she was not a virgin?) and then he slid in easily. Neill moved slowly and, what he thought was expertly, trying to employ his tool for its design, which, at least partly, was to arouse females. Soon, though, he forgot Misso's pleasure and began to pump her in pure animal heat, a solipsistic venery. As his tool filled, it occurred to him that they had not discussed birth control. (They had not discussed anything of any consequence.) So, right before he came he pulled out (O how difficult it was, enwrapped as he was in her silky quim!) and unloaded across the white dessert of her fundament. He grunted and shivered and shook. He made noises like a tarnished sackbut. Then, he flopped down next to her. She did not move. She did not say a word. Neill thought about shaking her shoulder to see if she were awake....or alive. But she opened her baby blues and they twinkled at him.

"Hi, you," Neill said.

"Will you get me a washcloth?" Misso Anthill said.

At Shomo's

"I can't believe you're seeing Doddy Anthill's daughter. She's what? Ten?"

"Um, 23. I think. Maybe 22. You know Doddy?"

"And you're 24."

"Thanks. 29."

"Misso Anthill. That's very interesting. A little less so that she is my new neighbor."

"Surprise! You like having Helen so close? She talks about you a lot these days."

"I think she wants to be a groupie. I don't want groupies."

"What's wrong with you?"

"How much time do you have?"

"Anyway. Misso. She's, I don't know. I can't pin it down, what is drawing me, what I find so intoxicating about her."

"She's very cute. Did you know her name is an anagram for Millionth Ass?

"Oh, her ass."

"I forgot you're an ass man."

"God's finest work, the female ass. Better than meerkats or Turkish hash."

"Yeah, well. I don't want Helen here as much. I write in the mornings. My friends understand that."

"She comes over in the mornings?"

"Seemingly right after my wife leaves most days."

"Uh oh."

"And I can't ignore someone knocking on the door. I can't. Something in me, some vestigial politeness."

"Does your mind do that?"

"What? Make me answer the door?"

"No, turn words into anagrams."

"Doesn't yours?"

"No. I'm not that smart."

"Shmontses."

Misso Comes to Holmes Circle

"Later on, feeling expended, he lay again in kindness gently rooting in soft clefts, rocking and drifting on smoothness, afloat and basking in softness. He clasped a waist, his penis nestled between two gentle mounds and he was filled with kind nowhere."

—Alasdair Gray

Their third date occurred at Holmes Circle. Neill cooked them dinner (spaghetti and jarred sauce and Texas Toast) and he rented Bergman's *The Serpent's Egg*. The dinner was fine. The movie seemed to bore Misso. But during their viewing, she sat snug up against him and in the brain-splatter scene she grabbed his hand and they held hands for a while. Her proximity was working in Neill like a narcotic. He wanted to see her naked again. He wanted to love every inch of her.

And so he did.

They moved gracefully to the bedroom after the film and Misso, still reticent, still almost *indifferent* to what was happening, did manage to get aroused once their clothing had been cast aside and their bodies touched forehead to forehead, and toes to toes.

Misso had breasts like a young Charlotte Rampling, perfect teacups with dark pip nipples.

So, Neill decided to introduce her to cunnilingus. He was relatively sure she had never had that done before (he *intuited* it). They had also discussed the birth control dilemma and it turned out Misso was on the pill. She admitted it reluctantly.

Misso's beehive dripped. It did more than drip. It flowed, it flooded, it ran like a river past Eve and Adam's. It was an embouchure. Neill was surprised and took this to mean her level of excitement was greater than she could let on with words or body language. And when he drank, there it was the most pleasurable pussy he had ever explored with lips and tongue. It was as soft as a shadow, and as warm as light through a gem, and it was as wet, O my friends, as seafoam. And when Neill brought her off with some fairly proficient clitoral action, Misso gripped a handful of bedspread in both fists and squinched up her pretty face as if electricity had just run through her.

Slowly, Neill rose from the site of his triumph and moved toward her mouth. He kissed her with her own juices fresh on his lips. She kissed back with a fervency that had been missing in action. Neill's dick slipped into her almost unnoticed by either of them. This time, Misso spread her legs and held Neill around the neck. She would not meet his eyes but she made little kittycat noises that were pleasant and helped Neill reach the finish line. When he did, it was with a youthful stream that drained him. He was literally dry-mouthed afterward.

That night Misso slept next to him. He held her and he fell asleep and he dreamed something that, in the walking-around world, became just as true as in the sleeping fantasy. He dreamed that he loved Misso Anthill. And when he woke the next morning, he knew that it was so.

Should he tell her this soon? His MO had always been to lead with his heart. He was too fast and loose with his emotions. He was emotionally extravagant. He cautioned himself to take it slow. He recognized his own problematic ways. Misso woke slowly and seemed to be disoriented and unsure how she arrived in Neill's bed.

"Mm, that was nice," Misso said.

Neill thought she meant the sex. She meant the sleep.

Neill thought it was the warmest thing she'd said to him yet. And he wanted to tell her he loved her but he did not. His editor was working. It was holding his ape in its cage. It was beating his ape with a baton.

"Bathroom," Misso said. She rose and put on a t-shirt of Neill's. Her brown legs squeezed Neill's heart like some kind of sinning. The ape stirred but returned to his straw.

When she was in the bathroom Neill tried to straighten his covers. He never had learned how to make a bed. Blame his mother. No, blame Neill. He was a lazy bastard.

In shaking out the sheets and coverlet, he discovered a circular moisture stain about the size of a basketball. He put his nose to the already drying spot. The smell inebriated him. It was Misso's essence. It was her myrrh, her ichor. It was her vaginal flow. Neill brought it to his nose again and wrapped it around his face. He wanted to die. He wanted to live forever.

"I used someone's toothbrush in the bathroom," Misso said, re-entering.

"I love you," Neill said.

In Love

Neill was in love. He was a gudgeon. This tall, slender artiste, with her blowaway hair and peppery skin, her long legs and pouty ass, her insouciance and her quiet ways, had bewitched Neill. He saw her flaws and forgave them all. He was a fool. He was brave. He opened his heart as if it was a screendoor and the Memphis heat a dragon. (This is a terrible metaphor, ed.)

Neill convinced himself that this was the way Love worked, with lightning bolts not gradual warming. He was in love for the first time. Such was the fervency of this feeling. (Poor gongoozler, how many times has he said it in just the limited confines of this narrative?) It practically sickened him, but not like the sickness he experienced in the bathroom of Circuit Playhouse because his date was too beautiful for him. This was a soft anxiety, a jumping ahead to a future he was sure he had finally discovered and, like a pilgrim, settled. Misso Anthill was his forever love. He knew it as surely as he knew his apprenticeship with lesser women was behind him.

Neill had already forgotten Chara Winsky and the transformational trip to Birmingham, Alabama.

For her part, Misso was warming up. The conversations were richer, the sex more mutual, the camaraderie developing. Misso was blooming.

A Delicate Subject

"It is a curious odor,/a moral odor,/that brings me/near to you."
    –William Carlos Williams

We've touched on this but here we will comment further and, in doing so, try to figure out why this was so important.

The aroma of Misso's love juices acted upon Neill like catnip to a cat, smack to a junkie, the hooch to a bousy goop. Neill would not wash his bedclothes; they were so thick with the bouquet. Whenever he was alone—and he hated the nights Misso did something other than see him (recall the conversation with Marcane about this subject—the desire of the lover to spend every moment with his beloved vs. the idea that 'space' is occasionally a good thing [someone smarter than us said that the enemy of love is not hate but indifference])—Neill spent time in his room lying face down on his counterpane, which was really a tie-dyed drape, a lovely piece of cloth that was a gift from his sister when he first moved into the house on Holmes Circle. That aromatic counterpane became a drug for Neill. The odor spoke of Misso. It was Misso, the deep-down fluid that oiled her cogs and gears.

She had a kitchen between her legs.

(Later in life, Neill could never conjure up the smell nor explain what it resembled. He knew he longed for it but the actual detailed recollection of it was lost to time. This was as it should be or Neill might have ended up another of the jumpers from the Frisco Bridge.)

We will come back to this. It is the leitmotif of Neill and Misso, Neill and Misso's Theme. Rather than an air by Rodgers and Hart this theme exists in the same realm as ittar, The House of Worth, ambergris, and *Institut supérieur international du parfum, de la cosmétique et de l'aromatique alimentaire.*

[ISIPCA: International Superior Institute of Perfume, Cosmetics and Aromatic Food., ed.]

(It was around this time that Patrick Suskind's novel, *Perfume*, was published. Neill carried that book around with him for months. And the number of copies he personally sold at The Book Shelf, many to his loves, The Gorgeous Young Housewife's Book Club, nudged the book onto the New York Times Book Review. In an interview at the time, Suskind remarked to his interlocutor, "This novel broke me out, of course. I could not have predicted its success or why it's become this season's hot book. There is a curious spike in sales directly related to Memphis, Tennessee. My publisher told me they would look into it.")

{Also, years later, Neill was to tell his female therapist, "Forgive me for this indelicate description, but my heart was smashed to pieces by the smell of one woman's vulva sauce."}

["*My mouth fills with the pure perfume of the waters of her stream./Twilight comes, then moonlight shadows, as/we sing fresh songs of love.*" –Ikkyu]

The First Visit to the Anthill

The house on Goodbar Avenue was umbrellaed by trees as tall as Yggdrasil. They seemed to hang over the ramshackle house like the hand of God, either in benediction or in a godly attempt to hide it from the workaday world. The house was gothic, straight out of Hawthorne or Charles Addams, and it seemed to spire up into the heavens as if every time you thought you reached the top floor you would find another hidden staircase and upward you would continue. It had about it a Tower of Babel essence of magic (and doom).

It was called simply The Anthill. It had a badminton court in the front yard, a wraparound porch where one imagined darkies delivered mint juleps to retired Colonels of the First Zouaves. The front door, behind a screen that squeaked like summer itself, was as thick as a tree and there was a small window in the middle, the kind one expected in a speakeasy. The driveway had four cars, all gleaming, all exotic as Tuckers. One car sported a trailer which housed the woven wicker basket of a hot air balloon.

Around back, an area darkened by leafy branches and tall trees, was a small swimming pool, built to resemble a grotto, complete with waterfall and the songs of happy frogs who understood their great luck landing in this peaceful paradise free from giggers. Off the eastern end of the back yard sat a strange box, a little larger than an outhouse. Its wooden beams were covered in tinfoil, and its door was decorated with playful runic symbols apparently devised by Doddy Anthill. The walls were built of alternating layers of organic and non-organic substances. Some were created by Doddy in his Kalpi Kauldron, the name given to his paper-making lab at MCA. Neill was later told that this box was an Orgone energy accumulator. Inside was a single chair, a plain oak chair similar to the ones used in school. ("The name comes from *org*, meaning life force as in *org-asm* and *ozone*, meaning '*the neutral principal*'," the eldest brother Ram explained to Neill, virtually daring him to crack wise.)

Neill was nervous about meeting the parents, intimidated, of course, by Doddy Anthill's reputation and renown. He was greeted at the door by the mother, Sister. ("Please call me Sis," she sparkled.) She took Neill by the arm and showed him much of the ground floor of the house, excluding a room off the large, darkly paneled living room, whose closed door bore a sign: "CLOUDBUSTER: Do not Abandon all Hope. Nevertheless, Ye Do not Enter." Neill learned later it was Doddy's workshop, full of vats and dyes and twists of metal and paper, and tools too numerous to mention but, *in toto*, they seemed like miniature torture devices, or alien medical instruments.

Doddy emerged from this Cloudbuster, blinking as if he'd been in a cave, as Neill and Sis were entering the kitchen, which resembled the gargantuan kitchen in Gormenghast. Sis turned and said with a soft pleased exhalation, "Ahh, here he is," as if the day were designed to introduce Neill to the great man.

Doddy Anthill was soft spoken, wry, pleasant, intelligent, and gentle. Neill liked him immediately and their initial conversation put Neill mostly at ease (though the devil in Neill wanted to say, "I love your daughter's hoohoo"), but it was to the mother Neill was drawn.

Sister Anthill was full of soul. She was Gaia. In her home, she was the heart and the heat and the calming influence amid a sea of high-strung artistic types. That first afternoon she and Neill discussed books as if they had been reading together for decades. Lunch was lemonade and finger sandwiches and fresh vegetables, and a whipped dessert Neill devoured without ever finding out what it was. Doddy sat among them as if still wrestling the duppies in his lab. Once he did interject a non-sequitur into the conversation. The exchange student from Saudi Arabia was nowhere to be seen, while the brothers Anthill, never sat down but entered and re-entered like ghosts in a Shakespeare play.

"Neill," he said. "You're a book man. You ever read Wilhelm Reich?"

Neill said, "No, sir. I haven't."

That was all. Doddy went back to his cucumber sandwich, which he chewed meditatively like a cud.

As Neill and Misso left that day, Sister took Neill's hand in both of hers and said, with warmth, "To be continued."

Neill loved Sister Anthill after that day and, apparently, she loved him, too. Later, Misso admitted that her mother had told her, "If you let this one go I'll never forgive you."

Shlomo Good and Bad

As Neill and Shlomo were talking about the publication of Shlomo's new book by Viking Press (its logo a sailing ship by Rockwell Kent) (a book of stories entitled *Just the Unjust*) Shlomo seemed jumpier than usual. He kept tapping his front tooth with the fingernail of his pointer finger.

"What are you doing?" Neill asked.

Shlomo looked at the nail as if it had offended him. "An addition to my bag of tics," he said.

"You're no Felix," Neill said.

"I'm no Shlomo," Shlomo said.

"What's up, Buddy? We're talking about your next book coming from Viking Fucking Press and your upcoming signing at my bookstore and you're miles away in Oz. Ozymandias in Oz."

"Daisy threw me out."

"Fuck. Whatever for? Jesus, Shlomo, when did this happen?"

"Well, it hasn't exactly happened yet."

"So, you're not on the streets. What did you do?"

"I didn't do anything. I am no philanderer."

"I know that about you."

"I wish I were a philanderer. Teach me how to be a philanderer."

"Shlomo. Tell me what happened."

"I can't be married. I told her that from day one. I told her the night of our wedding. I told her I could only *try* to be a husband, because that's what I thought she wanted."

"She didn't throw you out at all."

"What? Oh. No, she didn't. I am moving out."

"But you love her."

Shlomo gave Neill a withering look and began to tap his tooth with a ragged tattoo.

"Sorry. What's love got to do with it?"

"I'm moving out. I have to find an apartment. I started looking yesterday."

"My couch is yours, you know, anytime. I wish I could offer you a bed."

"Seriously? I mean. Do you mean it?"

"Of course, I mean it."

"It would only be a night or two until I find a place."

"Stay as long as you want. Really."

"Neill, you're a mensch. You're also a ninny. I'll drive you bats."

"Ok," Neill said.

So that night Shlomo arrived with a beat-up, brown grocery sack full of clothes and necessary items. When he spread the stuff out on the coffee table it seemed a poor exemplification of a life. Shlomo looked at the contents with disdain and sorrow. His face looked like Lincoln's in its midnight madness. Shlomo tapped his tooth a few times.

"Two nights max," he said.

"No matter," Neill said. "And don't call me Max."

Shlomo was there a week at the end of which Neill helped him move stuff (mostly boxes of books and sprung furniture) ['Hello, slug,' Daisy greeted either Shlomo or Neill—Neill assumed himself] into his new residence, a second-story garage apartment about as charming as a cough, a placeless place.

Setting the last box of books down, Shlomo, without inflection said, "Home." Tap tap tap.

And so Back to Harbert

Harbert Avenue now had one less attraction.

One Spring Saturday morning Neill arrived at Misso's early. They had made plans for a picnic by the river. The previous night, Misso had gone to some circus thing with her oldest brother. It rankled because Neill wanted Misso every night. Every. Goddamn. Night. He wanted her by his side, and he wanted her sexually. Neill did not pout or make Misso feel bad about her odd family evening and he stayed home by himself, sure that the entire world was having a better Friday night. He rented a Bergman film, ate a fried chicken TV dinner. He was miserable.

Saturday morning, Neill found Misso already outside. Dressed in a loose t-shirt and man's pajama pants, she was sitting on the front porch blowing bubbles. It was a childish thing unless you meant it ironically. Even better if one meant it as irony, yet still found joy in it. Misso existed along this spectrum, somewhere between childish joy and nose-thumbing adulthood. Was she propped outside for Neill's benefit? Was she posing? Was she saying, here I am, Neill, simple, pleasurable, diffident Misso Anthill? Are you sure you want me, this simple puerile me, as your mate?

Let's not overthink.

"Hello, Love," Neill said. He kissed her. She offered up her lips while her hand still sent the dipper into the soap. As Neill unstooped, a jet-trail of bubbles rose around his face.

"Tee hee," Misso said.

"Who's out there?" The voice from inside was Helen's.

"It's Neill," Neill said.

Helen came out onto the porch. She was wearing a loose dress that was so short her cotton-covered vulva winked at Neill.

"Coming with us?" Helen said, bussing Neill's cheek and holding her lips there a beat too long.

"I'm sorry," Neill said.

"It was only a kiss on the cheek," Helen said, gliding away, elegantly smirking.

"Going where?" Neill said.

"We're going to go look at Voodoo Village. Misso is too chicken to do it at night."

"I thought we were going to have a picnic," Neill said.

"Helen's been planning this for a week," Misso said, as if Neill were mistaken. As if Neill was a vulgarian to bring it up.

"Ok," Neill said.

"Oh, now, Bunky," Misso said. She finally rose and took Neill's arm. "Can we all picnic afterward?"

"Who is all?"

"Who's all in there?" Misso asked Helen.

"Kristi, Misty, Richie, Chella—is Hank still here?"

"Richie," Neill said.

"Hank spent the night, I think," Misso said. "Go pound on Chella's door. I certainly heard them both in there last night."

"I'll pass," Neill said. He turned and moved toward his car waiting for Misso to call him back or follow him to the car. He rounded his car and looked back. The porch was empty. In the air between him and the house one iridescent bubble floated like a broken promise.

Misso in Bed

A section called 'Misso in Bed' could just as well be about her sleeping, her ability to make sleep an art, an *occupation*. Instead, we will talk about how Neill initiated the inactive artist into sexual ways that were, at that time, outside her ken.

The evening of the broken picnic playdate, Neill stayed home by himself and tried to read. He tried to watch nitwit television. He tried to watch highbrow films. He tried to write a poem but it was dead before it left his pen; it wasn't written in blood but in embalming fluid. He ended up spread-eagle on his bed inhaling the redolent lees from their congress of days ago. Neill had not washed the bed clothing since the first time he detected what would become for him a narcotic. (He did not wash them for over a year after they split up, ed.)

The next day, Misso called and was eager to see her 'boyfriend.' Neill responded coolly.

"Come on, Teddy Bear," Misso cooed.

"What do you want to do?" Neill asked.

"I don't know," Misso answered as he knew she would. Just once, please, *passion*. Just once *desire*.

"Go get deli fried chicken and watch a movie?" Neill offered.

"Yes, let's do that."

"Ok," Neill said. "I'll come by around five."

"Ham," Misso said.

"Pardon?"

"I don't want fried chicken."

So, they ate together on Misso's futon and watched *Born Yesterday*.

"She's funny," Misso said. Neill was pleased by this simple affirmation for his choice.

After eating, propped on pillows, they lay side by side. Misso was wearing a faded Janis Joplin t-shirt and men's boxer shorts. Her long copper legs were as enticing as the coming of spring and as natural. Neill wanted to lie between them.

It was Misso who made the first move, such as it was. She put her hand on Neill's stomach and rubbed it idly, the way one pet's someone else's cat. Neill put a hand to one of Misso's thighs.

Soon, they were kissing, Neill's tongue attempting to fill the watery chasm of Misso's mouth. Misso even used a little tongue back.

Neill looked at his love. "You're so freckly," he said.

"Ugh. I know. I hate it."

"You're beautiful, Misso. So beautiful."

When they were naked and the movie had reached its apotheosis, Neill clutched Misso to him, gripping each cheek of her ass and pulling her half on top of him. He could feel the fire between those burnt sienna thighs. Her pubic hair was dripping. From the rear he put a finger inside her, pulling her closer.

Meanwhile, Little Neill was straining against Misso's flat, smooth midsection like a mad dog on a leash. So far, Misso had not even touched the cur.

When this occurred it was difficult for Neill to say why. It was partly his frustration that he wanted to force her, ahem, hand, and partly Misso had apparently entered the evening with a new goal in mind: if they were going to continue with this tomfoolery called sex then she was going to learn a bit about it.

At any rate, at this point Misso's hand wrapped Neill's rigid cock. She just held it the way a five-year old would his bat at t-ball. She just held it firmly. They both were still for a moment or two.

Neill found her Caribbean eyes and looked into them.

"Can I show you what to do?"

Misso smiled. Neill put his hand gently over hers and coached her gently.

"Like this, up and down, lightly at first. Play with the head a bit but—carefully. It is most tender."

Misso did as instructed.

"Mm," Neill offered further.

"Is this right?" Misso said and she laughed that laugh of hers, which was a cross between rain and the silverware drawer turned upside down.

"Very right," Neill said.

Then, boldly, possibly just to really see what it was all about, she moved her hand to Neill's balls and squeezed them.

"G-gently," Neill said.

"Sorry."

"Keep going."

She did. She began to alternate ball action with pinion action. And the more she did it the more interested she became. She lifted her head to watch what her hand was doing as if it was a trick being performed by someone else.

Neill was enjoying the roughshod handjob—it was inexpert but the more fascinated Misso became the more Neill's prick shook. He debated about a blowjob lesson, too, but decided that this was plenty for one night. He was surprised really, and pleased, and unsure how they got here.

"Fsshhhhh," Neill said. Misso's hand stopped. "K-keep going, God, keep going."

She did. And soon, Neill's little fountain was putting on its show. Misso watched every drop of sputum erupt and shower down again. It was like a slow-motion explosion in an action film. When Neill had jerked his final jerk—and sometimes Neill really went into spasms—Misso smiled and put her finger in the viscous puddle in Neill's little patch of belly-button hair.

"Whoa, Nelly," she said. She looked at Neill. Was she seeking approval for so elementary a response?

"Great handjob!" Neill said.

Now Misso grew shy—or bored again. "What do you want to do now?" she asked. "Maybe we should go to sleep since you have to work tomorrow."

"Or I could eat you till you come," Neill said.

"Oh yes! Let's do that first," Misso said. She was feigning childlike joy but it worked for them both. That night was one of the best times together they ever had. As she was falling asleep, Misso whispered, "I love you, you know."

Neill was pretty sure she was awake enough to mean it.

Sex Curricula

To say that Misso wanted to learn about sex from Neill has two flaws. First, Neill, despite his experience, did not feel pedagogical toward his paramour. He felt love for her, he felt stirred by her, he felt compelled by her. He entered an emotional territory that he had never ventured into before, not with Victoria, nor Dinah, nor his darling Syrie, nor Marcane and certainly not with Chara Winsky, who, in retrospect Neill felt had bewitched him. She was black magic.

Secondly, Misso was already a formidable young woman with power of her own and her own vision of what life should or could be. (Did Neill really believe this part? It nagged at him.)

Nevertheless, their lovemaking now took on a pattern. Misso was much more engaged and was using her hands and mouth to make love in ways that even surpassed Neill's tender admonitions.

Once Misso found out how to take a cock into her mouth, things changed for the better. They became closer. Like lovers before them, when feeling that a line of propriety had been crossed, they were a club of two, insulated and apart from the rest of the world, which streamed by like a bad radio playlist.

"Misso, my love," Neill said into Misso's aromatic shoulder. "What about oral sex?"

Misso laughed (perhaps) a nervous laugh. "I love what you do."

"That's a good thing."

"I know what you're asking. I don't know."

"You don't want to."

"I don't know. That's what I mean. I don't know how to do it and I guess I fear it a little."

"Would you like to try? "

"I know it's very pleasurable for you."

"It is."

"Take it slow."

"Of course. I love you. This is not a test. There is no danger of failing."

"Ok," Misso said.

They lay there naked, side by side like sarcophagi.

"I guess you want me to try now."

Neill laughed.

"Come here." He took her in his arms. "Put your hand around me."

"Jesus, you're so hard. This is unprecedented hard."

"Perhaps in anticipation."

"Oh Jesus."

"Go slow. Use your lips and tongue to start. If you don't like it, quit."

Misso sighed. He rose onto her elbows and eyed her prey. It was mocking her with its cyclopean visage. It was daring her. *Damn you*, she thought.

She glanced back once, her dimples like quotation marks around her dying words, spoken with pluck and aplomb. "Here we go," she muttered.

She put her lips on the head of Neill's penis. She ran her tongue around it. Neill's sigh filled the room. It threatened to drown out the REM record on the stereo.

Holding the club near the bottom, she slowly put it into her mouth. She went a millimeter too far and gagged slightly. Neill petted her naked shoulder, which shown like dusky golden fleece in the candlelight.

Misso went down again. This time she moved it around a bit. Neill felt tongue. He felt lips. He felt a slight suction and then Misso began to push it in and out of her mouth. Neill groaned and spread his legs wide, as if to let the world see what was happening, as if to hang his balls in the wind, in pride and celebration.

Misso found a tempo. It was working. Neill couldn't tell if she was enjoying herself but Misso could tell Neill was. And then the age-old conundrum: does the man go ahead and come in the woman's mouth when it's the first time?

Neill was contemplating this as he began to shoot warm jets down sweet Misso's throat. Neill flipped and flopped. He tossed and turned. He tossed again, hesitated and then flipped and flopped again. His twitching lasted about 30 seconds.

Slowly Misso raised her head. A trickle of semen exited her mouth. She was intent on Neill's face.

"Are you ok?" she whispered.

"Wait," Neill said, raising a hand as if it weighed too much.

After a repose, Neill spoke: "Sweetheart. That was—it was—"

"I did ok."

"Y-yes. You did ok. You got into the spirit of the thing anyway."

"Well, Neill, I mean, how could I stop? No way I was stopping in the middle of those animal sounds."

Neill laughed and then Misso laughed. She lay back down beside him.

"You're sleepy now," she said.

"You're a wonderful lover," Neill said. And they slept in each other's arms, while suspended above them were the infinite masks of God.

The next morning, as Misso bathed, Neill spent the entire time with his nose buried in his bedclothes. The pungent salmagundi there was now ineradicable. It was beyond human understanding. Diabolism had entered in.

The Pattern Established

Here is the pattern that was established. Forgive its clinical and graphic elucidation. Know this: love bloomed between Neill and Misso. Misso now said, "I love you," almost as much as Neill. (No lover Neill ever had—*in his entire life*—said "I love you' to him as much as he said it to them. Why not? Kurt Vonnegut said that saying "I love you" to someone was like holding a gun to their head because they *had to* answer and answer only one way. Kurt was a little, how shall we say, cynical?)

And now, Neill and Misso were together almost every night (including dinner with Neill's parents on Sundays [more on this later]) and the desire seemed mutual. No, it *was* mutual.

And every night, after whatever they did, dinner, movie, play, concert, they went to bed and slept together and woke together.

Between the sleeping and the waking, this is the program they established:

- (1) Foreplay once they were both naked and aroused. Hands and French kissing.

(2) Neill licked down Misso's body, either from the front or the rear, and ended his tongue's journey in Misso's musky and warm and sopping cunnicle.

(3) Just before Misso came she would touch Neill's shoulder.

(4) Neill rose and, straddling Misso's impeccable pocket-sized breasts, he placed his peacemaker inside Misso's mouth.

(5) Misso gave with some gamarouche until Neill was about to come.

(6) Neill quickly switched positions and entered Misso in standard missionary fashion. (Sometimes, if the urgency of their inner storm allowed it, Neill turned Misso over and achieved his favorite sex position, the rear entry, where he got to stare at Misso's back, which was so eyesome sometimes he wept, not to mention he got to hold her by her well-rounded bunchy.)

(7) They worked that action until they both came.

(8) And they saw that it was good.

Shlomo, Crow, Bidden, and Neill

"Sad bastard bachelor club now in session."

"Speak for yourself, Shlomo," Neill said.

"I do. I always do."

"Crow's married—*still*—and Bidden, my man, has a new woman."

"Is this true?" Shlomo asked. He was genuinely interested because, despite his solipsistic posturing, he really cared about his friends. (On the subject of solipsism, Shlomo once said, "A man who doesn't look in the Kleenex after he blows is not very interested in himself.")

"I don't know," Bidden said. Because he never does.

"Godia? Isn't that her name? I've seen her and she is a peach. Beautiful, I'd even say," Neill was feeling expansive.

"She is a peach," Bidden admitted.

"With jugs."

"A peach with jugs. Yes, that's Godia. Why aren't you with Misso tonight? I thought you were inseparable."

"She's doing something with the MCA crowd. I wasn't invited."

"And that rankles."

"No, not really, not much anymore. Things are—things are truly great."

"I'm hearing a love song."

"I'm hearing bells."

"I'm hearing the final gavel."

"And you're happy too, I guess?" Shlomo asked Crow.

"Married," Crow said. "Sure, happy. Wife, child, husband. Father, son, and Holy Ghost."

"How is the holy ghost? How is my namesake?" Neill asked.

"He misses you," Crow said, and then finished his beer.

"I know. I'm coming over. Invite me and my woman for dinner, and I'm there."

"We'll do that. She won't want to come though."

Neill was provisionally stunned.

"What do you mean?" he asked. "She loves you guys."

There was a consensual silence.

"What aren't you saying?" Neill asked. Now, he couldn't finish his hamburger.

"Nothing," Crow said. "Forget it. We'd love to have you."

Shlomo looked at Neill. It was that caring friend look again.

"Neill, she doesn't—well—she doesn't really *like* your friends much, does she?"

Dinner at Crow's?

"Crow says little Neill misses me. He wants us to come to dinner."

"He wants you to come to dinner."

"No, why would you say that? He specifically said both of us."

"Ok. We'll go to dinner. His wife doesn't like me."

"I don't know where that's coming from. All my friends like you."

Misso sniggered. "Ok, Boyo. They love me."

"They like you. Only I love you."

Misso shot a glance at Neill. He smiled his rascal smile. Everything was ok.

Dinner at the Folks'?

There had existed at the Rhymer's house, for Neill's entire life, a quotidian ritual called Sunday Dinner. Everyone took it very seriously. (Though Neill's mother threatened almost every Sunday to end the ritual, complaining to all how ungrateful everyone was.) Neill had run a sequence of girlfriends through this gauntlet. Some did well:

Virginia had been part of the family and everyone assumed, though they were young, that a marriage was in the offing.

Syrie reveled in it and was beloved (as previously indicated).

Marcane only went once. She was embarrassed. "They were looking at me with only one question in their minds: who is this old woman and what does she really want?" "They were not," Neill countered, though she was right. "I can't believe you came from them." "Why?" "Well, Bunny, they're so...*traditional.*"

Chara hated Sunday night dinners. Sometimes she went and sometimes she did not.

"Mom's making spaghetti and meatballs this Sunday," Neill said. "It means she is really trying. Her spaghetti and meatballs should be insured by Lloyd's of London."

"I've had the spaghetti and meatballs," Misso said.

"Then you know."

"I might be doing something with Helen this Sunday."

"Might be," Neill said. He suspected that this was spur-of-the-moment invention.

"Yes. I'll let you know later."

"Ok," Neill said. He was irritated.

In bed that night Misso was only going through the motions. Her pussy got wet enough however (when did it not?) and everything came off, though most of the enthusiasm was generated by Neill. When it came to step 4 Misso reluctantly took Neill's persistent peepee into her mouth. When he moved toward step 6 Neill put it into Misso a tad aggressively. It was part anger and part prayer. He wanted her to get excited. He wanted her to want him. He was fretting.

Misso came like a kitten. It might have been feigned. Neill dismounted post spasm.

As Neill began to cover them for the night and turn out the light Misso spoke, softly, "Neillo, I need to go home tonight."

Neill's apoplexy rose instantaneously. He tried to control his voice.

"Of course you do," he said.

"Never mind. I'll stay if you're going to throw a fit."

"I'm not throwing a fit."

"You're upset. I'm sorry. I don't want to upset you. Forget I said anything."

"Why do you need to go home?"

"I don't."

Misso settled under the covers. Neill turned out the light and they moved together because it was habit. Neill held onto her like she was a crucifix. Like he needed a fix. Like he needed fixing. His mind jumbled and he slept. His dreams pell-mell.

Around 1:30 Neill woke suddenly. What was the matter?

He moved upward and it was as if someone had stabbed him in the eye with a knitting needle. He rarely got headaches this bad but when he did they were monstrous. He sat up and tried to hold his head perfectly still.

He squeezed his eyes shut tightly, though he knew it was better if he relaxed.

Behind his eyes a supernova exploded. The pain almost made him whimper.

"What is it?" Misso said, stirring.

Had he whimpered? "A goddamn headache," Neill whispered. "A bad one."

Neill was sitting up, propped up by his reading bed pillow. Misso stroked his temple, then his arm. She was genuinely concerned.

She put her head on Neill's stomach, resting it there lightly, and stroked his arm. Neill began to relax some.

Then Misso began to touch Neill's flaccid penis, poking it gently with one finger, petting its little head. She ran the finger down its soft length. It stirred.

She covered it and Neill's scrotum with her soft hand. She was treating it as gently as one would when blanketing a baby.

As it stiffened, Misso moved slowly over Neill. "Shh, shh," she whispered. Then, she did something unprecedented. She leaned over Neill and placed his willy between her small but pliant breasts. She looked up at Neill, whose eyes were now open. She smiled sweetly and bade Neill to move softly against her while she pinched her breasts together. She licked the head until it was damp and slid more easily.

Neill followed her lead (she *never* lead!) and soon he was close to orgasming between her tits. Misso's blue, oceanic eyes opened wide. The tide was coming in.

Neill began to spurt over her neck and tits. He came a nice quarter cup and Misso stayed in position for a while as the white flow moved down her dark, freckled chest. Then, she lay against Neill's chest and they were stuck together with Neill's juice.

"Thank you," Neill said, quietly.

Misso was already back asleep.

A Bad Night at the Ridgeway Four

Neill and Misso had plans to see *The Cotton Club* at the Ridgeway Four. Misso was, naturally, as natural as light or kidney stones, tolerably tolerant of their plans. What would she rather do? That is a good question. Take photographs perhaps. (Though photography was, at this time, her medium, she never once took a picture of Neill. This is curious in itself. In another book it would be worth discussing.)

During the car ride Misso was practically speechless. She sat with her pretty knees against the dash, hugging herself as if for comfort or security.

Neill had written yet another poem about his patootie. It sat, folded like a newspaper, between them. He had not mentioned it yet. Perhaps, it would break through the indifference. Who wouldn't want a love poem written for them?

"I wrote this for you," Neill said. He handed her the folded poem.

She gave him a quizzical smile. It could have said, "Oh honey how sweet." It equally could have said, "You burden me with your literary love."

She read it. Neill concentrated on his driving. He had never driven so carefully, so mindfully, so fully invested in the beauty and strength of his ability to drive a car.

"It's beautiful," Misso said.

"Do you really like it?" Neill said. Why couldn't he have just nodded? Or said, simply, "Thank you."

"I don't know why you see me this way," Misso said.

This shut Neill up. He patted her thigh and turned off Poplar onto the loop that would take them directly into the movie theater parking lot.

The movie was good. It was colorful and bright. The music was Jubal-ation. It filled Neill with imaginary and inexplicable currents. And there was Diane Lane.

On the ride home, Neill felt good despite his semi-comatose love-of-his-life.

"I loved that," Neill gushed. "The music was so—" Neill waved his hand around in the air. Misso smiled.

"Did you like it? I felt like I was witnessing, partly, the birth of jazz."

"It was kinda violent," Misso said.

"Yeah," Neill agreed.

The streetlights turned orange and then yellow and then a kind of citrine putrefied uncolor. The streets were wobbling.

"Do you really like your poem?" Poor Neill.

Birth (and Death) | 425

Misso didn't look at him. Her face wore clouds for powder.

"I left it in the theater."

Neill was now himself speechless. He started to sputter a response. Then, he bit his tongue. Literally. It hurt like hell and brought tears to his eyes.

"I'm sorry," Misso said. "I don't deserve your poems."

They returned to Neill's. Neill pouted. Misso sat sunk in her own Misso-ness.

Finally, Neill said, "It's late. Let's just go to sleep. I have to work in the morning."

"Neill," Misso said. "Can I sleep at my house tonight?"

Neill still had his keys in his hand. He heaved the keys against the wall where they shattered the glass of his glass-and-clips framed Brueghel print, "Children's Games." Misso flinched. Neill's hand was, inexplicably, in a fist. Furthermore, his fist was in the air between himself and Misso.

"Go ahead," Misso said. "Hit me. You want to hit me."

Neill looked at his fist for the first time. Was it his? Like Lady Macbeth, he did not recognize his own weapon.

He moved around Misso, found the keys in the shards of glass, and picked them up.

"Let's go," he said.

It had started to drizzle. Neill was driving angry. At McLean and Peabody, he did not stop in time and gently slid into the car in front of him, the way the male hippo sidles up to the female. It was enough to jolt both Neill and Misso and, unfortunately, the driver of the other car.

"FUCK!" Neill said.

Misso put her hand on Neill's arm. "Are you ok?" she said. Her first impulse was more selfless than Neill's. She was genuinely concerned that Neill had hurt himself.

Neill got out and the other driver got out. Neill thought he was going to throw up. The other driver was a woman about Neill's age. She wore a scowl as she exited the car. She looked at her fender. There was no damage.

"I'm so sorry," Neill said.

"It looks to be ok," the woman said. "No harm no foul."

"Thank you," Neill said.

"It's ok," the other woman said. "Neill."

She got back into her car. Only later, after he had calmed down, Neill realized that she was a member of The Gorgeous Young Housewives' Book Club. He thought her name was Donna.

At Misso's, Neill and Misso sat at the curb, the car running.

"I'm sorry, Neill," Misso said. "I'm not good enough for you. Really. You're wonderful, you know."

Neill looked into her pellucid blue eyes, cornflower blue if the cornflower had been plucked and left on the porch railing in the sun.

"I love you, Misso. I love you more than I have ever loved anyone in my life. I want you to marry me and I want you to have a child with me. I want a little girl with your eyes and freckles and spring-loaded hair. I want her to have your dimples, cut by a jeweler. I love you. I don't ever want to be without you."

Misso began to cry quietly.

"I love you, too, Neill," she said. "I really do."

"It's gonna be alright," Neill said. He was willing it.

"I know," Misso said. She leaned over and kissed Neill hard, pushing her tongue into his mouth, a small treat she rarely offered.

"You still want to sleep alone?" Neill asked, lowly gink.

"Just for tonight," Misso said.

She was irresolute about some things, Neill thought, for such a passive woman. As she got out of the car, he thought, Fuck you, Misso. Fuck you and fuck you.

Out to Eat and then the Orgone Chamber

"You're chewing the hell out of that," Neill said.

"I don't eat a lot of meat. It's—sticking in my mouth."

"I thought maybe you were a Fletcherite."

Misso got the bite to go down the chute. She looked at her date, her boyfriend, her lover, her papa gateau.

"Just one more thing I don't understand." She sat slope-shouldered, almost slatternly. "Tell me again why you like me."

Neill started to explain Fletcherizing but bit his tongue. Instead, he took Misso's hand. He rubbed her pretty fingers between his as if they were made from fine material. They were made from fine material.

Eating out was a treat. The evening held great promise. Misso's parents were at a hot air balloon show in Missouri with the male siblings, and Mehrnoosh and Misso, who wanted to go with them but decided at the last minute to stay behind (Neill wanted it to be because of him—perhaps this is small of Neill), so they were housesitting. They had the Addams Family house (The Anthill) to themselves.

Walking into its dark, cavernous, and enveloping aura after dinner felt transgressive. And, for Neill, transgressive meant sex. They went into Misso's room where she tossed her bag onto the bed. The room was still decorated as if Misso had not left. It was a younger version of the now adult artist, a room whose breasts were just developing. No pinks but some snapshots of Michael Stipe and Bob Marley.

Neill put his arms around Misso and kissed her. She kissed back almost hungrily, what passed for hungrily in Misso Anthill. She wanted sex. This was promising and Neill was as giddy as a teen.

"Your bed?" Neill asked.

"No, let's look around," Misso said, and took Neill's hand, leading him into the forest in search of the witch's candy house.

Of course, the art room was off-limits (it was locked anyway) and no one else's bedroom seemed proper. There was a large den with a good size TV and a couch off the Queen Mary. Neill made wide eyes and nodded toward the couch. Misso looked at it, appraisingly. Eventually she shook her head, no.

They went to the upper floor. It was like something from *The Haunting*. Neill expected a corpse to descend from above at the top of the old staircase.

They walked back down the stairs in a bit of a funk. The kitchen, which always seems adventurous, can be very uncomfortable. They stood leaning against its shiny wood counter and Neill waited for Misso's ruling. He was both apprehensive and enlivened.

Misso's gaze traveled out the sliding glass door to the backyard, which glowed silvery in the moonlight. And Neill's gaze followed hers, and they both settled in the same place. The Orgone Chamber glimmered eerily. It was lit with spooklight.

"Might be fun," Misso said.

Running outside like kids about to jump in the pool, Neill grabbed at Misso's pleasing backside before him and caught a handful of sweet cheek. She squealed and did a 360 turn. Her dress, which was more like a large, gauzy scarf, came off in Neill's hand and she was there, in God's grey backyard, clad in a t-shirt and thin panties. Her legs were the legs of ur-woman. They were so shapely Neill almost tumbled like thrown dice, snake eyes.

Misso opened the door still facing Neill and backed into the chamber. There was a single seat, like an outhouse's, and she settled there, reaching out for Neill's hand. Neill entered also and closed the door behind him. There was very little room to move, which was a challenge, and there was also a stillness inside that came perhaps from some mystical place. It was very hot inside. The inner walls were decorated with lunatic pictograms that meant nothing to Neill. He put his finger to one and felt its ridged surface.

"Paint?" he said.

"My dad's runes," Misso said. "Come here."

Neill sat in Misso's lap. She put her arms around him and held him still. His heart, once beating a jagged foxtrot, began to calm. Misso's lips sought Neill's and found them easy enough, eager enough, hungry for her. Their kiss slopped slobber over the sides the way one settles into a bathtub that is too full.

Misso began to undress Neill. This was unique. She *wanted* it.

Neill pulled Misso's shirt over her head. After some bumping and maneuvering they managed to unclothe each other. They were standing, Misso's flaming legs straddling the chair. They kissed again. A current ran through them. Neill couldn't remember ever feeling that powerful before. His erection was anthracite.

Misso reached down for it.

"Jesus," she said. "What is in there?"

"Love juice," Neill said, and Misso laughed. "The magic of the leprechaun. The power of Cenote. The strength of Easter Island. The turgidity of Angkor Wat. Or Some Wat, anyway."

Misso let him riff. She was smiling.

"I feel it too," she said.

And so she turned and put her hands against the wall and presented Neill with her archetypal backside and, legs akimbo, began to cantillate softly under her breath. It was not words exactly. Neill was unsure what was going on. It was almost music. He tried to listen but instead he saw that vaginal juices were running down Misso's thighs. She was literally dripping with lust. Her singsong drew Neill's magic erection into that velvety, wet, fragrant place. It slid into her like the sword going into the stone. For a strange, mystic moment, Neill thought perhaps he would never be able to pull it out. He thought, in a flash of sexual *presque vu*, that Misso's enchanted pussy was going to catch and hold him there until he withered and died.

Neill prayed that he would go in exactly this way.

As they swayed and bumped and shook, enjoined like a pegged loghouse, Misso kept up the strange chant which was half breath and half prayer. Misso came once, shaking against the wall, her hands drumming to her mouth's tune, shivering in her nakedness, but their bond held tight. Hours passed. They had the power of Medieval European sacerdotalism. They were stronger than death. They were full of life-force.

Misso came three more times. Neill's eyes rolled back in his head and when they returned he could only watch the elemental beauty and power of his unbreakable prick going in and out of the hot cave below Misso's supernal ass. He watched sweat run down Misso's bowed back and dive off the ledge of her rump. When it hit the chair below, it formed rainbows.

Finally—and it might have been at the witching hour—Neill felt his sputum ascending. It traveled from his heart to his kidneys to his spleen, where it veered sharply to the left, rode the top of the large intestine, formed a knot of lightning at the base of his spine and finally—finally—finally—burst forth and sprayed the godlike insides of beautiful Misso Anthill's climbing immaculate body.

They collapsed slowly onto the Orgone chair, tangled like new kittens. At some point, they formed a marble pieta, froze there with Neill's mouth suckling a tough little nipple. Their bodies lit briefly like the summer's first fireflies, faded out and returned them to golden, humming flesh.

Like sleepwalkers, they exited the Orgone Chamber naked as crystal just as the sun rose in the East, far away over Stonehenge and the Omayyad Mosque and Kyöpelinvuori (The Flemish Ghost Mountain) and the Nazca Plains, and lit our lovers with godlight, as they stumbled along the Earth's vortices and into Misso's childhood bed, where they fell asleep in each other's' arms and slept straight through a whole day and half.

When they awoke, they did not speak immediately about what had happened. They looked into each other's eyes, eyes now bottomless and photic.

"I want our daughter to have your baby-blue peepers," Neill said, not for the first time.

"Neill," Misso said. One junkie heartbeat separated his name and her next thought. "I love you, Neill Rhymer."

Confab and Consanguinity at Shomo's Garage Apartment

Shlomo's new digs were a tad depressing. Austere, as if by design, the place held what the writer called "all I really need:" a bed, a desk with a typewriter, a few pots and pans, dishes and cups, a closet half-full of Shlomo's indifferent clothing, and a small bookcase of 'essentials,' mostly Dickens, Joyce, and the American Jewish writers.

"I'm not cutting into writing time, am I?" Neill asked. It was 11 a.m. and Neill knew to never disturb his friend in the mornings.

"I'm pretty much done for the day," Shlomo said. "I'm pretty much done for good."

"Balderdash," Neill assured him.

"Actually, I was going to call you," Shlomo said, handing Neill a dash of weak ice tea in a jelly glass. "I ran into someone last night."

"Here is where I ask who. Or is it whom?"

"Chara," Shlomo said. He tapped his front tooth, once, twice.

"Chara?" Neill said as if Shlomo had mentioned Bigfoot.

"Isn't that her name? Your ex?"

"Oh yes, quite right. Chara. It's just not a name I was prepared to hear from you today."

"It gets better. Or worse. Things seldom get better."

"You fucked her."

Shlomo tapped his tooth once. He bit his thumb. He was not looking at Neill.

"Wait, you mean I am right?"

"No, no," Shlomo said. "Of course, I didn't."

"Where did you run into her?"

"At the North End. I went down to hear Sid play and she was there with a girlfriend. The girlfriend knew you, too, but I can't remember her name."

"Who were you with? Or is it whom?"

"Locker. You know Locker?"

Shlomo had a large coterie of old friends, most of them reprobates or drunks or other varieties of lost sheep. Locker was the one who, at the last signing Shlomo did at The Book Shelf, ran from the front door yelping like a maniac, headed straight for Shlomo and grabbed his balls in a monkey-grip. Neill hated Locker.

"Did you talk to Chara?"

"I did (tap tap), which is why I wanted to call you."

"Get to it."

"I wanna ask her out."

"Shit, man, you don't need to ask me that, though you are a gentleman and a pal to do so."

"It's ok then?"

"More than ok."

"It's just that I'm—I'm—to borrow your phrase—*flesh-lonely*."

"I understand."

"You're good with it. Of course, you're good with it because you have Misso keeping you slaked."

"Well."

"Oh no. Trouble in paradise? I thought it was going so great. I saw the two of you walking hand in hand the other day and I thought you looked like Hero and Leander."

"I want to marry her," Neill said. He said it as if he was talking about a death sentence.

"Then?"

"I don't know. She's so—passive. So—*not there* sometimes."

"She is a little ethereal. Hell, she's only 14."

"I know she's young. It's more than that. It's like loving someone on TV, like falling for Gidget or Bailey Quarters. I can burn with real passion but she's not—*real*."

"Perhaps it's not the best time to talk about bedding your ex."

"Doesn't matter. You want sex from her? That's all?"

"I'm a shitheel."

"No, I think it's ok. She is very, very sexual. When she's not being mean."

"You told me she was a tiger in bed."

"She'll strip your gears. She could suck the eyes off a die."

At The Book Shelf

"Do you have romance novels?"

"Yes, ma'am. Back there in the mass market paperbacks."

"Hm, no, not like these. I don't know these authors."

"Who do you like to read?"

"Barbara Cartland. You carry her books?"

"No, ma'am. Nor Harlequins. But I understand that Kathleen Woodiwiss and Rosemary Rogers are very good."

"No, young man. Those books are too thick. I don't like it when the words get in the way. Plus—there's the other thing."

"The other thing?"

"The bedroom thing."

"Ah. Well, I can't advise you there. I mean about books without such things."

"Barbara Cartland. Now, there's a writer. No smut. But great stories and interesting heroines."

"Yes ma'am."

"Of course, she is not always great. I read the first one and fell in love with her. The second one was good too. I didn't like the third quite as much but numbers four and five were up to par. I don't know about number seven. I am still thinking about that one. Numbers eight through eleven were just ok. I really loved number twelve. You'd like that one I think—"

"Yes'm—"

"But thirteen was, oh my, it was so good. I didn't like fourteen or fifteen but I think sixteen is one of her best. Seventeen I don't remember too much about. I think I had a cold when I read that one. Eighteen and nineteen I read in one sitting back to back because it was when Mr. Fortner was out of town. When he came back he brought me numbers 20 through 30. Let me tell you about number 20...."

Wednesday Night Ball

"Are you playing basketball tonight," Misso said into the phone. She sounded as if she had just awakened, or was just about to conk.

"I am. Though it's starting to be that time of year when the gym is like the devil's kitchen," Neill said, as he bagged a paperback copy of an Anthony Burgess novel for a pimpled teen and his rail-thin girlfriend. "Thanks," he said.

"For what?" Misso yawned.

"Not you. A customer. So, yes, basketball. Be over as usual afterwards for a shower and a sandwich and a snog?"

"Maybe not this time," Misso said.

Neill felt a familiar thump in his cardiac chamber.

"You have plans?"

"I might. I might have plans."

"With whom?"

"I might just sleep."

"It's 3:30."

"I mean, I might just sleep and then make plans. I am too sleepy to make plans now."

"So you don't have plans yet?"

"What?"

"I said. Never mind. I'll play basketball and call you after."

"I might not be here."

"I'm getting that."

"Ok then."

"Ok," Neill said, and he took a deep breath.

The line went dead.

In the Dark Room

A few nights later, Neill visited Misso while she was working in the dark room at Memphis College of Art. She didn't exactly invite him but she didn't say not to come and, at this time, to Neill, that felt like fervor.

"That familiar dark room smell," Neill said. He was sitting on a tall stool with no back and he felt off-balance. He curled his legs around the legs of the stool but this made his vertigo worse.

"You've been in a dark room before," Misso said, without looking up.

"Sure. Crow used to have one in his home."

"Mm."

"So, are you hungry? Do you want to grab some food when you're done here?"

"It's kinda late."

"Have you eaten?"

"No, I haven't. Fuck."

"What?"

"This is—this is shit. Too much time."

"Sorry. Is this crucial?"

Misso looked up. She seemed to not recognize Neill. She moved from developing tray to enlarger.

"So, you hungry?" Neill tried again. He was really trying to keep some modicum of light-heartedness in his voice.

"Yes. But I am gonna be a while here."

"Ok," Neill said. Was anything just decided?

He watched her again for a while. She didn't look at him during this time.

"Want me to go fetch some food and we can eat it here?"

She didn't answer.

"Misso?"

She looked up, swimming to the surface, her saucery eyes wide as if she were tripping.

"I want to finish this," she said, in sepulchral tones.

"I should just go then," Neill said. She didn't look up.

"I said I should just go then. Got the new Paul Auster I am eager to start."

"I'll talk to you tomorrow," Misso said.

Neill stood.

"Call me in the morning," Misso said.

Neill stood by his stool.

"You can open the door now," Misso said.

A Sea Change in Neill

Possibly, probably, we should have mentioned this earlier. A sea change had come over Neill. Neill, who before time wanted only to sleep with as many women as possible, to stay on the move, to keep the future at bay through sheer willpower and desire, suddenly found himself wanting something more stable: marriage, children.

He began to think this way before his aborted love affair with Chara. She just happened to be there at the wrong time (or the right, depending on your politics). He thought he wanted to marry her because he was ready, suddenly, as we said, to get married, and he was with Chara.

Thank God for her reliable volatility.

So, is this the case with Misso? She is just there at the right (or wrong) time?

No, Misso was a Grand Passion. She entered Neill like a drug and he was dizzily in love with her, body and mind and heart (o defective heart.) Neill, poor cat's-paw, thought she was his one and only perfect mate because he was so turned-on by her (not just physically, though he was certainly physically—he could get excited just glimpsing her ankle). He was not the first human to fall this way. He will not be the last. But, it still begs the question: why does this happen and what does it mean? (That's two questions. On its knees on the rough chancery floor it begs both.)

An Afternoon Party

Helen and one of the transient roommates decided to throw a backyard party one Saturday afternoon. Misso seemed noncommittal about it.

"You don't have to come," she told Neill.

That afternoon turned out to be a lovely day, the notorious Memphis humidity temporarily drained. And there were a lot of people. Some guy, perhaps the boyfriend of one of the transient roommates, fired up a grill on which there were more veggie burgers than cow meat, more tofu than wieners. Someone else bought a tin tub full of corn on the cob. There was punch. There were tables of various dishes set upon the back lawn, just below the large wooden deck. The yard, as often is found in Midtown, was long as a bowling alley. At the back trees shaded a small area where a couple was locked in an avid enfoldment on a Topcat beach towel.

When Neill arrived Misso was sitting on the deck, talking earnestly to her brother Ram.

"Howdy," Neill said.

Misso half-turned. "Hey, Neillo. Grab a seat."

Neill scanned the yard first. He knew most of the folks, Midtown hippies and sons and daughters of older hippies, art-types, a few musicians (one a member of Panther Burns, Neill believed, and Rob Jungklas, who Neill was quite fond of), a few MCA students. He sat next to Helen and nodded to Ram, who chose to ignore the nod.

There was a tall, bosomy woman standing under a shade tree. She looked like Cher with big tits.

The story about her, Neill remembered, was that she had done adult films and also played fake bass in the female punk band, Twot. "You don't really want to watch someone you know in a porn film," Helen had said.

There was a stoner, a friend of Helen's, who, though white, sported sullied Rasta dreadlocks. His faded t-shirt said, inevitably, "Old pirates, yes, they rob I." Neill thought his name was Dreadful Gate. He recognized Neill through bleary eyes, and sauntered toward him.

"Hey, bookstore man," he said, handing Neill a muddy paw.

"Mr. Gate, right?" Neill said.

"You ever read Velikovsky?"

"Um, no, I haven't," Neill said.

Dreadful thought about this. He was disappointed in Neill.

"You read much?" he asked.

"I do," Neill said.

"He knew it all."

It took Neill a second to realize he meant Velikovsky.

"Tall order," Neill said.

"I don't follow you."

"Don't," Neill said, with a smile. "I'll have you arrested."

"You're a man," Dreadful said and moved away.

"I think you meant *the* man," Neill said to his back.

Neill began to feel out of sorts. He had no extra sorts to take their place. All his sorts were used up. Misso was practically ignoring him and his attempt to take her hand or arm was met with gentle dissuasion. She was moving away from him.

Then Sue Goorile arrived, some drugged-up youngster at her side. She greeted Neill with more enthusiasm than Misso had (strangers did as well, so...) and hugged him and Neill once more recalled her body made of snow and Johnson's baby powder. She was as white as an opal. She was an opal.

"Long time no viddy," Neill said.

"I've moved back. Did you hear?"

"I had." (He hadn't.)

"I wondered if you would be here today."

"You know me. Any excuse to party."

"Ha. You don't use party as a verb so I know you're lying."

"Check."

"I gotta tell you. I am a little surprised."

"At my being here?"

"At you're being with Misso Anthill."

"You know Misso, my wayward paramour?"

"Not well. I know how old she is."

"Don't give me any shit."

"I'm not. I just assumed after I was such a fiasco that you would date women closer to your age."

"Not a fiasco."

"Well, whatever it was."

Neill was nonplussed. A little ticked, perhaps. He wanted to talk about Marcane. He wanted to prove he wasn't just a cradle robber. But why sound defensive? Instead, he sat in a lawn chair, a tight smile on his face.

Sue's sister, Goneril, sat beside him for a while and they talked music and Tiger basketball. Goneril was one of the few women Neill knew who loved the Tigers as much as he did, good team or bad.

Someone started a badminton game. Neill loved badminton and joined in readily. Each time he zinged a shot by a younger opponent, or feathered a birdy just over the net out of reach, there were grumblings and some small admiration. Neill could play some badminton. He honed his game in his backyard with his sister AJ, his older brother and, sometimes, with his Uncle Larry, who was once upon a time the 2nd highest rated badminton player in Canada.

"Hey, hit one to me," Dreadful Gate called out, springing to his young feet.

Neill lobbed the birdy over the net. It landed at Dreadful's feet and he looked down at it for a moment.

"You ever read Richard Brautigan?" he said, looking up.

"I have," Neill said.

"Oh," Dreadful Gate said. He seemed disappointed in Neill all over again.

Neill sat down afterward, sweaty and appeased. All his bad feelings were left on the lawn. He took Misso's hand. She pretended there was something on the horizon that was engrossing, a black sun, or the long goose necks of the Martian War Machine.

The Marbleized Car

"You sound sleepy," Neill said, one morning on the phone. Misso always sounded sleepy so this was phatic conversation.

"You kept me up last night."

"Then you went home to sleep the sleep of the just."

"Still I had to get up early."

"Why?"

"'I told you. This is the day we're marbleizing the car."

"You did not."

"I meant to. We're gonna take that old Studebaker and marbleize it. Dad's got it all mapped out and we've got gobs of MCA students to help."

"You don't even drive."

"I will learn. Especially if I have a marbleized car to drive."

"Um hm."

"Are you mad?"

"No. I just. Never mind. I just thought we were doing something today, my day off and all."

"You can come help."

Neill went but he did not help. Misso was in her element. There were about a dozen fresh-faced students (Neill was sure that at least 3 of the strapping, shirtless, long-haired men were in love with Misso) helping with this strange alchemy, utilizing vats of paint that, magically, created a marbled pattern on the car's old, rough exterior. Even after he had seen it, Neill didn't understand how it worked. He had to admit the car looked pretty groovy. It looked like elegant endpapers on whitewalls. He also had to admit that he was jealous of the car, the students with their youthful grace and simple joy, and the whole Anthill world that excluded him.

Neill Confides

"It's going wrong," Neill said. "I don't know what to do."

"How is it going wrong?" Shlomo asked. "She's awfully young, you know."

Neill looked at Shlomo with a face as long as Secretariat's.

"I'm sorry, Neill. I just meant you've brought her a long way. She was inexperienced, sexually and emotionally and, for her, these aspects of her life are still in their infancy."

"You're right, I'm sure."

"Give her some time. I think she really loves you."

"Do you?"

"I really do. She's gaga for you."

"You don't use words like gaga."

"I know. I don't know where that came from."

"She has never seemed gaga. Yet, she tells me she loves me."

"Then."

"I want to marry her, Shlomo. I want to have blue-eyed Nazi children with her."

"This is the first I am hearing that."

"I've been ashamed or something to admit it. I am not sure why. It's been long coming to me, the desire to have one woman for the rest of my life."

"And you think Misso is that woman?"

"I really do. I can't imagine myself post-Misso. I think I would rather die."

"Neill."

"I know. Sorry. I just—don't know what to do."

"Don't ask me about marriage. Or even relationships."

"Still you're wiser than Time or Silence."

"Pfft."

"You're a *hochem*."

"Don't do Yiddish."

"Right."

Across Canada by Train

She chose the rosy light of afterglow to punch forward her dark agenda. It had been a rousing coupling, one of their best, Misso's hellbroth adding luster to the already pungent counterpane that Neill vowed never to launder. Misso, when flooding, could turn Neill inside out. O how his core warbled for her!

"Remember the trip I told you about?" Misso asked, her hand idly turning the curlicues of Neill's sodden belly hair.

"Mmf," Neill said, drunk on ardor.

"Across Canada by Train?"

Neill was returning to the surface.

"You're taking a train across Canada?"

"I'm sure I told you."

"I am sure you didn't."

"Well I am leaving in a week. I fly to Halifax on Saturday."

"Wait. You're flying to Canada and then taking the train—where?"

"All the way across Canada. Ends in Vancouver. Stops wherever that big rodeo thing is. I really want to see that."

"You're leaving?"

"Yes. In a week. Didn't we talk about this?"

She knew they hadn't.

"How long does this take? How long will you be gone? Wait—first—who's going with you?"

"No one."

"Alone. Across Canada."

"Yes."

"Jesus, Misso. Jesus."

"It will pass quickly. I'll miss you."

"How long will you be gone?"

"I'm not sure exactly. Three weeks?"

"Fuck."

"I'm not sure the exact time. When I get off in Vancouver, friends are picking me up and we're going to bike from Vancouver to Portland. I'm gonna stay with them in Portland for a while. Might be closer to four weeks?"

"Fuck."

"I know. I'll miss you."

"You said that."

Misso stopped talking. She took her hand off Neill's belly. Neill was tensed as if waiting for a rectal exam.

"I've always wanted to do this," Misso said, quietly, after a while.

"So you should."

"I know. It's a great opportunity," Misso said, missing the irony in Neill's voice.

"Jesus, Misso. I don't know." Neill's throat was constricted. Everything he'd ever eaten was assembling under his glottis.

Misso turned over and presented her golden, dappled shoulder to Neill. "I love you," she whispered.

She was asleep when Neill answered a moment later, "I don't know."

Missing Misso

"It's to read on the trip. See it's *Strangers on a Train*," Neill was standing anxiously by as Misso was being hustled into her father's car for the ride to the airport.

"My bag is so full," she said. "I've got two Calvinos."

Misso loved Italo Calvino. Neill suspected another man had turned her on to the Italian's enchanted word worlds.

"Ok," Neill said. Neill let the present drop to his side.

Misso was distracted, anxious. Her blue orbs were catching the pale morning sun and they seemed to glisten as if tears welled there.

"Let's go," Daddy Doddy said. "See you, Neill."

Neill was about to cry himself. Misso was halfway in the car when she turned back. She sighed (even the sigh seemed rushed) and stepped back out, kissing Neill lightly on the lips.

"Call me tonight," Neill said. "And write. Write a lot."

"I'll try," Misso said. She stepped back toward the car and then, quickly turned and said, "Here, give me the book. Thank you."

And she was gone.

Neill worked that day. He was a zombi. Not the kind who move spastically and have sunken cheeks and tear flesh off unsuspecting necks, flesh that looks like bloody spandex, but the kind whose soul has literally been absquatulated by the obeah man. He bumped into things. He came within a split second of squeezing a woman's ass as he passed her browsing through the greeting cards all because her pants, harem pants, looked vaguely like Misso's pajama bottoms and her bottom looked vaguely like Misso's bottom.

At home, he went to his room, closed the door, left the light off and lay down on his bed, his nose wrapped in the basketball-size ring of Misso's vulva lather. Have we tried to describe the scent? Neill tried, when it was clearer and not sunk into its thaumaturgic olfactory funkification.

It was woodsmoke and piss and sumac, humus and hummus, long pepper and perspiration, blood and anardana, tender pork smoke and syllabub, lemongrass and *pasilla de oacaca chile*. And, underneath that olio something plutonic, something *dark*, almost malevolent, certainly something deliciously sinful, immoral, and criminal. It was to Neill what doojee is to a junk devotee.

Did Misso call that night? She did not.

Neill stayed up till 2 a.m., grew frantic and antic and confused about time-zones and where his true love was. Amazonia?

Did Misso call the next day or night? No, again no.

Did Misso call on the third night?

You get it.

Neill was despondent.

"She'll call. She's just wrapped up in herself right now," Bidden said.

"She'll call. She's probably just overwhelmed with the logistics of getting around in a new country," Shlomo said.

"Do you believe that?" Neill asked, anxiously.

"No," Shlomo said.

A week later a postcard came from Quebec City. It was a picture of The Plains of Abraham. There was one line quickly scrawled on the other side. "*Went to Musée national des beaux-arts du Québec. love, Misso.*"

Neill, like Jesus before him, wept.

Missing Misso (2)

Neill's friends tried to console him. They paid him a lot of attention and they kept inviting him out, to dinner, to the movies, to go record store shopping. Nothing stuck to him. He was walking around inside himself and finding no joy, no outlet, no reason for doing anything. He was reading (by coincidence?) Graham Greene's *The End of the Affair*. He loved it. He hated it. He wanted to die in an opium den.

Bidden was steady. Hardly a day went by he didn't call and invite Neill out, even though Bidden was enjoying the first flush of new romance.

After two weeks and one other postcard: picture of someplace called Sioux Lookout, on the back of which Misso had scrawled, "*I saw a used bookstore today. It made me think of you.*"

This was unbearable.

Finally, Helen would not take no for an answer and told Neill one Sunday morning that they were going to spend the day together. Neill was to drive to Helen's house (Oh, it was Misso's, also, *alack*) [Helen's bug was in the shop, down with a bug] and they were going to spend the whole day running around downtown, people-watch by the river, walk the corpse of Beale Street (still rumblings about reanimating the desiccated thing), and eat at the new restaurant that was an open-air boat moored at the river's edge.

Neill drove to Helen's as if he were driving to his own execution. The house—the tarnal house—was haunted. From outside it looked malign. The windows were mouths. The front porch an abattoir. Neill didn't want to go inside. The door was open and Neill hollered through the screen, "Helen? You ready?"

"Come in, Neillo, come in. I'm almost ready."

Neill crossed the threshold, a vampire now given permission. The house smelled like dead love. Neill wanted to taste blood.

"Where are you?" Neill said.

"Back here."

Neill shuffled along the hallway, passed Misso's room with averted face, and walked in the open door of Helen's room. Helen was emerging from the bathroom in a robe, a towel wrapped around her head.

"Almost ready?" Neill said, sarcastically.

"Hey, I just need to get dressed."

"Ok," Neill said.

"Jesus, you have to wear that face?"

"Believe me, I wish I had another."

"You just gonna stand there?"

"Oh, you wanna get dressed right here."

"Neillo," Helen said. The moment froze (it can happen). Helen stood there with a comical smirk on her pretty face. "Neillo, do you just wanna *stand there*?"

"Helen," Neill said.

Helen undid the sash of the robe. It fell open. There was nothing underneath but Helen.

"Ok then. Here goes," Helen said, as if this were Neill's idea.

The towel dropped from her head. Her brown squiggly hair sprung out like a flower dehiscing. The bathrobe was shrugged aside. There was Helen, the body that crashed a thousand ships. There were those tits that Neill hadn't seen since Helen was 16. They were peachy and unimpeachable, so full and so perfectly round and taut, standing up even firmer than Neill's little soldier.

Neill just stared. He could not move or change the expression on his face.

There was Helen's Aunt Annie. Her pubic hair was sparse, wispy, a spray of light brown filaments. The folds of her vulva were more apparent than on any other woman Neill had ever seen.

"Well?" Helen said.

"You're beautiful," Neill said.

"Thanks, young swain. You seen enough?"

Neill raised his eyes to Helen's face. Her brown eyes were moist with—what? She was smiling. Was this charity? Did Helen really want him for himself or was this part of the whole strange rivalry she felt with Misso?

"I'll wait outside," Neill said.

He went and sat on the porch. He remembered the day he sat on this same porch with Misso while she blew bubbles as bright and versicolor and pointless as dreams. Helen joined him, dressed in a short summer skirt and white man's dress shirt (not just for white men...you understand).

"Ready?" she sang. "Let's let the day lead us. Let's become what the day wants us to become."

And they did. And neither of them ever again mentioned Neill's up close and personal viewing of Helen Guru's consummately shapely body. (She looked like Venus skateboarding on her half shell.) (Though Neill could conjure it mentally whole for the rest of his life.)

And Neill went home that night, a cur, and, as a cur, he fell asleep with his face in the diabolic circle of mephitic power upon his now beloved and accursed bedspread.

That Summer

That summer went by like a creeping shadow of pent-up lust and love, like a dead man walking. Neill, our Neill, worked by day and read and wrote by night. Misso called once from some midpoint in her wanderings. The conversation didn't go well. While Neill tried to keep the whiny child out of his voice (failing...*failing*), Misso tried to inject something into the conversation that she felt Neill wanted or needed. The disingenuousness worked like a poison on Neill's weak system.

So, he wrote. He wrote short fiction now, while still pecking away at trifling poems full of self-pity and metaphors for death, loss, decay, demise by neb and tail.

Sometimes, he talked to pretty women in the store but, without his heart, his wit withered. Without his heart he was as charming as a scarecrow made of mud.

Once, he went out to lunch with Sue Goorile. She had grown up to be even more beautiful. Where Neill thought her exquisite, like an untouched template for young womanhood at 17, now the world saw the bloom from the bud. She wore her white-blond hair longer and her adult body moved the way the spheres move, intricately astonishing while seeming meet and modest.

They went back to Neill's house afterward. They talked over the old times. Sue's line, oft repeated, was that she was too young. She wasn't offering regret for leaving him behind but, instead, offering a buffer for his aching core.

At the end of their talk, they kissed for a long time. Did their bodies remember? It's hard to say. Neill was an insect.

"I wondered how that would feel after all this time. You were my first real lover, you know?" Sue said, stroking his stubbly cheek.

"How was it?"

"You were there."

They laughed their old laugh. Neill's heart went kachunk.

"I like kissing you. You always were a great kisser," Sue said. Her eyes twinkled.

"I like it, too. I miss you still. I think I always will."

"You won't. I was a short stop on the way to Neill becoming Neill."

"You were more than that."

"Flatterer."

"Go to bed with me."

Sue jerked her head back but held her smile. Now the smile became more feline as it crept across her cheeks.

"Do you really want that?"

"Yes."

"You don't, Neill. What about Misso?"

"I think she has joined the Inuits."

"Is that a religion?"

"Like Eskimos."

"I know what the word means. I was batting the birdy of your joke back."

"Forgive me."

"Canada does not have Eskimos. Wait, do they?"

"How the hell should I know?"

"Because your mom is Canadian?"

"Oh yeah."

"No Eskimos in Canada."

"And no Sue Goorile in my bed."

"I think not, Neill. Misso will come back. You will be reunited and the summer of pain will be forgotten."

"You've not only gotten prettier but wiser, too."

"Sweet Neill."

"Sweet Sue."

"Kiss me one more time then I have to go."

With Bidden

"You hear from Misso today?"

"—"

"Sorry."

"I no longer know what to do if I ever knew what to do."

"Try to relax? It might not be as bad as you're thinking. Anticipatory anxiety is one of the most lethal kinds."

"Do you believe that?"

"No."

"Me neither. It's always as bad as you think it is."

"I'm sorry."

"Me, too."

This is Unbearable

We have to cut to the chase, to resort to a cliché which enables us to cut to the chase. We find this long summer of bereavement and misgiving unbearable. So this is the end, more or less, of this crucial and excruciating segment:

On Neill's 30th birthday, July 20, 1985, he received some small tokens of affection from friends. Albums, books. Bidden asked Neill to go to a Chicks game with him, but Neill said he had to stay by the phone for Misso's call. So, instead, Bidden and Pas brought dinner and a VHS of *Broadway Danny Rose*. If anything would make Neill feel better, it would be this very funny Woody Allen movie.

Nothing would make Neill feel better.

Misso didn't call.

And it gets worse from there as you will soon see in the next chapter, which we call...

Cuckold Clocked (False Start)

The narrator does not want to continue.

The story lies doggo.

We need a break.

The narrator is just like you. We are only flesh and blood.

Wait.

Cuckold Clocked (False Start 2)

Eventually, she must have come home. Was she changed by her travels, by finding herself a small animal traveling across a large country, by rail, by bike, by God?

We must assume she was though it was hard to tell. She is like a cloud.

She is home.

Neill is there the first night.

Things have changed. It's like the atmosphere has thickened. It's like the sun has dimmed. Neill is afraid.

They kiss.

Misso is still missing.

Cuckoo Clocked

"The cuckold is ridiculous; everyone knows that. The cuckold, ribald figure of fun in a thousand bedroom farces...baffled, injured, impaired, impotent cuckold—the last to know, always complicit in his own deception, living in a dream world of his own making, a cartoon figure."
     –Ward Just

"You don't have much to say to me after all those weeks alone, all the time away, all the things you've seen?" Neill and Misso are sitting on the futon, upon which, once upon a time, Neill entered Misso for the first time, from behind while she lay beneath him as still as a bag of oats.

"I'm tired. I wrote you some."

"Scant words. Scratches."

"Neill, do we have to talk about this now?"

"You'd rather sleep."

"Yes."

"You'd rather sleep alone."

"I *did* miss you."

She said, "I *did* miss you." It hurt like fire.

"I'll go home if you want," Neill said. His insides were threatening to become outsides.

"Neill, I'm just wrung out. I have too much on my mind and I can't formulate articulately."

"Tomorrow will be better."

"Yes."

Neill did not move. He could not move.

"I ached for you all summer, Misso. I don't think you know what your lack of communication was doing to me."

"I'm sorry. Seriously. You deserve better."

"Don't start that again."

"You do. I'm not good enough for you. You are a really good person, Neill."

"A good person."

"I've learned so much from you."

"Misso, is this a wrap-up?"

"I don't understand."

"Is this some kind of summing up? You're writing the memoir about this part of your life with me being over and being, in the long run, a *positive* experience?"

"You tangle me up, Neill."

"Why didn't you call more, write more?"

"I was on a train. I wrote some postcards."

"Two."

"No, I mean I wrote some postcards and then couldn't find mailboxes and I guess I lost them."

"You wrote me more than I got?"

"Yes."

"What about when you got to Portland? With your friends? They didn't have a phone? Misso, you were in Portland when I turned 30. You know. I turned 30 without a word from you."

Misso looked at Neill. Her face crumpled. She looked away and a tear ran across her round, freckled cheek.

"What is it?"

"Neill. I was with *people*. Calling would have been—awkward."

"Who were these people? Do I know any of them?"

Again, the look and then the look away.

"Who were they Misso?"

"Helen told you. I know she did."

"Helen told me—what?"

"Who I was with."

Neill thought for a moment. He was teetering. He was about to fall. God, the God of Abraham, gripped Neill's stomach like the grippe.

"Was it an old boyfriend?"

The tears came without words. Misso just sat, still as Buddha, and let tears take the place of language. After a while she spoke.

"I'm so tired."

"Misso," Neill started. He could not make a sentence. It was a life sentence and he could not make it to the end.

"Did."

"You."

"Sleep"

"With"

"Him?"

Misso now turned completely away, her back to Neill. Neill stared at the back of her head. He stared at the wall. The wall was solid. It might fall anyway. The back of Misso's head might fall also. Anything could happen. These were the endtimes.

"You slept with him on my birthday." Neill spoke his questions declaratively. He had already written the script, or someone had, someone who knew more than he did. The we. The editorial we.

"You fucked him while I sat up all night waiting for you to call."

Misso's sobs grew louder.

"You were fucking some guy while I was at home dying because you forgot my birthday. No wonder you—" Neill was crying now, too. "Forgot me."

Misso was out of words. Neill was alone. He was talking to the wall. The wall had a picture on it. The entire wall was this picture. The picture was of a cell, a holding tank, a cage. Neill traveled into the picture. Inside it was Hell. Hell is other people. Hell is strangers who are young and hip and carefree and fuck your lover 2000 miles away without a qualm. They do it because they are Hell.

Neill knew to walk away right then. Misso didn't care. Would his walking away hurt her? No, Neill decided. Did he want to hurt her?

He did. Of course, he did.

He unfolded himself and stood up. He was an empty suit of clothes. His soul was in the cage with the strangers who fuck your lover.

He took a step. He wanted to look back. He wanted to turn to salt. He did not want to be Neill anymore. He did not want to be Neill ever again.

He moved outside. The night was as black as Charon's heart.

Somehow he drove home. Somehow he found his bedroom.

He picked up the phone.

He should not call Misso. He was defective. He called Misso.

She did not answer.

Somehow, later, another day began.

The Most Shameful Day in Neill's Life

Having slept for no hours Neill ventured out. (He called Ianthe at home and told her he couldn't make it into work because his heart was shattered.) Neill woke and drove. He only had a vague idea what he was about. His chest was raw, his eyes burnt holes in a blanket. He drove westward, warily, slowly, like a car with a broken axle. He was headed toward Misso.

Neill did not go to Misso's. His life might have turned out differently had he. Who is to say?

Neill drove to The Anthill.

What was his plan?

He had none.

What was he going to say?

He had planned nothing.

Sister answered the door. She was perplexed by the death mask Neill was wearing.

"Neill, for God's sake, what's wrong?"

"Can I come in?" Neill began to sob. He sobbed through his entire visit with HER parents. This visit would haunt Neill for the rest of his life. Just thinking about it made him ill.

Sis and Doddy sat together on a loveseat, a sort of Victorian thing with fabric that looked like a Watteau painting. Neill sat a few feet away in a comfortable chair. He sobbed.

Mehrnoosh entered the room, spun and exited.

"I love her so much," Neill said. "I want to marry her. I want her to have children with me. I've never felt this way about anyone. She is everything to me."

So far so good. Doddy and Sis watched the tears fall and they empathized, though they had no idea where Neill was taking them.

"Would you like some tea?" Sister asked.

"She fucked some guy in Portland, some old boyfriend," Neill sobbed. His face was red, angry, fallen in. It was the face of tragedy, the face of a fiend.

"On my birthday she was sleeping with her old boyfriend," Neill sobbed.

"She doesn't care. She doesn't love me. She fucked this guy and I love her so much. I am dying, I think. I think I am really dying of heartbreak. You know her. How could she do this? How could she do this? How could she spit on me? How could she be so horrible, so unloving, so heartless? How how how? She is a snake. She is a monster."

"I love her so much. I'm sorry, I'm really sorry. This is terrible," Neill sobbed. His heaving and his blubbering made the text of his speech, at times, indecipherable, but the gist was apparent.

The speech, the crying scree, the outpouring, the logorrhea lasted for days. It was Biblical in proportion. Neill emptied himself. The Anthills sat by, stunned. They did not know what to say.

After a while, Neill wound down. His spring was going limp. His energy was bleeding from him in a torrent of tears. He was dissolving like a retted witch.

"I'm so sorry," Sister said, when she sensed Neill was through.

"We're sorry," Doddy said. He was embarrassed. He wanted to be miles away from this. He did not want to hear his daughter, his beloved only daughter, denigrated even if she had done something terrible. Had she done something terrible? Doddy found himself asking this.

Meanwhile, Neill's voice had grown so soft it was made of breath, except Neill couldn't breathe. It was the voice from the inside of a toadstool. It was a voice used after the sorceress has taken your human voice.

"I'm sorry," Neill said. He meant to stand up. His body was a puppet's.

"I'm sorry. This was appalling. This was an appalling thing to do."

Sis and Doddy strained to hear. They didn't strain too hard. They wished him gone.

Finally, Neill stood. He looked around the room as if he didn't know where he was. His vision rested at last on The Anthills.

"I'm sorry," he whispered one last time.

And then he left.

That night he managed a few hours' sleep. He took 4 Tylenols. They did nothing but he had no other medicaments to aid him. He rolled around in his own disgust. He hated Neill. He hated what Neill had done, crying like a child in front of the Anthills, the last people on Earth who wanted to hear about the duplicity of Misso. A grown man does not cry that way. He does not cry as if he has no inner resources.

Neill awoke the next day and dressed for work. He worked. Nothing happened. He went home again. Goffredo was gone. Neill was so alone he thought the world had lost some of its population.

Sister Anthill called Neill at home that night. She asked if she could have lunch with Neill the next day. Neill said, yes, yes, that would be good.

Then, he cried again for 6 hours straight.

The Lunch with Sister Anthill

Sister came by The Book Shelf and took Neill to a small vegetarian restaurant that had opened next door to the CK's on Poplar. It was called The Pea Green Boat. Sister was dressed in her crisp, white nurse's uniform. Neill was comforted by her appearance, an almost angelic mien.

Neill had some soup and a roll that was made from cornmeal and something sweet. Honey?

"How are you, Neill?" Sis said. Her face was kind, composed. She was genuinely concerned.

"I'm ashamed. I'm so sorry for showing up at your house and subjecting you to that."

Neill's voice choked once, like a car on a cold morning. He would not cry.

"Forget that," Sis said. "Take care of yourself."

Neill thought about that.

"I can't live without her," he said.

"Ok," Sis Anthill said. "Start with that. You must have in mind forgiving her."

Neill thought about that.

"I don't know. Yes. I think so. I don't—"

"You don't have to decide anything today, you know," Sister put her hand over Neill's. It was warm. The gentle gesture made Neill's heart slow its ragtag pulsation.

"I've talked to Miss," Sister said now. "She feels terrible. She wants you to talk to her."

Neill thought about that.

"I don't think I know how," he said at last.

"You do, Neill," Sis said.

"I don't know."

"She loves you."

Neill felt himself stiffen as if someone had tied him to his chair. Love? his heart asked. Misso loves me?

After a while, Sis realized Neill wasn't going to respond.

"Trust me on this, ok? I know Miss and she loves you."

After they ate, as they walked outside, Sister Anthill slipped her arm through Neill's like a young lass on a first date. "I want you to know I am on your side," she said, delicate as air. Back at the Poplar Plaza shopping center, Sister parked the car and got out. She moved to Neill and put her arms around him.

"It's going to be alright," she said. "I told Misso that she could not let you go that easily. Ok? Call her."

Neill smiled tightly. Sister put her Earth Mother's hand on his cheek.

That night at home, Neill sat sunk in contemplation. He did not fix dinner. He did not read or watch TV. He thought about what he was going to do next and what he was going to do next scared the pee out of him.

Sometimes You Just Have to Sit Still and Hold Hands and Wait for the Bad Part to be Over

"I'm just so sorry I am miserable," Misso said.

They were sitting on The Anthill's front porch. It was a late summer evening and the air was full of humidity and the buzz and drone of crickets and cicadas.

Neill was silent. He had set up this tête-à -tête and he did not know entirely why except that he was convinced he could not exist without Misso. Without Misso he would be spit. He would be pee.

"I told you I wasn't good enough for you," Misso whispered.

Neill looked across the lawn where the badminton net was standing at half-mast. He feared speech because he thought he might cry more. He was tired of being such a sop. So he took her hand and held it in his and began to examine it as if it were something he had found on the beach. He spread the lovely, long fingers. He rubbed the palm with his thumb as if there were Lady Macbeth's blood there. Misso stared at her own hand. This homely activity drew all the attention the actors in this poor drama could muster.

"I don't want to go on without you," Neill said, finally.

Misso didn't answer for a while. Neill thought that her next words would turn his heart to ice before throwing it into the street to smash.

"I want *us* back," Misso said, finally.

Neill looked up and Misso looked up. Neill moved closer and put his lips on hers. It was an old kiss, a lingering buss whose momentum came from a shared past.

After it ended Misso said, "My mother says that sometimes in relationships you just have to sit still and hold hands and wait for the bad part to be over."

"Your mother is a treasure."

"She says that about you. She and Mehrnoosh think you are a treasure. My treasure?"

Neill Talks to the Boys

"I'm happy if you're happy," Shlomo was saying.

"Of course, I am too," Bidden said.

"Are you?" Crow asked.

"I am. I think this is it. I think we turned a corner, relationship-wise."

"You've been watching *The Apartment.*"

"She said something interesting. She said her mother told her that sometimes, in relationships, you just had to hold hands and be still and trust each other."

"Hm," Bidden said.

"You don't agree?" Neill tried to keep the shrill out of his voice.

"I do agree, whole-heartedly," Bidden said. He dipped a thoughtful French fry into a thoughtful dollop of ketchup. Or maybe it was catsup. "I wish a woman would say that to me."

"Bidden, I thought you were in love," Shlomo said. "Pass that ketchup."

"I thought so too."

"Or maybe it's catsup," Shlomo added.

"She wanted to do it prairie dog-style," Bidden said.

Everyone laughed.

"Then she asked if I had read *Return of the Screw*?"

"Ha, that's funny but—what? You ended the relationship?"

"No, not exactly. It was just—*untenable* after that."

"I get it," Neill said.

"You do?" Crow asked.

"Sure."

"Because you had that sort of thing with—with Syrie."

"Oh damn. Sweet Syrie."

"You loved her though," Bidden said, as if this were a corrective.

"I did. I still do. Syrie."

"Anyway," Shlomo said, bringing the conversation back around. "I believe in you and Misso. You know, I believe it's right for you."

"Do you really? Man, that's good to hear."

"I know the Anthills. They're good people."

"Not sure about Ram."

"Who's Ram?"

"One of the lesser Anthills."

"You set yourself up, didn't you?"

Neill laughed.

"Anyway, they are," Neill said. "Good people. And I shamed myself for all time in front of them. Will they ever forgive me?"

"They already have," Shlomo said. "Relax. Not all of us get to start over with real faith."

Did Neill have real faith? It was the question bedeviling him. He wanted to test it. He wanted to be with Misso every minute.

Was that how it had gone bad?

Naked Again

Neill thought that when he lay with Misso again his mind would torture him with thoughts of the other guy, the dick whose dick was most recently in the formerly secret place that Neill now wished to re-enter. But, his mind gave him a pass. Maybe not a get-out-of-jail-free pass but it did not deter his desire, his machinations, his *love*.

He bore down hard.

Misso came and he came and he told her too many times, "I love you so. I love you so much, Misso."

Afterward they fell asleep, Misso's hand resting on Neill's shirtless chest, as weightless as an angel in a child's dream.

And so they started again.

Surprisingly, Things Went Well

Neill was surprised at how smoothly they glided back together and how stress-free their time together seemed to be. They resumed as if the summer had never happened. Misso even began to go regularly to the Rhymer's Sunday night dinners. She even seemed to enjoy herself.

At the bookstore, Neill had gotten a raise and he was once again fully engaged with his work. Romantic distractions and their concurrent black moods were, for the moment, put aside. Neill laughed and joked with his clientele. He even found some time to talk in a friendly manner with Iago. He invited Iago to one of the P&H get-togethers. It didn't go that well. Iago sat there like a silent stormtrooper waiting for someone in the group to reveal his Jewishness.

In October, Ianthe, the owner, published a children's book with St. Exupery Press, Memphis' sole publishing concern. It was a child's history of Beale Street entitled *The Night Elvis Came to Beale Street*. The Book Shelf threw a huge party for her, which was attended by every moneyed family in Memphis. It was gangbusters. Neill was nominally in charge and he was running around frantic. He was stressed, worrying that the bash might not be everything he had hoped it would be. He loved Ianthe and wanted her to be pleased.

By night's end, it was an obvious success. And, as the last stragglers were leaking out the door, Neill looked up to find Misso standing off to the side thumbing a paperback book. He was so pleased she had come. This was a new committed Misso. She was taking an interest in Neill's life and Neill vowed to himself to make sure he took an interest in hers as well.

"Hello, Kitten," Neill said. "I'm happy to see you."

"I'm hungry," Misso said. "Take me to dinner? Want to eat Chinese around the corner?" She reached for Neill's hand. Public affection. This was Misso, Mach 2.

"There was some talk about us all going out to eat with Ianthe and her husband and all the employees and friends. Would you be interested in that?"

Misso made a vague moue.

"It would be a paid dinner at a nice place," Neill added with a smile.

Misso smiled too, and her pellucid blue eyes watered with affection.

"Yes, thank you," she said, softly.

So, they all went to Justine's, a tony restaurant that Neill thought was mythical, or perhaps only appeared every 100 years like Brigadoon.

The meal was remarkable. The company convivial. Misso at Neill's side, a truly happy-making thing. They shared an oyster appetizer.

"I think this has gone straight to my Timmy," Neill said.

Misso snorted and put her mouth next to Neill's ear. "I want to go straight to your Timmy."

Neill put a hand on her thigh and slowly rubbed it through the thin material of Misso's pants, working his pinky as close to Arcadia as it dared.

Though they were filled with rich food and Misso was a little tipsy from wine, and the hour was very late, they managed to find their way into Neill's bedroom, where they stripped each other, and before they could even lie down, Neill kneeled and sucked at Misso's masterpiece, until juice ran down his chin, an aromatic juice like myrrh that accompanied the oysters' powerful element, blending along the dark path to the tip of Neill's cockalorum. Neill wanted to bathe in Misso's funk-nectar. He wanted to smell like Misso from head to heel.

But Misso had other ideas. Before she began to climax, she pushed Neill's head away, in a gesture both intimate and inflamed. She threw herself face-down on the bed and raised her beautiful, biscuity rear-end like a pooch in heat. Neill almost fainted at the sight. She really had the noblest ass and legs Neill had ever seen. And, with her legs spread like that, even in the dim, Neill could see all the way to Elysium.

Still on his knees, he crawled to her and waggled his tongue a bit in and out of her two abysses.

"Neill, quick. Quick!"

Neill stood like the good soldier he was and impelled his jocum inside her, slowly, slowly, sinking, sinking, sinking down.

"Ahh," Misso said.

They both came.

They fell together. If it was not the world of men it was the world of afreets and centaurs and basilisks, where they belonged.

They pulled the sheet over themselves though the room was sticky-warm because the ancient window unit never cooled efficiently.

They snuggled up tight.

"When someone asked Casanova what made him a great lover," Neill spoke into Misso's shoulder. "He answered, 'The tenderness afterward.'"

Misso hummed.

"I wish that had made a baby," Neill said. He was speaking as one in a dream. "It was so intense, so perfect, so mutual. I wish it had made a baby and we would remember that this night, this enchanted night, was the one that made junior, or Elspeth, or Lilith. He or she would walk out to the edge of every day, all the way to the brightest horizon, and he or she would teach us that the answer is never to be found in the questions."

He wasn't even sure he had spoken out loud.

He had.

"Me, too," Misso said. And then, she was asleep.

Neill followed her down that rabbit hole, as he would follow her down any.

The Monkey's Wedding

Neill and Misso sat on the porch of the house on Linden Street and watched the rain spatter the street like a toy drummer beating a toy drum. The fall weather in Memphis should be bottled along with Rendezvous Barbecue Sauce and sold around the globe. It was that kind of early evening. The sun, before it set, was shining through the falling rain, red klieg light through a shower curtain.

"The monkey's wedding," Neill said.

"What's that?" Misso was tying a bracelet onto her wrist. It was made of sack cloth and pieces of the savior's robe.

"When the sun shines and it rains."

Neill watched his love's attention to what she was doing. It was childlike. It went through Neill like a lance.

"I heard it called the devil beating his wife."

"I guess, like with many things, there is a sacred and secular version."

Misso looked up to see the expression on Neill's face.

"Which one is yours?" she asked with a half-grin.

"Well, it's not mine. It's been passed down in my family, like the sacred pessary, Mesler to Mesler, down through the generations. It is time-worn."

Misso smiled her fay smile and returned her attention to her bracelet.

"Actually, we don't really have a sacred pessary," Neill said. He looked westward to where the sun was the color of blood being washed off macadam.

"I made that part up," he finished, softly.

Fall Leads to Winter Inexorably as Summer Leads to the Fall

Misso and Neill stayed strong through the autumnal changes. The leaves of trees, brilliant in their dying throes, spoke to Neill in a distant, dusty language. Something in him ached, a fear, a seer's curse.

They had some rows, balanced by the best sex of their relationship and balanced by times of sweetness and determination. Neill sometimes felt as if he were watching Misso through the wrong end of a telescope. She was so close, yet she was shrinking.

They went out to the movies a lot. Misso tolerated Neill's obsession with films, and sometimes, she liked a movie as much as he did. Those were good nights to Neill.

Neill wrote her poems. He believed, he really believed, that if he wrote well enough, powerfully enough, succinctly, acutely, precisely, forcefully, inspired enough, that he could hang onto Misso. Surely, she would love him if his poetry were worthy.

They had the same fights. Neill wanted to be with her always. She wanted to make art, spend time with her (younger) friends, be by herself. It drove Neill crazy. Neill was crazy.

One evening, it came to a head again.

Sex wasn't on. When sex wasn't on, Neill felt as if he would never be loved again. He felt loveless, bereft, and alone.

"Neill, I'm just tired," she said. Tired was code. Neill knew what tired meant.

"Sure," Neill said. His hurt feelings made things worse. He knew that and he was powerless to stop. When he was in 7th grade, and he would find the darkest room at the party in which to hide and wrap himself around his own pain, he was really aching for someone to come to him—he could not go to them, surely that was obvious—for someone to come and say, "Neill, you are not alone. We all love you. I love you." This current poseur's pose was not much different and found itself aligned with 7th grade angst along the maturity scale.

"Just take me home," Misso continued. "We'll talk in the morning."

"I wrote you a new poem," Neill said.

The room was pregnant with silence. The baby was due and it was a monster.

"Can you give it to me tomorrow?" Misso said after an entire opera of silence had passed.

Neill looked at his love. He looked hard at the woman he wanted above all women.

"Sure. Or not at all."

"Ok, not at all." Misso, now, was making for the door.

"What are you going to do, walk?" Neill said to her back.

"Yes," she said back. The three simple letters were laced with poison.

"Wait, dammit," Neill ran to her. "Just wait. Come back. Come to bed."

"No, Neill. No."

"Fine, fuck it," Neill spat. "Go home. Go to sleep. Do something you're good at."

Now, in a mirror replay of an earlier battle, Misso was the one whose fist was brandished. She was going to punch Neill in the face. Something held her back. A scrap of pity, a scrap of love. Amity reigning? The dove stronger than the hawk? Who can say?

The fist was balled. It was cocked and loaded. Then Misso lowered it slowly, a weapon put away but shown. Once shown the weapon has power.

Neill drove her home that night.

It was only another spat, Neill told himself later, alone, in bed.

It wasn't. It was the beginning of the end.

Fall, the Fall

It was cooler. The nights were tired and the chill went through everyone.

There was a raw-bone feeling.

There was Neill and there was Misso and the world seemed to be dry and all the changes seemed adamantly precarious.

It was the season of mold.

It was the season of revolution and chaos and entropy.

Another Book

"I brought you something," Neill said.

"Something?" Misso asked. "Another book."

"Oh well."

"No, I didn't mean it like that. I haven't read the last one you gave me."

"What was the last one?"

"You don't even remember. You give me too many books and then you expect me to read them."

"You're right. I am an oaf. Sorry."

"No, don't do like that. What is it?"

"*The Sot-Weed Factor.*"

"Which I don't understand at all."

"The title?"

"Right."

"You'd understand if you read it."

"For Godsake, take it from behind your back and give it to me."

"You don't have to read it." Neill handed her the package wrapped in Book Shelf paper with a Book Shelf seal.

"Cripes, it's thick."

"You haven't opened it."

"I can still tell it's thick."

"Right."

Misso carefully undid the paper.

"It's thick."

"It is. I'll take it back."

"No, I want it. Thank you. I know the author's name."

"John Barth. He wrote *The End of the Road.* I gave that to you when we first started dating."

"Right."

"Have you read it?"

"Neill."

"Right, sorry. Forget it."

Misso kissed Neill. On the cheek. Misso kissed Neill on the cheek.

Later that night, they slept in the same bed. They had sex. It was the last time.

Helen Calls

"Where are you?" Neill asks.

"Maine. On the beach."

"There is a phone on the beach?"

"Neillo, the house is on the beach."

"Of course, it is."

"What's up with you?"

"Nothing. Same. Reading, writing, loving."

"That's my boy."

"Things are ok. Misso and I –we've reached some kind of plateau."

"A good plateau, or a plateau on the threshold of damnation?"

"A good one, I think."

"I'm happy for you, Neillo. You've matured."

"I wouldn't go that far. And I shouldn't listen to that from a child."

"I ain't no child. I was a child when I was sixteen."

"Ok."

"You and Misso, I don't know. I don't think I thought it would work. But I thought you would be good for her."

"Neill the proctor."

"No, Neill the thinker, the carer, the poet."

"Thank you."

"You got through all that bullshit in Portland and that really showed me I was wrong. You guys are good together."

"I still—well, I am happy, yes."

"The guy in Portland—you never should have worried about him. He's—he's arty, but kind of a drip. Like Pollock."

"Ok."

"You should never have cared but I know it hurt. It was just a stupid thing, a transient stupid thing."

"Ok."

"You're better than him. You're past him. You don't care that he moved back to Memphis?"

"Excuse me?"

"He lives in Memphis again. Surely Misso told you."

"We're not that mature."

"Did I say something wrong? You've got that catch in your voice."

"How long has he been here?"

"I don't know, Neill. Sorry. I could be wrong. I think he's in Memphis maybe not."

"How long?"

"A week. Ten days. Something like that."

"Misso has been with him."

"What? What do you mean?"

"She told me she had late-night developing to do, twice this week."

"I'm sure she did."

""

"Neillo?"

""

"Neill? Talk to me."

The First Death of Neill Rhymer

"Helen has always been so—something with me. Competitive. Destructive. She slept with both my brothers, you know?

"You're saying she is lying?"

"Neill."

"Is she lying?"

"About Paul being here?"

"Yes."

"No. He moved back."

"You didn't tell me."

"I know how you get. You don't trust me."

There was silence, like the interval in the movie between when they show you the bomb and when it detonates.

"Have you seen him?"

Misso turned her face away. They were sitting together on the futon, where it all began, their backs against the wall.

"You've seen him."

"Neill. He just wanted to have a drink."

"Which night was this?"

"Pardon?

"Which night of the nights you told me you were developing pictures?"

"Wednesday."

"You lied to me."

"Because I know how you get."

"Did you—"

"Neill!" Misso barked his name. Her voice carried venom, anger, shame. Tears gathered in the tiny triangles at the edges of her linger-on pale blue eyes.

"You slept with him." Neill said it without inflection. It wasn't a question. It was a death sentence.

In an *Outer Limits* episode, a milquetoast character, played by Donald Pleasance, discovers he has the ability to generate an electrical vortex with his anger. It appears like a small tangle of cloudy voltage in the upper corner of the screen, and it wields a destructive energy. This vortex now appeared.

"Neill, I told you. I am not good enough for you. You are so great. I can't keep up. I am not mature enough, not smart enough." She was sobbing now. "You can do better. You will do better."

"I—wait—I—you want—you're saying." Neill sputtered. The alien was about to burst out of his chest. "We're through?"

"Neill." Now Misso just cried. She sat there and cried.

"You don't love me," Neill tried.

She cried.

"You must love me, too. I love you that strongly. It must mean something." Now, Neill was crying too. "It has to mean something. I've never loved anyone like you. It has to make you love me, too."

"I'm sorry," Misso said.

That was the most destructive 'I'm sorry' in the history of the phrase.

Neill stood. He couldn't see. He fled.

Thought of you as my mountain top,
Thought of you as my peak.
Thought of you as everything,
I've had but couldn't keep.
I've had but couldn't keep.
Linger on, your pale blue eyes.
  -Lou Reed

Where Neill Went and Where he Ended Up

Neill drove blind. His car guided him. He was without volition or reason. He was blinded by tears and discombobulated by a pain in his chest like the stroke of an adze.

Neill's car found a home, a Midtown apartment wherein lived Gulley and Victoria Jawell, friends from a past that was unstable and precariously constructed, friends who would understand, who could possibly save Neill, though Neill thought, no, salvation would not be possible that night, or ever.

Gulley answered the door. Neill was a quivering pudding.

"Pal," he croaked.

Gulley found Victoria and put her on the porch with Neill. Neill fell into her arms. He was inarticulate; he was mad with grief; he was a warrior dead already in a battle, lengthy, disheartening and bloody. Dis-heart-ening.

Eventually, Victoria talked Neill inside where there was a cat which Neill was allergic to. With alarming swiftness and completeness, a stuffed nose, plugged ears and a scratchy throat, were added to Neill's already sodden, red eyes, and the rampant sickness in his soul. Not to mention his aphasia nor the blood pouring from his broken heart.

"Take this," Victoria said. In her palm Neill could make out, like bleary light from a star long dead, a small round white medicament.

"What—what—" Neill blubbered.

"It's gonna knock you out. You'll sleep till noon tomorrow."

Neill threw it back. Oblivion, yes that was what he wanted. He wanted oblivion.

Victoria led Neill to a bedroom. She sat with him for a while and watched his heaving chest slowly subside.

"Oblivion," Neill said, druggily, unfeelingly. "I want. Oblivion. I want it."

Victoria screwed up her face in wary judgment.

Neill did not sleep till noon. He woke 6 hours later and the sickness was all over him like a beast, a formication. He was still in the world, in the world that contained Misso Anthill. Misso Anthill, whom he would never again hold, naked and shivering. Neill began to keen.

Victoria opened the door. Gulley was behind her.

"I want to die," Neill said.

Victoria and Gully huddled quickly. They made plans.

Thanksgiving on the Thirteenth Floor

There is a thirteenth floor to St. Dymphna Hospital. Of course, they don't call it the thirteenth floor. It is called the fourteenth, so that there is no thirteenth. And on this fortuitously renumbered floor, they put the psychiatric cases, the flip-outs, the suicides, the moonstruck, the nuts. It was here that Neill spent Thanksgiving, that liminal Thanksgiving, after which his Pilgrim soul was never the same.

What happened is not remarkable in any way. Broken love led Neill to say that most despondent of phrases, *I want to kill myself.* Of course, he did not really want to kill himself but at that time he was the only one who knew that. His friends, in whose home he chose to have his wig-out, thought they saw signs of the Final Desperation. They thought in Neill's simplistic, narcissistic phrasing, they saw an endgame. This is admirable in friends. This is what we would wish of our friends. God bless them.

The breakup was standard fare in that Neill really thought he could not live without this woman. She had entered his bloodstream like heroin and like heroin it was not gonna be pretty getting rid of her. Like many partings, this one came in stages. There was the stage where a lengthy separation, by miles and weeks, was instigated. There was the stage where Neill was cuckolded—on his 30th birthday!—cuckolded for no better reason than boredom, sweet 20th century ennui. And, there was the stage where Neill went raving, weeping, hysterical to her parents to convince them that he loved their daughter more than any man in the history of civilization was capable of loving their daughter.

But the blow of mercy, the unambiguous, terminal guillotine blade was delivered after they had presumably patched things up. It was then that she decided that Neill was not good enough for her, a formulation given this way: she told Neill that *she* was not good enough for *him.* He recognized grim resolve when he heard it. It was the finality of this—black like imagined death, her *tone*—that sent him spiraling. Neill would admit to not being the most stable youth. He was not the guy you trusted with the church secrets. And hence, this spiraling, this unspooling, did not surprise too many of his friends or loved ones.

Vaguely, he remembered friends putting him to bed in their home with a pill. A sleeping potion. He remembered waking early the next morning with the horror all over him again, as fresh as the night before. Sleep had solved, had resolved nothing. And he remembered that it was then that he uttered that fateful phrase. He believed part of him understood that this would lead to his being put someplace safe. He believed that this was at least partly why he said it. Was Neill bringing drama into play, so to speak, as a sort of drastic action to signal his own seriousness, his own heartfelt loss? Yes, part of him knew *that*, too. He seemed to have been split into many parts: the Steppenwolf brain.

At any rate, to the hospital he went, cowering, crying like a squonk dissolving in its own tears. He wanted to be free of the succubus tearing about inside him, but the succubus *was* him. Vaguely he remembered being admitted, and an interview with a psychiatrist who readily agreed that he was possibly suicidal, possibly a danger to himself.

And then, his little room on the 13th floor. And into a hospital bed as if he had broken a bone instead of a heart. It was Wednesday, the day before Thanksgiving.

Neill remembered then that afternoon and evening, contemplating the pain in his, um, soul that led him to this ignominious rest cure. The psychiatrist came by again to look at him with melancholic discernment—or so he read it—Merlin's smile on her Cheshire mouth. She told him that since it was a holiday he would pretty much be left alone until she could return sometime during the weekend. Immediately, this whole adventure seemed off-beam—a miscalculation somehow. Neill felt as if he had done something wrong—a ready enough default function—as if occupying that bed had been a decision he had made, akin to choosing an elective in college, or deciding between working full time or finishing school.

Of course, it hadn't been a *decision*. Yet, he felt as if he could have done something else—anything else—and would have felt better about myself. Partly, this was due to the fact that he was sitting alone in a hospital room watching *The Rockford Files*, eating hospital victuals, trying to read *The Sheltering Sky*, which seemed impenetrable. In other words, he felt guilty about taking up hospital space, without having internal bleeding, that is, literal internal bleeding. What was wrong with him? All he needed was a little time to get over the end of a stormy relationship. Was he looking to psychiatry to solve a problem that went back, at least, to Man's second generation—say, Seth and his wife, who didn't seem to share the same interests, Seth with his shepherding, and his wife with her book group? Or perhaps, they argued about Enosh's seeming indifference to his homework.

Ok.

Neill lay there, institutional covers up to his goozle, and knew that he had to make at least one phone call. He had to tell his parents that he wouldn't be there for turkey at their house tomorrow (and neither would Misso—ach, *Misso*.) Instead, he had decided to see what kind of festivities the Booby Hatch had to offer. This was a tough phone call. Neill wept. Max and Lolly wept. ("Goddammit," she said, choking on wrath and shame, "Wouldn't that rot your socks?") Maybe only Lolly wept. Neill's father, stuck with his entire generation's inability to show emotion, gave stolid strength, implied empathy, and then he exited the phone call quickly. Neill feared their approbation. He feared their disappointment. What did they do to deserve such an unstable son? Well, perhaps a few ill-considered things here and there, but that's the subject of another narrative [ed.?].

Actually, Neill was surprised by his mother's show of solidarity. And, at the time, he didn't really think of it as commonality. He did not realize that his mother was suffering with clinical depression, untreated her whole life. She did empathize. She knew the parameters. But, that's skipping ahead. Back to Wednesday night, post phone call.

Now, Neill had to admit to being slightly disappointed with the Psycho Ward at St. Dymphna Hospital. Where were the men picking imaginary nits off their skin? Where was the nymphomaniac who entered rooms slavering and concupiscent? Where was Renfield? Where were the guys with the straightjackets? The firehose? He wanted a Snake Pit. It fit his inner prison. All he got was a quiet floor with a few eccentrics. Neill was disappointed because he fancied himself a litterateur—or at least he fancied himself *becoming* a litterateur. He needed gritty experience. He needed a good schizophrenic to conspire with, a nymphomaniac to turn over his little apple cart. Instead, he got James Garner's wry, world-weary smartass, and hospital jello.

All this is embarrassing. One wants to ask at this point, hey, Jocko, were you really suffering or just overly theatrical?

Neill was really suffering. He did think that he might hurt myself. Not kill but hurt. Because the pain inside needed an exterior emblem. He fancied that the entire city where he lived was suffused with the image, the imprint of his now erstwhile lover, the woman who, he imagined, just spurned him and was now pleasuring some other guy, some more stable, sexier, younger, artier, more accomplished guy. He imagined that he could not walk around in his hometown because everything would remind him of her. He would have to leave Memphis for Samarkand, or Green River, Utah, or Satu Mare, Romania. He needed her. It was an addiction in that it was physical. His *body* needed her. (It would be a long time before our protagonist would give her up, even through subsequent relationships. She was hooked into all his senses. Sexually, she was a harsh and crucial biologic. Forgive us, but he could not get the smell of her sex—that heady, chemical cookery of delights—out of his head, out of his system. He thought he would die if it were taken away from him permanently. It was a longing of the flesh, *and* of the heart.)

Neill managed a short walk around the corridor that night—he had kitchen privileges, which meant he could go into the scant provisions in the little fridge there. He took a pudding cup. The only other denizen of his new Laughing Academy was a soldier in the room next to his. Neill passed his door and saw the poor squaddie sitting on the foot of his bed, spine as straight as a column of fire, staring straight ahead. Neill assumed that he had worse phantoms in his head than did Neill.

Neill slept very little the first night. Who sleeps well in a hospital? The nurses came in periodically even though there was on no medication, no drip. Neill thought perhaps he would be awakened by Billy Babbit's screams, but the ward was peaceful, almost dreamy. And the next day dawned like a rag-end of tattered dream. He was alone in a hospital. And the woman who loved him, loved him no longer.

It was Thanksgiving Day in the Bughouse!

Neill met a few more of his fellow inmates. A number of them wandered the floor, doctors home with their loved ones and a roast turkey or duck. There was Sally who looked like Sally

Struthers, tits and all (maybe it *was* Sally Struthers), and there was Hank who had hit his kid with a tennis racket and could not forgive himself. There was Susan who perished from fits. There was Creole Myers, a writer whose writer's block was so severe he tried to carve his way out of it with a skiver. And there was Sonny Lemontina, an old man, who once played for the Memphis Redsox in the Negro Leagues ("I played alongside Charley Pride and I got to pitch to Willy Mays once"), who was dying of loneliness, no family, no friends.

There was a game room where no one was playing games. The pudding cups were going like water. And word spread among the inmates like a conspiracy: the dinner tonight would be turkey. It was as if someone had told them they were all going to Paris! The exhilaration, the anticipation! Turkey!

Neill passed the soldier's room and in about 12 hours it seemed he had moved 12 inches. He was now standing at the foot of his bed, at full attention, TV flickering.

Neill retreated to his room. Bidden and Shlomo came to visit. They sat at the foot of the bed and the jokes came fast and furious. I have funny friends, Neill thought. This sometimes saved him. They laughed, and Neill made with the self-deprecating sallies and he felt, briefly, as if everything was beautiful again. Sure, he was going to be alright—he was *laughing*. Not graveyard humor, but Bedlam humor. He had friends. What was he doing in the psycho ward on Thanksgiving?

"What's taped up there above your bed?" Shlomo asked.

"Rumi," Neill said.

"I'll room with you but not here," said Bidden.

"Rumi, look." Neill grabbed the small paper which had these words typed on it:

"What keeps you alive without me?

How can you cry?

How can you know who you are?

How can you see?"

    —Rumi

"Hm," Bidden said. "Is this healthy? Does your doctor think this is healthy?"

"What doctor?" said Neill. "I haven't seen a doctor."

That evening his parents and AJ brought Neill leftover turkey, dressing, gravy, potatoes, green beans. Now, Neill's mother's roast turkey and gravy would be enough to pull anyone out of a trance. It could make Hyde Jekyll. And the sweet, comforting expressions his family wore—well, they broke his damn heart further. The smashed pieces ground to grit.

After they left, Neill felt bereft, lonely. He called a woman whose affection for him had always been a constant and a great boon, her unflagging affection. For whatever reason, she kept a pilot light burning for Neill, if not a flame. It was, of course, Dinah Mist, beautiful, sexual Dinah. Neill asked her to come see him. She did, she came right away. Ah, sweet friendship! He didn't deserve it. When she visited, all nurture and concern in her lovely face, Neill felt lighter, enriched. She smiled sweetly, and placed her palm on his cheek. Such tenderness is vouchsafed few men.

She sat on the edge of the bed and they made little murmurs meaning nothing.

"Dinah," Neill said. "Oh Dinah."

Dinah moved her hand down his cheek and across his chest. She rubbed there as if she was resuscitating a dying man. In a way, she was.

"Oh Dinah," Neill said again. And he sighed.

Dinah looked him in the eyes and slowly slid her hand to his cock. Neill was not given a hospital gown so he was wearing his own underwear. His erection surprised even him. With a steady, firm, slow movement, all the time holding his eyes with her deep, caring eyes, she brought Neill off under the flimsy hospital bed sheet.

"Dinah," Neill said one more time. "I love you."

"I love you, too, Neill. I always will."

And yet—and yet—the next day, Neill awoke on the ward and felt like an astronaut abandoned on a desert planet. It was the *Twilight Zone* episode where the poor sap is stranded all by himself on a faraway planet. Was it Robert Duvall? (Check?) He was all alone in the world, unloved, unlovable, inconsolable. Perhaps you have felt this way once or twice. Perhaps you can relate.

Neill determined that he had to go home. He asked for a doctor, for the shrink who had admitted him. He had a plan. And when she came later that day—business face on—Neill outlined his plan. He would leave the hospital. He would stay with his parents until he felt better. He would be fine. Time heals, etc. She looked at Neill the way Apollo looked at Orpheus, when Orpheus summarized his proposal to follow his dead wife.

In short, it was agreed that if he still felt ok he could leave on Saturday. She recommended that Neill make serious plans to begin seeing a psychiatrist. He made her an empty promise that he would.

Lolly and Max came to collect him Saturday morning. He rode home in the family Buick, feeling as if he were six years old again, as if he were being picked up from the sleepover where he'd gotten homesick. He felt small. Voiceless and microscopic.

He stayed with his parents who were remarkably accommodating, helpful, remedial. When he finally went back to his home—where dwelt the ghost of Misso Anthill—he was still as sad as if steering toward dim eternity. He had not healed. His very house cursed him. His kitchen stank of all the meals they had eaten together. His living room was an antechamber outside Perdition. The TV only showed movies she loved. And his bed, his bed with a memory like the moon's, still smelled of her sex. He wanted to rend it slat from bedpost. He wanted to burn the sheets as if they were tubercular or ancient dangerous texts. He felt like Poe's tell-tale heart sufferer. Tear up the bedclothes—it is the lingering aroma of her deep, dark sex!

He also wanted it to never disappear, that aroma that he had helped concoct. Perhaps, when it lost its potency so would Misso's autocratic hold over his heart.

Eventually—well, you know what eventually means. He slept in his bed again. It did not try to kill him. It did not liquefy and swallow him like the beds in *Nightmare on Elm Street*. Eventually, it succored him again, allowing him to sleep peacefully, somewhat.

Eventually—slowly, slowly, like a bird sharpening its beak on Ararat—he recovered from his addiction to his difficult and seductive ex-lover. Of course he did. Humans do. Humans heal. Erratically, measurably, and by increments.

But, still, after Misso Anthill, something was broken in Neill.

Where do We go From Here? [There was some discussion about this part being a fifth book, ed.] or The Via Dolorosa

Where do we go from here?

Somewhat downhill. Not seedily downhill (time's ravaged wino), but as if the snow was now hard-packed and the erratic Rosebud, upon which Neill was perched, was speeding into the future, careening as skeigh as a muirland filly, come what may, like it or not.

Valhalla, I am Coming

Neill walked around. He was mobile. His bones were weak and his flesh scored, but he faced the everyday anyway. What other choice did he have?

(No, he didn't, not *that*.)

The bookstore was a place of palliative and consolation. Neill attempted to switch his passion from the fleshly (oh, aromatic Misso) to the sacred (Barth, Percy, O'Connor). It didn't work. Neill hurt. He wrote sad, ugly poems, poems full of rancor and starch and loathing. Poems made of pepper and dust. He didn't sleep. He wondered if it were possible to get pharmaceutical help. He imagined that would entail going to the doctor.

"Doc, I have a broken heart."

"Here, Neill, take these little boats of calm. They will help you sail away from the world of pain."

Beautiful women shopped at The Book Shelf, but Neill had gone blind.

Once Luna (the doyenne of The Gorgeous Young Housewives Book Club) (see earlier notation) came in. Her flushed cheeks were surrounded by the snowy fur inside her hood (see earlier notation). She looked like an Icelandic princess. She looked carnal and delicate as rose. It almost stirred Neill. She spoke gently, kindly to Neill as if she could see his ache. Perhaps she could.

Christmas was coming. The bookstore was busier than usual. This was good.

Christmas missing Misso.

Christmas with his parents and siblings, (actually only AJ and her hubbie, because Brack had moved with his fiancé up to frozen New England, a small berg in Connecticut that had an old mill with a working waterwheel—imagine that) who would treat him kindly, the way one wraps an old family heirloom in corrugated cardboard for shipping.

Christmas with new LPs. New books.

Christmas with Mom's turkey, one of the Seven Culinary Wonders.

Christmas with a heart of darkness.

Valhalla, I am coming.

If This Were a Novel

If this were a novel one might expect Neill to close the shabby circle of his life by getting back together with Syrie Hardwood. A *Manhattan* ending, in a way.

It's not going to happen, so stop waiting for it.

At The Book Shelf

An old fellow entered the shop early on a Monday morning He was a business type, wire rim glasses and a bow tie, but he wore a befuddled expression.

He was apparently on a mission he did not relish.

"My son needs a book for school," he said, and dug a crumpled piece of paper out of his pocket. "*Pigmania*, by George Shaw.

On another day, Neill might have laughed. Instead, he gave the baffled father a wry smile and went to get the book. He returned with the Penguin edition of *Pygmalion*. The fellow looked at it, did not register that he had made a mistake and sighed, superciliously.

"Why he has to read this for school I'll never know."

Perhaps, it was just bad small talk and Neill let it go.

Later, one of the semi-regular customers came in, a man Neill knew by sight but not by name. He seemed a pleasant enough man and often engaged Neill in chitchat. Today, he was buying the new Robert Ludlum.

"You read this, Neill?" he said.

"I haven't yet," Neill said.

"Ludlum's good. He's damn good."

"I believe you. That'll be 15.33."

The guy paid but did not move off. It was just as well. Neill didn't really want to work very hard and would just as soon talk with a near stranger. Betty was meeting with a greeting card sales rep in the middle of the store.

"Who do you read, Neill?" the customer now asked. "We've never talked about that."

There was so much they hadn't talked about. And they were so close!

"Oh, fiction. I like fiction."

"Me too, yes, fiction, Neill," the guy busted in.

"Barth, Doctorow, Iris Murdoch, Anne Tyler."

The guy's brow wrinkled. He was perplexed. "I don't know any of those names, Neill. Would you write them down for me?"

Neill did.

"Thanks. Hey, even better. Let me buy something. Tell me something to start with. Gimme one of your favorites."

Neill thought for a moment, held up a 'stay right there' digit, and went storeward. He returned with Walker Percy's *The Moviegoer*.

"This is good, eh?" The man was studying the rear cover, perhaps looking for a loophole, something to get him out of buying some egghead literature.

"Ah, a Southern boy," the man said.

"Yes, friend of Shelby Foote's, as a matter of fact."

"Shelby! Really?"

Neill was pretty sure that this man didn't know Shelby Foote well enough to call him Shelby.

"I'll take it."

He paid—and still didn't move.

"I was talking to my wife the other night about the Civil War. Shelby's bailiwick, you know?"

Neill nodded his encouragement without adding a smirk which said, *no kidding, Sherlock*.

"Helluva thing, the Civil War. Still being fought of course."

Neill was losing interest. He was looking out the plate glass window at the shopping center parking lot. The winter light was dancing on the car windshields, sparking back and forth between them and the storefronts. It was a mid-day photic display. There were people out there moving about. They looked like wavy aliens.

Neill lost the first part of the next sentence but the end jerked his attention forward.

"And that's mostly the fault of the niggers, I am telling you."

Neill's blood boiled. It happened that quickly, zero to whatever the boiling point of blood is, in a split second. Even among pinheaded bigots, you rarely heard the n word used in public and Neill's ire was mostly sparked by this bozo's assumption that because Neill was white and a Southerner that the word would not offend. He just *assumed* Neill's collusion in his pinheadedness.

Neill gathered himself and, with quiet dignity, replied, "You know—my wife is black?"

"Oh, Jesus," the man said. His embarrassment, his shame, was immediate and heartfelt. "I didn't mean it *that way*."

Neill didn't let him off the hook. He remained silent, letting the guy stew, letting him search for the phrases that might save his cracker ass.

"Neill, how can you forgive me? I am not a bigot. I am truly sorry. You know what I meant though, right?"

The guy continued to dig. His grave was almost deep enough.

"I don't know how to apologize. I don't know what to say."

More bubbling silence.

"I'm sorry, Neill," he said, with some finality and in a voice certainly more diminutive than when he began. He hoped to make a graceful exit and, along those lines, he stuck his hand out.

Neill looked at the hand. He perhaps should have refused to shake it. But Neill, even among the despicable, still hoped to avoid all bad feelings.

He raised his hand slowly, trying to make eye contact the whole time. The guy was staring at his own hand, perhaps praying Neill would take it soon and, hence, release him from this conversational purgatory.

Neill shook the asshole's hand.

Betty had dismissed the sales rep, Neill had gone to lunch and returned, and Iago had come to work the late shift, 1 to 8.

"How's it going, Neill," Iago said.

"Fine, fine," Neill said. He imagined Iago had heard about Neill's terrible break-up and didn't know what to say. As far as Neill knew, Iago had never had a girlfriend.

"I'm doing ok, too," Iago said.

The best part of the afternoon was when the Ingram box came. Neill would never, in his long, lifetime career as a bookseller, get tired of opening a new box of books. And in this shipment was the new Graham Greene novel. Neill put a copy in his personal basket, to live there until Neill could come up with the cost (with his 30% discount) and take it home. Ah, Mr. Greene, Neill said under his breath.

Later, about fifteen minutes before Neill was to leave, Iago came hustling out of the stockroom to find Neill at the front desk.

"Neill," Iago said, breathlessly. "You're not gonna believe this."

Neill waited. Apparently, he had to fill in his conversational blank. "Try me," he said.

"I think that young couple who was just in—did you see them?"

Neill had. Young hipster with a beard and his skinny blond girlfriend. Neill had done more than notice them. He could not stop looking at the blond's legs, put on glorious display by the brevity of her skirt. They were shapely for such a thin woman. Neill also thought she was a bit of a ninny to come out on such a cold day with bare legs.

"Yes," Neill said, so Iago would, at some point, reach the point.

"I think they used our bathroom—to fuck."

"What?" Neill said, involuntarily. "Why do you think that?"

Now, Iago had the power he felt his story deserved. He crooked a finger and motioned for Neill to follow him. At the bathroom door, Iago stepped aside to let Neill pass him in the narrow doorway.

And there on the sink, looking like an alien's moist and severed body part, was a used joybag.

"Fuck," Neill said. "Has Betty seen this?"

"God, no," Iago said.

"Throw it away and clean up a bit."

Iago looked at Neill as if Neill had asked him to take his only son to Mount Mariah and throw him into traffic. Iago hated that Neill was his boss.

"Right," he said. "I'll handle it."

Neill was already in his coat and hat when Iago returned to the front of the bookstore. Neill waved and moved out into the biting air.

It had been quite a day.

Goffredo Moves Out

When Goffredo delivered the news to Neill that he and his girlfriend were moving in together, with plans to marry in the Spring, Neill experienced a mixture of joy and trepidation. Have we mentioned before about Neill's penurious ways, his fear of the poorhouse? [Yes, in earlier chapters about Lolly's hand-wringing paranoia about losing all their money, her anile surety about how destitute they were.]

Neill reimagined the house inside his head to contain only him and his books and albums. And the whole house to entertain women—sex in the living room, amorous congress in the bathroom, hogmagundy in the kitchen, convivial society in the empty room that was once Goffredo's bedroom, blanket-hornpipe in the back yard. Simultaneously, he totted up financial figures in his head and reached the conclusion that it would be tight but he might very well make it.

Of course, *tight* scared him.

Shelby Foote

You probably already know some Shelby Foote lore. If you do, you probably already know at least two of his famous quirks. He did indeed compose with a quill pen. Imagine writing that Civil War Trilogy, all gazillion pages of it, in long hand. With a pen dipped in ink.

And he was equally famous for not autographing copies of his books. (Don't tell, but he did sign a copy of his novel *Shiloh* for Neill—we're not sure why.)

Once, Neill took a phone call from a woman who asked if the bookstore would hold all three Civil War volumes, in hardback, at the front desk for her.

"Of course," Neill said, welcoming the large sale.

"Shelby will be by to inscribe them for me," the woman said.

"Are you sure, ma'am?' Neill asked, gently. "Mr. Foote doesn't like to sign his books. We try to protect him as much as—"

"He'll do it for me," the woman cut Neill off. "I am a friend of his ex-wife's."

The ex-wife, Neill thought, after he'd hung up. She was—*peculiar* would be a nice way of putting it.

Neill told Betty about the phone call. Betty chuckled.

"This should be good," she said. She and Shelby had known each other since they were kids back during the Andrew Johnson administration.

About twenty minutes later, Shelby Foote stormed into the store.

"Hi—"was about all Neill got out.

"Where are these goddamn books that goddamn woman wants me to sign?" he roared, like the literary lion he was.

"Now Shelby," Betty said.

Neill placed the three volumes on the counter. Shelby Foote brandished a pen (not of the quill variety) and dutifully inscribed all three volumes. He muttered, scowled, and left.

"That went well," Betty said.

It was also about this time that a new woman came on board at The Book Shelf because Maude was retiring and hence an extra hand was needed. This woman, who was the daughter of one of Memphis's most famous and wealthy families, would become, over the next few years, one of Neill's best friends.

Her name was Smithy. If she doesn't figure prominently in the pages and years that follow, it is our fault. She was dear to Neill if not central to the story as we have decided to tell it.

Smithy became confidant and companion, in store and out. Her sense of the ironic was as deeply seated as Neill's. It was how they related to the agley world.

[Some chapters relating to her have, unfortunately, been excised.]

Enter Mink Risk

Listen: here coincidence lolls.

Harken back to the early 70s when our hero and his pal Mick were tooling around the greater Raleigh-Bartlett area in Mick's top-down red convertible, kicking Buddha's gong and chasing all the pretty women. Ofttimes Neill found himself a willing witness to Mick's conquests. Mick liked sex. He liked it the way koalas like eucalyptus. And he was good at it. So he had plenty of willing participants in the Mick Allen Four Legged Frolic and Goat's Jig.

On one such afternoon Mick picked up, almost literally, a young brunette with buck teeth, whose name is lost to the annals of this wobbly history. Mick and this toothy youngster did some daytime canoodling in Mick's car, and Neill found himself in the backseat with the gal's sidekick, who seemed slightly embarrassed at her friend's tentiginous impulses. This friend was blond like a cowslip, with radiant, dappled, and pallid skin. She was...*cute*.

Fast-forward now to the 80s and we shall recommence with the straight-ahead narrative.

Put Neill, Shlomo, Bidden, and Pas (just returned from a year working with the Yupik in Alaska) into their customary booth at the P&H. Run the conversation, which consists largely of different synonyms for forlornness and withdrawal.

Neill: "Just once I want to be the person whose situation doesn't tip over into its worst possible outcome."

Shlomo: "You know, not *everybody* loves the cha cha cha, but it seems churlish to disagree with Sam Cooke."

Bidden: "My entire knowledge of British culture comes from Dickens, Mike Leigh, and Benny Hill."

Pas: "Sometimes I take Pepto Bismol recreationally."

Neill: I've got a crappy week ahead. Dentist on Tuesday. Car inspected on Wednesday."

Bidden: "I hate going to the inspection station. I always feel like I am going to be examined in myriad ways. I dress nice. I put on extra deodorant. It's like I expect the guy to stick his head in and say, 'You missed a spot shaving there. And hey, you've been abusing yourself again, haven't you?"

Shlomo: "I had a two pee night. That's not fair. Better than a teepee night...or a toupee night, I guess. Or a To-Pay night. But better than a Pay-to-Play night and not quite as good as a Two Play night."

Neill: Sometimes I pee just to pass the time.

Shlomo: What color should your pee be? Mine looks like orange juice.

Neill: I think it's supposed to be lemonade.

Shlomo: At least it's not cranberry juice.

Etc.

Enter a group of people, returning perhaps from a play at Circuit Playhouse. Perhaps A

Sickness at the Center with Chris Ellis and Carla Binnage. Or A *Whirly-gig World* with Norm Degair and Uma Shikuma. Perhaps that light-hearted romp, *The Third Wilhelm Reich* with Claire Obscure, Michele Somers and Ransom Stoddard. They were well dressed and glittering like Richard Cory's chums. Or perhaps, Professor Irwin Corey's.

And there, like a firefly in a cave, in the middle of the gaggle, there was a woman all in white. She was paley as Grace, graceful as a snow leopard. Her hair was Tupelo Honey and her face Helen's before the ship sailed. She was, simply, the most stunning woman Neill had ever seen.

Had. Ever. Seen.

"Jesus," Neill said.

"I see what you see," Shlomo said.

"I have to talk to her."

"Why?" Shlomo backhanded.

"She's the most stunning woman I've ever seen."

And Neill rose like Indian smoke. He made his way through the fusc to the large table of strangers. The blond goddess was seated next to another blond woman, as pretty as the proverbial older sister who turns out to be the mom. She was the mom. They were both the color of lions, a blond found only in nature.

It didn't matter. Neill only saw her and her tractor beam drew him.

"I have to know you," Neill said.

The blond tittered the way some women do.

"I'm Neill," Neill said. He put out his paw. "Neill Rhymer."

"Mink Alpan," the vision spoke and from her vortex of light extended one pale, speckled hand. It felt like rose petals.

"You're lovely," Neill said like every nimrod before him.

She retittered.

"I don't want to disturb your evening further, but if you would perhaps consider going out with me sometime I work at The Book Shelf in Poplar Plaza. Call me if you're interested."

Neill handed her a business card. She took it and nodded like, you know, Grace.

Neill bowed to the table of faces all turned in his direction. Were some of them scowling? Neill couldn't tell. Maybe it was the light that had blinded him.

"You have Godzilla balls," Bidden said when Neill resat down.

"Jesus," Neill said.

"She is beautiful," Shlomo said.

"She is," Pas said.

"Her name is Mink."

"Sure it is."

"It is. And that rings a bell for some reason."

"That ringing is the bells in your belfry."

"I know her."

The table waited for what Neill would say next.

"The way Adam knew Eve. That kind of immediacy."

"What did you say to her?"

"I can't remember but I think we're going out," Neill said. His head had gone all swimmy.

Another Pinter silence descended, perhaps because it was Thespian Thursday at the P&H.

"Shit, I'm not ready to get laid. I just cut my nails," Neill added.

"What—"

"You know. The day you cut your nails your fingertips feel strange. I won't be able to get maximum tactile appreciation of her body."

"You're getting a little ahead of yourself," Shlomo admonished.

"I am. Thank you. I am. All the same, I need to go home and start a ritual cleansing."

The Phone Call

The next morning began with a bit of fairy-tale serendipity.

A young swain came in, nervous like a poet, pimpled and stuttery, tall and sweet. He did not look up when he said to Neill, "Can I ask you something?"

Neill braced himself.

"I want to propose to my girlfriend in the bookstore."

Neill smiled. "Ah," he said.

"This is her favorite place in Memphis."

"That's nice. You don't really need permission to ask her in the bookstore."

"Well, I wanted to do it, uh, cleverly. I wanted to put the engagement ring in a book she is coming in to pick up."

"Oh," Neill said. "How can we work that?"

"Her name is Kathy. Kathy Curtis. You have the book already on hold for her."

Neill turned and stooped to the special-order shelf and quickly found Kathy Curtis's book. He stood up with a big smile on his face.

"*The Day of the Locust*," Neill said. "She has good taste."

The fellow looked up from under his bangs. He blushed as if Neill had mentioned the connubial congress he and his intended were planning.

"May I secure the ring inside?"

"Of course," Neill said. "How?"

The fellow pulled out a small white envelope. Inside, it must be inferred like Schrodinger's Cat, was the engagement ring. He handed it to Neill.

"Good," Neill said. "Now what?"

"Put the book back."

Neill laughed a quick bark. He stooped and reshelved it. "I meant what will happen next."

"Oh," the swain said. There was an awkward silence.

"I'm bringing her to the store this afternoon after she gets out of class. We'll take it from there."

"Good plan," Neill said.

"Ok," the fellow said.

Neill put out his hand. "Neill," Neill said.

"Right," came the answer along with a damp handshake.

Neill was relating the story to Ianthe and Smithy and was only halfway in when the phone rang.

"I hate to try and tell a story when I am working," Neill said. "Hello, Book Shelf."

"Neill Rhymer, please," she said.

"This is Neill," Neill answered, rightly.

"Um, this is Mink Alpan. We met last night."

Neill felt faint. Suddenly, both Ianthe and Smithy were looking at him with concern. What was his face communicating?

"Yes," Neill said. "I remember."

"I was thinking that, yes, perhaps we could go out on a date."

"Wonderful!" Neill boomed. Neither Ianthe nor Smithy had ever heard Neill boom.

"Ok," Mink Risk said.

"You really called."

"Um, yes. Because. Um...I've never been called *lovely*."

Neill wondered about the guys in this gal's past. If Neill knew lovely, Mink Risk was lovely.

"Yes, yes, tomorrow night. Great. I'll come get you. Dinner, maybe? I can be there at 6 or so." It all came out in a burst.

"Good," Mink Alpan said.

"Thanks," Neill said and grimaced. "I mean, I'll see you tomorrow night."

"You want my address."

"Oh. Yes," Neill said.

After he hung up, he stood there for a moment to gather himself. Then, almost to himself, he said, "She didn't even wait 24 hours."

Neill walked away. Later, when the young couple were hugging and squeaking and jumping about at the front of the store, Ianthe and Smithy were not clear about what was going on.

"Oh, they just got engaged. In the store," Neill said. His head was full of taffy.

Back to Raleigh

The address Mink Alpan gave Neill was off Yale Road in Raleigh. His old stomping grounds. The itch that began when he first heard her name was becoming an uncontrollable rash. He needed the steroids of unpolluted memory.

Then, it hit him. This was the blond from the convertible double date. That little girl became one of the prettiest women on The Pale Blue Dot. It happened. Not exactly the ugly duckling story—she was cute when a teen—but a transformation, worthy of the best legends, a Hans Christian Anderson or The Arabian Nights.

Mink Alpan was Mink Risk.

Which meant she was a nee. Which meant a husband. Where was this unlucky fellow? Dead perhaps. Killed in a car wreck. Born with a defective heart. Beaten and left in a ditch.

Neill's head was full of carom shots and lightning. He had to calm down. Then, it struck him that he could no longer speak. He wasn't sure when it had occurred but he was sure he had total aphasia. Mink Alpan would never fall in love with a mute. Neill tried to talk aloud to himself. He tried to sing along to Tommy Roe on the radio. All that came out was the silence of shadow on a standing pool.

He might as well turn around and go home.

A block from her house and Neill stopped the car. He wasn't really mute, he didn't think. He was just trapped in his own attic.

He turned the radio down so he could see the address better.

Ok, he told himself. You are an interesting fellow. Mink Risk will understand that immediately. I can talk and I have things to say, he said to himself as he rolled up the curb in front of her house.

And, what flashed across his inner screen, as he exited his automobile, was a perfectly preserved sepia snapshot of Misso Anthill, brown-back naked, face down, her textbook fanny shining in his head like a gallows made of the fires of sunset.

Neill trudged forward.

The Date

"You're the fellow from the P&H," Mrs. Risk said. "Mink tells me you run a bookstore."

"Yes ma'am," Neill said. "In Poplar Plaza."

"I think I've been in there. I mostly shop at The Book Rack. I like the 2 for 1 trade in."

"Yes ma'am."

"I like to read, too," Mrs. Risk said, and then turned away. She was not as lovely as her daughter, who stood by dressed entirely in white, a princess in waiting, but she was a good-looking woman, still. The house seemed to contain only the two women. A father who had done a bunk? Neill guessed.

"I figured out that I did already know you," Neill said.

They were seated in Jade East, an Asian restaurant on Austin Peay, recommended to Neill years ago by Dr. Lucas.

"You did?" Mink drawled. She sounded a bit like Elly May.

"Years ago, my friend Mick and I took you and a brunette friend out in his red convertible."

"I don't remember you," Mink said, deflating the balloon that used to be Neill's heart.

"You're Mink Risk."

She laughed, placing a demure hand over her pink lips.

"You must have married."

Mink Risk rolled her eyes. "Don't get me stahted," she said.

"A bad one, yes?"

"Right out of high school. An old story."

"I see. And so, you had him shot."

"Ha ha," Mink laughed. It was a tintinnabulation that would have given Poe pause.

"I'm glad he's out of the picture."

"He's way out of the picture," Mink said. "This is nice soup. What is it?"

"Goat eyes, I think."

She laughed again. Neill's balloon reflated.

As they were talking Mink's attention was slightly drawn to Neill's left. Neill turned his head just as a young football type approached the table.

"Hey you," he said and sauntered slowly by.

"You know him?" Neill said, pleasantly.

"No," Mink Risk said. She hid her smile behind her napkin.

"An admirer, I guess. I forgot I had my cloak of invisibility up."

"I don't know. Tell me about you, Neill. Tell me about books."

Neill was warmed.

On the Horn with Bidden

"You mean the guy hit on her with you sitting there?"

"Yes, as if I didn't exist."

"What did you do?"

"I took him out back for a dust-up. I slit him up a treat."

"Ok, right. What could you do?"

"Suffer in silence."

"But the date went well, otherwise."

"She's too pretty for me, isn't she?"

"Of course not," faithful Bidden said.

"I don't know. She—she's made of cathedral light."

"She is quite beautiful. Not more so than Syrie I would say."

"True. But, it's of a different quality. Mink is—otherworldly. It's like being out with one of Charley's Angels."

"You gonna see her again?"

"Yes. Isn't that amazing?"

"Good. When?"

"Tonight."

"Jesus, that's great."

"I know."

"Ok then."

" "

"Ok, the phone is turning into a toad in my hand."

"You have to ask one more question," Neill said.

There was a pause.

"Cripes, Neill, you didn't sleep with her already, did you?"

"Oh, no, no. I took her home after dinner and we sat outside for a while."

"Oh. I get it. Did you kiss her?"

"I did, Bidden. I kissed her good."

The Rise of Mink Risk (The Next Night)

So, they went out to eat again. Neill could not think what to do on the sophomore date. He suggested Coletta's on Summer Avenue. It wasn't Asian, but Italian, so he felt like a man of the world.

The talk over dinner was small, sometimes so small it almost went away. They established that Mink didn't read much and that Neill would recommend some things. And Neill found out that Mink was a graphic artist and was making pretty good money for an advertising firm whose offices were on Covington Pike in Raleigh.

The conversation dwindled, went astray, stalled at times. But Neill made her laugh once or twice and that helped.

"You're funny," Mink said, her laugh spreading her delicate pink mouth wide, revealing teeth carved by ancient ivory artisans. Her smile could flat out stop your heart, and your lungs and kidneys.

"Do you like the spaghetti?" Neill asked.

"I do. Not a very original choice. I haven't eaten out much."

"Their spaghetti is especially good."

"What is that you're eating?"

"I can't remember. It ends in a vowel, too."

No laugh. Mink Risk looked around the dark, cozy restaurant. Perhaps she was hoping another stranger would hit on her.

"What do you want to do after we eat?"

This was bold of Neill. He was suggesting something beyond just taking her home.

"I don't know. What can we do?"

Neill's mind went ribald. But he held his tongue. "Watch a movie at my place?"

"Sure," Mink Risk said. Just like that.

The movie was some Italian thing (a theme date?), which both Neill and Mink lost interest in as they began to kiss. Soon hands were under shirts. Soon Neill was going gaga.

Mink pulled her own shirt off and then grabbed Neill's. Her grip was strong, almost manly. She practically tore the shirt. (Later, Neill found out that Mink was an athlete, a helluva shortstop.)

"Do you—heh—want to—heh—go to the—heh heh bedroom?" Neill said, as Mink threw her bra aside and revealed small coral breasts, about the size of the cups under which the elusive pea hides. They were small but, of course, perfect. And Mink's skin was alabastrine and as smooth as a billow.

She did want to. They went there.

When they were down to just their lower skivvies, a sudden, terrible thing occurred. Neill's bowels began to sway and pulse.

"Um," Neill said, as Mink ground her cotton-covered crotch against Neill's cotton-covered penal area. "I've got to. Um, I'll be right back. Excuse me."

He bounced off the bed.

He made it to the head. He was reminded of a date with a dishy volleyball player and the ignominy of hiding in the Circuit Playhouse restroom, while the play went on and his nervous bowels howled. Yet, he could do nothing else. What came, came. He was angry and embarrassed. He used a hot washcloth to finish the cleanup, and as he re-entered the bedroom, his nausea subsided a bit. But Little Neill had subsided, too. He may have even inverted.

Neill lay back down next to Mink, who was still clad only in panties. She was reading the back of the album that Neill had put on (Amazing Blondel).

"I've never heard of them," Mink said.

"English. Pretty stuff."

"It is."

"Where, um, were we?" Neill said, his confidence flagging with his wiggle-stick.

"We were about to take our underwear off," Mink said, and she laughed a short bark.

"Ah," Neill said.

"Neill," Mink now said. "I gotta say something."

"Ok," Neill said. He propped himself on one elbow, kissed her quickly, and set himself to listen.

The tale Mink told involved her ex-husband. They had only been divorced about three weeks. But the marriage had been bad from the get-go. He was dull and mean. Neill let the story unfold, saving his questions for the end.

"He wasn't, you know, physically abusive, but close. He was just an old redneck. Anyway, we—you know, didn't have much sex."

"Oh," Neill said. He didn't know where this was going.

"So, I'm not on the pill or anything."

"Oh!" Neill said. "Oh, I see. Well, sure, that's ok."

"Is it?"

"Of course, it is. We can just fool around. That might be best anyway, right? We hardly know each other."

"But, Neill...."

"Yes?"

"I want to."

Neill was gaga. Did we say gaga?

"Me too. Of course," Neill said. He leaned in and the kiss was passionate, intimate, friendly, liberating. "Do you know about the Today's Sponge?"

So, with that taken care of, they re-engaged.

Neill, when it came time, pushed her panties aside and fingered her into orgasm. She huffed and puffed and it was a wonder Neill's house still stood afterwards.

"Wow, you're good at that," Mink said.

"That? Oh, I can do better than that," Neill said, with what he hoped was a jocular tone.

"Now, I'm intrigued."

"I mean, you know. With my mouth."

"Oh."

"No good? Not what you want?"

"I have no idea."

Neill could only wonder.

"No one has ever, you know, eaten you?"

"God no."

"Come here, Sweetheart."

Neill lowered her panties. Mink Risk was as naked as a ghost in sunlight. She was as pale as a candle. Her pubic hair was the same honey shade as her beautiful mane. Mink tensed her body as Neill spread her legs. Neill stared like a gapeseed.

"Relax," Neill said.

"Sorry."

Neill kissed each knee. He ran his fingers up her thighs, followed by his tongue. As he got close to heaven, he went slower, circling that frothy little patch, until finally his tongue entered the tall grass and found her clit, already glistening with dew. Gently at first, then more firmly, he licked until he put his mouth hard over her mound, while he snaked a finger inside her. It didn't take long.

"Oh FUCK!" Mink Risk said. And Neill had to hold her hips to keep from being thrown from the bed. She shuddered like an old car.

After the tremors, Neill lay back down beside her. His little friend had rediscovered his purpose and Neill took it out of his underwear and rubbed it against Mink's thigh.

"That was," Mink Risk said. "Unexpected. I guess. I guess, I am really inexperienced next to your otha women."

"Mink, I gotta tell you," Neill said, putting a hand in her hair. "You're a vision. I am already smitten."

"I think I am too."

"Oh my," Neill said.

"Neill?"

"Mink?"

"I don't know what to do with yours."

Neill laughed. It just came out, fast and loud.

"Sorry," Mink said.

"It's ok. It's all ok," Neill Rhymer said to his new lover.

Today's Sponges

When Neill had taken Mink home that night he asked her if she wanted him to get some sponges. She said she would take care of it.

"When?" she asked.

"When, you mean, to use them?"

"Yes. Can we do it tomorrow night?"

So that next night, back in Neill's bedroom, no dinner included, they stripped each other naked once again.

Then, Neill had to go to the bathroom.

This was awful. Again his bowels shook and shimmied and emptied him. Again, he felt a little better afterwards and washed himself thoroughly.

The path up there, Neill thought, is so precipitous, it is a conquest every time you scale it.

"Neill, why do you go to the bathroom?" Mink asked, shining on the bed like a painting by Botticelli.

"Sorry," Neill said.

"I put a sponge in," Mink said.

"Good girl."

"But, Neill, before that?"

"Yes?"

"Will you—um, you know—again?"

"Eat you?"

"Yes."

"Lick your clit."

"Mm, yes."

"Suck you and finger you till you come?"

"Ok, stop."

"Yes, yes, I will do that," Neill said.

And he did. It was an encore performance and left Mink as flushed and satisfied as the night before.

This time Neill kissed her hard afterwards. Her liquors ran down both their chins.

"Do you want to show me how to—um, you know, do that to you?"

"I can do that," Neill said, gallantly.

"I'm ready."

Neill gave her his thumb and described what to do.

"Act like the tip of the thumb is the most sensitive part. Lick it, lick down the sides, put it in your mouth and use your saliva and lips and tongue to play with him. Let me stress this part: be careful with your exquisite white teeth."

Mink laughed. She did as he instructed with the thumb and then began to suck on it. Hard.

"Oh, one more thing. The names 'sucking' and 'blowjob' are misnomers. Do not suck—well except lightly. And, of course, do not blow."

"Ok," Mink said. "Oh, your thang is soft."

"Thang?"

"Stop. What do I do?"

"It will respond."

Mink put her honey-colored head over Neill and lowered her face toward him like a helicopter landing in a marsh. For a few seconds Neill couldn't tell if he was actually inside her mouth. She was being overly chary.

Then, as it grew in her mouth, she found a nice pace. Neill was watching, and studying her strong and perfect blond body. She was a vision, truly an angel.

"Oh, wait," Neill said suddenly.

Mink unpopped her lolly. "Did I do something wrong?"

"No, too right. I was about to come in your mouth."

"That's a good thing though, right?"

"It is. But, if you want to test that sponge, perhaps we should move onto that."

Neill didn't want to admit that the two-orgasm night for him was a rarity.

"Ok," Mink said. Now, she took some control herself.

She pushed Neill back on the pillows and climbed on top of him. Jesus, Neil thought, she has a chiseled body, without being overly muscular. And her skin was—eerily fine, as if it were not human. She could actually squat over him, holding her honeypot directly over his erection, her feet planted on either side of him, her strong thighs shining with health. She looked at him and smiled like a bad child.

Then, he was inside her. Neill Rhymer was inside Mink Risk and all Neill could think was, *"This is happening. No matter what else happens in my life no one can ever take this away from me. I am parallel parking with Mink Risk."*

Neill thought Mink had another orgasm while riding him. And, better than usual, he was keeping a good tight erection and not coming too soon. He decided to make good use of it. He swung her off him and she landed on the bed with a comical 'oof' sound.

He entered her, missionary style. She knew this position well, apparently, and made good use of it. At one point, she put one ankle on Neill's shoulder. Then, she put her other ankle on Neill's other shoulder. Neill pressed so deeply into her, he thought he might disappear inside her. He could live in her pussy forever.

Mink knew how to make herself come in this position and so she did. And still, Neill had more to do. "Thank you, Little Neill," he solemnly intoned .

"Turn over," Neill said. Mink looked at him funny.

She slowly turned. Neill wanted to eat her ass. It was made of white cake. He rubbed it until it shone. It was wet from her pussy.

Neill spread her legs.

"Um," Mink said.

Then, he slowly inserted himself inside the sponged cave.

"Oh," Mink said. Instinctively she raised her ass.

Neill pushed hard against her. Her strong thighs were supporting them both. Neill rocked there for a few minutes, hitting her ass harder and harder with his groin. Then, only then, did Neill feel it coming. He grasped Mink's milky cheeks, holding them so hard he left red hand prints, and shot off inside her for about 3 hours.

Well, seriously, it was a lot of come.

They fell together.

They lay still.

The music had ended long ago. They listened to the crickets outside.

Neill kissed her softly on her pink lips.

"Hoo. Neill," Mink said, in what Neill was thinking was her conversational gambit. "That was wild."

"It was awfully, awfully good," Neill said. He hoped she understood irony because he meant it was life-changing.

"Neill."

"Yes, Mink."

"We did more things the past two nights than I ever did in ma three years of marriage."

"Glad you got rid of him," Neill said, and they both laughed.

"Mink," Neill said, trying it on for size. "Mink?"

"Yes, Neill?"

"Can you spend the night?"

"I can, Neill. I was hoping you'd ask."

"Your mother won't worry?"

"She's probably passed out in front of the TV. Or her skanky boyfriend is over, and she and he will be making animal noises to beat the band." She said it like "bay-and."

"Spoon me," Neill said.

And Mink snugged her godly ass up against him and after a while she drifted into sleep. Right before she went out, she said, one more time, "Neill?," so soft it was more breath than language.

And Neill thought, "I am the luckiest man in what's left of the world."

Larry Csonka and the Invisible Man

Larry Csonka, Jim Kiick, and Paul Warfield came from the vaunted Miami Dolphins to join the newborn World Football League and the Memphis Southmen. This was a big deal for Memphis at the time. They had no pro sports team and constantly built rickety dreams on fly-by-nights like the WFL.

But Csonka, Kiick, and Warfield were not too far removed from a Dolphins team that was almost unstoppable. They were, as sports fans say, awesome.

So, the first game at Liberty Bowl Stadium was something of a happening in the little burg on the bluff. Tickets went fast. Neill scored a couple from a shady friend. Why? Because his gal, his new gal, she of the unearthly magnificence and fondness for the innovative gymnastics of sex, was a sports fan. Neill was, somewhat. He loved his Tiger basketball teams and he loved professional tennis and professional basketball.

"Oh boy!" Mink said into the phone. "Professional football in Memphis!"

"I'll pick you up around 10 a.m. Parking will probably be a bitch and the game kicks off at 11:30."

"You want me to drive to your house? You're already close to the stadium?"

"Yes," Neill said. "Yes, that would be great."

So, on a temperate Saturday afternoon, they went to see the Southmen play. The game was of passing interest. Csonka and Kiick didn't do much. They were, perhaps, past their prime. Neill couldn't concentrate on the game anyway. His girlfriend, in halter top and a short skirt, made critters come alive in Neill's conker. He wanted only to get her into bed. It was all he ever wanted. Everything else was preparation or celebration.

On the drive home, a few blocks from Neill's home, a convertible pulled up next to Neill and Mink at a stoplight. The 'gentlemen' in it looked as if they had just come from the game, also.

"Hey," the sandy-haired fellow driving hollered. "Hey!" He may have been Biff Loman.

Neill looked. Mink looked and then looked back at Neill. Her face was an apology.

"You look like the chick on *Bewitched*," the passenger in the convertible said. Both men looked like frat boys, with that kind of swagger and that sense of entitlement, and with that kind of haircut.

Mink did not look like Elizabeth Montgomery except that they were both blond. It was probably as deep a cultural reference the guy could make. He was trying to impress. He was positively pavonine, spreading his multi-hued ass feathers.

"You're prettier than her," the driver now countered.

The light changed. Neill eased ahead and the convertible matched his moderate speed. Neill speeded up. The convertible speeded up.

Eventually, they moved on but not before offering some more Neanderthal praise.

"Does that happen to you often?" Neill asked. He tried to keep the injured child out of his voice.

"Sometimes," Mink said. She put her hand on Neill's thigh. Everything was suddenly alright.

"I'm invisible when I am with you."

"It's nothing to do with you, Sweetie."

"Do it to me again from behind," Mink said a little later. "I've discovered I really like that."

"It's a wholesome discovery," Neill said.

"I love you, Neill," Mink Risk said, not for the first time.

"I love you, too, Pumpkin. So much."

"And Neill?"

"Hm?"

"You really like my white ass, don't you?"

Neill Speaks of His Love

To Bidden: "She's so—*real*. You know? I am getting my hopes up. I think this is the real thing. I can't see it going moldy."

"Good for you. You deserve it. There is nothing inevitable about dissolution in love."

"Right, right! It's not inevitable. It's totally evitable."

To Shlomo: "You have to meet her, Shlomo. She's not—well, she's not a reader much, but she's not had much opportunity. She's been through it. Bad upbringing, bad marriage, abusive husband. She's a real survivor."

"Like Jimi Jamison."

"And, God, is she beautiful. You won't believe it."

"Why wouldn't I?"

"Because—because she loves me. She really loves me."

"You're messed up. Of course she loves you."

"She shits peppermints," Neill said.

To his boss, Ianthe: "She's an amazing woman. She's come through so much and is really tough and, you know, she has these secret smarts."

"Why secret?"

"Because unexpected, I guess. She's so—grounded. Unlike some of the flibbertigibbet women I've dated."

"This sounds serious."

"I think I want to marry her."

"Oh my."

"I know. This is a new me, I think. Do you think that's possible?"

"Of course, it is, though I don't see why a new you is necessary. You've always been pretty great."

"Thank you. Imagine me married. Imagine me married to someone like Mink Risk."

"Uh huh."

"I mean Mink Risk herself, of course. Not just someone like her."

More and More Mink

Mink came to Sunday dinner at the Rhymer's. There exist photographs of Mink and AJ and Neill playing cards in the Rhymer's backyard. Mink shines like sea-born Cythera. Neill's expression says, "I can't believe she's with me. I am glad pictures are being made. Please let me keep her. Please may I keep her?"

Mink and Neill went to the movies. Mink said she wanted Neill to teach her about good movies, but honestly, she would rather see the latest Meg Ryan film. She thought Meg Ryan was the epitome of screen glamour. Meg Ryan made Neill's eyes weep blood.

Once Neill went to watch Mink play softball. She was stupid good, a terror at shortstop, and a single and double hitter like the best who ever played her position. She was the star of the team. Neill was dazzled watching her and his heart was full.

Alongside Mink, Neill recognized the woman playing second base. In moments of delay she would look from Neill to Mink, her face a squinchy fury. What the hell? Neill thought at first. Then he recognized her.

Years ago, Neill met this woman at a book signing. She was short, well-built, and cute, with a pageboy haircut. She was also whip-smart, and she and Neill hit it off, each laughing at the other's humor. Her name was Radical Foyer. Neill asked her out and they dated a bit. The first date was to see *Hiroshima Mon Amour* at the main library on Peabody. Neill pronounced Hiroshima with the accent on the second syllable and Radical made a point of pronouncing it on the third. Nevertheless, the date went well, with a kiss at the door and a promise to get together again soon.

Which they did. And after dinner, they went to Radical's apartment and she read some of the poems Neill was working on. Radical taught English at a chichi East Memphis high school and Neill was anxious about her opinion.

"Phew," Radical said, after reading a handful.

"What?" Neill said, his voice rising.

"You know. I was so worried that it was going to be crap and then what would I say?"

"Oh. Oh, so you like?"

"I do. Let me read some more."

That night they kissed on the couch. It was like a kiss between a puppy and a fence. There was no spark. Neill sensed that Radical was holding back, yet Neill couldn't figure out why. Radical was a few years older than Neill, so it surely wasn't inexperience.

They went out a few more times but it just wasn't on. Neill let the relationship, such as it was, die on the vine.

Later, he heard that Radical Foyer had come out of the closet. Ah, Neill said to himself. *Ok, then.*

Now, here she was playing softball with Neill's beloved.

After the game Neill stood off to the side, by the bleachers, waiting for the players to say goodbye to each other and praise each other's play.

Mink and Radical left the group together, walking toward Neill like gunslingers.

"Rad says you already know each other," Mink said.

"We do," Neill said. "I recognized you out there. Good game. That was a mean play you made on the blooper to right."

"Hello, Neill," Radical Foyer said. If two words could drip venom they did.

"What was wrong?" Mink said, in the car.

"I have no idea," Mick said. (Just let me get you home and into bed, Neill finished to himself.) (But the curtness bothered Neill. He wanted everyone to like him and didn't understand anyone who did not.)

"I'm all sweaty," Mink said.

"Shower at my house?"

"That would be great," Mink said.

They showered together of course. The soap had startling, slippery, aphrodisiacal powers, and lathering each other, they became so aroused they almost tumbled out onto the floor. Instead Neill entered Mink from behind while she leaned under the hot spray. It was so sublime (Welcome to our porno movie!), Neill forgot about that poison moment with Radical Foyer. He also forgot to remind Mink to put a sponge in.

He couldn't forget Rad Foyer for long though, because the next day she called Neill at the bookstore.

"Neill, what are you doing with Mink?" she said without greeting.

"Hello," Neill said.

"Well?"

"We're planning to blow up the doughboy statue in Overton Park. Don't tell, ok?"

"She's too –young for you." Neill knew she had bitten off the phrase "too *good* for you."

"Not really," Neill said.

"Not in years perhaps. But she is fragile. She's been through hell."

"I know the history, Rad. What is this about? I love Mink, you know."

"You don't love her. You're too shallow. You just want to fuck her."

Neill hung up.

Only afterwards did he realize he missed the opportunity to retort, even if it implied he had checked up on Radical Foyer. He recognized only after he hung up that Radical Foyer was choleric with jealousy. She was also in love with Mink Risk.

The Sponge Was in the Next Time

More outings and more couplings occurred and Neill was feeling pretty puffed-up and grateful that borborygmus had not continued to haunt his attempts at entering the temple of his beautiful Diana. He had fucked Mink Risk. He told himself this often and, often, it worked as a talisman which propped him up. His adulation of her splendor was both pathetic and grand. But she was also *fun*, he kept telling himself.

The bedroom passion was as physical as it could be and it shook and rattled the little cage around Neill's heart. Mink Risk stirred him and, so, he loved her. He was convinced his fierce feelings were undying and remarkable.

So, it had to happen. This center would not hold.

When naked, she was astonishing. She had skin like silk and marble. It took Neill's breath away. It took it away and kept it in a closet of dark mysteries. Plus, for those keeping score, Mink liked sex, which was mostly a novel and stimulating recreation for her. Mounting her, Neill became a young god, one of the lesser deities who still kept his ties with the homeland. After coming again inside the humid apiary between Mink's eternal thighs, again with her athletic legs resting on his shoulders so that she appeared an open door (a door to heaven often looks like a door to the other place, Shlomo had once told Neill), Neill gazed down at her delicate, freckled face, haloed by honey hair, and he spoke the intemperate words that would alter everything: "Will you marry me?" Neill said, earnestly, with impatient hope, with the desire for these days of fire to never end.

Mink's face went cockeyed. Her eyes flashed. Her mouth became a distant horizon. Madame Defarge knitted her brow.

Slowly those powerful legs slid from Neill's shoulders, and slowly Neill slid out of heaven and slowly Mink began to move away, emotionally, assuredly, and with damning resonance. It was as if Neill had changed, in that one moment from The Beloved into Old Harry.

Such is the power of words. Of one badly timed phrase.

Mink made an excuse and went home early. At the door Neill said, "Is everything alright?" (It was like saying it as the deck chairs began their 45-degree slide over the mezzanine of the Titanic.)

"Of course," Mink said, kissing Neill with measured pressure. "I'll talk to you tomorrow."

To his Friends for Succorance (And then I go and Spoil it all by Saying something Stupid like I Love You)

To Shlomo: "I fucked up."
To Bidden: "I fucked up."
To Crow: "I fucked up."
And, afterwards, dripping lachrymosely onto the lined page, which swam beneath the overflow, Neill wrote, "It is dangerous to overestimate your importance to someone. It is more than dangerous. It is fatal."

So it all Went Strabismal

"What do you want to do tonight?" Neill said into the phone, which felt like some obscene toy in his hand, something with which DeSade might have worked his demonianism.

"I can't tonight," Mink said. "I'm going out with the softball team."

"Radical?"

"She'll be with us, yes."

"How about tomorrow? There's that Fellini film at the library?"

"Tomorrow? Maybe. I might have to work late. We're on a deadline with some artwork."

"Ok," Neill said.

When he called the next day, his eagerness, his anxiety even, repulsed himself.

"I can't tonight. Mom's having a rough time."

"I thought you were going to work late."

"Yeah, that too."

"Ok," Neill said. "Tell me when next."

"Tomorrow night for sure."

"Ok," Neill said. "What do you want to do?"

"I'm not sure. How about I come by your house as soon as I am done."

"Done?"

"Done with—whatever , work and stuff."

"What time?" Already Dead Neill asked.

"I'm not sure. Certainly by 8."

"Eight?" Neill screeched like a macaw.

"I'll come as soon as I can, ok?"

"Ok," Neill said. "I love you."

"I love you, too," Mink Risk said, for the last time.

That Next Night

Neill looked at his watch again. She was now one hour late. He knew what this meant. She didn't care. Mink was showing him that she didn't care.

And he knew why. Because he had been precipitant. Because the marriage proposal had come too early, and with too much heat. But, she was so beautiful—she could knock you down with her smile—he was trying to secure her. Instead, she ran. This was conventional human behavior.

After another half hour Neill left his house. He left his house so that when she did show up—*if* she did show up—he would not be there. Instead, he walked up into the cove and sat on the curb, looking down at his own house, a small yellow glim in the darkness. It was late at night. In his heart, his ashy heart, every moment was more tenebrific than the last. In his ashy heart blackness.

Neill had been sitting there fifteen minutes when Mink arrived. She pulled up to the curb, as opposed to pulling into the driveway the way she used to. He tried not to read anything into that.

She stood underneath his porch light, knocking on the door. Her knocking was not very convincing. She stepped back, scanned the neighborhood. Her face was as calm as the breast of a lake.

Neill hated her at that moment. His hate burned in him like the crashing of stars. Neill was all alone in the world, his love washing away in the insouciant gaze of his erstwhile lover. Still, she was so damned beautiful. O how his heart sang!

It sang as Mink Risk drove away, forever, forever, and forever.

He Thought of Sue, He Thought of Misso, and He Thought of Mink Risk

And he declared himself a failure at love and life. He would never love again. These three formidable and wonderful women did not want to be with him. It meant he was unlovable. It meant he was an invertebrate, left to squirm around the muddy bottom of some dank lake.

Neill's self-hatred boiled to a degree formerly unimagined.

He didn't answer his phone. He missed the next three days of work.

When, eventually, he returned to The Book Shelf it was as if everyone knew of his ignominy, his shame. Even Iago tiptoed around him with a tight smile.

Neill spoke to no one. Not even customers, beyond an inhuman grunt as acknowledgement of their incarnate selves.

Neill went home alone and told himself he would never love again. All that was good in him had been extinguished. All that was nice had been distorted. All that was human had been putrefied.

And Then Something Worse

A few weeks later Neill was having lunch with a sales rep in the Asian restaurant across the street from Poplar Plaza. They were laughing because Neill, in his nervousness being with someone he didn't know very well, was employing his usual coping method: wiseassness.

Just as a roll of mutual laughter subsided, Neill looked up to see Smithy standing by the table. Her face was drawn and fearful.

"Neill," she said, voice timorous, "Your sister just called. You have to come quick."

"What—?" Neill began.

"It's your dad," Smithy said. "He's had a heart attack."

Of course, he's had a heart attack, Neill thought, his throat constricting and tears running. He's old and he's smoked since he was 16.

Neill made the drive to the new Methodist Hospital in Raleigh sobbing openly. As self-conscious as always, he thought about the other drivers observing him. Let them see the pain of human loss.

He parked in the emergency lot and quickly found his sister and mother in the waiting room. They all hugged and let the tears fly. When they were able to talk, Neill gleaned this from his family: the heart attack was bad. He had died in the emergency room and been revived by electric paddles. They were going to fly him in the helicopter to the Methodist Hospital on Union Avenue because the heart facilities there were better.

Neill absorbed all this and they agreed to drive in two cars back to Midtown and the other hospital. AJ's husband Dan, who coincidentally worked at Methodist North, had pushed the ER people to act quickly and get Max to Midtown. This might have saved his life.

Congregated in the small waiting room at the other hospital the family tried to make small talk but the air was too thick. It was difficult to forget the purpose of the small room where they were squatting.

There was another family in the waiting room. A serious surgeon pulled them aside (though aside still left Neill and his family in hearing distance) to deliver bad news.

"Your husband," he said to the middle-aged woman, who was nodding before she was even addressed, "is in bad shape. We can operate but he will not be able to live without life support. I need your permission to operate, but again, I stress that afterwards he will not be functioning. He will be in a coma, hooked up to life support."

The woman, nodding, said, "Operate, please, keep him alive."

Another man, possibly the woman's brother, stood behind her, hands on her shoulders. He began to nod, too, to support the wife's decision. The two children, around 8 to 10 years old, just stood sullenly and silently clinging to their mother's dress.

"Let me be clear," the surgeon said. "He will be in a coma afterwards. The brain damage is that significant."

"Ok, doctor," the woman said. She stuck out her lip like Mussolini. "Operate."

They all left.

"Jesus," Neill said. "He was begging them to pull the plug."

"Neill," Lolly said, signifying nothing.

Soon a surgeon visited them. He was Cary Grant handsome, later-Cary with silvered hair.

"Your husband is a tough old bird," the matinee idol said. "We're anticipating a triple bypass." And he told them, typically surgery like this could last ten or more hours.

The family settled in.

"I better call Brack," Neill said, and went to look for a pay phone.

"Fuck," Brack said. "I'll call the airlines. I should be there before he wakes up."

The surgeon was back in the room when Neill returned. He was smiling like old Cary Grant.

"I was just saying you can talk to your dad for a minute before we wheel him in."

The family followed Cary Grant down the disinfected corridors.

Max Rhymer was wheeled in front of them before a bank of elevator doors. He was about to be pushed into an elevator and the attendants seemed impatient to get past the family greeting so they could get on with their jobs.

Lolly kissed her husband's whiskered cheek. AJ did the same and then Neill followed. His father's cheek, which had always been immaculately shaved, was stubbly, and his breath unpleasant. Neill squeezed his hand and said, "How you doing?"

"Pain," Max said. He closed his eyes as if to demonstrate. "This is a fucking mess," he said, reopening them. It was the first time he'd heard his dad say the f word.

"Max," Lolly said.

The attendants gave us tight smiles and began to move toward the open elevator door.

"Lolly," Max rasped, taking her hand again. "Call Dipper and tell him I can't drive carpool tomorrow."

Later this became a defining moment for Neill, a moment that he realized something about his father and, hence, something about himself. Max Rhymer was the most responsible person Neill had ever known. And Neill later realized that he too aspired to be that responsible.

The Family Gathers

Brack got there early the next morning. The surgery was over. The surgeon had already given the family the thumbs up.

"We had to do a quadruple bypass once we got in there but we think he's going to be ok." Lolly hugged him and, God bless his pretty ass, he hugged her back.

We related this to Brack when he arrived, frazzled and hagridden, but ready to take over the role of most accountable male (up to this point that role had been taken by Dan).

They all had brunch together in the hospital cafeteria. Dazed from lack of sleep and drunk on relief, it was one of the nicest gatherings the Rhymers had ever had.

Later when they got to see Max, briefly, he smiled at them.

"They. Tell. Me. I'm. Going. To. Be. Ok." he susurrated.

The doctor standing by cautioned Max about talking, about doing anything but recovering.

"I told him he'd had his last cigarette," the doctor said.

Max smiled and nodded his head as vigorously as possible.

And it was true. He never smoked again.

Later, even this horrific happenstance could not dissuade Lolly from smoking. At first, she smoked outside the house but, gradually, as they returned to some kind of normality, she began, once again, to smoke whenever and wherever she wanted.

So Every New Day was a Temporary Stay Against Extinction

So, every new day was a temporary stay against extinction. Gradually, the Rhymers returned to what passes for regular life. The near-tragedy had made them all closer. Brack returned North but he and Neill began talking regularly on the phone, and AJ and Neill also talked on the phone, saw each other every Sunday at the parents' home and even began going out occasionally to bars to talk privately, brother to sister.

"Even though it makes me laugh I hate to hear you call yourself Bobo the Unmateable Gorilla," AJ said, sipping her umbrellaed something.

"Ach, I dunno. I can't make love stay. How do you make love stay?"

"I don't know, Brother of Mine. Work at it?"

"Is love work? Really?"

"I guess so."

"Is it for you and Dan?"

"No, not so much. We've had some rough times, mostly due to my jealousy. I am convinced he is going to run away with a nurse. He is surrounded all day by pretty nurses who think he's the berries."

"But they're not you."

"You're sweet."

"I mean it. He loves you. It's easy to see and it's hard to see that you really have to work at anything."

"People say that though."

"People say what?"

"That you have to work at love."

"Misso said that. Right before she stuck a steak knife through my heart."

"Misso. Pfft. She can't carry your shoes."

"Is that an expression?"

"Isn't it?"

"I don't know. But I understand the sentiment. Thank you. My body aches for love, if you're excuse the earthy reference."

"Been a long time, eh?"

"I can't even remember sex. I can't even see it from here. It must have been made in the days of King Wamba."

"You'll find someone. You're funny. You're handsome. And you're as smart as Poindexter."

"Felix the Cat's friend."

"Yes. He was very smart."

"He was."

"Anyway. Hang in there. Love comes when you're not looking. Someone will fall into your, um, lap."

"My track record includes many votes against that kind of happy ending. Women like me but they don't want to stay with me. They think I am funny and atypical for a while and then they go on to marry lawyers, or dentists, or PhD candidates in Socio-biology."

"Nah. You're the real thing," AJ said, putting her umbrellaed something down. "What the fuck am I drinking?"

"Zombi killer?"

"Seriously. Is that what I ordered?"

"I don't know. I'm sticking with my girly drinks."

"You've always been a Kahlua man."

"I have. And I am damn proud of it."

There was this Woman from Oxford, Mississippi

Neill met her at a signing for Willie Morris at The Book Shelf. She had driven up with friends. She was short, blond, and cute as a stack of kittens. She also had amazing Mary Poppins. She was built like a miniature Marilyn Monroe.

Her name was Mopsy Dowd. It probably still is.

Neill thought she was delicious and he made with the google eyes.

She made some google eyes back.

So Neill tracked down her phone number through bookstore connections. It turned out she worked at Square Books in Oxford.

Neill made plans to visit her. Bidden went with him.

Mopsy Dowd was in the bar she said she would be in. She brought along a sidekick, also, a skinny, tall gal, whose name Neill never did catch.

The foursome took a little tour of Oxford. They ate cheesecake at The Hoka. They visited Roanoke, Faulkner's home, and they visited the great man's grave. It was a lovely day, and as the sun went down, they all agreed to stay together and have some dinner. They returned to The Hoka. After dinner they strolled some more. As if agreed upon beforehand, the couples split up. Bidden and the friend wandered away, and Neill and Mopsy were left alone in a darkened parking lot behind a church.

They leaned against Neill's car. They kissed. Mopsy kissed very well and her compact little body felt like seven kinds of bliss. This is more like it, Neill thought.

They made out for about an hour. Neill put his hands under Mopsy's shirt in the back and felt her young womanly flesh. Neill grabbed her tight buns and pulled her close against him so she could get the point. The point was prominent.

They exchanged phone numbers and addresses, and the boys went home.

"How was your day?" Bidden asked.

"Blissful," Neill said. "Jesus, can she kiss."

The car was quiet except for Creedence singing "Fortunate Son."

"God, I love Creedence," Neill said. "How was *your* day?"

"I think she's gay."

Neill hated the telephone, and the couple times he tried to talk to Mopsy it was awkward and horrible. She seemed unexcited, to put it mildly. Perhaps, she is gay, too, Neill thought to comfort himself.

But he tried a new tack. He began to write her letters. He attempted to court her through letters. This went considerably better.

"Your letters are terrific," Mopsy said, after a flurry of them. "Really terrific." They were back on the phone and the tracks had been greased.

"Come see me," Neill said.

"I will. How about this weekend?"

Yes, that would do fine. Neill was eager. He was too eager. He told himself to temper his enthusiasm, a lifelong refrain, and one he had great difficulty following. He would not, he vowed, ask her to marry him.

She arrived on Neill's doorstep in a tight, patterned shirt that she must have been told emphasized her bosom, and a short skirt, also tight.

"You look delicious," Neill said. Fuck, he told himself.

They went out to the Knickerbocker restaurant and ate. Mopsy had a house salad and some vegetable thing. Neill had a steak.

"Steak, huh?" Mopsy said.

"Yes. Good meat. Meat good."

"Ha ha," Mopsy said.

"You're not vegetarian, are you?" Neill asked.

"Oh no, no. Just trying to watch my girlish figure."

They went back to Neill's after dinner. They went to the bedroom. The letters had worked their magic. When Mopsy took off her shirt and bra, Neill was treated to just how grandly orbicular and celestial were those breasts. She was crackling.

"Woof," Neill said.

"Ha ha," Mopsy said. She wore only white cotton panties.

Neill was naked.

"God, you feel good, Mopsy," Neill said. "Your body is—amazing." Words failed him.

Mopsy took a good hold on Little Neill. She knew how to give a handjob.

"Mm," she said. "Better take care of this."

She bent over him. She knew how to give a blowjob.

"Nnnggggm," Neill said. "Mopsy."

"Mmm," Mopsy said.

"Mopsy?"

She raised her blond little Marilyn Monroe head. "Hm?"

"Let me do you before I...you know."

"Lie back down, Cowboy."

So Mopsy finished her skillful blowjob, sucking up Neill's coconut juice and finishing with a loud, comical slurp.

"Ah, that was good," she said.

She was still wearing panties.

When Neill had recovered himself enough, he began to stroke her.

"Now, let's do you," he said.

He put his hands inside her panties. He found her crack, her anus, her clit, her vagina. They were all where they were supposed to be. When he put one, two fingers inside her he tried to simultaneously take her panties off.

"Mm," she said. "Keep doing that. But leave my panties on."

Neill worked his hand the best way he knew. He knew he could bring her off with his mouth but she didn't want that this time. There will be other times, he thought.

Finally, she came on Neill's hand.

"Mm, thank you," she said like a good houseguest.

"You're very welcome," Neill said like a good host.

"Sleep here?" she asked.

"Oh yes," Neill said.

In the morning, they woke and they kissed and Mopsy began to get dressed.

"I've got to get back," she said. "I have to work this afternoon."

Neill watched her dress. It was quite pleasing. He wanted that body some more. He wanted to show her he was as talented orally as she was. When they kissed at the door Neill told himself, there will be other opportunities.

He never saw her again.

His letters went unanswered. His phone calls were even more painful than before. Mopsy Dowd had already moved on.

"I don't get it," he told Bidden. "What am I doing wrong?"

And So He Toiled Long into the Night

...Working on his loneliness, burnishing it, rubbing it like a lamp with no genie or genius. He was a worn-out lobcock, with a streak of broken romances. He wanted to give up. He told himself that that was what he was doing. He could no longer go the vole. He was giving up on Love.

But, of course, he didn't. Neill, like most humans, had an infinite capacity for hope, and an unshakeable desire for company, for romance, and for building something long-lasting.

Neill wrote a lot during this period of his life. He was now writing short fiction as well as poetry. None of it was very good but he had apprenticed himself to Calliope, and some nights he felt that he was on the road to find out. That perhaps, one day he may be able to call himself a writer without embarrassment.

He wrote this:

The Men at P&H, sans Shlomo

After the success of Shlomo's book with Viking, he began to cast about for ways to make some money at his chosen profession. He also wanted out of Memphis, out of the land of ghosts and regicide. He accepted a position at Skidmore College in New York.

"I miss Shlomo," Neill said.

"Yeah," Crow said. "This beer tastes funny."

"You knew him better than I, but I miss him, too," Bidden said.

"It tastes like licorice. Is that possible?"

"Guess who's on the faculty with him?"

"T. C. Boyle," Bidden said.

"Nope."

"Franz Kafka."

"Nope."

"Dr. Seuss."

"Nope. But did I tell you I met him once and made him laugh."

"Yes. Just tell me."

"Maybe it's anise," Crow said.

"Maximilian Calvada."

"Jesus, that's the big time. Our own American fabulist."

"Shlomo loves him. Says they're like brothers already, mopey, self-deprecating brothers."

"I can see that."

"Maybe it's because of the gum I was chewing."

"Did you hear about Mookie?" Neill asked.

"Pop Tunes Mookie or Mormon Mookie?" Bidden asked.

"Pop Tunes."

"Y'all know two guys named Mookie?" Crow asked.

"What?"

"He killed himself," Neill said.

"Shit," Bidden said.

"He'd had this bad week, I am told, and at some point on Thursday someone mentioned that it was Thursday and Mookie had been thinking it was Friday and that it was the end of the week. He went behind the store and shot himself."

"Shit."

"I know."

"There but for the grace of Mookie."

"So, you and the new gal are spending a lot of time together?" Neill asked Bidden.

"Kayla. I don't know. She's alright."

"I thought you were head over teakettle."

"We are. Were. I don't know. She's—what's the word? Pretentious."

"Really?"

"She drags me to these things called 'happenings,' where it's out on this abandoned farm in the middle of the night and there's a lot of light and noise and zero coherence."

"Signifying nothing."

"Exactly. She takes me to plays in places I didn't even know they performed plays. We went to something the other night. It was in a warehouse downtown. Something about abuse, or self-abuse, or selfish boots. I think that was the name of it. Selfish Boots."

"Avant-garde. She loves avant garde stuff. That's not all bad."

"Oh, it was *avant* avant garde. The stage was at the back of the auditorium and all the seats faced a giant mirror which sometimes reflected the play proceeding at your backs and sometimes, through some kind of mechanical lever system, reflected the audience's bewildered faces in circus mirror fashion."

"It's this throat lozenge," Crow said. "Smell this."

"It smells like throat lozenge," Neill said.

"But mixed with the beer—"

"You had a date since the spy from Oxford?" Bidden asked.

"Spy?"

"I don't know. I thought maybe she was a secret agent. I can't explain her behavior."

"Right. She had a secret. Her secret was that she only wanted to sleep with me once."

"So, you're masturbating a lot?"

"Just trying to keep my hand in."

"It's not the throat lozenges either," Crow said. "It's a mystery."

He Sees Her Running

In these waning days, each night, as Neill left through the rear door of The Book Shelf, he was treated to a vision, perchance a flight-of-fancy vision. Every night, at that exact time, there was a jogger who went round and round the block west of Poplar Plaza. She was short, small-breasted, with powerful thighs, a mop of curly dark brown, almost black hair, and impish dimples as deep as ether.

You're thinking: Old Neill is not quite dead yet if he is noting this shimmering, galloping afternoon eyeful. And you'd be right. Venerate the hominid heart. It gets back up off the canvas time and time again, always ready for another blow, but hoping against hope, that this time, *this time*, it would be oh so right.

So, what to do?

Perhaps, this was born of despondency. Perhaps, Neill was remembering how bold he had been to show up on Dew Drynow's doorstep, lo those many years before, when she didn't know him from Adam's off ox. (Is that the expression? ed.)

Perhaps, he was also remembering how staggeringly badly that had gone. Perhaps, he didn't care.

Enough.

His plan was this. After watching her for weeks, counting on her being there for weeks and never being disappointed, he decided to simply step in front of her and say hello.

And this, he did.

As she rounded off Poplar, passing the Taco Bell on the corner (O Ring that Taco Bell!), and turned down Prescott heading North, Neill placed himself on the sidewalk like Ozymandias. This cute, brunette jogger was heading toward a new future. She was heading toward a collision with Neill Rhymer.

As she got closer, her face wore a querulous expression. Neill stood there grinning like an asshead.

She slowed. Neill put up a traffic cop's paw.

"Hi," Neill said.

"Yes?" she said, curiosity and wariness mingled on her pretty face. She had a turned up nose and a thimble-full of freckles, sown by a clever Appleseed.

"I've seen you jogging every day, same time, like clockwork. Every night I get off work, you're here."

"Yes?" she said, again. She began that kind of jogging in place thing that runners do, impatience mixed with a show of bravado. *I am serious about this running thing*, the motion says.

"Well, I work at the bookstore here." Neill jerked a thumb over his shoulder. "I just had to stop you because, well, shucks, you're so damn pretty that I couldn't pass up the opportunity. I couldn't have lived with myself had I done nothing."

Maybe he didn't really say shucks.

Now, the impish runner smiled.

"Ok," she said. "I am stopped." She ceased running in place.

"Would you like to, you know, go out sometime?"

She closed one eye. She looked at this jaunty pirate in her path.

"May—*be*," she said.

"Neill. Sorry, my name is Neill. Neill Rhymer."

"You write poetry."

Neill's eyes goggled. She'd read him?

"How—did you know?"

"You mean you really write poetry?"

"Oh," Neill said now. 'Because of my name."

"Right."

"Yes, I write poetry. I'll write a poem for you."

Neill had to stop himself. He was driving off the cliff.

"What's your name?"

"Lucrezia Enough," the pixie said.

"Enough?"

"Don't."

"Ok, Lucrezia." Neill put his hand out. Hers was as small as a chaffinch and sweaty.

"Sorry," Lucrezia said.

"I'll never wash it," Neill said.

Stop, Neill, please, for God's sake, stop.

"You live around here?"

"Right here," Lucrezia Enough said. She indicated the apartment complex behind Poplar Plaza.

"Ah. So. Will you?"

"I can go for a drink. Can we start with a drink?"

"Of course," Neill said. "Oh, wait. God. Do you have a boyfriend?"

Lucrezia closed her studious eye again. "No," she said, softly.

"Ok, wonderful."

"When?" she asked.

"Oh yeah. Tomorrow?"

"I guess so."

"Wonderful."

"You said that."

"After your run, after your shower, I'll call on you?"

"Lemme come to you," Lucrezia said.

They exchanged phone numbers and Neill gave her his address on Holmes Circle.

"Ok," Neill said. "See you tomorrow night. Same Bat-time."

She laughed. The puckish pixie laughed and rolled her eyes.

"Ok then," she said.

Neill exhaled on the way home.

A Square at the Circle Café

There was a popular bar/restaurant next door to the Taco Bell at Poplar and Prescott. It was called The Circle Café and it was there that Neill joined Lucrezia. He had called her and she had said she'll walk down and meet him. "Just for a drink," she added.

She was standing outside when Neill drove up. His heart went bang. His heart gunned the motor, spun on the ice, and nearly ended itself by crashing spectacularly. She really was quite attractive, now that he saw her for the first time in something other than t-shirt and running shorts. She was wearing a short-sleeve white shirt and blue jeans. She was callipygian in a way sure to send Neill over the edge. Neill would have to try to walk that edge with more grace this time. This he vowed, though, readers, honestly, he was already getting ahead of himself. He was getting ahead of both of them.

"Hi," Neill said, getting out of his car. She was walking toward him.

"Neill," Lucrezia Enough said. She had a twinkle in her eye. Maybe it was a twinkle.

They sat at a table by the window looking out on Poplar.

"Gin and tonic," Lucrezia said to the waitress, who was about 25 but looked 40.

"Ice tea," Neill said. He smiled at the waitress and as he moved his smile downward to his date he saw her bemused annoyance.

"Ice tea," she said. "A teetotaler. A careful man."

"I don't drink."

"But you couldn't very well ask me out for tea."

"Exactly. I would sound like Arthur Treacher."

Lucrezia Enough laughed. She had a great laugh. It came from her chest and burst from her mouth like a snatch of song.

"Or Benny Hill," Lucrezia said.

Now, Neill laughed. This was going well.

The drinks came. The waitress, who might have aged another 6 months while away, said, "Anything else?"

"Let's get an appetizer," Neill said. "I haven't eaten."

"Mozzarella sticks," Lucrezia said.

"And fried mushrooms," Neill said.

"And chips and dip," Lucrezia said, and she and Neill laughed.

"Did you know that mozzarella comes from water buffalo milk?" Neill asked Lucrezia.

"I did not. It sounds like bullshit over drinks."

"Might as well call it dinner," Neill said.

"Then this becomes a dinner date and not just meeting for drinks."

"Does that ruin it?" Neill asked. "Is this too heavy too early?" He was smiling.

"I think it'll be alright."

"I gotta tell you. I've been watching you a long time. I was trying to get my courage up to stop you."

"I'm impressed that you did," Lucrezia said. She seemed to be looking Neill's face over as if it were a tarot card. "I have to say that your confidence is what intrigued me. Confidence is a real turn on."

"Are you turned on?"

Lucrezia barked a short laugh. "Maybe," she said.

"Check," Neill said.

Lucrezia laughed harder. It was like Pan's pipes.

The waitress came over. "You don't want the apps?"

"Just kidding," Neill said.

"Great," she deadpanned, walking back.

By the time the food came, the conversation was flowing. Neill found out that Lucrezia worked at one of the downtown banks, not as a teller, but in an office. And Lucrezia found out that Neill had published a few poems and short stories and was a voracious reader.

"Will you recommend books for me?" she asked. "I mean to read more but don't know what I like."

"We can fix that," Neill said.

By the time they had eaten, the talk and laughter were so animated that Neill already knew the answer before he asked but he asked anyway. When the bill came he paid it.

"My place for a while?" he said, glimmering.

Lucrezia glimmered back. Her face really was pixyish and her nose and mouth particularly beautiful. Her lips made a small bow. Neill wanted to unwrap it.

They sat on the couch. Soon they were sitting closer. When Neill bent in to kiss her she matched his enthusiasm. They tongue-wrestled. Torridness arose. Torridness.

When Neill took her shirt off and bent her backwards over the couch arm he found her boyish breasts with their long nipples quickly with his mouth and sucked hard. Lucrezia's head hung over the edge and blood rushed to it. Her neck grew mottled with desire. Her breathing was like Ginger Baker's drumming. She was in heat.

Neill was turned-on himself. He wanted to continue. Instead, he stopped and, slowly, Lucrezia raised her head, still panting.

"What happened?"

What did happen? Neill was scared. He knew he was prone to diving into the deep end without, first, learning to dog paddle. But, Lord, he wanted to paddle this eager puppy. Lucrezia Enough's cheeks shone with want.

"I want to go slowly," Neill said.

"Oh," Lucrezia said. "Do you really want me to put my shirt back on?"

"I do and I don't," Neill said. Now, he was worried that this was going the wrong way. If she thought him a poltroon so much for being turned on by his confidence. But, dammit, he didn't want a repeat of the Mink Risk file.

"You're quite a gentleman," Lucrezia said. She turned her shirt back right-side out and pulled it over her head.

"I want to see you tomorrow night," Neill said. "Let's really call it a date and see how that goes."

"Ok, Neill Rhymer," Lucrezia said. "This time I'll choose the place and I'll pay."

For once, Neill thought, I played it right. So far, I've played it right.

Bidden on the Horn

"I did it," Neill said. "I stopped the jogger."

"The beauty you saw every afternoon at the same time?"

"Yes."

"You're King Kong, you know that?"

"As opposed to Bobo the Unmateable Gorilla."

"That's me."

"You—womanless again? Wait. Yes ma'am."

"You know an Arkansawyer woman writer, does poetry and essays. Lives here I think."

"I'm sorry. I am not sure who—"

"She has a press here. A religious press. St. Mark's or something."

"Oh. St. Luke's. Phyllis Tickle. Yes, we have some of her books. Hold on just one minute. I don't think she's from Arkansas, but I think she is who you mean."

"She certainly is from Arkansas. Phyllis Tinkle, right."

"Ok. Hold on just a second."

"You're at work."

"Obviously"

"Phyllis Tinkle. That's funny."

"Yeah. I better go see to her. She's wandered into the sex section."

"Yes. Of course, I'm womanless. Tell me about this jogger."

Neill told the story, with more self-deprecation than necessary, but with relish for the part where she said his confidence was a turn-on.

"It is?" Bidden said. "That explains a lot. I'll never have a woman."

"Oh, stop."

"You seeing her again?"

"Tonight."

"Damn. Ok. Neill."

"Yes?"

"Go slowly."

"I'm telling myself that. I could have had her last night. I really could have."

"You turned it down?"

Neill hesitated.

"I'm stupid. I'm stupid as any stoon. I'm stupider than Dr. Watson."

"You mean the Nigel Bruce Dr. Watson. In the books—"

"Yes, yes."

"Sorry. You're not stupid. You may have played it right."

"What if that was my one chance with her?"

"Then you're stupid as a stoon."

"Tickle!"

"Yes, ma'am."

"It just came to me."

"Gotta go, Bidden."

"Call me tomorrow morning."

The Second Date which, This Time, is Called a Date

They ate at Ireland's, a place Neill had been a few times with Victoria, many years ago.

"Have you eaten here before?" Lucrezia asked as they got out of the car.

"Long time ago."

"Oh."

Was she disappointed? "I don't remember it well," Neill added.

"Get their steak fries. They're amazing."

Neill looked around. This was a part of Memphis he did not know well, almost downtown but not quite. Across the street from the restaurant was a church. Its signboard said, *Masturbation is the devil's typewriter.*

Neill pointed it out. Lucrezia collapsed with laughter, leaning against Neill in an affectionate and oddly moving gesture. Neill held her small body against him and relished her soft bones.

Dinner was nice and the conversation even livelier. There was rapport. Neill thought rapport and mutual senses of humor meant a lot. He thought, feasibly, that it was the secret, the key to what made relationships last.

Neill was jumping ahead again. Didn't everyone? Apparently not.

They went back to Neill's.

"You gonna let me see your apartment sometime?" Neill asked. "I'm not even sure which door is yours."

Lucrezia ignored the question. "You got any tea?" she asked.

They started on the couch. Neill put a movie in the VCR. It was *Repo Man*, a particular favorite. They saw almost none of it.

By the time Harry Dean Stanton arrived, our young couple was shirtless and dry-humping on the carpet.

"Bed. Quick," Lucrezia said.

"Birth control," Neill said, putting his tongue back in Lucrezia's ear.

"Taken. Care. Of."

In the bedroom, on the bed, their passion was like a tidal wave. Lucrezia Enough was one sexed up woman. Neill was just trying to keep up.

Lucrezia pulled her own pants off. She pulled off Neill's and then his briefs. She wrapped her hand around his crimson drumstick. "Ahh," she said, and she seemed genuinely pleased with it. She weighed his dinky bag next. "Ahh," she said, again. Neill was as hard as a Greek puzzle. Then, she began to suck him with wild abandon, as if driven wild by what she had discovered, but with a skill that only comes from practice.

Neill groaned. Lucrezia Enough looked up.

"Groan for me," she said, and squeezed Neill's balls as if they were a wet sponge.

Neill groaned again.

Lucrezia stopped the scoffing and leapt upon Neill, her strong thighs spread over his now wet and fully prepared willy. She was still wearing small white panties. She rubbed them against the tool and was working herself up to a real frenzy. She seemed to want Neill to penetrate the cotton membrane separating them.

"Neill, Neill," she rocked.

"Jesus, you're beautiful," Neill said. "Your ass is incredible."

"Say more," she said, rocking, rocking.

"Let me get my hands on you."

Neill grabbed her still swathed ass, his fingers digging in, one hand slipping inside.

"Tear them," Lucrezia said.

"Really?"

"Fuck, Neill. TEAR THEM!" she said, rocking harder.

Neill grabbed one side and pulled.

"Ow," Lucrezia said.

"Sorry."

Lucrezia grabbed one side and, somehow, with a nail and a crooked finger, she got the tear started. Neill sensed it was his job to do the rest. He pulled them hard and damned if they didn't tear away. He threw them aside.

"Ah, ah, ah," Lucrezia said, grabbing the pole vigorously and putting it inside herself. Neill was almost a spectator for this wondrous sexual athlete. She was going at it, hammer and tongs. She was lost to the frenzy.

Then, she opened her eyes and found Neill's face.

"Fuck me, Neill. Do it harder. Come on. Do. It. Harder."

Neill bucked.

"Yes, yes, give it to me hard, Neill. Your dick is amazing. Your gorgeous dick, Neill, give me all."

Readers, Lucrezia came five times before Neill finally let his own come. By that time, they had run through various positions, including a few Neill thought perhaps Lucrezia had invented. Neill came in his favorite way, up against her magnificent ass, which he grabbed in frantic handfuls as he pumped away. She kept up a stream of obscenities that spurred them both on. It was the most intense dirty talk he'd ever heard (and for the rest of his life he would be turned on by words more than actions, or visuals) surpassing the blue streams of verbiage that Chara Winsky used to contrive.

"I feel you filling up," Lucrezia said over her shoulder. "You like my ass, don't you, Neill? You like fucking my ass, don't you? I feel it, Neill. I want you to shoot your load in me. I want to feel that hot come rising up and exploding in me. It's gonna make me come one more time, Neill. Yes, I feel it. We're gonna come together, Baby. Come on, here we go. Let's come together. Gimme your spunk, Baby, gimme it all. I want to...FEEL...IT.....OH....I'M GONNA...COME....IF YOU'LL SHOOT INSIDE ME....NEILLLL!!!!"

And they did. They came together.

As dates go, it wasn't bad.

"You come?" she joked.

"As the writer Peter DeVries said, 'it was the kind of orgasm unjellies the eyeballs.'"

Lucrezia spent the night. In the morning, she dressed quickly.

"Fuck, I'm gonna be late. You're a tiger, you know that?"

"I think you wore me out."

Mm," she said, distractedly as she looked for her belt.

"Yet I want you some more. Tonight?"

"Mm," she said, smiling at him. Those eyes. That mouth. "Maybe. Lemme check and I'll call you later."

Dressed, she leapt upon the bed and kissed Neill thoroughly.

"You're alright, Neill Rhymer. You are definitely alright."

Neill is, Of Course, Besotted

If Neill had ever been in control, he relinquished it now. Not consciously, but his heart came on as if by occultism, like a chandelier suddenly bursting into light in an abandoned house. Neill's heart was haunted and haunted, it made Neill one of the walking dead, a revenant, a ghost, a man in love.

O how his soul sang! He was alive again. Mink Risk did not kill him. Misso Anthill did not kill him (though she came closest). No one and nothing had killed him. He was alive and he was smitten like a 12-year old with his first stiffy.

At work the next day, he was full of ardor, and full of himself.

He loved the beautiful young housewife who came in for her book-club book, Willie Morris's *The Courting of Marcus Dupree*. He loved the little boy who came in with his sickly mom who wanted *The Poky Little Puppy*, because he had worn his copy and the pages had fallen out. Neill even loved the unpleasant old lady who castigated him for not knowing the word *Pensees* was pronounced *pahn-seyz*.

"Anyone who works in a bookstore should be multilingual, you know, young man. Can you not speak anything but a bastardized form of English that most Southerners accept? The entire culture is going to pot. When I was young..." Etc.

Neill's impulse was to say, "I speak Pig-Latin. Uckfay ouyay." Instead he said, "Yes, ma'am, you're right, my education is sadly lacking. Thank you for correcting me."

Neill was Love. He was Gandhi. He was St. Sebastian.

Because, he was going to fuck that little dark-haired sprite named Lucrezia Enough again and soon. Neill was Love.

And So it Began

And so, they began to see each other, almost every night. The sex was rousing. Neill loved Lucrezia (whom he began calling Lucky) for her sly, dimpled wit, her enthusiasm, her elfin mop of hair, and her absolutely stunning and muscular corybungus. Mounting her from behind was about as stirring as sex got. He felt the strength of Pan. And he was becoming addicted to Lucrezia's bedroom vocabulary.

Once, sitting astride him, riding his erection for her 3rd and 4th orgasm, Neill sucked one of her extended nipples into his mouth.

"Bite it," she said.

Neill gently raked his teeth across it.

Bite it, *harder*," she said.

Neill bore down on it slightly.

"Bite it, dammit," she said.

Neill bit. He was afraid of drawing blood. Lucrezia didn't instruct him further (for she was lost to her convulsion), but Neill worried a bit about the frenzied command. Did she really want to be hurt?

One fine morning Neill woke to find her pulling on his sleepy willie, sitting astride him, her succulent rump facing him.

"Morning," Neill mumbled.

She was too busy to answer. She was attempting to form a little rocket out of Neill's initially inactive, limp clay. When it was sufficiently rocket-shaped, she mounted it. And Neill was introduced for the first time to, what the manuals call, 'the reverse cowboy position.' He liked it. Especially because of Lucky's great gift, those Imperial Cheeks.

They also went out. They had dates. They saw movies and ate in restaurants. Neill thought she was a perfect fit for him, the most perfect fit, moodwise, temperamentwise, sexwise, and witwise, since Sue Goorile. And she was multi-orgasmic like Sue. Was there a connection?

They went for walks. Neill gave her mix tapes and books. He gave her a tape of love songs which ended with The Velvet Underground's "After Hours:" "If you close the door, the night could last forever...."

Lucrezia was moved by the gift. On a walk they stopped and sat on the curb to watch the sun set and she slipped her hand around his thigh and they sat there quietly in the empurpling gloaming.

"You're awfully wonderful," she said.

"Oh, Lucky. I'm ok. I am having such a good time," Neill answered, temperately. "You're—I don't know—just right for me, I think. You're cheeky and sardonic and cute as a kitty."

"Neill," she said. And the pause made Neill's heart beat like Dino Danelli on horse. He was braced. "I think I love you."

"Lucky!" Neill expostulated. "What are you saying?"

This time Neill was not the more careless, profligate one.

"I've not met many men like you. You give me books. No one has ever given me books. You write poems to me. Needless to say, no one has ever written poems to me."

"Lucky," Neill said. "You deserve all those things and more."

"Really, Neill? I am not so nice."

"You are."

"I'm not nice like you."

And Neill said this: "I love you, too, Lucky."

She turned to him and tilted his head and kissed him with passion and tongue.

"Mm," she said, laying her head on his shoulder. "It's lovely out tonight."

"Lucky. Look what your kiss created."

"Oh, Good Little Kiss," she said. "Can we make it home in time?"

"I'm not sure."

"Is there a dark cove in this neighborhood?"

"Let's find out," Neill said.

They both sprang to their feet and began a rapid amble around the neighborhood, like rascally fairy tale children. If only they had not strayed so far from the house.

"Look, there," Neill said.

"Between those houses?"

"It's dark enough."

"We'll have to be quiet."

"You'll have to be quiet, my vocal lover," Neill said.

They skipped between the houses, in amongst the shadows. There, next to the drippy hum of a window-unit air conditioner, and the muted musical gargle of a television from one of the windows, they kicked off their pants, stripped off their undergarments, which they spread over the AC unit, and they began to fuck fiercely against a damp brick wall, only to finish tumbling onto sod and soil, both coming like feverish raccoons. Neill put his hand over Lucrezia's mouth when she came. A muffled rumble was caught in his palm.

Afterward, they walked home.

"Thank you for taking the bottom," Lucky said, laughing.

"I think I have Ortho weed killer in my crack."

Lucrezia laughed harder. "I can't believe we made it work."

"We're good together," Neill said, and just like that, he believed it.

"Oh, Neill. This weekend. I have to tell you. I am going to be out of town."

'The whole weekend?'

"Yes, till Sunday evening. Bank thing. I'm sorry."

"Shit," Neill said. He was like a little boy at the end of the birthday party who was just been told that he had to give back some of his gifts.

"I'm not sure I can go two nights without having you," Neill said.

"I know," Lucky said. "I might be back in time Sunday night."

"Ok," Neill said, sulking.

"Here, sulky, kiss me."

"I love you, Lucky."

"I love you, too, Neill."

Saturday

Saturday Neill did not work. This meant that he stayed home, brooding over his love being away, until he took his brood and tried to make of it something resembling poetry. He instead made something resembling a collapsed flan.

He also pondered the age-old question. The one called *How to Make Love Stay*.

Was this love? Was he really ready to re-engage the old pumper? He thought so, yes. The glue, he thought, the difference, he thought, was that Lucky was funny. She was as funny as Sue Goorile. She was as funny as Dinah Mist. A funny woman, Neill thought, was just what he needed, what would make him complete and make the relationship work.

Did he like expressions like 'make the relationship work?'

He did not.

Sunday

Sunday was much like Saturday except that, after sleeping fitfully, he roamed his empty house like a stink. He wandered into the bedroom that used to be Goffredo's, which now seemed like an emblem of loss. It was 90% empty and the other 10% was a box of old sweaters, a couple stacks of dusty books, and a lava lamp that hadn't worked since 1979.

But Sunday was different in a profound way: Neill believed he would see Lucrezia that night.

Sunday was infused with Hope and Anticipation.

Neill, readers, did not forget the night he waited for Mink Risk, the night he, ignominiously, waited in the cover of the cove, and watched her come and go. How drear. How desolate.

So, could Neill short-circuit the anticipation, temper the hope, bypass the desire? Need you ask?

By five o'clock he was nervously sitting on the couch with an open novel (*Think Fast, Mr. Moto*) on his lap and the TV turned on (The Packers and somebody) but muted. He could neither concentrate on his book nor give a damn about the football game. He did not know whether to make dinner or wait for Lucky.

Isn't waiting an extremely difficult human endeavor? Surely, it is easier to bounce a signal off a satellite ten-thousand miles away, easier to make Apple Pan Dowdy, easier to split an atom or an infinitive or a milkshake, than it is to sit and wait. Walk around and wait. Lie down and read and wait.

Franz Kafka's motto, written above his bed, *Warte*. (Wait.)

A prescriptive magic phrase, like an 'open sesame' for turning inner demons into pussycats: "Now, wait a minute."

At 5:46, precisely at 5:46, Neill's phone rang.

It was Lucrezia.

"Who loves you, baby?" she said.

"Oh, Lucky."

"I hope you're free," she said.

By the time she got there Neill had ordered a pizza and set up the VCR with *McCabe and Mrs. Miller*.

She did not knock. She entered. She looked at Neill and Neill looked at her.

She looked like ambrosia. She looked like Apple Pan Dowdy.

She literally jumped onto him. Neill, having ordered his Charles Atlas instructional booklet from the back of *Grit* when he was a child but never having read it, was somewhat weak (no upper body strength, in the words of his college tennis coach, if you recall), but he managed to only stumble backwards a step or two with Lucky's mouth pasted onto his and Lucky's legs wrapped around his torso. With Lucky's eely tongue dancing over his molars. With Lucky's astonishing buttocks gripped tightly in his hands.

When they finished kissing and petting, Lucky noticed the pizza.

"I'm famished, fa—ham—ished." She threw her purse aside and jumped onto the couch as if it were her childhood bed.

"I've got a movie set up to watch with dinner, a favorite of mine. *McCabe and Mrs. Miller.* Seen it?"

"Shut up and eat," she said.

Neill started the movie anyway.

After a few Leonard Cohen songs Neill was in an oneiric state. He ate two pieces of pizza to Lucrezia's four. Lucrezia wiped her mouth with the back of her hand like a sailor in a bar.

"Look," Neill said. "Just as Leonard Cohen says, "curling like smoke above his shoulder," the smoke curls above his shoulder. When Robert Altman finished this movie he didn't have a soundtrack. But then...."

"Neill?"

"Hm"

"Shut up."

"I want to share this with you."

"Ok, Bucko," Lucky sighed. She pretended to watch the movie. Meanwhile, her hand ran up Neill's thigh. Neill was wearing shorts and her cool little hand worked its way all the way up to his Balzac, where it ticked and bobbled. By pushing harder upward, it found Neill's cockadoodledo, hard as kryptonite.

"Oh, Jesus," Neill said.

"I've missed this," Lucky said, unzipping Neill's shorts. "I mean I've missed you, of course," Lucky said, pulling Little Neill out and starting to suck on him with exaggerated noise.

Neill flung his head back.

Neill pulled his shorts and underwear down so she could have full access.

She used it wisely.

And, somehow, like a contortionist in a magician's box, Lucrezia managed to strip herself naked without taking her mouth off Neill's yum-yum. And, taking the opportunity of Lucky unhooking to take a breath, Neill pushed her down onto the carpet where he spread her legs and began to suck and lick her already slick panocha.

They did it in every position, Lucky getting off six times, and Neill finally coming while Lucky was doing the splits on the couch. Neill stooped to enter her bottomless cave, and shot off with the fury and fizgig of a bottle rocket. He would almost hear it ricocheting inside her. Then they fell to the floor, sweating and sated.

"I didn't know you could do the splits," Neill said.

Lucky looked at him, her eyes all googly like an obscene puppet.

"I didn't either," she said, breathlessly.

There Were these Inexplicable Gaps

The weekend apart led to this shivaree of sexual undertakings. If absence makes the heart grow fonder, it also makes the sex organs more penurious and lubricious. But Neill did not want to be apart. He wanted to see Lucky every night, to sleep next to her little brownie body, to have her say things to him that no woman had ever said, words that inflamed and invoked, words that drew the inner Neill out into the open and shot him full of buckshot.

This is part of the pattern, as you've already guessed after 600 or so pages of Neill and Neill's ways. Neill Rhymer wanted an all-the-time lover.

But, there were these inexplicable gaps, nights when Lucky did something else that was explained as 'going out with friends from work' or 'having to do this for my sister's sake' or 'my day was so draining, I am just going to stay in.'

Why did Neill not accept these logical explanations for a simple night without his paramour? It's hard to say. Neill had either become sensitive to the female's capacity for deceit (which might mean misogyny, based on Misso and Mink) or he was paranoid (which might mean cracked).

Now, Neill began to wonder if the weekend away had indeed been 'bank business.'

Neill and Lucky Step Out

Weeks went by, a month, two. Neill and Lucky went many places together. He proudly showed her off at P&H, where she shone like Snowlight. ("She's stuff," Bidden said.) Neill proudly took her home to the folks where her Southern manners and sweetness melted even Lolly's refractory heart. "These are the best meatballs I've ever eaten," she said. (AJ pulled him aside, "This is a good one," she hissed in his ear. "She makes you happy, I can see it.")

Neill took Lucky with him to a friend's party. Smithy and some of her rich, raucous friends had rented the roof of the Peabody Hotel for someone's 30th birthday party. Neill, generally, did not like parties, especially with countless strangers, but it was Smithy and for Smithy, Neill wanted to be more outgoing.

The night was cool and the sunset as colorful as the mind of a small boy. Standing at the edge of the roof (but not too close because it gave Neill the collywobbles: "It's not fear of falling. It's fear of jumping," he quoted someone) and looking out over the city's broad, tree-filled landscape, and the boulevards with their cars full of speeding monsters just now turning on their headlights as if it were group-mind at work, Neill felt a power in himself. The world is variegated and ceaselessly interesting, he decided, and standing next to Lucky, who was sparkling with charm and wit, he further decided that he was as happy as he had ever been. He believed, if only for the duration of that *presque vu* flash, that Lucky was his future.

That night they did it five different ways and Lucrezia came in each of them, as if marking their trail with bread crumbs. Neill orgasmed with his face buried in Lucky's poozle and his tommy-gun deep in Lucky's mushmouth.

In the afterglow, which lit them like the sulfurous numerals on the bedside clock, which read 2:53, Neill pulled his petite lover close to him, relishing the cool fit of her body locked onto his. Yin/Yang. Sonny/Cher. Ball/peen. Ball/glove.

"We're so good together," he said, not for the first time. His voice was airy, his words made of cobwebs. "These past months have made me so happy. My friends love you. My family loves you. And, I love you."

The room was as still as a sleeping boa.

"You're sweet, Neill," Lucrezia Enough said, and then fell headfirst into dreamland.

More Confab at Night

"Do you read on the toilet?" Bidden asked.

"What else am I going to do?" Neill said. "Balance my checkbook?"

"I read that it's bad for you because it promotes staying on the john longer with your cheeks spread. It leads to hemorrhoids."

"Where did you see that?" Crow asked.

"In a magazine I was reading in the bathroom," Bidden said.

"Ok."

"I've seen that shirt," Bidden said.

"It's what I was wearing in the photo that poetry magazine used," Neill said.

"Right. That's a good picture."

"I have to throw the shirt away," Neill said. "It's in a photo now. I didn't realize or I would have already gotten rid of it."

"Because it's stuck to eternity via this small zine?"

"Well, yeah. You take a picture in a piece of clothing you don't want to ever be seen in that again. People will think it's what you wear when you want to appear—I don't know, cool or something."

"I can see that," Crow said.

"Who is this new woman?" Neill asked Bidden.

"I don't know."

"Stop it. You said she was really sexy."

"That was before I met her."

"She's not sexy now?"

"She's too sexy?"

"Is that possible?" Neill asked.

"I can see it," Crow put in.

"She's too sexy for me. She's got tattoos."

"Ooh, tattoos. Plural. Where are they?"

"One across her shoulder blades that looks like Peaceable Kingdom. And a rose on each cheek."

"Ass cheek."

"Of course."

"You dog."

"I don't know."

"Give yourself a chance. As the shrinks say, give yourself permission to be happy. Or at least sexually satisfied."

"The sex is good. She's kinda kinky."

"Whips? Leather? Blisbos, boots, and bullwhips? Small animals?"

"No, just. Forget it."

"Talk to me."

"She's so confident sexually, she's like an instructor."

"Hm."

"She's hot, really hot. I find myself fantasizing about her and my fantasies are as wild as anything she introduces into the bedroom but then, when I am with her, I find myself just following her."

"You want to lead?"

"Sometimes. I guess. Who knows?"

"Who knows is right," Crow said.

"Tattoos though. I'd like to see them."

"I can send her to your house."

"I'm sorry. That's not what I meant. I've never been with a woman who had a tattoo. Not strictly true, I guess. Misso had a small colophon on her ankle. Jesus, her ankle. She had the sexiest ankle. Jesus, I miss her. Bidden, I miss her like hell."

"I'm sorry, Neill. No woman since has assuaged that grief."

"I guess not. I think the tattoo was 666."

"How are you and Lucky?"

"Good. I think. No, really good. I'm pretty sure."

"Ok."

"I wish she had a tattoo.

"Stop."

"Hey, here's an idea. Get a tattoo yourself. Perhaps it will lend you a certain sexual power over her."

"I have a tattoo."

"You do not."

"I have a tattoo on my heart. It's in the shape of my bicep."

What is Love? It is Not Red Bricks

What was going wrong? The smooth-running train that was Neill and Lucrezia was chuffing black smoke, choking, jerking, threatening to jump the rails. It was Neill's cursed foe.

Indifference. Implosion imminent.

What was once so hot and mutual was now stumbling and lukewarm. Neill began to flounder. Losing a lover is horrible, as terrible as the curse of a dead man's eye. But losing a lover for no apparent reason will make you as crazy as a shit bug.

"How about tonight?" Neill found himself saying.

"Are we still going to get together?" he found himself saying.

"Look, just lemme come by," he said.

"I'm on my way to a party," Lucky said. "You can't come here."

"I can't?"

"Neill, lemme call you tomorrow."

"Lemme come give you one kiss and I'm history. One kiss and I am a ghost, wafted away by foul winds."

Lucky laughed. "You don't even know the apartment number," she said. And then, because Neill made her laugh she gave him the number. "One minute."

"Yes. I'll kiss fast," Neill said.

Neill drove the one and one-quarter mile as if it were LeMans.

He knocked on Lucky's apartment door and it swung open. He could hear her talking on the phone. He slipped in and called quietly, "Here."

Lucky's apartment was small and messy. Like Lucky.

In the next room, her attempt at muffling her voice was not working, possibly because she was speaking with such heat.

"I am not. Dammit, you listen. I am not. I –I can't tell you now. I will see you. Yes, soon. Yes, Dammit. I said I would. No, no, of course he's not here. Ok. Ok."

She came into the living room wearing a mask made in one of the outer workshops of Abaddon. Her already pale face was chalk white and set. Her mouth was a nasty straight line.

"Happy now?" she said.

"I don't understand," Neill said. He was terrified.

"You heard me. It's why you can't come here."

"Who were you talking to?"

During Lucky's long hesitation, Neill prayed for release. He prayed for time to stop and for this day on the calendar to disappear like Judge Crater. He prayed that he would be a stronger chap, a chap who stood up to adversity and said, *Fuck you.*

"It's a man I've been seeing."

"Oh." Neill microfied his voice. It was an atom made of the end of the world.

"Neill. I tried to make this not happen. I tried to tell you. I suck. I am rotten."

"Because you're seeing two men at once?" Neill was trying not to upchuck.

Lucrezia Enough measured him with a long, grim expression. She was grinding her teeth.

"Because this will drive you away forever if I tell you this. Because it will release you and you won't want to ever see me again."

"Luck," Neill started.

"He's married. Ok? I've been seeing a married man. A man 20 years older than me with a wife and two kids. Good, yes? Happy? That weekend away I was with him at his cabin. This is me, Neill. This is why we could never come here. He's insanely jealous and has recently found out about you. Though he has told me I am only for sex, right? I am his whore. Anyway—" Lucky waved a hand in front of her face as if this conversation were made of gnats.

"Fuck," Neill said.

"Now you have to go. I am sorry. I am really sorry, Neill. You're too good for me. Go find someone nice. You deserve it. Forget me. You're a good guy."

Neill hated her right then. He hated her, himself, the married asswipe, the floor on which he stood, the ceiling over his head, the mile and a quarter he had to drive home, and most of all, he hated being told once more that he was too good for someone. It was disingenuous. It was a downright lie, the sort of thing one uses to not feel bad about one's poor behavior.

Neill could not talk, so he walked. He turned and he heard the door close behind him and he drove home. When he reached his little home, he sat down on the couch in the darkness and cried. He cried because he would never be loved. He cried because love does not last. It is not red bricks.

I'm Sorry

"I'm sorry," Bidden said.

"…"

"Neill?"

"I know. Thank you."

"It's just gonna hurt until it stops. But it will stop."

"…"

"Neill."

"I know."

"Want me to come over?"

"No. But thank you."

"Ok."

"…"

"Neill."

"I can't make love last longer than three months now. It used to be a few years, then six months. Now, it's down to three months."

"It won't be right until it's right," Bidden said.

"…"

"Neill."

"I know, Bidden. Thank you."

Once More Around the Block

Neill stewed and fretted and wrung his little Dwight Frye hands. He felt sorry for himself. He abhorred himself. He needed something but all his pacing and moping got him no closer to what it was.

Some time passed. Lucky wouldn't answer her phone. Neill wrote her a letter. He might as well have burned it in the fireplace and hoped the ashes would fall on her.

At the bookstore, the others avoided him. They pitied. Esther offered Neill part of her Vienna sausage sandwich. Betty offered some of her soup, which meant it was Wednesday. They must believe, like Jewish mothers, that food can cure anything, including heartache.

One afternoon, Neill called Lucky's number from the bookstore. He pushed the numbers carefully as if they were some telegnostic code that just might open the mummy's tomb. Lucrezia answered.

Neill croaked. "Lucky."

There was a moment of silence and then, "Hi, Neill." No inflection, the voice of a machine.

"Lucky, can we talk?"

This time silence felt like an opening.

"Go for a walk with me after work?"

"Ok, Neill. I'll come to your house."

"Oh, great," Neill said. He tried not to sound like a ten year old. "Why are you home from work?"

"I'll see you around 6."

After he hung up, Neill felt sick to his stomach. He found Ianthe in the back and asked if he could go home for the day.

"You don't have to ask," she said. "Neill," she added as Neill turned. "Take care, ok? Take care of your heart."

"Thank you, Ianthe," Neill said.

Once home Neill took a shower, not because he was soiled but to pass the time and in hope that the warm water would calm him.

By six he was sitting in the living room, three feet from the door. He feared she would not come. That would be worst case scenario. That would be cruel.

She pulled up at the curb a little after six. She got out of the car. She was dressed for the recent downturn in temperature so that her pretty, runner's body was swaddled in puffy, sexless clothing.

"Hi," Neill said, opening the door. Her face was too beautiful. It cut Neill like a laser.

"Come out and let's walk," Lucrezia said.

They began a slow motion stroll around the quaint neighborhood. The sky was the color of a filing cabinet. The air had a nip to it like the bite of a puppy.

Lucrezia took Neill's hand and they walked in silence for a while.

"I'm sorry," she said, after a while. Neill was concentrating everything he had on her hand. He was trying to send her a coded message through his palm, one that would act like a spell and reverse her insouciance.

"It's not too late," Neill said.

"It is, Neill."

"Lucky. Lucky, I love you. I'm not sure I'll ever love anyone the same way again."

"You will, Neill. And soon. You're so funny and charming. You bowled me over. If you hadn't bowled me over I would never have opened up to you at such a terrible, mixed-up time in my life."

"You're going to stay with this married man? You're going to hope he leaves his family?"

Lucky didn't answer. They walked further.

"Lucky, we're so good together. We're like—I don't know. Stiller and Meara. My friends told me that we were so funny together and I thought, I think, that means something. We had fun, real fun together."

"You don't have to try to convince me of that."

"What then? Why are you leaving me?"

"Neill, I shouldn't have come tonight."

They were closing the circle, rounding the block. Neill's house was within sight.

"I shouldn't have given you any hope."

"Fuck," Neill said. He should have let go of her hand but he did not. He could not.

They stopped by Lucky's car, a rust-red Saab.

"This is it?" Neill asked like a spoony.

"Bye, Neill."

"There's no chance you'll change your mind? You won't miss me?"

She smiled a patient smile and let go of Neill's hand. Neill thought to grab it back but did not. He watched her get into her car without looking at him. He heard the motor start.

There must be something I can say to stop this, he thought. If there was, it was lost to mankind for all time. She drove away and they never talked again.

After Lucky Time

After Lucky, time was out of joint. A day felt like a week and an hour felt like a minute. Weeks collapsed into other weeks; night was only the dark hallway toward another door which would *probably* open to reveal another day.

And it would all start again.

Around this time, Neill found a puppy in his front yard. It had no collar and it seemed to be sick. He called his friend Dinah and she drove over and helped him get the dog, a female mutt, part Weimaraner perhaps, part retriever, to a vet. The vet said she had worms and kennel cough but that otherwise she would be fine. She gave the dog some shots and sent them back home.

"Should I keep her?" Neill asked the vet.

"Of course. Someone probably dumped her in a nice neighborhood because they couldn't afford the bills of fixing her, hoping a nice person would take her in. And that's what happened," the vet said and smiled.

Dinah and Neill stopped and bought a bowl, some dog food and a chew toy.

Once inside the house, the gray beauty put her head in Neill's lap and fell asleep. She knew who saved her. Neill stroked her soft/coarse hair.

"She's so pretty, isn't she?" Neill said.

"What are you gonna call her?"

Neill had a name already. He'd been thinking about it.

"Una," he said.

"Una. Yeah, that's nice. But why?"

"Three reasons."

"You've been thinking about this."

"On the car ride to the vet, yes. One, una is Spanish for one and she is my first dog, the first dog that is all mine. Then, there is Chaplin's wife and Eugene O'Neill's daughter, Oona, one of the world's most beautiful women. And, finally, after the little fairy in the movie *Legend*."

"That little fairy was hot."

"You and I are on the same page as usual."

"Ok then," Dinah said. "Una, welcome to your new life."

Una was a Dog, Not a Symbol

Beautiful, gray-browed Una, dog from the mist, dog sent to help assuage Neill's broken heart. Loving, sweet, grateful Una.

When Neill had to go out of town to another book extravaganza he now had someone to worry about back at home. Having no backyard Neill was using a stake and a long line to tether Una under the walnut tree in his front yard. He often sat out there and read while she lay lazily by, occasionally looking up from her sleepy haze, to smile at Neill and wish him well.

(Neill would show her his book, Bellow's *More Die of Heartbreak*, for instance, and Una would nod knowingly.)

The day before Neill was to go to Chicago for the book convention, he put Una out as usual. She settled down in the shade.

Neill was packing for his trip, which t-shirts? which jeans? which books? to last 3 days. When he had filled his tote bag, the leather one which was a gift from Marcane, the one with the "Abbie Lives" button on it, Neill fixed himself a fried bologna sandwich (yellow mustard and white bread, ah Sweet Jesus), and took his book (*Nabokov's Quartet*, now) outside to sit under the tree with Una.

She was gone.

The collar with her tag on it sat on the lawn still attached to the long piece of clothesline. Neill dropped book and sandwich and began to jog around the corner. This was foolish, he realized. She could have gone either way. He grabbed his keys and, in his car, began the slow journeys around his neighborhood. Surely, she could not have gotten far.

Readers, Neill did not find her.

He called AJ, who worked as a Vet Tech now, and asked her what to do. She lined up the proper agencies. By the next morning, Neill was sick leaving Memphis behind, the large, sprawling city, now seemingly a dangerous playground where his dog wandered like a hobo.

In Chicago, Neill could not shake his blues. The first night's activities went by in a blur. He talked to friends, ate some indifferent chicken, met some authors. It was awful.

The next morning, he went to the hotel restaurant for breakfast. He met a friend there and they ate together. Neill told his tale of woe. The one about his dog, not the one about Lucky. His friend commiserated. People understand that attachments to pets are deep and fulfilling and, hence, fragile.

He returned to his room to see what his itinerary for the day was. The light on his phone was blinking.

He punched the right numbers to get the message. The message was from AJ:

Found Una at Humane Society. Will keep her till you return. Love you, Sis.

Neill was ecstatic. He wanted to go home right then. Instead, he endured the rest of the convention (he did meet Joan Baez so that was good) and flew home Sunday night. AJ and Dan picked him up at the airport with Una in the back seat. Neill joined her there and Una wet Neill's face thoroughly before settling into his lap and falling into a sleep safe as houses.

"How's Dad?" Neill asked, because he was strong enough to.

"Good. He's good. He's got home oxygen now."

"I'm gonna start giving him fat novels again."

At home Una seemed so pleased to be back. She found her food bowl, her water bowl, her wubbies, and her toys, and settled right back into her routine. Now Neill walked her instead of employing the stake method. Una had some accidents.

For a week, life quieted to a dowie blankness. Neill was not exactly happy but he was not as lonely with Una around.

Then Una stopped eating. She peed on the floor more than outside. She had a slight cough. Neill called AJ and she asked pertinent questions. She suggested another 24 hours (she may just have a stomach ache, she said, might just be kennel cough) and then, if no improvement, she would take her into her vet's office.

The next morning, Neill found Una in the kitchen in convulsions. Neill tried to hold her. Then, he called AJ. "Take her to the nearest vet right now," she said.

Neill did. The vet told Neill to go back home and he would call once they had a good look at her.

An hour later, he called and told Neill she had advanced distemper.

"What do I do?" Neill said.

"There's nothing to do. I am sorry. We can put her to sleep here if you'd like and you can be with her if you'd like."

Neill burst into tears. He hung up. He cried. Then, he called AJ.

"Oh shit," AJ said. "Do you want me to take care of it?"

"What—what do you mean?"

"I'll go to the vet, take care of the body. You won't have to see."

Neill didn't know what was best. Did he want to see her die? No, he did not.

"Ok," Neill said.

So Una disappeared as if she had never existed.

"I managed to keep a relationship with a dog for 4 weeks. That's worse than my romantic record," Neill snuffled into the phone.

"I'm sorry, Buddy," Bidden said. "Want me to come over?"

"Sure," Neill said, because he did not want to be alone.

Bidden arrived with Taco Bell and Pas.

"You guys are great," Neill said.

They ate.

Afterwards, Pas said, "Neill, this is rotten timing. Can I show you something that might upset you?"

"Of course," Neill said. "I can't go any lower."

It was a clipping from the daily newspaper. It was the announcement of Lucrezia Enough's wedding. She married someone else. Did she maintain him, too, along with Neill and the married man? It would appear so.

"I was wrong," Neill said. "This is awful. I feel poorly."

"I shouldn't have brought it," Pas said. There were tears on her sweet, round, brown cheeks.

"It's ok," Neill said, starting to snuffle again. "I'm tired of being alone."

"Maybe you need a roommate," Bidden said. "I worry about your being alone sometimes."

"Oh, I'm ok alone," Neill said.

He wasn't. He did want a roommate. Who could that be?

Neill Wants to Stop Writing about Lucrezia

"Nympholepsy"
  I stopped her running.
  She had thighs
  like hell-roosters.
  I wanted her so badly
  I ignored her sins
  and crafts. I was ensorcelled
  but by my own desire.
  She couldn't make it
  to the end of a movie
  without grabbing my
  central nerve. Sex was like
  some vexed and angry sea.
  When she left I cried
  like a squonk. I tore my
  breast open. I left the
  ground sodden with my blood.
  This was too recent.
  The devil-devil won't fade,
  nor will it ever burn off.
  Its root is deep,
  and when I try to extricate it
  I am half-hearted and weak.
  God help me, I am half-
  hearted and weak, a maniac.

Love and Unlove

For the male of the species (and perhaps for the female too), there is only one comfort that helps assuage the end of a relationship: Neill was free to go to bed with any woman who wanted to go to bed with him. He could yet make love, even in the unlove.

Neill did not cut his hair. He did not know if Lucky had cut hers. He assumed not. She did not take the relationship seriously enough to be saddened at its demise (and it didn't last long enough for Enough), and she had a better life-change than a simple haircut to signal her independence: she married some guy. Some dude. Some other man. Some *better* man.

So Neill was at least alive to the idea that, perhaps, maybe, somehow he might find another woman to take to bed, in the dark of the unlove.

At the Subterranean Grotto with Smithy

Cattycorner to The Book Shelf, just next door to Kroger, was the Poplar Plaza Bowling Alley. It was below street level so you gained entrance down a long, narrow, linoleum-covered stairway that smelled faintly of plastic and sweat. This made the place seem recondite, a place where hugger-mugger took place, *sub rosa* meetings of Clubs Arcanum and back-alley deals, things done as secretly as what a lion might accomplish in his private den.

Perhaps, the Masons met there, one felt as one descended. Perhaps the Thuggees, the Russian Castrators, The Organization of the Order, The Garduna, The Illuminati, Sam the Sham and the Pharaohs, The Decided Ones of Jupiter the Thunderer, The Skopzi, The Wolf River Society, The Cult of the Black Mother, The Loyal Order of the Water Buffalo, Mystics and Rosicrucians. Perhaps it really was The Underworld.

(Perhaps, it was just a bowling alley for those who *will not see.*)

And in this underground emporium, adjacent to the lanes so that you could dine while watching one of the Greatest Sports Ever Devised by Evolved Apes, dine while around you pins crashed like ivory surf, was a café. Perhaps café is too fancy a word. But griddle hamburgers, hotdogs, crinkle-cut French fries, and BLTs are not just simple foods. They are modes of super-reality understood by only an elect few.

Smithy loved The Subterranean Grotto (and, of course, she had named it...its more prosaic name was something like The Poplar Plaza Bowling Alley Grill). She loved it in her post-ironic understanding of what is real and what is merely veiled.

Some days Smithy and Neill went to lunch there together. These were good days. These were reminders of the value of genuine amity.

One such lunchtime happened shortly after the untimely passing of Una. Neill had the burger and fries. Smithy, a chilidog and a milkshake.

"My sister's done it again," Smithy said. She had a sister who was as wild as a tameless horse of Tartary. The sister was a constant source of conversation.

"What's she done this time?" Neill said, relishing how the ketchup clung to the crinkle cut, amid its spackling of salt.

"Well, you know she has seizures?"

"I thought our constitution protected against those."

Smithy snorted some Dr. Pepper through a nostril.

"Stop. Listen, *Chief.*" Smithy called Neill Chief, and always with Jane Hathaway's inflection.

"She was dancing with some guy at The Antenna. Turns out he was a mobster's son."

"Mobster? We have mobsters in Memphis?"

"Quite. Anyway. She broke their embrace and signaled to her friends she was ready to leave. He did not want her to leave."

"Oh no. He didn't hurt her."

"No. Not then. But the next day she woke to find a horsehead in her bed."

"*Trés amusant.*"

"No, not really a horsehead. A whippet."

"The head of a dead whippet."

"No. A live whole whippet. Tied to the bumper of her car. My mother went nuts."

"Sorry, it's sorta funny."

"It is. Except it's my sister and her escapades end up not being funny."

"Right. Sorry. I sympathize."

"You don't want the whippet, do you?"

"Oh. Oh no, I guess not."

"I thought—"

"I know. Because of Una. I don't see another dog in my life right now. Though, hell, I miss her."

"You grew attached to her quickly."

"I did. Have you ever noticed that people tend to repeat what they say to pets?"

"What?"

"Have you ever noticed that people tend to repeat what they say to pets?"

"I'm not sure."

"Like you say to your dog, 'Are you hungry now? Are you hungry?' Or, 'Is Fizzy clean after her bath? Is my Fizzy clean'?"

"I guess it's to fill the silence in the conversation where their answer would be. It's to fill in the blanks. We do that in conversation."

"We do. Like how one finishes conversations in one's head. You supply the missing voice. Because one is the loneliest number, as the Holy Trinity told us."

"Like that, yeah."

"Except Una could actually talk. She had mastered human speech."

"What did she tell you?"

"I'm not sure I am supposed to say. It might break the owner/pet confidentiality covenant."
"Right."

"She said, 'Stop sulking about your lost Lucky and get back in the game'."

"Smart dog."

"I told you."

Some More Chinwag with Neill, Crow, and Bidden

P&H nights often devolved to men-only nights. Hence, the topic of conversation was often women. With or without mates the men felt that life was not giving them a fair share. In particular, Crow and his wife were having trouble and talking of splitting. Crow was threatening to leave town like we all do when a relationship goes bad.

Neill told him to just cut his hair instead. Or grow a beard.

"I can grow a beard overnight. That's not dramatic enough."

"Right. Shave your eyebrows."

Sometimes other subjects were touched upon.

"I have to laugh at Memphis meteorologists. A storm comes through and it's like it's their Christmas or Easter service. Even the unbelievers are watching."

"God is watching," Bidden said.

"It's a real shaggy god story."

"I sometimes tell my wife she didn't rinse the bathtub between her bath and mine. I mean, you have to have some rules, some mutual respect," Crow said.

"Not rinsing the tub isn't that big a deal."

"Well, I don't mean she doesn't rinse the tub. I just say that to her because, obviously—"

"Even Stevie could see that," Neill interjected.

"– she can't remember whether she rinsed it and in her doubt is my advantage."

"It was my mother who told me there was no such thing as a weekend," Neill said. "She told me Saturday you were still exhausted from work and thinking about work and Sunday you spent worrying about Monday. I remember one Labor Day weekend I thought I had her. On Sunday, I said, now this is a weekend, right? a 3 day weekend? And she said, it's just a Sunday like any other Sunday. The holiday doesn't start till tomorrow."

"At which time you start worrying about work again."

"Right."

"Though no momist, I'd defend my mother still. Against all odds. Against all comers."

"It's a slippery slope. You start out denying the Holocaust and pretty soon you're defending Bobby Knight, or your mother's verbally abusive methodology."

"Methodology?" Crow said. "That's a fancy word for parenting, isn't it?"

"There's a word for being good with words but I can't remember what it is," Bidden said.

The talk grew inconsequential. It shrank as though Death were passing in Sivad's hansom.

"My dad, on the other hand," Neill said, "was empirical to a fault, if he encountered a problem he immediately began to search for the solution while I, whenever I encounter a problem, throw up my hands and say, 'It's the end of the world!' A more existential response of course and utterly useless. He tried to teach me about car engines, but it was like trying to teach a monkey how to write a sonnet."

"There often is not a good solution," Crow said.

"The ocean is the ultimate solution," Neill said.

"Ha. That's good."

"Frank Zappa. I can't take credit for that one."

"Where did you hear him say that?"

"I don't remember."

"So much of success is knowing where things are," Crow said.

"Who wants to succeed?" added Bidden.

Movie Night with Bidden and Pas

Bidden brought the movie, *Interiors*. Pas brought a casserole she made. Neill provided the home in which these things were enjoyed. It was as close as they came to having parties.

The reason for the get-together, partly, was to help Neill through his lonesome time.

"This is a beautiful movie," Pas said. "The set decorator should get an Oscar."

"It's so miserably sad it makes me happy," Bidden said.

"Why is it so sad?" Pas asked.

"Pas hasn't seen it," Neill said.

"Sorry. Not sad, just, um, serious."

"This is dynamite casserole," Neill said. "What's in it?"

"You mean there is something about it that is mysterious and questionable?" Pas asked with a smile.

"No, it's just—interesting."

"Turkey sausage," Pas said.

"They make turkey sausage?"

"Neill, leave your house sometime."

"You watch Jeopardy?" Bidden asked.

"Working," Neill said.

"The final question stumped all three of the geniuses. It went something like this: She said her father's extensive collection of hats led him to write his next book. I think they gave a date, like 1938 or something."

"Dr. Seuss," Neill and Pas said together.

"See."

"Have I told you my Seuss story?"

"About meeting him?"

"No, about Bartholomew Cubbins."

"I've heard it," Bidden said.

"Not me," Pas said.

"Ok. This was at Waldens. A woman came in looking for *The 500 Hats of Bartholomew Cubbins* and we were out of it. So I told her we could special order it and she asked me to do that. I asked her name and she said, 'Hope Cubbins.' I laughed and said, 'Funny coincidence. Is that why you want the book?' And she said, 'My father was Bartholomew Cubbins. We lived next door to the Geisels, and my dad and Mr. Geisel were good friends.'"

"Wow, that's cool," Pas said.

"Yeah, it makes for a good bookselling story. So little happens in our job that is very exciting."

"Did you ask her out?" Pas said, with a similar smile to the one mentioned above.

"You think I ask every woman out?"

"Yes," Pas and Bidden said.

"I did not."

Shlomo on the Horn

"I might be the stupidest published writer in America," Shlomo began with one of his most common tropes.

"Why do you say that now?"

"The other writers in this department. They're talking Guggenheims, NEA grants, PEN Faulkners."

"Those are just awards."

"Someone used the word 'turgidity' about the plant in their office. I said, I think you mean something else. Turgid is like slow-moving prose. Turns out turgidity in plants means how well they stand up or something."

"Huh."

"I know nothing. Why do I write books?"

"Shlomo, you're the smartest man I know."

"Poor you."

"Tell me about Maximilian Calvada. I just finished *Cozy Pavich: Kid Genius.* By the way, can I send my book to you again for his inscription?"

"Sure. Maxy says when he sees his mailbox stuffed with a package his initial response is excitement. Someone has sent a gift. Inevitably it is a book to be signed."

"So I shouldn't send this one?"

"No, of course send it."

"I love his writing. I can't believe you're friends."

"I know. He's one of the top dogs but he doesn't know it. I go over to his apartment and visit with the wife and kids. His wife writes crossword puzzles for the L. A. Times, you know?"

"Huh."

"And there he is down on the floor wrestling with the kids, who love me, and they're calling him 'poopyface' and I am thinking, this is one of our best writers. Poopyface."

"As he shall henceforth be known."

"Just ran across a word you need to know: zouch. It means either an 'ungenteel man,' or 'a bookseller.'"

"Guilty on both counts."

The Essay

So Neill was single again and, again, feeling Unmateable. Ever since Misso (the record of Chara's time expunged like the Final Four appearances of cheating coaches) Neill had been meditating on marriage and children. He was a little late to the game. A wild oat sower was his default function for a long time. But, having fallen seriously in love with Misso, and seeing his children in her wide blue eyes (*linger on...your pale blue eyes....*) Neill was now thrust back upon his own emptiness.

If he loved Misso that much and wanted to spend the rest of his life with her and wanted her to be the mother of his pale blue-eyed children, what did it mean that she did not want him in the same way, or, indeed, in any way?

So, again, he concentrated on his job, which he still loved as if he were the fox put in charge of the chickens, and his writing, which occasionally made him feel ecstatic, but more often made him feel inadequate. He would read Graham Greene. He would read Iris Murdoch. He would read John Crowley, James Tate, C.K. Williams, Sylvia Plath, Mark Strand. And he would think: never. I will never be any good.

Still, in the messy smithy of his soul, he found some words that he strung together, awkwardly, like a juggler who can't even keep two beanbags moving. He pecked a few small poems onto sheets as blank as his generation, little black marks that meant only that he was trying. He also cobbled together some sentences into funky little short stories that pleased him but did not resemble anything like the short fiction he loved, the short fiction that was appearing in journals like *Paris Review, Epoch, Transatlantic Review,* and *Fiction.*

Then, for no good reason, Neill decided to do something he had never even considered before. Neill decided to write about Neill.

So, he wrote an essay about what he loved most, after coitus: books and bookselling. He wrote it and he called it "Melville, Malamud and Me." And then, he did something even bolder: He sent the damn thing to *Memphis Magazine.*

And then, he forgot about it.

Another Bookstore Signing

In September of that year, The Book Shelf hosted a signing for Memphis poet, Camel Jeremy Eros and his newly published collection of poems, A *Spotless Kip* (Monkey Fat Books, 1985). Camel was an old soul in a slightly younger body, a guy who had been through all the wars, literary and literal, in the 60s. He knew the beats, the New York Poets, the folk music scene. His longest friendship was with Richard Brautigan, whom he slightly resembled. He was tall, with a stoop, and a copious and unruly moustache. His moustache looked like a misplaced fur.

Neill had known Camel from as far back as his Waldens days. Camel and Shlomo had spent time together at a commune in South Mississippi called Peace Meal, together with novelist Budd Insky, songwriter Fly Stevens, and sculptor Mason Avalanche, whose dung constructions caused quite a ruckus back in the day. Shlomo said that Camel was the most laid-back person he'd ever known, so impassive, it was a wonder he was ever published. He was known to have thousands of sheets of poems in his Midtown home lying under furniture, plant stands, bed, and pizza boxes. There was a rumor he also had written a novel.

Camel arrived a full hour early.

"I know I'm early," he said, putting his soft hands around Neill's outstretched palm. He held the hands there as if about to speak an incantation over them.

"That's ok. You want anything," Neill asked. "Soda, water?"

"Got any grass?"

It was hard to tell if Camel was joking.

"Uh, no, didn't think to lay some in."

"That's ok," Camel said. "I brought some."

Camel stood there and the conversational ball came to rest in a deep indentation.

"Sorry I'm early," Camel said again. "My car."

"Having car trouble? I would have come to get you."

"No, the car's fine," Camel said. "Have you got Eloysias Ferragut's new collection, *Poems of Urine and Blood?*"

"No, I don't think so," Neill said. In truth, he'd never heard of him.

"It's shit," Camel said. "I love him though."

"Ok."

"Who do you read, Neill? Have we talked about this before?"

"Um, Fowles, Anne Tyler, Doctorow," and then, just to show off," Joyce, of course."

"Poets, Neill. Poets."

"Oh. I like, uh, Strand and Merwin a lot. Ginsberg."

"Ahh," Camel said. He went into a reverie.

"Who's your favorite, Camel?"

"I slept with Allen once. But only once."

"Huh," Neill said.

"I love the guy. He was trying to make Peter mad, I think. Peter. That was his name, wasn't it, Neill?"

"I think so, yes," Neill said.

"Ever meet Ginsberg, Neill?"

"No. My friend Crow and I tried to call him one night when we were really high. He was listed in the New York phone book."

"He wouldn't talk to you?"

"No one answered."

"Yes," Camel said.

"Get you a soda?" Neill said again.

"I think I'll sit on the couch here and wait for the party to start. Is anyone coming, Neill?"

"Of course," Neill said. "We expect a good crowd."

Camel adjusted his large frame into a sitting position on the green leather couch. Within 30 seconds he was fast asleep.

Smithy came out of the back.

"Oh, Camel's here," she said.

"Yes, where were you? It was hard playing conversational pinball with him."

"I can still hear you," Camel said.

"Right," Neill said.

"I might just close my eyes now," Camel said.

The party, once it got going, was a success. All of the Memphis literati were there. The Tickles, Bunny Glazer, Bill Page, Gordon Osing, Reynard Kane, Sissy Peters, whose dress was so short every male eye, and some of the female, was on her during Camel's reading. How was she going to sit and not show what she has was the unspoken question. She sat. She showed gossamer white panties. The party was a complete success.

During clean-up Neill turned, with a stack of sticky plastic wine glasses in his hand, to find a small blond woman standing severely close to him. She was as tall as a complete set of Britannica and her yellowy hair was cut with a weed-whacker.

"Hi," she said. "My name is Pepper Pimwell."

Neill nodded because he didn't have a free hand. "Hi."

"I've written some poems," the young woman said. She looked a bit like Louise Brooks, if Louise Brooks was blond and five foot two.

"Ok," Neill said. He tried to smile nicely because the woman's face was fierce with determination. For what, Neill could not imagine.

"Would you read them?" Pepper Pimwell asked.

"Sure," Neill said. "But I am not Camel Eros, whose signing we just had."

"I know. I was here. I love his stuff but mine is so different. I think you might like them better."

"On what are you basing this?" Neill asked. His curiosity was piqued and he felt free to take whatever tone he desired.

"I've read your stuff."

Neill looked at her and wondered if she ever smiled.

"Ok. Chara Winsky showed me some of your poems. She said you wouldn't be happy to hear her name again."

Wine was dripping. Neill's hands were tacky with it.

"Follow me to the back," Neill said, gesturing with his head toward the stockroom.

"Said the spider to the flea." Pepper Pimwell stayed where she was.

"Fly," Neill said.

"You want me to leave because I wouldn't go to the stockroom with you?"

"No," Neill said. His exasperation was showing. "Spider to the fly, not flea. And I have to go to the stockroom to throw these away and wash my hands. You can wait here."

"I'll come with you," Pepper said, as if allowing Neill this.

Neill, once his hands were washed, felt less awkward. And a little pissy.

"Tell me what you want," Neill said.

"Read my poems. Tell me if they're shit."

"I'm not really very good at that."

Smithy came back into the stockroom, saw the diminutive blond, mugged foolishly at Neill, and backed out.

"You won't do it. I understand."

"No. I will. Gimme what you got. But I am not sure I am expert enough to give you any pointers."

"I've read you. You're good," Pepper said. She reached into her backpack and pulled out a red folder, the kind you did your school projects in.

"My phone number is written inside."

"Ok," Neill said. "Ok, Pepper Pimwell."

And she left.

"Who was that?" Smithy said, as Neill emerged from the stockroom.

"Crazy person, I think," Neill said.

"You wanna talk crazy people," Camel said, from the couch where he was now stretched out, his big feet hanging off one end. "Herbert Huncke was crazy. I loved Herbert."

The Poems of Pepper Pimwell

Neill was tired when he got home that night. He had a Hungry Man's fried chicken TV dinner waiting for him. This was what he was looking forward to. He also wanted to watch a movie that Crow had dropped off, the film version of Peter Carey's *Bliss*.

There was a note tacked to his front door.

"I am looking for you. Call me. Dinah."

Neill called after he got his dinner in the oven, and got himself settled. Dinah's husband answered. Neill hung up.

During dinner Neill put Pepper Pimwell's folder of poems next to him. He began to read them without much interest. The word 'darkness' appeared a lot, in almost every poem. There were some four-letter words, some copped Plath, some spitballs aimed at just about everything except Charles Bukowski.

What could Neill say about them? He tried to find a glimmer of wit or any small love for the language she was using to limn her despair. Neill recognized the method. He had a drawer full of similar scribblings. He would call her in a few days and offer something positive. He should call Shlomo. Shlomo was always encouraging, in clever and smart ways.

The phone rang just as Neill was about to watch *Bliss*.

"Sorry," Dinah said.

"Hello," Neill said.

"I mean, sorry. I mean, hello, sorry, I wasn't thinking. You got my husband on the phone."

"I did."

"I've left him."

"Oh shit."

"Yeah. So, stupid of me. I wasn't there because I don't want to live there anymore."

"I'm sorry, Dinah. You wanna come over and talk."

"Yes. You need a roommate?"

"What?"

"Bidden said you needed a roommate."

"Oh. Yes. You mean—*you*?"

"It could work. Listen. It wouldn't be sexual at all. I've always loved you as a friend, too, you know?"

"I do. The feeling is mutual."

"We can do it. We can be roommates without anything getting fucked up."

"Bidden told you."

"That's another thing. Bidden and I have been seeing each other."

"What?"

"We've been seeing each other. An affair if you want."

"I don't want. I mean, I didn't know. He didn't tell me."

"He's not proud of it."

"You're leaving your husband for Bidden?"

"No. God, no. That's what he doesn't want to think. No. When you talk to him tell him how much I wanted away from my husband anyway."

"That's true."

"Tell him that. I have but he'll listen to you."

"So, you still want to come over?"

"Yes. Can I sleep there tonight?"

"Really?"

"Yes. Bidden is about to move out of his mom's."

"I know. He's renting a place around the corner from me."

"I know."

"You don't want to move in with Bidden because he'll think you left your husband for him."

"Exactly."

"Ok, sure. Come spend the night. I'll sleep on the couch."

"Thank you, Neill. I love you. And I'll sleep on the couch."

She Came to Stay

Dinah came that night with a paper sack full of clothes and soaps and coffee and other necessary items. She burst through the door as if Neill had been trying to keep her out.

"This is the worst night. The worst! But, Neill, you're so great, really. This is going to be great. This really is. The best thing I could have done. I already feel better just getting out of the house. Really. I am so happy. This is so good of you. I'll be a great roommate and you will, too. Neill, this is going to be great, isn't it?"

"What happened today?" Neill asked.

Dinah grabbed the nape of Neill's neck and pulled his face to hers. She kissed him hard.

"I'm going to bed. I am so frazzled."

"Look," Neill said. "I put a pallet and some extra blankets on the floor in what used to be Goffredo's room."

Dinah spun into the nearly empty room.

"Yes. This is where I will live. Good night, Neill."

And she shut the door on him.

The Next Morning

Neill woke late the next morning. He didn't have to work. It dawned on him slowly that there was another human in the house. Neill lay in bed and thought about what had happened. He loved Dinah, of course. It could work. Certainly financially it would help.

Neill slowly unfolded himself. He smelled coffee.

That was a plus already. She is awake and has made coffee. He wondered, just for a second, if she would be in dishabille. Perhaps, a sheer nighty. Then the thought police hit him with a truncheon. She was Bidden's now.

Not to worry. Dinah had already left for the day.

Next to the Chemex was a note: "I love you, Neill. Bidden and I will be back tonight with my stuff. SMACK!"

So, the day opened before him like a door into nonexistence. He had nothing to do.

He made some toast to help absorb the coffee's acidity and read the paper as he ate.

Pepper Pimwell's poems still sat on the table. He picked them up and flipped through them. They weren't terrible, he decided. His eye fell to the sticky note with her name and phone number. Her handwriting was cramped. It was like dark spider web on the page and she had dotted the i in Pimwell with a circle.

Neill showered and shat and felt pretty good. Nothingness seemed almost welcoming.
He called Pepper Pimwell.

"Yeah," she answered.

"Uh, Pepper?"

"Yeah."

"It's Neill. Neill Rhymer."

'Neill! Fucking-a! Thanks for calling."

"I've read your poems. They have a real—something. Gravitas, perhaps. A real realness."
Neill sounded like an idiot.

"Brilliant!" Pepper said. "Can I come over?"

What? Neill thought. Come over?

"I guess so. Sure. Do you know where Holmes Circle is?"

`   "I know where you live. I'm coming now."

Even in her enthusiasm, her tone held something of the sepulchral.

She hung up without a goodbye, and Neill sat down with his copy of Bellow's *Herzog* and tried to read. He was distracted. His head was full of swill.

Neill heard her car pull up and went to the door. He stepped onto the porch. Her car was a Rambler that had seen better days. It seemed to be held together with rust and twist-ties. Pepper emerged, cigarette dangling moll-style from her lip. She raised a hand in greeting. Then, she proceeded to push and kick the car door until it stayed closed.

"Hi, Pepper," Neill said. "Come in."

Pepper walked by him. She was so tiny. She reminded him a bit of Harness Myers, a slight but curvy body clad in a bare minimum of clothing. Pepper's Ramones t-shirt used to be full-sized but she had razored enough of it away to make it barely qualify as a midriff. And, she wore the same miniscule skirt from the night before. There was a fresh coffee stain on it today, a circle marking the exact location of her female parts.

"Nice," Pepper said. She threw a small crumpled brown bag on the couch and followed it there. Neill took the chair catty-cornered to the couch. Neill couldn't help but think, *how old is this child?*

"So, I read your poems."

"Yes," Pepper said. She was still seriously smoking her cigarette. She was giving it her all. She held one hand to her mouth. Her nails were bitten to the quick and once had been painted black.

"There are some really good things in your writing, directions you should follow."

"Where?"

"Well, I am not sure I can be that specific. I think, perhaps, and, of course, you don't have to listen to me or anyone else, perhaps, you should curb the death wish."

"Death wish."

This was a conversation in need of oiling.

"You are, perhaps, I say, a little too gloomy."

"Life is shit, Neill."

"Sometimes," Neill conceded.

"I've been screwed over so many times I can't tell you." Her mirthless laugh sounded like the bark of a jackal.

"We all have."

Pepper thought that over. She squinted behind her own smoke.

"We all have," she repeated. "Hm."

"Sure," Neill offered just to have something to say.

"You been screwed over, Neill?"

"Of course. Many more times than you, I'd wager."

"Why not write about it?"

"I do."

"But you said."

"I meant, it's not the only subject. If you want readers to follow you, you have to offer a choice of doors." Neill had no idea what he was talking about. He was no teacher.

"Can I read your ex-girlfriend poems?"

"Pepper, we're getting off the point."

"What's the point?"

"Listen. You are brave to write through your pain. And, you're working fertile ground. Keep at that. But allow yourself the transcendent thought that there is more than just loss."

"Fertile," she said. She tipped over sideways and lay on the couch with her knees pulled up. Her cigarette dropped from her fingers.

Neill rose and picked up the cigarette and tossed it into the fireplace. He returned to his chair. Pepper Pimwell lay still as if unconscious. She was staring into otherness, or perhaps she was just in a stupor. Neill couldn't take his eyes off her hairy but pleasing legs and her little rounded butt with its ridiculous green panties.

"You ok?" Neill said.

Pepper didn't move.

"Pepper, did I upset you in some way?"

"Are you looking at my ass?"

"Oh. You're ok."

"I said, are you looking at my ass?"

"No," Neill said.

"Liar."

"Pepper, sit up. Do you want to talk some more?"

"You got someplace to be? I brought some grass." She lifted the brown bag.

"No place to be, no."

"Look, Neill."

Pepper flopped onto her back. She slowly opened her knees. The green panties over her crotch also were stained. Neill did not want to guess with what. Yet he was—naturally—stirred.

"Pepper," he said, weakly.

"You've been nice to me. I can be nice to you, too. Wouldn't that be fair?"

"You don't owe me."

"But your eyes keep going to my...."

"Numnum?"

"I was gonna say my dick alley."

"I know a Dick Alley."

"I'll bet you do."

"Pepper, I *am* a man." Neill tried a laugh for punctuation.

"Ha," she barked. "Because a poet can be a man, too."

"Yes, just so."

"Then, Neill, I want to fuck you as a man. Not as a poet."

"That—while pleasant—isn't necessary."

"Or desired?"

Neill didn't answer.

"Pleasant? You think it would only be pleasant?"

Neill sat back in his chair. He didn't realize he had been sitting forward. Pepper rose slowly, like a column of smoke. She sat up straight and took off the tattered sail of her shirt. Her breasts were large for her proportions. Her nipples were brick colored, almost red.

"Ok," Neill said. "Ok. Pepper, you should really be more careful."

"Because there are bad men out there?"

"Yes."

"You're not a bad man." Her tiny skirt had an elastic band and she flipped it off quickly.

"You don't owe me, Pepper." Neill was talking in his sleep. He was already under.

"Oh, oops, damn," Pepper said. She put a hand to her panties. "Fucking period."

Hence, the stain.

"That's ok," Neill said.

"Fuck me on my period?" She made a face, half aversion, half intrigue. She was so young.

"It's been done. But I meant it was ok. We don't have to see this through."

"Just take your cock out and shut up, Neill."

"Are you 18?"

"Neill, I am a lot older than 18." Neill doubted it. "Take. Out. Your. Cock."

Pepper got on her knees. Neill hesitated but then opened his pants. It sprang upward like the little gymnast it was.

"Mm," Pepper said, in her grave way. "It's not big but it's pretty."

Then: "You come pretty good," she said, ticking off the boxes on her report card. "And it tastes pretty good, too."

Julia *Child*, Neill thought.

"Thanks," Neill said. "You suck good."

"Yeah, I do. I fuck even better."

"Next time," Neill said.

"Oh, there probably won't be a next time, Neill. I'm sorry. My boyfriend wouldn't like it."

"You have a boyfriend."

"Yes, of course." She was already redressing.

"Then, why are you here?"

"Poems, Neill, poems. Jake said I could fuck you if you read my poems and liked them."

And then she was gone, leaving the air polluted with smoke and her body pong. Neill

imagined the funk was still in the air when Dinah and Bidden arrived that night with two
carloads of Dinah's belongings.

Roommates

Time passed. Neill grew lonely and horny, lonelier and hornier. Meanwhile, his new roommate
and her boyfriend were going at it like a bottle rid of its cork. Some nights, Neill took to
wearing earplugs. Nothing sounds worse than the flailing of your fellow humans in wild
venereal boogie when you are bereft. What might be music at better times is a tune even a
bear would not dance to.

And they were loud. Neill had never noticed how loud Dinah's voice was, just in plain
conversation. Sometimes, it grated on him. Sometimes, the lovebirds monopolized the living
room with their movies and popcorn and cuddling. They always asked if Neill would join them.
They were always polite.

Neill was growing fangs.

Some nights, he would drive around and convince himself that he had no friends. One of
his best friends and one of his best girlfriends had found each other and erased the world for
Neill. Neill felt like he was ten years old and no one had shown up for his birthday party.

The drives invariably took him past the homes of past lovers. He was cursed as the Ancient
Mariner and the bird around his neck, Unmateable foul fowl, began to stink.

The homes he passed included Sissy Chastain's, Misso Anthill's, Mink Risk's, Kat Dix's, and
on and on, the drive that follows the peripatetic human heart.

Some nights he spent at home if he knew the lovers would be absent.

Once they came back early. Neill was in mid-movie: Hitchcock's *Foreign Correspondent*. Joel
McCrea had just returned to the old mill to find that the baddies had skedaddled.

"Howdy, Roomie!" Dinah boomed.

"Hey Neill," Bidden said.

Neill only looked at them. They were terrible.

"Anything wrong?" Dinah asked. She bussed his cheek.

"No. Everything is peachy," Neill said through grit teeth. He snapped the TV off and went
to his room. Once there he realized the book he was reading—Christina Stead's *The Man who
Loved Children*—was still in the living room. He could not now exit his room. He sat on his bed
in the dark, in the silence, and stewed.

An hour later, he crept out to get the book and pee. Someone was in the bathroom.

He drove around.

Memphis Magazine

In September, he got a call from the editor of *Memphis Magazine*. The editor said, "We love
the article and want to run it next month."

Neill's head swelled. He wanted the attention. He dreamed of the whole city marveling at his deathless prose. He dreamed of fame starting from the October publication and spreading out in concentric circles until all of America was aware of him.

"What is it?" Smithy said.

"Hm?" Neill said.

"Bad news? You look like you've been poleaxed."

"Hm? Oh, no. Good news."

Ianthe appeared. "What's the good news?"

Iago stood behind her. He wore a lean and hungry look.

"*Memphis Magazine* called. They're publishing the essay I wrote."

"Hey, that's wonderful!" Smithy said.

"You are launched," Ianthe said.

"Thanks, thanks," Neill said. "The news today. It is not so bad."

Crane Open

The Book Shelf did their banking at a branch in Poplar Plaza, just down the sidewalk, past the cafeteria and the furniture store (where are you now, Lula?). The morning walk to the bank with a paper sack full of the store's meager earnings from the day before was one of Neill's duties, one he enjoyed because he liked walking.

He had become friends with some of the bank tellers. There were two women there who made Neill's palms sweat. One was a young blond who couldn't be more than 23. The other, a chocolate-colored woman who looked like Lola Falana. Her name was Beatrice.

This morning he got Beatrice. This always pleased him.

"Morning, Beatrice, my darkling darling," Neill said.

"Good morning, Neill. You watch what you say to me."

"Because I was daring with darling?"

"You silver-tongued type. My boyfriend will slap you silly."

"You don't have a boyfriend."

"Why would you think a fox like me wouldn't have a boyfriend?"

"Because no man is good enough for you."

Beatrice laughed with all of her luscious self.

"You're right, Neill. When you're right, you're right. You need change?"

"I could use change, yes."

"Uh huh."

"Oh yes. Two quarters, two nickels. 35 ones."

While Beatrice was getting Neill's money, Neill became aware of some attention from another of the tellers. She was dishwater blond with Twiggy freckles and she was looking at Neill the way nuns look at handsome priests. She seemed familiar.

And, just like that, it came to Neill who she was.

Her name was Crane Open. She had been a year behind Neill at Nicholas Blackwell High School. She was a freshman cheerleader when Neill was a sophomore. Back in the day, Neill thought she was cuter than new saucepans. Too cute for him, surely. He vaguely remembered asking her out and being turned down. Did that happen? It might have.

"She's new," Beatrice said.

"I know her," Neill said. Crane was now waiting on a customer and not looking their way.

"You wish you did. You're a skirt-chaser, Neill. I know the type."

"I bet you do. *Darling*," Neill said.

Beatrice tittered and waved Neill away.

Neill walked toward Crane's window and, when she finished with her customer, Neill said, "Crane Open!"

"Hello, Neill," Crane said.

"How are you?"

"It's Crane Closed now."

"What?" Had Neill misremembered her name?

"Closed because I am old and I have a new last name."

"Oh, I see. You're married."

"Franks."

"You're welcome."

Crane laughed. "Same old Neill. Franks is my new last name."

"Like Ballpark."

She laughed again. "Like Larry."

"Larry Franks from high school?"

"Married him."

"Nice," Neill said.

"Excuse me," a huffy, heavyset woman in line said. "Are you open?"

"Franks," Neill said to the woman as she pushed past him to Crane's window.

"Good to see you," Neill called over his shoulder as he walked away.

More Memphis Magazine

Memphis Magazine sent a photographer to The Book Shelf. The photographer took Neill's picture. Neill leaned against the New Fiction shelf with a wry smile on his still young puss. The photographer praised Neill's easy grace in front of the camera.

Neill liked this compliment.

Later, he thought the photographer was accusing Neill of being a ham, a lover of the spotlight. A shallow man. Most ambitious.

When the issue was published, the photograph pleased Neill. Underneath it ran the caption, "One for the Books." This pleased Neill, too.

Neill fielded some calls about his article. The essay was mostly a cheerleader's account of the Big Game, that is, Bookselling.

Bidden liked it.

Crow liked it.

Shlomo called from New York. "Thanks for sending me your wonderful article. You're a mover, if not a shaker. I loved everything you had to say except for your championing of the over-praised and mawkish Christopher Morley."

Though Neill and Shlomo had been through much together, though they had traveled together, and though Shlomo had slept on Neill's couch, Neill remained intimidated enough by his brilliant friend that the criticism stung.

All in all, though, he was gratified.

And when he got a check for $100 from *Memphis Magazine*, he was sure that he was now on the road that led to literary recognition.

This good feeling lasted about 24 hours.

At Home

Things remained tense at home. The lovers still made Neill feel like a poisoned cat behind a hanging corpse. Then, he felt guilty for feeling that way and for not being able to celebrate his friends' love. He was angry at his own petty jealousy and he was angry at being angry. Self-loathing bubbled in Neill like dyspepsia.

"You doing anything tonight, Neill?" Dinah asked one morning. She was already dressed though it was only 8 a.m. It rankled Neill that she did not run around in panties.

"I'm never doing anything," Neill said, sourly.

"Right," Dinah said. She was beginning to slowly cool on Neill. She was growing tired of his outright disdain for the situation. She was sorry he was lonely but, fuck, he needed to grow a spine and act like an adult.

"You guys staying in?"

The way he asked made Dinah put down the coffee filter she was fiddling with. She looked at Neill for a long time. The morning air crackled.

"Whatever," she said. And she left.

That night Dinah and Bidden stayed in Dinah's room. They played their Bowie too loud and their passion sounded like they were eviscerating small animals with power tools.

Neill left. Neill drove around.

The Second Heart Attack

Max Rhymer went into cardiac arrest a second time. Neill's parents had moved from their home on Kenneth Street (this was another thing that broke Neill's heart—his old family home now housed strangers) to white-flight Cordova. They bought a house on a golf course because, since Max's retirement from DuPont (forced out at 63 so they wouldn't have to pay full pension at 65), golf was the thing they cared about most.

An ambulance took Max from his home to Methodist North.

They did not need to operate again. Instead, they did an angioplasty and loaded him up with Lasix and in three days he was back home.

Neill had gone to the hospital every day. Now, he visited both his parents in Cordova. AJ and

Dan, who had also moved out of Raleigh and bought a home in the same neighborhood as Max and Lolly, were there, too.

"Thanks for the book," Max said, weakly. His shortness of breath made Neill tremble. He had always been a rock, a strong, stoic rock.

"John D. MacDonald. It's his new one."

"Thank you, Neill."

"He's your favorite."

"I know. Thank you."

Everyone watched the football game.

"How's the bookstore?" Max asked, softly.

"Oh fine. Financially, I am not sure. We've been hurt by the competition."

"Sure."

"You sleeping ok?"

"Better than in the hospital. Are you still seeing—Latitia?"

"Lucretia. No, no I'm not, Dad."

"What happened?"

"I don't know."

"Ok."

"I guess I better go."

Neill kissed his dad on his whiskery cheek. His breath was stale.

"I'll call tomorrow."

"Ok. I'm ok, Neill."

"I know you are."

In the kitchen, he pulled his mom aside. "Is he eating healthy?"

"We're following the heart diet they gave us," Lolly said.

"No cheeseburgers."

"Well, Neill. He's so stubborn."

"You're cooking him cheeseburgers?"

"He has to have his Wendy's bacon cheeseburger. He gets too grouchy if I say no."

"Mom. You have to. Are you cooking healthy stuff for him here?"

"Yes. We're following the heart diet."

"Less meat?"

"Well, Neill, now your father is not going to turn vegetarian."

"You going easier on the salt?"

"Neill. I'm old. I don't need you to tell me."

"Ok. You're not still smoking?" Neill's father had not had a cigarette since the first heart attack.

"I smoke outside."

"Sheesh. Ok, ma. You take care." Neill bussed her cheek as well.

As he was getting into his car, AJ hustled out.

"She tell you he's eating healthier?"

"Of course she's telling me that."

"They haven't changed a damn thing. She still smokes in the house."

"I figured. What can we do?"

"I thought they would listen to you. Mom thinks I'm an idiot."

"She doesn't listen to me any better."

"I called Brack and asked him to speak to them."

"And he said they wouldn't listen to him either."

"Right." AJ's eyes got misty. She had a loose trigger when it came to tears.

"It'll be alright, Sis."

"Until it's not," AJ said.

"Until it's not."

Again Crane Open

"I read your article," Crane Open said as she counted Neill's money and, slowly, put together his change.

"Ok," Neill said. He was smiling.

"You're a big shot writer now."

"Hardly. One essay in a local magazine. I'm working on a 2nd essay about higher education. I want to call it 'On Collegey'."

"You write poetry too, though, right?"

"I do. Poetry, a little fiction."

"Wow."

"It's not really a wow. But thanks for propping me up a bit. What are you doing these days?"

"I work in a bank."

"That must be pleasant. Which bank?"

"Dope."

"Yeah. So, you're married, new name and everything. You got kids?"

"One. A son. Christian."

"His name mean anything?"

"It means follower of Christ."

"Right."

"Here's your change. Anything else?"

"No, thanks. Good to talk to you again, Crane. It's really nice our working so close."

"Ok. Bye Neill."

Neill turned, and then turned back. There was no one else in line.

"I had a big crush on you in high school," he said.

"Well!" Neill thought Crane was going to fan herself. "You never told me."

"I thought you were out of my league."

"Neill! No one was out of your league. You had every pretty girl at Bartlett in love with you."

"I wish I saw the world with your eyes."

"You should."

"You have beautiful eyes."

"Ok, go on with you now."

"Right. Sorry, Mrs. Franks."

Life is Hard

Neill was not the only one in turmoil, in transition. There was trouble brewing between Bidden and Dinah.

Neill found Dinah in the kitchen making gazpacho when he got off work one day.

"That for Bidden?" Neill asked. He tried to use his affable voice. His affable voice was in the shop.

"Nope," Dinah said, never looking up.

Neill went to his room. He stewed.

He came back out.

"Dinah, I'm sorry. I'm trying to make polite conversation."

"Stop trying," she said.

Neill went back to his room and tried to read.

Around 3 a.m. he was awakened by a combination of strange sounds. It was raining pretty hard. It might have been hailing. And there was another dimension to the sound, a human voice blubbing like a voice in the wilderness. Like an animal caught in a trap in the wilderness.

Neill got out of bed and crept down the hall. He could see light under Dinah's door.

The sound was coming from Dinah's room though it sounded muted. Neill stood as still as a disembodied spine. It was Bidden's voice. He was howling. He was howling outside Dinah's window.

Before Neill could beat a hasty retreat and hide back in his own bedroom, Dinah jerked the bedroom door open. She brushed past Neill as if he were the villain in a domestic melodrama. She opened the front door. In came Bidden, soaked to the skin. There were tiny ice pellets in his hair and his face was more terrible than the mask of Tragedy.

Neill nodded and went back to bed.

The next morning, there was no sign of Dinah or Bidden.

Neill dressed and went to work.

The Note

Neill's day at The Book Shelf was nice. He saw one of his favorite sales reps and had lunch with him at the cafeteria. He got a shipment from Ingram, which always pleased him. Neill was like a kid on Christmas morning whenever he opened a new box of books. [In his lifetime of bookselling, Neill never lost this joy.]

The new John Barth came in.

These were nice things, small compensations for the rough patch Neill had been going through. He meant to call Bidden all day and his cowardice prevented him. He was a poor friend. He was a quakebuttock.

Smithy invited him out with her friends to see a movie. She was kind.

Instead, Neill went home. If he'd known what was waiting for him he would never have gone home. He would have left the state and lived under a pseudonym.

The house was as empty as a politician's speech.

There was a note lying on the couch. Neill's eye found it just as he entered. Its whiteness—two typewritten sheets in an envelope—was like a stain. There was something incongruous, even evil about the way it swallowed all other light in the room.

Neill opened it.

It was from Dinah and this is what it said:

I have moved out. I took all my stuff already. This was a disaster and it was your fault. You are a selfish asshole and a self-involved prick. You don't really care about anyone. All you care about is how someone can help you, not ever how you might help someone. The way you treated me and your supposed best friend Bidden was unconscionable. I am sorry we were having a good time while you were lonely. Grow up, asshole. I know we've had a checkered past but you have never loved me except when I was sucking your dick. I have watched you treat other women the same way. I was only good enough for you when your dick was full. Well, now Neill, I am leaving your house so I won't bother you anymore. I don't ever want to see you or talk to you again. You're a whore and you suck. I hope you learn how to suck yourself because no woman is going to stick with you.

Don't call me.

Dinah.

Neill called her. She hung up.

Neill was as hurt as he had ever been in his life. Was he like what she described? Was she right about him and this was the end? Neill's chest hurt. He thought about his father's bad ticker. He thought he might be going to die and he wanted to. He sat on the couch and cried. He cried for himself, for Bidden, and for Dinah. He cried for the decades of wasted romance that left him washed up here in his 32nd year without a woman in his life, and now, nearly friendless.

Neill came to an end. Not The End, perhaps, but an end just the same.

Did the mean justify the end?

An Opening

Neill sulked for a few days. A week. The house was as empty as eternity.

The house was empty because there was a space where there was formerly a human being, a beloved human being. And that absence was Neill's fault. It would be over a decade before he saw Dinah again.

Work was a sleepwalk. The Gorgeous Young Housewives' Book Club was now reading Peter DeVries' *Tunnel of Love*. This was Neill's suggestion.

He explained to each GYH what was special about Mr. DeVries. It was good work but Neill's heart was blasted cold.

Luna came in. Neill had the novel in his hand when she came in the door.

"How do you know I wasn't just coming to see you?" Luna teased. She glowed. Luna glowed.

"Because Peter DeVries is real and I am a hollow log."

Luna pursed her pretty lips and looked at Neill.

"What's wrong with my Neill?" she asked.

Her Neill? Neill's cinereous heart sent off one tiny spark.

"I'm a waste of harvestable organs," Neill said.

Luna laughed despite herself.

"Perhaps you'd let me buy you lunch."

"Oh, I would," Neill said.

"I can't today. Later this week?"

"That would be grand," Neill said.

After Luna left Neill felt a bit better. Glowing women can do that to a lonely man.

"I gotta run to the bank," Neill shouted back to Iago. "We're out of quarters."

"Why didn't you get some this morning?" Iago shouted back.

Neill let that go.

Walking down the sidewalk on this bracing late November day Neill almost felt human again. Maybe someday he would see Luna naked. Absurd, his inner demon said back to him. She's happily married to a rich man.

At the bank Neill got Crane Open's window. Speaking of attractive married women.

"Hello Neill. Didn't I see you in earlier?"

"Yes," Neill said. His smile was apelike.

"Ok," Crane said. She figured Neill was going to be all business today. That was fine.

"I read your *Memphis Magazine* piece," she said, handing him a roll of quarters. "You're really smart, aren't you?" (Neill had not the heart to tell her she'd already said this. Was she nervous for some reason?)

"I wish you weren't married," Neill said. He had not prepared, obviously.

Crane laughed a laugh louder than she intended.

"Neill, darling Neill of Bartlett High, I am divorced." She smiled that kind of smile.

"I think my day just got better," Neill said.

"I think mine did, too," Crane said.

"Should we—get together?"

"We should. I gotta tell you something."

"You have a kid, I know."

"That's true but not what I meant. I read that article and, well, I sorta set my hat for you. Your picture was so cute. It reminded me of how cute you were in high school." (Neill always got 'cute.' He never got 'handsome.') "I mean, you're still really cute, is what I meant."

Neill was charmed. Charmed by her beautiful freckled smile and by her use of such a quaint phrase as 'I set my hat for you.'

"I am charmed by your freckled smile and your use of such a quaint phrase," Neill said.

"My smile is freckled?"

"How about Friday night?"

"How about tonight?" Crane said.

"Yes!" Neill said. "Even a better idea. What do you want to do?"

"I can't get a sitter this quickly. How about I cook for you?"

"I would love that," Neill said.

Crane wrote out her address and directions to it on the back of a bank slip. She lived off James Road in Raleigh. Neill hadn't been back there in a while.

"Fantastic," Neill said. Just hours ago Neill thought he would never say fantastic again.

"I make a mean beef stew," Crane said.

"I eat mean beef stews. I eat mean things. I eat almost anything except beets."

"I love beets."

"I'll eat them, too," Neill said.

Dinner at Crane Open's

Crane Open lived off James Road, up a long gravel driveway, tented by overhanging trees, making it seem a small country road. Her house was practically a cabin in the woods. Neill thought the night had suddenly become adventurous as if he was Richard Halliburton and Crane Open was a Chinese junk.

Neill knocked on a flimsy white screen door. A small boy with unkempt brown hair opened the inner door. He just stood his ground and looked at Neill through the screen. The night was dark and the music of crickets predominated.

"Hi," Neill tried.

"Mom!" the boy yelled without taking his eyes off Neill. He was a good cop.

"Christian, I said to greet our guest and let him in." Crane came to the door with a dish towel in her hands.

Neill stepped inside and put his hand out for Christian to shake. Christian did not shake his hand.

"Well, it's nice to meet you, Christian," Neill tried.

"I'm sorry," Crane Open said. Her pretty blondish hair was damp with perspiration. "He's not usually this shy."

Christian went to his room and Neill followed Crane into the kitchen.

"Hi," Neill said.

"Oh, sorry," Crane said, putting down the wooden spoon she just picked up. She put a hand on Neill's shoulder and kissed his cheek.

"How forward!" Neill said.

"Shit. I'm sorry. I'm off to a bad start."

"I'm kidding. Give me another."

Crane laughed. "I guess I'm trying too hard to make a good impression."

"Stop trying. You've already made an impression."

"Oh. A good one?"

"I had such a crush on you in high school."

"You had a crush on everyone."

"I assure you I did not."

"Well, thanks. That was a long time ago."

"Not too. You're still as lovely. And I am happy to be here."

Crane gave him a sidelong, suspicious glance, but smiling.

"I can't believe you're here." She laughed at herself.

"Yet I am. Why is it hard to believe?"

"I don't know. My life's been messy. Two divorces, one kid, one deadbeat dad."

"I'm sorry. I have a rough road behind me, too."

"Married?"

"No, not that."

"Come close?"

Neill thought about this. "I guess not."

"Anyway, I swore off men. And when I saw your picture in *Memphis Magazine* it—I don't know. It rang a bell or something."

"An alarm."

"No, ha. Just the opposite."

"Thanks. I think I understand what you're saying."

"I'm sorry. I am putting pressure on this evening already and I vowed not to."

"It's all fine. Can I help?"

"No, I've just about wrestled this into edibility."

"It smells delicious."

"Pot roast soup. I think I made it up."

"So, you read?" Neill asked as they ate. There was a small bookcase with dog-eared paperbacks.

"I read all the time," she said. "I always have a book going."

"That's the real definition of a reader, someone who is always reading."

"I guess I'm a reader."

"What are you reading?"

"I can't remember the name of it."

"Who wrote it?"

"I can't remember."

"Ok," Neill said.

"Thorn something?"

"Birds?"

"Yeah, that's it."

"This soup is exquisite. You really make it up?"

"It's not fancy."

"Christian doesn't eat with us?"

"Normally, he and I eat early. He's six and has school in the morning, so he's eaten. I think he's doing homework but he might be just watching TV."

After dinner they sat in the living room, which was really the western end of the dining room. This cabin in the woods was really the size of a cabin. The room was already decorated for Christmas.

"You start early," Neill said, gesturing at the lights.

"Christian insists."

"I see. Where is he?"

"He went to bed."

"Quietly."

"Yes. He should have come said goodnight but I think he's wary of you. New man, you know."

"Uh huh." Neill had no clue. He didn't know much about children.

They talked about how they each got to where they were. They talked about Crane's going back to school to get her nursing license. She was unsettled now but expected the road to level off for her.

"Neill, I can't believe you don't have a girlfriend. You were so popular in high school."

"I didn't feel popular. And, you know, it's easier back then. Small pond fishing."

"I hadn't thought of it that way. I didn't have a boyfriend in high school."

"Seriously? You were—*gorgeous*."

"I wish you'd asked me out."

"I did. I was rebuffed."

"You mean, turned down? I turned you down?"

"You did."

"It must have been shyness. I was so shy. I don't remember even talking to you."

"Funny, the walls we build."

Crane seemed to be thinking this over. "I'm glad you're here now."

"Me too."

They looked at each other. I guess this is ok, Neill thought, as he leaned in.

The kiss was gathered greedily. Crane's mouth was wild and slushy, and her tongue a downed wire, sparking. It was so arousing Neill quickly began to use his hands to explore Crane's womanly body. Crane followed suit and her hand found its way to Neill's bare stomach and its little isle of hair. This was one of Neill's hot spots (we have mentioned this earlier?)

Neill put his hands under Crane's light sweater and found a receptive Crane. She arched her back like a cat in heat.

"Take your sweater off," Neill whispered between wet osculations.

Crane didn't even pause. The sweater hit the ground. She was wearing a white bra that was simultaneously childish and sexy. Neill took it off her. Her breasts were small, tight swellings.

As Neill began to suck her nipples, Crane's hand went to Neill's zipper. She was good. Precipitously, Neill's yang sprang into view. Crane was grabbing it as if it were a lifesaver.

Both were breathing heavily.

"Will Christian get up?"

"He never does. Want to go to my room?"

"Yes."

Neill held his pants up with one hand. He followed Crane into a small room just off the living room. Really small room. Like the berth on a ship. Dresser, bed. As they moved into the bedroom, Crane unzipped her own jeans and let them fall. Her ass in sheer aqua panties was a wonder, round like a tun. Neill, good sport that he is, dropped his own pants. He also wrestled his way quickly out of his shirt.

They began to dry hump through their underwear. More sparks flew.

"Birth control?" Neill panted.

"Yes," Crane panted back.

Neill whipped Crane's panties off. He began to finger her and she got good and wet. Then, he left the small bed and knelt on the wooden floor, positioning himself between Crane's beautiful legs. (She had beautiful legs!)

He gave it his all. Crane was enthusiastic. Her crotch was loose and extremely wet. There was a lot to lick and suck. When she came the first time, Neill was sure she had woken the child. But he did not stop and no child appeared.

Neill rose, intending to get back into bed but the picture of Crane Open, well, *open*, her cheerleader legs spread, her bush fulsome and sodden, was too much of an incitement. Instead, Neill unsheathed his jimmy and entered her missionary style. Crane did the dance with him. They were good together. Neill grabbed her ass. Crane grabbed Neill's balls. She came once more. Then Neill did, hard and surging, and as he did, he bore down hard, pressing his pubic area against hers the way you use silly putty to lift a picture from a comic book.

Then, he fell back beside her.

They kissed and murmured and said sweet things to each other. Neill knew he had to drive home but he did not want to. He had to work in the morning but he didn't care. This was refuge. This was Eden.

"Neill, you're as wonderful as I thought you would be."

"You mean in the sack?"

"Ha ha, no," Crane said, mock-swatting him. "But that too. You're good in bed."

"Hm hm, you too. You're so—so pretty."

"Am I Neill?"

"You're one of the prettiest things I've ever seen."

"Neill."

They lay quietly. Neill was dropping off.

"Neill," Crane whispered. "You can't sleep here."

"Huh?" Neill said.

"I'm sorry. I know it's awful."

"No, I understand. I didn't mean to fall asleep."

Crane began to knead Neill's wet, limp dingus.

"That feels good."

"One more orgasm before I send you on your way," Crane said and began to massage in earnest.

"Oh, I can't come twice that quickly," Neill said.

"No?"

"Never have." Neill thought of the king/knight joke but he did not say it.

"Wanna bet?"

Crane Open threw the covers aside and moved between Neill's legs. She started a first-rate course in genitalese. She began with gentle tongue swirls and gentle fingering of balls. Soon, Neill offered her a half-mast salute. Only then did she lower her mouth over the whole thing. It was the gentlest, sweetest, soggiest blow job Neill had had in years. And, even though his wac-a-mole was sore, it rose, hardened, filled, and pumped.

Crane Open swallowed it all, held her mouth there a moment, and then raised her pretty face. In the half-light, Neill saw her smile of triumph.

She snuggled back next to him. He kissed the top of her head and held her as if they were man and wife and about to fall asleep together.

"First time twice?" she asked, softly.

And Neill lied: "Yes, Crane. You are miraculous."

Crane Visits

A few nights later Crane brought dinner to Neill's house. It was a crockpot full of potato soup which she announced was perfect comfort food for chilly nights. It was.

Neill had provided the movie. He had rented *Rear Window*, his favorite Hitchcock film.

After the toothsome soup, they cuddled on the couch and watched Jimmy and the ravenous Grace and the murderous Raymond Burr, but both of them were thinking about the bedroom. The previous coupling was obviously splendid for them both. The fact that Crane had paid for a babysitter meant this was going to be a night to remember. It was.

Even as the credits began to roll Neill had his tongue deep in Crane Open's open mouth. They both were hot to get undressed and feel the press of each other's naked flesh. This they accomplished in short fashion.

Neill again brought Crane to a powerful orgasm with his mouth.

"Gosh," she said, afterwards.

Neill crawled up the bed, straddled Crane's torso, gently set his ass down on her erect nipples and put the tip of his cock on her lips.

Crane did work that surpassed the previous piccolo concerto. But Neill removed his now wet and solid penis and backed slowly off. He put his hands on Crane's pretty hips and helped her turn onto her stomach. He ran his cock down her crack. She arched her back, a natural enough reaction.

Neill entered her from behind, pulling himself up tight against her rounded base and then began a slow thrusting tempo. It was more the building, acoustic opening of Zep's "Gallow's Pole," than the raucous end of same. Gradually, he increased his speed as his own pleasure increased ("Hangman, hangman, wait a little while"). Crane was making little hedgehog noises. As he started to go in and out faster, Neill grabbed Crane's cheeks to aid his near frenzy. She let out a long exhale.

So Neill began to knead her bum, slapping it tenderly. Then, he ran a finger down her crack and hesitated outside her little mudeye, just discernible in the shadowiness. He touched it with the tip of his index finger.

"Unh," Crane said. It was a good sound.

Neill switched to his pinky and slowly inserted it. Crane began to buck. She pushed her pretty ass so high in the air it almost threw Neill off. Neill pumped her harder while wiggling his finger inside her anus.

"JESUS!" Crane said. It was a kind of prayer, or hymn. "NEILL!" she further explained. And then, "OH GODDAMN!"

This was Crane's orgasm.

Neill's followed shortly thereafter, spurred on by Crane's extraordinary outburst.

In the afterglow, Crane scooched her comely face up close to Neill's. She kissed him lightly on the nose and lips.

"You have amazing talents."

"Oh, Crane. You're just so sexy."

"No. The things you come up with. I...I'm speechless."

As if Neill had invented the use of anal probing to increase pleasure. Neill decided to let her think he had.

Crane and Christian Come to the Bookstore

"Christian wanted to see where you work," Crane announced not three feet inside the store.

"Hello!" Neill fairly bellowed. This was a pleasant surprise.

"And, he wants a book," Crane continued.

Neill sidled up to them. He did not know whether a kiss was a good thing at this point. He settled for bussing Crane's speckled cheek. She was wearing one of those puffy sleeveless winter things, so Neill could not have gotten closer if he wanted to. It was as if she was wearing armor.

"Let's look back here, big guy," Neill said, in a chummy voice.

"He likes pictures still," Crane said, as if in apology.

"Who doesn't?" Neill said.

They stood around in the kids section while Christian glumly fingered a few books. He didn't want a book. He could care less about books.

Betty walked by and Neill made introductions. Betty was as sweet as a grandmother.

"What would you recommend?" Crane asked Neill. Her eyes twinkled. Neill had never noticed before how her eyes twinkled.

"Do you know about Choose Your Own Adventures?"

Christian looked up at him but did not speak. Neill proffered a few books in that series.

"Let's see," Crane said.

Crane looked at the books with about as much interest as Christian had.

"Yes, these are fun. We'll take a couple of these."

They paid at the register and Neill walked them out. The air stung slightly as if filled with tiny ice crystals.

"Such a nice surprise," Neill said.

"Was it?" Crane said. Her voice was tinged with anxiety. "I didn't know whether to just pop in or not."

"Why not?"

"I don't know." Crane chewed on the inside of her cheek.

"I thought maybe you had a girlfriend, maybe that woman you work with," Crane continued.

"Betty? No, we're just good friends."

Crane laughed.

"Though some days I can't keep my hands off her."

"You know I meant the other woman."

"Smithy. How do you know about Smithy?"

"You've mentioned her. Twice, no three times. She's come in the bank. I thought—"

"No. I have no girlfriend. Will you be my girlfriend?"

Crane looked into Neill's face. Her gaze was intense. Her gaze was trying to eat Neill's gaze.

"Really, Neill?"

"The position is open."

"Yes, please. Yes, thank you."

"Ok, girlfriend."

"You gotta work."

"Eh."

"Now I'm really happy I popped in."

"Me too."

"See you tonight?"

"Let me check my appointment book." Neill looked skyward, made as if he were totting up figures in his head. "Nope, looks like I'm clear."

"Idiot," Crane said. Then, she kissed him. The armor allowed just that much contact.

That Night

That night Neill took Crane out to dinner at Sandy's on Summer Avenue. He also paid for the baby sitter. It was a celebration of sorts. Crane was loving, misty-eyed, silly. She laughed a lot, grabbed Neill's hand often, touched his cheek. Neill echoed every bit of affection.

It was a splendid meal.

They went to Neill's though time was short. The babysitter had to leave at 10:00.

They started to make out as soon as they stepped inside the door.

"Coats off!" Neill said.

They kissed some more. Heat rose like lava.

"I have an idea," Neill said.

"Tell me," Crane said. "What kind of idea?" she emended.

"Do you have any sexy underwear?"

"Not really. It's mom underwear."

"Oh."

"I'm sorry. I've disappointed you already."

"No, no."

"I have on the prettiest pair of panties I own. It's just been so long since anyone cared."

"Did you used to have sexy lingerie?"

"No."

"Ok. So you have nice panties on. That's good. I want you to go in my bedroom, find my white dress shirt in the closet, and come back out with just that shirt and the panties on."

This had become one of Neill's favorite fantasies. See earlier application.

"I don't know. I'm not exactly a runway model."

"Crane. You're prettier than a stack of cats."

Crane laughed. "Ok."

While she changed, Neill stripped down to his briefs and t-shirt. The house was warm, almost too warm. With floor furnaces one never knew what to expect, tropical heat or tepid sputterings of near-warmth.

The bedroom door opened. Neill watched her walk down the hall. She was not walking sexy. She did not sell the performance.

"I don't know," she said as she stepped into the overly bright living room.

"Crane, you're goddamn beautiful. Your legs are perfect. God. You're so beautiful."

"Really, Neill?"

"Unbutton the shirt."

Crane hesitated, then smiled. She unbuttoned the top two buttons quickly, then slowed. She discovered her inner stripper. Gradually, her lovely golden skin was revealed, the swell of her breasts just under the white material.

"Turn slowly," Neill said.

Crane was engaged now. She turned in small increments. It was driving Neill wild and she knew it. When she had her back fully to him, she raised the hem of the shirt slowly. The panties she had on were not Victoria's Secret but were of a thin material so that her ass looked wonderful and her crack deep and dark.

"Oh Jesus," Neill said. "I love your ass."

Crane let the shirt fall.

"You're so beautiful," Neill said again. He lost his eloquence to his randiness.

Crane looked over her shoulder. "Want me to turn back around? Or you want me to lose the panties?"

"Either," Neill said. He was mesmerized.

"You gotta pick, Bucko. But first turn one of those lamps off."

Neill did. Now the room had a buttery glow.

"I can't lose either way," Neill said. "Take the panties off."

She did. They slid down her shapely legs like the snake exiting Eden.

They lay on the dusty carpet in front of the fireplace, where a weak flame spat. Neill was thinking: this is perfect. This is—*cinematic*. Neill often thought of scenes in his life as if a great director in the sky was blocking it out and recording it. Neill's idea of Heaven was that his life had been composed into a well-made film, directed by Bergman, perhaps. Or Fellini.

They did the usual preliminary stuff. It was more erotic than ever given the good meal out, the girlfriend/boyfriend situation, the strip, and the fire.

When Neill turned Crane onto her stomach again. Crane sighed. This time she was anticipating Neill's great sex trick.

In the orange glim, Crane's ass looked like a peach. Neill put his teeth into one cheek. He nibbled, then he bit.

"Ooh," Crane said. She arched her back. It was an invitation.

Neill bent closer. He kissed one cheek and then the other. Then, he licked both. Then, he licked slowly down her crack, starting at the small of her back, dragging it deliberately down toward his goal. When his tongue found her little anal opening, Neill licked around its rim.

"Uh huh uh," Crane said.

He put his tongue in. For him, it was an old trick, this anilingus. He had done it with Akin in 10th grade. For Crane, it was the forbidden door thrust open. It was raw, pure SEX.

When she came, she used language Neill had never heard her use. It was so sexy Neill was tortured with lust. He turned her over and ate her once more from the front. She came again and screamed so loud Neill was sure the sweet old lady next door had heard.

Afterward, as the logs creaked and hummed, Crane was like a piece of driftwood tossed by waves, beached.

"Oh my, Neill," she sang. "Oh, my, my Neill."

"My beautiful Crane. My Cranesong."

"Neill, I think," Crane began.

"Shit!" Neill said. Responsible Neill said. "It's 10:15."

"Shit," Crane echoed. She jumped up and ran toward the bedroom where her clothes were. The drive to her house seemed to take forever.

"She's gonna kill me. She'll never babysit for me again and she's the best I've found."

"I'll pay her some extra," Neill said. He was a little freaked out by her anxiety.

The babysitter really was pissed. She really did say she wouldn't sit for Christian again. She took Neill's extra ten dollars, got into her beat-up Pontiac, and scratched out.

"I'm sorry," Neill said. He felt bad because Crane's face seemed so careworn.

Then, Crane let her shoulders slump and she laughed a quick laugh.

"Fuck her," Crane said. "It was worth it."

They kissed for a long time.

"I want that tongue," Crane said. "If you ever leave me, I'm taking custody of your tongue."

Bidden on the Horn

"You still talking to me?"

"Of course," Bidden said. He sounded tired.

"I'm sorry, Bidden."

"Ok."

"What's the news? Wait, I'll go first. I'm seeing someone new. Believe it or not, a woman who I went to high school with. Freckly, pretty freshman cheerleader, when I knew her back then. Or didn't know her since I thought she was out of my league and didn't talk to her much. She, believe it or not, was titillated by my *Memphis Magazine* article. First time I've won a woman with my writing. I think it's the first time. Did you read my piece?"

"I did. It was very nice. Nice enough to melt a woman's heart."

"So, what's new with you? I'm sorry we haven't talked. I feel awful about what happened. I behaved boorishly. I should be horsewhipped."

"We all behaved badly."

"I guess."

"I do have news."

"Ok then. Let me have it."

"I've been a tad worried how you would take it."

"Uh oh. Tell me fast."

"Dinah and I are getting married."

Neill swallowed his heart. His heart landed in his stomach with a thud, indigestible, and tough like bully beef. His heart made him sick. He could not speak through the bile. He wanted to warn Bidden about Dinah's previous marriages, though certainly he already knew about them. He wanted to say, I've been with Dinah, she's wonderful. He wanted to say, Dinah is right for you. He wanted to say, Dinah is so wrong for you. He wanted to say so much, and here he sat, saying zilch.

"I'm sorry," Bidden said. "I didn't want to tell you this way. I guess I've been avoiding you."

"No, Bidden, come on. This is great news. I love you both. When are you thinking?"

"Two weeks."

"Seriously?"

"Yes, I'm sorry."

"No, it's fine. Two weeks. Yeah, my calendar is clear."

"We're not inviting anyone. We're driving to Covington and getting married by a judge there. Then, we're driving to Myrtle Beach for our honeymoon."

"Oh," Neill said.

"You know, if we were doing it the other way you'd be invited."

Neill did not know this at all. He half-believed that they were sneaking away just so they didn't have to deal with him.

"Of course," Neill said.

After the call, Neill had a premonition that he and Bidden would drift apart. It hurt him like the pain of dissolution. He was losing his best friend. It hurt him as much as Brack's estrangement. He counted his remaining male friends and came up with two. The number two. Crow and Shlomo.

Did they still love Neill?

Neill was woeful enough to ask himself that question.

Back in Crane's Arms

"We have to be quiet. Christian has a cold. He's in bed but he might get up."

"Ok, sure," Neill said, shrugging off his coat.

"Are you hungry?"

"Are we having dinner together?"

"Yes."

"I'm hungry."

"What's wrong? You seem sad."

"Nothing's wrong. It smells good. What is it?"

"Kentucky Fried Chicken."

"Oh."

"I mean a homemade version. I found the recipe in the paper."

"Oh, good. I love fried chicken.:

"I know. You told me so I made it."

"Great."

"Neill, what's wrong?"

Later, Neill would reflect that his inability to share with Crane Open meant he didn't trust the relationship. Or that he was only partly invested in it.

After dinner they made out on the couch in front of a rerun of *The Rockford Files*.

"Maybe we better not, you know, go all the way, what with Christian sick and all."

"Of course," Neill said. He couldn't keep the disappointment out of his voice.

"I'm sorry, Neill. I'm not helping your funk, am I?"

"It's ok. It's nothing."

"It's not nothing to me. I mean, I love having sex with you. Did you know that? I love it. It's the best sex I've ever had."

"Poor you." What a dumbass thing to say. Neill immediately wished he had not said it.

"Meaning you've had much better." Neill had not seen Crane mad. Her anger flashed like sheet lightning.

"No. I'm sorry. I feel the same way. I think about it all day."

"Really, Neill? You think about me all day?"

That wasn't exactly what he had said. "I do."

"What do you think?"

"I think your ass was made by spirits of deep soulfulness. I think your blowjobs are masterful. I think thinking about being inside you is just about the hottest thought I can have."

"Oh, Neill," Crane said, putting her hand on his chest. "Maybe Christian won't wake up."

"I don't want to if you're worried about it."

"I have an idea."

Crane jumped up and left the room. Neill watched TV. It was an Angel episode. Angel episodes were the best Rockfords, followed closely by Gandolf Fitch episodes.

"I'm naked under this," Crane said in an undertone.

Crane returned dressed only in a robe. It was not a sexy robe. It was thick and it seemed dirty, almost greasy, but the thought of her sweet body underneath it was indeed stirring.

"Now," she said, happy to be in charge. "Lemme take Little Neill out and see what he wants."

Crane rarely said the words 'cock' or 'dick,' and, when she heard Neill refer to his roger as Little Neill, it became her pet name. Her first grade teacher voice made Neill laugh. She unzipped Neill's jeans and pulled them aside a bit, felt around in his briefs, as if playing Feely Meely, and found what she desired. Having found it, she brought it out of its cage.

"And what does Little Neill want?" Crane asked. She was laughing at herself as she put her ear down to Little Neill's tiny, pinpoint mouth.

"Sometimes he lies," Neill said, with a grin.

"Now, can I remember all that Little Neill wanted?" Crane asked, still holding him, but looking into Neill's eyes with a melting cluster behind her gaze.

She did remember. And, it all went very well.

Until Christian came out just as Neill was coming inside Christian's mom. He was *almost* finished squirting.

"I think my feelings still hurt," Christian said. He rubbed his eyes like a movie version of a child emerging from his bedroom with a cold.

"Erp!" Crane said, hopping off Neill, while Neill quickly covered his retted, liquescing dingum with a couch pillow.

Crane took Christian to the bathroom for some aspirin. Neill took Little Neill in his hand and whispered to him, "You were a good boy tonight."

Thanksgiving Dinner at the Rhymers

"My mother makes the best turkey in all of Christendom," Neill said on the ride to the Rhymers.

"How big is Christendom?" Crane said.

Neill was unsure if she was joking or asking a very specific question.

"Bigger than you and me," Neill said, and put his hand on Crane's jean-covered thigh.

Crane smiled and put her hand over Neill's. She stared out the windshield with a small satisfied smile, a secret smile that only she knew the reason for. Or perhaps, she didn't.

Cooking odors wafted toward them as they entered Neill's folks' house. AJ and Dan were already there.

"Everyone, Crane Open," Neill said, presenting her as if she were a big fish.

"Welcome," Lolly said, scooting toward her. She was wearing an apron over her polyester shirt and her pale green polyester pants.

"Thank you," Crane said, softly.

In the kitchen, Neill, Crane, and AJ stood around waiting for the caramel-colored bird to emerge from the oven. When it did, AJ and Neill shared the pieces of bacon that Lolly draped over the turkey as it cooked.

"Bacon?" Neill said, holding up a crispy strip.

"No, thank you," Crane said. She was smiling like a kid.

When Max came out to carve the turkey—because fathers did that—AJ and Neill continued a long-held ritual at the Rhymers: they picked pieces of the bird off even as their father bore down on it with sharpened knives.

At dinner, the talk turned more personal but by then some camaraderie had been established. And the soporific meal: turkey, heavy gravy, whipped potatoes, yams, cranberry sauce, made everyone feel a little drunk and overly friendly.

"Where is your family?" Lolly asked Crane.

"I don't see much of Mom and Dad," Crane said. "I have a son but this was the year he went to his dad's for Thanksgiving. I get him at Christmas."

"How old is he?" AJ asked.

"Six," Crane said. "He's a handful."

"Kids are," Lolly said.

"He's allergic and all."

"So was Neill," Lolly continued, warming to the repartee. "He was so sickly and pale and scrawny I thought for sure he wasn't long for this world."

"Let's drink a toast to Neill's staying power," Neill said.

"Here, here," AJ said, raising her water glass as well.

After dinner Crane helped Mrs. Rhymer clean up. AJ and Neill took a walk around the block. AJ was pregnant at this time, early still, but they knew they had a boy on the way.

"How you feeling, Sis?"

"I'm not bad. Mornings a little rough."

"Uh huh." Neill blew out his breath to observe the white cloud.

"She's stuff," AJ said.

"I knew her at Bartlett. She's a peach."

"I don't remember her from high school."

"I didn't know her well. She was in Orbit's class, a year behind me. I asked her out once but she said no."

"I can't believe that."

"She did. She says she was shy. I just assumed she was too beautiful for me."

"No one was," AJ said. AJ was Neill's biggest fan.

"Ach."

"I'm glad she's here. You look good together. She's got stars in her eyes for you."

"I don't know."

"Uh oh. Trouble already?"

"No, not really."

Neill hesitated so AJ waited.

"She's got that kid."

"You don't want to be a step dad, even a dating one?"

"That might be what's wrong. I just feel—fuck, you know—that it's never gonna be right. I am not even sure how one decides it's ever right."

"Suddenly it just is."

Neill liked AJ, four years his junior, taking the proctor's role.

"I will wait for that *suddenly*."

On the way home, Crane was practically intoxicated with cheer.

"Your family is SO wonderful. No wonder you are. They are really super."

"It was nice of you to help Mom in the kitchen. She liked you, I could tell."

"We had us a talk," Crane said, that little half-smile returning.

"Uh oh."

"No, nothing much. She thinks you're the brightest star in her constellation."

"Ha. She said that?"

"Those were her words."

"Funny," Neill said. But he didn't really think it was that funny. He thought it was calculated to test Crane. Neill wondered if she passed. He then wondered whether he cared.

A Movie and its Consequences

"Christian is going to his grandmother's," Crane said with as much lasciviousness as she could inject into her sweet, simple voice.

"I'll rent a movie," Neill said. "What shall we eat?"

"I'll make some meatball sandwiches. You like meatball sandwiches?"

"Of course I do. I am a man and men eat red meat."

"Are you joking?"

"I'm not sure. But I love meatball sandwiches. Yes, ma'am. That's the new one."

"Wait. What?"

"Sorry. Customer. Anyway, yes I get off at 6. Come as soon after that as possible."

Neill rented a movie from the supermarket. It was called *Betty Blue*. He didn't know a whole lot about it but he thought he remembered hearing good things. It was subtitled. Would Crane like a subtitled movie? Crane asked himself. Then, he admonished himself for underestimating her.

"That smells good," Neill said, holding the door for Crane.

"I didn't do much. The meatballs were leftovers."

"Ok. Wanna put them down in here?"

"Are we going to eat in the living room?"

"I thought we would. We can eat and watch the movie at the same time."

"That sounds like fun."

So, with sodas and meatball sandwiches (on Kaiser rolls, which Neill thought a tasty choice) and potato chips they settled in front of the TV.

"This is in French," Neill said as the previews were running.

"I don't speak French," Crane said.

"No, they put the English down below. You have to read it."

"Neill. I was joking. I've seen a foreign film before."

"Of course."

Then, *Betty Blue* began. And how it began. The very first scene, before even one whole meatball had been digested, was a scene of high-geared fucking, the like of which Neill had not seen since *Last Tango in Paris*. It was graphic. It was shocking. And it was so arousing Neill thought he would have to abandon his meatball sandwich. He didn't even want to chance a look at Crane. He wanted to shove the food out of the way and take her on the carpet.

He chanced a look.

Crane Open looked stricken.

She was looking at her lap. Her sandwich lay on her plate with one bit taken out of it.

"You ok?" Neill asked.

"Sure." Her voice was that of a mouse if a mouse could mix embarrassment and fear into its tiny piping.

"What is it?" Neill persisted. He was a bit stricken himself—and a bit put out.

"Did you rent a porno movie? Did you think that would make me sexier, wilder, or something?"

"Crane," Neill said. He had to swallow and modulate his voice properly. "I've never seen this before. I was surprised by the opening scene too."

"Is the rest of it like this?"

"You're not hearing me. I've not seen this before. You think I calculated that seeing a sex film would improve our own relations?"

"Do you not think so? I know you think I am uptight. You've done so many more things than me. And, and." She just stopped.

"None of that matters. We're good together. Do you not think so?"

Crane sat so still she seemed made of glass.

"I don't know."

"Do you want to turn the movie off?"

"I guess so. No. You do what you want."

"I'll do what we want."

He turned the movie off. They sat next to each other in silence. The red sauce looked like blood. The air was full of the screeches of invisible bats. The night was scabbing over.

Later, they went to bed.

Neill was gentle and, when they were both unclothed, he kissed her shoulders and arms and chest. He kissed her nipples which were not erect. They were soft pink declivities. He kissed her velvety stomach.

"Neill, wait," Crane said. "Come here."

Neill stopped his ministrations and lay face to face with her.

"I'm sorry."

"What are you sorry about?" Neill said.

"About stopping that stupid film."

"It doesn't matter."

"But the reason does, doesn't it? I thought maybe that you wanted that actress, or someone more like that actress. I don't know. It bothers you that I am not more— lustful."

"I assure you that is not the case."

Crane lay quietly in Neill's arms. Her breathing was slowing as she calmed. Neill thought she might fall asleep in his arms.

He thought she had gone to sleep before she said, faintly, "I'll do anything you want to."

"Crane," Neill said.

"I will. I love having sex with you. Though it scares me sometimes."

"How so?"

"Just the level of your experience."

"You're exaggerating it. It's not like I am a sexologist. I just do what seems to feel good or to make you feel good."

"Ok."

"Besides there are not really sex experts. No one knows how any lover is going to respond so every new lover is a new way to learn about other humans."

"That's true," Crane said. She thought for a minute. "Like when I gave you your first second orgasm."

"First second."

"Right," she laughed.

"You better now?"

"I'm ok."

They re-started foreplay and moved quickly beyond it. It went well. It was almost love.

And Then it All Began to Diminish

Though he could not say why, it all went south for Neill, and by Christmas he was no longer seeing Crane Open. She was hurt but recovered quickly. It was, as the saying goes, not meant to be, and Neill comforted himself with the thought that she saw it that way too.

Neill did Christmas in his overalls.

The next year went quickly, then slowly, then its gears jammed, and it stood still. Then, repaired with twist ties and spit, it lurched toward its conclusion. We shall follow in parts.

The Expiration of the Mom and Pop Bookstore

It was happening all over the country. This was no comfort to anyone faced with the closure of their bookstore.

In Memphis, Pluto and Persephone's, a mega-store compared to its competition, having positioned itself geographically between two small independent bookstores, was sucking the life out of both stores. The first to drop was The Roundtable, further East off Poplar Avenue. The owner closed the door, locked it for the last time, and walked away to pursue a career in social work.

At The Book Shelf, there were meetings filled with hand-wringing and portents of gloom. Could they downsize, cut staff, and survive?

Ianthe called in her husband, a prominent banker (or some other kind of heartless quaestuary) and a man richer than God, to handle the 'transition.' It soon became clear that the transition would be from Nice Little Store to Dustheap.

Neill clung on with faith in the rightness of what they were doing. They had been in business over 50 years!

Smithy saw the writing on the wall and wanted to jump the wall into a more rewarding career. She was promised a job at Ianthe's husband's bank, if she stuck around. So, she stayed on, a femur in the skeleton crew. She kissed Neill on her last day, the first and last time they kissed. It was also years before Neill saw her again.

Things were changing and Neill hated change. This is why he was still working every shift at the store, even after Betty retired.

"I'm tired," she said. "And, as of today, I am retired."

The Poem

Neill was not a happy man. He was as low as he was when the whole Bidden-Dinah thing blew up in his face. His world had demassified.

He was as lonely as Crusoe.

He was as horny as a married man.

And he felt as unattractive, witless, and dim-witted as he had ever felt in his life. He would never attract another woman. All the women in his past hated him. He was adrift, as loose as a nickel rolling down an ugly alley.

He wrote poetry. He wrote about all the women he loved who loved him not. He wrote about all the women he wanted but could not have.

Including Luna, his luminous Gorgeous Young Housewife Nonpareil.

He wrote a particularly bad poem about her called "What Good is It if I Can't Even Sing it to You?" Remember?

One day Luna came book shopping. It was Spring. She shone like dew on a rose petal.

"You're still sad," Luna said.

"I am," Neill admitted. They were still not telling the public about the possible demise of The Book Shelf so he could not use that to garner pity. "I am a lonely, lonesome man."

"Got to lunch with me," Luna said.

And they did. Neill sat across from his Angel Vision and tried to press food between his tightened lips. They chatted amiably. Luna knew Neill had a crush on her. She was sweet. She was pitying him and Neill knew it but he still enjoyed himself.

The next time she came in (twice in one week!), he followed her to her car.

"I wrote this for you," he said, catching up to her.

"What is it, Neill?"

"A poem. A poor poem. But heartfelt."

Luna only glanced at it. "I can't," she said, thrusting it back at Neill. "No," she said, and drove away. Neill felt as frustraneous as fat on a monkey.

His loneliness increased like a rise in temperature for a man sick in his head.

The Pianist

There existed, at this time, a woman in Memphis who was known as a world-class pianist. She could 'transmit the Preludes through her hair and fingertips.' And, in typical Memphis fashion, she chose not to live in New York City and make boodles of money, nor travel Europe playing Chopin and Scarlatti for the sophistos. She chose to stay in Memphis and be a local celebrity. She was an artist, true and pure.

She was also as lovely as a new toy on Christmas morning. Her small eyes sparkled. And her smile could knock down birds from trees.

Her name was Forecast Older.

Neill knew her only marginally. He'd seen her at parties. She was seven or so years older than Neill and this was a large enough gap that he did not see her often.

She was, however, starting to come into The Book Shelf more often.

"I just moved to the neighborhood," she said one day to Neill, as he rang up her purchase of the new Peter Lovesey mystery.

"Ah," Neill said.

After a few more visits Neill began to feel a frisson. Was this attraction? Was it—possibly—mutual? They talked. She knew a lot, was a wise woman.

"I know about you and Misso Anthill," she said.

"Oh," Neill said. This was a deflating subject. Neill deflated.

"It's ok, Neill. We've all done it."

"What? All done what?"

"Had our hearts broken, beaten our fool heads on impossible walls."

"Yes," Neill said. "I was a fool. I made a fool of myself."

"Ach," Forecast said.

"She just—you know—got inside me. Like a virus."

"Forgive her, Neill."

"Forgive her?"

"Forgive her for not loving you."

This hurt. But Forecast Older was smiling. Her cheeks were ripe fruit.

She smiled a lot. Her laugh was a cheery tubular bells.

Neill took a chance.

"You wanna go out sometime, see a movie, have some dinner?"

Neill's heart was doing the Anvil Chorus.

"Neill, are you asking me out on a date?" she hammed on wry.

"No. Not if it's absurd."

She looked at Neill and her pretty smile slid sideways a millimeter or two.

"It's not absurd. Absurd why?"

"Because I'm younger. Because I am not in your league."

She laughed. "You are well within my league, Buddy-Boy."

"Oh," Neill said. It was a very small o.

"I am on the run from my second husband. Does that scare you?"

"On the run? Is he—violent?"

"No, no. Just wrong."

"Then it doesn't scare me."

"Ok. Let me think about it."

"Ok," Neill said. "Lemme know when you make this momentous decision."

She laughed again and was gone in a poof of colorful smoke.

Shlomo Has Something to Say about Forecast Older

"I've known her my entire adult life," Shlomo said. "If I've had an adult life."

"Your tone sounds like you're warning me off her."

"No, I wouldn't want to do that. She's just—well—she's marvelous, of course. Beautiful and smart and funny. She's also flirtatious and—not *insubstantial*—but untrustworthy."

"I don't understand."

"For instance. She would occasionally hand me a line like, 'I dreamt of you last night,' and would give with the bedroom eyes."

"Flirtatious, I get. Why untrustworthy?"

"Because it was all for show. She was, if I can put this inelegantly, a prick tease."

"Meaning she never followed through."

"Right. If I pressed the issue she laughed and absquatulated."

"I see. Like the Rascals' song."

"Groovin'?"

"*You can get any man you want going and you do it and don't say you don't know you do it.*"

"Yes, like that. She flirts with anyone and everyone, including a gargoyle like me."

"Stop."

"But, it wasn't just me she didn't follow through with."

"I see."

"Not to burst your bubble, if you are making a bubble."

"No, it's ok. I am still waiting for her to decide whether she wants to go out with me. I am sure after 10 days the decision did not go in my favor."

"Who knows? But I have to hang up now. There's a thing coming on PBS about Bruno Schulz."

"Later for you," Neill said.

Neill turned on PBS. It was a pledge drive and a show about 60s pop groups.

A Surprise

Again, Luna Wildfowl showed up at The Book Shelf. It was about 3:30 in the afternoon and she was sans kids.

"Neill, I'm wondering if you can take the rest of the afternoon off," she said, as if out of breath. As if she had galloped in from a far-flung corner of the globe to ask Neill this important question.

"I guess I can," Neill said. "Let me check."

Neill told Smithy and Iago he was taking the rest of the day off. Smithy looked at Luna Wildfowl with the stink eye.

"Have fun. See you tomorrow," she said.

Once outside, Luna said, "May I come to your house?"

"Um, sure," Neill said, caught unawares. "It's dirty. But it's also dimly lit enough that you can't tell."

Luna laughed the way some women do.

"I'll follow in my car," she said.

At Neill's they entered together. Neill's hand was shaking a bit and his stomach was full of moths. Luna moths.

"This is it," Neill said.

"It's nice," Luna said in a neutral voice. "Lots of books."

"Of course. You want something to drink?"

"Yes. Do you have wine?"

"Uh no. I don't drink. Let's see what we've got."

They bent together to peer inside the refrigerator.

"Have you seen 9 ½ *Weeks*?" Luna asked.

"No. Do I want to?"

"Hm, soda or soda."

"Yes, but one is Mountain Dew!" Neill mocked.

"I've never had Mountain Dew. Open one for me."

Neill did a Dew apiece. They moved to the couch.

"This is good," Luna said. "It's got a kick."

"It used to be called Kickapoo Joy Juice. I think they doubled up on the caffeine."

"Good. I need a jolt."

"So—what's the plan? Why did you coax me away from the bookstore?"

Neill was talking to try and calm himself.

"Let's sit here a minute and then I'll tell you."

"Ok," Neill said. He drank.

They made small talk. Books, her kids, her older husband, Neill's loneliness.

"Ok," Luna said. She put her Dew can on the coffee table. The moment had, apparently, come.

"You've got a crush on me," Luna said. It wasn't a question.

Neill looked at the small opening in his pop can. He put a finger there and felt how sharp the edges were.

"Neill, it's ok. I love it that you do. You might not believe this but I am very lonely myself."

"How can that be? You have kids, husband." He started to say "and more money than God," but held himself in time.

"My husband is much older than me. Our sex life is in the past."

Neill wasn't sure he wanted to hear this.

"So, I am more than flattered by your attention. I've thought long and hard about it and I think we can be good friends. I enjoyed having lunch with you. I think we should do that more often."

"Oh," Neill said. A bit of comfort returned to him. "That would be nice."

Yes," Luna said. She looked at her hands which rested in her lap like tired doves.

"There's more?"

"Y-yes," Luna said. "I want you to do me a favor."

"Anything," Neill said. He was trying to keep his puppy tongue in check.

"Will you go sit on the edge of your bed down the long hallway there?" She gestured with her hand as if Neill needed a guide to his home.

"Ok," Neill said. He started to smile.

"What's funny?" Luna said and laughed.

"This is all so—mysterious."

"Ok, Cut to the chase. I want you to sit on the edge of your bed and I am going to slowly walk the length of your hall, away from you, so you can see my backside. I want you to tell me if my ass is still pretty. I used to get so many compliments on it and they've sorta dried up and, since I can't see it myself, I thought you would help me."

"Uh huh," Neill said. He feigned thinking about it. "I already know you have a great ass. Is that all you want me to say? Or you want the clinical exactitude?"

"I meant to say I am going to take my skirt off. I'm not wearing panties."

"Jesus God," Neill said.

"And I guess I thought you might enjoy it too."

"Oh yes," Neill said. His palms were sweaty.

"But, Neill. You can't touch me. You just watch and then give me the thumbs up or the thumbs down."

"Jesus God."

"This is not a good idea?"

Neill looked at her face, a Botticelli face.

"C'mon," Luna continued. "It'll be fun. Then after I'll take you for a treat."

"If I'm a good boy."

Luna laughed so Neill laughed too. She took his hand and walked him down the hall.

"Sit right here," she said.

"I get the concept," Neill said with a smile.

"Ok," Luna said. She backed off a few steps and stood in the bedroom doorway. She took a deep breath and turned around. Two beats later she had unzipped her skirt and let it fall. Neill was about 3 feet from her naked ass.

It was certainly pretty. Neill thought it quite pretty. He watched it as it undulated down the hall. It was a nice show.

But, oddly, Neill did not even get a twinge in his rocket. This was Luna Wildfowl, the Angel from his Dreams, Luna of the Poem. And she was very attractive, and this was a nice gift, but Neill could not help but wonder what was wrong with Little Neill. Had he croaked?

Afterward, they went to Jerry's Sno-Cones and sat at a little outside table and sucked the overly sweet, brightly-colored ice. Luna kept putting her hand over Neill's. It was a loving gesture and it was so public. Neill was a little troubled.

Subsequently this Ensued

One night, a few days later, as Neill was locking up the bookstore, Luna appeared next to him.

"Hi," she said, rushing to him like a schoolgirl.

"Hi," Neill said.

"Happy to see me?"

"You know I am."

"Thinking about me?"

Now Neill gave her the one-eyed squint and saw her eyes were moistly animated.

"Uh huh," Neill said.

"Thinking about my ass?" Luna said. She laughed so Neill laughed.

"Many times," Neill lied.

"What are you doing right now?"

"Nothing. Going home to a TV dinner."

"We can do better than that."

Luna drove Neill in her gray Mercedes to Folks Folly Steakhouse. It was a place Neill had never been because he couldn't afford it.

While they ate Luna was like a giddy lass, drunk on her own attractiveness. She was dressed in fashionable scarves and what Neill imagined was expensive jewelry. She chattered away about anything and everything. She kept touching Neill's hand and, again, Neill was agitated by it. Did she *want* people to see her out with a young man they would, of course, assume was her lover?

"You like the steak?" she twittered.

"Very much," Neill said. "I'm not sure I can eat it all."

"Red meat," Luna said.

On the drive back, Luna rested her hand on Neill's thigh as she drove. Her fingertips did a subtle typing on Neill's leg. Now Neill could feel the familiar solidifying essence.

In the Poplar Plaza parking lot Luna turned off her car. She looked at Neill intensely.

"Do you have a key to the store?" she asked.

"You know I do."

"I guess my question was *can we go inside*?"

"Oh!" Neill said. Did he want this? With a married woman?

"Neill, I want to give you a blowjob. Would you like that?"

Once inside the store, they had to move to the stockroom at the rear because of the large glass window at the front. In the stockroom, there was a faint red glow from the Exit sign. It was like an industrial darkroom. The floor was cold, hard linoleum.

"Hm," Luna said. She was problem-solving.

"I guess you lie down right here," she directed.

Neill lay on his back on some broken-down cardboard boxes. It was chilly and unforgiving, like a bed of rime. In Neill's fantasies about Luna Wildfowl, the rutting was accomplished with something like superhuman exuberance and talent. Once, Ianthe had joked with Neill about his crush on Luna and said, "I've heard from the many men she's been with that she is a wildcat in bed." This fueled Neill's longing for her. And now, he was prostrated before her beauty and she was about to perform Neill's favorite delicate operation: the pricknic.

"Are you hard?" Luna said, undoing Neill's belt.

"Um," Neill said.

"There it is," Luna said. "Yes, there it is."

She put her hand around its intermediate erection. Her hands were cold.

"Get hard for me," Luna said. She was speaking directly to the penis.

"There we go. There it is," she said. She smiled at Neill as if she had turned water into chuff and chutty.

Neill was prepared for the wildcat. He was prepared for the services of a World Class Fellatrix.

"Neill, I don't want to swallow, ok?" she said, as she brushed her hair behind her ear.

Neill nodded. That was slightly disappointing, coming from a wildcat. He was craning his head upward so he could witness and forever remember the moment that his wee-wee entered the honeyed mouth of Luna Wildfowl.

He watched. It *was* a nice moment.

But the blowjob was so uninspired. He'd had better blowjobs from Akin in high school and they were kids playing in the adult lab. Neill worried that he might not even come.

He concentrated on Luna's lips. He thought about how his tickler might feel in her throat. Maybe this was a real turn-on for her. In this way, he willed his sap to rise. When he began to come Luna pulled her head back and left Little Neill hung out to dry.

Neill finished himself off with a few well-placed jerks.

"Sorry," Luna said. "Is there any on my clothes?"

"I can't see."

"You were supposed to warn me," she said, but it was only mock-scolding.

"I thought you could feel it."

"I guess I wasn't paying attention."

"That was—wonderful," Neill said, shrugging his ass back into his pants. It really wasn't that wonderful.

"Tell no one," Luna said. "No. One."

"I know," Neill said, as if he were an old hand at extra-marital affairs.

"If you're good maybe we can do something like this once in a while. But you have to remember that I am a married woman with a standing in the, you know, community."

What was she prattling on about? Neill thought.

"Of course," he said.

The Next Morning

The next morning Forecast Older called Neill at home while he was getting ready for work.

"I've decided yes," she said. Her voice. It was like her music. It did something inside of you, the way birdsong sometimes can seem like the soundtrack to your day.

"Oh," Neill said. "Ok then."

"A date, right? We start with a date?"

"Naturally," Neill said.

"Are you free tonight?"

"Yes," Neill said. His penis was raw from Luna's mishandling.

"More enthusiasm," Forecast said.

"I'm very enthusiastic," Neill said. "I can't believe I won."

"Ha ha," Forecast Older said. "Have you ever eaten at Folk's Folly?"

Instead they go to La Montagne

La Montagne was a new, swank health-food restaurant on Park Avenue. Forecast picked Neill up in her beat-up, ragtop Karman Ghia.

"This is nice," Neill said, looking around at the candlelight and flutes of wine, and the other diners, a motley bunch of well-dressed, hippie-fied Memphians.

"Have you not eaten her before?"

"No," Neill said. "A vegetarian hamburger?"

"It's great," Forecast said.

The meal was good. Very good. And worth the money, ever cash-conscious Neill thought.

Afterward neither of them knew exactly what to do.

"What should we do?" Forecast said.

"What should we not do?" Neill said.

This made Forecast laugh and that helped Neill relax.

"My place is pretty close," Neill said.

"Ok then."

When Neill began to make-out with Forecast, he could not stop his mind from saying, 'You're doing it. You're kissing Forecast Older, one of the most sought after women in Memphis.' When they moved to the bed Neill begged his brain to shut up. It turned its back but kept up an obscure murmuration.

Prone they did pretty well for first-time lovers. Forecast was a great kisser and a great—*spirit*. She was fun. She was delicious. She was frabjous. She was butter.

Foreplay was aces. Forecast foreplay.

They lost some outer clothing, coats and vests and shirts, but mostly accomplished their friction while both wearing jeans. When Forecast took off her bra, Neill was astonished to discover, on such a willowy frame, such large Manchesters.

"Surprised?" Forecast said. Her smile was spritely.

"Ha, I am, a bit," Neill said.

"Uff-da! Look what Forecast was hiding!" Forecast said.

Neill loved those breasts. He loved every square inch of them. They were full with small nipples and they were a heap of fun.

Forecast seemed to be having a good time. She kept that teasing little smile on her face throughout, even as she bent her head backwards and sighed while Neill suckled.

When Neill's hand went to the hot place between her jeaned thighs, Forecast did a little laugh and said, "Eh eh eh. Not on the first date, Whoa Neilly."

When they kissed at the door, they lingered in each other's arms.

"I'm a little afraid, Neill," Forecast said. The ironic smile was now only half-there.

"How so?"

"I don't want to hurt you. I have hurt people."

"Forecast, you find me at the bottom of life. Nothing matters now. I have nothing. I'm just another word for nothing left to lose."

"But I could give you something you come to like a lot, come to count on, and then I could take it from you. That would hurt you. I don't want to hurt you."

"I'm a grownup," Neill said for the first time in his life. He didn't even believe it as he said it.

"Ok, Neilly," Forecast said. "Ok."

They kissed one last, full-mouthed kiss.

"When?" Neill said.

"Soon."

Shlomo's Prognostication Bothered Neill

Neill considered Shlomo's depiction of Forecast Older. If she was just leading him on, bringing him to the edge of delight (O those mammaries!) only to let him fall off alone into the slough of despond, it seemed a gamble worth taking.

"You're seeing her again?" Shlomo said, on the phone.

"Yes."

"That's a good thing. Forget what I said. What do I know, a warped, frustrated old man? You go have your fun. You're the man to pass Go and collect."

"Ok," Neill said. "Even if it all goes sour it's going to be worth it."

"That's the spirit."

"It's the giddy talking."

"Hey, how's Bidden? I missed him last time I was in town."

"I guess he's ok."

"Still not talking over that roommate fiasco."

"It'll be alright."

"Of course."

At the Midtown Home of Forecast Older

Her home, situated between the bohemian enclaves of Cooper Young and the posh gated community of Central Gardens, was beautiful. Its interior was tastefully arranged. Her walls were graced with art by Memphis' finest painters, weavers, and collagists. And her music room was dominated by its Mason and Hamlin piano—a beautiful, dark wood instrument that was a work of art itself. It was the only shadow in a room full of light. One whole wall was glass, outside of which was a lush garden with palms and wildflowers. On the white walls were framed scores, one signed by Arthur Rubenstein and another by Myra Hess.

Neill whistled through his teeth.

"This is certainly very nice," he said. He tried to take it in whole. It intimidated him.

"This is where the magic happens," Forecast said. The ironic smile was in place. It dominated her pretty face the way the piano dominated the room.

"Will you play for me?"

"Ach."

"No?"

"Something quick. I didn't want you here to impress you with my virtuosity." The smile slipped a millimeter but righted itself quickly. "My musical virtuosity."

She sat down and bowed her head for a minute.

"Why *did* you bring me here?" Neill teased.

Now Forecast looked up. She smiled directly into Neill's eyes. As she held his glance, her hands, seemingly by themselves, ran through a deeply resonant Bach piece which quickly morphed into "Let it Be."

Neill laughed. Forecast laughed also and stood up.

"I brought you here to feed you," she said, taking Neill's hand.

"You cook too? You are the Renaissance woman."

"I am going to stuff you on cake."

"Ah."

"The cake is me."

They stopped in the hallway. They kissed deeply, softly. The bedroom door was open and the bed was capacious and comfortable and full of colorful pillows. It looked like a bed in a *Bonanza* bordello.

"Delectable," Neill said.

"I hope you will think so. Take all your clothes off."

Neill began to undress and Forecast sat on her bed holding a golden pillow on her lap.

"You joining me?" Neill asked. "Or am I eating you through a straw."

Forecast laughed her ringing laugh. "I want to watch you first."

Neill dipped a shoulder. Swiveled and hip. Grew self-conscious.

"C'mon, Cowboy. Drop 'em," Neill's soon-to-be bedmate said.

Neill shrugged off his shirt. Unbuckled his pants. Stopped. Bent down to remove his shoes and socks. Stood back up.

"Slower," she said.

Neill smiled but it was not a cocky smile. It was—*hesitant.*

He unzipped his jeans and they fell. He was now wearing only his white briefs.

"Uh huh," Forecast said.

"You want to see zee rest?" Neill said.

"Slowly. I've never had a man strip for me before."

Neill liked that idea, being the first. He turned his back to her. He put his thumbs in the waistband of his briefs. Slowly, he slid them off the small domes of his buttocks.

"Oh yeah," Forecast said. "Slower."

Neill held them at the bottom of his ass. He took one hand and gently swiped a buttock as if he were using a chamois. His voyeur groaned. This spurred him on.

He moved the briefs slowly down his legs. They pooled at his feet and he kicked them aside. Then he turned—slowly. Just before he faced her, he slipped his hands over his privates. He smiled his most lascivious smile.

"What have you there, honey?" Forecast said. She put the golden pillow down and spread her legs, still encased in denim.

Neill slowly opened the fingers of one hand to reveal about 1/3 of his cock and ½ of his padlock. Then, he stopped.

"I want it," Forecast said.

"I only show it to naked women," Neill said. "Women made of cake."

Forecast rose to her knees. She knelt on the bed and began throwing clothes in every direction in a comic parody of excitement. Which, in turn, led to excitement.

When those breasts emerged again, Neill sighed.

Forecast was out of her pants in a heartbeat. Neill wanted it all. He wanted to see the Older Pussy. He wanted to prove Shlomo wrong.

"Now show me," she said.

Neill opened his other hand. His erection—thank God—was formidable.

Forecast looked. She looked for a long time.

"Ok," she said. And the panties were removed also. And, once removed, Forecast lay back and opened her thighs. Her bush was as dark as an unexplored continent. Neill thought it was so beautiful that his heart cramped. It pulled up lame in the stretch. Dear heart, Neill beseeched, just send blood to the penis, post haste.

He slithered up the bed and rested his head on one thigh. He brushed her pubic hairs with his fingertips, tickling them, looking at them closely. Forecast sighed.

He bent. He ate.

But before he began to really chow down he looked up at a Forecast without irony and he spoke to her. "Mm, sponge cake," he said.

Then he gave her the best plating he had ever given.

She came, and after she came, she grabbed at Neill. She almost bodily hoisted him on top of her. Neill put his dick right on the outside of her secret place. This was another moment he wanted to remember forever: the exact second he entered Forecast Older, who was no prick tease. As slowly as a bell tolls, he slid inside her.

The rest was as grand as the grand piano. Neill Rhymer came inside of Forecast Older. It was one of the happiest moments in his life. He could not believe that this remarkable and beautiful woman was his, in that moment, *his*.

And, in the morning, waking beside her, he knew something else.

He had fallen deeply in love with her and, thus, she had given him something that, forever more, it would wound him to lose.

And he prayed again, do not take *that new thing* away.

Neill's New Spring in His Step

Smithy laughed at Neill. He was practically capering around the store. He flirted with every woman customer. He was helpful, funny, energetic.

In a moment of calm, Smithy said, "I can guess why you're so chipper. You dog."

"Live in the moment, Smithy. Live in the moment."

"Yeah, that's the Neill I know."

"I know. You'll forgive me. Let me ride the wave."

"I'm sorry. I'm not poking fun. I love you when you're this *on*."

"Thanks, Smithy. I love you, too."

The moment froze.

Smithy added quickly. "She is married, you know. So be careful."

Neill hesitated. What was she talking about? Then it occurred to him that he thought he had bedded the wedded Luna Wildfowl.

"Oh no, Smithy," Neill said. But he stopped himself. Perhaps, it was not a good thing to make public his new love. Perhaps, Forecast did not feel the same way (it was highly probable that she did not), and perhaps, Forecast would be ashamed—no that's too strong— uncomfortable with people knowing she took Neill to her ample bosom.

"It's ok," Smithy said. "She deserves scrogging from what I hear. You know, it's a time-honored thing, the younger woman marrying a rich old man and then having an affair with a younger, freer fellow. It's almost—*right*."

Autumn, also Known as The Fall

The air was chilly now. Neill lamented the heavier clothes on women. Summer in Memphis meant short skirts, short shorts, halter tops. Young women with their first shapeliness still intact, parading for the adoring eyes of young men.

"Book Shelf," Neill said into the phone. He wondered how much longer he would be saying that.

"Neill Rhymer, I want your body," a woman giggled into her end of the phone.

"Of course you do," Neill said, laconically.

"I really do. But first I want to take you to the movies."

"Luna!" Neill recovered. "How are you?"

Luna had not been to see Neill in a week or so. And Forecast seemed to be busy—a lot. Neill tried to retain his faith in Forecast's affection.

"Are you busy tonight?"

"Um, no," Neill drawled out.

"Can you get off work early? The movie starts at 4."

"I guess so," Neill drawled out.

"Neill. You do want to see me?"

"Of course I do. You are my unattainable goddess." But he said it without conviction. It used to be true.

"Neill, it does wonders for me to hear that."

Luna picked Neill up at this house and they went in her car the few blocks to the Malco Quartet.

"Two for 9 ½ *Weeks*," Luna said, and cast a libidinous grin at Neill.

They got popcorn and cokes and sat in the back row. Luna was wearing the coat with the white fur collar. Her cheeks were blushed with cold.

"9 ½ *Weeks*?" Neill said. "You've seen it."

"Yes. I thought it would get you warmed up. I want you horny."

"Ok," Neill said. "What are you warming me up for?"

"My husband is out of town."

The lights went down. After the previews, the movie began. It was so awful. So stupid and soft-porn silly. Neill was a long way from being turned on. And, with Luna constantly casting glances at him during every prurient moment, he was squirming.

When they got to the infamous refrigerator scene, Luna leaned over and whispered, "Watch this."

It was, of course, inane.

But it was helped by Luna, who had taken off her expensive gloves, who snaked a hand along Neill's thigh and ran her pinky finger over Neill's nutmegs. Neill let out an involuntary sigh. Then Luna, with her left hand, began to knead Neill's now prominent prow.

"Jesus," Neill said. "Don't make me come in the theater."

Luna laughed. "I could suck you right now. We're in the back row."

"Um," Neill ummed.

"I won't, Neill. I am saving you for my house."

"Did you like the film?" Luna said on the drive from the theater.

"Sure. It was kind of stupid."

Luna made with a mock pout. "But it turned you on."

"Yes. It did," Neill fibbed. Her hand on his stuff turned him on despite the insipid movie. Now Neill was nervous about entering the home her husband bought for her.

It was on Central, west of Chickasaw Gardens, a red brick mansion that seemed to be hidden by trees. It was like a house in a movie. Even when he was dating Marcane and visiting the homes of the rich and influential, he had not seen a house like this. He imagined every knickknack on display was worth more than his house, car, and life.

Luna paid the babysitter, a brunette bombshell with dark bedroom eyes and a chest like Mamie Van Doren. She looked sideways at Neill. She wasn't flirting. She was disgusted.

Luna brought out a cheese tray and some wine and set things up in a small den off the main living room. The main living room was the size of a ski lodge. It was dark in the den, not just dimly lit, but the wood was dark, the carpet was dark, and the sofa they sat on a deep-brown leather.

"You must be hungry," she said. "Just popcorn for dinner."

Neill took some crackers and cheese and a sip of wine. He hated wine.

"Where are your kids?"

"Asleep."

"Good sleepers, are they?"

"Count on it," Luna said.

They ate cheese and sipped wine and made small talk. They both knew these preliminaries were for show.

"These preliminaries are for show," Luna said. "What I really want is for you to fuck me."

"I kinda guessed that," Neill said.

"You're so smart," Luna said. She put down her wine glass.

"I don't know, Luna."

"You don't want to fuck me? I find that impossible to believe."

"Of course I want to. But here? In your house with your kids asleep, the house your husband bought you?"

"Kick that conscience to the curb," she said, as she slipped her tongue between Neill's lips. She was a good kisser, despite the fact that her lips were too thin.

They wrestled with each other while Neill wrestled with his integrity.

They undid some clothing.

"Are we going to get naked here?" Neill whispered as Luna opened her shirt and took her bra off."

"We can," she said.

"I'm not sure," Neill said.

"You don't want to see me naked?" Luna simpered as she unzipped her skirt and let it fall.

"Luna, it's been my dream for years."

`   "Let's go then, Neill. Time for you to step up."

In the end, Neill never took his clothes off. Luna had unbuttoned his shirt and undid his belt and unzipped his jeans and yanked them down to expose the tool she needed and, having accomplished all that, was satisfied to sit on top of Neill's toy and swivel. It was an ungracious coupling and almost uncomfortable. Luna wasn't very wet and Neill had to will himself to come. Which he did inside the woman who was once his sexual ideal.

It just wasn't there.

And after achieving that small goal, Neill realized he had no way home.

"I—I think I am stuck here," he said, zipping up.

"Nonsense, Lover. I'm not going to ask you to stay the night. I'm sorry. You know I'd love for you to but that's too much of a risk. I will call you a cab."

All the way back to his house, Neill felt like a louse. He was also amazed by how unsexy sex with Luna Wildfowl was. What was wrong?

Autumn, also Known as The Fall, Part Two

On Sunday afternoon, Forecast had time for Neill. She invited him over for lunch.

They had cheese and sprout sandwiches on thick whole wheat bread on the deck in her backyard. The day was unseasonably warmer and they were both dressed in short sleeves.

"This is so pleasant out here," Neill said.

"I love my backyard," Forecast said. Neill looked around. She had some nice sculptures by local artists.

"I've been kinda missing you," Neill ventured.

"Kinda?"

"Well, I've been missing you."

"I've been missing you, too, kid."

"Really? Because I kinda thought you were avoiding me. Though the phone conversations have been sweet."

"You don't believe in us, do you?" Forecast said. The smile put parenthesis around her question.

"I want to," Neill said. He felt as if he were not on solid ground.

"Why would you not?"

"Are we dating? Are we a couple?" Neill tried to keep the anxiety out of his voice.

"What would you call it?"

"I'm not sure. I think I am letting you lead."

"I don't sleep with strangers," Forecast said.

"I know. Of course not. It's just—I think about you all the time."

"This is the dangerous area, right? You're thinking about my warning."

"I am."

"Neill, I don't know. I really like you. I might even love you."

"I hear a 'however' in there."

"No, I mean, I have this bad record. You've probably heard."

"No."

"I've been married twice. I can't seem to hold onto any man for very long."

"This is giving me confidence."

"What—what bothers you about us?"

"I'm not sure. I guess I believe I don't deserve you. I guess I also believe you're going to continue to travel around the world playing and being toasted in far-flung places. I can't compete with that."

"You can't picture yourself traveling with me? Maybe with a bambino in tow?"

"Seriously? You mean—a child—of *ours*?"

"Why not, Neill?"

"I can't think of one good goddamn reason why not."

Neill, like a teenage tourist, had brought his camera. He took a few pictures of Forecast on the deck. Then, he held the camera away from them and took a picture of them kissing. This will end, Neill said to himself, but I will have this photographic evidence that once, just once, Forecast Older was mine.

"I want to interosculate you," Neill said. He put his hand over the crotch of her jeans. It felt warm there. "I want to interpenetrate you."

"Keep talking big dirty words," Forecast said.

They barely made it into the bed before Neill was back inside her. This time it was more erotic, as they explored each other more fully. When Forecast sat on Neill and her breasts moved with celestial grace, Neill knew a happiness he had not known in a long time. He was in love. And when he came inside her, he half-hoped she had forgotten her diaphragm. He imagined his long white spurt traveling upward to meet and greet a round, musical egg, and he thanked his long white spurt and he loved his long white spurt and he wished only for more of this.

On One of the Nights Forecast Older was Busy

Neill assumed when Forecast was busy she was practicing. She played with the Memphis Symphony, often as a headlining guest artist. Neill wasn't sure if she had such a concert coming up because Forecast rarely talked about her playing and, except for that first day, she never played for Neill. Neill was the most unmusical person on the planet. He was the only kid in fourth grade who could not learn the simple song on his tonette. So, he really wanted Forecast to play pretty songs for him.

On one of the nights Forecast was busy, Neill was at home with a Hammer horror film and a big bag of cheap cheese puffs. It was stoner food that he never quite outgrew.

When the telephone rang, Neill's heart leapt. Perhaps Forecast was suddenly unbusy. He hadn't seen her in four days.

"Hello, Lover," Luna said.

"Hello, Luna."

"What are you doing?"

"You don't want to know."

'You're not masturbating, are you?"

"No."

"Come out with me."

"You mean now? Tonight?"

"Yes. I left the kids at home with their father."

"What do you want to do?"

"I want you to pick out lingerie for me at Victoria's Secret."

Neill laughed. "Right," he said.

"You wouldn't want to do that?"

"Oh. Seriously? Yes, I guess I would."

"I'm on your street."

Off they went in Luna's expensive auto to Oak Court Mall. Neill was nervous walking beside her. She was so uninhibited. It seemed again as if she were showing him off.

Once inside the porny, pink atmosphere of Victoria's Secret Neill felt even worse. He tried to make himself small. He tried to make himself invisible. He wanted to be Kaspar Hauser, the Feral Ghost.

Luna kept calling out to him, in a voice that was teasing and showy. "Neill, what about these?" And she would hold up the skimpiest pair of panties in the store, panties made of cerise cobwebs. "Come here!"

"They're very nice," Neill said, feigning partnership with this loud, ostentatious woman.

"Ooh, or these," and she held a pair of black panties that looked almost demure.

"Those are nice," he said.

"Nice? Nice? Look." And she put her hand through the open crotch.

"Oh I see. Wouldn't they be *uncomfortable*?"

"Neill, what's wrong with you? I'd wear them just with you. What do you think?"

"This is a little embarrassing."

"Ok," she said, shoving the panties back onto their shelf. "If you're embarrassed. I wanted to turn you on. I wanted you to visualize me in them."

"I know."

"Forget it," she said and made for the exit.

"It's just that, you know, you don't need to show me movies or underwear to make me visualize you sexually," Neill said, catching up with her.

She thought this over.

"Ok," Luna said, slipping her arm under Neill's. "I like that."

In the car, Luna had another great idea.

"Hey, you wanna go parking? I haven't been parking since I was a teen."

"In this car? What if we get sperm on the leather?"

"You think too much."

Luna drove around and around the mall and surrounding properties. It was country dark and there were many places of shadow and concealment. She pulled into a church parking lot. This seemed the worst choice possible.

"Here?" Neill said.

"Relax, Neill."

"Right."

"And undo your belt."

"Ok." Neill unbuckled his belt. Luna laughed.

"I meant your seatbelt."

"Oh yes."

"But as long as this is open."

Luna began to massage Neill's penis through his underwear. He was decidedly hard. He thanked the gods for that. Any more embarrassment tonight would have been a poor showing.

They kissed and wrestled, at every move thwarted by the car's unforgiving space. Neill's whacker was hanging out and Luna's skirt was hiked up around her waist and her panties hung on the turn signal lever.

"This was much easier when I was younger," Luna said.

"We were smaller."

"Ha ha. Maybe so. Let's see. You want to fuck outside?"

"It's chilly."

"Neill!"

"Sorry. Of course. Lead the way. Lemme snap my pants back."

They found a small playground behind the church. The air was nippy and the light outside was grayish, the way light looks through a fine mist, though there was no mist. Distant streetlights glowed but halfheartedly. The cloud cover was soft as night-swollen mushrooms.

"Hmm," Luna said. "How about there?"

"In the swings?"

"No, there. Underneath."

"Ok," Neill said.

Luna practically skipped toward the space, a dirt dugout made by the scuffing of a thousand young children. "C'mon," she said, as if she had found a leafy bower.

"Lie down on your back. This is going to work."

Neill lay in the cold, brown dirt. He was wearing a thick coat, as was Luna. She re-unbuckled his belt and pants and found the formerly stiff and willing willy now diminished.

"You wanna see my pussy. Would that get you going?"

"Of course," Neill said.

Luna stood over him. She lifted her skirt until Neill could see it all, a fancy little quim in its bed of beard. It did look pretty.

"Ah, you're growing. You wanna keep looking?"

Neill didn't answer. He ran a hand up her naked leg.

"Mm, Neill. I want to fuck you now."

She squatted over him but had to tickle his scrotum, spit on her palm and rub him, and make cooing noises before Neill's armament was loaded.

"Oh yes," Luna said. The descent was painful. Her pussy was dry again. Why was she always dry if she was so sexed up?

They achieved the coupling. It was rough going. Neill closed his eyes and thought about Forecast's great breasts. In this fantasy, he was able to aim and fire.

"Good job," Luna said, as if Neill had just done a watercolor that was fridge-ready.

Neill stood and wiped the brown dirt off his ass. He was cold. He was spent. And he was miserable.

The drive back to Neill's house was quiet. As they turned onto Holmes Circle, Luna said, "Penny for."

"Hm, nothing," Neill said.

"Neill. This is Luna. Right? We're friends. I love you."

"I know."

"Talk to me."

It came out as if it were bile. "I can't do this," Neill said rapidly before he could think too much.

"Oh," her smile disappeared. "I see."

"Look. It's just that—I can't with a married woman. If not for that, Jesus, you know how attractive I find you. I can't believe you're even with me."

It was all bushwa. Neill wanted his former fantasy to leave him alone. Married or not. It wasn't ethics, though Neill appreciated being able to use that as an out. It was—*disappointment*.

"You don't want to have sex with me anymore?"

"I do. You know I do."

He didn't.

"But I am married."

"Yes."

Luna sat there and stared out the windshield.

"Get out, Neill," she said.

"Luna."

"Get the fuck out of my car. You're a liar."

"Ok," Neill said, and opened the car door. Just a few steps and he was home and it was all over.

"And you're a lousy fuck too," Luna said, as he walked away.

And Neill thought this, along with other sickening thoughts: we've just lost another customer of our dying bookstore.

The Next Morning

The next morning Neill woke with only one thought.

(Why do people say that? No one has only one thought at any one time ever. Change?)

He wanted to see Forecast Older. He wanted to take her in his arms. He wanted to strip her and kiss her all over. When the phone rang, Neill was sure it was her.

"Neill, this is Dewitt, Ianthe's husband," Dewitt said. (As if Neill knew another Dewitt.) "Can you meet with us over breakfast?"

"Sure," Neill said, tasting bile, tasting failure.

"The Barksdale in 30?"

The Barksdale in 30. Jesus. This guy thought in meetingspeak.

At the restaurant, Dewitt and Ianthe were already there. They waved Neill over.

"Good morning," Ianthe said.

"Neill," Dewitt said. He put a hand out but did not stand up.

"Good morning," Neill said. "Though I feel it might not be."

Neill ordered eggs and bacon and toast but by the time it came the grease was nauseating to him.

"We're closing the bookstore," Dewitt said. Ianthe was hiding her face. She was studying her plate.

"When?" Neill croaked.

"As soon as possible. It's bleeding cash."

"When?" Neill repeated.

"Ianthe and I think we should announce a sale, 30% off everything, starting Monday. And we would shut the door the next Monday and begin returning all stock that didn't sell."

"Shit," Neill said.

"We would like you to stay on and help us pack up. We think only you can really do it right since you know the inventory and the publishers."

"Ok," Neill said.

(To skip ahead [I know, I know, we said we wouldn't skip beyond the end of our narrative. Just this one last time.]....Neill did stay. It took him 3 weeks of 8 hour days to return all that was returnable. Neill figured he would get a nice severance check for his loyalty. Instead he was thrown upon a bad job market with only the pay those 8 hour days would have garnered anyway. Money men, rich money men like Dewitt Smith, are the cheapest SOBs on the planet.)

Neill went home. He wanted to cry.

He cried.

Return to Forecast Older: The Reality Police

"The reality police have arrived, Neill Dear," Forecast said, almost the minute Neill walked into her house.

"I don't like the sound of that."

"No, you shouldn't."

Forecast sat on her burnished throne with a mug of hot tea in her lap. She was wearing a thick, white robe. She was also wearing her half-cocked, cocky smile. The one made of irony like steel.

"I guess you're through with me," Neill said. His head was full of tar.

"Neill," Forecast said. It was not ungently put.

"May I sit?"

"I'm sorry. Yes. Would you like some red zinger tea?"

"No, thank you. Do you have coffee?"

"No."

"Ok." Neill sat across from Forecast in a hard wooden chair. He crossed his legs in a manner suggesting someone baring his neck for the guillotine.

"You're thinking this couldn't have lasted because I am older, because you are not good enough, because, oh I don't know, because we are star crossed."

"One or two of them," Neill said. He looked at Forecast. She was beautiful. Neill's eyes burned from sorrow and lack of sleep.

"Neill, you should know this. This is your lesson."

"Don't. Don't lecture me."

"It's not a lecture. It is a bald truth. You cannot sleep with two women at once when they are best friends."

Neill was confused. He might have actually tried shaking his head to clear it.

"What?" he asked with a croak.

"Luna tells me everything. I tell her everything. You are lucky we hadn't seen each other for a while. I knew she was seeing someone but she had kept a low profile about it. Until yesterday."

"Wait. Wait. You and Luna Wildfowl are best friends?"

"Neill. You knew that."

"I assure you I did not."

"Well, well. I can choose whether or not to believe you, of course."

"It's the God's truth. I had no idea."

"Oh, Neill. Neilly. Well, hm, live and learn."

"Please don't talk down to me."

"I don't mean to. But the reality police have arrived. It's time for both of us to get on with our lives."

Neill put his head in his hands. Despite the chill his forehead was damp with sweat. He felt feverish.

"Forecast. You are so beautiful."

"Don't, Neill. Don't do that."

"So. That's it?"

"It is. I had a good time."

"Oh, me too," Neill said, biting off his words. "I had a great time. Thanks for the access to your body for 3, or was it 2 times. We were really lovers."

"Goodbye, Neill." Forecast didn't move. She was no longer looking at Neill. After a few moments, Neill rose and silently left.

Cicisbeo

Neill wrote this poem. He formed it from the clouds of his rage, his loneliness, his desperate disappointment.

    "Lunacy"
She drove me to a playground
behind a church.
There underneath the rocking
swings she sat
astride me, taking my root
roughly into her
body like a philter. I bucked
against her, the
ground was hard and cold.
Later she would be too.
But, for a while, illicitly she
carried me around like
a stone. She was in love with
my smile, my talk,
my ability to not be her husband.

Three-Months or Less

Neill now believed his attractiveness had entered a fugue state. He was diminished and diminishing. He was not desirable. He was barely hominoid.

For a time, he could not make love last for three months.

Now it was down to a few weeks.

It was the endtimes. It was Doom stepping on the accelerator.

One More Self-inflicted Wound

It was in this same spirit of desperation that Neill went driving around, like water circling a drain. One night, because he was thinking about Misso again, remembering only the good parts, the parts of tenderness, the parts in bed, he drove to her house. He had learned from Helen Guru that Misso was sharing a house on Vinton Avenue with another ex-MCA student. Neill drove there. Because his feelings about her were still so strong, Neill felt that it was right—it had to be right—to see her again. He still loved her.

It was about 9:30 p.m. The lights were on.

Neill parked on the street and, his heart thudding, he approached the house.

He stepped onto the porch. It was Misso's house alright. The semi-enclosed porch was full of old canvasses, paint cans, bicycle parts, cat dish, dog dish.

He rang the bell.

He waited but no one came. He could hear someone inside, tinny music from an inner room. It started to rain, lightly, a mist that haloed the streetlights.

He knocked and no one came.

He walked around the house. It was a stupid move. Even as he did it he hated himself, cursed his seemingly self-destructive instincts.

At a lighted window, he stopped. He tiptoed up to it. He meant to knock on the window or scratch on the screen. Instead, he froze.

Misso was inside. She was naked. And she was sitting on a naked man. She was riding him the way she used to ride Neill.

Neill stumbled away. He fell over a crappy shrub and hit the driveway on his hands. He made it to the car. Inside him a tornado raged. His hands were abraded and the knees of his pants torn and wet. His heart throbbed. He was sure he would burst apart. He drove. The rain had picked up. He was blind. He was hoping he wouldn't make it home. He was sure that this was the end of the narrative of Neill Rhymer.

Calling Dr. Einstein

"Shlomo, I am heartsick. Literally, I think my heart is sick."

Neill ran down the activity over the past month or so.

"Jesus, Neill. Your life is complicated. Mine is so truncated. Write, teach. God, I hate teaching. Not really the teaching itself but the time away from writing. I resent it."

"Sorry, man. Gotta make the bread."

"I didn't mean to change the subject."

"The subject was my utter failure as a human being."

"Stop it. You'll get another job. You're a known quantity. Some other bookstore will snap you up."

"There are no more bookstores."

"What about Pluto and Persephone's?"

"Funny story. I applied there. It was like they knew I was coming. They had already hired an employee from The Roundtable, which they had also driven out of business. I filled out my application, sat in the waiting room outside the boss's office. Was ushered in. The boss was Heidi, the woman I replaced at The Book Shelf. Boy, had she been sharpening her knives."

"Fuck. This was a surprise?"

"Not entirely. I mean, I knew she was the boss. She pretended to glance over my application and then, with a satisfied smile, the kind the wolf wore right before he opened Riding Hood's gullet with his teeth, she said, 'But Neill, all you've done since we came to Memphis was run us down. You think we didn't hear what you've said'?"

"What had she heard? How had she heard it?"

"That's a mystery. I had run the store down. The same way the mead-drinkers had been running down Grendel. You know, they put my store out of business. But the karma caught up with me. I said to Heidi, 'You're not even going to consider me for this position'?"

"And she said, 'that's right'."

"Listen, here's an idea. Come see me."

"Come to Saratoga Springs?"

"Yes, why not? Between Christmas and New Year's it's dead here. We could go into New York, drink some flaming rum punch, catch up."

"Are you serious?"

"I am. You need to be distracted. You need to get out of town."

"I need to be with a friend who really loves me."

"Come then. And, as a bonus, better than seeing me surely, I have a neighbor across the street who undresses in front of her window every night at 9 p.m. You can set your watch by it."

"I'm coming," said Neill.

Shlomo was known as a—*liar* is too strong a word—mythomane. He took the stuff of his everyday life and turned it into Story. He was a mage this way. It made Neill doubt the naked neighbor fantasy but it didn't matter. He suddenly knew that going to Saratoga Springs over the holidays was exactly the thing he wanted to do. He wanted to shake the beasties out of himself.

"Great. Give me your flight information when you get it. You need to fly into Albany and I'll pick you up there."

"Albany. Ok. I'll call them now."

The Christmas Get-Together

Prior to the family things, Neill asked a few people over to decorate his Christmas tree and drink some eggnog and watch It's a *Wonderful Life*. His list was small. It made him a little sad.

Bidden did not return his phone call.

Attending were Crow, his wife Sarah and their youngster, Little Neill, Smithy with a new boyfriend, Gulley sans Victoria (she begged off with a migraine), Thistle Sharer and her husband, AJ and Dan.

It was a punctilious affair. They laughed (especially at the Menorah ornament Shlomo had donated last year which became a permanent decoration for Neill's tree the rest of his life), they drank some nog, they cried when the druggist hit young George's ear.

At the end of the movie, as if on cue, everyone rose and began to put on their coats. The appropriate bussers bussed Neill at the door. They hugged him and told him Merry Christmas. When they had gone Neill sat down in the multi-hued light of his tree and he cried as if over the birth of the Christ child. The world had been changed that utterly.

Saratoga Springs and Beyond

Reader, you have been patient at this extended expatiation. We are nearing the end. The end, as they say, is in sight. We thank you for your attention so far and beg you to stay with us a bit longer. The saga of Neill Rhymer, while not heading toward the conclusion (for he lives, he still lives), is nearing its apotheosis, its critical point, where it shall stop like an old coal burning locomotive which is soon to be replaced by—whatever they replaced coal burning locomotives with.

Shlomo met Neill's plane in the Albany airport. Albany, the capitol of New York, the home of William Kennedy. Shlomo looked thinner, if such a thing were possible. He looked like a slanted shadow.

The drive to Saratoga Springs was pleasant (though Neill had his slight travel flutters), the air chilled and spitting iotas of ice. The conversation moved as if they were finishing a conversation they started three years ago in Memphis.

Neill: You seeing anyone?

Shlomo: I see students. I see Maximilian and his family. I see the other teachers.

Neill: I see England. I see France.

Shlomo: And you've seen a lot of underpants.

Neill: Long ago in a kingdom far away.

Shlomo: How many women have you had?

Neill: Jesus, I don't know.

Shlomo: You do.

Neill: I don't—I think maybe, about 60 or so.

Shlomo: Oh. I thought you were in triple figures.

Neill: You're disappointed in me.

Shlomo: If I had had your looks—I don't know where this is going.

Neill: Still I am full of regret.

Shlomo: Thanks. That makes me feel better.

Neill: So am I gonna get to meet Poopyface Calvada?

Shlomo: Naw, he and his wife and kids are in Brunei for the holidays.

Shlomo's Apartment above a Garage

Shlomo's apartment was above a garage. It was small, a bedroom, a half-living room/kitchen, a bathroom the size of an airplane head. The couch in the living room was a hide-a-bed. This was Neill's 'room.'

"It's a shithole," Shlomo said. "I'm a teacher."

Neill and Shlomo went to a pub for dinner. The sky was still spitting tiny bits of icy snow but they walked there nevertheless. It was about a mile.

They had some pub grub, which was edible. But the real treat was the Irish Coffees they had for dessert. Only one was enough to give Neill, whose blood was thin enough that anything acted quickly on him, a nice buzz. The walk home was in the gloaming, the wintry skies now a deep purple bruise with ice-cream swirls of hazy snow clouds.

"We're supposed to get some snow this week. Of course, we always have snow so this is hardly news."

"Tomorrow we're going into the Enlarged Apple?

"Yeah, we'll catch the train in Albany and ride down the Hudson. It's quite an experience."

"Groovy," Neill said.

"Yeah, groovy."

They watched a little TV on Shlomo's crappy TV set, some PBS thing about The Beach Boys.

"I hate The Beach Boys," Neill said.

"I do too," Shlomo said. "Oh, wait, what time is it? Almost nine. Almost time."

"For what?"

"I told you about my neighbor across the way. She strips in front of her window every night at nine."

"I just assumed you were lying."

"Hang on."

Shlomo turned off the lights in his living room and they gathered in front of his one window. It looked out on a bosky courtyard and a weedy parking lot. Across the parking lot was a three-story apartment complex, with four windows on each level facing Shlomo's.

"Second window from the right, middle floor," Shlomo said. He was using his Marlon Perkins voice. "It's right about now."

Neill, dubious Neill, was finding the game a charming cheat until the woman's light came on and they watched her moving about her bedroom. It was hard to tell from their vantage point but she looked attractive, black hair, straight shoulders, shapely. She was wearing a shirt and trousers.

"She's alright," Neill said.

"Shh," Shlomo said. "You're breaking my concentration."

Neill started to say something. Neill wanted to laugh but he played along.

Then, the woman began to unbutton her shirt.

"Holy shit, Batman," Neill said.

"Shh," Shlomo said again.

The woman unzipped her pants and let them drop. She must have been about a foot from the window. This was meant for show. This was meant for Shlomo and Neill.

She unhooked her bra and her breasts fell plumply downward.

Gk," Neill said.

Then the panties were removed. She had a deep, dark bush. She stood still for a moment, stretched, just for show, and then turned her light out.

"Fuck me," Neill said.

"I told you," Shlomo said, nonchalantly. He was used to the show.

"How often?"

"Almost every night. When she misses a night I worry."

"Who is she?"

"I have no idea. I've never seen her anywhere except in that window."

"That you're aware of."

"That I am aware of."

"Might she be one of your students?"

"I think I would recognize her. Maybe, maybe not."

"Wild."

"I know. So to bed then with something to dream about."

"You go to bed this early?"

"It's my disciplined routine. My mornings are always for writing."

"Oh yeah. I guess I am spoiling that."

"Nonsense. We're on vacation."

"Right."

"You want some of this?" Shlomo was holding out a fat doobie.

"Naw, I can't smoke anymore."

"This is a banano, mostly tobacco with a little pot. This and a Tylenol every night and I can sleep. Otherwise the voices keep me awake."

"Ok," Neill said. He picked up his small grip and began to look for his pajamas.

"You have a book to read?"

"Shlomo."

"Sorry. Stupid question. I meant, what book are you reading?"

Neill held up his copy of Alasdair Gray's *Lanark*.

"I love that book," Shlomo said.

"What are you reading?"

"*Ada*."

"A Nabokov I have been meaning to get to."

"It's grand."

"Ok."

"Good night then," Shlomo said. He closed the accordion door between his bedroom and the pull-out couch. It took Neill a long time to get to sleep but he was happy where he was. Memphis, with its phantasms and incubi, was far away, and his good friend, Shlomo, was only a few feet away, behind a thin contraption of wood and rubber.

The Empire Service

The train ride up the Hudson on The Empire Service was awe-inspiring. Neill tried not to sound like a Clampett on holiday. Shlomo was a gentle dragoman.

Neill's favorite part, apart from disembarking in Grand Central Station, was the Castle on the Hudson, twenty-five miles outside the city. Neill wanted to live there. They also passed West Point, whose river-facing wall seemed to Neill a medieval fortress, better suited for a prison than a military academy (if there is any difference, Neill thought).

Shlomo's New York City (With or Without Lorrie Moore)

One couldn't say that Shlomo had an agenda, exactly, but he knew New York City and Shlomo's New York City was the one Neill wanted to experience. It consisted of mad jumping on and off subway trains, crisscrossing the great metropolis to visit every important bookstore. This was the plan.

They began with lunch in a Russian deli where they had egg creams and Reuben sandwiches. The Reuben Neill would talk about for the rest of his life. (What was the name of the deli? Is it important?)

Then a bookstore.

Then a train ride and another bookstore.

Then a train ride and another bookstore.

They visited The Strand, of course. Neill bought a Wallace Stegner novel, *The Spectator Bird*, and a book of Pauline Kael's reviews, *Reeling*. Shlomo bought a John Cowper Powys' novel, *Maiden Castle*. They visited Gotham with its 'Wise Men Fish Here' sign and its autographed copies of all of Edward Gorey's enchanting, arabesque play-pretties. This was a particularly delightful store for Neill. He bought a very nice edition of Joyce's poems. They visited the bookstore where the film *Crossing Delancey* was shot. (Find out which one? ed.) Neill had just seen the film and loved the films of Joan Micklin Silver.

"I have something in my pocket that might interest you," Shlomo said as they muddled along the cold sidewalk.

"Hashish?"

"Lorrie Moore's phone number."

"Oh my. She's, well, the eyebrows, she's, you know."

"You love her."

"I do. She writes well, too."

"But you would be afraid of meeting her?"

"Yes. No, I don't think so. Why do you have her number?"

"We have teaching gigs in common. I got a nice letter from her and she said if I was ever in the city to call her."

"Any city."

"I think she meant this one."

"Ok."

Shlomo pulled out a crumpled piece of envelope on which the number was written. They stopped at a pay phone and Shlomo, making with the Groucho eyebrows, dialed.

He prolonged the drama of the moment as long as he could. He seemed to be listening for an hour.

"Got her machine."

"Oh, well. I am sure I'll meet her somewhere else."

"Yeah, I'm sure of that."

They ended up having dinner at Umberto's Clam House, the clam bar where Crazy Joe Gallo was gunned down. It was packed. It was hot and the food was tasty. It was New York City and Neill was happy.

"I think this is the exact table," Shlomo said.

"Seriously?"

"No. I have no idea."

"But this is the dish he ordered that night?"

"So I am told."

"I hope someone shoots us."

"Not really. You're still a pup."

"I'm a broke down piece of man."

"How's your dad?"

"He's good. But, you know, once the heart goes bad you're never really healthy again. The heart is too important, yet too fragile."

They were quiet for a while, enjoying their oily food.

"Lemme get this," Shlomo said, when the waiter dropped the check on the table on his way by.

Neill fought with Cheap Neill who normally directed his every move. He was, after all, out of work.

"I got money," Neill said, and he paid his share. He let Shlomo add the tip.

As they emerged back on Mulberry Street in Little Italy, they decided to walk a bit. They still had time to catch the last train to Albany. It was now snowing in earnest, snowing like it meant it. The city, with its holiday lights yet everywhere, seemed a fairyland to Neill. He was aching inside but he felt unusual. It was hard to put into words so he didn't try. He and Shlomo walked in companionable silence, through Soho, by galleries and beautiful people. Neill wanted to imagine he walked the same sidewalks Frank O'Hara walked. He had recently developed a passion for the great New York Poet.

The snow. The colored lights. The buildings lit and decorated. Life.

The Rockefeller Plaza Christmas Tree. Weighted with cliché yet still somehow epiphanic.

The train ride back was anti-climactic. Neill was tired but full of himself. He talked on and on about an idea he had for a novel.

"I didn't think you liked the long haul," Shlomo said. "I thought you were a sprinter."

"I know. I am. I am trying to not let it limit me. Listen to this idea."

Shlomo was a good friend, a good man. He listened to Neill's half bullshit plot and he nodded encouragement and laughed in the right places. It was just a wild fantasy that was based on other wild fantasies. Gently, Shlomo tried to steer Neill back to earth. He wasn't a big proponent of 'write what you know,' but he knew grounding would help Neill.

"You know, Neill, you've had a wonderful life," he began.

"Am I fixing to die or am I fixing to get a lot of money dumped on me by the townsfolk?"

"I was thinking about this when you were talking about how many lovers you had."

"You were talking about how many lovers I had."

"Just listen to me. Why not write about that? You've had the kind of experience with the human heart that I have never come close to. I have these few little pissy romances and you've had grand passion and wild sex. Maybe that's a book."

"Sure, under the pseudonym, Bill Dungs Roman. Who would want to read that? Henry Miller fans? Charles Bukowski fans?"

"Maybe."

"You hate Bukowski.:

"Outdo him."

"No one wants to read about my life. I am an ordinary loser from Memphis, Tennessee."

"Ok."

"It's just—"

But Neill could not finish the thought. He was feeling defeated again. He was reminded that he was to return to Memphis the next day, jobless, womanless, and hopeless. What would become of him? He was certainly not destined for literary fame, even the modest but well-respected fame of his friend, Shlomo Einstein.

His plot sucked. His love life an abortion. For every plot a marplot. For every woman he'd ever known a black mark on his soul, a chit for Old Scratch.

By the time they got to their car in the Albany lot the snow was coming down in flakes as big as quarters and as soft as the place on Misso Anthill's body where her beautiful shoulders met her beautiful neck.

"This is shaping up into a big storm," Shlomo said, as they crept toward Saratoga Springs. "What do you think, Rudolph?"

"I got no light. Let's cancel Christmas."

"You ok? I mean, we haven't really talked about it."

"I'm ok. Just ok. My life is not a tapestry of rich and royal hue."

"Women? Loneliness?"

"Failure, I think. I am he who fails."

"You're not, you know."

Neill watched the snow swirl against the car window, sometimes in the gentle maelstrom he thought he saw a figure out of myth.

"I miss Misso still."

"She stuck in deep."

"I guess so."

"Why her? She wasn't that good for you."

Neill looked at his friend with a world-weary expression, an expression that was a shrug.

"I know. Fatuous to even ask. It's always a crapshoot and an obscurity."

Shlomo kept glancing at Neill, even as he worried about the fogging windshield and the accumulation of snow and ice.

"I'm glad you came," Shlomo said, at last.

"Thanks. I am, too."

Back in his pull-out bed that night Neill spent some time worried about the snow storm because he was conditioned to worry about things like snow storms. But, tired and full of rich wanderings, he fell asleep and dreamed about a place he often dreamed about, a neighborhood that might be actual and might be fairy-cake, a neighborhood where he is walking toward something, a house with a light on, a house inside of which is a young woman waiting for him. She loves him and he is happy that he does not have far to go. The woman might be Akin Upspins. It might be Thistle Sharer. It might be Misso Anthill.

The Last Morning: It's Pitch White Outside

"the burial/of sleep, the down of winter, the negative of night."
    –Mark Strand

"Your flight's been cancelled."

Neill stuck his head out from under the covers. He had to cover his entire body to even approach warm on the pull-out. "What?" he said, though he had heard.

"Your flight's cancelled. Wait till you look outside."

"Do I have to?"

"What?"

"*What?*"

"Do you have to what?"

"Catch the plane?"

"Look. Wake up. I'm going to walk to the coffeeshop and pray they are open. We're out of coffee. I'm going to walk if I can get through this stuff."

"Ok."

"I'll be back. We'll make coffee. I'll get some croissants or bagels, too."

"Ok."

Shlomo stood at the door heavily swathed.

"Shlomo?"

"Yes?"

"Thanks. You know."

Shlomo looked at Neill. He shrugged and exited.

Neill was gradually coming up from what was a very deep immersion. The world was still fuzzy around the edges. Had he dreamed? Was that it? He couldn't remember a dream but he felt—*funny*, as if he had been someplace new, someplace unexpected. Maybe he had dreamed that he could not get back home.

After a long period of woolgathering, he wrapped himself in the light blue, pilled blanket and stood. He was slightly unsteady, almost as if he had a hangover. Except he felt splendid. He thought suddenly, I feel splendid. He didn't even ask himself why.

He moved toward the window.

The world was submerged. There was only white outside. The car in the driveway was buried. There was a sea of smooth whiteness stretching from where Neill was to the horizon, which was indistinct. The monotony was only broken by the occasional light pole and the wires which connect everything.

There were no footprints where Shlomo had walked to the store. Perhaps, he had gone another way. There weren't even the little Ys of bird tracks.

Neill was mesmerized. The white felt like blindness, or a new kind of vision. He felt that if he walked outside he could walk on top of the blanked-out world. He was light. He looked across the blank white sheet of the snow and he did not see a story forming there, the way Shlomo makes a story out of a trip to the bank or a slog to a bar for Irish Coffees. He saw emptiness.

But he thought that tomorrow would probably come anyway and he would either be here or somewhere else. He thought he might be heading home. It was going to be a new year soon. Neill thought that, yes, he would, at some point, go back to Memphis and it could all begin again or not. Neill thought that either way something profound was about to happen.

Today he was not going back to Memphis. Today he was not going anywhere.

"He wanted to publish a book, but it never came to that, for he kept changing his manuscript, changing it so often and to such an extent that nothing was left of the manuscript, for the change in his manuscript was nothing other than the complete deletion of the manuscript, of which finally nothing remained except the title, The Loser."
— Thomas Bernhard

Special thanks to my friends and family with superior memories and generous hearts: Sue Kennedy, Sadie Mesler, Trish Leathers, Christy Crouse, Melinda Fry, Angie Smith, Jay Wells, David Gaddie, Robin Burton, Richard Roberts, Mary Reynolds Price, Anna Hightower, David Tankersley, Sherri Williams, Larry Wells, Steve Stern, John Beifuss, Mark Whitaker, Cursey and Linda Roberson, Sue Jackson Williams, Richard Alley, Larry Wells, David Tankersley, Sam Tickle, Terry Chouinard, Teresa Angle-Young, Heather Minette, Eddie Burton, Debra Jones Jackson, Elise Crockett, of course Cheryl....and to everyone on Facebook who encouraged me along the way.

Part of this book appeared originally in *Memphis Magazine*, in, as they say, a slightly different form. And another part in *Hypertext Magazine*.

Books by Corey Mesler:

Poetry
For Toby, Everything for Toby (1997) Wing & The Wheel Press
Ten Poets (1999) editor, only Wing & The Wheel Press
Piecework (2000) Wing & The Wheel Press
Chin-Chin in Eden (2003) Still Waters Press
Dark on Purpose (2004) Little Poem Press
The Hole in Sleep (2006) Wood Works Press
The Agoraphobe's Pandiculations (2006) Little Poem Press
The Lita Conversation (2006) Southern Hum
The Chloe Poems (2007) Maverick Duck Press
Some Identity Problems (2007) Foothills Publishing
Pictures from Lang and Fellini (2007) Sheltering Pines Press
Grit (2008) Amsterdam Press
The Tense Past (2010) Flutter Press
Before the Great Troubling (2011) Unbound Content
Mitmensch (2011) Folded Word Press
The Heart is Open (2011) Right Hand Pointing
To Writing You (2012) Origami Poems Project
Our Locust Years (2013) Unbound Content
My Father is Still Dying (2013) Flutter Press
Body (2013) Chapbook Journal
The Catastrophe of my Personality (2014) Blue Hour Press

The Sky Needs More Work (2014) Upper Rubber Boot Books
The Medicament Predicament (2015) Redneck Press
Stone (2015) Origami Poems (chapbook)
Opaque Melodies that Would Bug Most People (2015) After the Pause Books
Mountain (2015) Fairfield Press
Home (2016) Fairfield Press
Among the Mensans (Iris Press) 2017
River (Fairfield Press) 2018
Madstones (BlazeVOX Books) 2018
Alphabeticon (Staring Problem Press) 2019
Dog (Fairfield Press) 2019

Prose
Talk: A Novel in Dialogue (2002) Livingston Press
We Are Billion-Year-Old Carbon (2005) Livingston Press
Short Story and Other Short Stories (2006) Parallel Press
Following Richard Brautigan (chapbook) (2006) Plan B Press
Publisher (2007) Writers Write Journal Press
Listen: 29 Short Conversations (2009) Brown Paper Press
The Ballad of the Two Tom Mores (2010) Bronx River Press
Following Richard Brautigan (full-length novel) (2010) Livingston Press
Notes toward the Story and Other Stories (2011) Aqueous Books
Gardner Remembers (2011) Pocketful of Scoundrel
I'll Give You Something to Cry About (2011) Queen's Ferry Press
Frank Comma and the Time-Slip (2012) Wapshott Press
The Travels of Cocoa Poem Lorry (2013) Leaf Garden Press
Diddy-Wah-Diddy: A Beale Street Suite (2013) Ampersand Press
As a Child: Stories (2014) MadHat Press
Memphis Movie (2015) Soft Skull Press
Robert Walker (2016) Livingston Press
Camel's Bastard Son (2020) Cabal Books
The Adventures of Camel Jeremy Eros (2020) Cervena Barva Press
The Diminishment of Charlie Cain (2021) Livingston Press

About the Author

COREY MESLER has been published in numerous anthologies and journals including *Poetry*, *Gargoyle*, *Five Points*, *Good Poems American Places*, and *New Stories from the South*. He has published over 20 works of both poetry and prose. He's been nominated for the Pushcart many times, and 3 of his poems were chosen for Garrison Keillor's Writer's Almanac. With his wife he runs Burke's Book Store (est. 1875) in Memphis.

About the Publisher

Whisk(e)y Tit is committed to restoring degradation and degeneracy to the literary arts. We work with authors who are unwilling to sacrifice intellectual rigor, unrelenting playfulness, and visual beauty in our literary pursuits, often leading to texts that would otherwise be abandoned in today's largely homogenized literary landscape. In a world governed by idiocy, our commitment to these principles is an act of civil service and civil disobedience alike.

9 781952 600104